WITCHBLADE
ORIGINS
VOLUME 3

Witchblade created by:
Marc Silvestri, David Wohl,
Brian Haberlin and Michael Turner

published by
Top Cow Productions, Inc.
Los Angeles

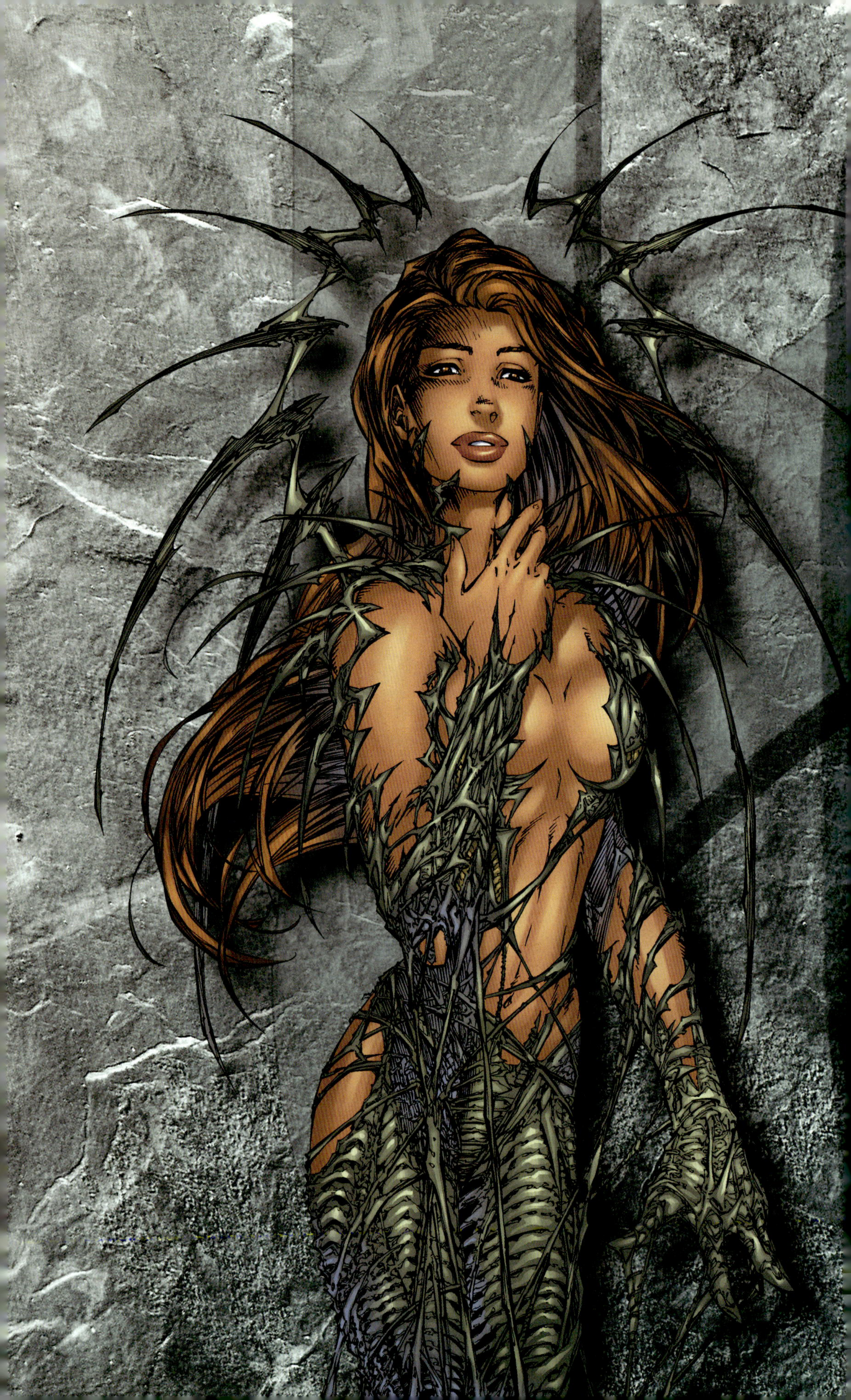

WITCHBLADE
ORIGINS
VOLUME 3

WITCHBLADE

letters for all issues in this edition by:
Dennis Heisler

For Top Cow Productions, Inc.:
Marc Silvestri - Chief Executive Officer
Matt Hawkins - President and Chief Operating Officer
Filip Sablik - Publisher
Chaz Riggs - Graphic Design
Phil Smith - Managing Editor
Adrian Nicita - Webmaster
Scott Newman - Production Lead
Jennifer Chow - Production Assistant
Bryan Rountree - Assistant to the Publisher
Rob Levin - Consulting Editor
Diana Siegel, Alex Galer and **Justin Bretter** - Interns

For this edition
Cover art by
Michael Turner, D-Tron
and JD Smith

For this edition
Book Design and Layout by:
Phil Smith

 for **image** comics publisher:
Eric Stephenson

 to find the comic shop nearest you call:
1-888-COMICBOOK

Want more info? check out:
www.topcow.com and www.topcowstore.com
for news and exclusive Top Cow merchandise!

Witchblade: Origins volume 3 Trade Paperback
July 2009. FIRST PRINTING. ISBN: 978-1-60706-047-5
Published by Image Comics Inc. Office of Publication: 2134 Allston Way, Second Floor, Berkeley, CA 94704. $17.99 U.S.D. Originally published in single magazine form as WITCHBLADE 18-25 and THE DARKNESS 9 and 10. Witchblade and The Darkness © 2009 Top Cow Productions, Inc. All rights reserved. "Witchblade," "The Darkness," the Witchblade the The Darkness logos, and the likeness of all characters (human or otherwise) featured herein are registered trademarks of Top Cow Productions, Inc. Image Comics and the Image Comics logo are trademarks of Image Comics, Inc. The characters, events, and stories in this publication are entirely fictional. Any resemblance to actual persons (living or dead), events, institutions, or locales, without satiric intent, is coincidental. No portion of this publication may be reproduced or transmitted, in any form or by any means, without the express written permission of Top Cow Productions, Inc. **PRINTED IN CHINA.**

ORIGINS VOLUME 3

Table of Contents

Witchblade issue #18  ———— pg. 7

The Darkness issue #9 ———— pg. 31

The Darkness issue #10 ———— pg. 55

Witchblade issue #19 ———— pg. 81

Witchblade issue #20 ———— pg. 107

Witchblade issue #21 ———— pg. 131

Witchblade issue #22  ———— pg. 155

Witchblade issue #23  ———— pg. 179

Witchblade issue #24  ———— pg. 203

Witchblade issue #25  ———— pg. 227

Witchblade  ———— pg. 252
Cover Gallery

FAMILY TIES part 1: *Witchblade*
issue #18

story: **David Wohl** and **Christina Z.**
pencils and co-plot: **Michael Turner**
inks: **D-Tron**
colors: **JD Smith**

ink assists: **Andy Kim, Marsha Chen, Jose "Jag" Guillen, Jeff De Los Santos** and **Viet Trong**

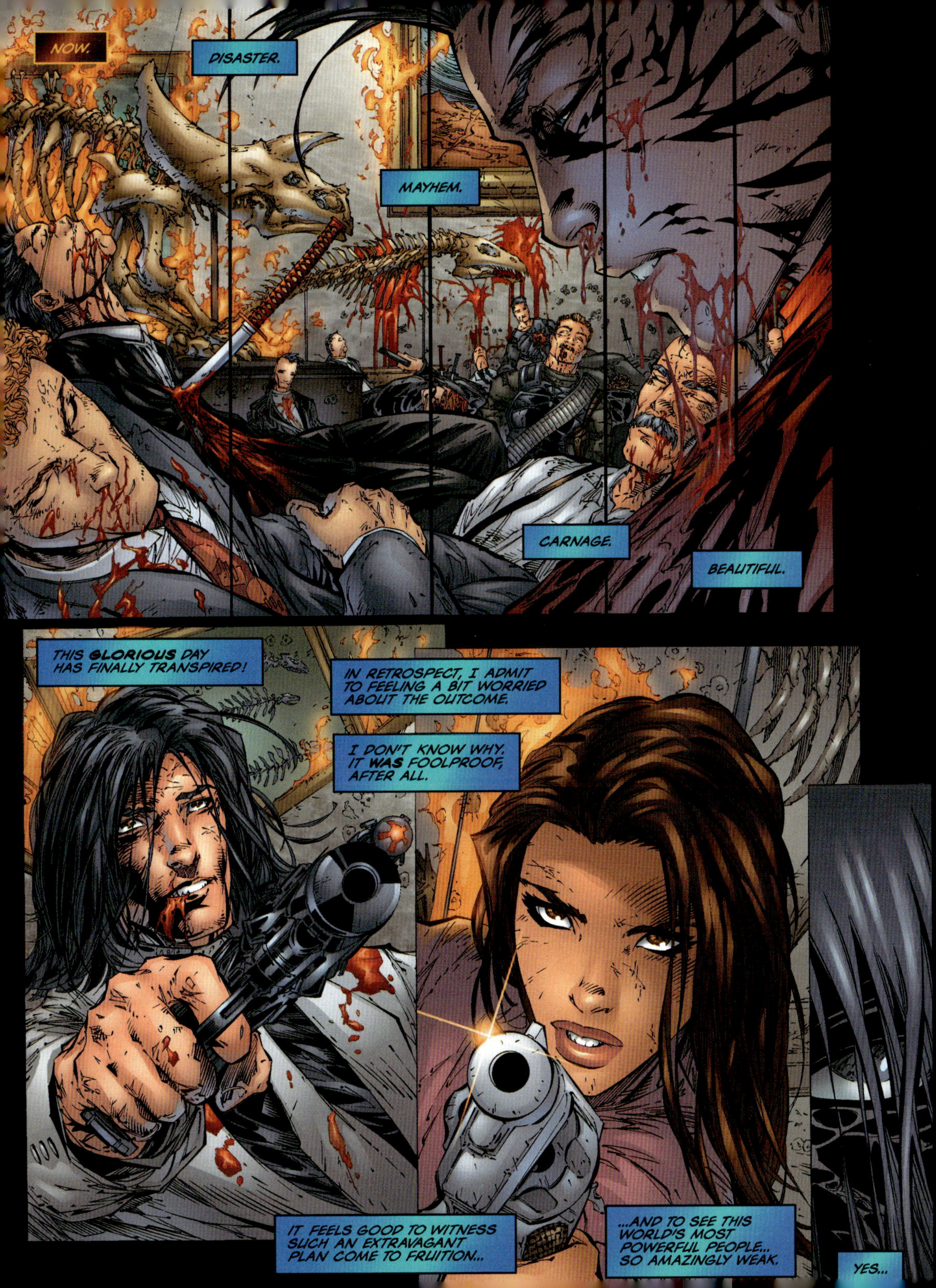
NOW.
DISASTER.
MAYHEM.
CARNAGE.
BEAUTIFUL.
THIS GLORIOUS DAY HAS FINALLY TRANSPIRED!
IN RETROSPECT, I ADMIT TO FEELING A BIT WORRIED ABOUT THE OUTCOME.
I DON'T KNOW WHY. IT WAS FOOLPROOF, AFTER ALL.
IT FEELS GOOD TO WITNESS SUCH AN EXTRAVAGANT PLAN COME TO FRUITION...
...AND TO SEE THIS WORLD'S MOST POWERFUL PEOPLE... SO AMAZINGLY WEAK.
YES...

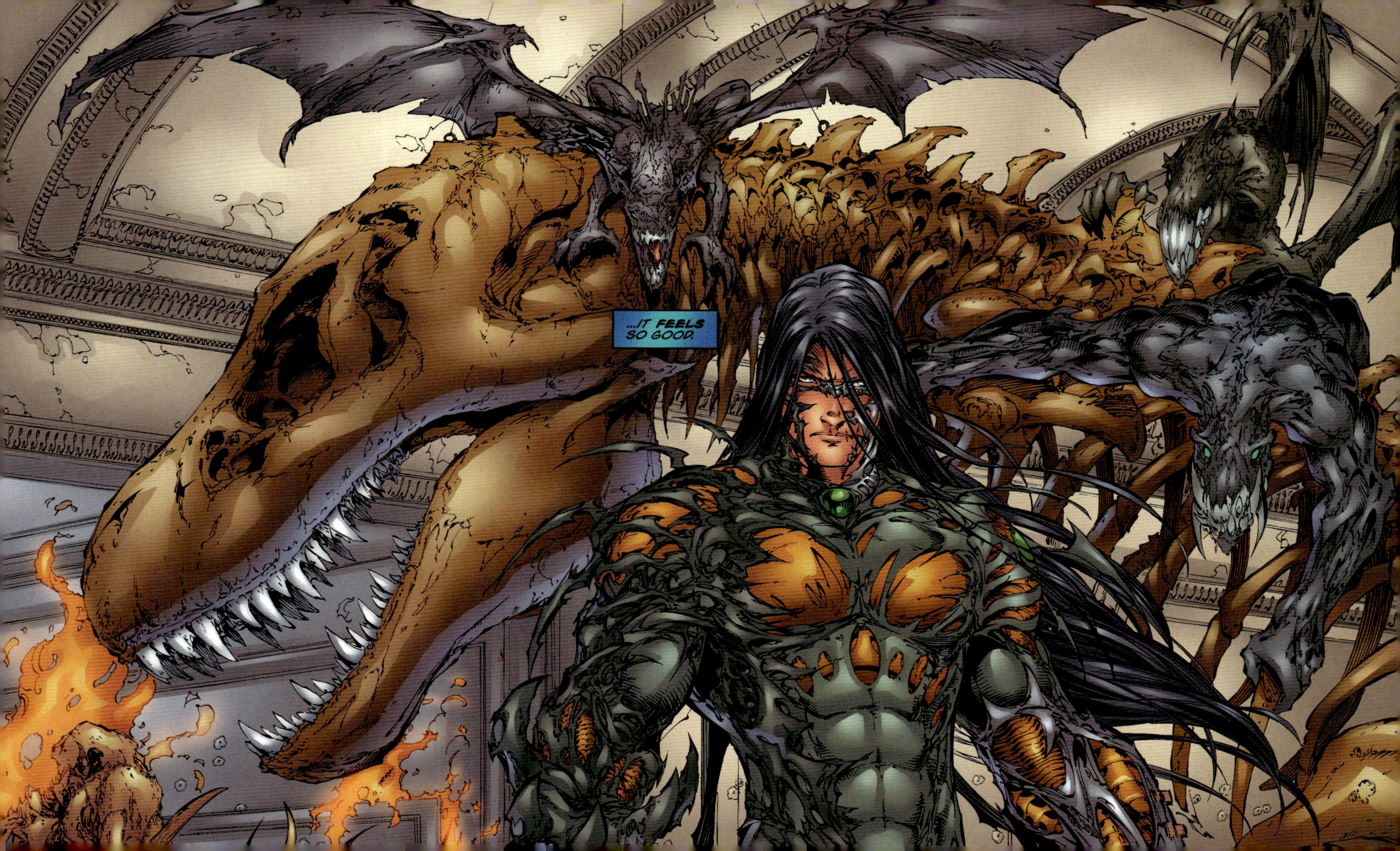
...IT FEELS SO GOOD.

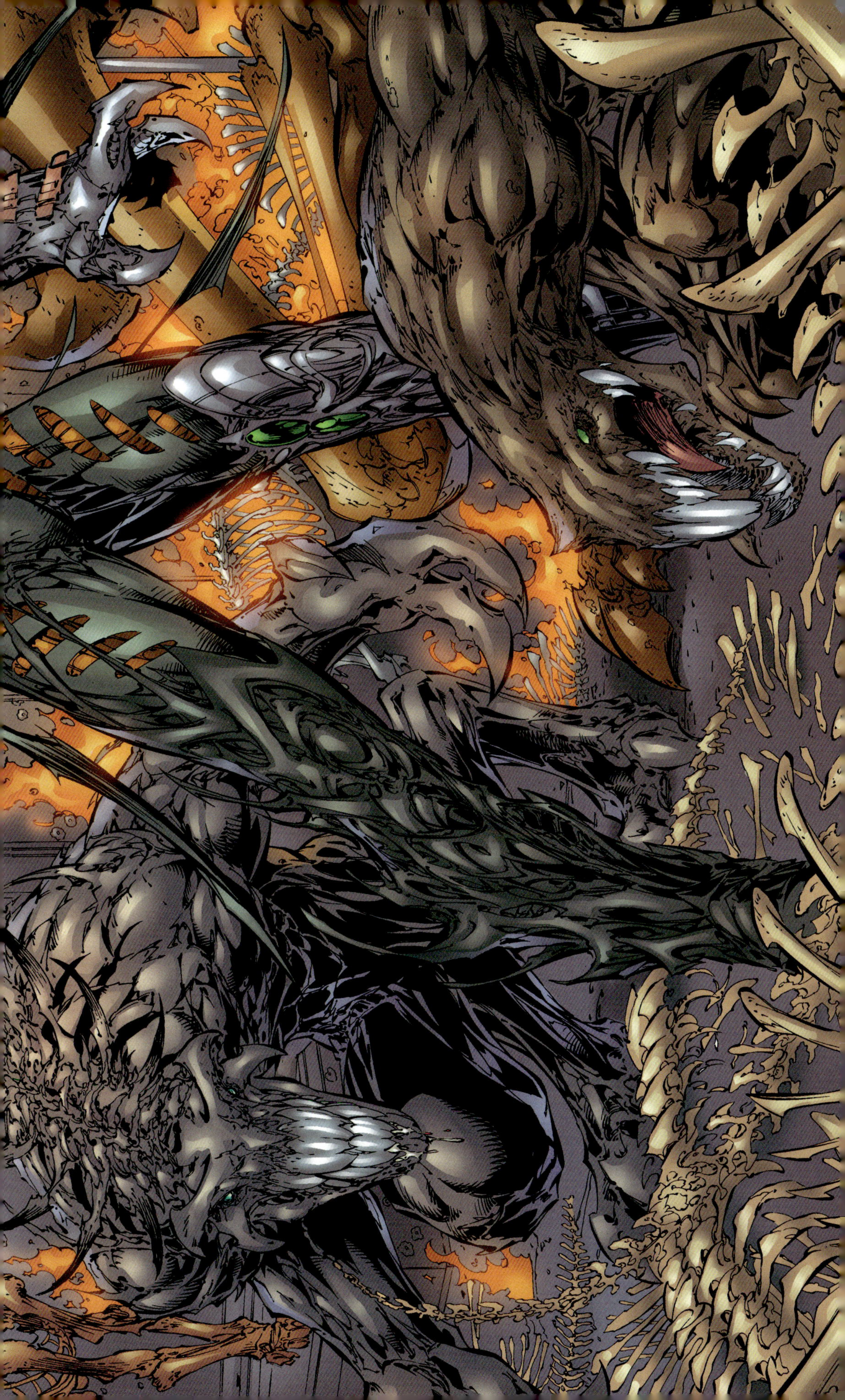

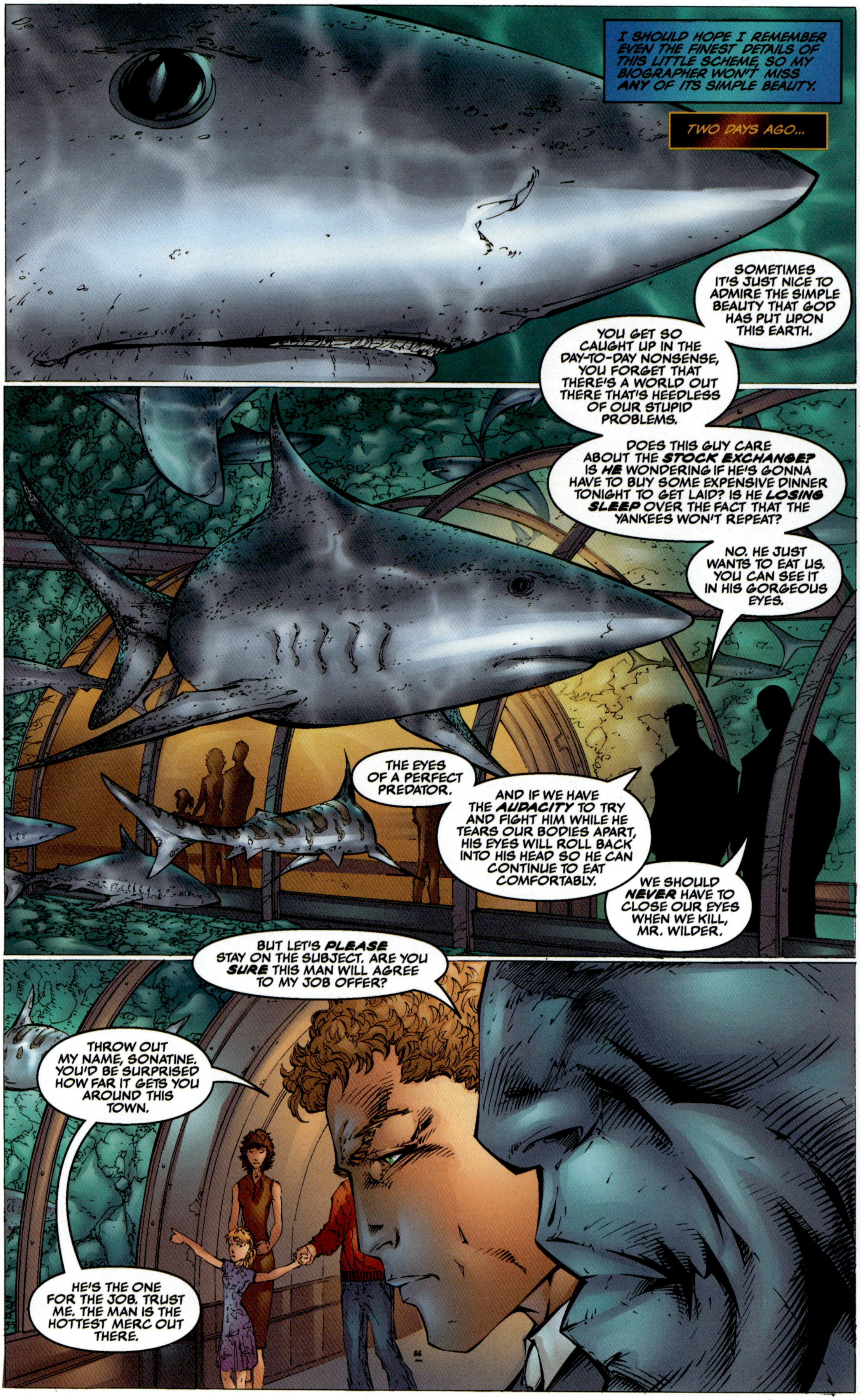

I SHOULD HOPE I REMEMBER EVEN THE FINEST DETAILS OF THIS LITTLE SCHEME, SO MY BIOGRAPHER WON'T MISS ANY OF ITS SIMPLE BEAUTY.
TWO DAYS AGO...
SOMETIMES IT'S JUST NICE TO ADMIRE THE SIMPLE BEAUTY THAT GOD HAS PUT UPON THIS EARTH.
YOU GET SO CAUGHT UP IN THE DAY-TO-DAY NONSENSE, YOU FORGET THAT THERE'S A WORLD OUT THERE THAT'S HEEDLESS OF OUR STUPID PROBLEMS.
DOES THIS GUY CARE ABOUT THE STOCK EXCHANGE? IS HE WONDERING IF HE'S GONNA HAVE TO BUY SOME EXPENSIVE DINNER TONIGHT TO GET LAID? IS HE LOSING SLEEP OVER THE FACT THAT THE YANKEES WON'T REPEAT?
NO, HE JUST WANTS TO EAT US. YOU CAN SEE IT IN HIS GORGEOUS EYES.
THE EYES OF A PERFECT PREDATOR.
AND IF WE HAVE THE AUDACITY TO TRY AND FIGHT HIM WHILE HE TEARS OUR BODIES APART, HIS EYES WILL ROLL BACK INTO HIS HEAD SO HE CAN CONTINUE TO EAT COMFORTABLY.
WE SHOULD NEVER HAVE TO CLOSE OUR EYES WHEN WE KILL, MR. WILDER.
BUT LET'S PLEASE STAY ON THE SUBJECT. ARE YOU SURE THIS MAN WILL AGREE TO MY JOB OFFER?
THROW OUT MY NAME, SONATINE. YOU'D BE SURPRISED HOW FAR IT GETS YOU AROUND THIS TOWN.
HE'S THE ONE FOR THE JOB, TRUST ME. THE MAN IS THE HOTTEST MERC OUT THERE.

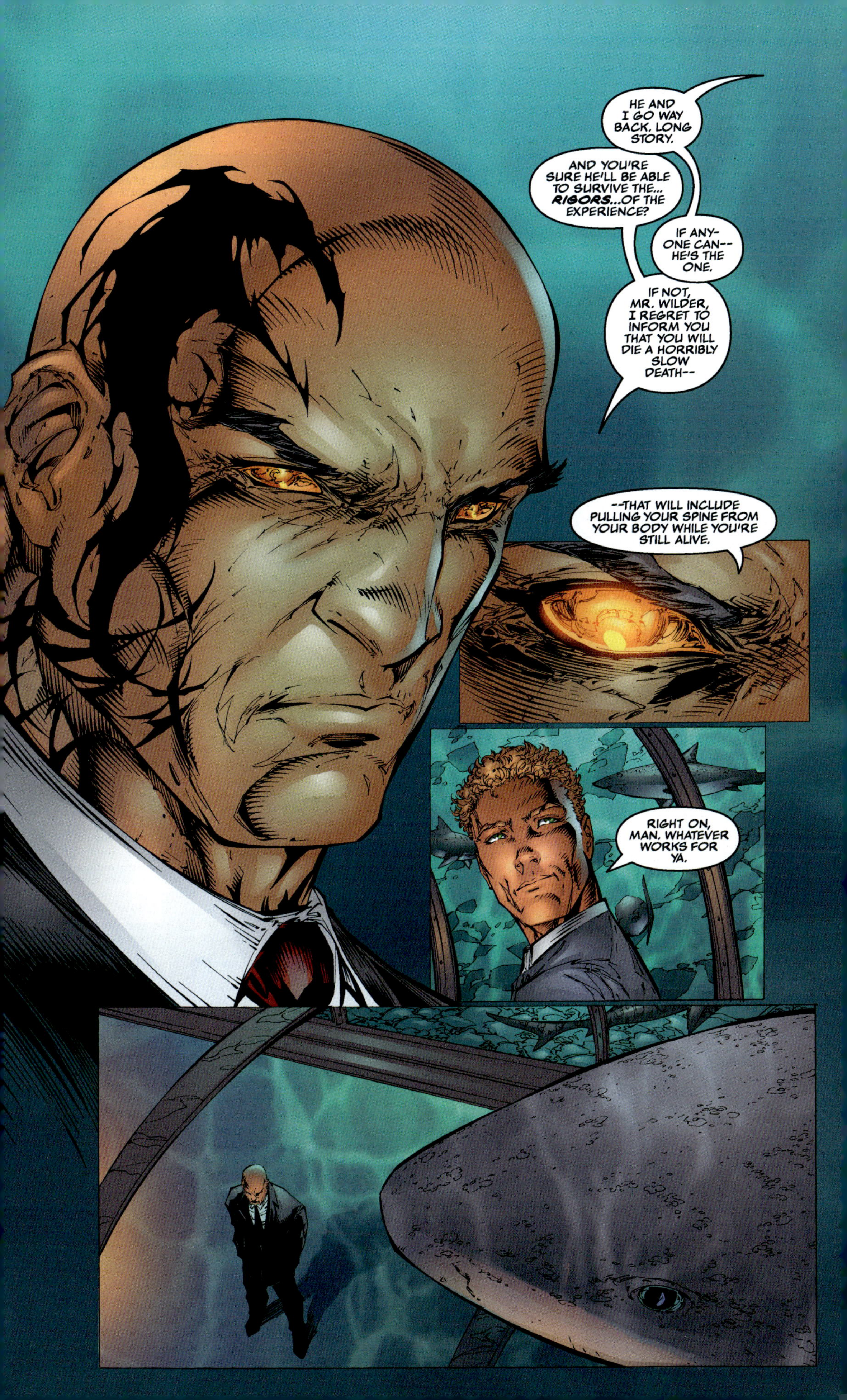
HE AND I GO WAY BACK. LONG STORY.
AND YOU'RE SURE HE'LL BE ABLE TO SURVIVE THE... RIGORS...OF THE EXPERIENCE?
IF ANY-ONE CAN--HE'S THE ONE.
IF NOT, MR. WILDER, I REGRET TO INFORM YOU THAT YOU WILL DIE A HORRIBLY SLOW DEATH--
--THAT WILL INCLUDE PULLING YOUR SPINE FROM YOUR BODY WHILE YOU'RE STILL ALIVE.
RIGHT ON, MAN. WHATEVER WORKS FOR YA.

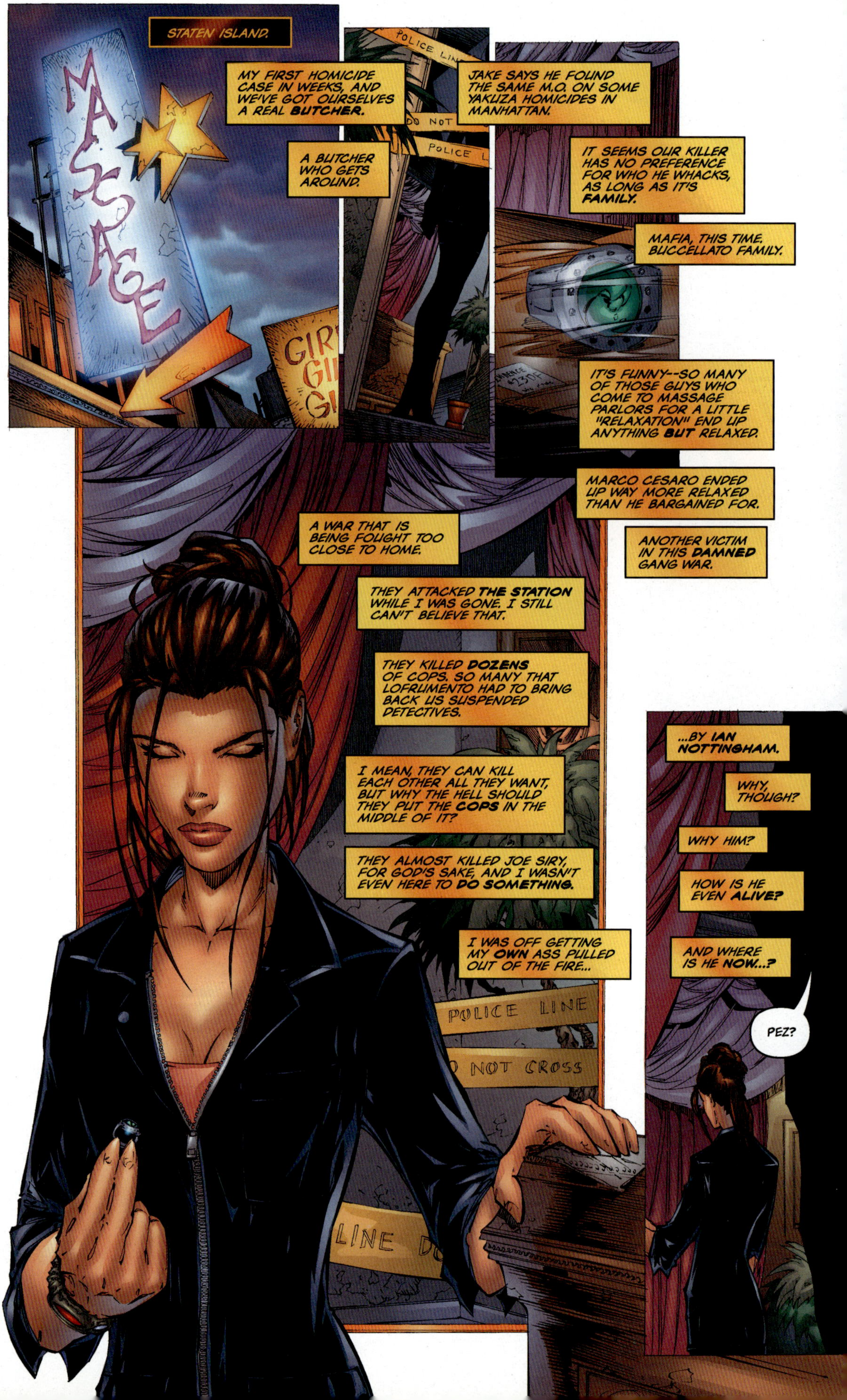
STATEN ISLAND.
MASSAGE
GIR
MY FIRST HOMICIDE CASE IN WEEKS, AND WE'VE GOT OURSELVES A REAL BUTCHER.
A BUTCHER WHO GETS AROUND.
POLICE LINE
DO NOT
POLICE L
JAKE SAYS HE FOUND THE SAME M.O. ON SOME YAKUZA HOMICIDES IN MANHATTAN.
IT SEEMS OUR KILLER HAS NO PREFERENCE FOR WHO HE WHACKS, AS LONG AS IT'S FAMILY.
MAFIA, THIS TIME. BUCCELLATO FAMILY.
IT'S FUNNY--SO MANY OF THOSE GUYS WHO COME TO MASSAGE PARLORS FOR A LITTLE "RELAXATION" END UP ANYTHING BUT RELAXED.
MARCO CESARO ENDED UP WAY MORE RELAXED THAN HE BARGAINED FOR.
ANOTHER VICTIM IN THIS DAMNED GANG WAR.
A WAR THAT IS BEING FOUGHT TOO CLOSE TO HOME.
THEY ATTACKED THE STATION WHILE I WAS GONE. I STILL CAN'T BELIEVE THAT.
THEY KILLED DOZENS OF COPS. SO MANY THAT LOFRUMENTO HAD TO BRING BACK US SUSPENDED DETECTIVES.
I MEAN, THEY CAN KILL EACH OTHER ALL THEY WANT, BUT WHY THE HELL SHOULD THEY PUT THE COPS IN THE MIDDLE OF IT?
THEY ALMOST KILLED JOE SIRY, FOR GOD'S SAKE, AND I WASN'T EVEN HERE TO DO SOMETHING.
I WAS OFF GETTING MY OWN ASS PULLED OUT OF THE FIRE...
POLICE LINE
O NOT CROSS
LINE D
...BY IAN NOTTINGHAM.
WHY, THOUGH?
WHY HIM?
HOW IS HE EVEN ALIVE?
AND WHERE IS HE NOW...?
PEZ?

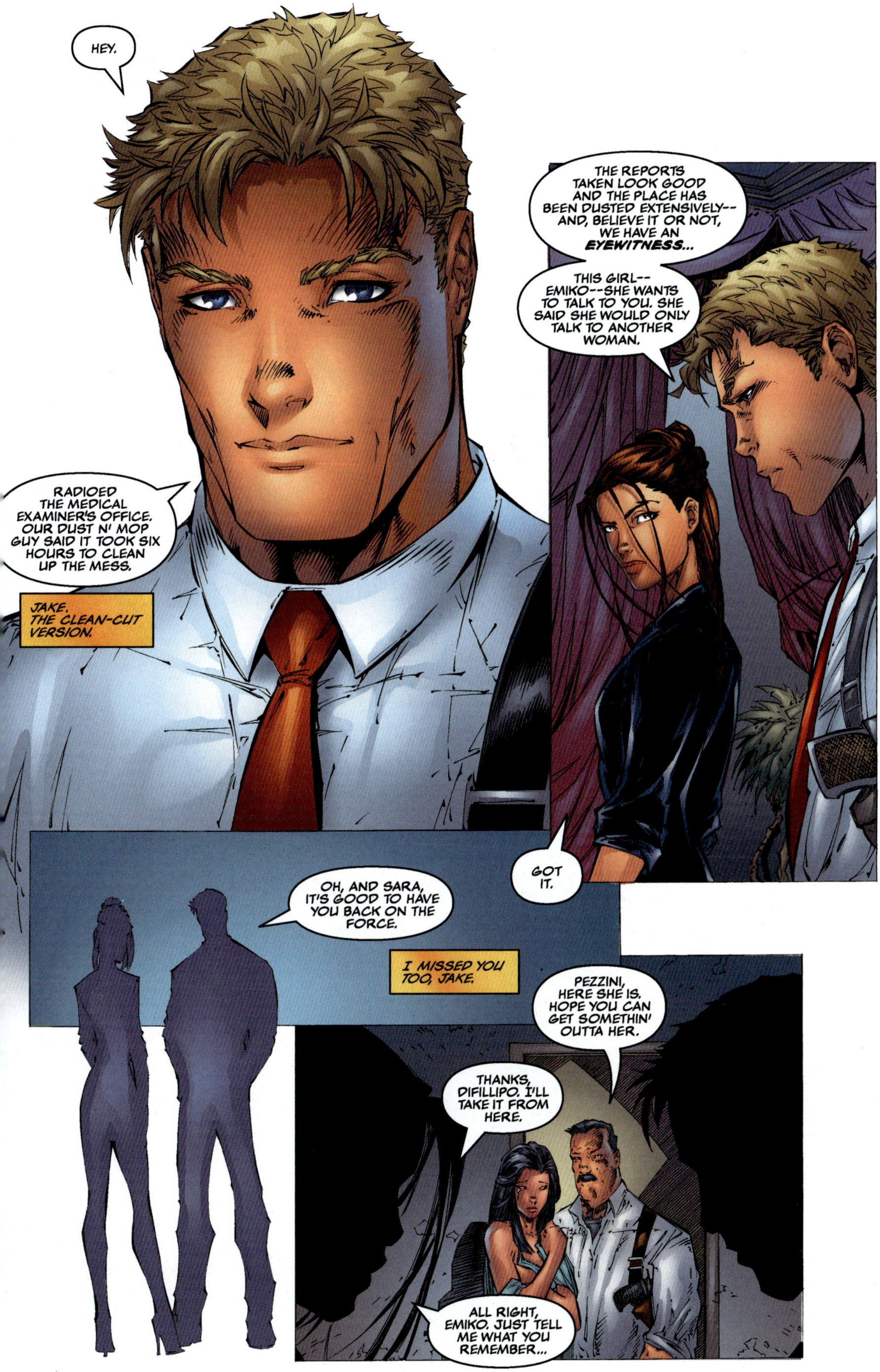
HEY.
RADIOED THE MEDICAL EXAMINER'S OFFICE. OUR DUST N' MOP GUY SAID IT TOOK SIX HOURS TO CLEAN UP THE MESS.
JAKE. THE CLEAN-CUT VERSION.
THE REPORTS TAKEN LOOK GOOD AND THE PLACE HAS BEEN DUSTED EXTENSIVELY-- AND, BELIEVE IT OR NOT, WE HAVE AN EYEWITNESS...
THIS GIRL-- EMIKO--SHE WANTS TO TALK TO YOU. SHE SAID SHE WOULD ONLY TALK TO ANOTHER WOMAN.
GOT IT.
OH, AND SARA, IT'S GOOD TO HAVE YOU BACK ON THE FORCE.
I MISSED YOU TOO, JAKE.
PEZZINI, HERE SHE IS. HOPE YOU CAN GET SOMETHIN' OUTTA HER.
THANKS, DIFILLIPO. I'LL TAKE IT FROM HERE.
ALL RIGHT, EMIKO. JUST TELL ME WHAT YOU REMEMBER...

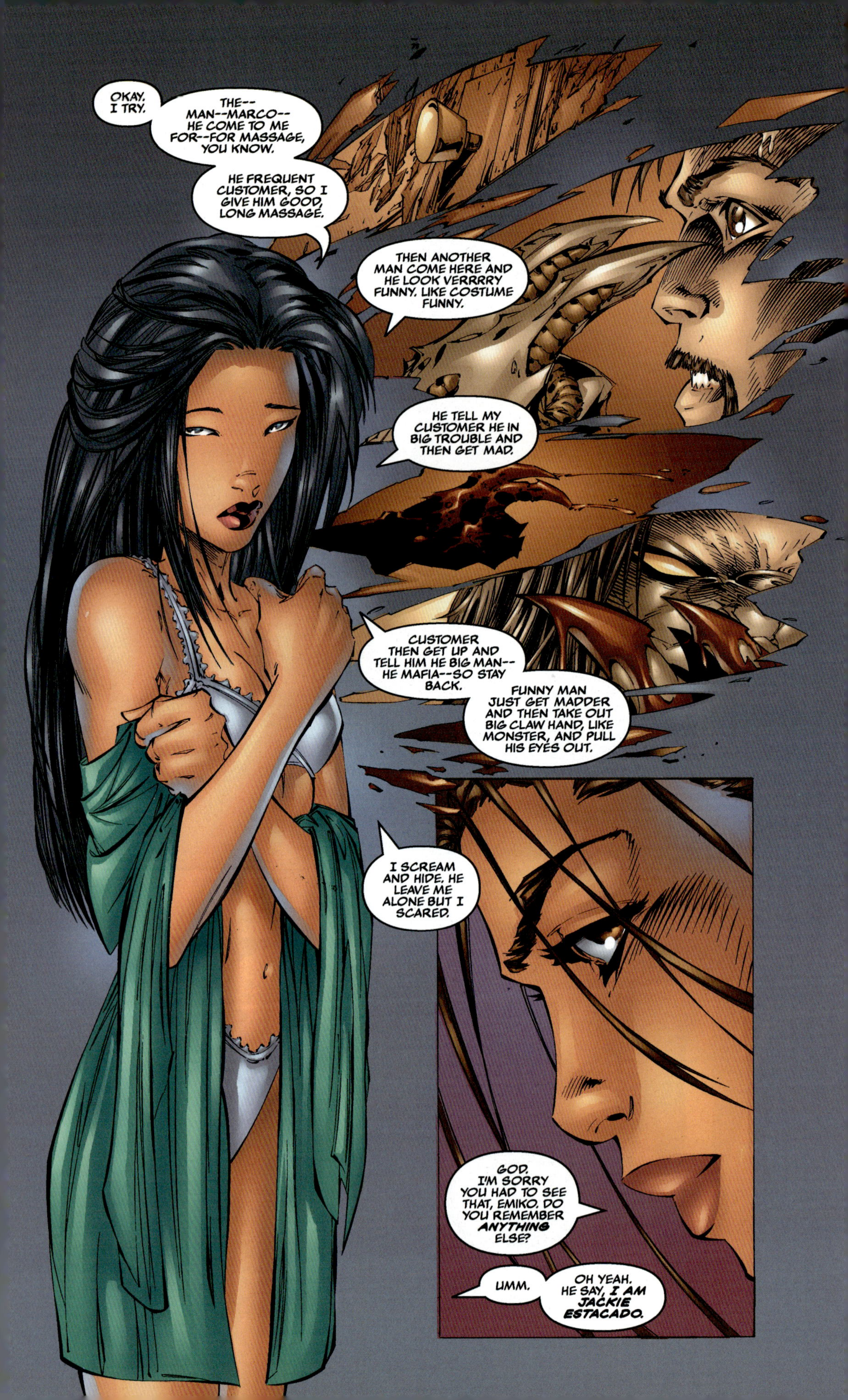
OKAY, I TRY.
THE--MAN--MARCO--HE COME TO ME FOR--FOR MASSAGE, YOU KNOW.
HE FREQUENT CUSTOMER, SO I GIVE HIM GOOD, LONG MASSAGE.
THEN ANOTHER MAN COME HERE AND HE LOOK VERRRRY FUNNY. LIKE COSTUME FUNNY.
HE TELL MY CUSTOMER HE IN BIG TROUBLE AND THEN GET MAD.
CUSTOMER THEN GET UP AND TELL HIM HE BIG MAN--HE MAFIA--SO STAY BACK.
FUNNY MAN JUST GET MADDER AND THEN TAKE OUT BIG CLAW HAND, LIKE MONSTER, AND PULL HIS EYES OUT.
I SCREAM AND HIDE. HE LEAVE ME ALONE BUT I SCARED.
GOD. I'M SORRY YOU HAD TO SEE THAT, EMIKO. DO YOU REMEMBER ANYTHING ELSE?
UMM.
OH YEAH. HE SAY, I AM JACKIE ESTACADO.

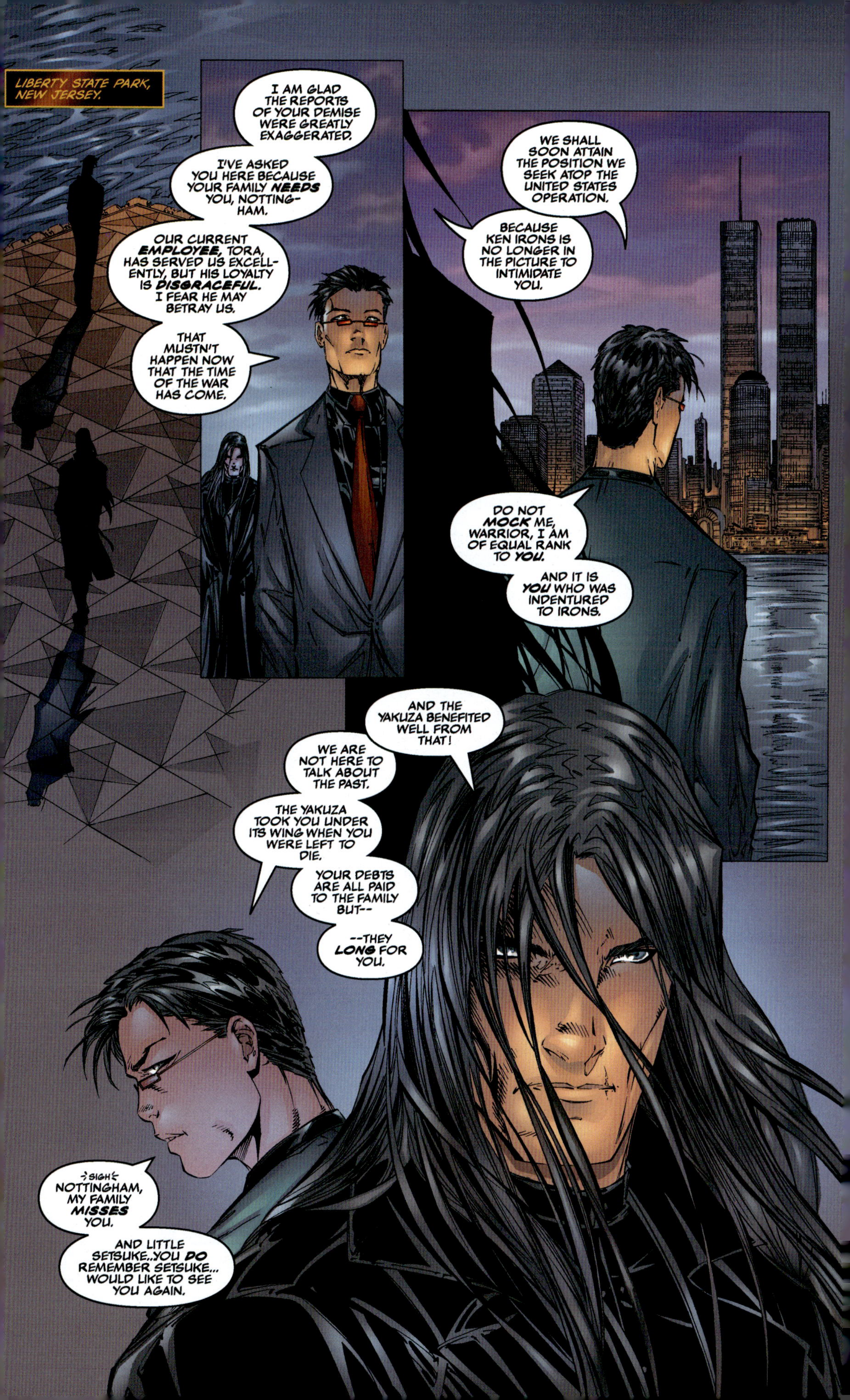
LIBERTY STATE PARK, NEW JERSEY.
I AM GLAD THE REPORTS OF YOUR DEMISE WERE GREATLY EXAGGERATED.
I'VE ASKED YOU HERE BECAUSE YOUR FAMILY NEEDS YOU, NOTTING-HAM.
OUR CURRENT EMPLOYEE, TORA, HAS SERVED US EXCELL-ENTLY, BUT HIS LOYALTY IS DISGRACEFUL. I FEAR HE MAY BETRAY US.
THAT MUSTN'T HAPPEN NOW THAT THE TIME OF THE WAR HAS COME.
WE SHALL SOON ATTAIN THE POSITION WE SEEK ATOP THE UNITED STATES OPERATION.
BECAUSE KEN IRONS IS NO LONGER IN THE PICTURE TO INTIMIDATE YOU.
DO NOT MOCK ME, WARRIOR, I AM OF EQUAL RANK TO YOU.
AND IT IS YOU WHO WAS INDENTURED TO IRONS.
AND THE YAKUZA BENEFITED WELL FROM THAT!
WE ARE NOT HERE TO TALK ABOUT THE PAST.
THE YAKUZA TOOK YOU UNDER ITS WING WHEN YOU WERE LEFT TO DIE.
YOUR DEBTS ARE ALL PAID TO THE FAMILY BUT--
--THEY LONG FOR YOU.
SIGH
NOTTINGHAM, MY FAMILY MISSES YOU.
AND LITTLE SETSUKE...YOU DO REMEMBER SETSUKE... WOULD LIKE TO SEE YOU AGAIN.

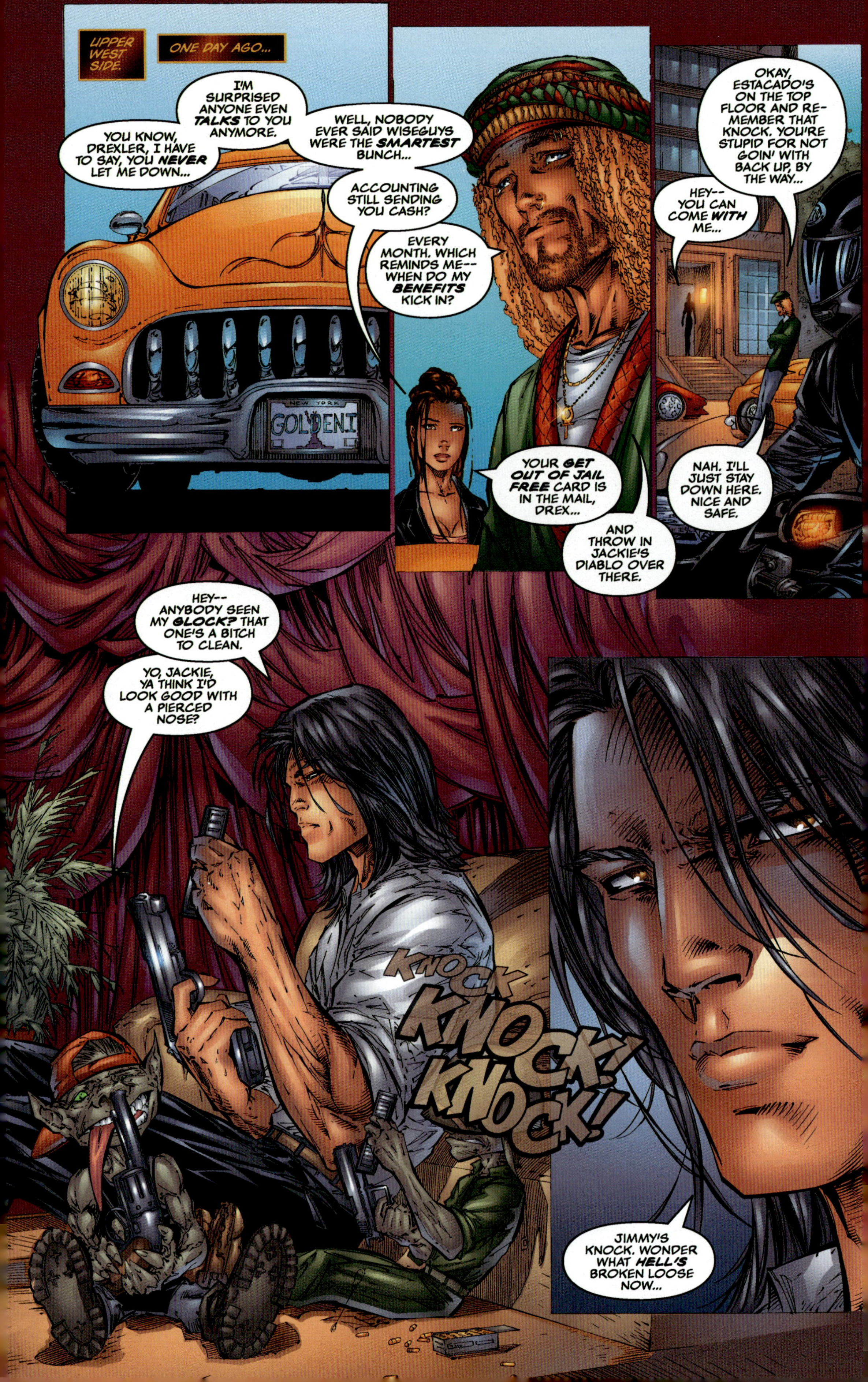
UPPER WEST SIDE.
ONE DAY AGO...
YOU KNOW, DREXLER, I HAVE TO SAY, YOU NEVER LET ME DOWN...
I'M SURPRISED ANYONE EVEN TALKS TO YOU ANYMORE.
WELL, NOBODY EVER SAID WISEGUYS WERE THE SMARTEST BUNCH...
ACCOUNTING STILL SENDING YOU CASH?
EVERY MONTH. WHICH REMINDS ME-- WHEN DO MY BENEFITS KICK IN?
NEW YORK
GOLDEN.I
YOUR GET OUT OF JAIL FREE CARD IS IN THE MAIL, DREX...
AND THROW IN JACKIE'S DIABLO OVER THERE.
OKAY, ESTACADO'S ON THE TOP FLOOR AND REMEMBER THAT KNOCK. YOU'RE STUPID FOR NOT GOIN' WITH BACK UP, BY THE WAY...
HEY-- YOU CAN COME WITH ME...
NAH. I'LL JUST STAY DOWN HERE. NICE AND SAFE.
HEY-- ANYBODY SEEN MY GLOCK? THAT ONE'S A BITCH TO CLEAN.
YO, JACKIE, YA THINK I'D LOOK GOOD WITH A PIERCED NOSE?
KNOCK
KNOCK! KNOCK!
JIMMY'S KNOCK. WONDER WHAT HELL'S BROKEN LOOSE NOW...

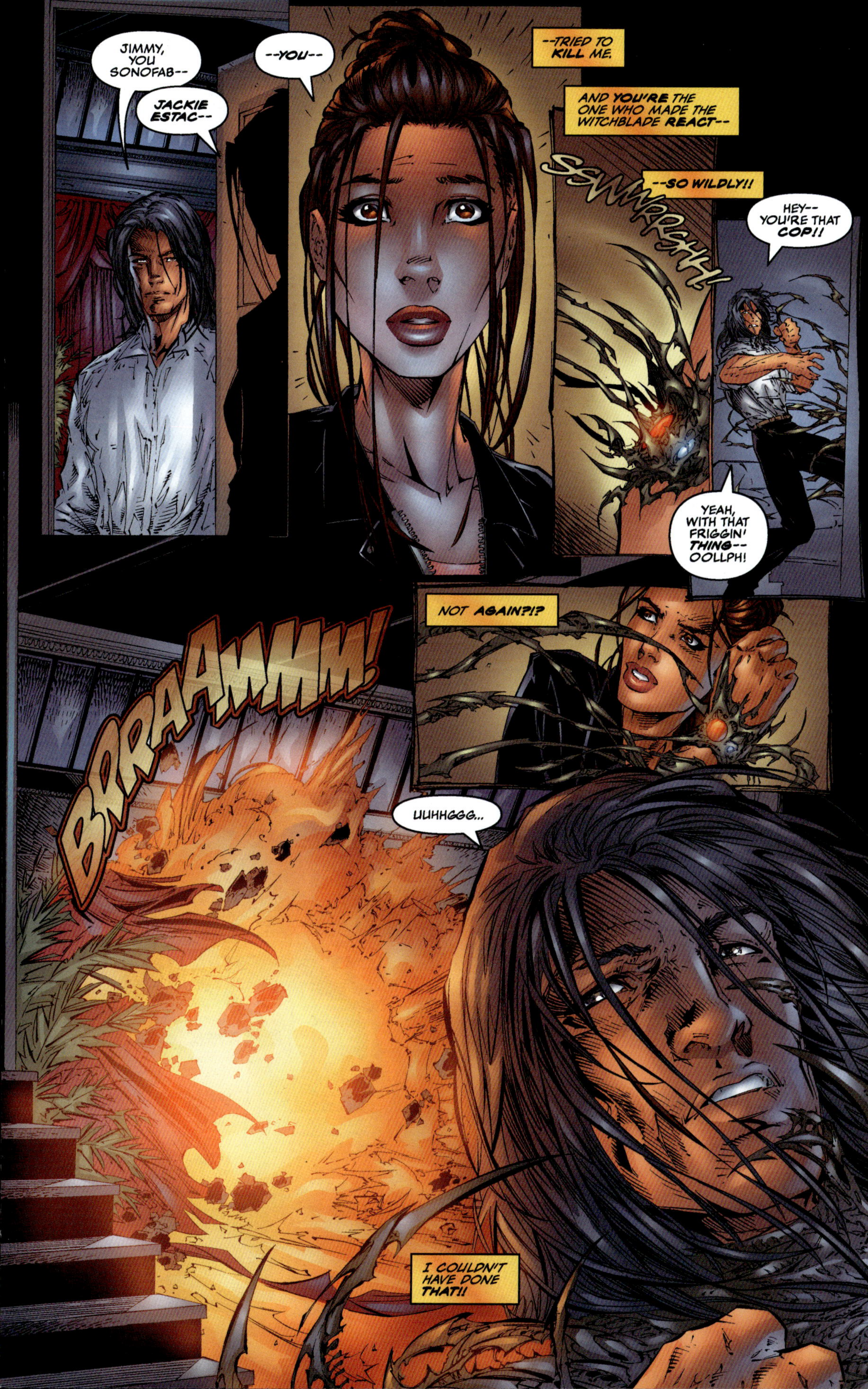
JIMMY, YOU SONOFAB--
JACKIE ESTAC--
--YOU--
--TRIED TO KILL ME.
AND YOU'RE THE ONE WHO MADE THE WITCHBLADE REACT--
SSWWRRSHH!
--SO WILDLY!!
HEY-- YOU'RE THAT COP!!
YEAH, WITH THAT FRIGGIN' THING-- OOLLPH!
NOT AGAIN?!?
BRRAAMMM!
UUHHGGG...
I COULDN'T HAVE DONE THAT!!

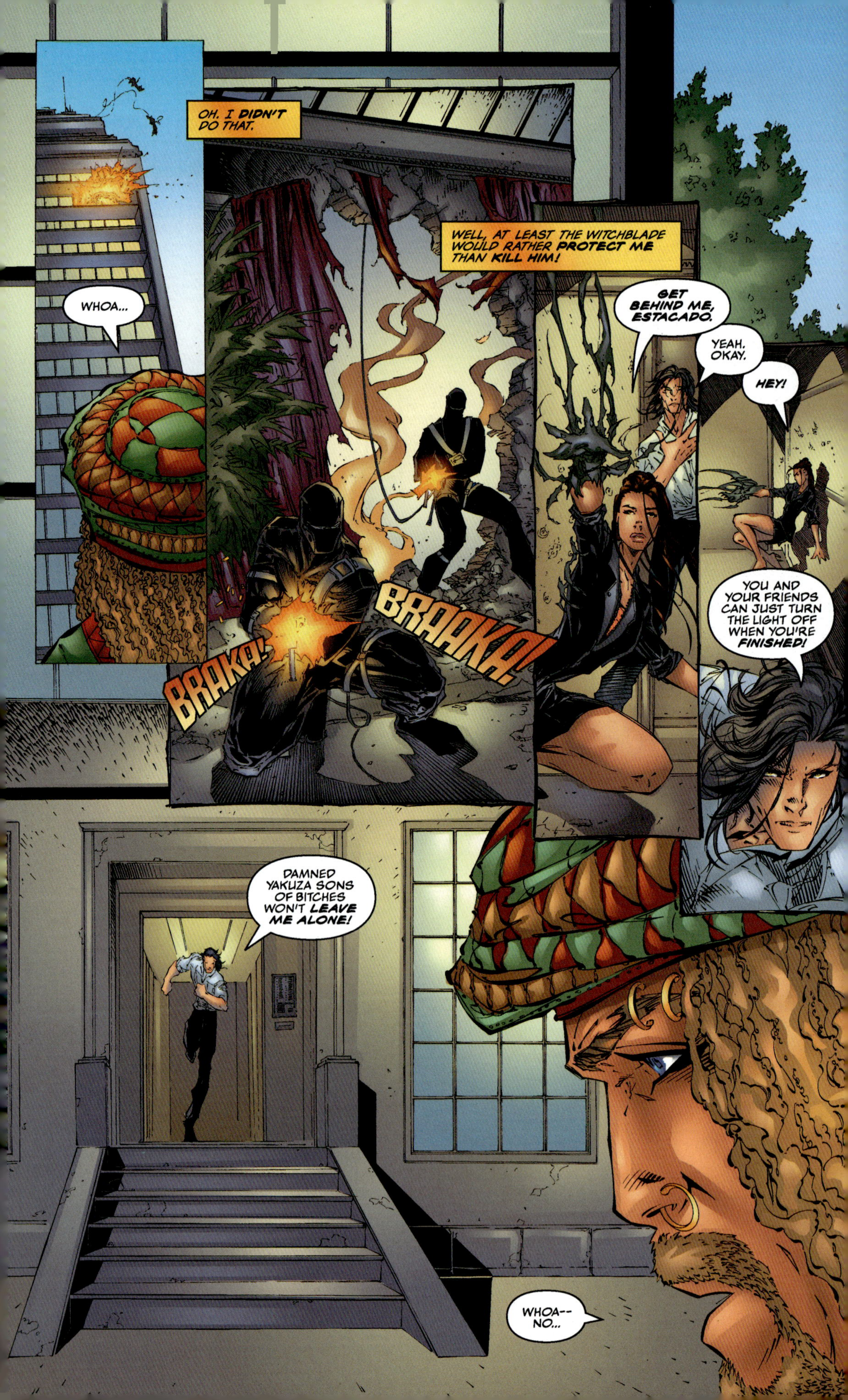
WHOA...
OH, I DIDN'T DO THAT.
WELL, AT LEAST THE WITCHBLADE WOULD RATHER PROTECT ME THAN KILL HIM!
BRAKA!
BRAAKA!
GET BEHIND ME, ESTACADO.
YEAH. OKAY.
HEY!
YOU AND YOUR FRIENDS CAN JUST TURN THE LIGHT OFF WHEN YOU'RE FINISHED!
DAMNED YAKUZA SONS OF BITCHES WON'T LEAVE ME ALONE!
WHOA-- NO...

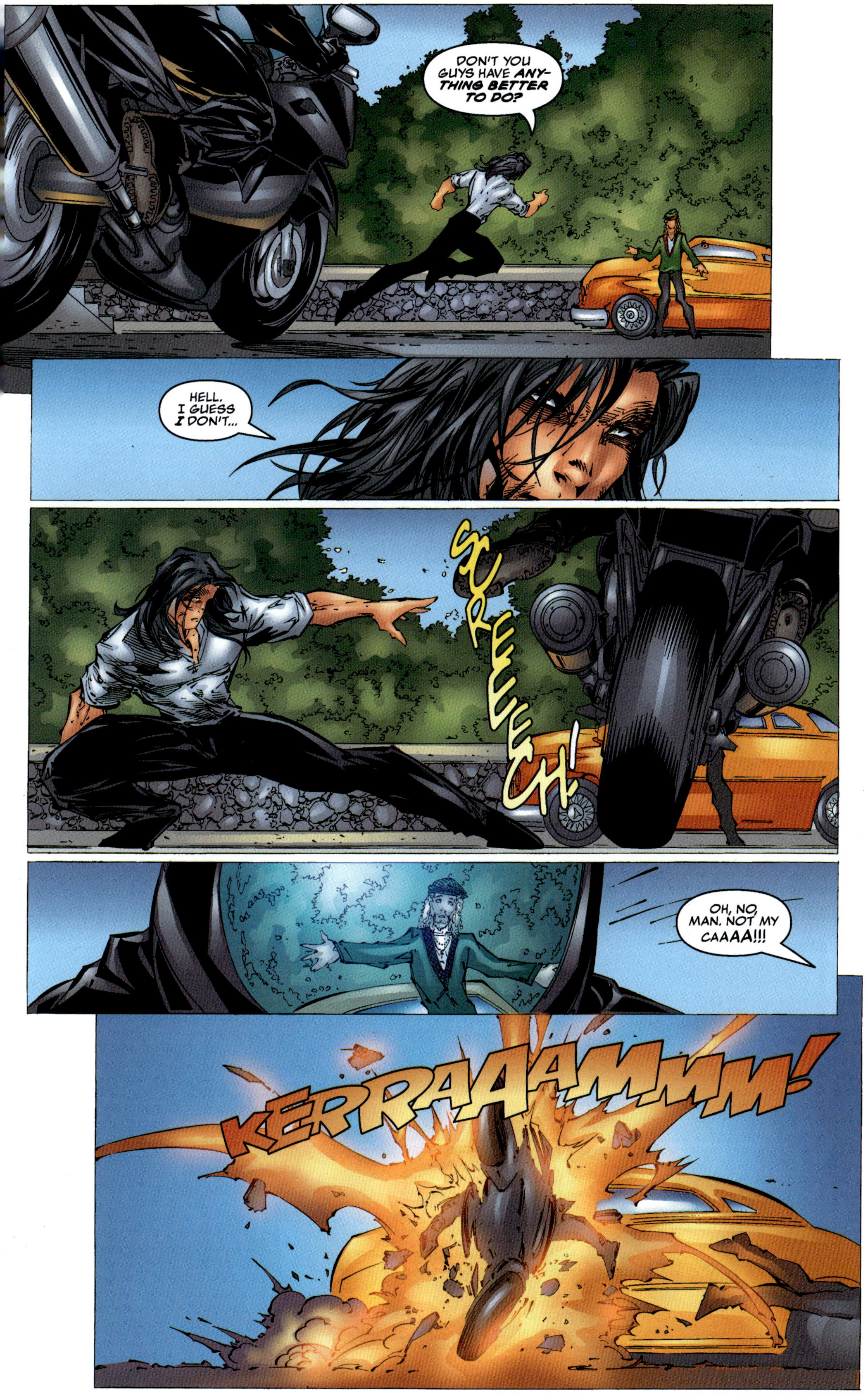
DON'T YOU GUYS HAVE ANY-THING BETTER TO DO?
HELL. I GUESS I DON'T...
SCREEEEECH!
OH, NO, MAN. NOT MY CAAAA!!!
KERRAAAMMMM!

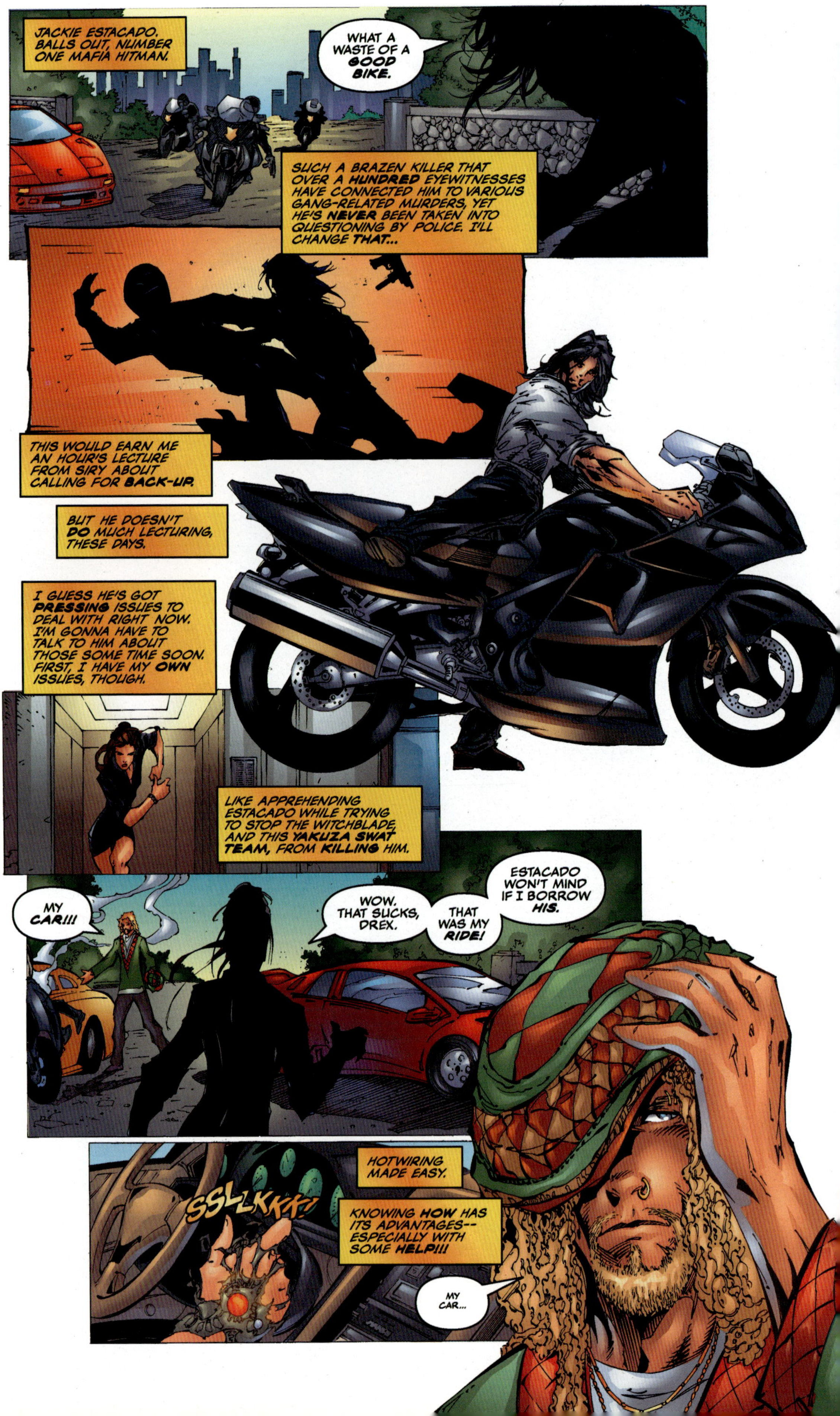
JACKIE ESTACADO. BALLS OUT, NUMBER ONE MAFIA HITMAN.
WHAT A WASTE OF A GOOD BIKE.
SUCH A BRAZEN KILLER THAT OVER A HUNDRED EYEWITNESSES HAVE CONNECTED HIM TO VARIOUS GANG-RELATED MURDERS, YET HE'S NEVER BEEN TAKEN INTO QUESTIONING BY POLICE. I'LL CHANGE THAT...
THIS WOULD EARN ME AN HOUR'S LECTURE FROM SIRY ABOUT CALLING FOR BACK-UP.
BUT HE DOESN'T DO MUCH LECTURING, THESE DAYS.
I GUESS HE'S GOT PRESSING ISSUES TO DEAL WITH RIGHT NOW. I'M GONNA HAVE TO TALK TO HIM ABOUT THOSE SOME TIME SOON. FIRST, I HAVE MY OWN ISSUES, THOUGH.
LIKE APPREHENDING ESTACADO WHILE TRYING TO STOP THE WITCHBLADE, AND THIS YAKUZA SWAT TEAM, FROM KILLING HIM.
MY CAR!!!
WOW. THAT SUCKS, DREX.
THAT WAS MY RIDE!
ESTACADO WON'T MIND IF I BORROW HIS.
HOTWIRING MADE EASY.
SSLLKKK!
KNOWING HOW HAS ITS ADVANTAGES-- ESPECIALLY WITH SOME HELP!!!
MY CAR...

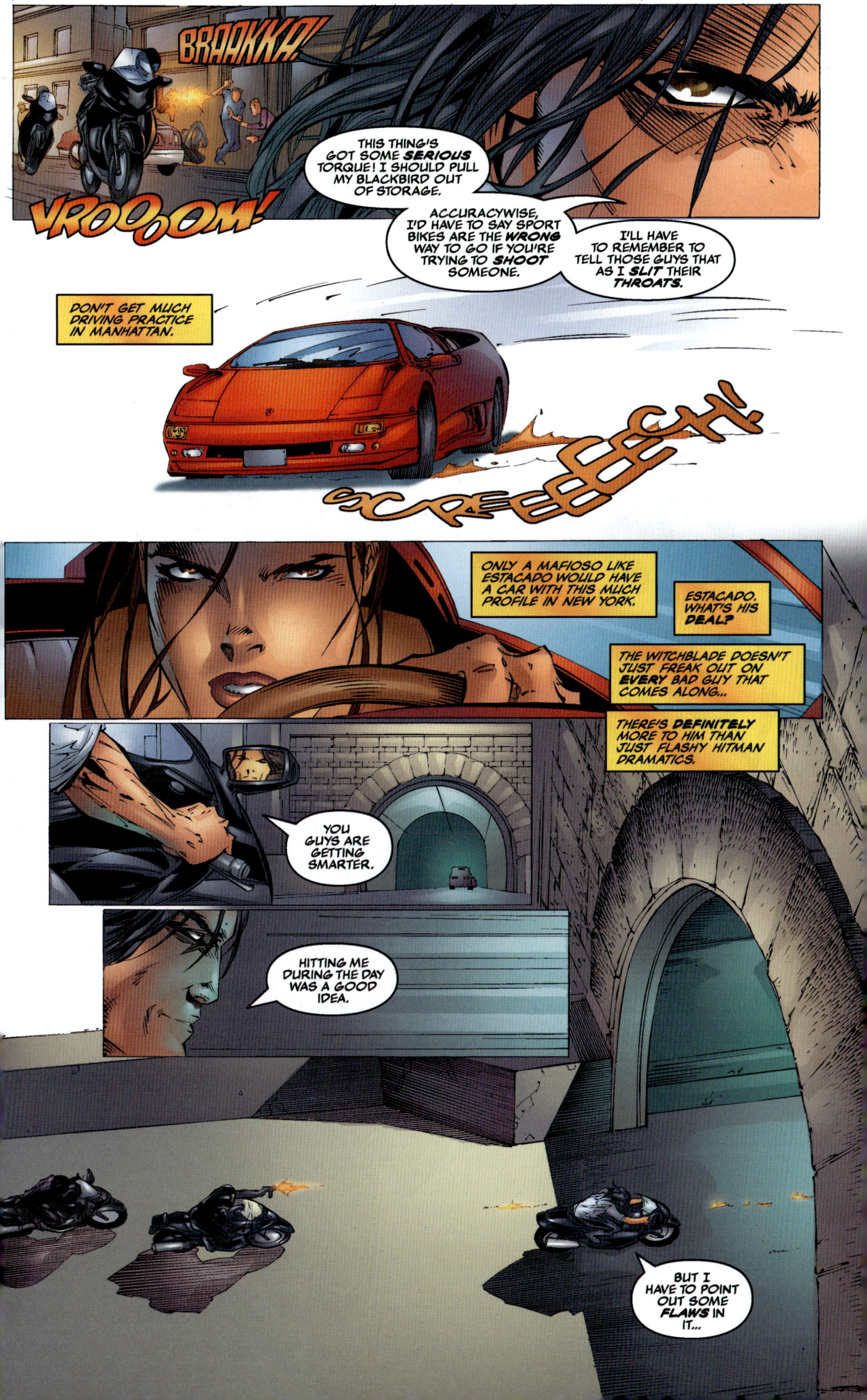
BRAAKKA!
VROOOOOM!
THIS THING'S GOT SOME SERIOUS TORQUE! I SHOULD PULL MY BLACKBIRD OUT OF STORAGE.
ACCURACYWISE, I'D HAVE TO SAY SPORT BIKES ARE THE WRONG WAY TO GO IF YOU'RE TRYING TO SHOOT SOMEONE.
I'LL HAVE TO REMEMBER TO TELL THOSE GUYS THAT AS I SLIT THEIR THROATS.
DON'T GET MUCH DRIVING PRACTICE IN MANHATTAN.
SCREEEEEECH!
ONLY A MAFIOSO LIKE ESTACADO WOULD HAVE A CAR WITH THIS MUCH PROFILE IN NEW YORK.
ESTACADO. WHAT'S HIS DEAL?
THE WITCHBLADE DOESN'T JUST FREAK OUT ON EVERY BAD GUY THAT COMES ALONG...
THERE'S DEFINITELY MORE TO HIM THAN JUST FLASHY HITMAN DRAMATICS.
YOU GUYS ARE GETTING SMARTER.
HITTING ME DURING THE DAY WAS A GOOD IDEA.
BUT I HAVE TO POINT OUT SOME FLAWS IN IT...

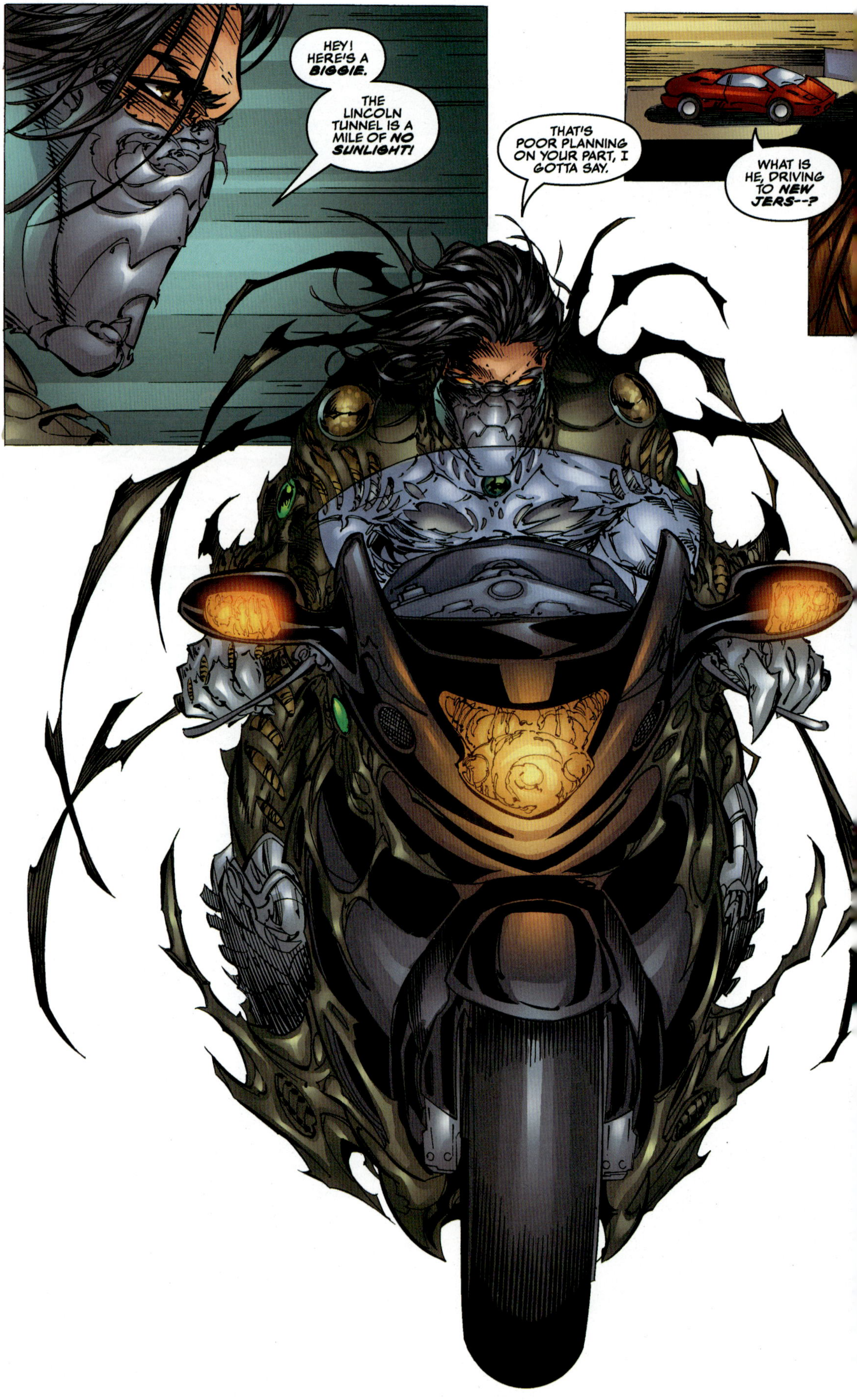
HEY! HERE'S A BIGGIE.
THE LINCOLN TUNNEL IS A MILE OF NO SUNLIGHT!
THAT'S POOR PLANNING ON YOUR PART, I GOTTA SAY.
WHAT IS HE, DRIVING TO NEW JERS--?

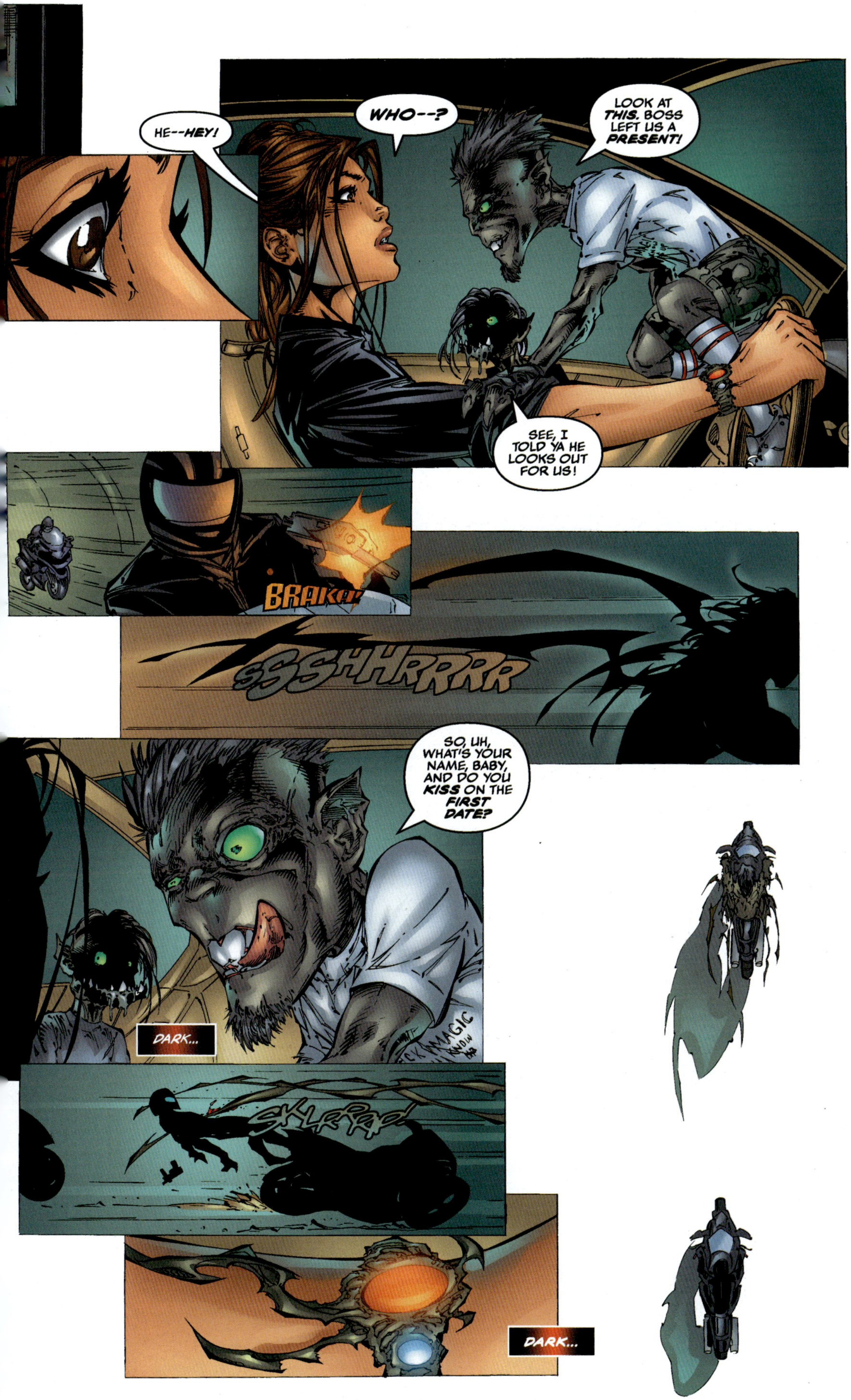
HE--HEY!
WHO--?
LOOK AT THIS. BOSS LEFT US A PRESENT!
SEE, I TOLD YA HE LOOKS OUT FOR US!
BRAKA!
SSSHHRRRRR
SO, UH, WHAT'S YOUR NAME, BABY, AND DO YOU KISS ON THE FIRST DATE?
DARK...
DARK...

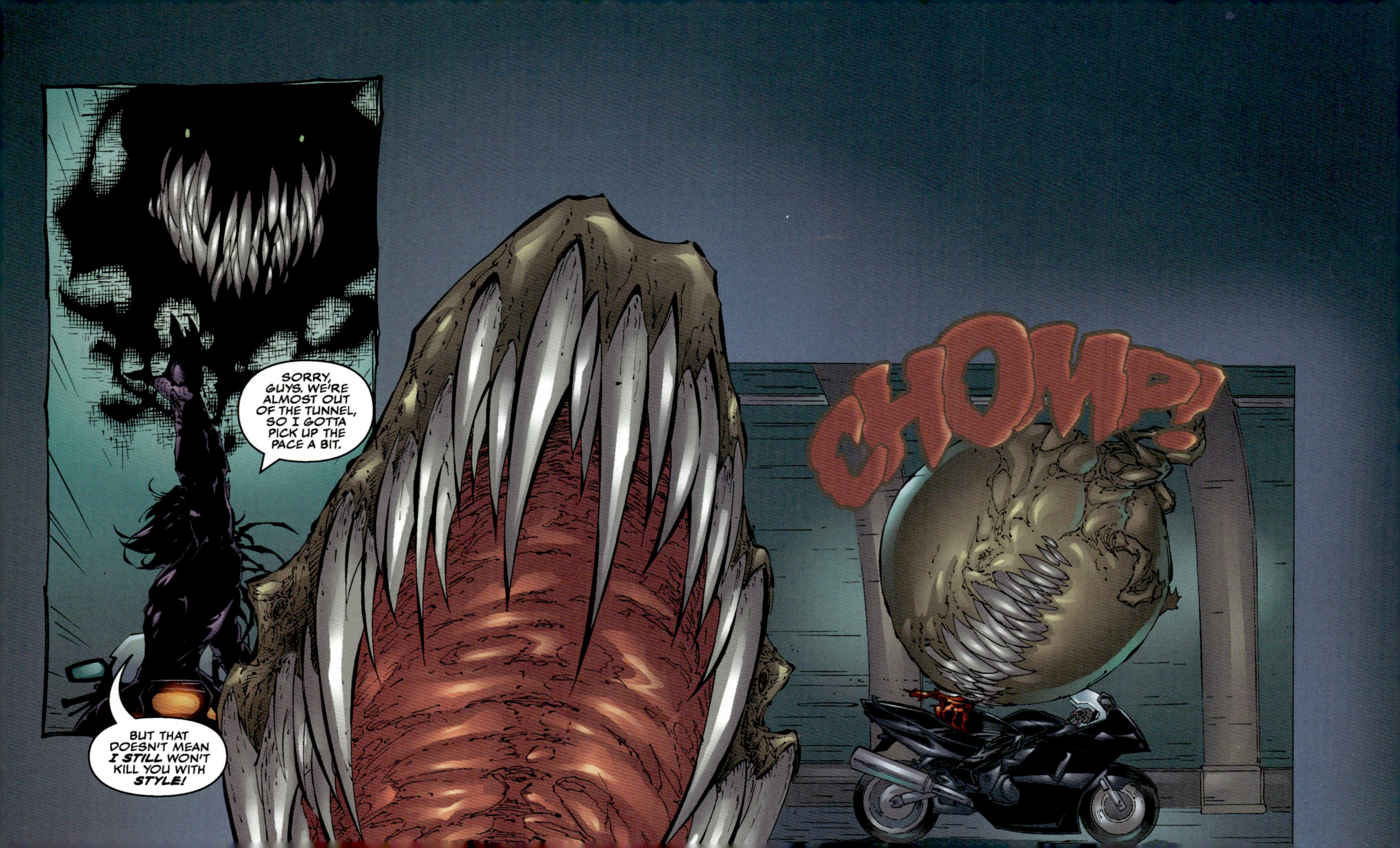
SORRY, GUYS, WE'RE ALMOST OUT OF THE TUNNEL, SO I GOTTA PICK UP THE PACE A BIT.
BUT THAT DOESN'T MEAN *I STILL* WON'T KILL YOU WITH *STYLE!*
CHOMP!

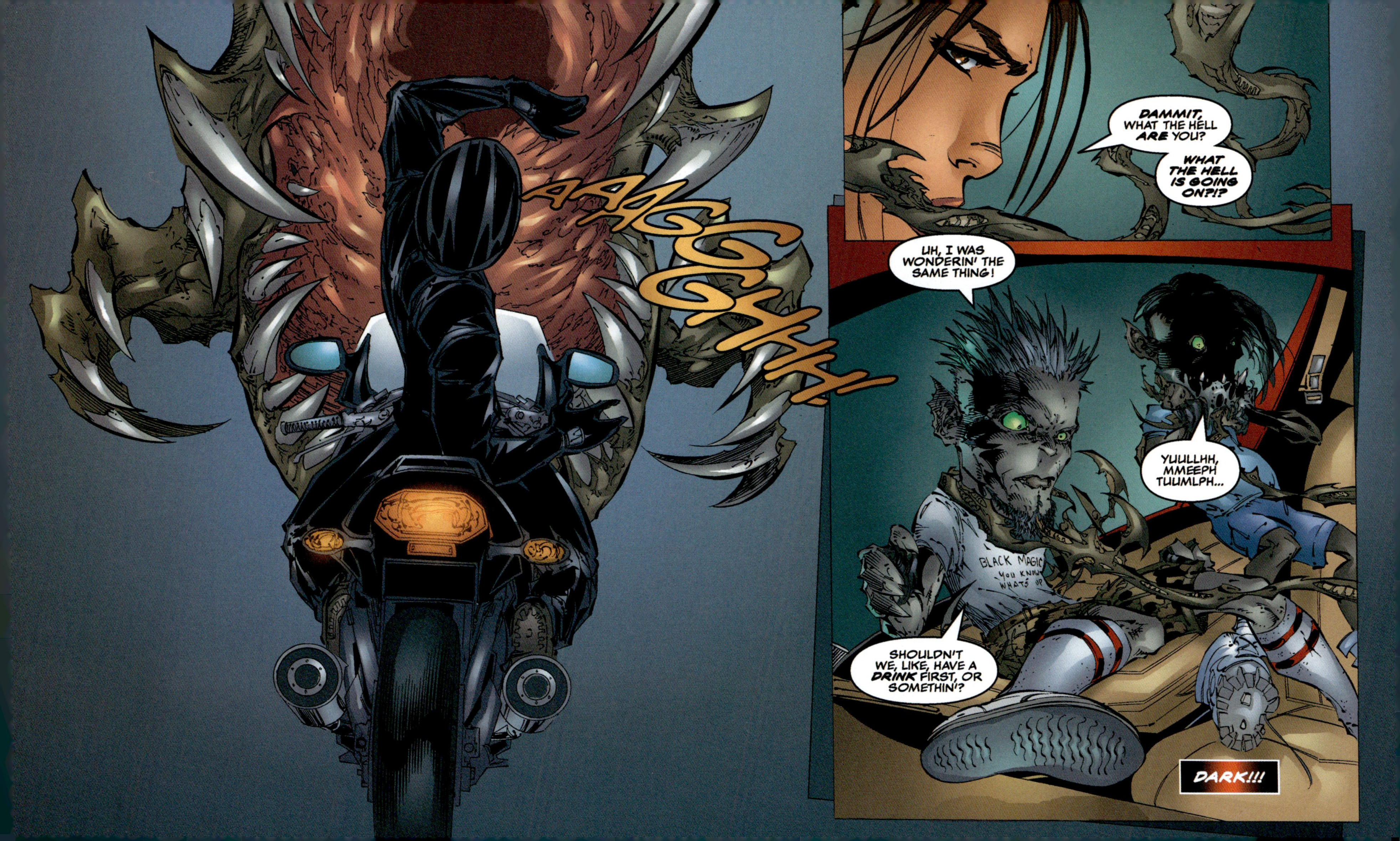
AAAGGGHHH!
DAMMIT, WHAT THE HELL ARE YOU?
WHAT THE HELL IS GOING ON?!?
UH, I WAS WONDERIN' THE SAME THING!
YUULLHH, MMEEPH TUUMLPH...
SHOULDN'T WE, LIKE, HAVE A DRINK FIRST, OR SOMETHIN'?
BLACK MAGIC
YOU KNOW WHAT'S UP
DARK!!!

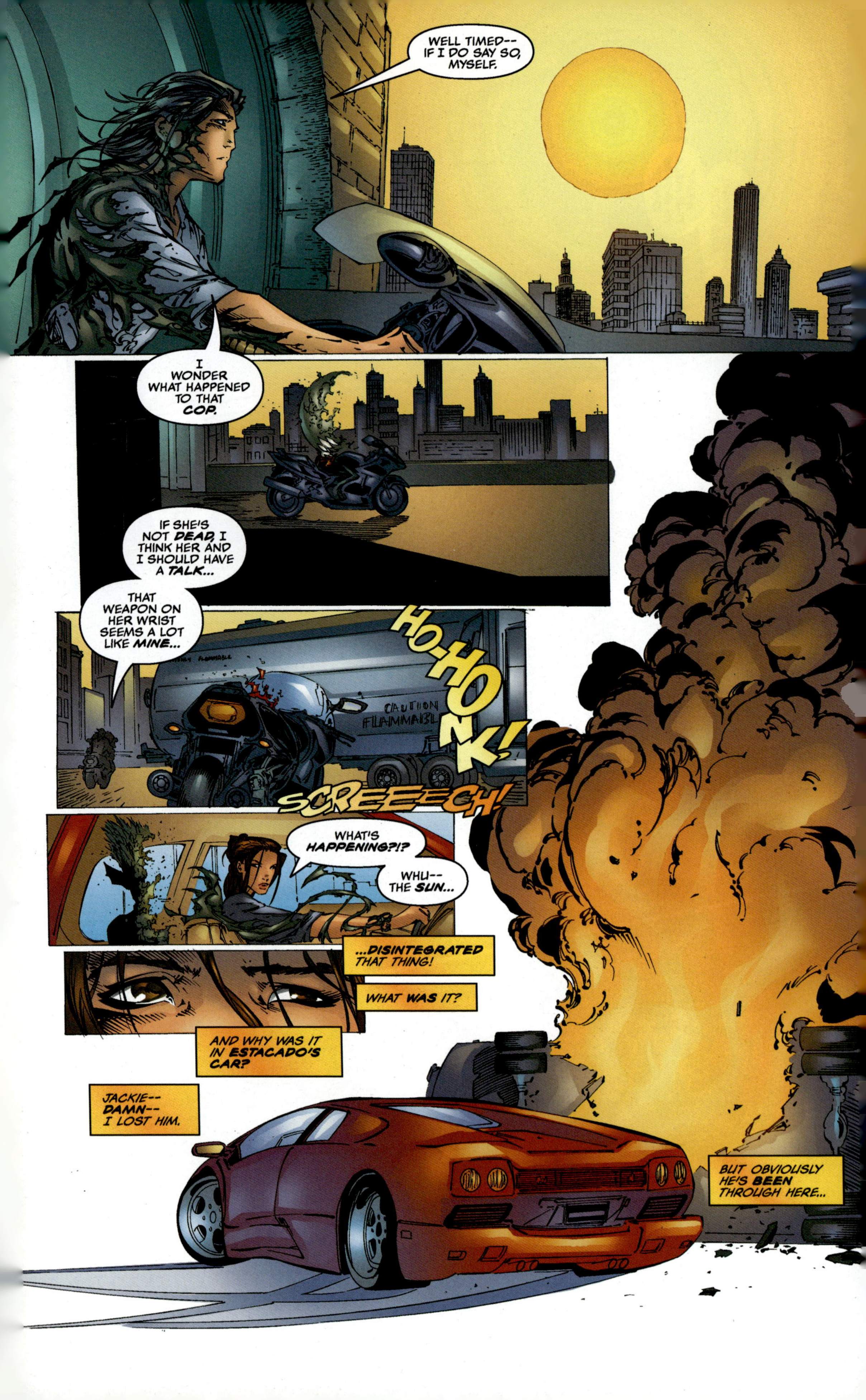

WELL TIMED-- IF I DO SAY SO, MYSELF.
I WONDER WHAT HAPPENED TO THAT COP.
IF SHE'S NOT DEAD, I THINK HER AND I SHOULD HAVE A TALK...
THAT WEAPON ON HER WRIST SEEMS A LOT LIKE MINE...
HO-HONK!
CAUTION FLAMMABL
SCREEEECH!
WHAT'S HAPPENING?!?
WHU-- THE SUN...
...DISINTEGRATED THAT THING!
WHAT WAS IT?
AND WHY WAS IT IN ESTACADO'S CAR?
JACKIE-- DAMN-- I LOST HIM.
BUT OBVIOUSLY HE'S BEEN THROUGH HERE...

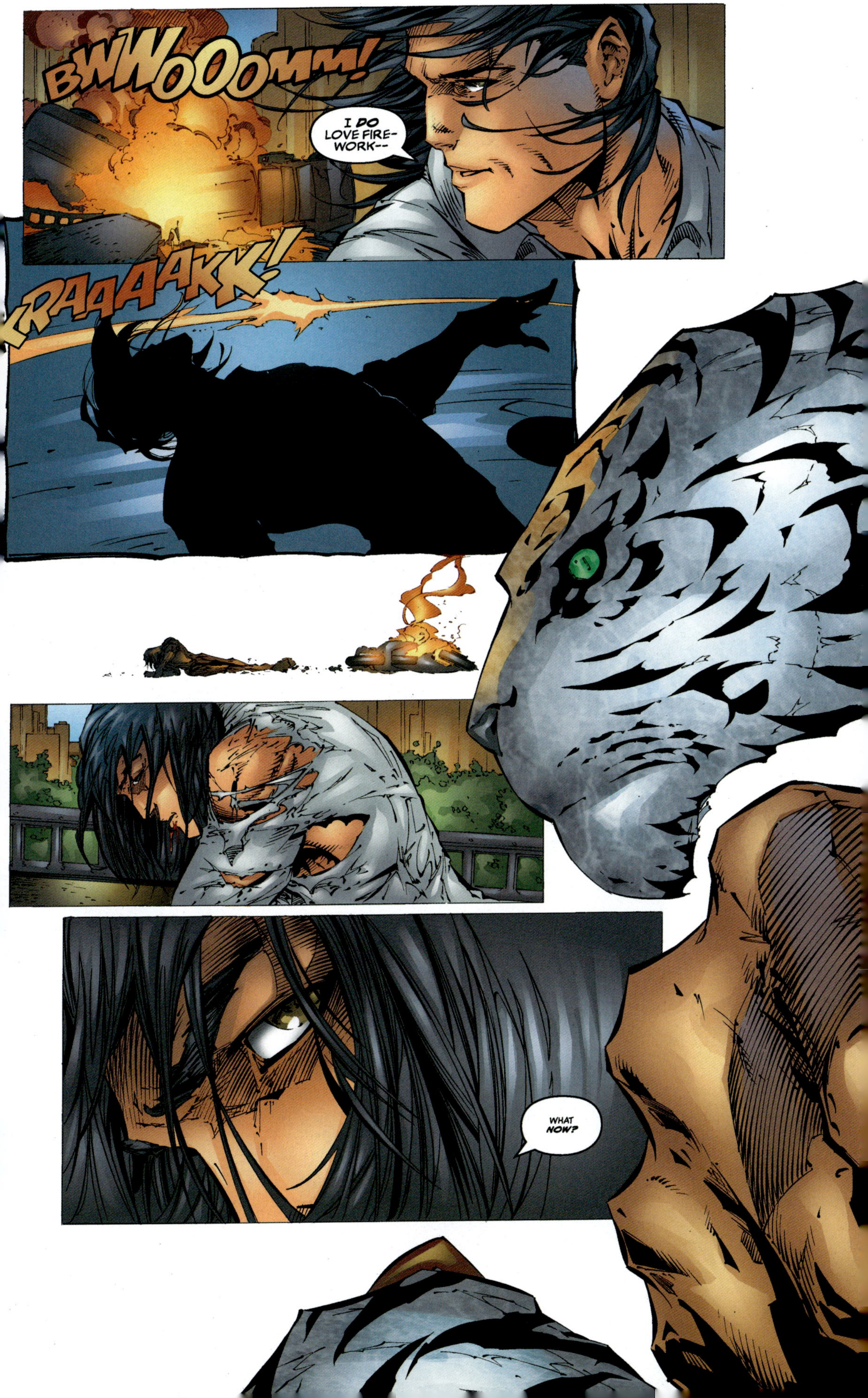
BWWOOOOMMM!
I DO LOVE FIRE-WORK--
KRAAAAKK!
WHAT NOW?

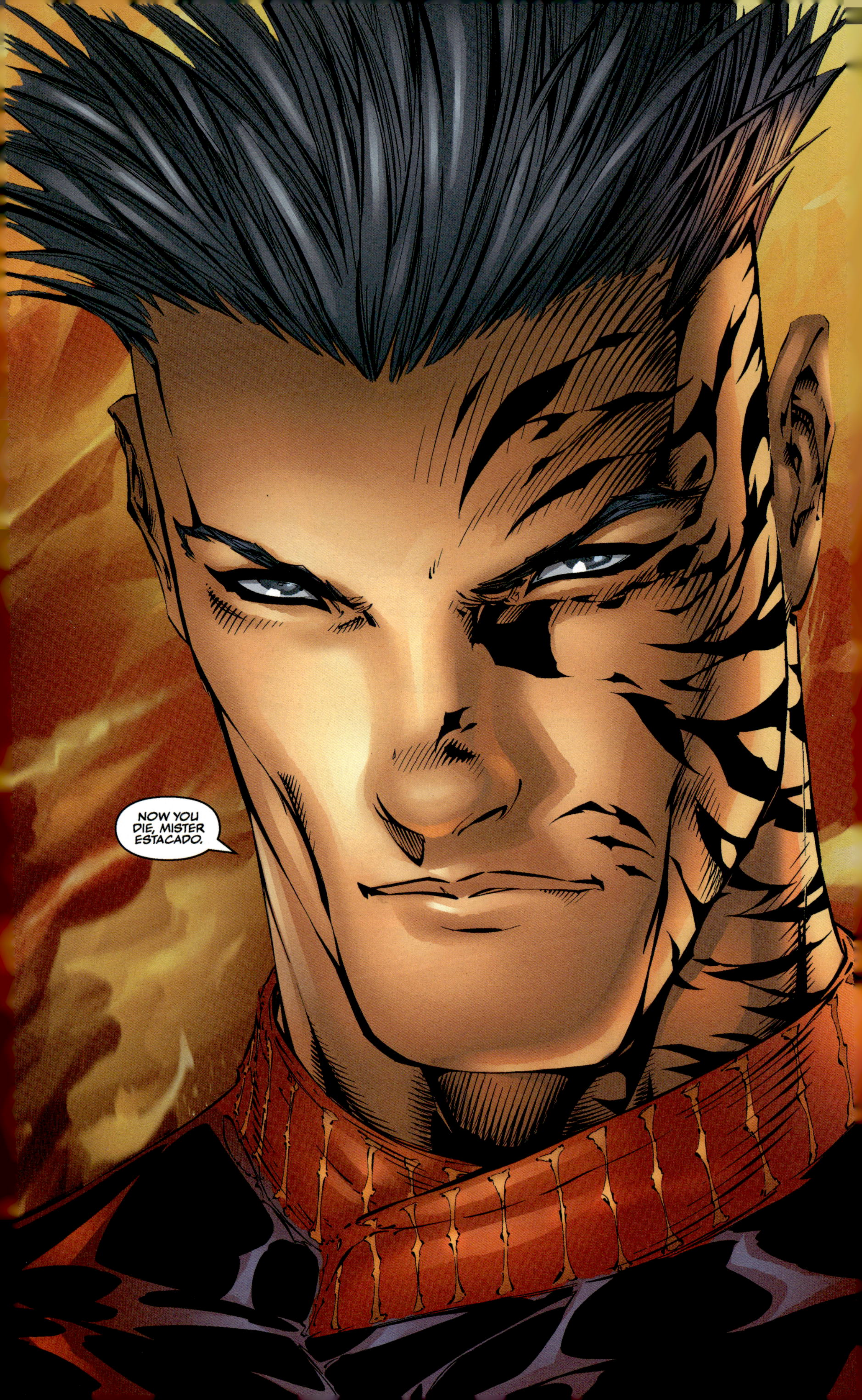
NOW YOU DIE, MISTER ESTACADO.

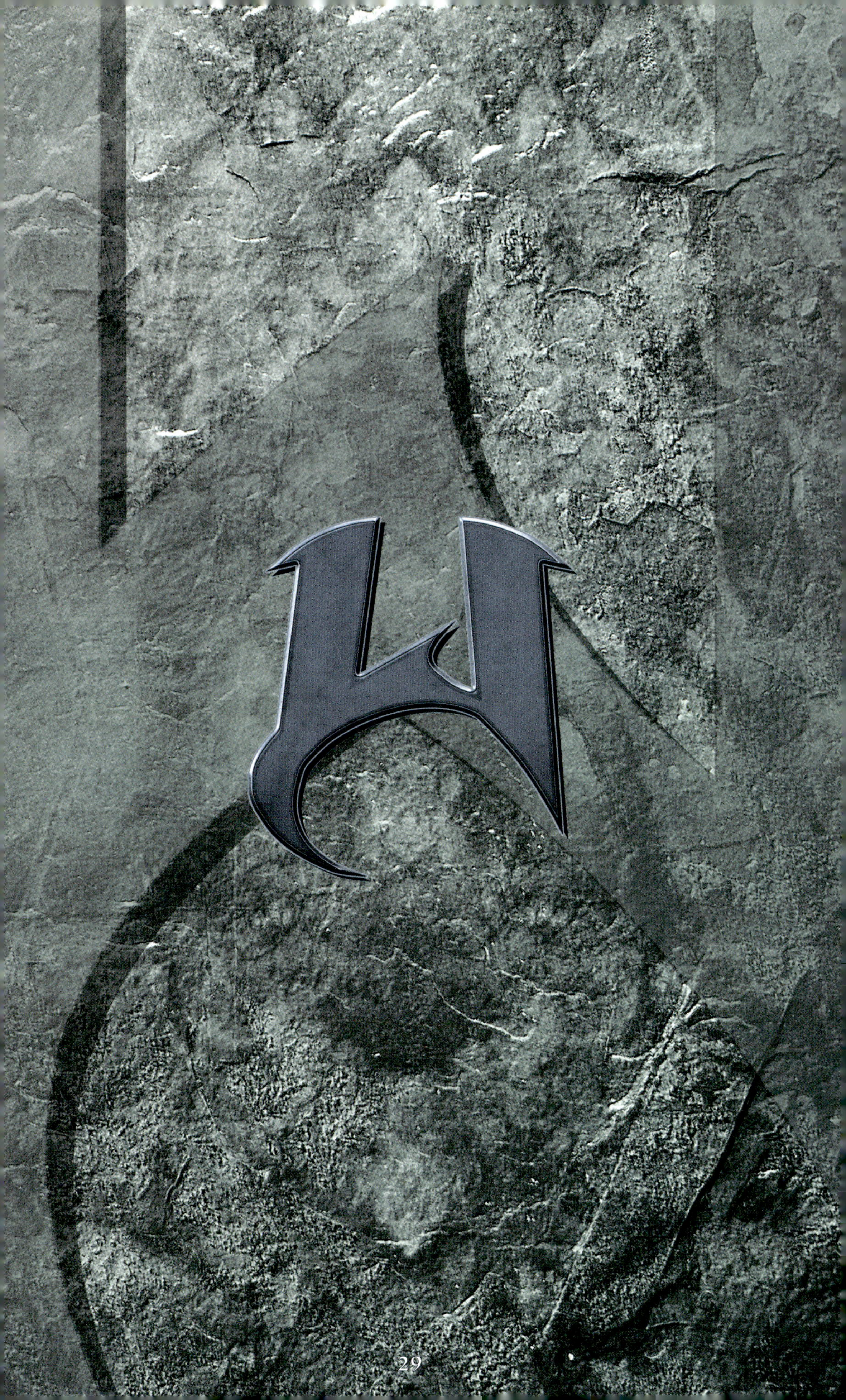

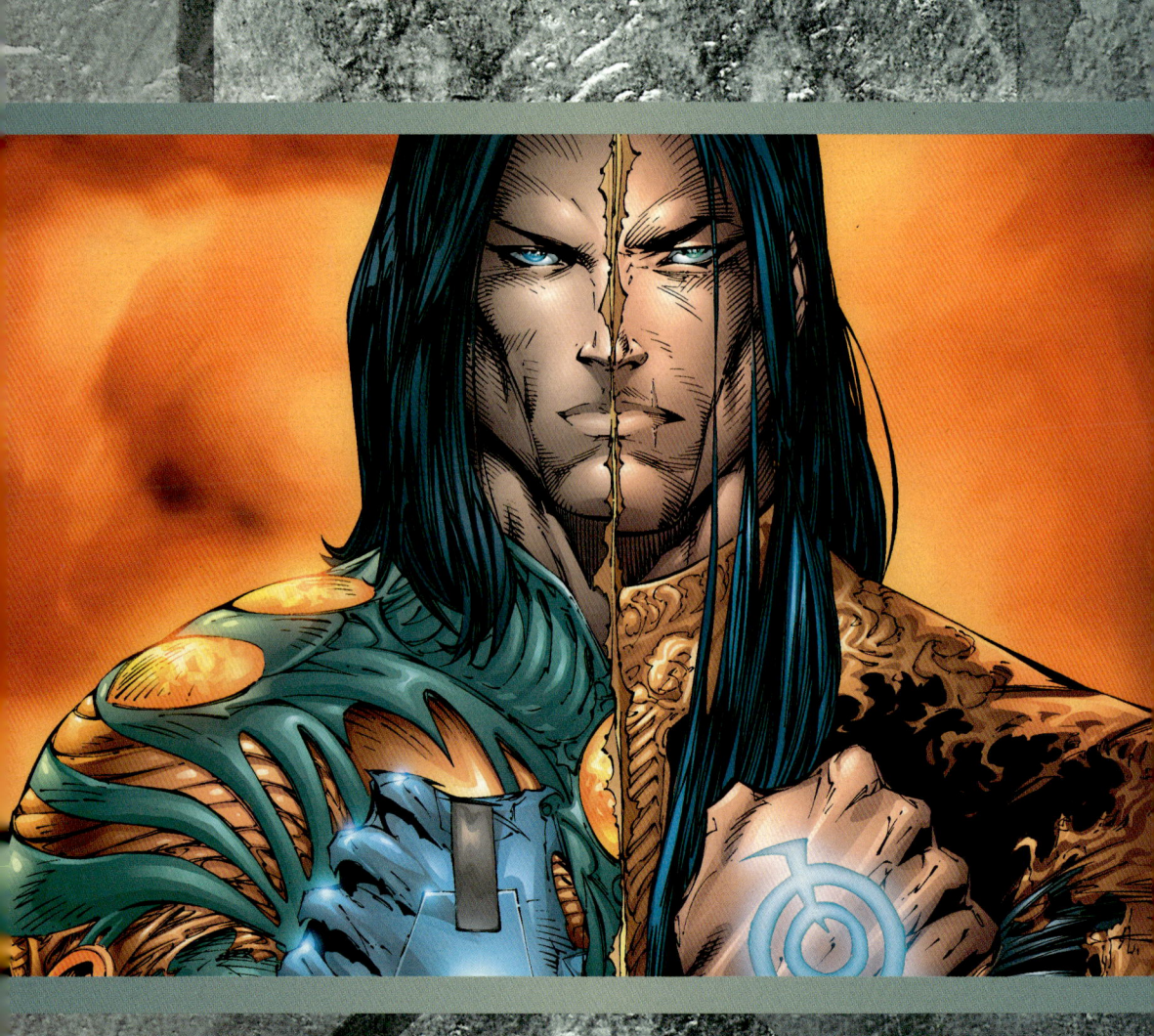

FAMILY TIES part 2: *The Darkness*
issue #9

story: David Wohl and Christina Z.
pencils: Marc Silvestri
inks: Matt "Batt" Banning
colors: Richard Isanove, JD Smith and Matt Nelson
pencil finishes: Richard Bennett

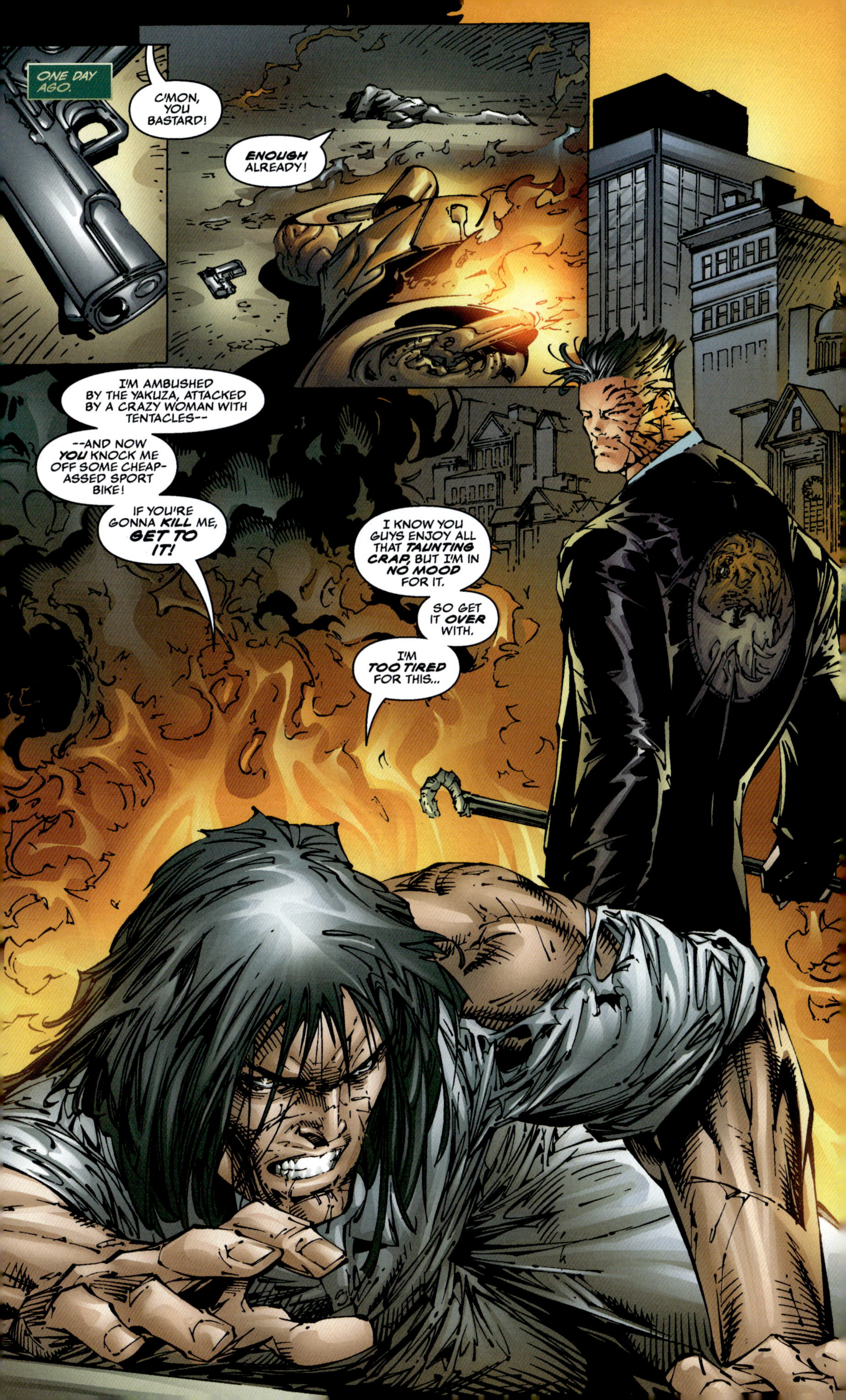
ONE DAY AGO.
C'MON, YOU BASTARD!
ENOUGH ALREADY!
I'M AMBUSHED BY THE YAKUZA, ATTACKED BY A CRAZY WOMAN WITH TENTACLES--
--AND NOW YOU KNOCK ME OFF SOME CHEAP-ASSED SPORT BIKE!
IF YOU'RE GONNA KILL ME, GET TO IT!
I KNOW YOU GUYS ENJOY ALL THAT TAUNTING CRAP, BUT I'M IN NO MOOD FOR IT.
SO GET IT OVER WITH.
I'M TOO TIRED FOR THIS...

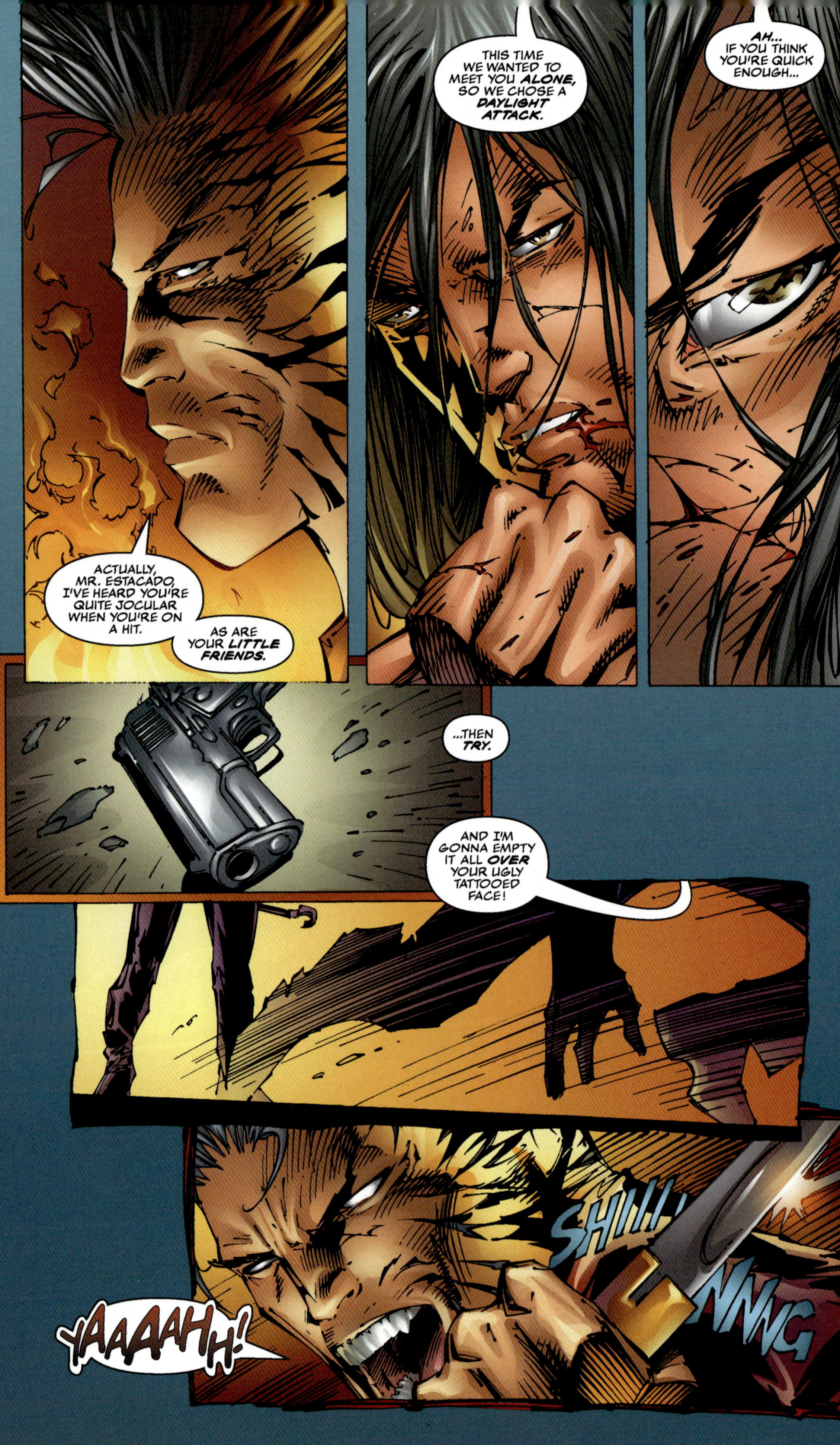
ACTUALLY, MR. ESTACADO, I'VE HEARD YOU'RE QUITE JOCULAR WHEN YOU'RE ON A HIT.
AS ARE YOUR LITTLE FRIENDS.
THIS TIME WE WANTED TO MEET YOU ALONE, SO WE CHOSE A DAYLIGHT ATTACK.
AH... IF YOU THINK YOU'RE QUICK ENOUGH...
...THEN TRY.
AND I'M GONNA EMPTY IT ALL OVER YOUR UGLY TATTOOED FACE!
YAAAAHH!

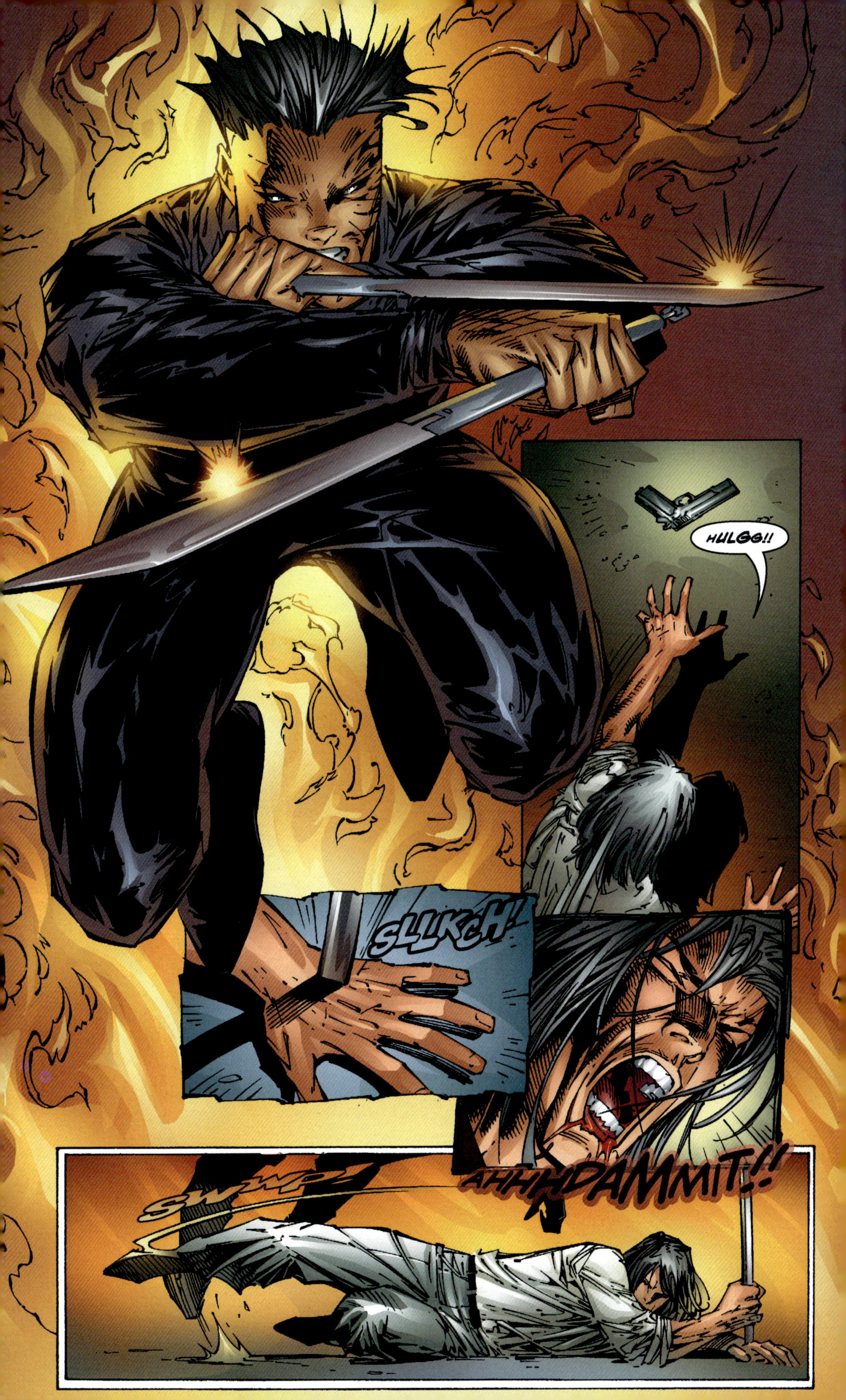

HULGG!!
SLLKCH!
SWPT
AHHHDAMMIT!!

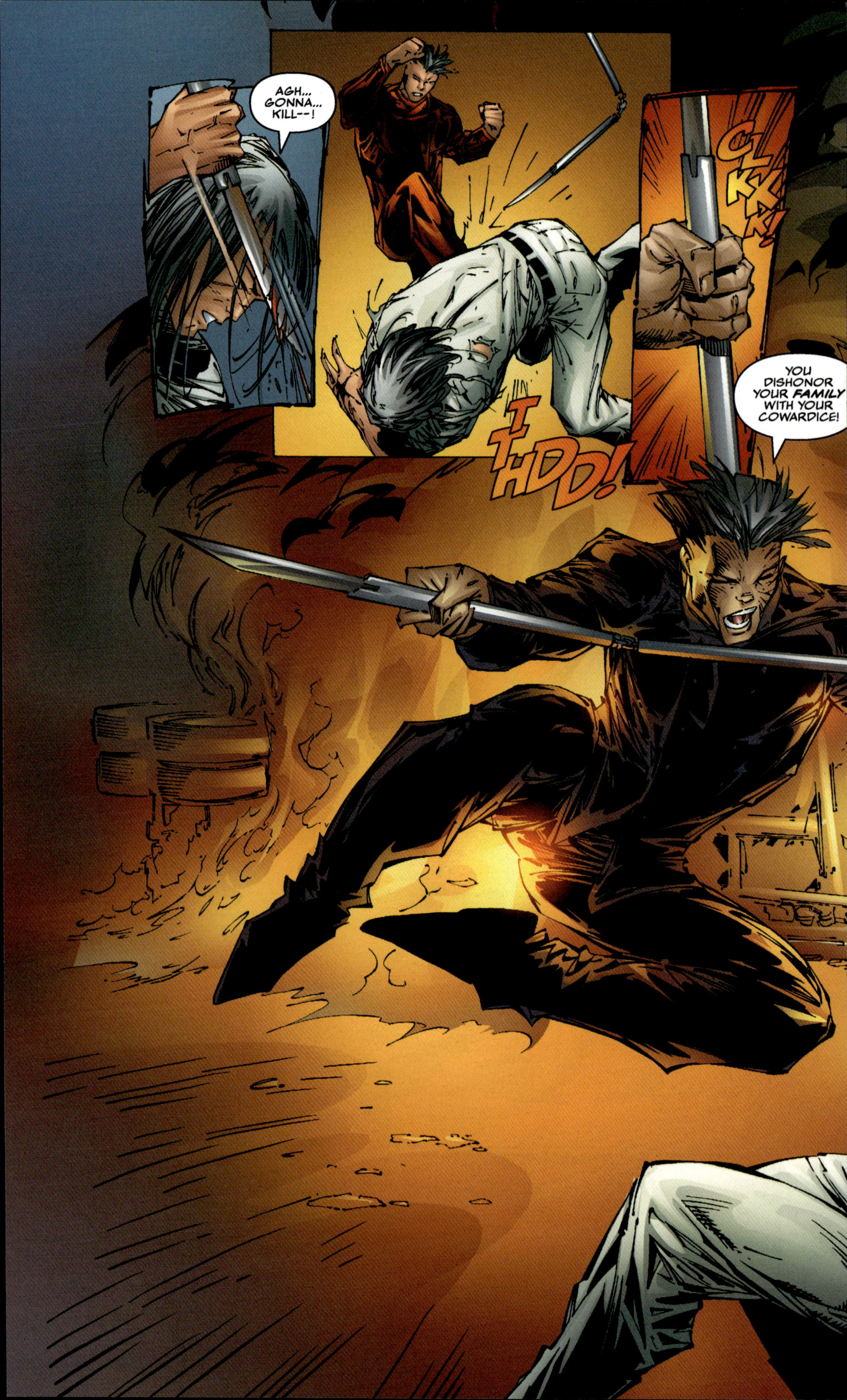
AGH... GONNA... KILL--!
THDD!
CLKK!
YOU DISHONOR YOUR FAMILY WITH YOUR COWARDICE!

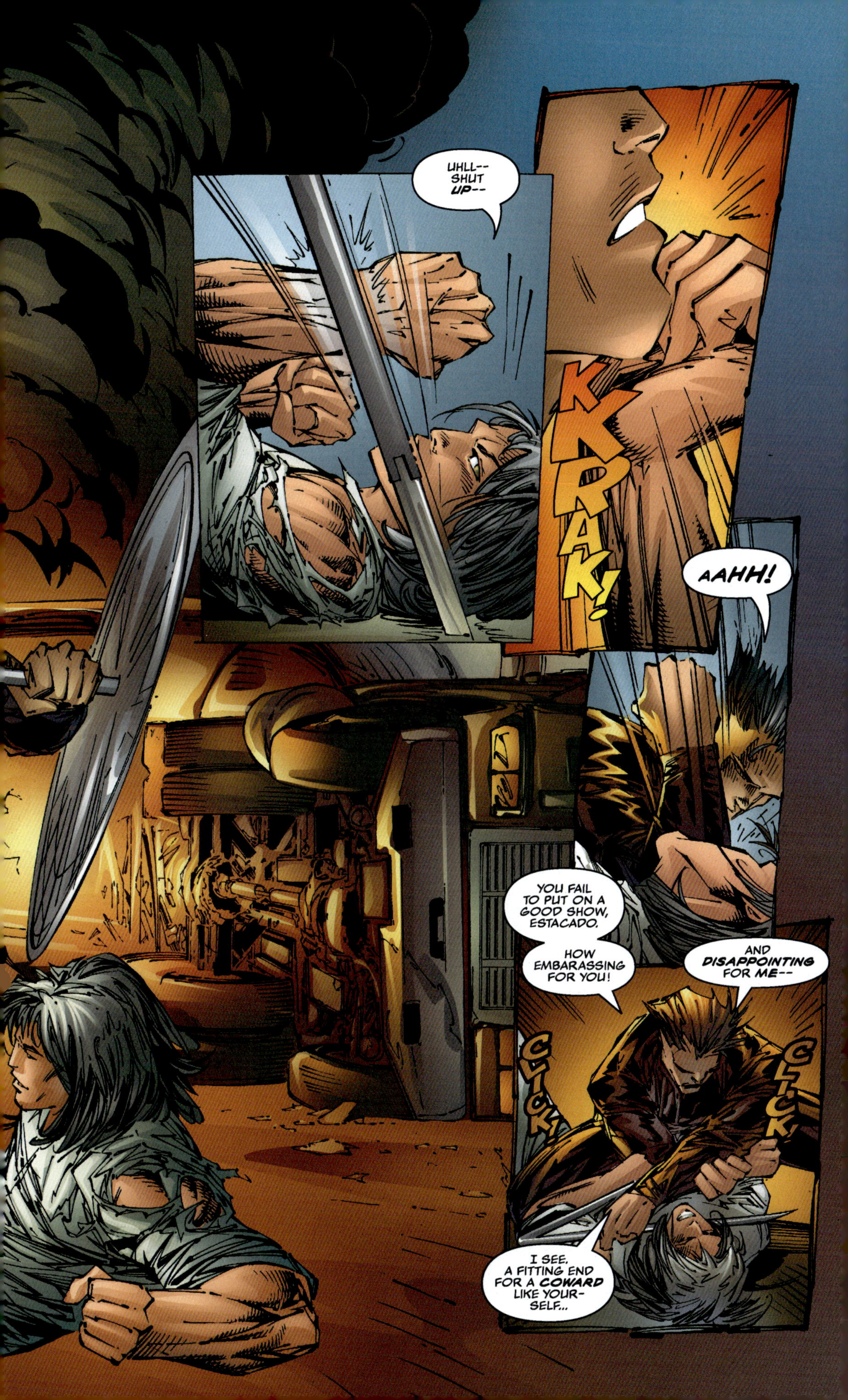
UHLL--
SHUT
UP--
KKRAK!
AAHH!
YOU FAIL TO PUT ON A GOOD SHOW, ESTACADO.
HOW EMBARASSING FOR YOU!
AND DISAPPOINTING FOR ME--
CLICK
CLICK
I SEE. A FITTING END FOR A COWARD LIKE YOURSELF...

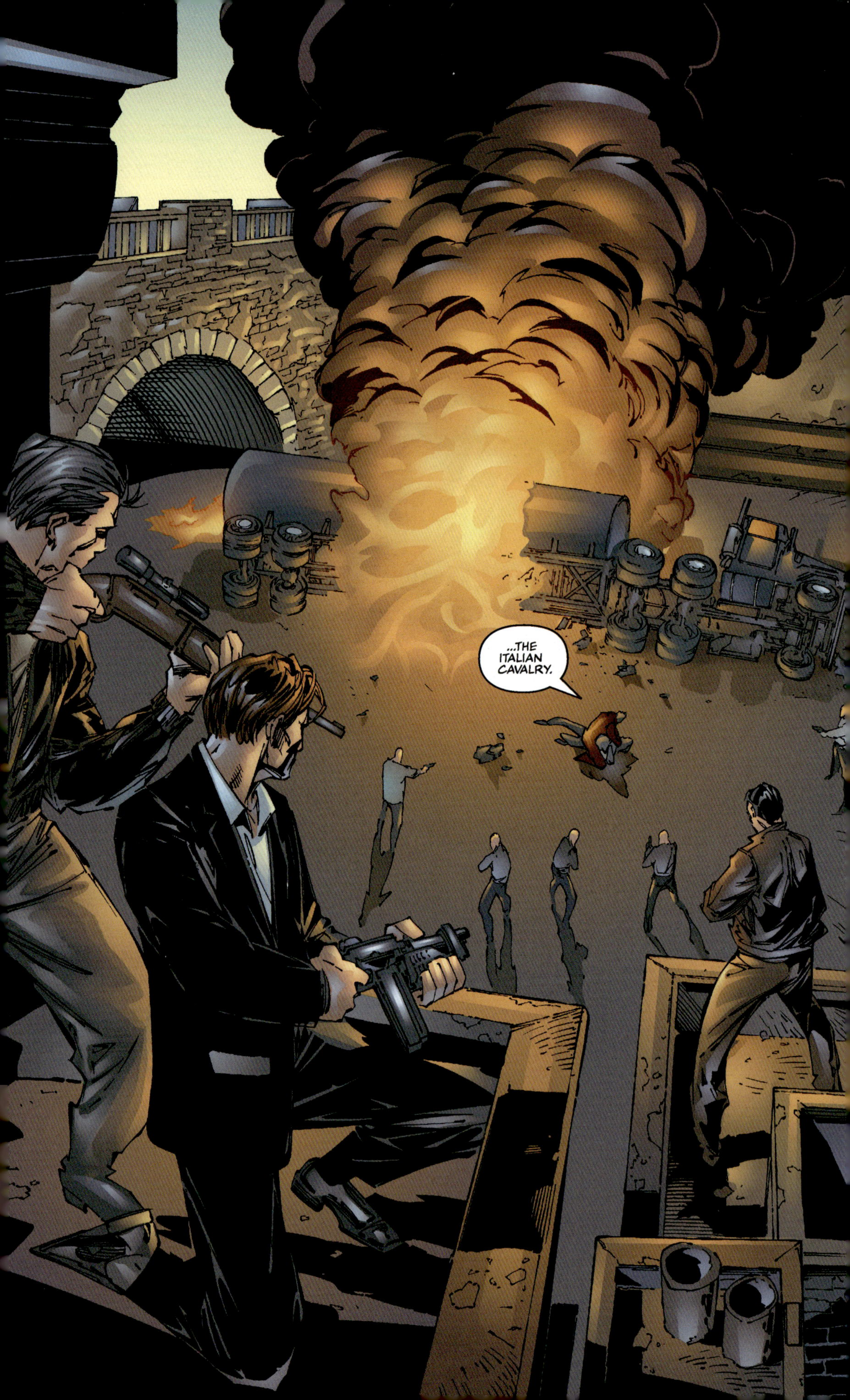
...THE ITALIAN CAVALRY.

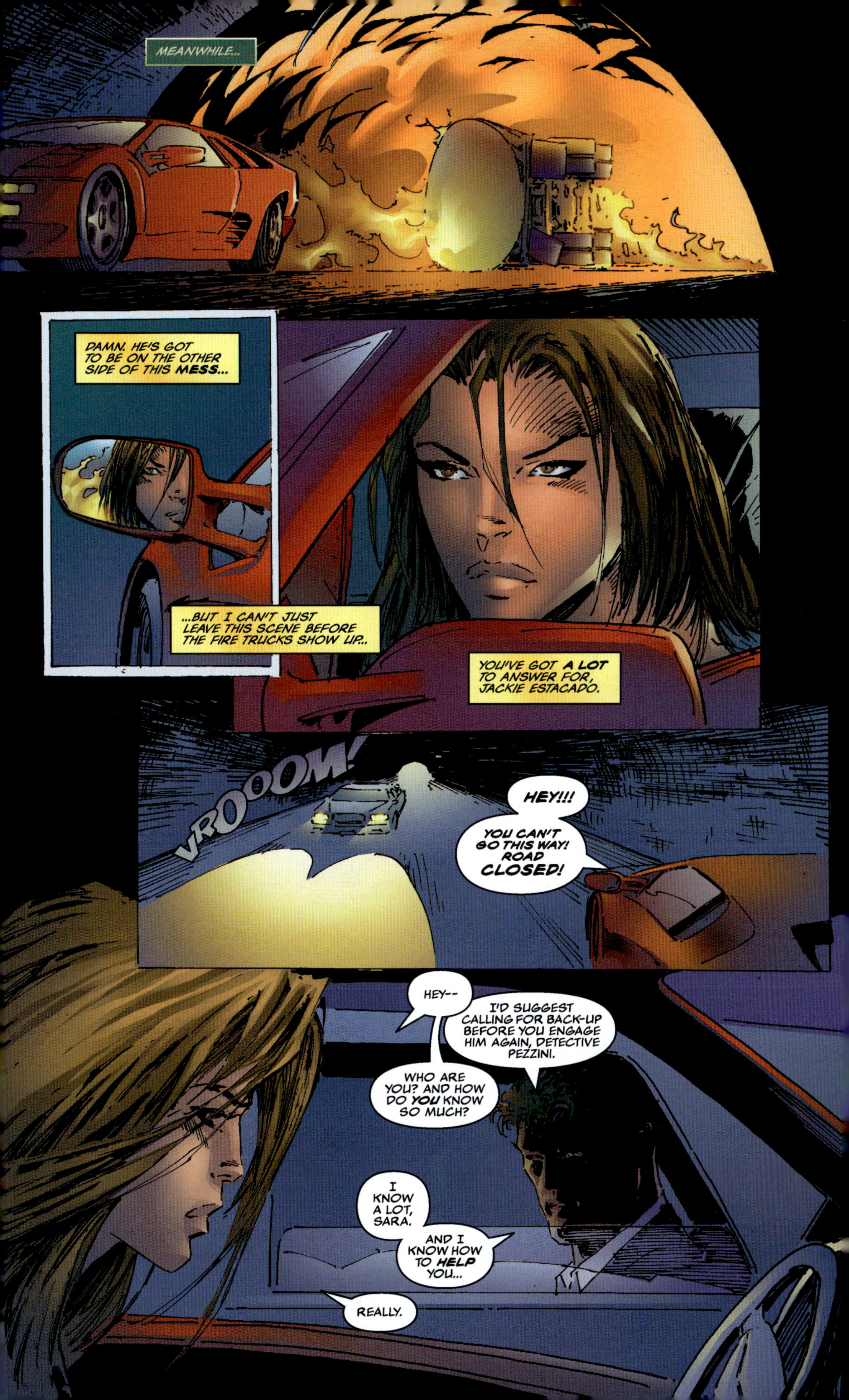
MEANWHILE...
DAMN. HE'S GOT TO BE ON THE OTHER SIDE OF THIS MESS...
...BUT I CAN'T JUST LEAVE THIS SCENE BEFORE THE FIRE TRUCKS SHOW UP...
YOU'VE GOT A LOT TO ANSWER FOR, JACKIE ESTACADO.
VROOOM!
HEY!!!
YOU CAN'T GO THIS WAY! ROAD CLOSED!
HEY--
I'D SUGGEST CALLING FOR BACK-UP BEFORE YOU ENGAGE HIM AGAIN, DETECTIVE PEZZINI.
WHO ARE YOU? AND HOW DO YOU KNOW SO MUCH?
I KNOW A LOT, SARA.
AND I KNOW HOW TO HELP YOU...
REALLY.

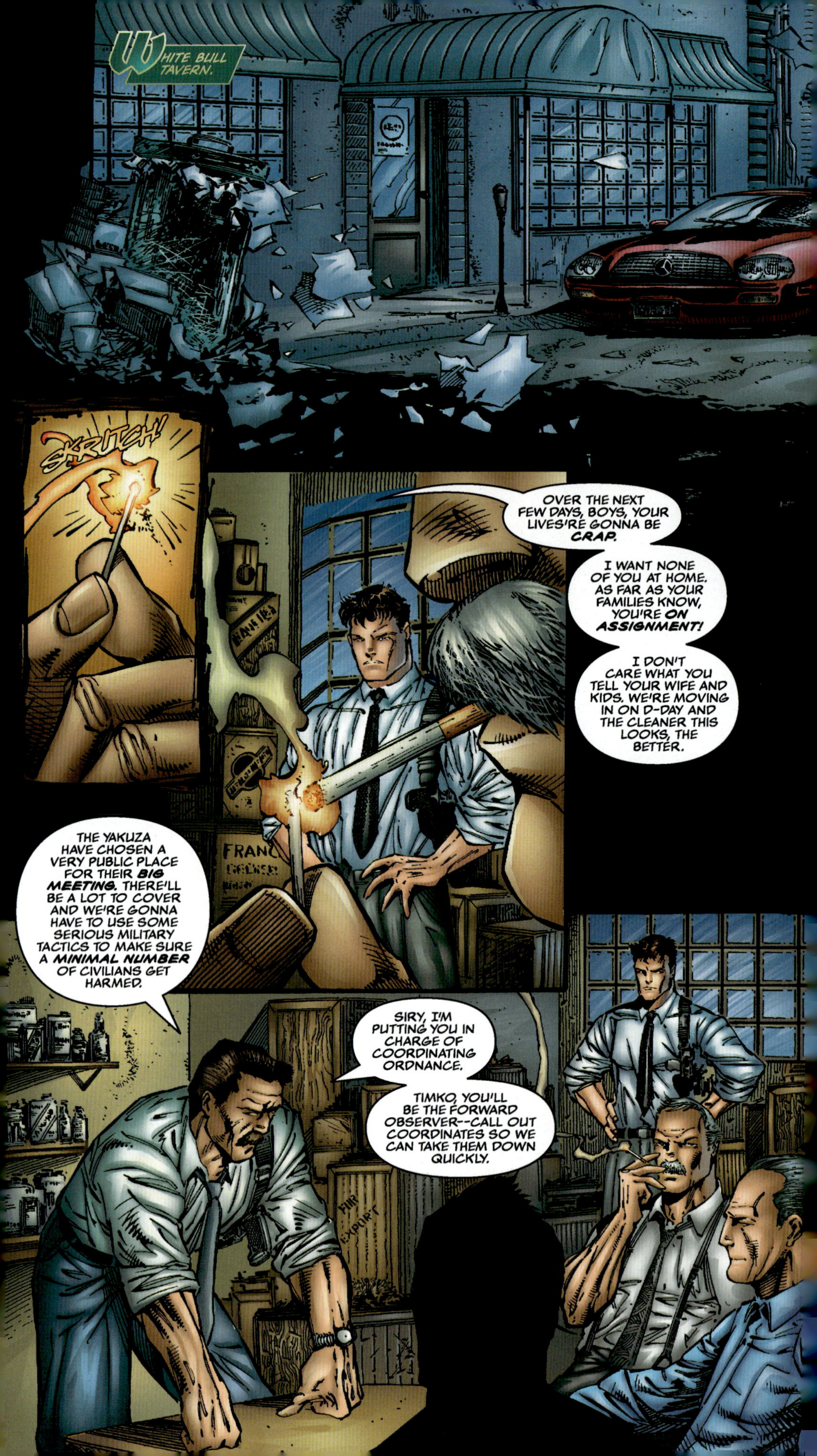
WHITE BULL TAVERN.
SKRITCH!
OVER THE NEXT FEW DAYS, BOYS, YOUR LIVES'RE GONNA BE CRAP.
I WANT NONE OF YOU AT HOME. AS FAR AS YOUR FAMILIES KNOW, YOU'RE ON ASSIGNMENT!
I DON'T CARE WHAT YOU TELL YOUR WIFE AND KIDS. WE'RE MOVING IN ON D-DAY AND THE CLEANER THIS LOOKS, THE BETTER.
THE YAKUZA HAVE CHOSEN A VERY PUBLIC PLACE FOR THEIR BIG MEETING. THERE'LL BE A LOT TO COVER AND WE'RE GONNA HAVE TO USE SOME SERIOUS MILITARY TACTICS TO MAKE SURE A MINIMAL NUMBER OF CIVILIANS GET HARMED.
SIRY, I'M PUTTING YOU IN CHARGE OF COORDINATING ORDNANCE.
TIMKO, YOU'LL BE THE FORWARD OBSERVER--CALL OUT COORDINATES SO WE CAN TAKE THEM DOWN QUICKLY.

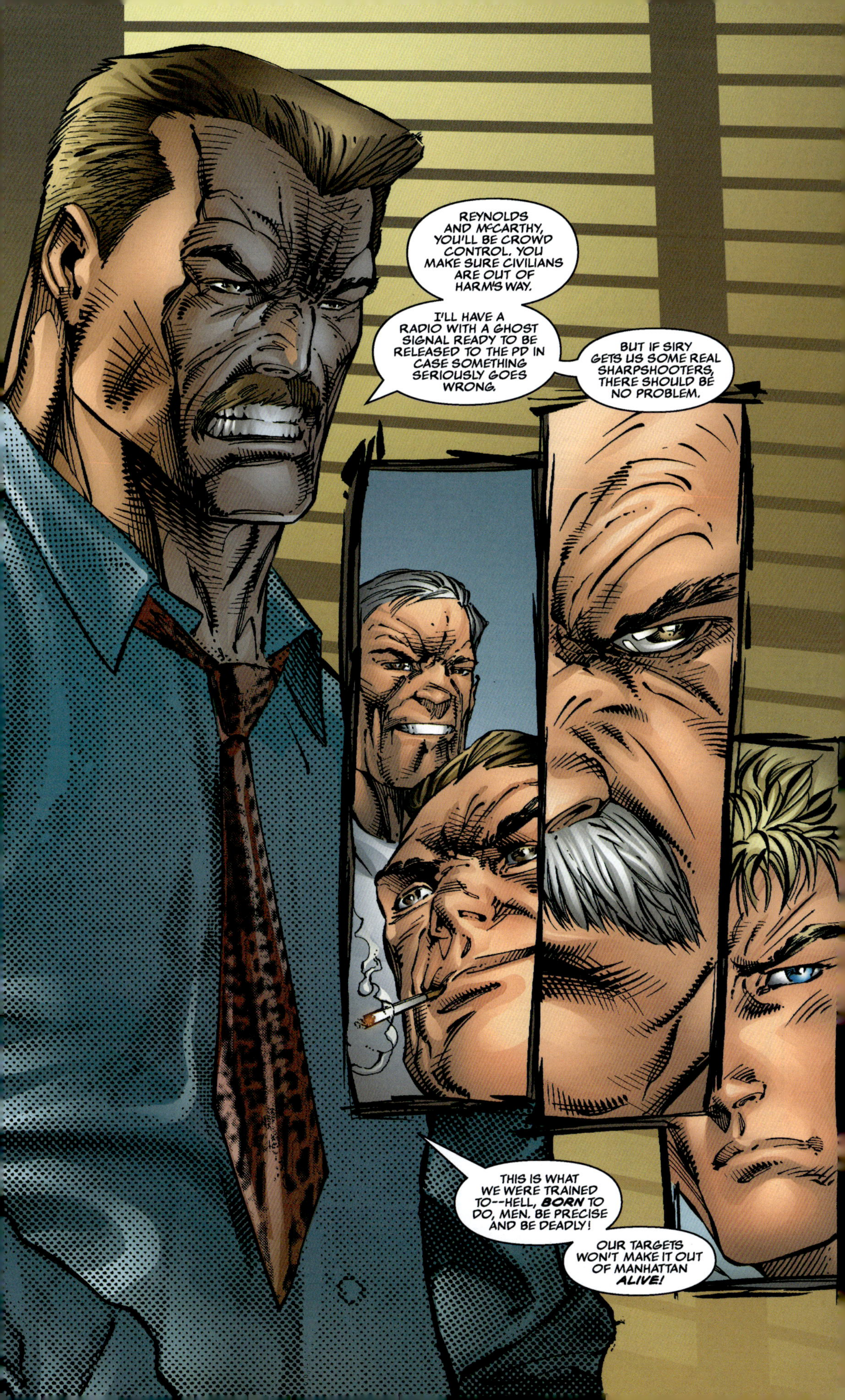
REYNOLDS AND McCARTHY, YOU'LL BE CROWD CONTROL. YOU MAKE SURE CIVILIANS ARE OUT OF HARM'S WAY.
I'LL HAVE A RADIO WITH A GHOST SIGNAL READY TO BE RELEASED TO THE PD IN CASE SOMETHING SERIOUSLY GOES WRONG.
BUT IF SIRY GETS US SOME REAL SHARPSHOOTERS, THERE SHOULD BE NO PROBLEM.
THIS IS WHAT WE WERE TRAINED TO--HELL, ***BORN*** TO DO, MEN. BE PRECISE AND BE DEADLY!
OUR TARGETS WON'T MAKE IT OUT OF MANHATTAN ***ALIVE!***

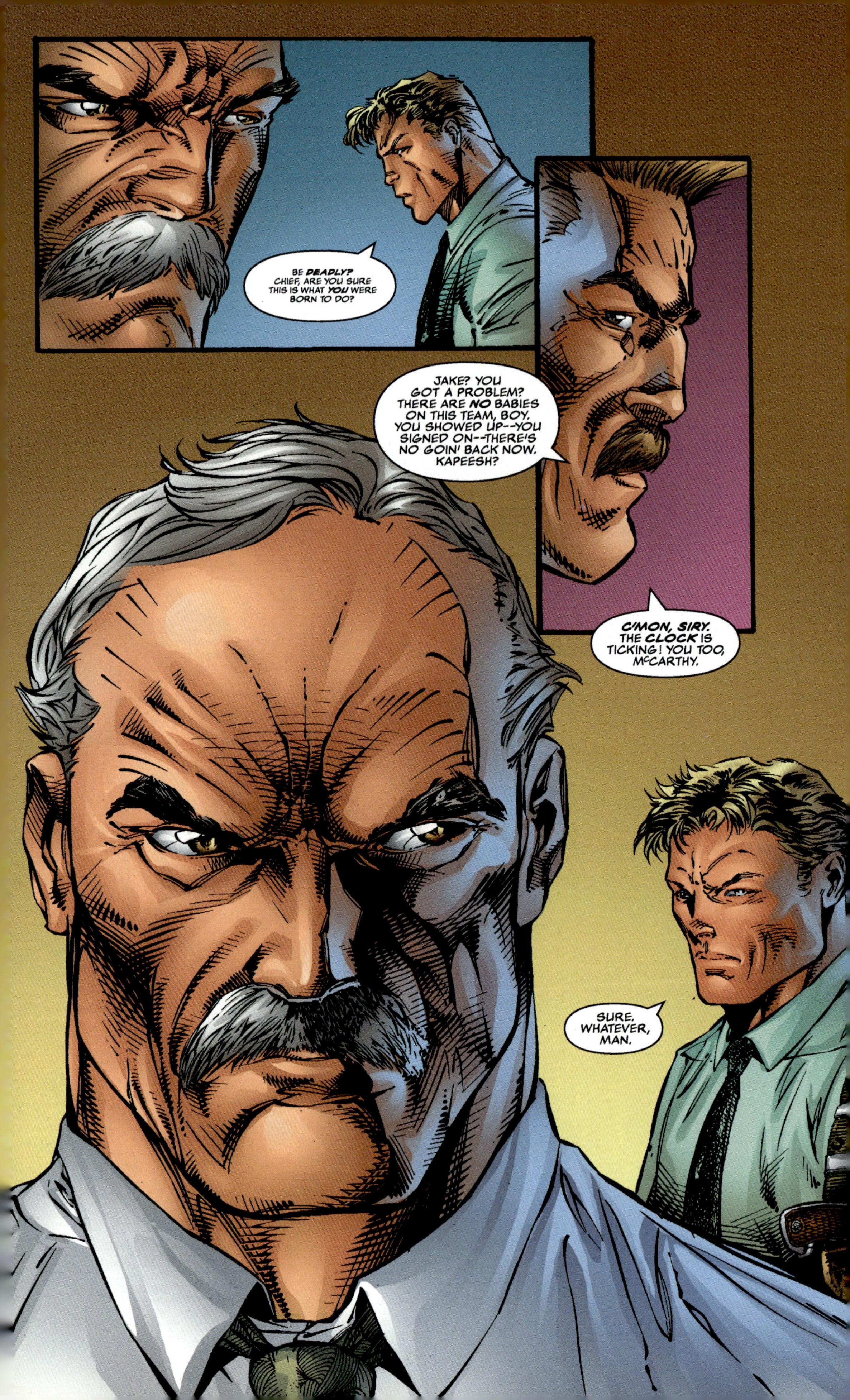
BE DEADLY? CHIEF, ARE YOU SURE THIS IS WHAT YOU WERE BORN TO DO?
JAKE? YOU GOT A PROBLEM? THERE ARE NO BABIES ON THIS TEAM, BOY. YOU SHOWED UP--YOU SIGNED ON--THERE'S NO GOIN' BACK NOW. KAPEESH?
C'MON, SIRY. THE CLOCK IS TICKING! YOU TOO, McCARTHY.
SURE. WHATEVER, MAN.

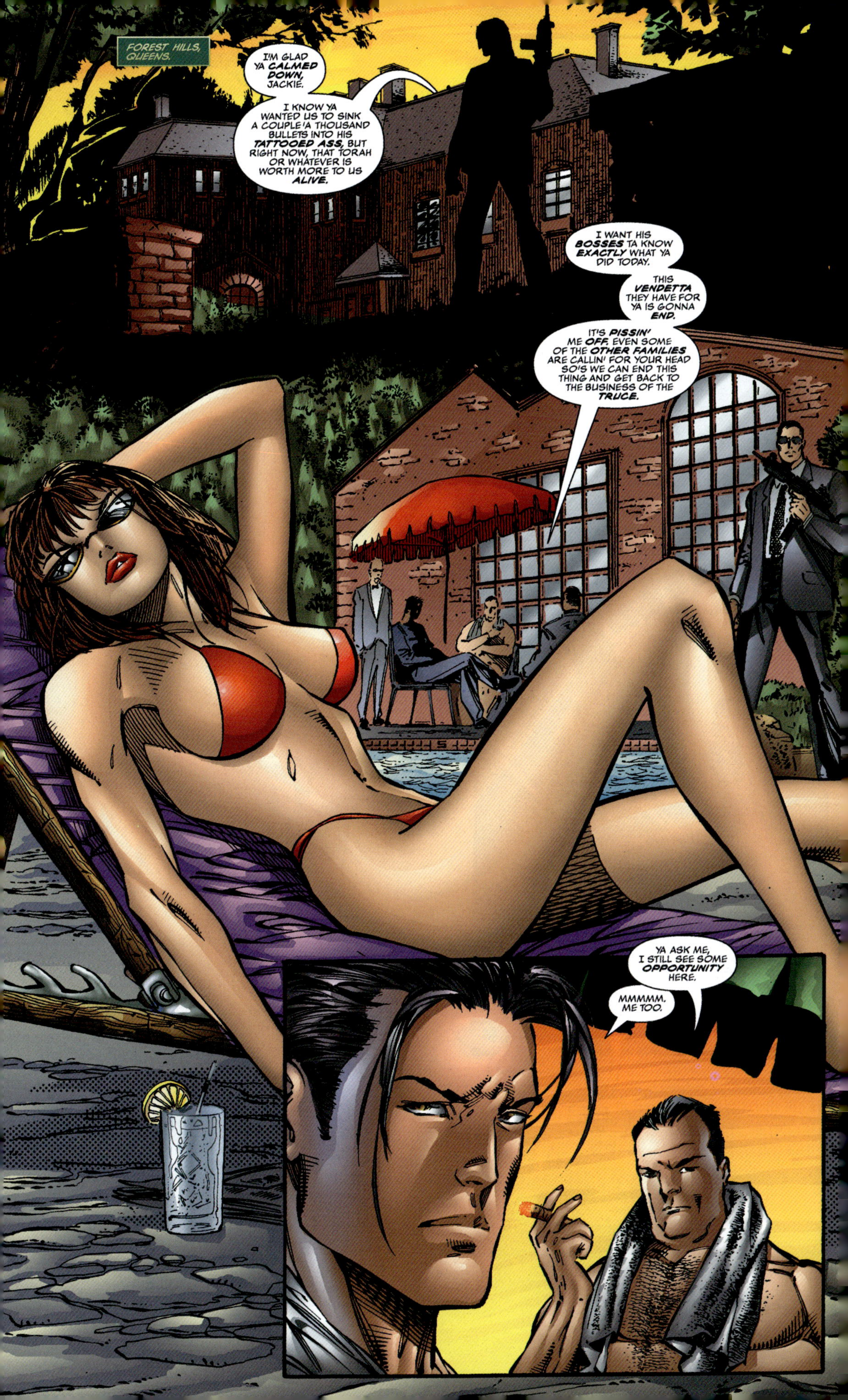
FOREST HILLS, QUEENS.
I'M GLAD YA CALMED DOWN, JACKIE.
I KNOW YA WANTED US TO SINK A COUPLE'A THOUSAND BULLETS INTO HIS TATTOOED ASS, BUT RIGHT NOW, THAT TORAH OR WHATEVER IS WORTH MORE TO US ALIVE.
I WANT HIS BOSSES TA KNOW EXACTLY WHAT YA DID TODAY.
THIS VENDETTA THEY HAVE FOR YA IS GONNA END.
IT'S PISSIN' ME OFF. EVEN SOME OF THE OTHER FAMILIES ARE CALLIN' FOR YOUR HEAD SO'S WE CAN END THIS THING AND GET BACK TO THE BUSINESS OF THE TRUCE.
YA ASK ME, I STILL SEE SOME OPPORTUNITY HERE.
MMMMM. ME TOO.

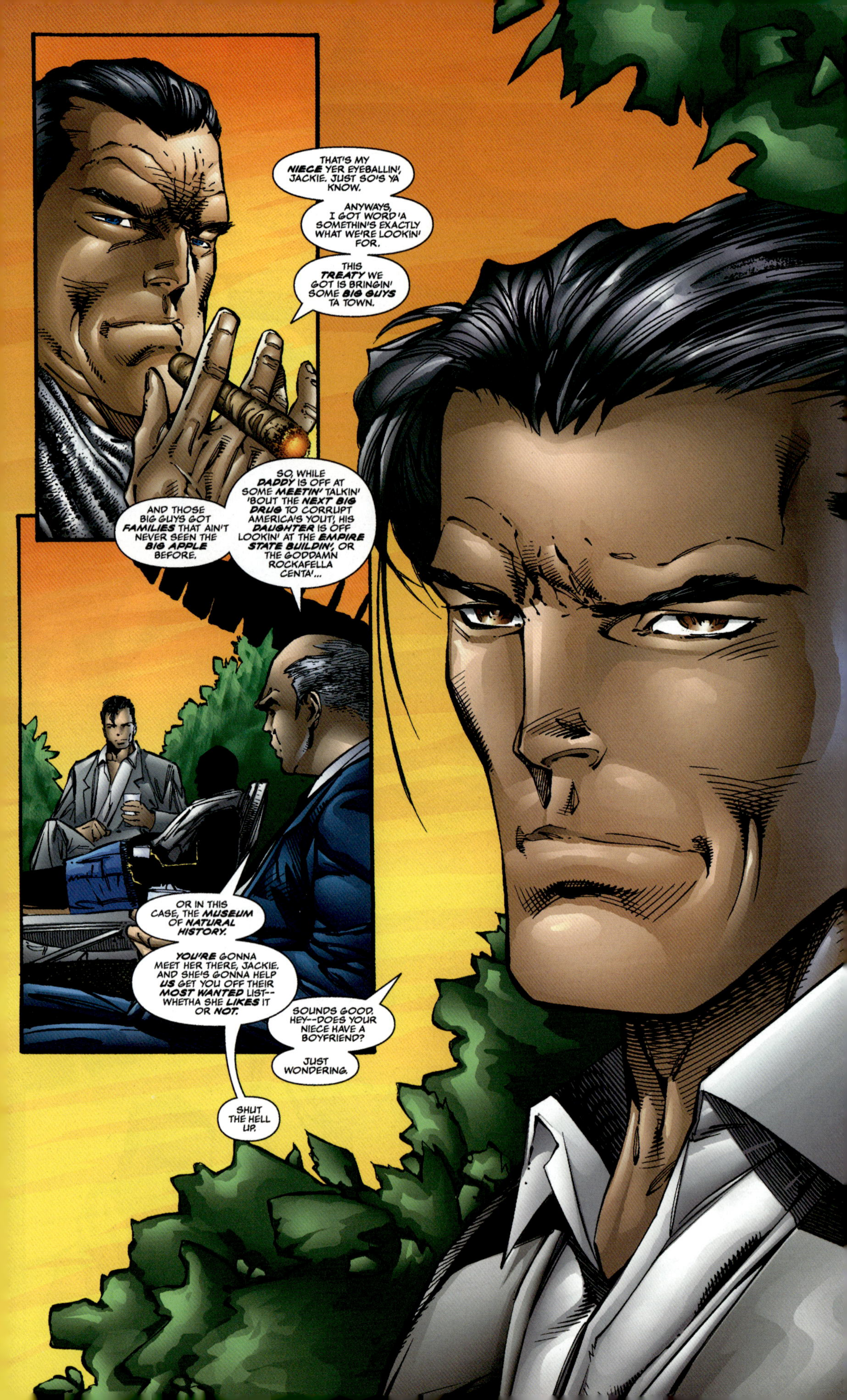
THAT'S MY NIECE YER EYEBALLIN', JACKIE. JUST SO'S YA KNOW.
ANYWAYS, I GOT WORD 'A SOMETHIN'S EXACTLY WHAT WE'RE LOOKIN' FOR.
THIS TREATY WE GOT IS BRINGIN' SOME BIG GUYS TA TOWN.
AND THOSE BIG GUYS GOT FAMILIES THAT AIN'T NEVER SEEN THE BIG APPLE BEFORE.
SO, WHILE DADDY IS OFF AT SOME MEETIN' TALKIN' 'BOUT THE NEXT BIG DRUG TO CORRUPT AMERICA'S YOUT', HIS DAUGHTER IS OFF LOOKIN' AT THE EMPIRE STATE BUILDIN', OR THE GODDAMN ROCKAFELLA CENTA'...
OR IN THIS CASE, THE MUSEUM OF NATURAL HISTORY.
YOU'RE GONNA MEET HER THERE, JACKIE. AND SHE'S GONNA HELP US GET YOU OFF THEIR MOST WANTED LIST-- WHETHA SHE LIKES IT OR NOT.
SOUNDS GOOD. HEY--DOES YOUR NIECE HAVE A BOYFRIEND?
JUST WONDERING.
SHUT THE HELL UP.

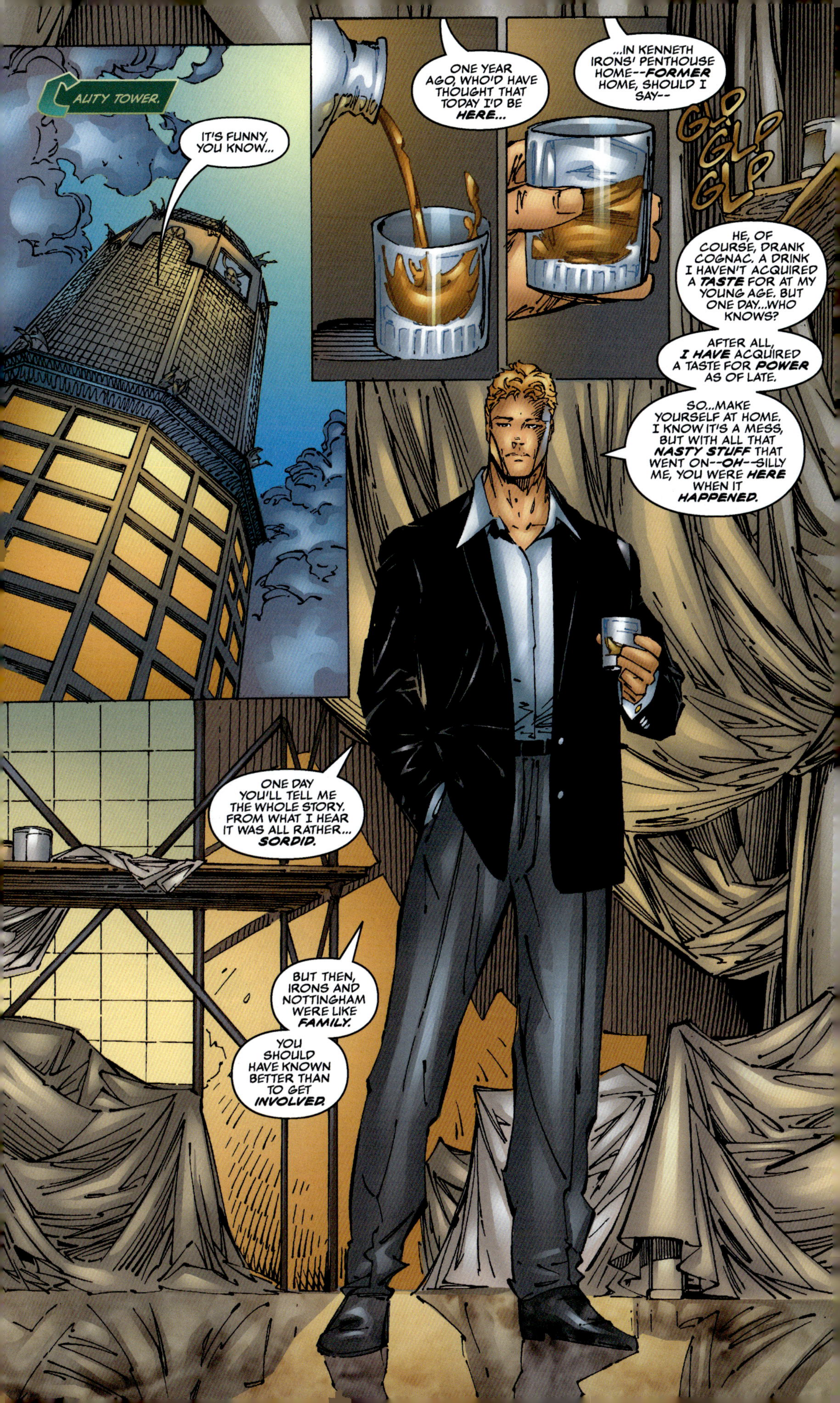

CAUTY TOWER.
IT'S FUNNY, YOU KNOW...
ONE YEAR AGO, WHO'D HAVE THOUGHT THAT TODAY I'D BE **HERE...**
...IN KENNETH IRONS' PENTHOUSE HOME--**FORMER** HOME, SHOULD I SAY--
GLP GLP GLP
HE, OF COURSE, DRANK COGNAC. A DRINK I HAVEN'T ACQUIRED A **TASTE** FOR AT MY YOUNG AGE. BUT ONE DAY...WHO KNOWS?
AFTER ALL, **I HAVE** ACQUIRED A TASTE FOR **POWER** AS OF LATE.
SO...MAKE YOURSELF AT HOME. I KNOW IT'S A MESS, BUT WITH ALL THAT **NASTY STUFF** THAT WENT ON--**OH**--SILLY ME, YOU WERE **HERE** WHEN IT **HAPPENED.**
ONE DAY YOU'LL TELL ME THE WHOLE STORY. FROM WHAT I HEAR IT WAS ALL RATHER... **SORDID.**
BUT THEN, IRONS AND NOTTINGHAM WERE LIKE **FAMILY.**
YOU SHOULD HAVE KNOWN BETTER THAN TO GET **INVOLVED.**

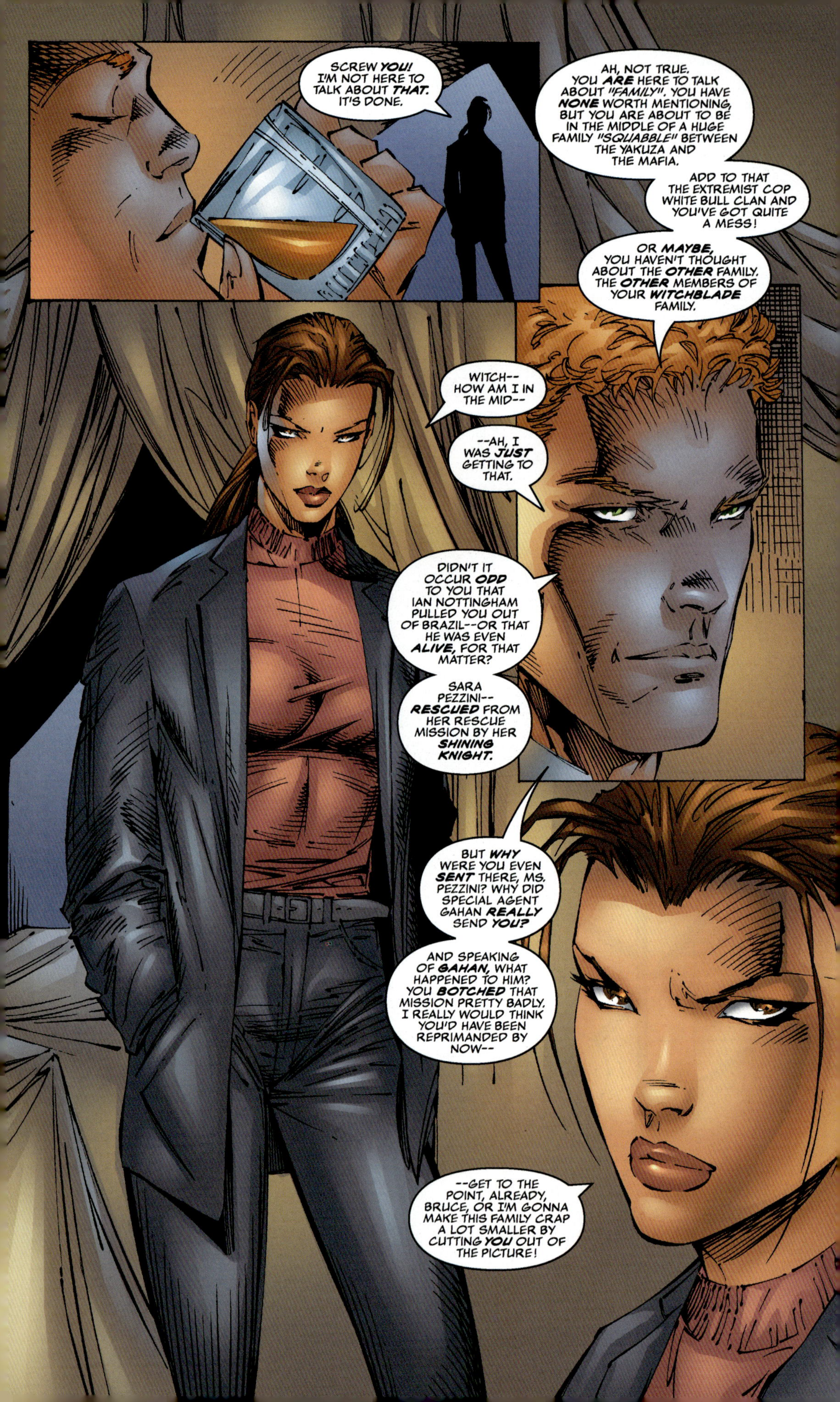
SCREW YOU! I'M NOT HERE TO TALK ABOUT THAT. IT'S DONE.
AH, NOT TRUE. YOU ARE HERE TO TALK ABOUT "FAMILY". YOU HAVE NONE WORTH MENTIONING, BUT YOU ARE ABOUT TO BE IN THE MIDDLE OF A HUGE FAMILY "SQUABBLE" BETWEEN THE YAKUZA AND THE MAFIA.
ADD TO THAT THE EXTREMIST COP WHITE BULL CLAN AND YOU'VE GOT QUITE A MESS!
OR MAYBE, YOU HAVEN'T THOUGHT ABOUT THE OTHER FAMILY. THE OTHER MEMBERS OF YOUR WITCHBLADE FAMILY.
WITCH-- HOW AM I IN THE MID--
--AH, I WAS JUST GETTING TO THAT.
DIDN'T IT OCCUR ODD TO YOU THAT IAN NOTTINGHAM PULLED YOU OUT OF BRAZIL--OR THAT HE WAS EVEN ALIVE, FOR THAT MATTER?
SARA PEZZINI-- RESCUED FROM HER RESCUE MISSION BY HER SHINING KNIGHT.
BUT WHY WERE YOU EVEN SENT THERE, MS. PEZZINI? WHY DID SPECIAL AGENT GAHAN REALLY SEND YOU?
AND SPEAKING OF GAHAN, WHAT HAPPENED TO HIM? YOU BOTCHED THAT MISSION PRETTY BADLY. I REALLY WOULD THINK YOU'D HAVE BEEN REPRIMANDED BY NOW--
--GET TO THE POINT, ALREADY, BRUCE, OR I'M GONNA MAKE THIS FAMILY CRAP A LOT SMALLER BY CUTTING YOU OUT OF THE PICTURE!

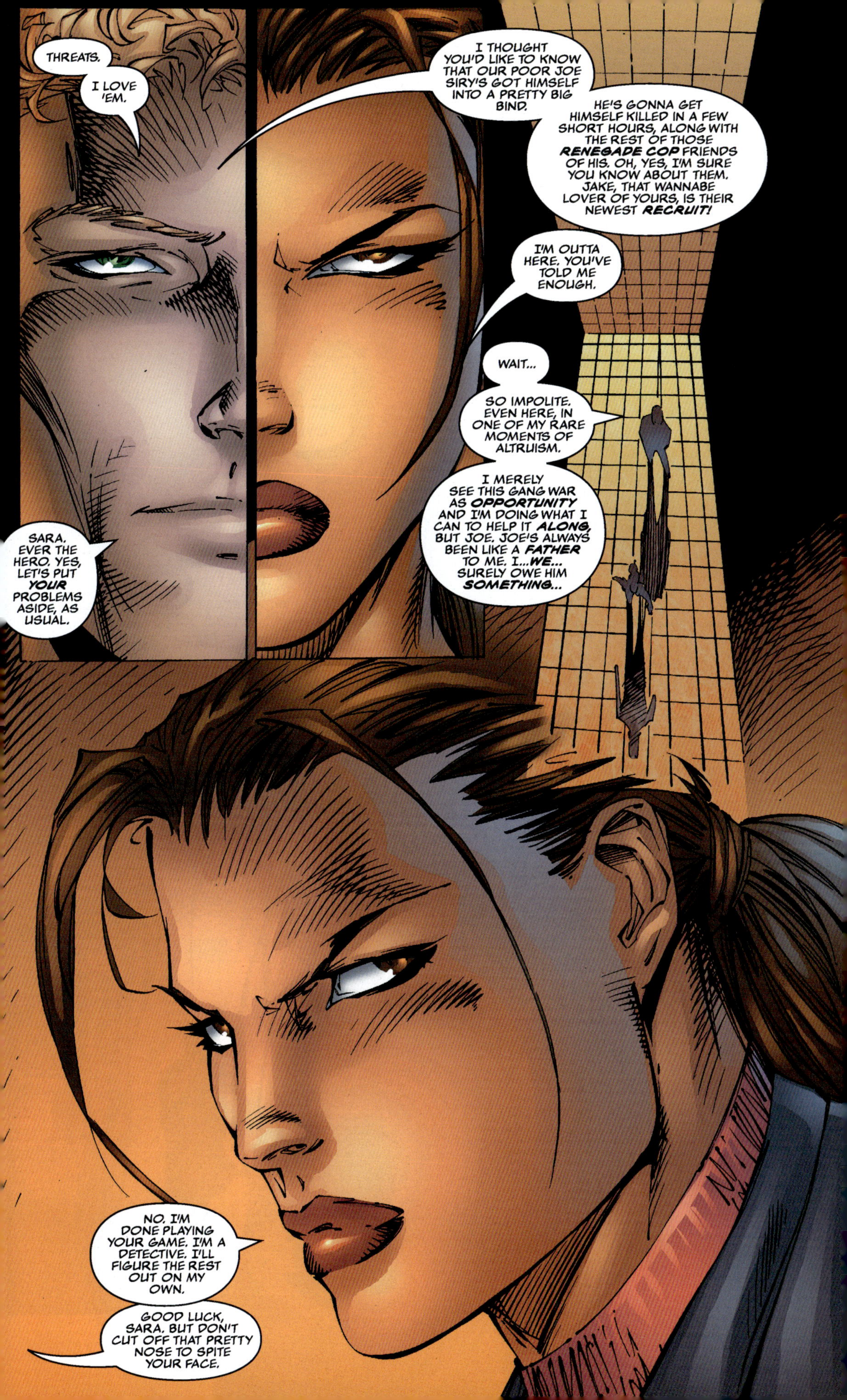
THREATS.
I LOVE 'EM.
I THOUGHT YOU'D LIKE TO KNOW THAT OUR POOR JOE SIRY'S GOT HIMSELF INTO A PRETTY BIG BIND.
HE'S GONNA GET HIMSELF KILLED IN A FEW SHORT HOURS, ALONG WITH THE REST OF THOSE RENEGADE COP FRIENDS OF HIS. OH, YES, I'M SURE YOU KNOW ABOUT THEM. JAKE, THAT WANNABE LOVER OF YOURS, IS THEIR NEWEST RECRUIT!
I'M OUTTA HERE. YOU'VE TOLD ME ENOUGH.
WAIT...
SO IMPOLITE. EVEN HERE, IN ONE OF MY RARE MOMENTS OF ALTRUISM.
I MERELY SEE THIS GANG WAR AS OPPORTUNITY AND I'M DOING WHAT I CAN TO HELP IT ALONG, BUT JOE. JOE'S ALWAYS BEEN LIKE A FATHER TO ME. I...WE... SURELY OWE HIM SOMETHING...
SARA. EVER THE HERO. YES, LET'S PUT YOUR PROBLEMS ASIDE, AS USUAL.
NO. I'M DONE PLAYING YOUR GAME. I'M A DETECTIVE. I'LL FIGURE THE REST OUT ON MY OWN.
GOOD LUCK, SARA. BUT DON'T CUT OFF THAT PRETTY NOSE TO SPITE YOUR FACE.

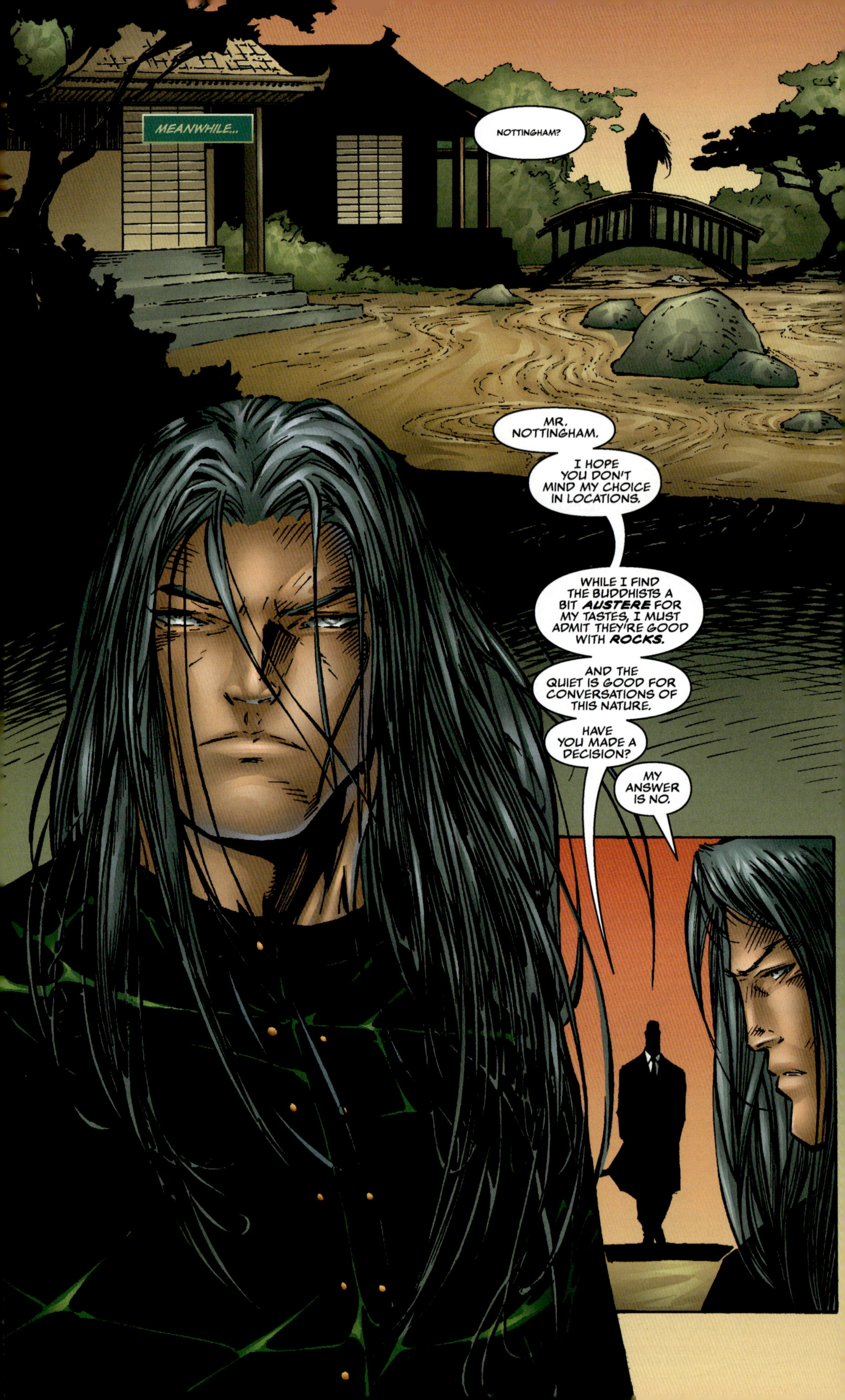
MEANWHILE...
NOTTINGHAM?
MR. NOTTINGHAM.
I HOPE YOU DON'T MIND MY CHOICE IN LOCATIONS.
WHILE I FIND THE BUDDHISTS A BIT AUSTERE FOR MY TASTES, I MUST ADMIT THEY'RE GOOD WITH ROCKS.
AND THE QUIET IS GOOD FOR CONVERSATIONS OF THIS NATURE.
HAVE YOU MADE A DECISION?
MY ANSWER IS NO.

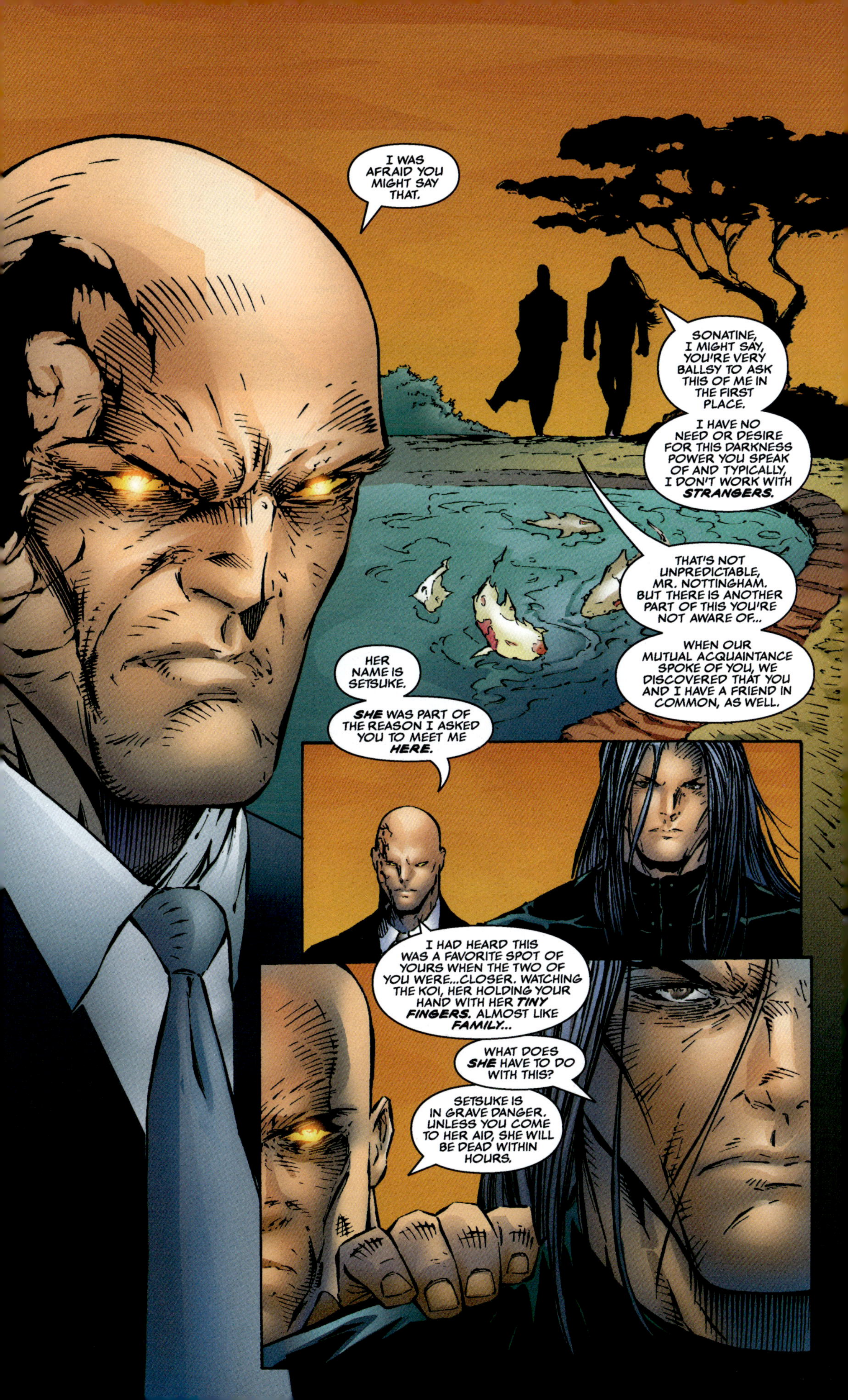

I WAS AFRAID YOU MIGHT SAY THAT.
SONATINE, I MIGHT SAY, YOU'RE VERY BALLSY TO ASK THIS OF ME IN THE FIRST PLACE.
I HAVE NO NEED OR DESIRE FOR THIS DARKNESS POWER YOU SPEAK OF AND TYPICALLY, I DON'T WORK WITH STRANGERS.
THAT'S NOT UNPREDICTABLE, MR. NOTTINGHAM. BUT THERE IS ANOTHER PART OF THIS YOU'RE NOT AWARE OF...
WHEN OUR MUTUAL ACQUAINTANCE SPOKE OF YOU, WE DISCOVERED THAT YOU AND I HAVE A FRIEND IN COMMON, AS WELL.
HER NAME IS SETSUKE.
SHE WAS PART OF THE REASON I ASKED YOU TO MEET ME HERE.
I HAD HEARD THIS WAS A FAVORITE SPOT OF YOURS WHEN THE TWO OF YOU WERE...CLOSER. WATCHING THE KOI, HER HOLDING YOUR HAND WITH HER TINY FINGERS. ALMOST LIKE FAMILY...
WHAT DOES SHE HAVE TO DO WITH THIS?
SETSUKE IS IN GRAVE DANGER. UNLESS YOU COME TO HER AID, SHE WILL BE DEAD WITHIN HOURS.

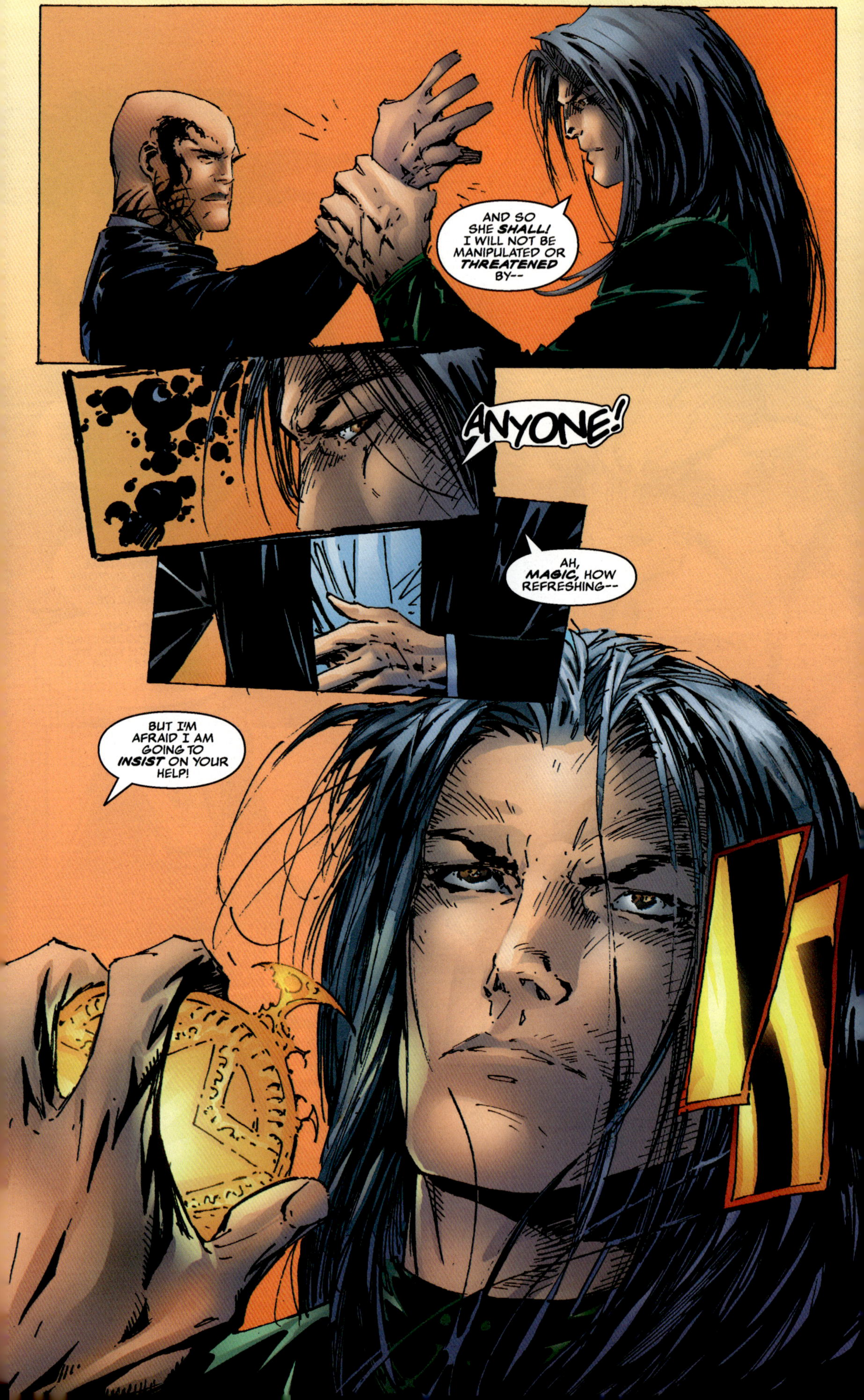
AND SO SHE SHALL! I WILL NOT BE MANIPULATED OR THREATENED BY--
ANYONE!
AH, MAGIC, HOW REFRESHING--
BUT I'M AFRAID I AM GOING TO INSIST ON YOUR HELP!

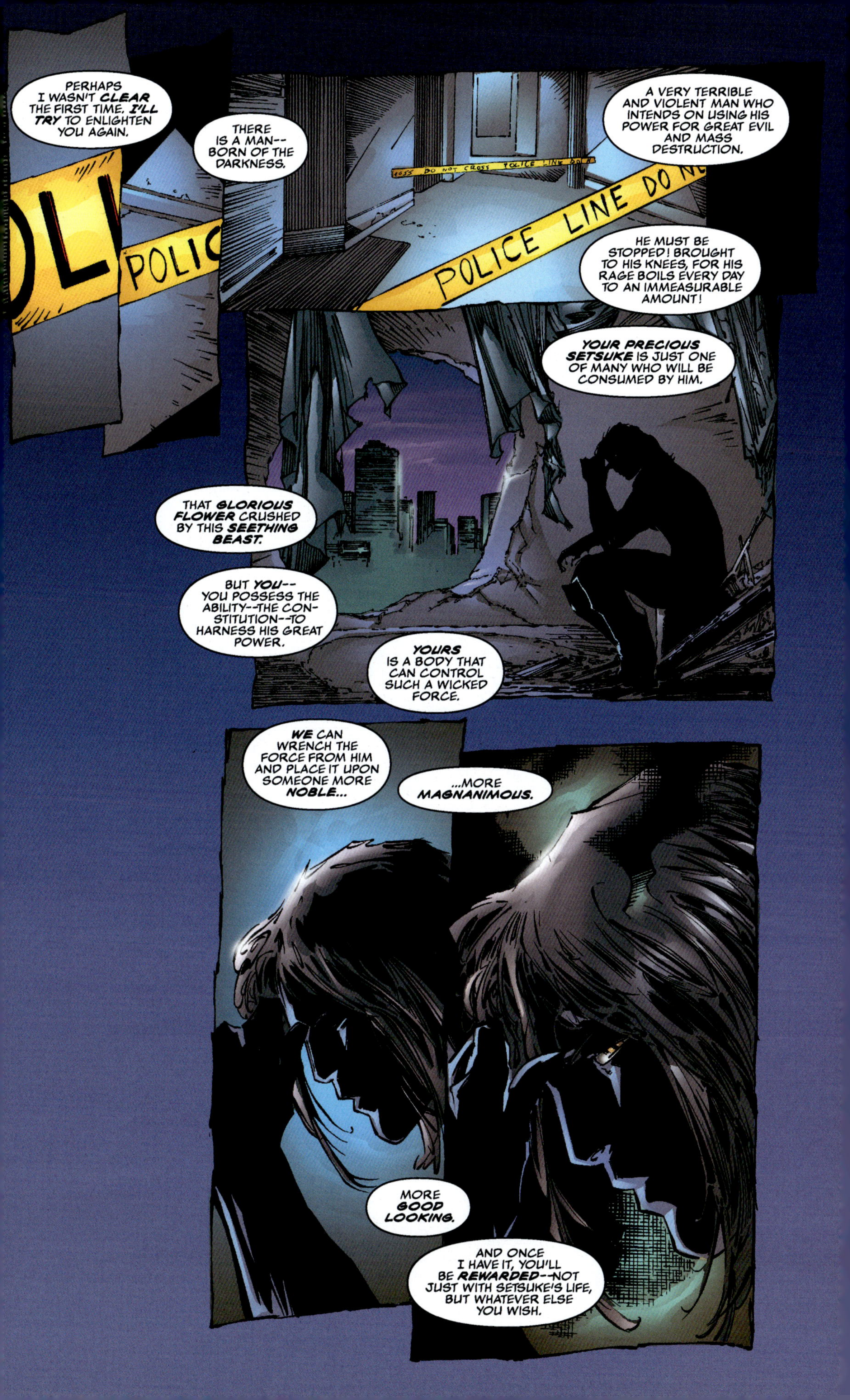

PERHAPS I WASN'T CLEAR THE FIRST TIME. I'LL TRY TO ENLIGHTEN YOU AGAIN.
POLIC
THERE IS A MAN-- BORN OF THE DARKNESS.
DO NOT CROSS POLICE LINE DO N
A VERY TERRIBLE AND VIOLENT MAN WHO INTENDS ON USING HIS POWER FOR GREAT EVIL AND MASS DESTRUCTION.
POLICE LINE DO N
HE MUST BE STOPPED! BROUGHT TO HIS KNEES, FOR HIS RAGE BOILS EVERY DAY TO AN IMMEASURABLE AMOUNT!
YOUR PRECIOUS SETSUKE IS JUST ONE OF MANY WHO WILL BE CONSUMED BY HIM.
THAT GLORIOUS FLOWER CRUSHED BY THIS SEETHING BEAST.
BUT YOU-- YOU POSSESS THE ABILITY--THE CON-STITUTION--TO HARNESS HIS GREAT POWER.
YOURS IS A BODY THAT CAN CONTROL SUCH A WICKED FORCE.
WE CAN WRENCH THE FORCE FROM HIM AND PLACE IT UPON SOMEONE MORE NOBLE...
...MORE MAGNANIMOUS.
MORE GOOD LOOKING.
AND ONCE I HAVE IT, YOU'LL BE REWARDED--NOT JUST WITH SETSUKE'S LIFE, BUT WHATEVER ELSE YOU WISH.

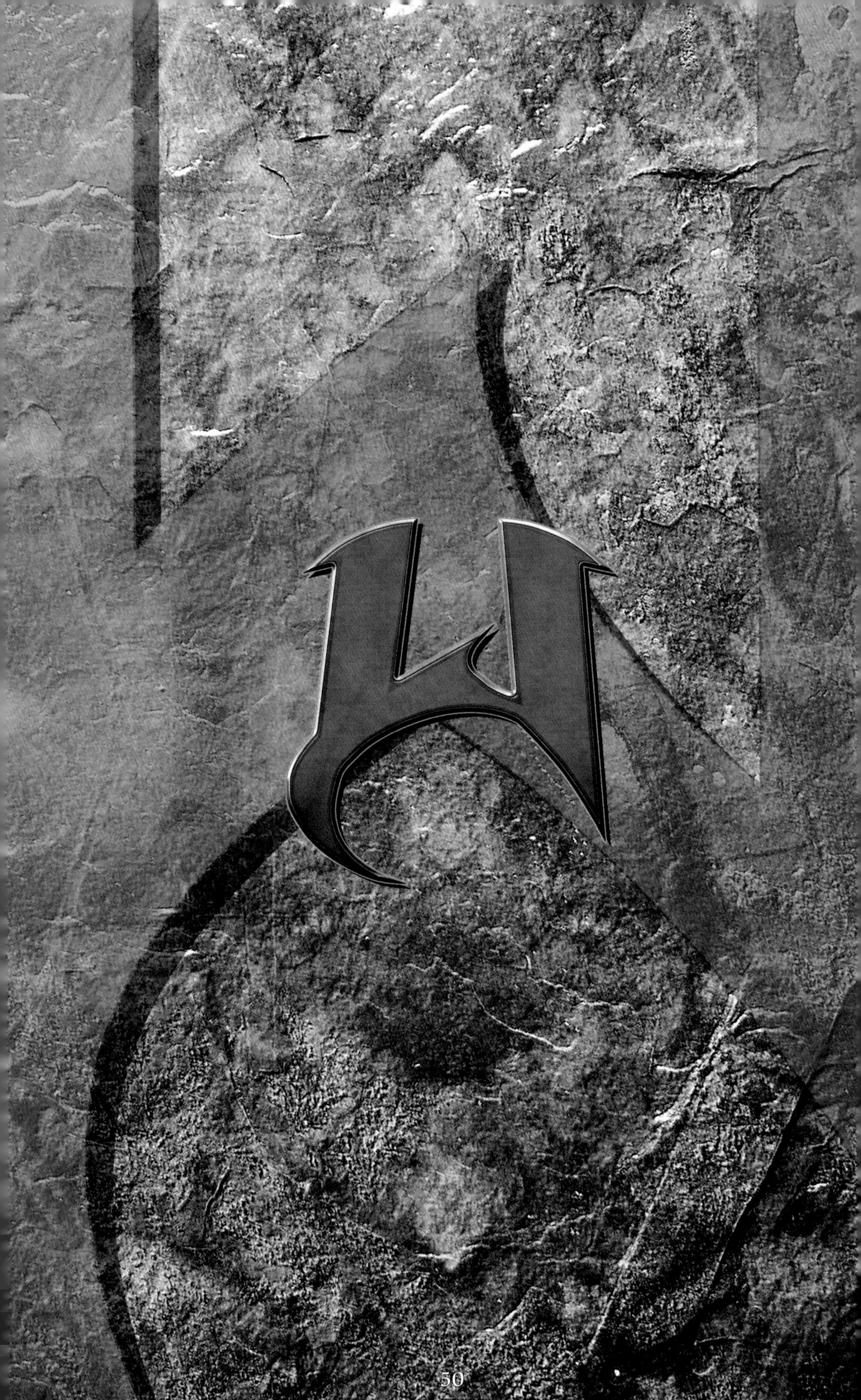

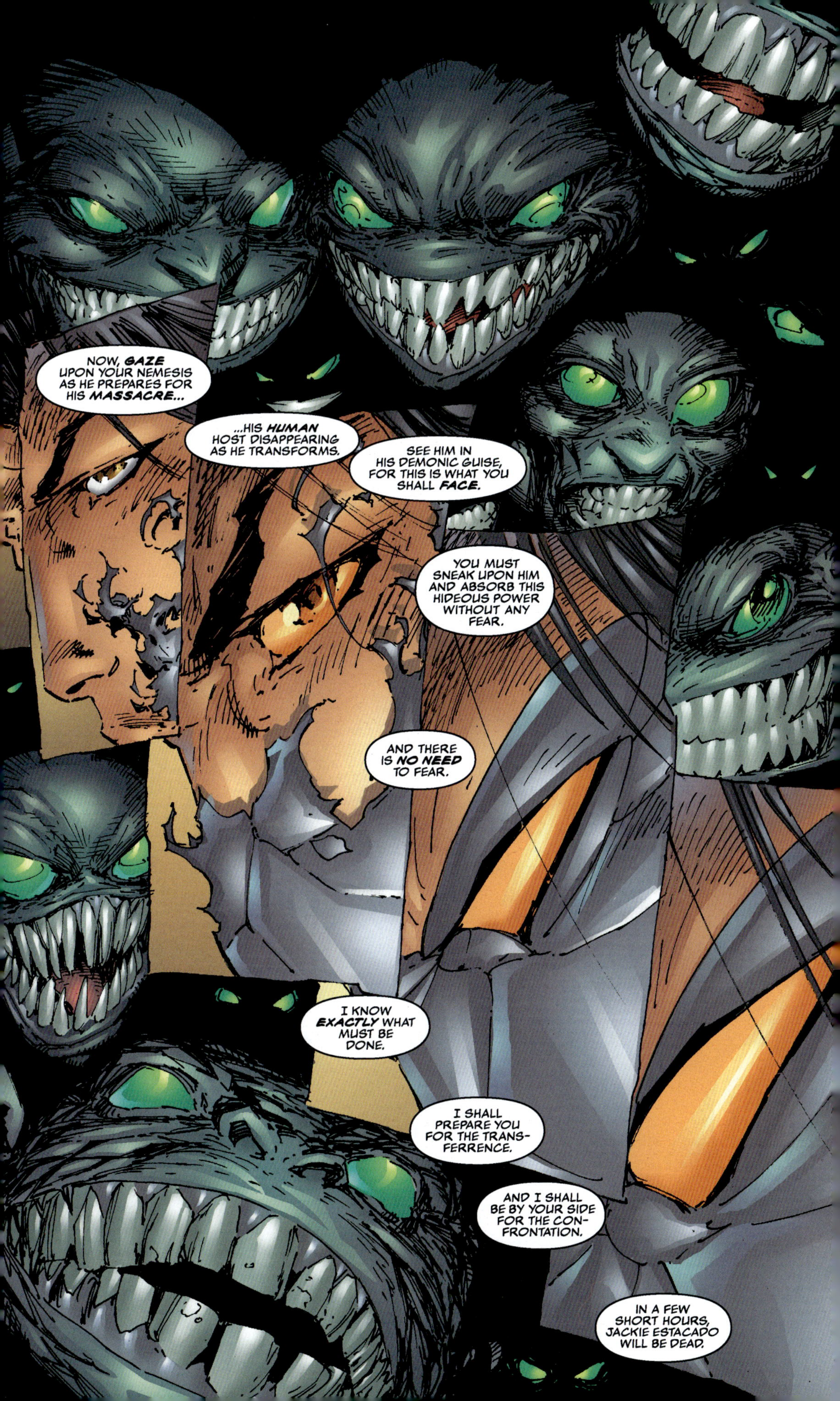

NOW, GAZE UPON YOUR NEMESIS AS HE PREPARES FOR HIS MASSACRE...
...HIS HUMAN HOST DISAPPEARING AS HE TRANSFORMS.
SEE HIM IN HIS DEMONIC GUISE, FOR THIS IS WHAT YOU SHALL FACE.
YOU MUST SNEAK UPON HIM AND ABSORB THIS HIDEOUS POWER WITHOUT ANY FEAR.
AND THERE IS NO NEED TO FEAR.
I KNOW EXACTLY WHAT MUST BE DONE.
I SHALL PREPARE YOU FOR THE TRANS-FERRENCE.
AND I SHALL BE BY YOUR SIDE FOR THE CON-FRONTATION.
IN A FEW SHORT HOURS, JACKIE ESTACADO WILL BE DEAD.

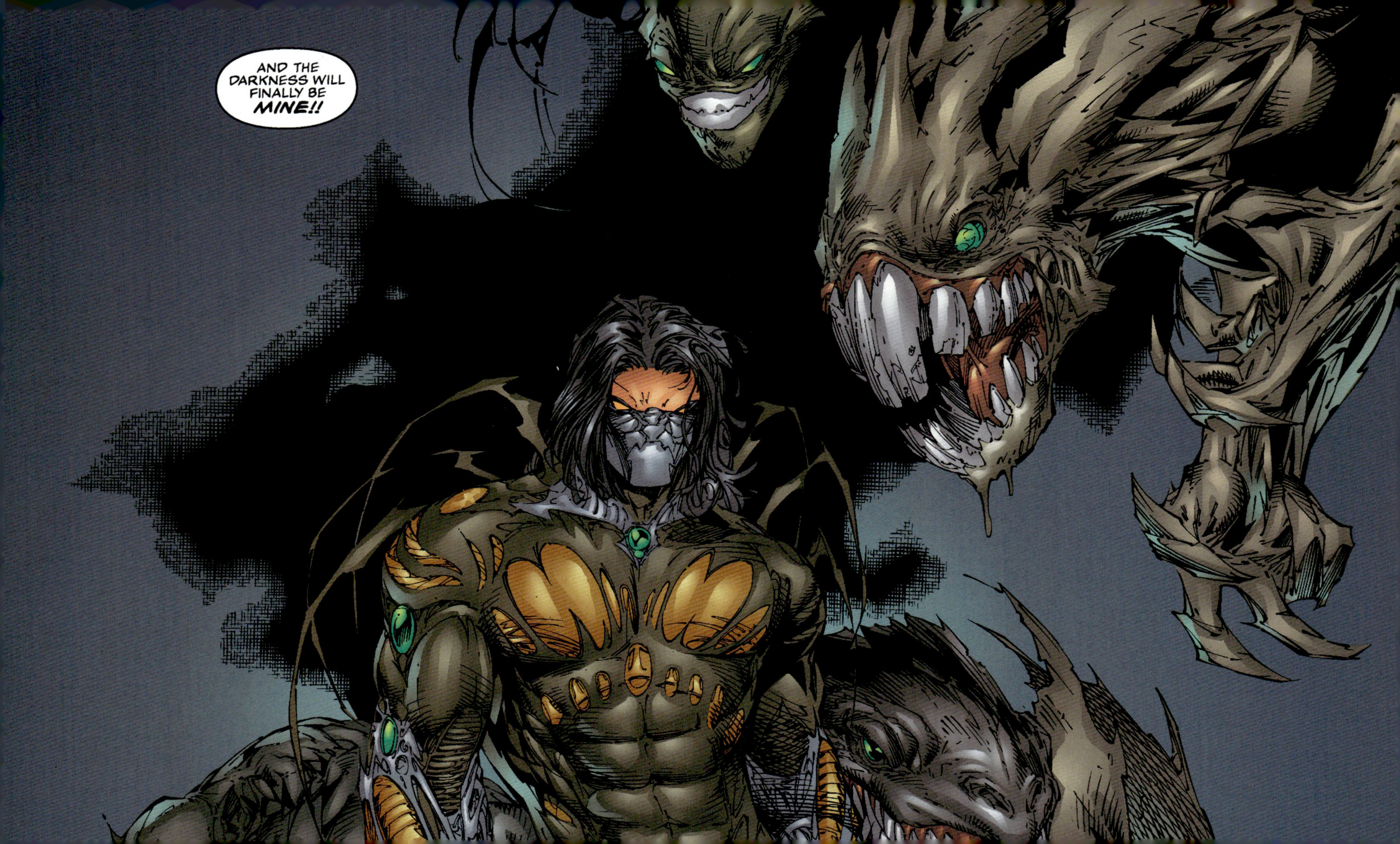
AND THE DARKNESS WILL FINALLY BE MINE!!

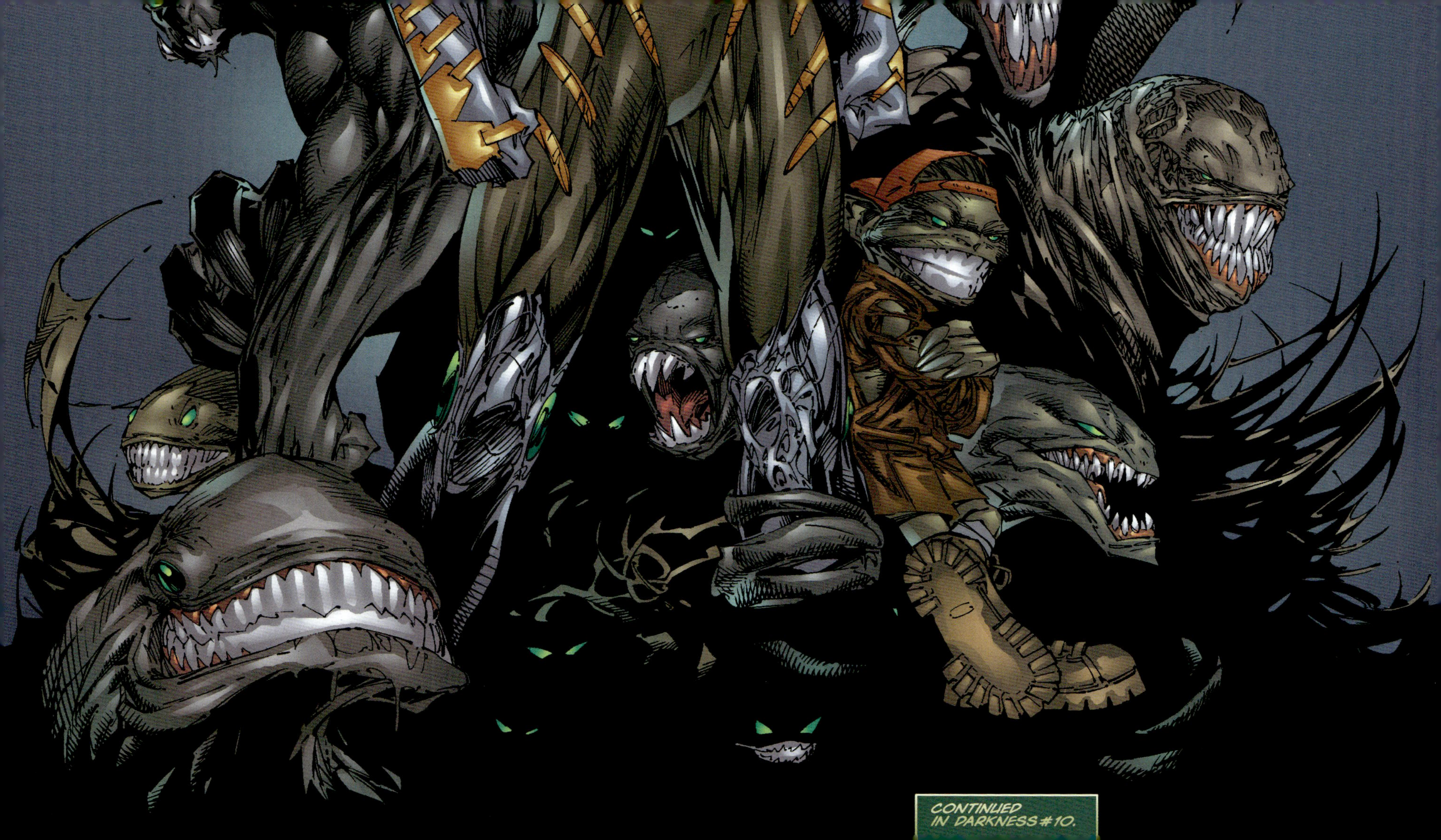
CONTINUED IN DARKNESS #10.

FAMILY TIES part 3: *The Darkness*
ISSUE #10

story: **David Wohl** and **Christina Z.**
pencils: **Marc Silvestri, Joe Benitez** and **Clarence Lansang**
inks: **Joe Weems V, Jason Gorder, Jonathan Livesay, Edwin Rosell, Marlo Alquiza** and **Richard Bennett**
colors: **Matt Nelson** and **Richard Isanove**

pencil assists: **Brian Ching** pages 19, 20 and 22
ink assists: **Marco "Madman" Galli** and **Victor Llamas**

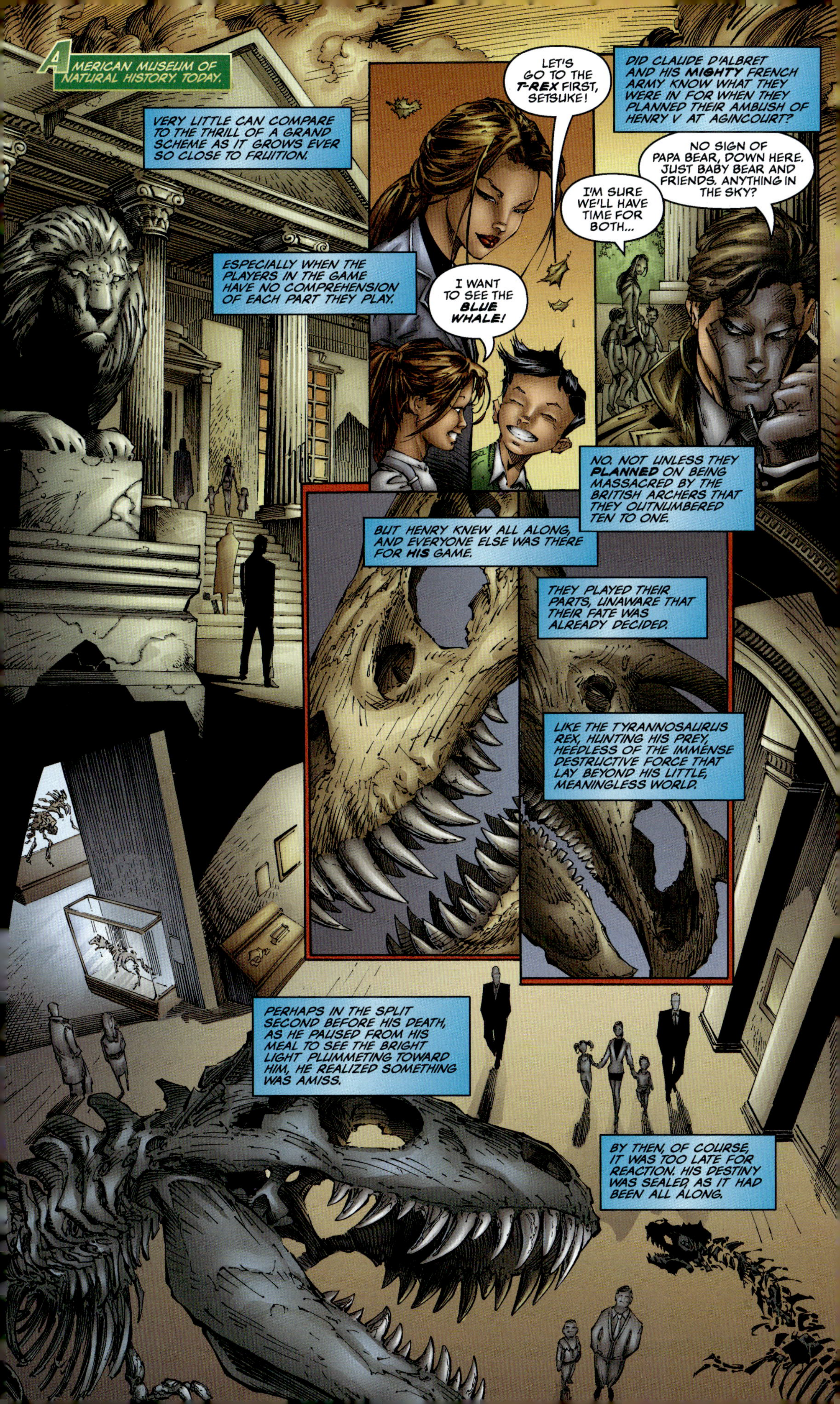
AMERICAN MUSEUM OF NATURAL HISTORY. TODAY.
VERY LITTLE CAN COMPARE TO THE THRILL OF A GRAND SCHEME AS IT GROWS EVER SO CLOSE TO FRUITION.
ESPECIALLY WHEN THE PLAYERS IN THE GAME HAVE NO COMPREHENSION OF EACH PART THEY PLAY.
LET'S GO TO THE T-REX FIRST, SETSUKE!
I WANT TO SEE THE BLUE WHALE!
I'M SURE WE'LL HAVE TIME FOR BOTH...
DID CLAUDE D'ALBRET AND HIS MIGHTY FRENCH ARMY KNOW WHAT THEY WERE IN FOR WHEN THEY PLANNED THEIR AMBUSH OF HENRY V AT AGINCOURT?
NO SIGN OF PAPA BEAR, DOWN HERE. JUST BABY BEAR AND FRIENDS. ANYTHING IN THE SKY?
NO. NOT UNLESS THEY PLANNED ON BEING MASSACRED BY THE BRITISH ARCHERS THAT THEY OUTNUMBERED TEN TO ONE.
BUT HENRY KNEW ALL ALONG, AND EVERYONE ELSE WAS THERE FOR HIS GAME.
THEY PLAYED THEIR PARTS, UNAWARE THAT THEIR FATE WAS ALREADY DECIDED.
LIKE THE TYRANNOSAURUS REX, HUNTING HIS PREY, HEEDLESS OF THE IMMENSE DESTRUCTIVE FORCE THAT LAY BEYOND HIS LITTLE, MEANINGLESS WORLD.
PERHAPS IN THE SPLIT SECOND BEFORE HIS DEATH, AS HE PAUSED FROM HIS MEAL TO SEE THE BRIGHT LIGHT PLUMMETING TOWARD HIM, HE REALIZED SOMETHING WAS AMISS.
BY THEN, OF COURSE, IT WAS TOO LATE FOR REACTION. HIS DESTINY WAS SEALED, AS IT HAD BEEN ALL ALONG.

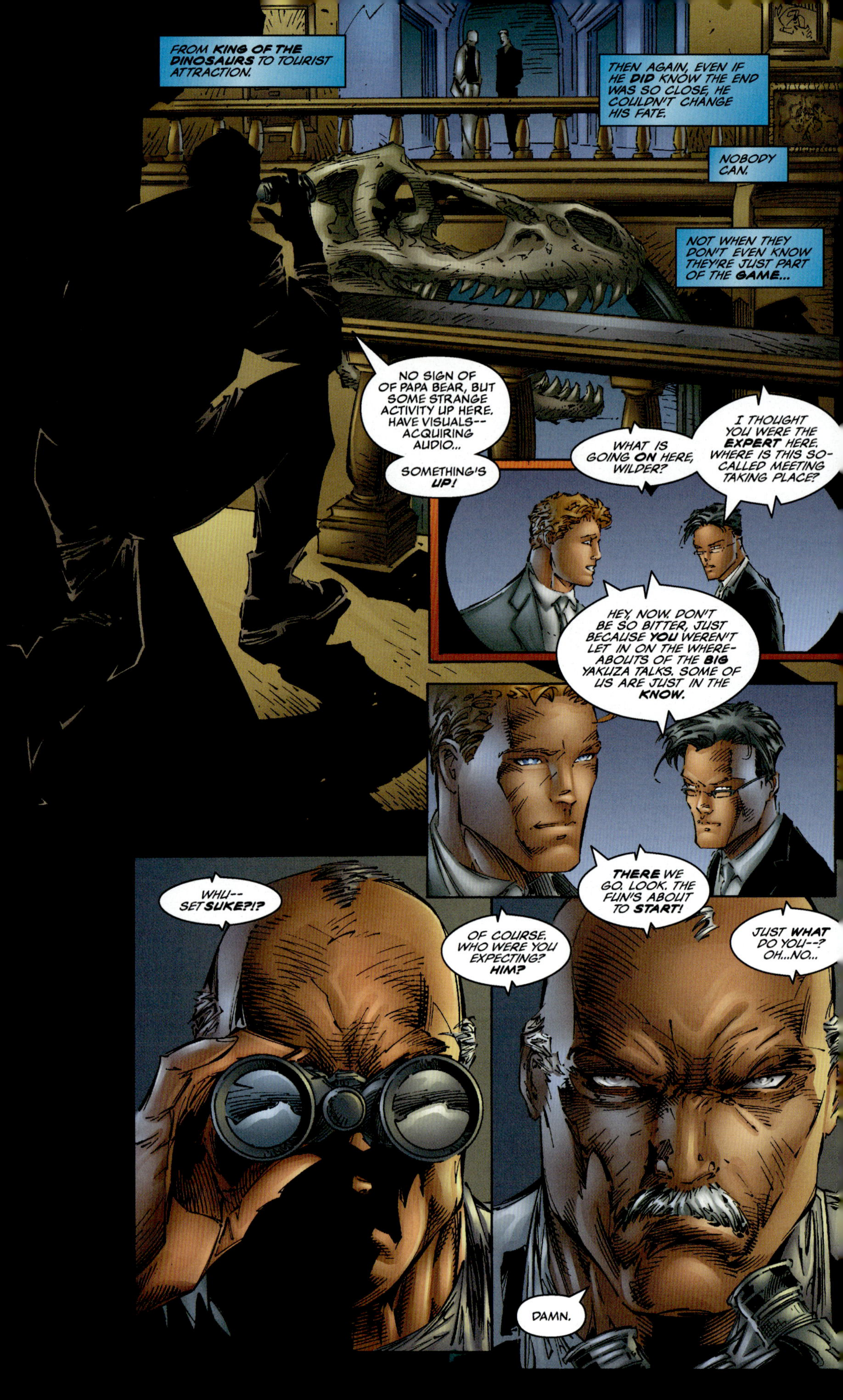
FROM KING OF THE DINOSAURS TO TOURIST ATTRACTION.
THEN AGAIN, EVEN IF HE DID KNOW THE END WAS SO CLOSE, HE COULDN'T CHANGE HIS FATE.
NOBODY CAN.
NOT WHEN THEY DON'T EVEN KNOW THEY'RE JUST PART OF THE GAME...
NO SIGN OF OF PAPA BEAR, BUT SOME STRANGE ACTIVITY UP HERE. HAVE VISUALS-- ACQUIRING AUDIO...
SOMETHING'S UP!
WHAT IS GOING ON HERE, WILDER?
I THOUGHT YOU WERE THE EXPERT HERE. WHERE IS THIS SO-CALLED MEETING TAKING PLACE?
HEY, NOW. DON'T BE SO BITTER, JUST BECAUSE YOU WEREN'T LET IN ON THE WHERE-ABOUTS OF THE BIG YAKUZA TALKS. SOME OF US ARE JUST IN THE KNOW.
THERE WE GO. LOOK. THE FUN'S ABOUT TO START!
WHU-- SETSUKE?!?
OF COURSE. WHO WERE YOU EXPECTING? HIM?
JUST WHAT DO YOU--? OH...NO...
DAMN.

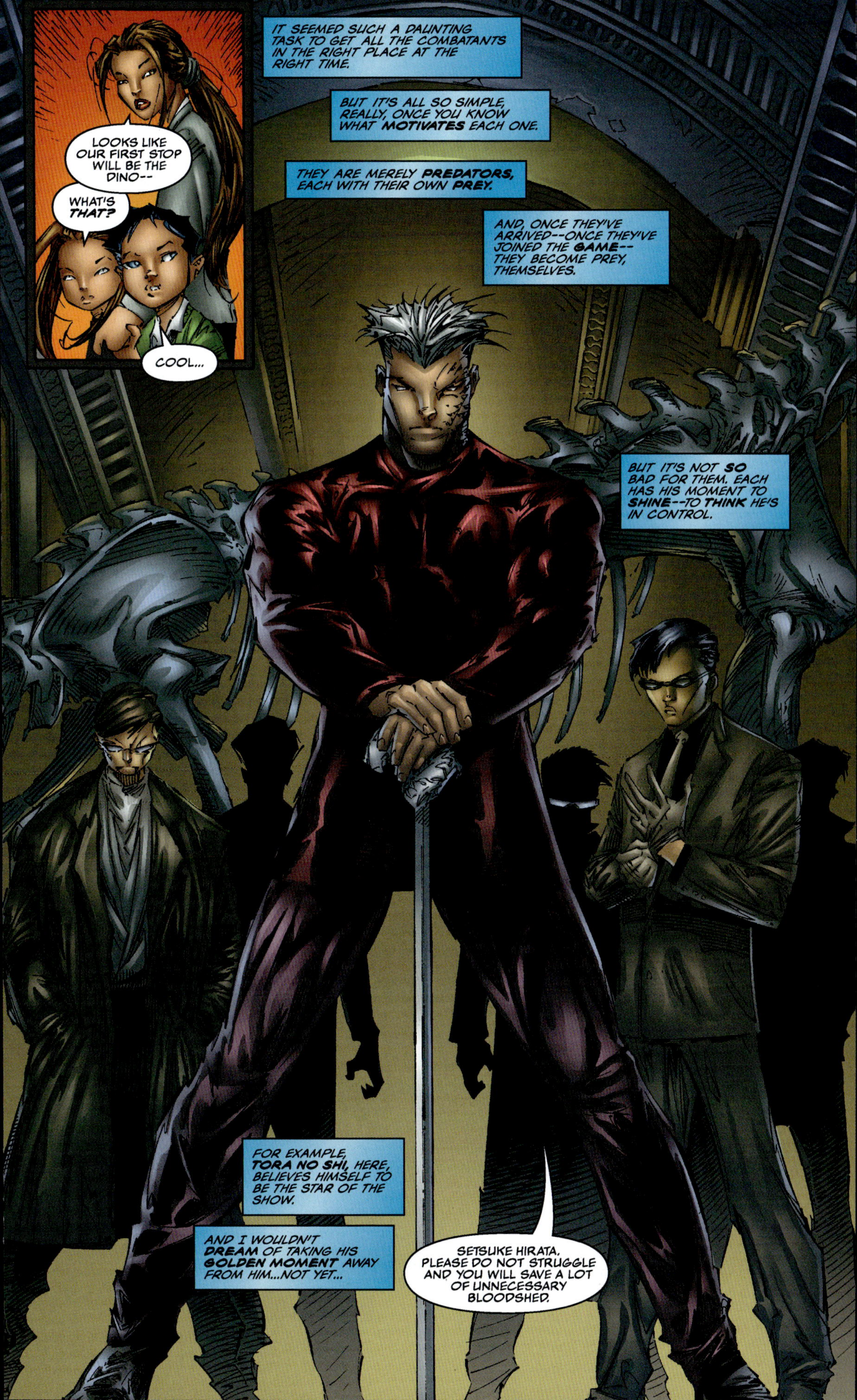
LOOKS LIKE OUR FIRST STOP WILL BE THE DINO--
WHAT'S THAT?
COOL...
IT SEEMED SUCH A DAUNTING TASK TO GET ALL THE COMBATANTS IN THE RIGHT PLACE AT THE RIGHT TIME.
BUT IT'S ALL SO SIMPLE, REALLY, ONCE YOU KNOW WHAT MOTIVATES EACH ONE.
THEY ARE MERELY PREDATORS, EACH WITH THEIR OWN PREY.
AND, ONCE THEY'VE ARRIVED--ONCE THEY'VE JOINED THE GAME--THEY BECOME PREY, THEMSELVES.
BUT IT'S NOT SO BAD FOR THEM. EACH HAS HIS MOMENT TO SHINE--TO THINK HE'S IN CONTROL.
FOR EXAMPLE, TORA NO SHI, HERE, BELIEVES HIMSELF TO BE THE STAR OF THE SHOW.
AND I WOULDN'T DREAM OF TAKING HIS GOLDEN MOMENT AWAY FROM HIM...NOT YET...
SETSUKE HIRATA, PLEASE DO NOT STRUGGLE AND YOU WILL SAVE A LOT OF UNNECESSARY BLOODSHED.

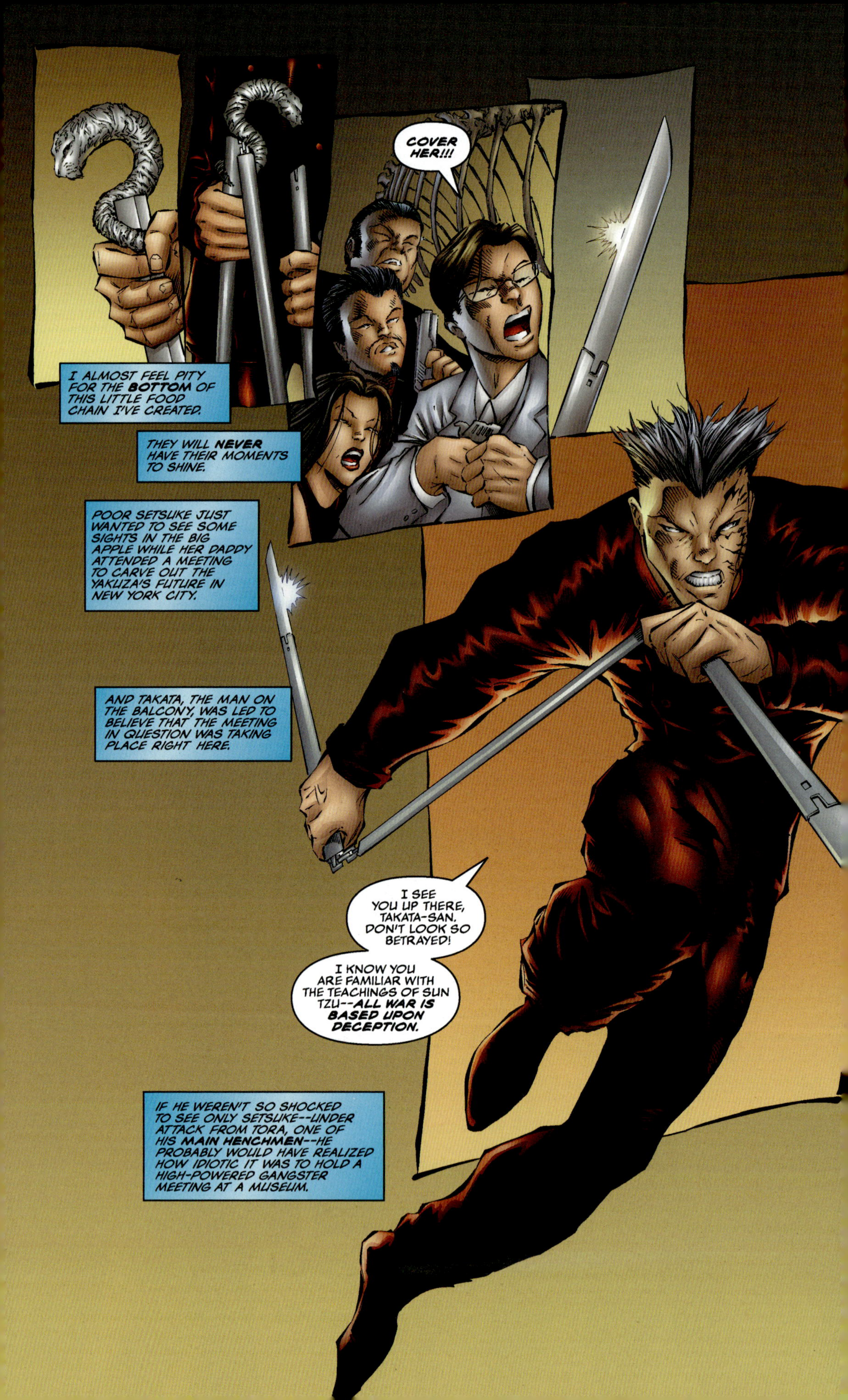
I ALMOST FEEL PITY FOR THE BOTTOM OF THIS LITTLE FOOD CHAIN I'VE CREATED.
COVER HER!!!
THEY WILL NEVER HAVE THEIR MOMENTS TO SHINE.
POOR SETSUKE JUST WANTED TO SEE SOME SIGHTS IN THE BIG APPLE WHILE HER DADDY ATTENDED A MEETING TO CARVE OUT THE YAKUZA'S FUTURE IN NEW YORK CITY.
AND TAKATA, THE MAN ON THE BALCONY, WAS LED TO BELIEVE THAT THE MEETING IN QUESTION WAS TAKING PLACE RIGHT HERE.
I SEE YOU UP THERE, TAKATA-SAN. DON'T LOOK SO BETRAYED!
I KNOW YOU ARE FAMILIAR WITH THE TEACHINGS OF SUN TZU--ALL WAR IS BASED UPON DECEPTION.
IF HE WEREN'T SO SHOCKED TO SEE ONLY SETSUKE--UNDER ATTACK FROM TORA, ONE OF HIS MAIN HENCHMEN--HE PROBABLY WOULD HAVE REALIZED HOW IDIOTIC IT WAS TO HOLD A HIGH-POWERED GANGSTER MEETING AT A MUSEUM.

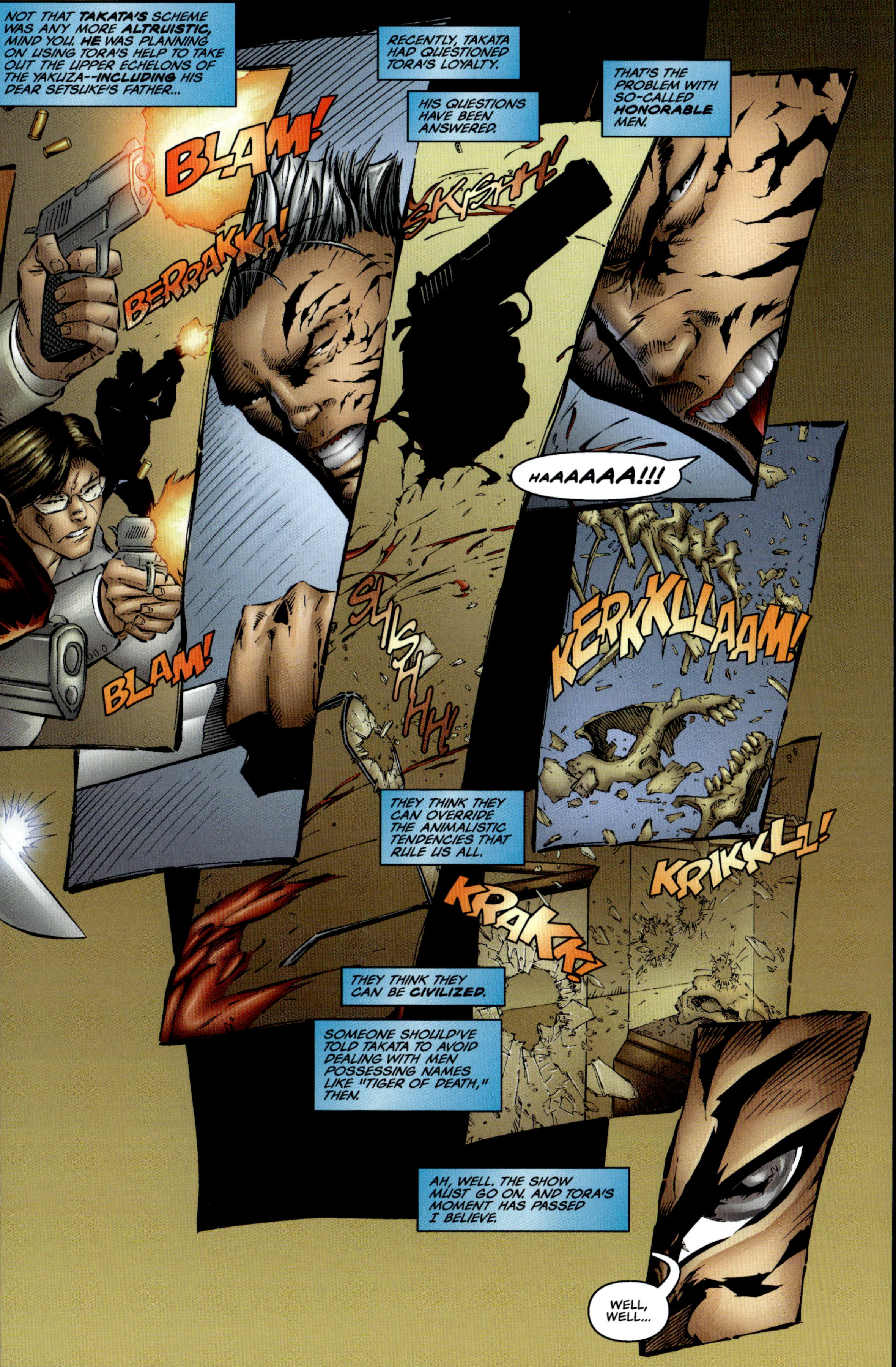
NOT THAT TAKATA'S SCHEME WAS ANY MORE ALTRUISTIC, MIND YOU. HE WAS PLANNING ON USING TORA'S HELP TO TAKE OUT THE UPPER ECHELONS OF THE YAKUZA--INCLUDING HIS DEAR SETSUKE'S FATHER...
BLAM!
BERRAKKA!
RECENTLY, TAKATA HAD QUESTIONED TORA'S LOYALTY.
HIS QUESTIONS HAVE BEEN ANSWERED.
SKRSHH!
THAT'S THE PROBLEM WITH SO-CALLED HONORABLE MEN.
HAAAAAA!!!
BLAM!
SLISHHH!
KERKKLLAAM!
THEY THINK THEY CAN OVERRIDE THE ANIMALISTIC TENDENCIES THAT RULE US ALL.
KRIKKLL!
KRAKK!
THEY THINK THEY CAN BE CIVILIZED.
SOMEONE SHOULD'VE TOLD TAKATA TO AVOID DEALING WITH MEN POSSESSING NAMES LIKE "TIGER OF DEATH," THEN.
AH, WELL. THE SHOW MUST GO ON. AND TORA'S MOMENT HAS PASSED I BELIEVE.
WELL, WELL...

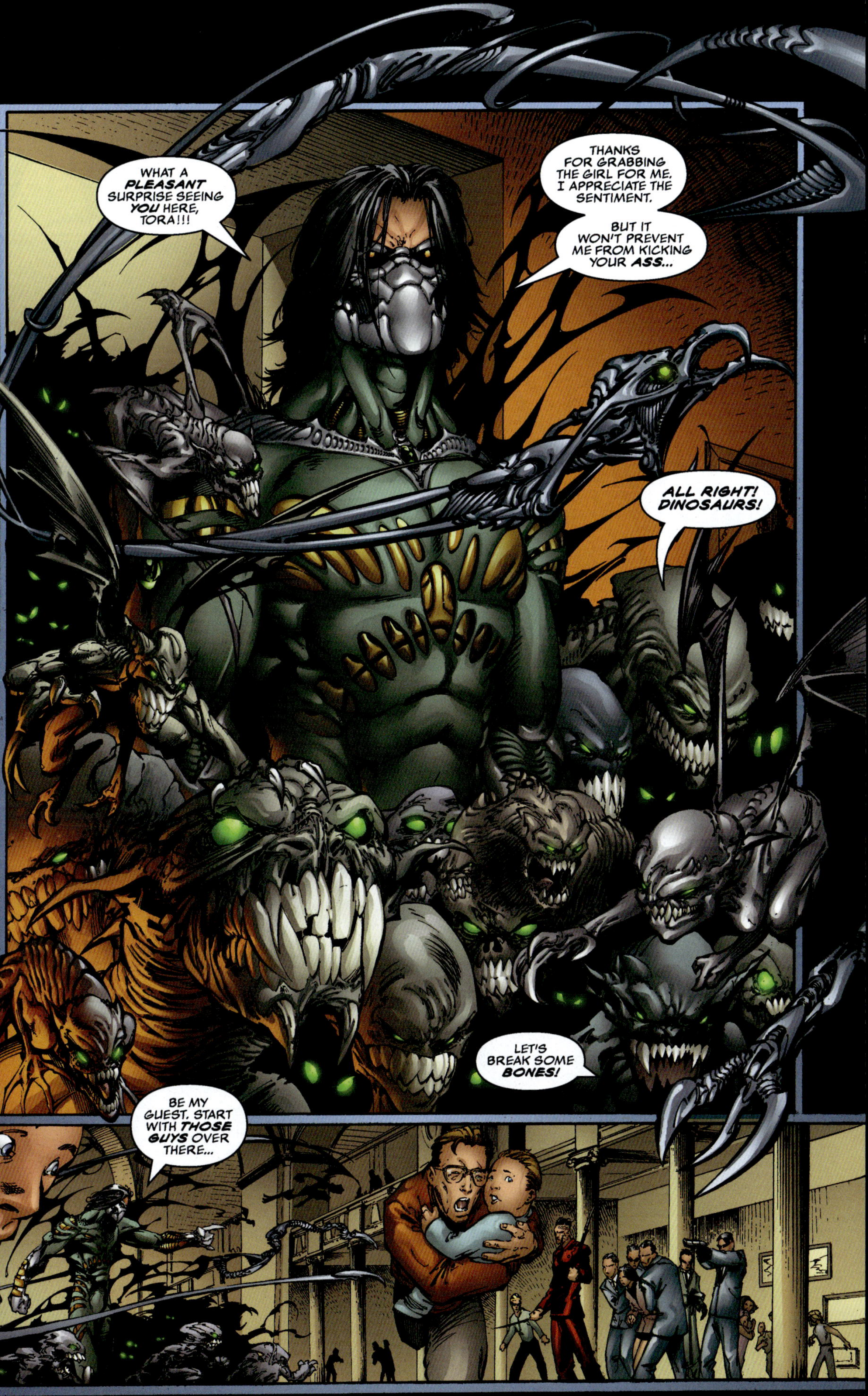

WHAT A PLEASANT SURPRISE SEEING YOU HERE, TORA!!!
THANKS FOR GRABBING THE GIRL FOR ME. I APPRECIATE THE SENTIMENT.
BUT IT WON'T PREVENT ME FROM KICKING YOUR ASS...
ALL RIGHT! DINOSAURS!
LET'S BREAK SOME BONES!
BE MY GUEST. START WITH THOSE GUYS OVER THERE...

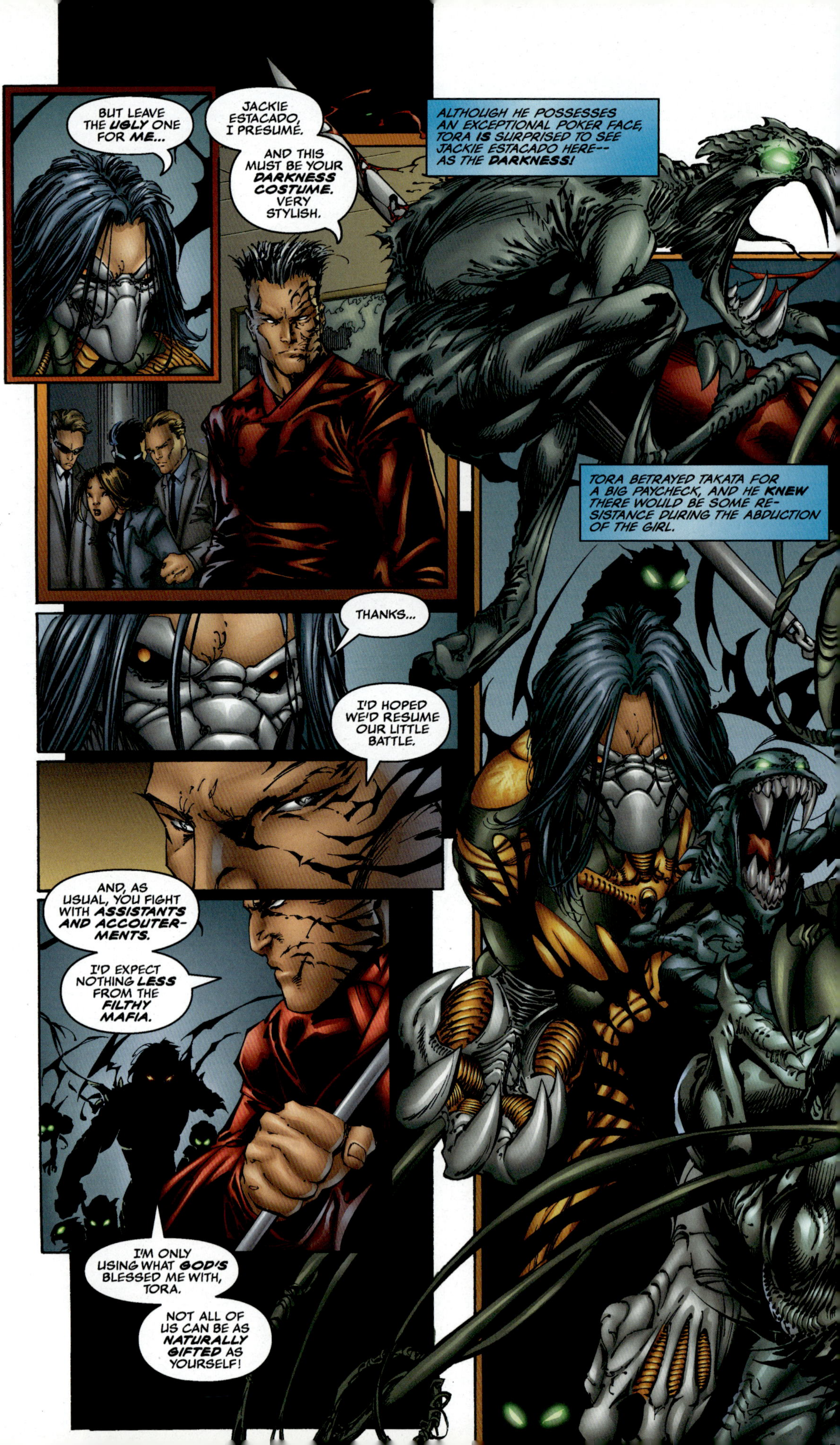
BUT LEAVE THE UGLY ONE FOR ME...
JACKIE ESTACADO, I PRESUME.
AND THIS MUST BE YOUR DARKNESS COSTUME. VERY STYLISH.
ALTHOUGH HE POSSESSES AN EXCEPTIONAL POKER FACE, TORA IS SURPRISED TO SEE JACKIE ESTACADO HERE-- AS THE DARKNESS!
TORA BETRAYED TAKATA FOR A BIG PAYCHECK, AND HE KNEW THERE WOULD BE SOME RE- SISTANCE DURING THE ABDUCTION OF THE GIRL.
THANKS...
I'D HOPED WE'D RESUME OUR LITTLE BATTLE.
AND, AS USUAL, YOU FIGHT WITH ASSISTANTS AND ACCOUTER- MENTS.
I'D EXPECT NOTHING LESS FROM THE FILTHY MAFIA.
I'M ONLY USING WHAT GOD'S BLESSED ME WITH, TORA.
NOT ALL OF US CAN BE AS NATURALLY GIFTED AS YOURSELF!

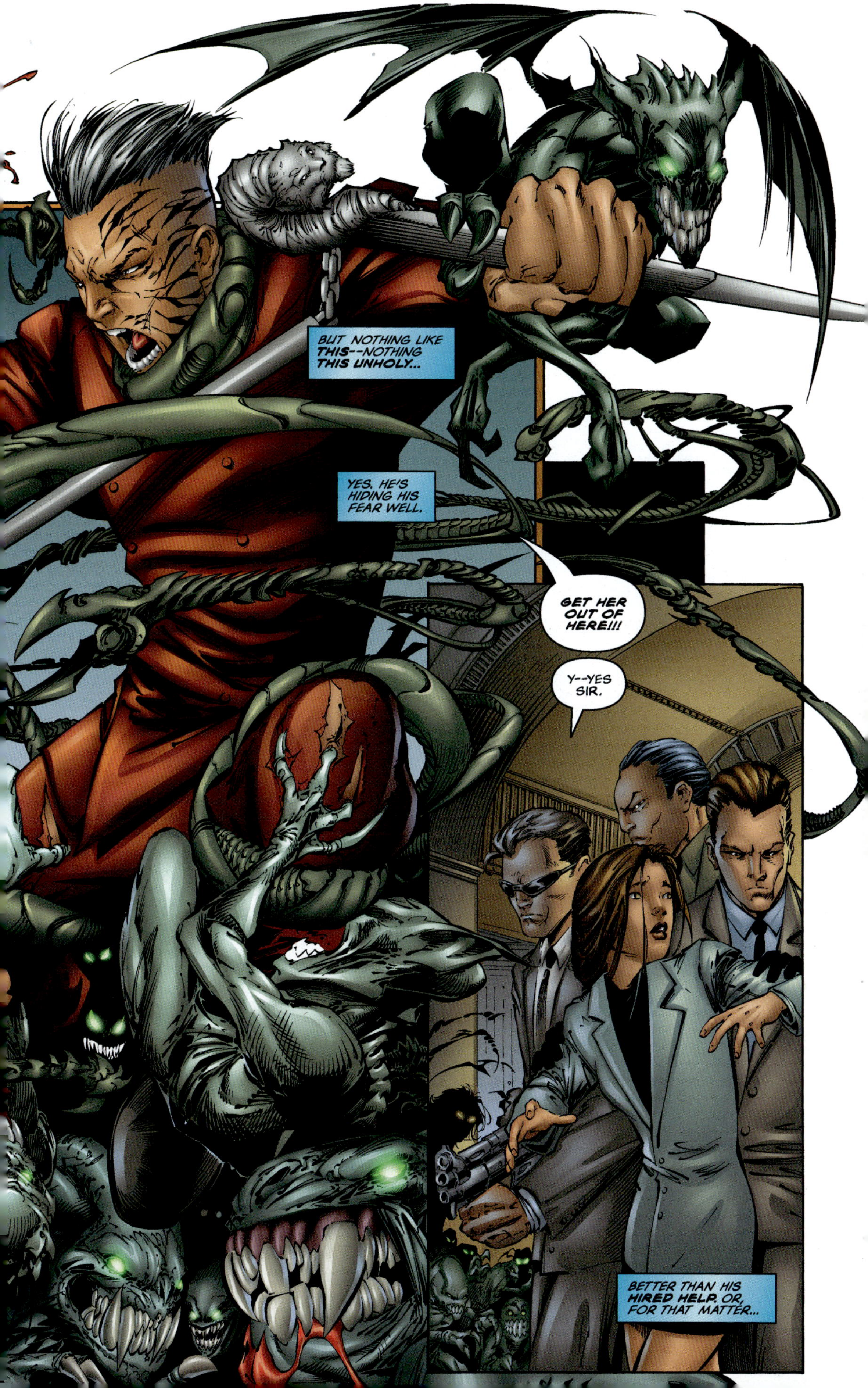
BUT NOTHING LIKE THIS--NOTHING THIS UNHOLY...
YES, HE'S HIDING HIS FEAR WELL.
GET HER OUT OF HERE!!!
Y--YES SIR.
BETTER THAN HIS HIRED HELP. OR, FOR THAT MATTER...

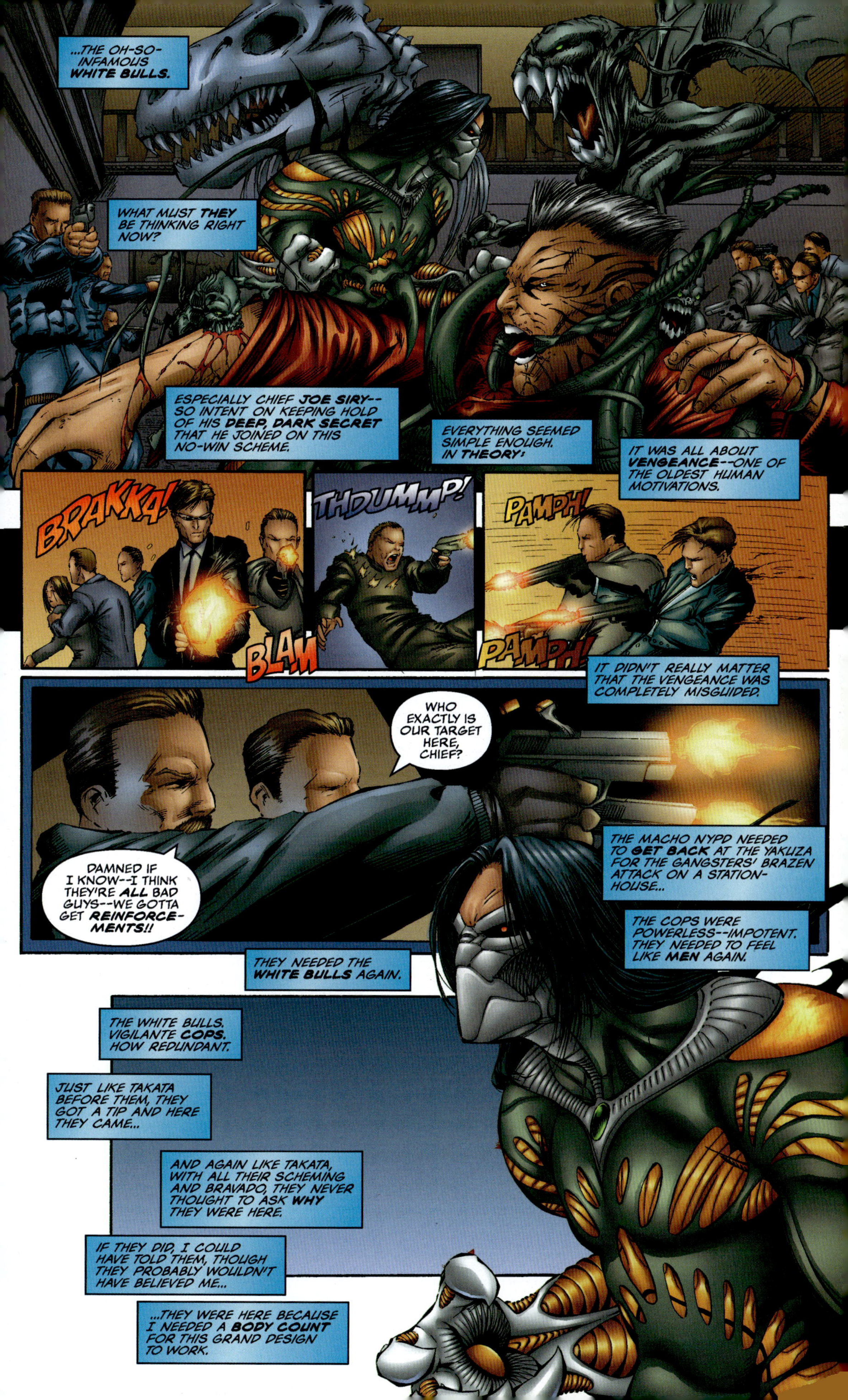

...THE OH-SO-INFAMOUS WHITE BULLS.
WHAT MUST THEY BE THINKING RIGHT NOW?
ESPECIALLY CHIEF JOE SIRY--SO INTENT ON KEEPING HOLD OF HIS DEEP, DARK SECRET THAT HE JOINED ON THIS NO-WIN SCHEME.
EVERYTHING SEEMED SIMPLE ENOUGH. IN THEORY:
IT WAS ALL ABOUT VENGEANCE--ONE OF THE OLDEST HUMAN MOTIVATIONS.
BRAKKA!
BLAM
THDUMMP!
PAMPH!
PAMPH!
IT DIDN'T REALLY MATTER THAT THE VENGEANCE WAS COMPLETELY MISGUIDED.
WHO EXACTLY IS OUR TARGET HERE, CHIEF?
DAMNED IF I KNOW--I THINK THEY'RE ALL BAD GUYS--WE GOTTA GET REINFORCE-MENTS!!
THE MACHO NYPD NEEDED TO GET BACK AT THE YAKUZA FOR THE GANGSTERS' BRAZEN ATTACK ON A STATION-HOUSE...
THE COPS WERE POWERLESS--IMPOTENT. THEY NEEDED TO FEEL LIKE MEN AGAIN.
THEY NEEDED THE WHITE BULLS AGAIN.
THE WHITE BULLS. VIGILANTE COPS. HOW REDUNDANT.
JUST LIKE TAKATA BEFORE THEM, THEY GOT A TIP AND HERE THEY CAME...
AND AGAIN LIKE TAKATA, WITH ALL THEIR SCHEMING AND BRAVADO, THEY NEVER THOUGHT TO ASK WHY THEY WERE HERE.
IF THEY DID, I COULD HAVE TOLD THEM, THOUGH THEY PROBABLY WOULDN'T HAVE BELIEVED ME...
...THEY WERE HERE BECAUSE I NEEDED A BODY COUNT FOR THIS GRAND DESIGN TO WORK.

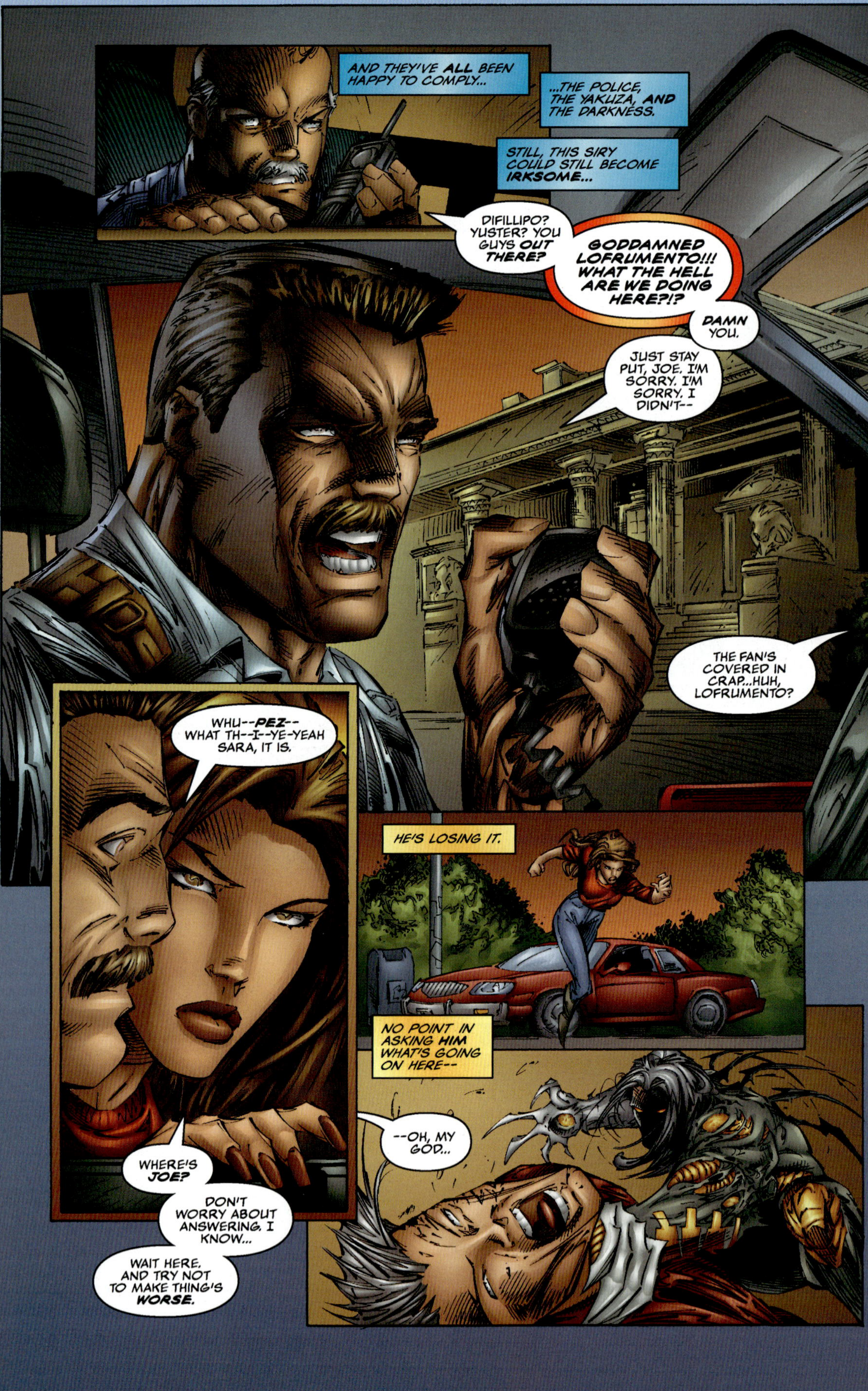

AND THEY'VE ALL BEEN HAPPY TO COMPLY...
...THE POLICE, THE YAKUZA, AND THE DARKNESS.
STILL, THIS SIRY COULD STILL BECOME IRKSOME...
DIFILLIPO? YUSTER? YOU GUYS OUT THERE?
GODDAMNED LOFRUMENTO!!! WHAT THE HELL ARE WE DOING HERE?!?
DAMN YOU.
JUST STAY PUT, JOE. I'M SORRY. I'M SORRY. I DIDN'T--
THE FAN'S COVERED IN CRAP...HUH, LOFRUMENTO?
WHU--PEZ--WHAT TH--I--YE-YEAH SARA, IT IS.
WHERE'S JOE?
DON'T WORRY ABOUT ANSWERING. I KNOW...
WAIT HERE, AND TRY NOT TO MAKE THING'S WORSE.
HE'S LOSING IT.
NO POINT IN ASKING HIM WHAT'S GOING ON HERE--
--OH, MY GOD...

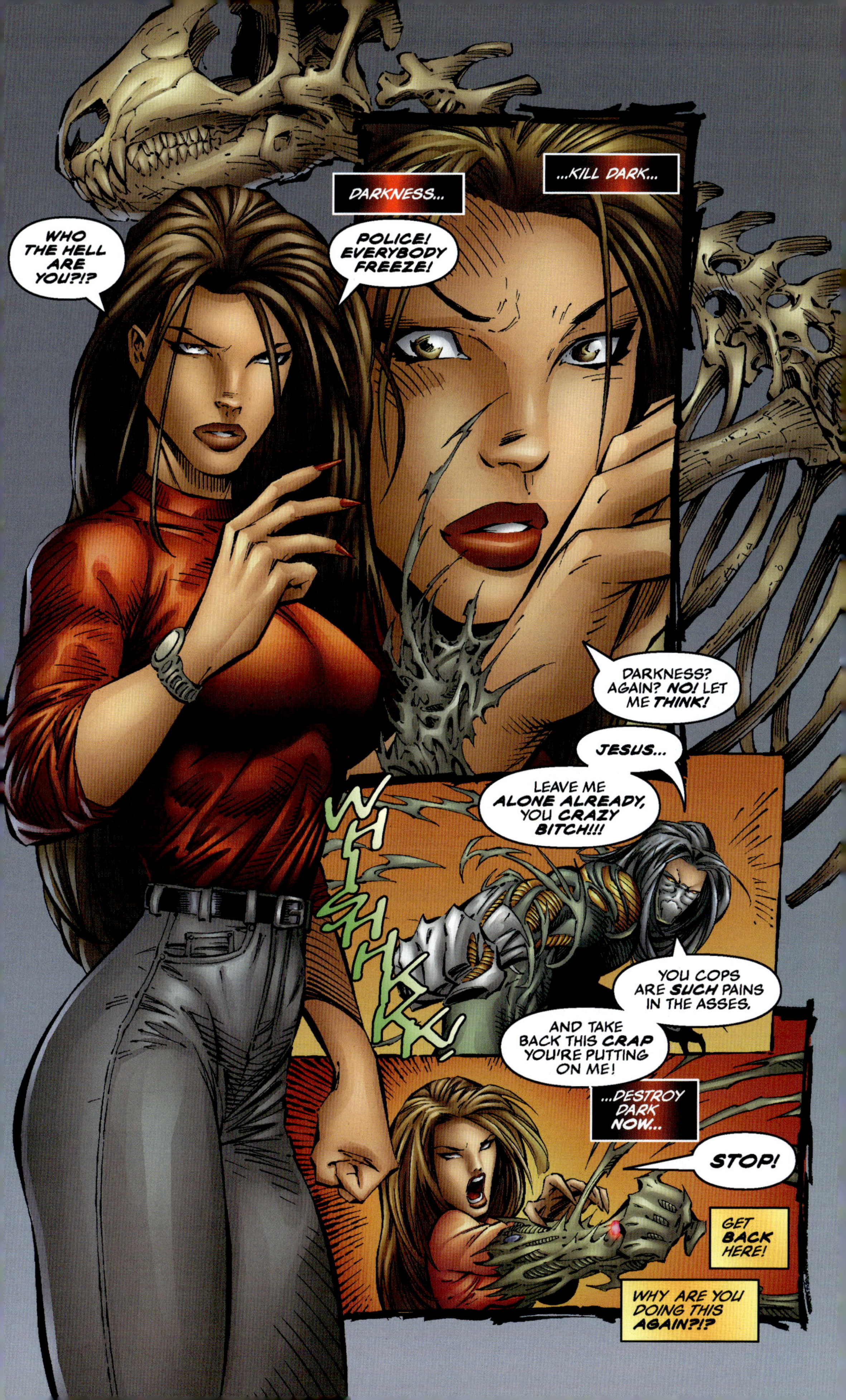
DARKNESS...
...KILL DARK...
WHO THE HELL ARE YOU?!?
POLICE! EVERYBODY FREEZE!
DARKNESS? AGAIN? NO! LET ME THINK!
JESUS...
LEAVE ME ALONE ALREADY, YOU CRAZY BITCH!!!
WHSHKKK!
YOU COPS ARE SUCH PAINS IN THE ASSES.
AND TAKE BACK THIS CRAP YOU'RE PUTTING ON ME!
...DESTROY DARK NOW...
STOP!
GET BACK HERE!
WHY ARE YOU DOING THIS AGAIN?!?

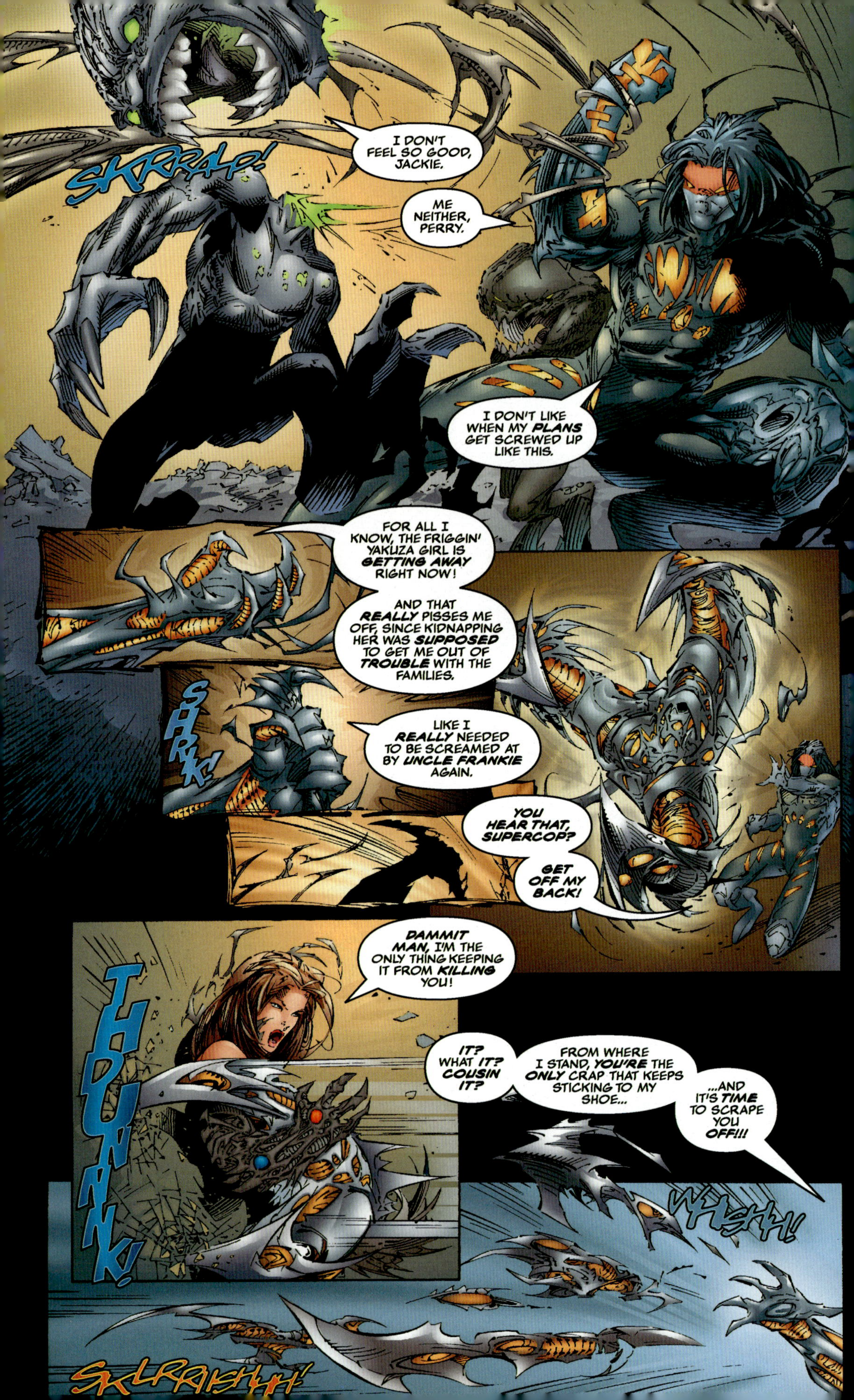

SKRRAAP!
I DON'T FEEL SO GOOD, JACKIE.
ME NEITHER, PERRY.
I DON'T LIKE WHEN MY PLANS GET SCREWED UP LIKE THIS.
FOR ALL I KNOW, THE FRIGGIN' YAKUZA GIRL IS GETTING AWAY RIGHT NOW!
AND THAT REALLY PISSES ME OFF, SINCE KIDNAPPING HER WAS SUPPOSED TO GET ME OUT OF TROUBLE WITH THE FAMILIES.
SHRAK!
LIKE I REALLY NEEDED TO BE SCREAMED AT BY UNCLE FRANKIE AGAIN.
YOU HEAR THAT, SUPERCOP?
GET OFF MY BACK!
DAMMIT MAN, I'M THE ONLY THING KEEPING IT FROM KILLING YOU!
THUNNNK!
IT? WHAT IT? COUSIN IT?
FROM WHERE I STAND, YOU'RE THE ONLY CRAP THAT KEEPS STICKING TO MY SHOE...
...AND IT'S TIME TO SCRAPE YOU OFF!!!
WHSHH!
SKLRRAISHHH!

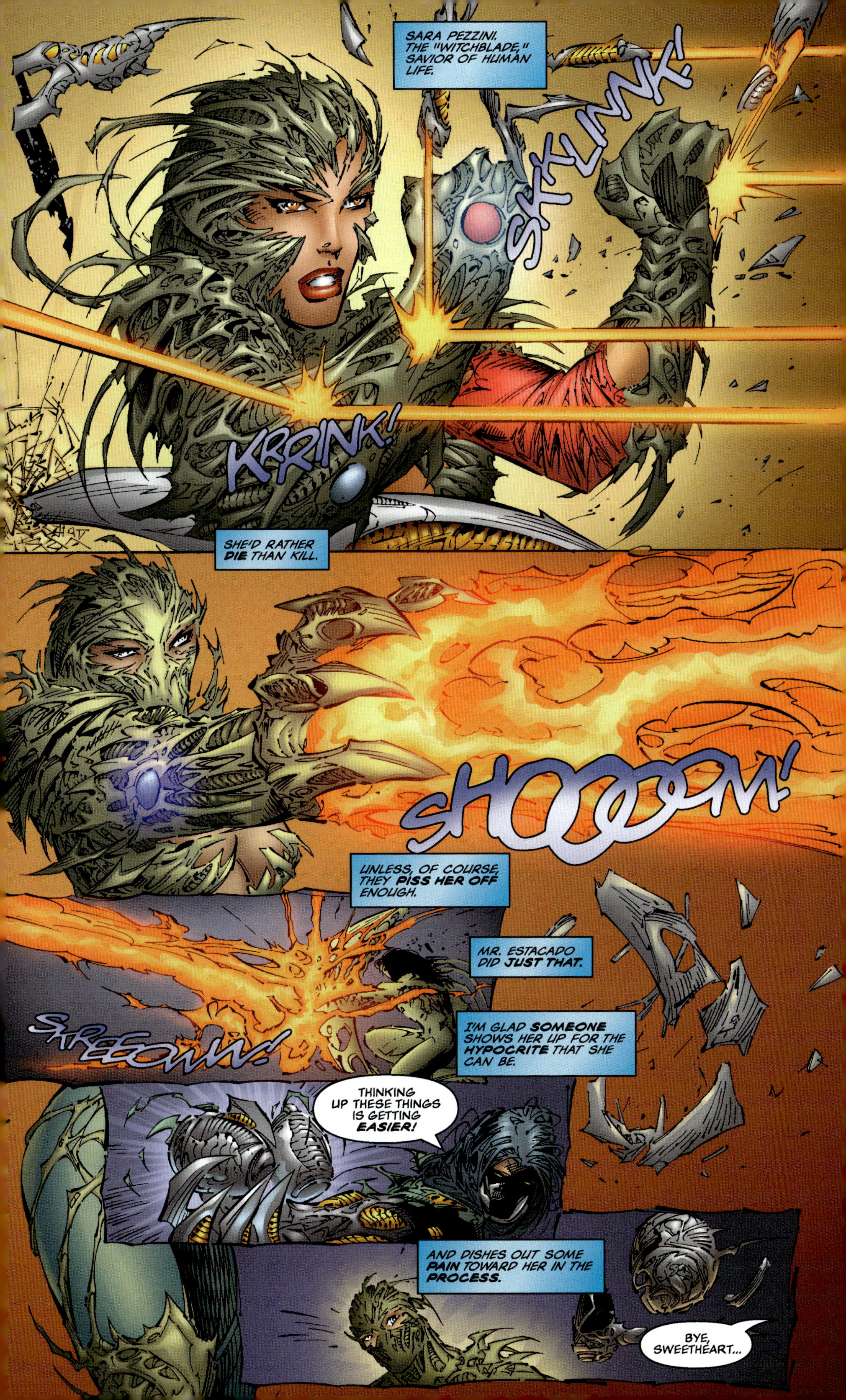

SARA PEZZINI. THE "WITCHBLADE," SAVIOR OF HUMAN LIFE.
SKLUNNK!
KRRINK!
SHE'D RATHER DIE THAN KILL.
SHOOOOM!
UNLESS, OF COURSE, THEY PISS HER OFF ENOUGH.
MR. ESTACADO DID JUST THAT.
SKREEOWW!
I'M GLAD SOMEONE SHOWS HER UP FOR THE HYPOCRITE THAT SHE CAN BE.
THINKING UP THESE THINGS IS GETTING EASIER!
AND DISHES OUT SOME PAIN TOWARD HER IN THE PROCESS.
BYE, SWEETHEART...

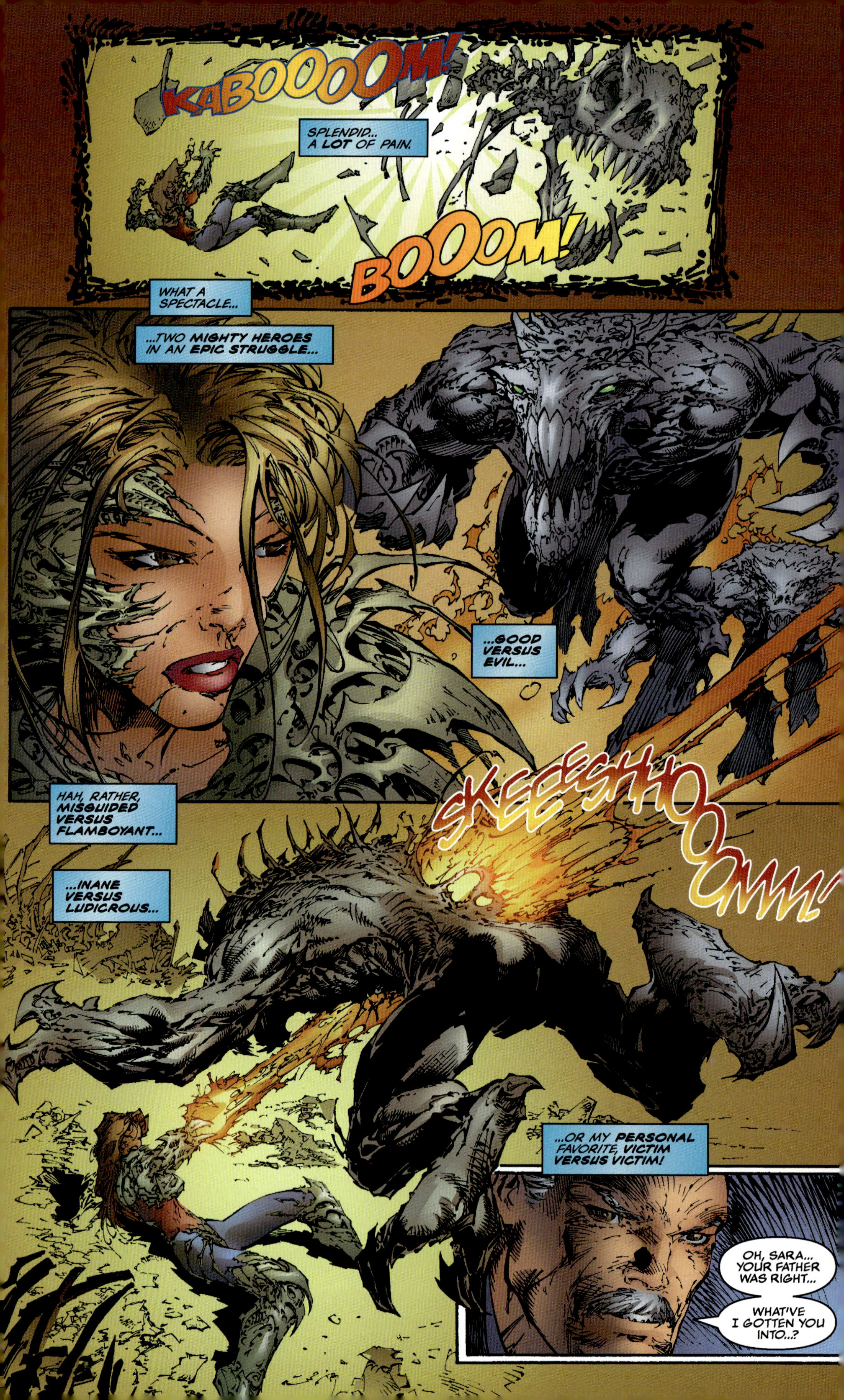
KABOOOOOM!
SPLENDID... A LOT OF PAIN.
BOOOOM!
WHAT A SPECTACLE...
...TWO MIGHTY HEROES IN AN EPIC STRUGGLE...
...GOOD VERSUS EVIL...
HAH, RATHER, MISGUIDED VERSUS FLAMBOYANT...
...INANE VERSUS LUDICROUS...
SKEEESHHOOOMM!
...OR MY PERSONAL FAVORITE, VICTIM VERSUS VICTIM!
OH, SARA... YOUR FATHER WAS RIGHT...
WHAT'VE I GOTTEN YOU INTO...?

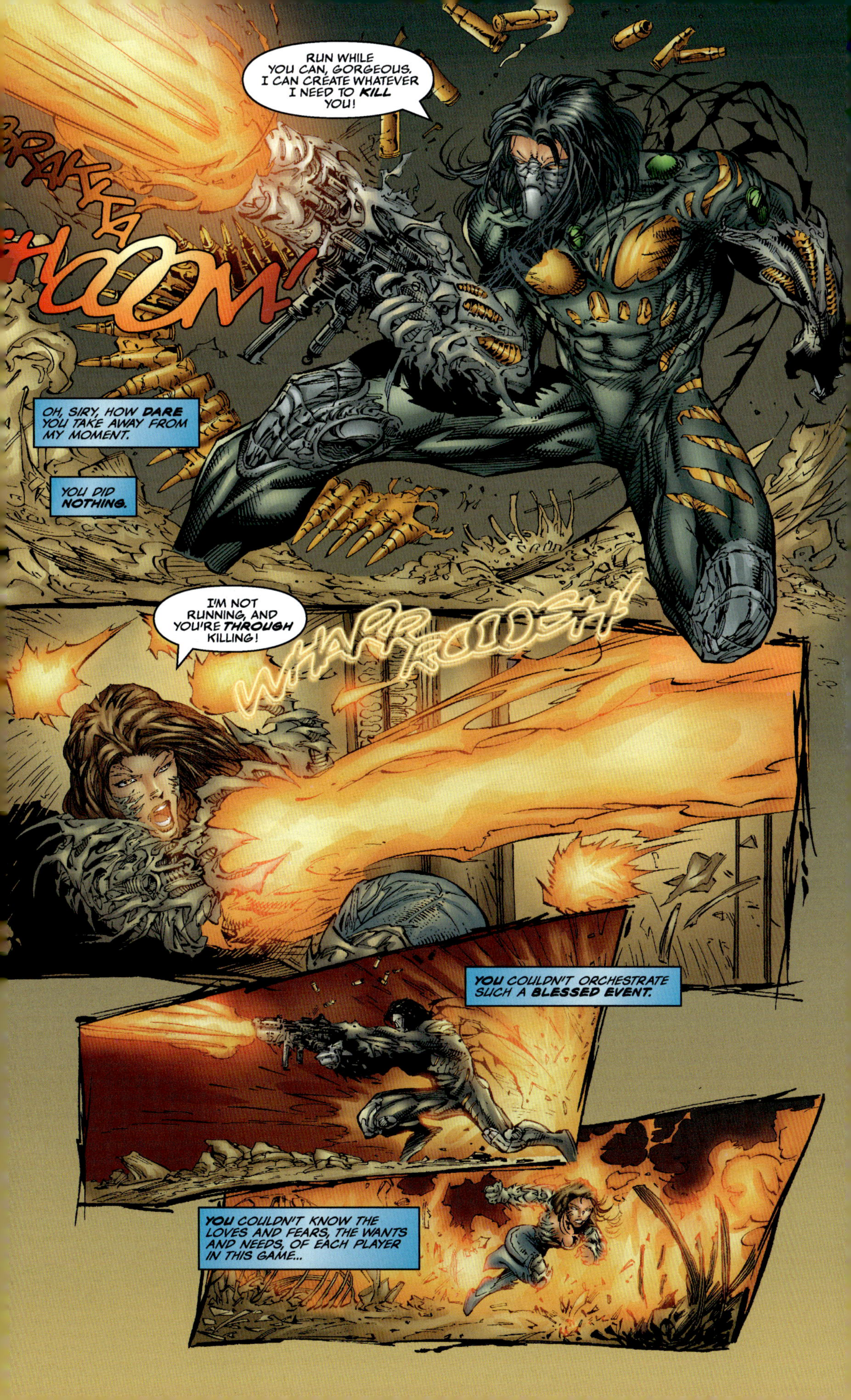
RUN WHILE YOU CAN, GORGEOUS. I CAN CREATE WHATEVER I NEED TO KILL YOU!
BRAKKA
THOOOM!
OH, SIRY, HOW DARE YOU TAKE AWAY FROM MY MOMENT.
YOU DID NOTHING.
I'M NOT RUNNING, AND YOU'RE THROUGH KILLING!
WHARRROOOSH!
YOU COULDN'T ORCHESTRATE SUCH A BLESSED EVENT.
YOU COULDN'T KNOW THE LOVES AND FEARS, THE WANTS AND NEEDS, OF EACH PLAYER IN THIS GAME...

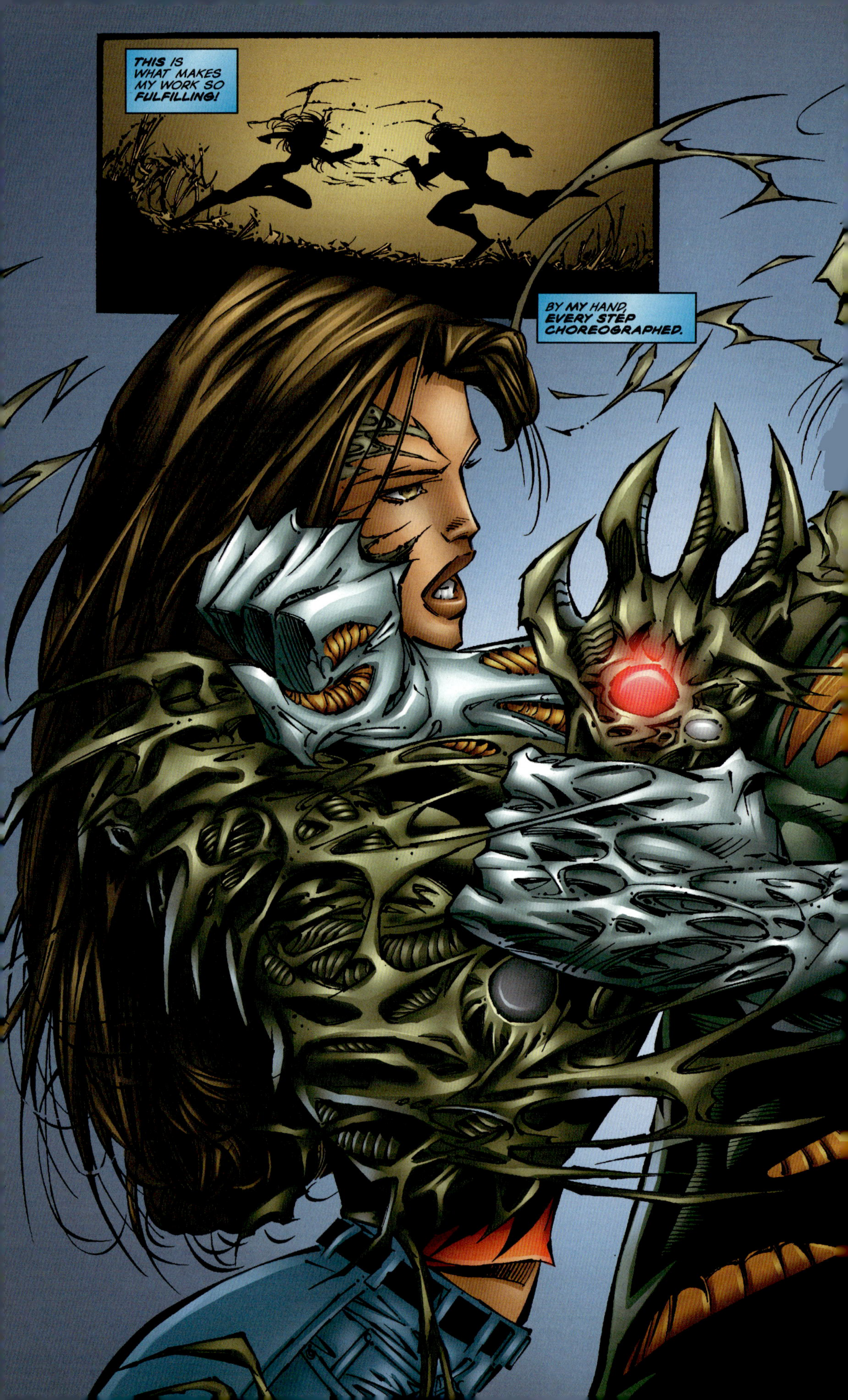
THIS IS WHAT MAKES MY WORK SO FULFILLING!
BY MY HAND, EVERY STEP CHOREOGRAPHED.

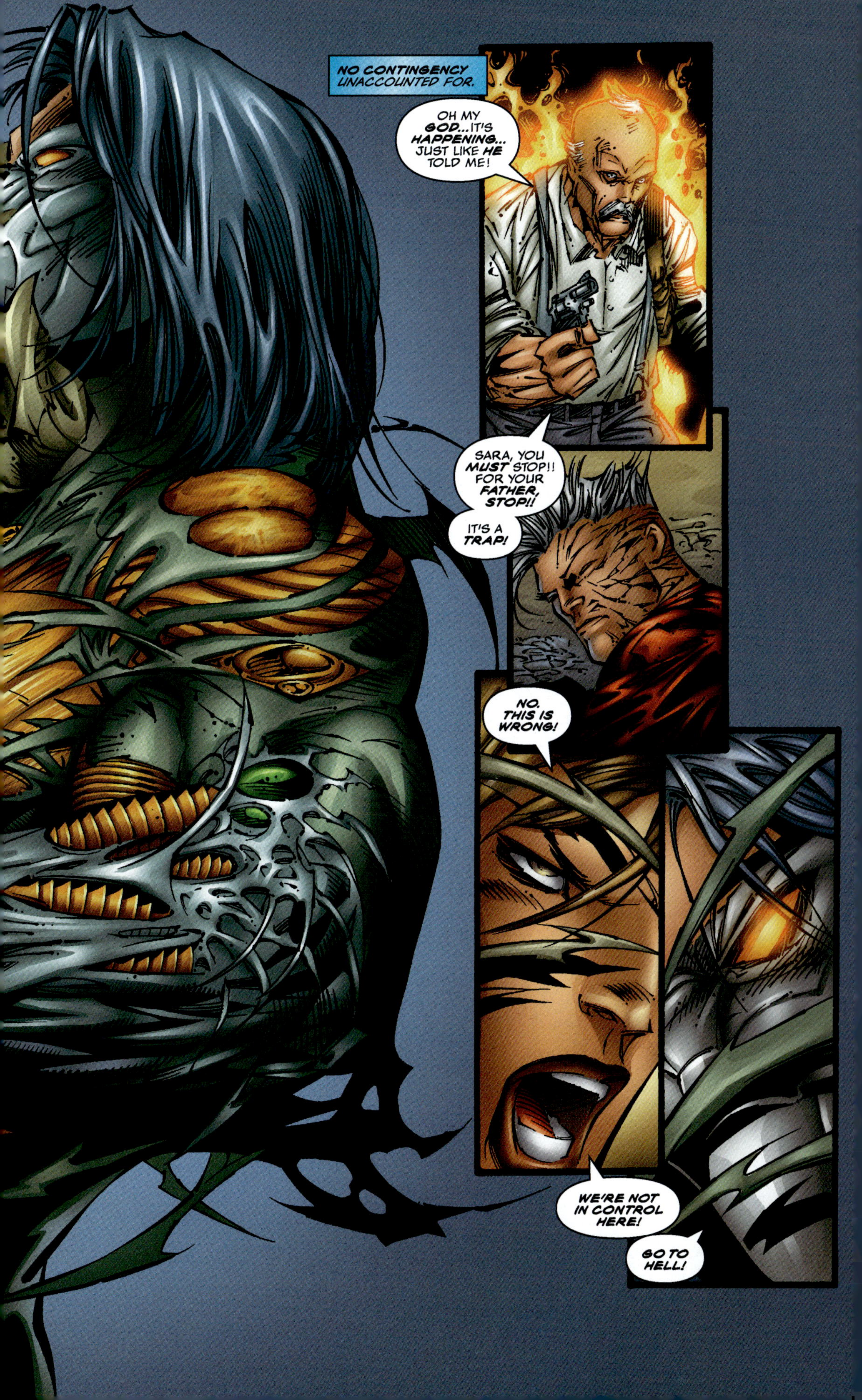
NO CONTINGENCY UNACCOUNTED FOR.
OH MY GOD...IT'S HAPPENING... JUST LIKE HE TOLD ME!
SARA, YOU MUST STOP!! FOR YOUR FATHER, STOP!!
IT'S A TRAP!
NO. THIS IS WRONG!
WE'RE NOT IN CONTROL HERE!
GO TO HELL!

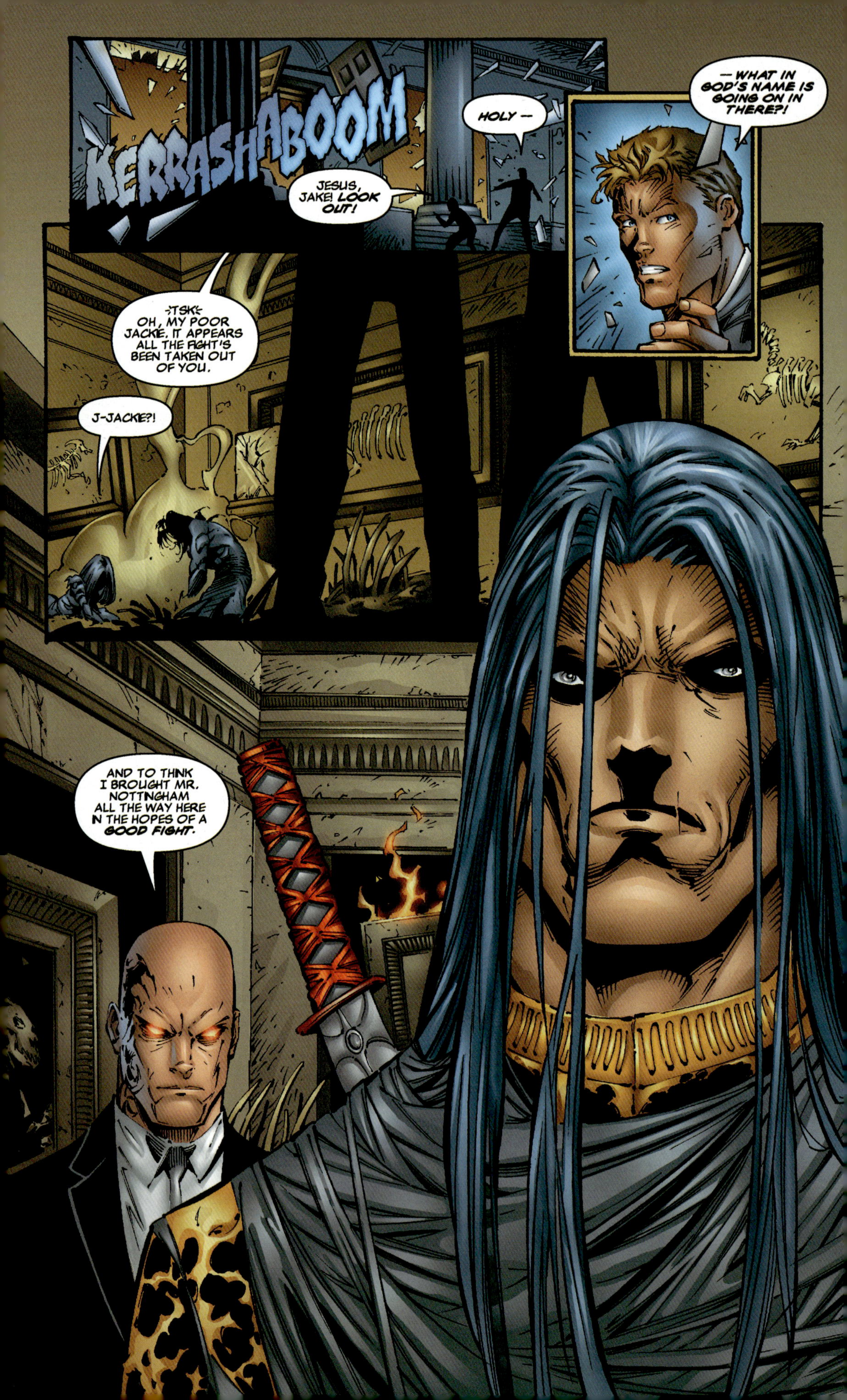
KERRASHABOOM
HOLY --
JESUS, JAKE! LOOK OUT!
-- WHAT IN GOD'S NAME IS GOING ON IN THERE?!
-TSK- OH, MY POOR JACKIE. IT APPEARS ALL THE FIGHT'S BEEN TAKEN OUT OF YOU.
J-JACKIE?!
AND TO THINK I BROUGHT MR. NOTTINGHAM ALL THE WAY HERE IN THE HOPES OF A GOOD FIGHT.

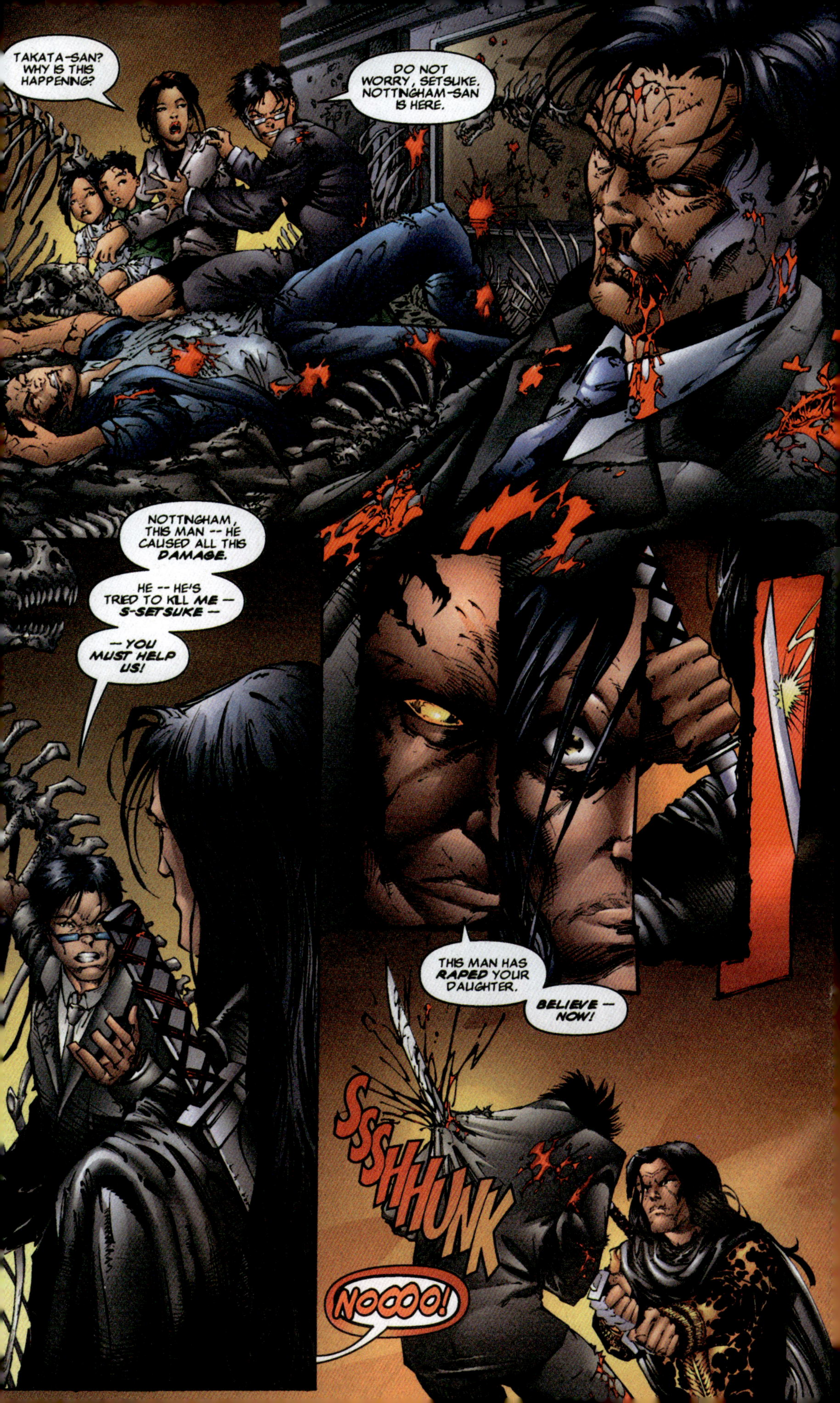

TAKATA-SAN? WHY IS THIS HAPPENING?
DO NOT WORRY, SETSUKE. NOTTINGHAM-SAN IS HERE.
NOTTINGHAM, THIS MAN -- HE CAUSED ALL THIS DAMAGE.
HE -- HE'S TRIED TO KILL ME -- S-SETSUKE --
-- YOU MUST HELP US!
THIS MAN HAS RAPED YOUR DAUGHTER.
BELIEVE -- NOW!
SSSHHUNK
NOOOO!

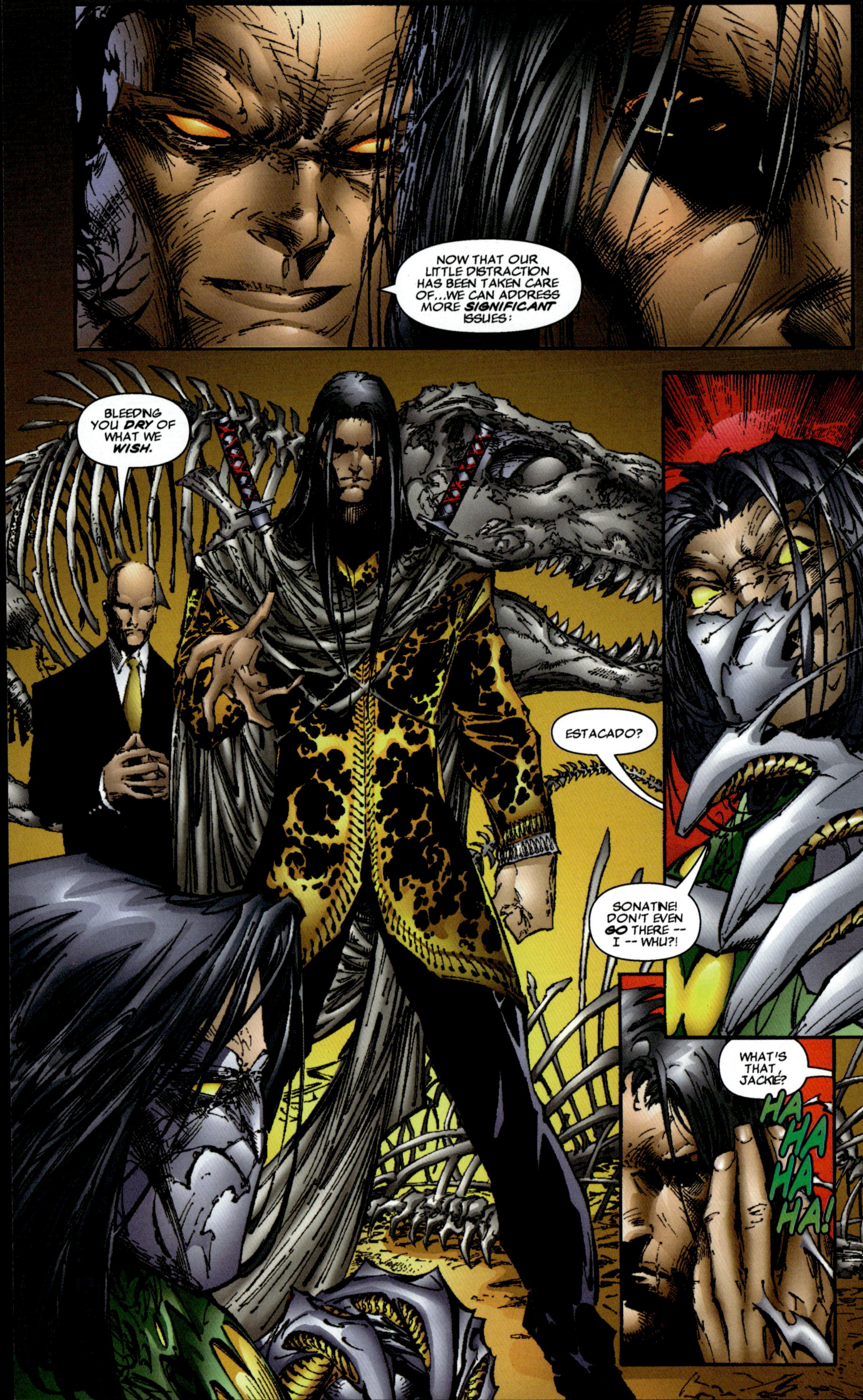
NOW THAT OUR LITTLE DISTRACTION HAS BEEN TAKEN CARE OF...WE CAN ADDRESS MORE SIGNIFICANT ISSUES:
BLEEDING YOU DRY OF WHAT WE WISH.
ESTACADO?
SONATINE! DON'T EVEN GO THERE -- I -- WHU?!
WHAT'S THAT, JACKIE?
HA HA HA HA!

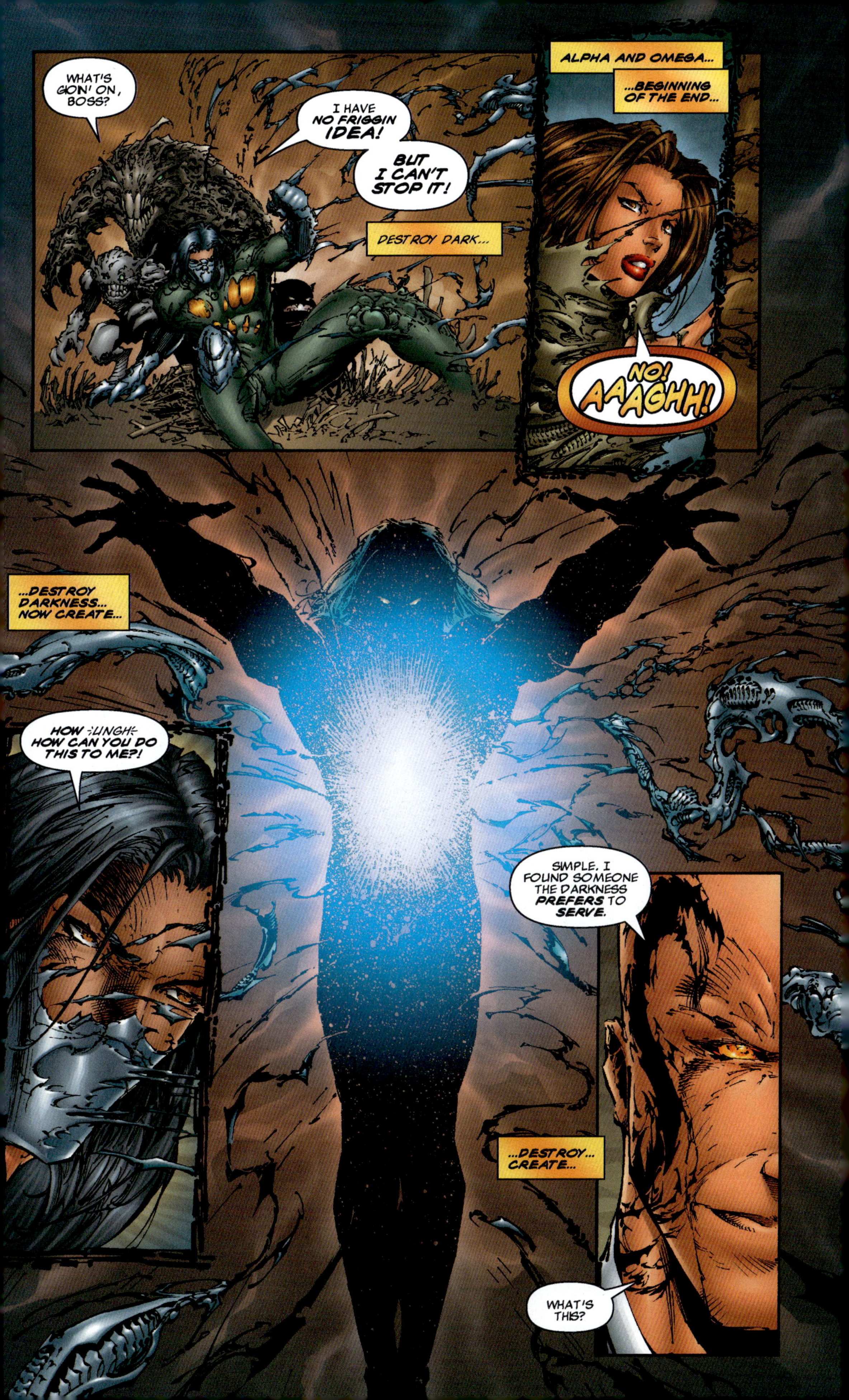
WHAT'S GION' ON, BOSS?
I HAVE NO FRIGGIN IDEA!
BUT I CAN'T STOP IT!
DESTROY DARK...
ALPHA AND OMEGA...
...BEGINNING OF THE END...
NO! AAAGHH!
...DESTROY DARKNESS... NOW CREATE...
HOW -UNGH- HOW CAN YOU DO THIS TO ME?!
SIMPLE. I FOUND SOMEONE THE DARKNESS PREFERS TO SERVE.
...DESTROY... CREATE...
WHAT'S THIS?

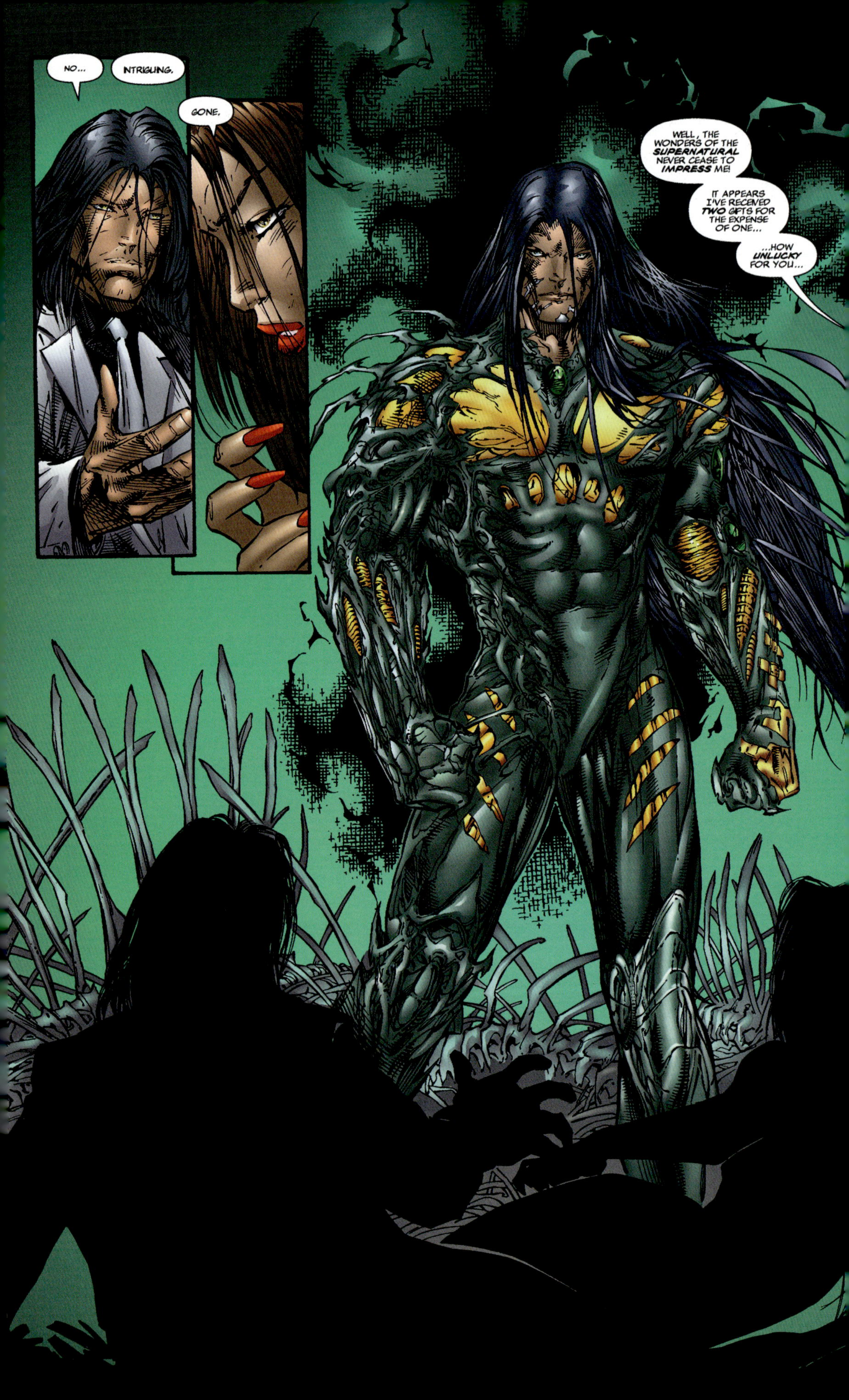
NO...
INTRIGUING.
GONE.
WELL, THE WONDERS OF THE SUPERNATURAL NEVER CEASE TO IMPRESS ME!
IT APPEARS I'VE RECEIVED TWO GIFTS FOR THE EXPENSE OF ONE...
...HOW UNLUCKY FOR YOU...

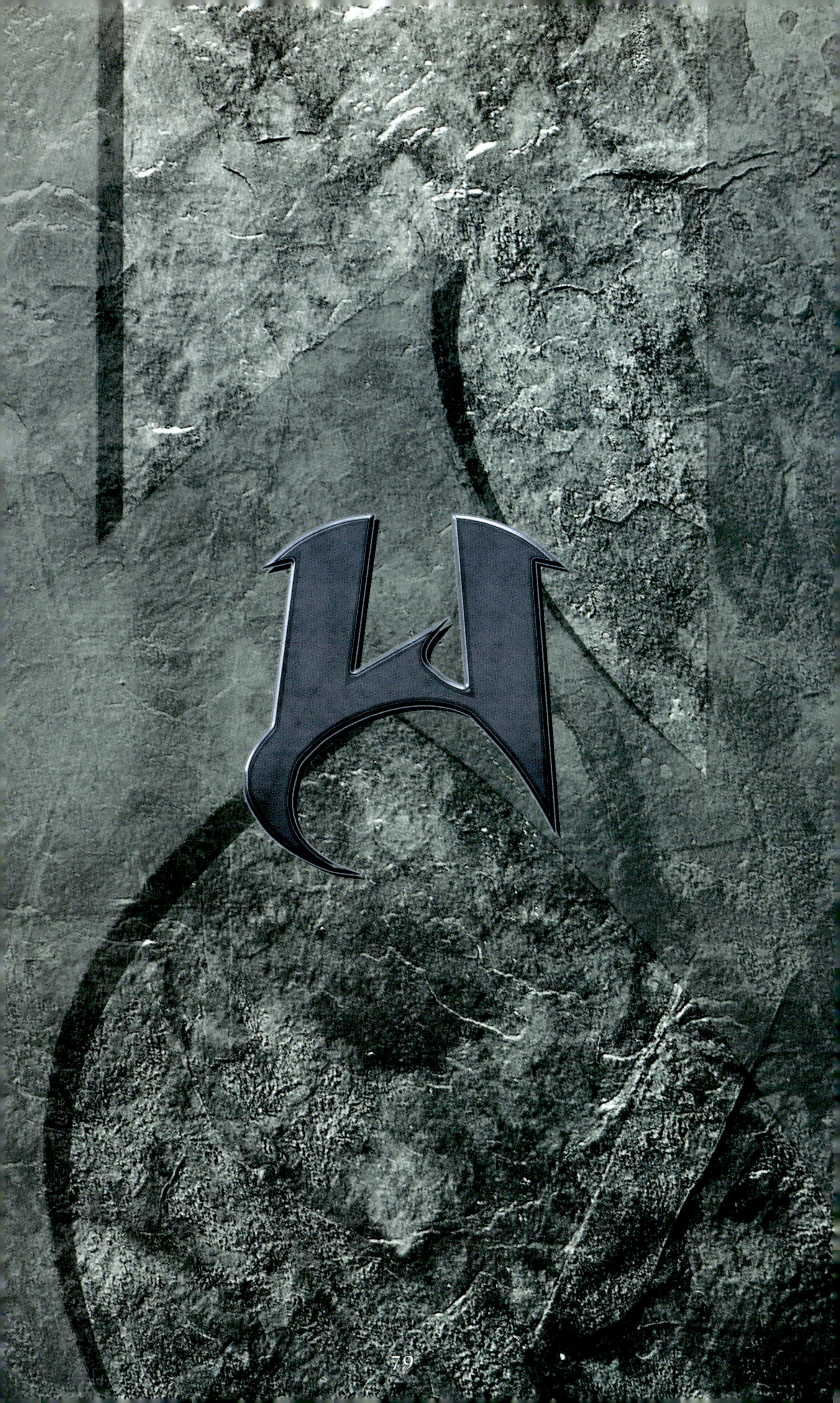

FAMILY TIES part 4: *Witchblade*
issue #19

story: **David Wohl** and **Christina Z.**
pencils and co-plot: **Michael Turner**
inks: **D-Tron**
colors: **JD Smith**

ink assists: **Jeff De Los Santos, Jose "Jag" Guillen, Marsha Chen**
and **Andy Kim**

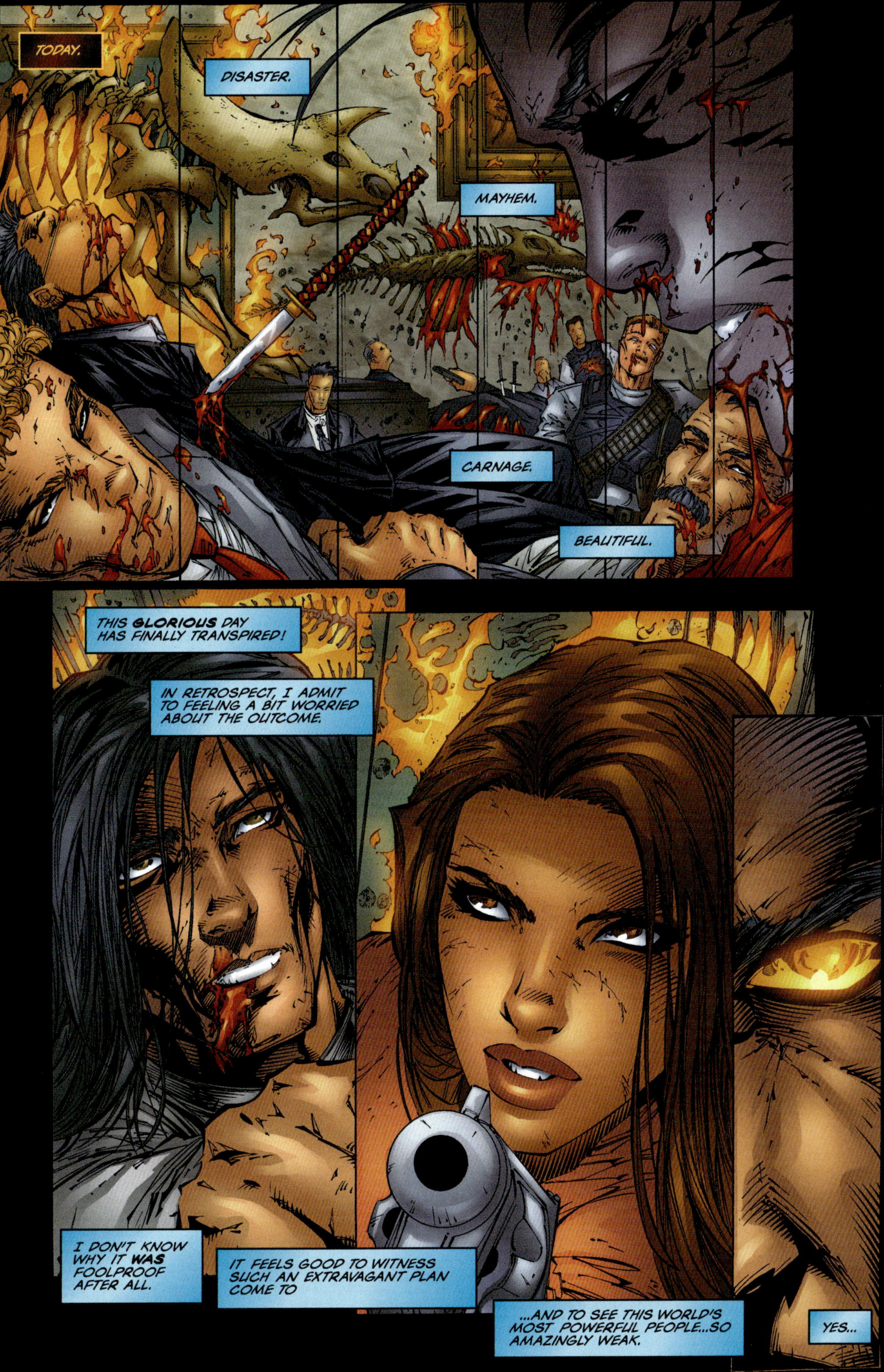
TODAY.
DISASTER.
MAYHEM.
CARNAGE.
BEAUTIFUL.
THIS GLORIOUS DAY HAS FINALLY TRANSPIRED!
IN RETROSPECT, I ADMIT TO FEELING A BIT WORRIED ABOUT THE OUTCOME.
I DON'T KNOW WHY IT WAS FOOLPROOF AFTER ALL.
IT FEELS GOOD TO WITNESS SUCH AN EXTRAVAGANT PLAN COME TO
...AND TO SEE THIS WORLD'S MOST POWERFUL PEOPLE...SO AMAZINGLY WEAK.
YES...

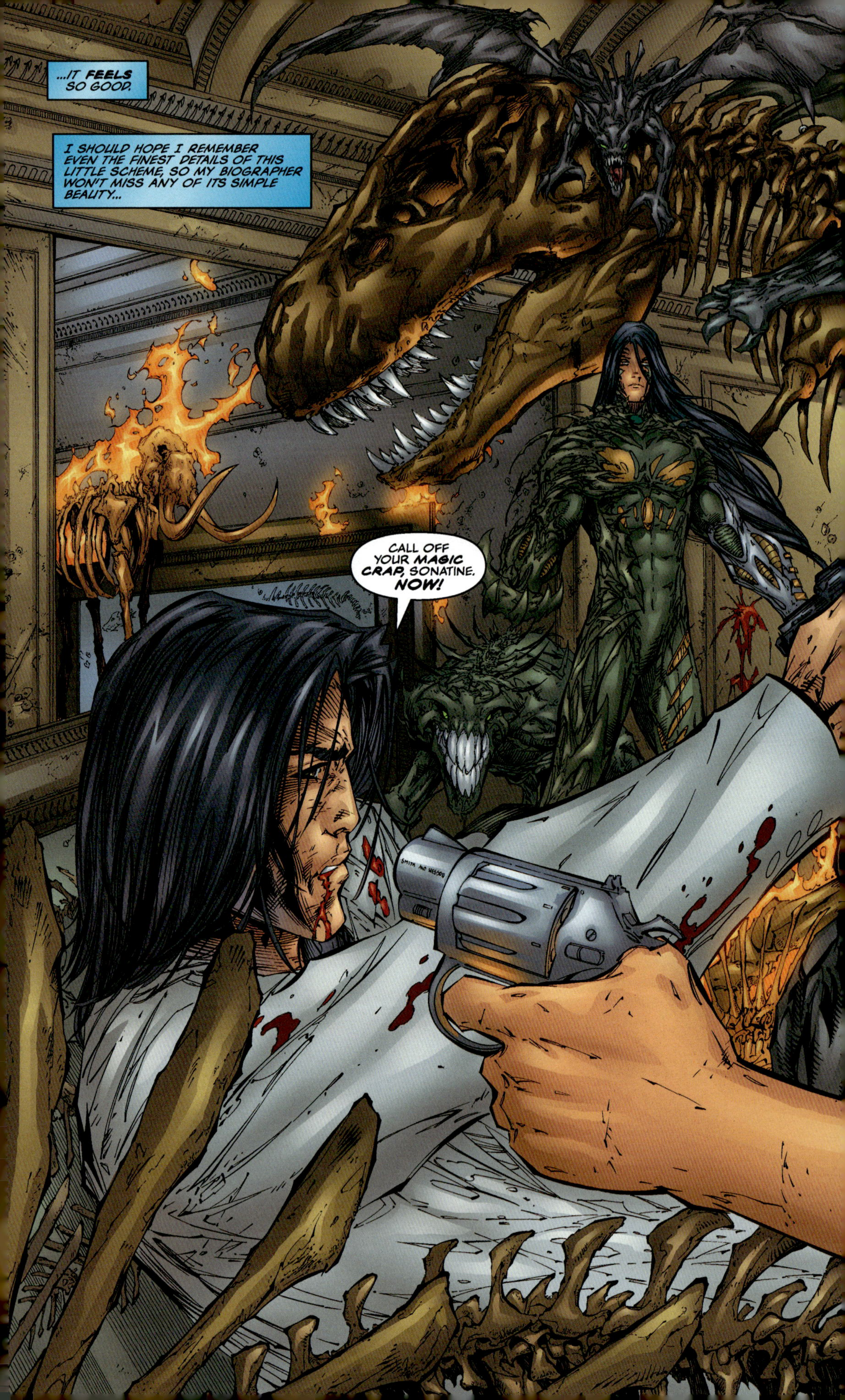
...IT FEELS SO GOOD.
I SHOULD HOPE I REMEMBER EVEN THE FINEST DETAILS OF THIS LITTLE SCHEME, SO MY BIOGRAPHER WON'T MISS ANY OF ITS SIMPLE BEAUTY...
CALL OFF YOUR MAGIC CRAP, SONATINE. NOW!

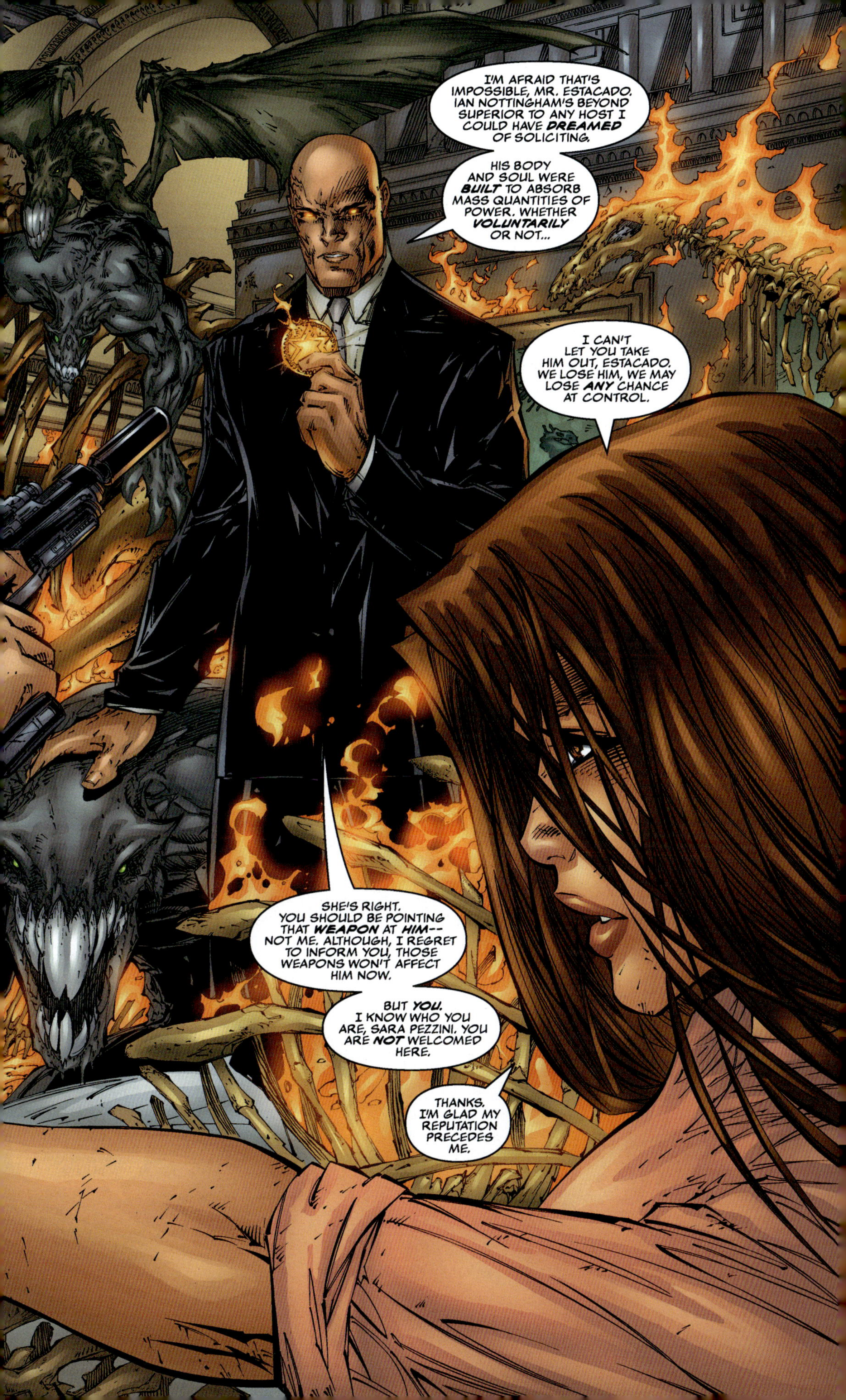

I'M AFRAID THAT'S IMPOSSIBLE, MR. ESTACADO. IAN NOTTINGHAM'S BEYOND SUPERIOR TO ANY HOST I COULD HAVE DREAMED OF SOLICITING.
HIS BODY AND SOUL WERE BUILT TO ABSORB MASS QUANTITIES OF POWER. WHETHER VOLUNTARILY OR NOT...
I CAN'T LET YOU TAKE HIM OUT, ESTACADO. WE LOSE HIM, WE MAY LOSE ANY CHANCE AT CONTROL.
SHE'S RIGHT. YOU SHOULD BE POINTING THAT WEAPON AT HIM-- NOT ME. ALTHOUGH, I REGRET TO INFORM YOU, THOSE WEAPONS WON'T AFFECT HIM NOW.
BUT YOU. I KNOW WHO YOU ARE, SARA PEZZINI. YOU ARE NOT WELCOMED HERE.
THANKS. I'M GLAD MY REPUTATION PRECEDES ME.

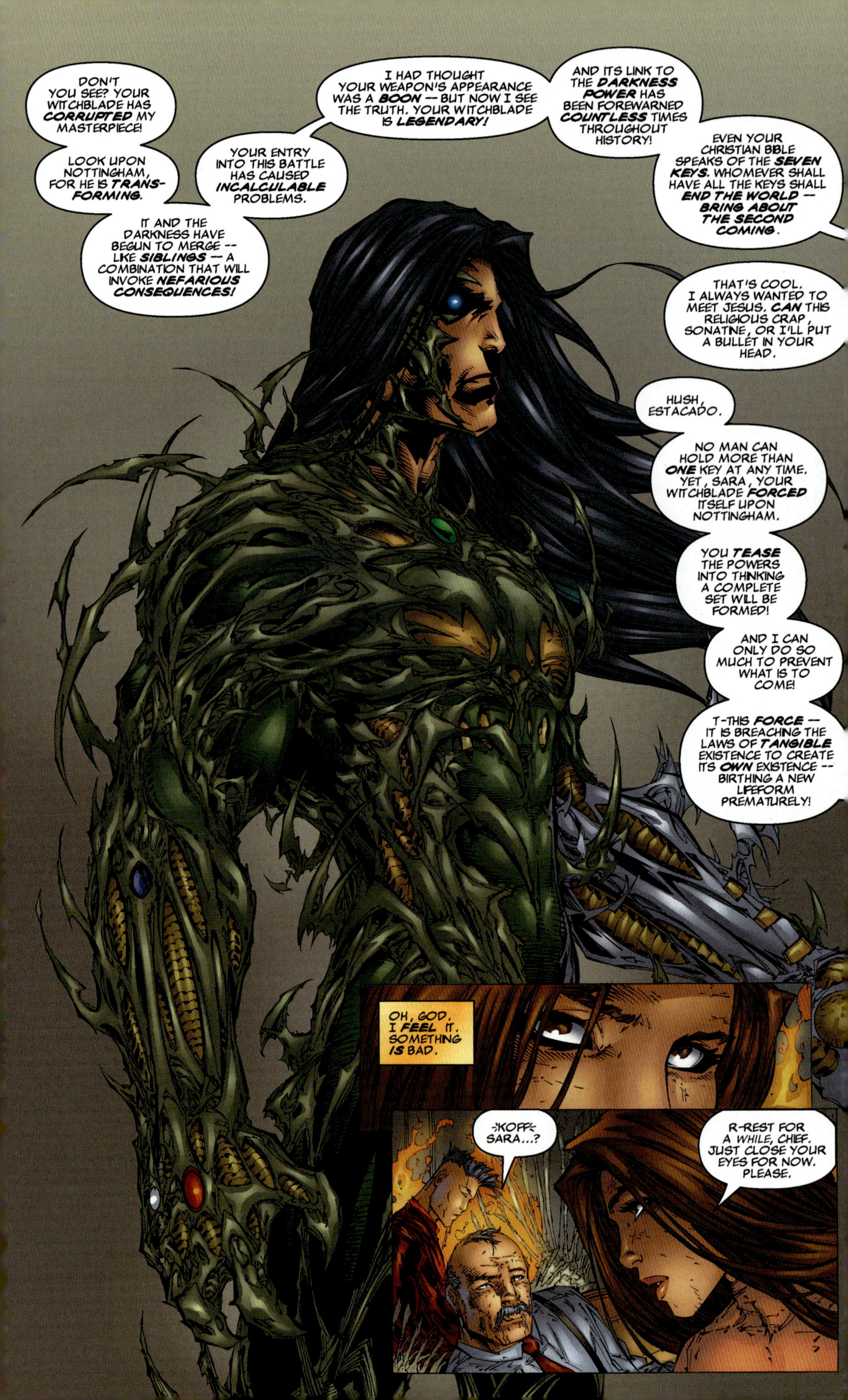
DON'T YOU SEE? YOUR WITCHBLADE HAS CORRUPTED MY MASTERPIECE!
LOOK UPON NOTTINGHAM, FOR HE IS TRANS-FORMING.
IT AND THE DARKNESS HAVE BEGUN TO MERGE -- LIKE SIBLINGS -- A COMBINATION THAT WILL INVOKE NEFARIOUS CONSEQUENCES!
YOUR ENTRY INTO THIS BATTLE HAS CAUSED INCALCULABLE PROBLEMS.
I HAD THOUGHT YOUR WEAPON'S APPEARANCE WAS A BOON -- BUT NOW I SEE THE TRUTH. YOUR WITCHBLADE IS LEGENDARY!
AND ITS LINK TO THE DARKNESS POWER HAS BEEN FOREWARNED COUNTLESS TIMES THROUGHOUT HISTORY!
EVEN YOUR CHRISTIAN BIBLE SPEAKS OF THE SEVEN KEYS. WHOMEVER SHALL HAVE ALL THE KEYS SHALL END THE WORLD -- BRING ABOUT THE SECOND COMING.
THAT'S COOL. I ALWAYS WANTED TO MEET JESUS. CAN THIS RELIGIOUS CRAP, SONATNE, OR I'LL PUT A BULLET IN YOUR HEAD.
HUSH, ESTACADO.
NO MAN CAN HOLD MORE THAN ONE KEY AT ANY TIME. YET, SARA, YOUR WITCHBLADE FORCED ITSELF UPON NOTTINGHAM.
YOU TEASE THE POWERS INTO THINKING A COMPLETE SET WILL BE FORMED!
AND I CAN ONLY DO SO MUCH TO PREVENT WHAT IS TO COME!
T-THIS FORCE -- IT IS BREACHING THE LAWS OF TANGIBLE EXISTENCE TO CREATE ITS OWN EXISTENCE -- BIRTHING A NEW LIFEFORM PREMATURELY!
OH, GOD. I FEEL IT. SOMETHING IS BAD.
-KOFF- SARA...?
R-REST FOR A WHILE, CHIEF. JUST CLOSE YOUR EYES FOR NOW. PLEASE.

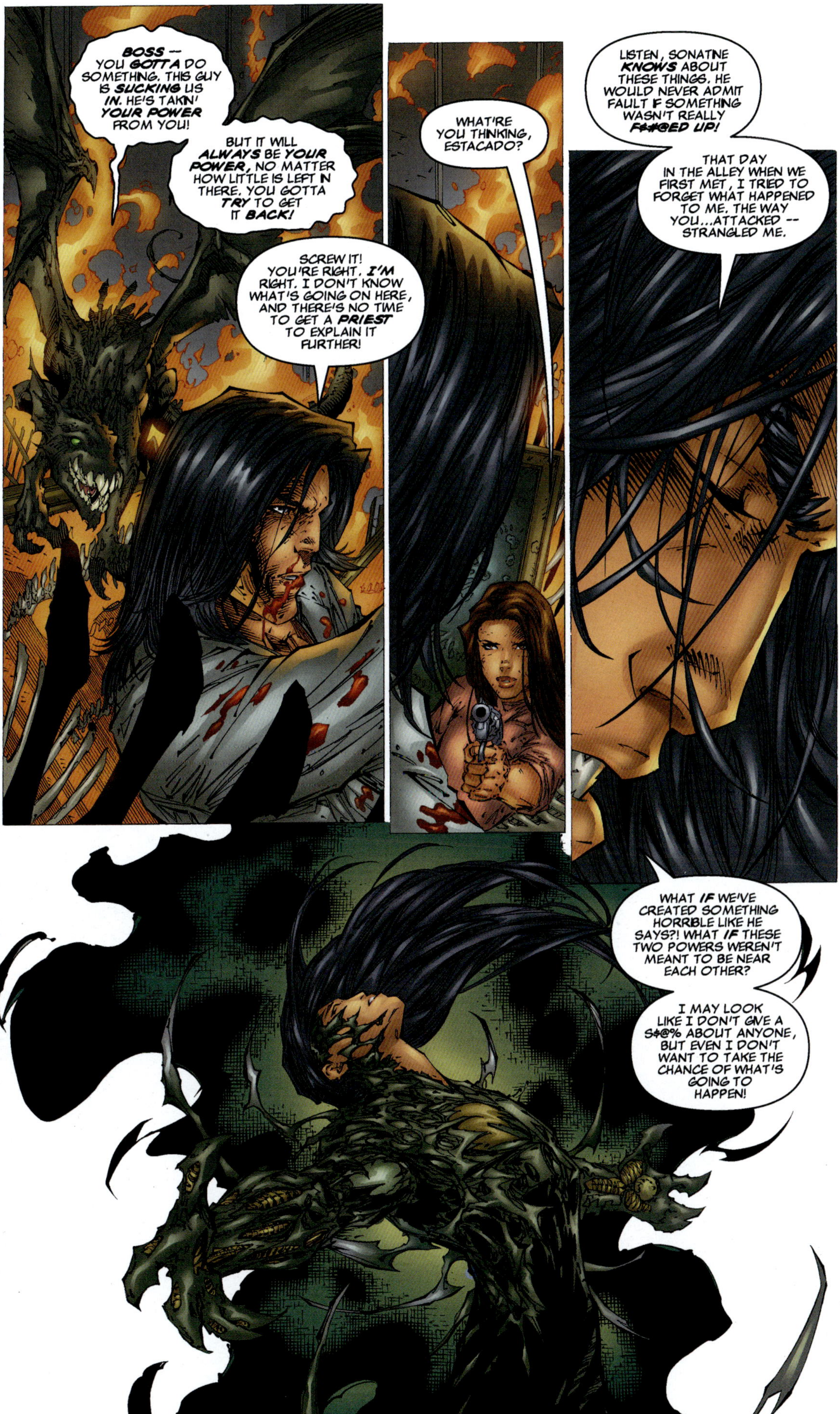
BOSS -- YOU GOTTA DO SOMETHING. THIS GUY IS SUCKING US IN. HE'S TAKIN' YOUR POWER FROM YOU!
BUT IT WILL ALWAYS BE YOUR POWER, NO MATTER HOW LITTLE IS LEFT IN THERE. YOU GOTTA TRY TO GET IT BACK!
SCREW IT! YOU'RE RIGHT. I'M RIGHT. I DON'T KNOW WHAT'S GOING ON HERE, AND THERE'S NO TIME TO GET A PRIEST TO EXPLAIN IT FURTHER!
WHAT'RE YOU THINKING, ESTACADO?
LISTEN, SONATINE KNOWS ABOUT THESE THINGS. HE WOULD NEVER ADMIT FAULT IF SOMETHING WASN'T REALLY F$#@ED UP!
THAT DAY IN THE ALLEY WHEN WE FIRST MET, I TRIED TO FORGET WHAT HAPPENED TO ME. THE WAY YOU...ATTACKED -- STRANGLED ME.
WHAT IF WE'VE CREATED SOMETHING HORRIBLE LIKE HE SAYS?! WHAT IF THESE TWO POWERS WEREN'T MEANT TO BE NEAR EACH OTHER?
I MAY LOOK LIKE I DON'T GIVE A S$@% ABOUT ANYONE, BUT EVEN I DON'T WANT TO TAKE THE CHANCE OF WHAT'S GOING TO HAPPEN!

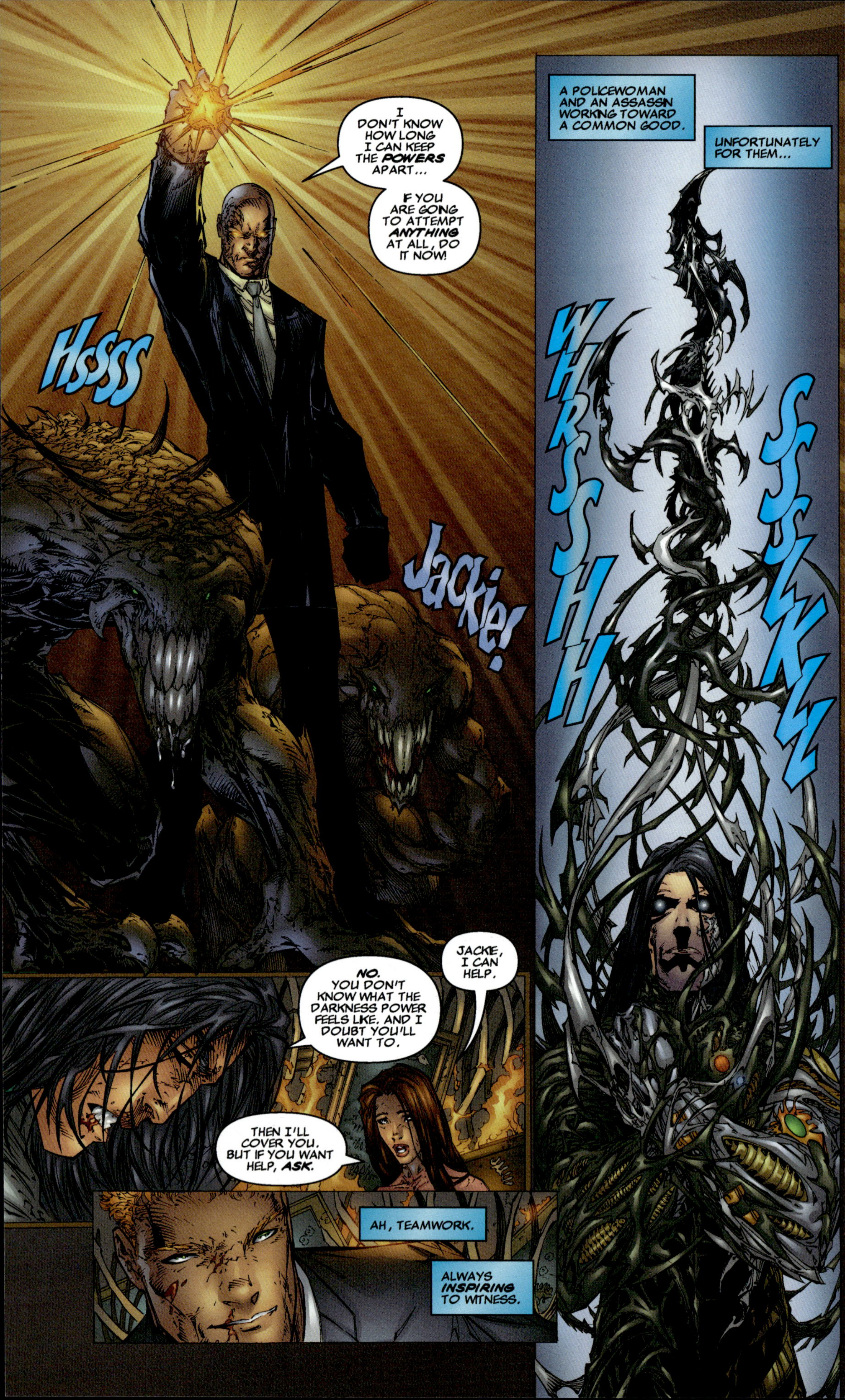
I DON'T KNOW HOW LONG I CAN KEEP THE POWERS APART...
IF YOU ARE GOING TO ATTEMPT ANYTHING AT ALL, DO IT NOW!
HSSSS
JACKIE!
A POLICEWOMAN AND AN ASSASSIN WORKING TOWARD A COMMON GOOD.
UNFORTUNATELY FOR THEM...
WHRSSHH
SSSLKKLL
JACKIE, I CAN HELP.
NO. YOU DON'T KNOW WHAT THE DARKNESS POWER FEELS LIKE, AND I DOUBT YOU'LL WANT TO.
THEN I'LL COVER YOU. BUT IF YOU WANT HELP, ASK.
AH, TEAMWORK.
ALWAYS INSPIRING TO WITNESS.

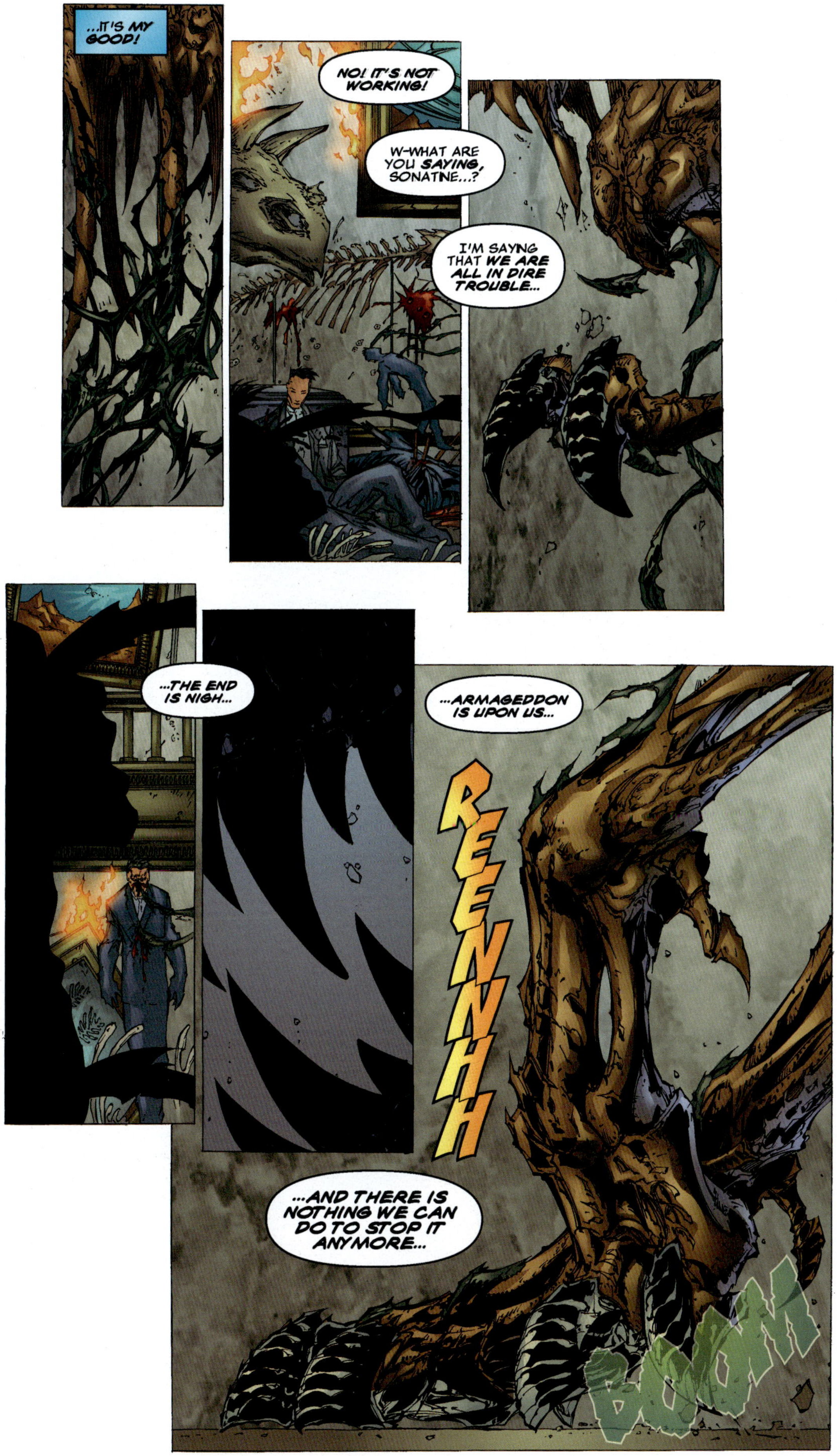

...IT'S MY GOOD!
NO! IT'S NOT WORKING!
W-WHAT ARE YOU SAYING, SONATINE...?
I'M SAYING THAT WE ARE ALL IN DIRE TROUBLE...
...THE END IS NIGH...
...ARMAGEDDON IS UPON US...
REEENHH
...AND THERE IS NOTHING WE CAN DO TO STOP IT ANYMORE...
BOOM

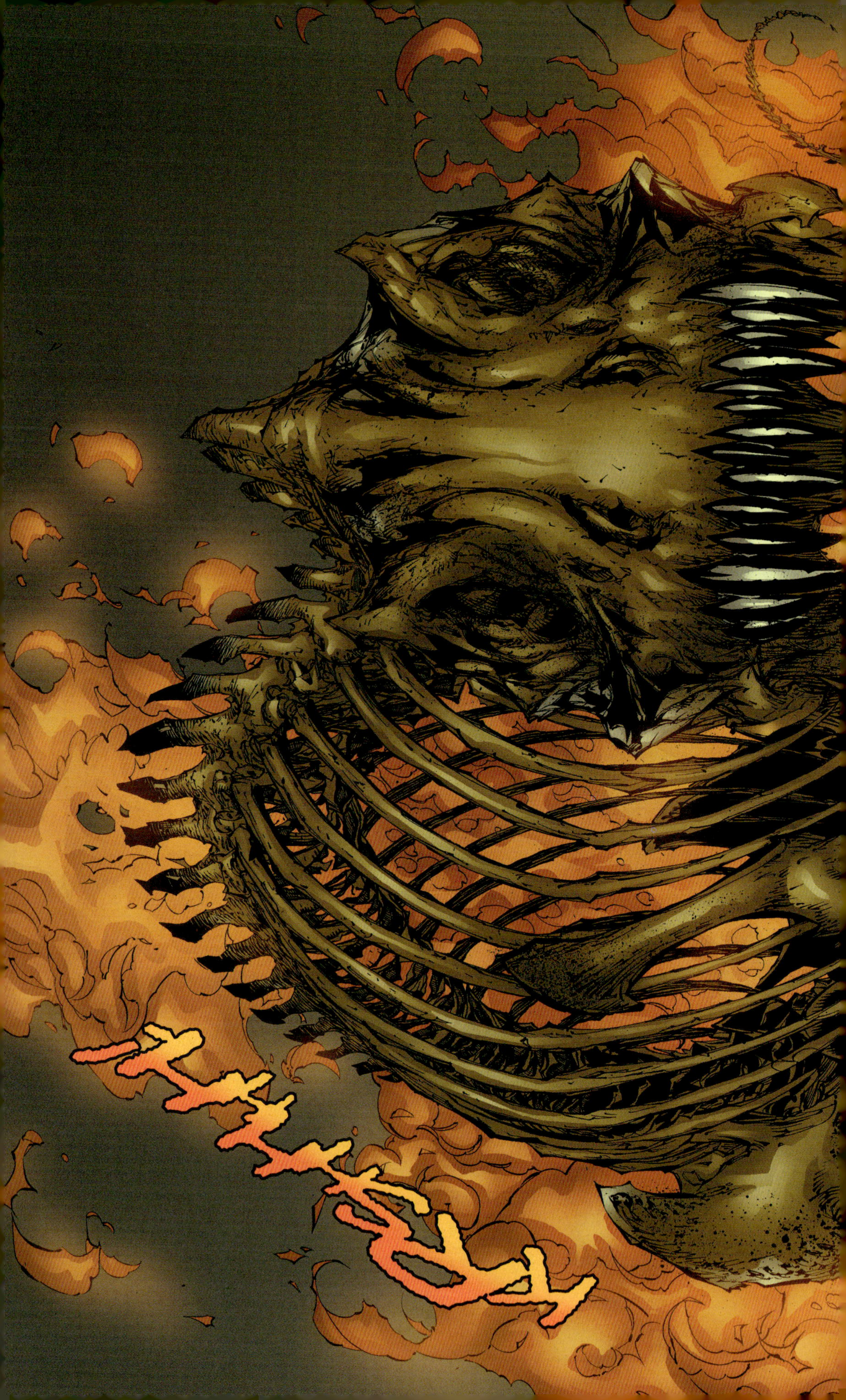

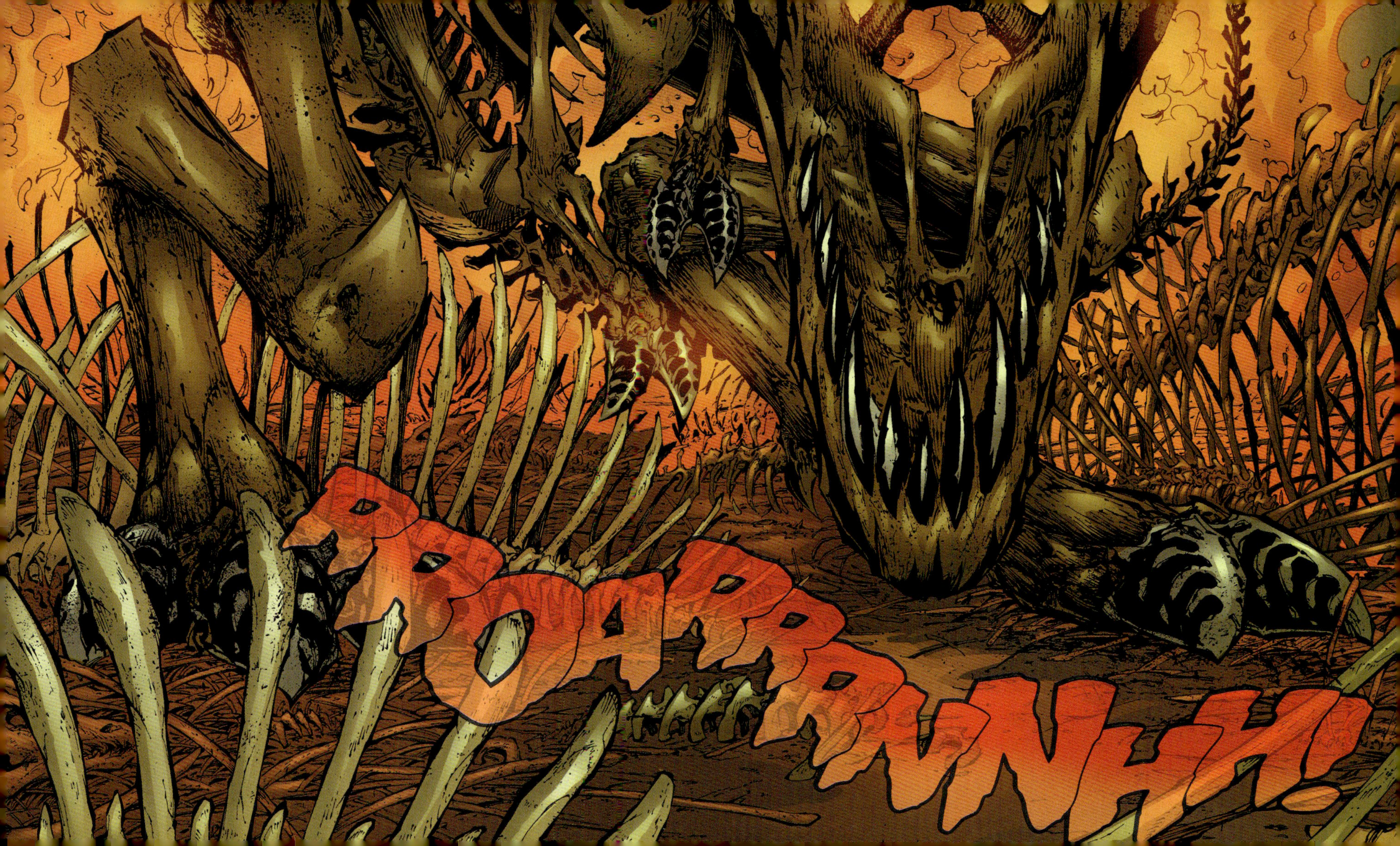
RROARRRRNHH!

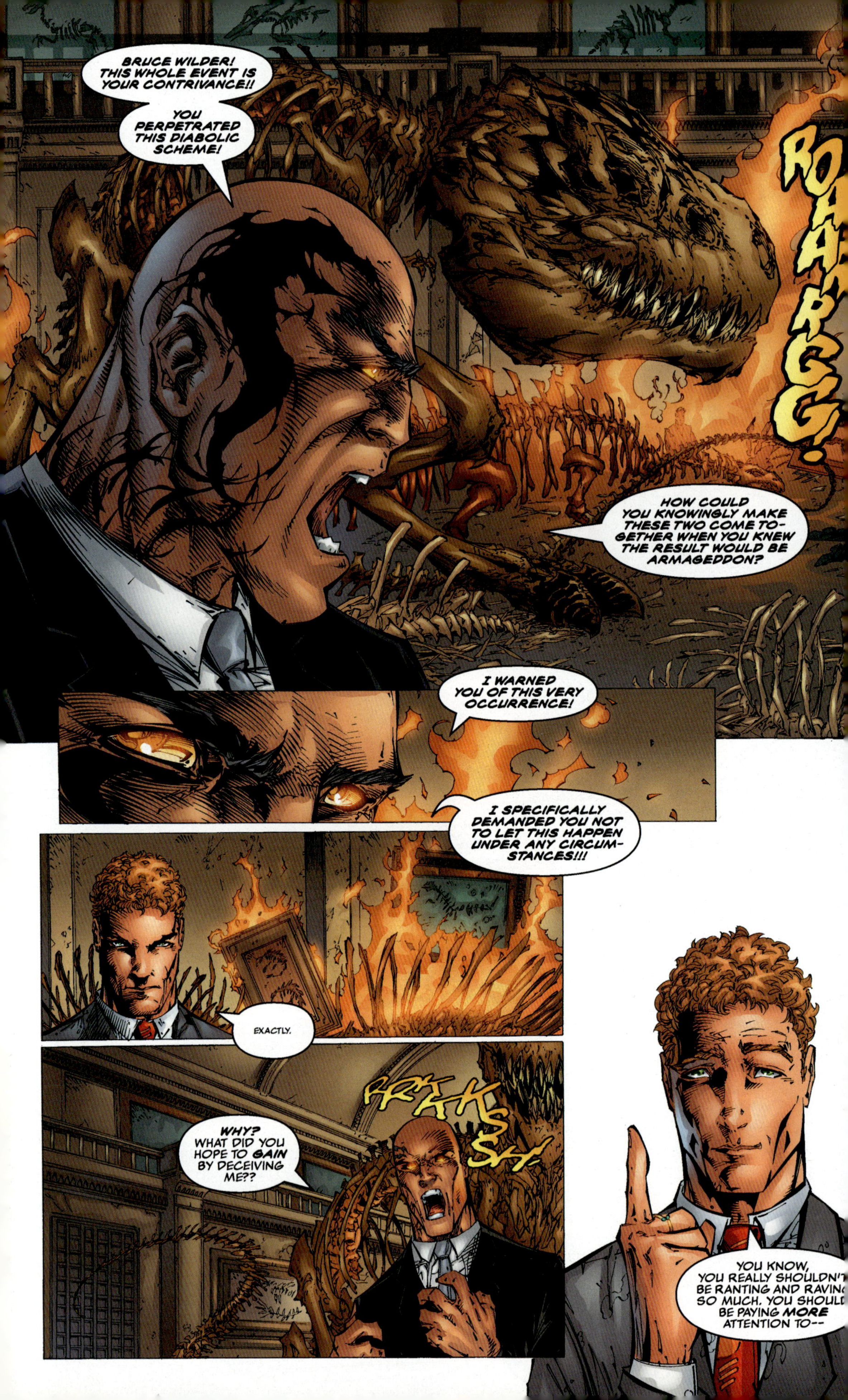
BRUCE WILDER! THIS WHOLE EVENT IS YOUR CONTRIVANCE!!
YOU PERPETRATED THIS DIABOLIC SCHEME!
ROAARGG!
HOW COULD YOU KNOWINGLY MAKE THESE TWO COME TO-GETHER WHEN YOU KNEW THE RESULT WOULD BE ARMAGEDDON?
I WARNED YOU OF THIS VERY OCCURRENCE!
I SPECIFICALLY DEMANDED YOU NOT TO LET THIS HAPPEN UNDER ANY CIRCUM-STANCES!!!
EXACTLY.
WHY? WHAT DID YOU HOPE TO GAIN BY DECEIVING ME??
YOU KNOW, YOU REALLY SHOULDN'T BE RANTING AND RAVING SO MUCH. YOU SHOULD BE PAYING MORE ATTENTION TO--

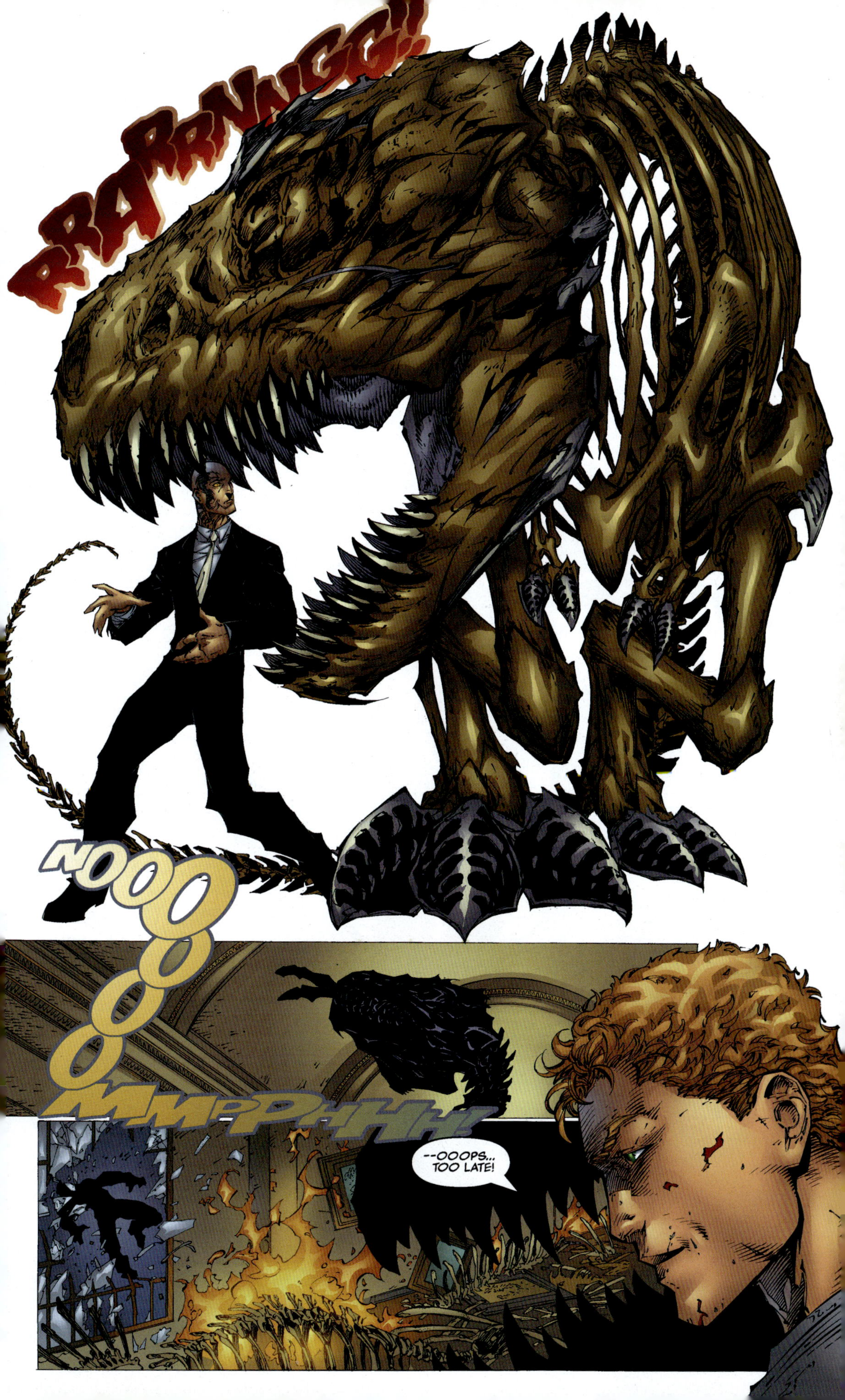
RRARRNNGG!!
NOOOOOOOMMPPHHH!
--OOOPS... TOO LATE!

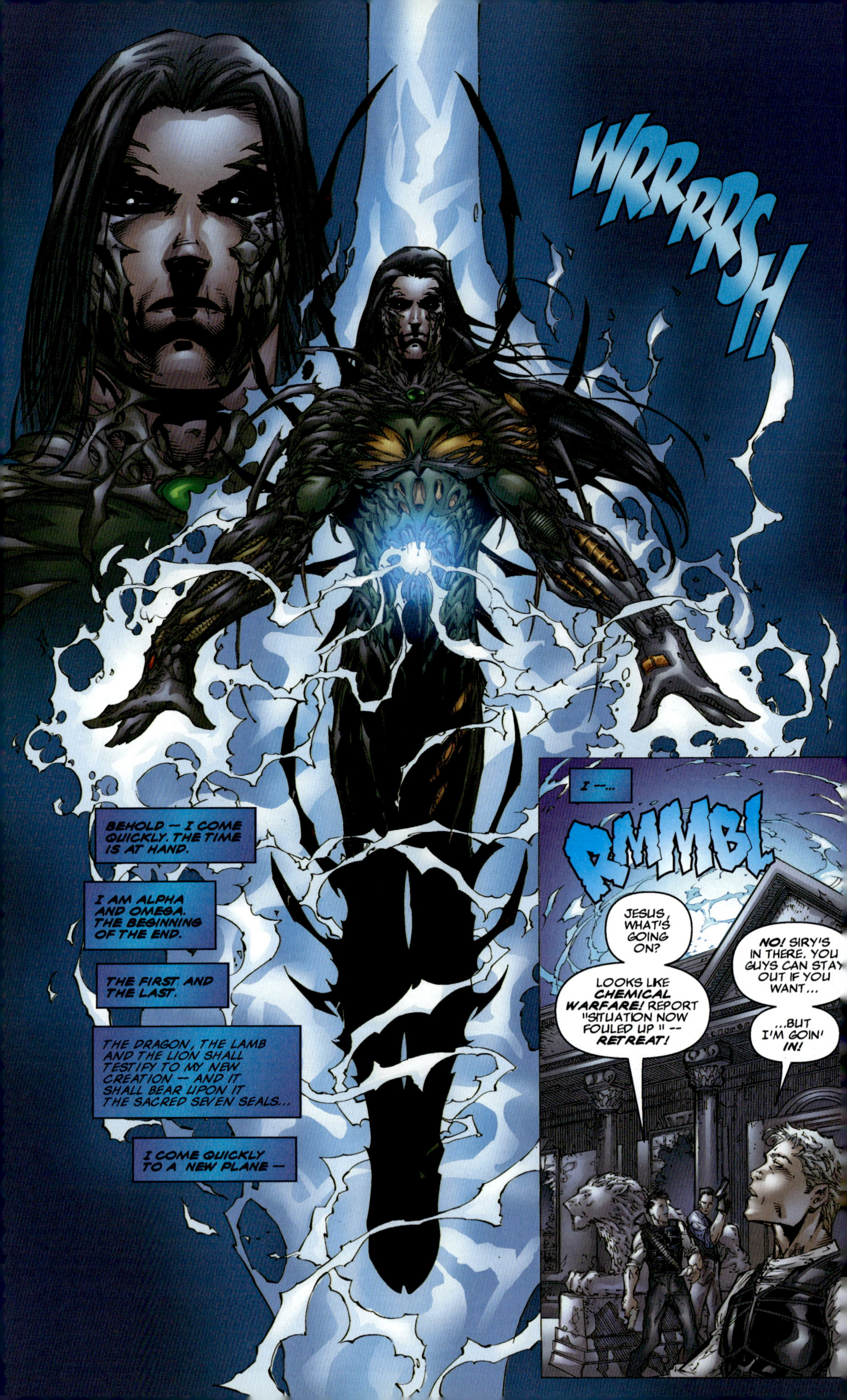
WRRRRSH
BEHOLD -- I COME QUICKLY. THE TIME IS AT HAND.
I AM ALPHA AND OMEGA. THE BEGINNING OF THE END.
THE FIRST AND THE LAST.
THE DRAGON, THE LAMB AND THE LION SHALL TESTIFY TO MY NEW CREATION -- AND IT SHALL BEAR UPON IT THE SACRED SEVEN SEALS...
I COME QUICKLY TO A NEW PLANE --
I --...
RMMBL
JESUS, WHAT'S GOING ON?
LOOKS LIKE CHEMICAL WARFARE! REPORT "SITUATION NOW FOULED UP" -- RETREAT!
NO! SIRY'S IN THERE. YOU GUYS CAN STAY OUT IF YOU WANT...
...BUT I'M GOIN' IN!

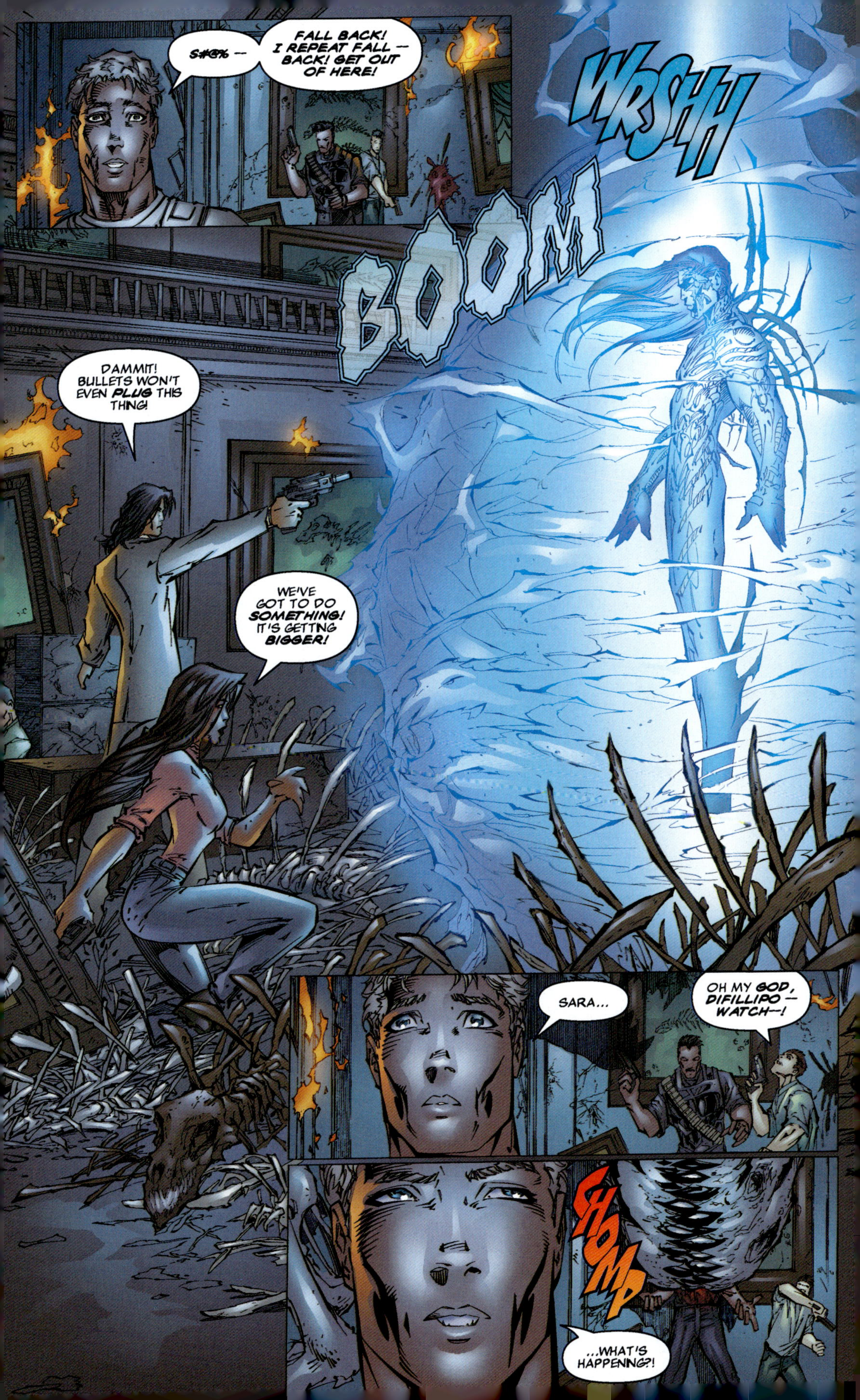
S#@% --
FALL BACK! I REPEAT FALL -- BACK! GET OUT OF HERE!
WRSHH
BOOM
DAMMIT! BULLETS WON'T EVEN PLUG THIS THING!
WE'VE GOT TO DO SOMETHING! IT'S GETTING BIGGER!
SARA...
OH MY GOD, DIFILLIPO -- WATCH--!
CHOMP
...WHAT'S HAPPENING?!

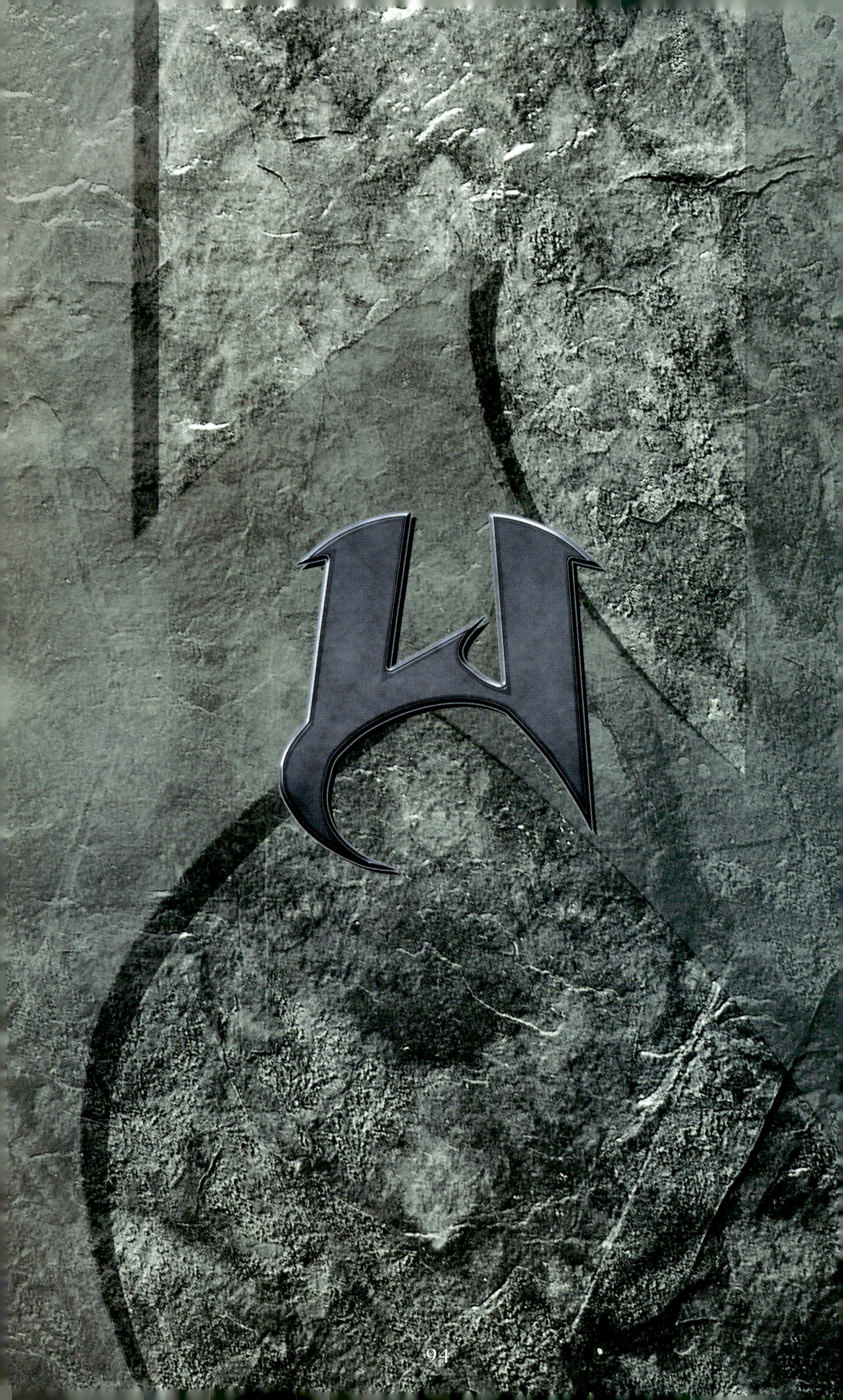

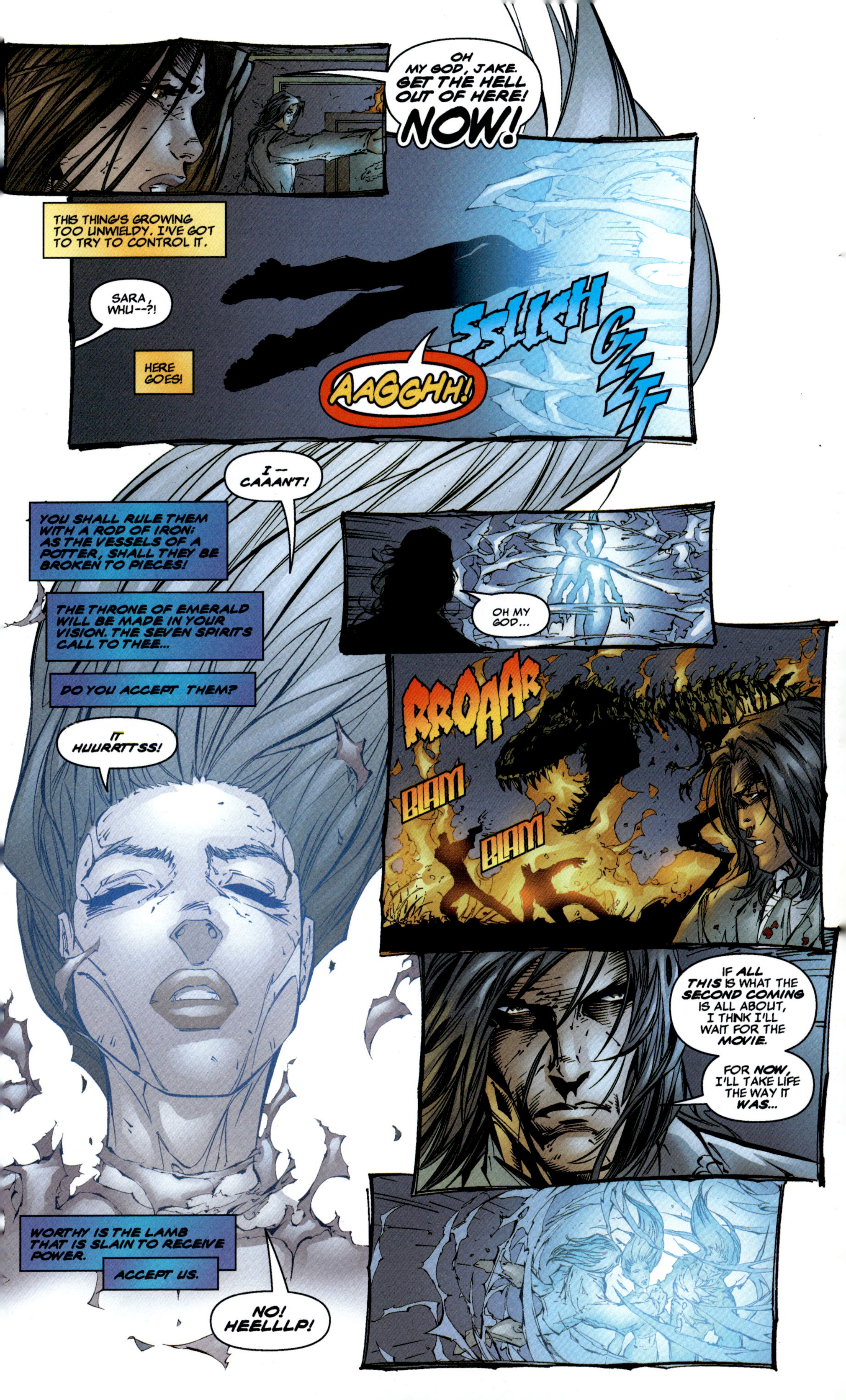

OH MY GOD, JAKE. GET THE HELL OUT OF HERE! NOW!
THIS THING'S GROWING TOO UNWIELDY. I'VE GOT TO TRY TO CONTROL IT.
SARA, WHU--?!
HERE GOES!
AAGGHH!
SSLICH
GZZT
I -- CAAANT!
YOU SHALL RULE THEM WITH A ROD OF IRON; AS THE VESSELS OF A POTTER, SHALL THEY BE BROKEN TO PIECES!
THE THRONE OF EMERALD WILL BE MADE IN YOUR VISION. THE SEVEN SPIRITS CALL TO THEE...
DO YOU ACCEPT THEM?
IT HUURRTTSS!
OH MY GOD...
RROAAR
BLAM
BLAM
IF ALL THIS IS WHAT THE SECOND COMING IS ALL ABOUT, I THINK I'LL WAIT FOR THE MOVIE.
FOR NOW, I'LL TAKE LIFE THE WAY IT WAS...
WORTHY IS THE LAMB THAT IS SLAIN TO RECEIVE POWER.
ACCEPT US.
NO! HEELLLP!

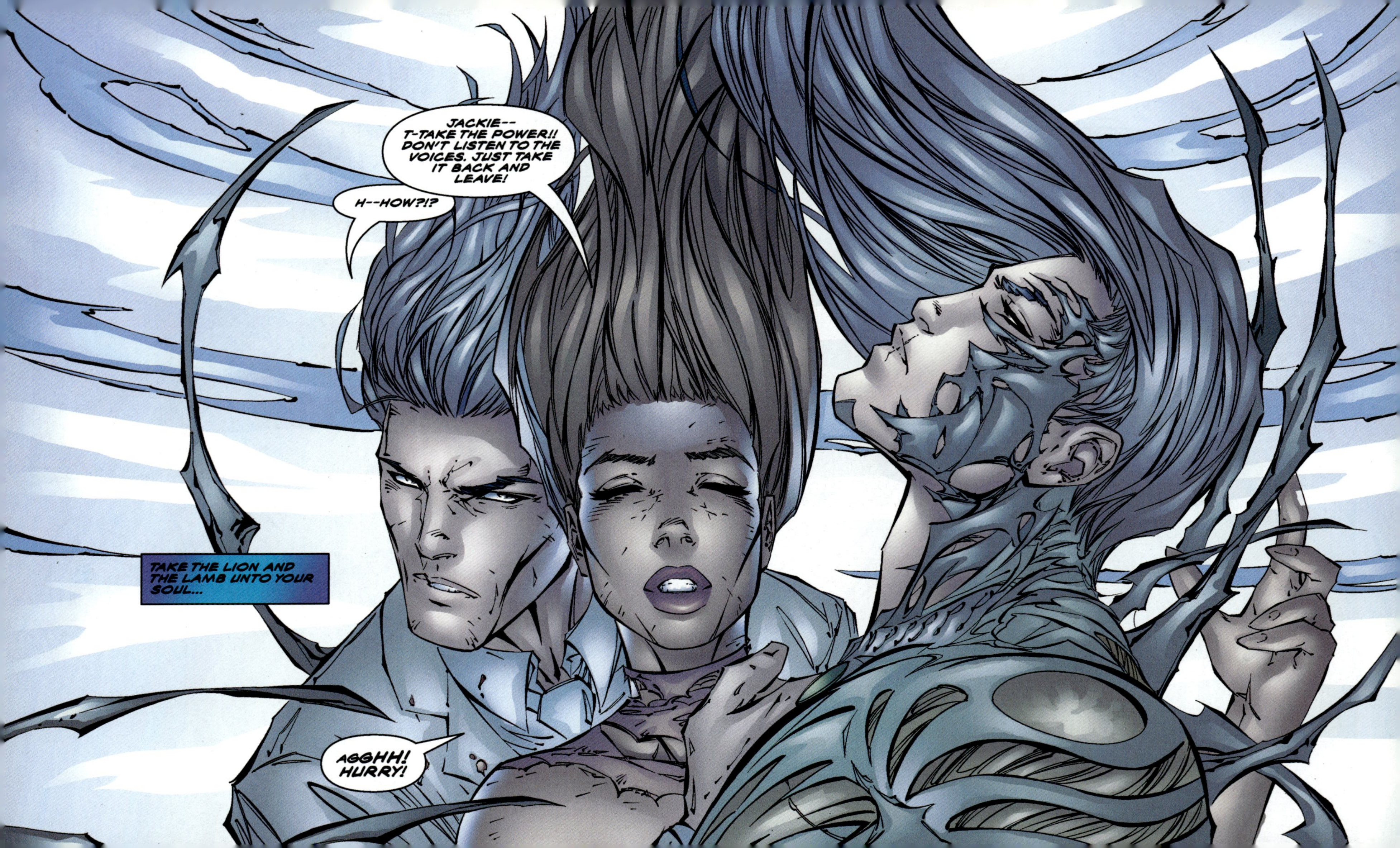

JACKIE-- T-TAKE THE POWER!! DON'T LISTEN TO THE VOICES. JUST TAKE IT BACK AND LEAVE!
H--HOW?!?
TAKE THE LION AND THE LAMB UNTO YOUR SOUL...
AGGHH! HURRY!

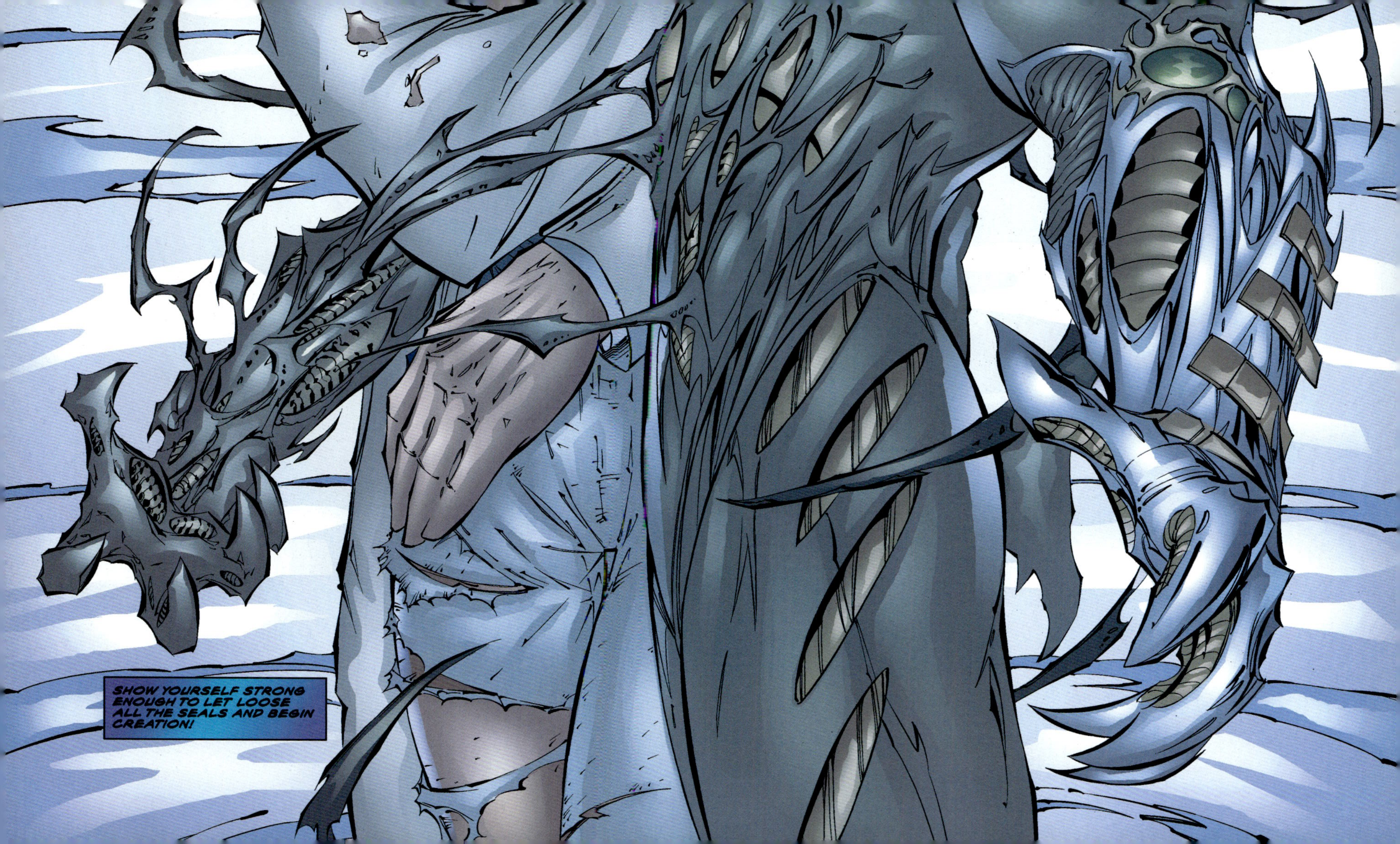
SHOW YOURSELF STRONG ENOUGH TO LET LOOSE ALL THE SEALS AND BEGIN CREATION!

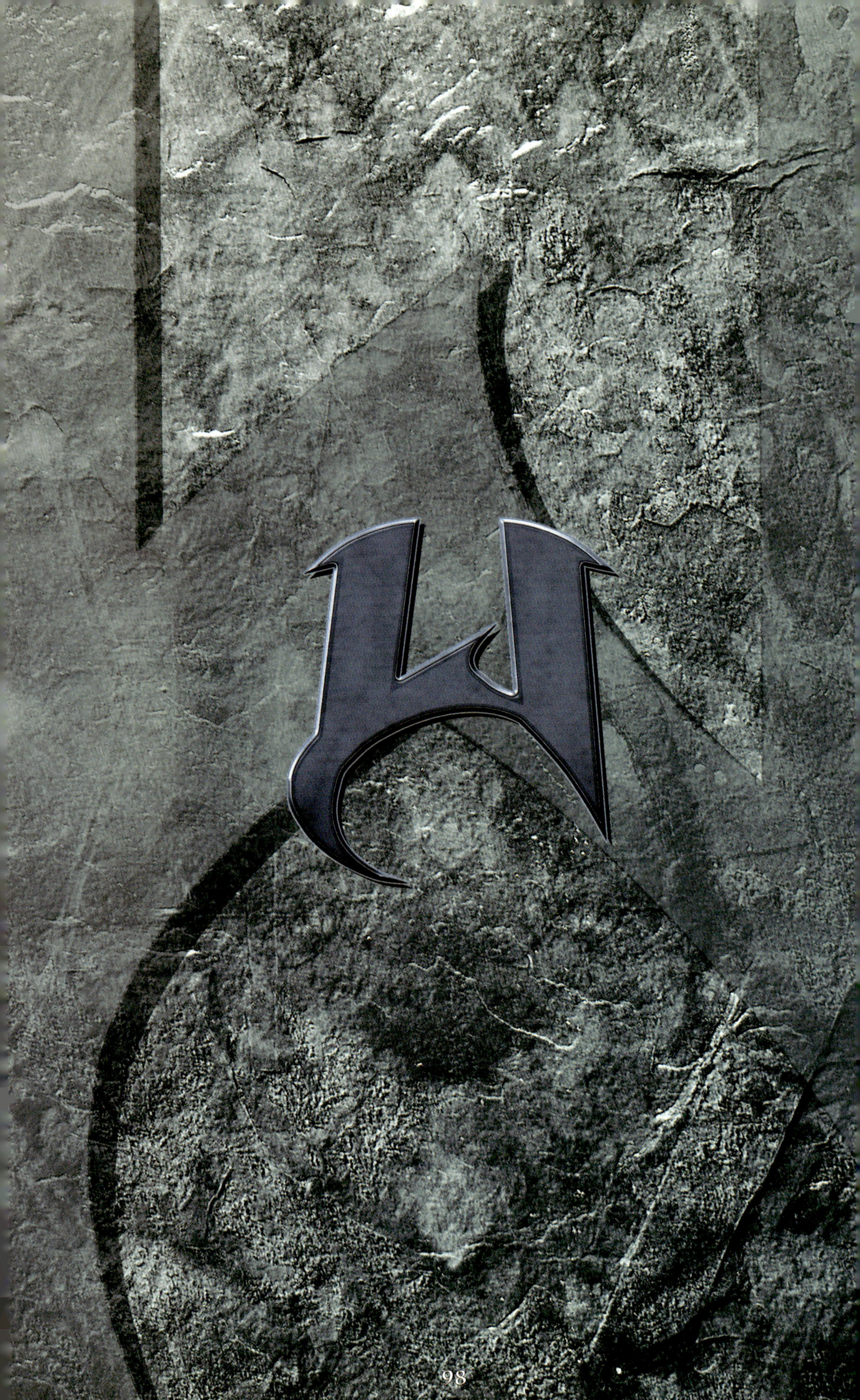

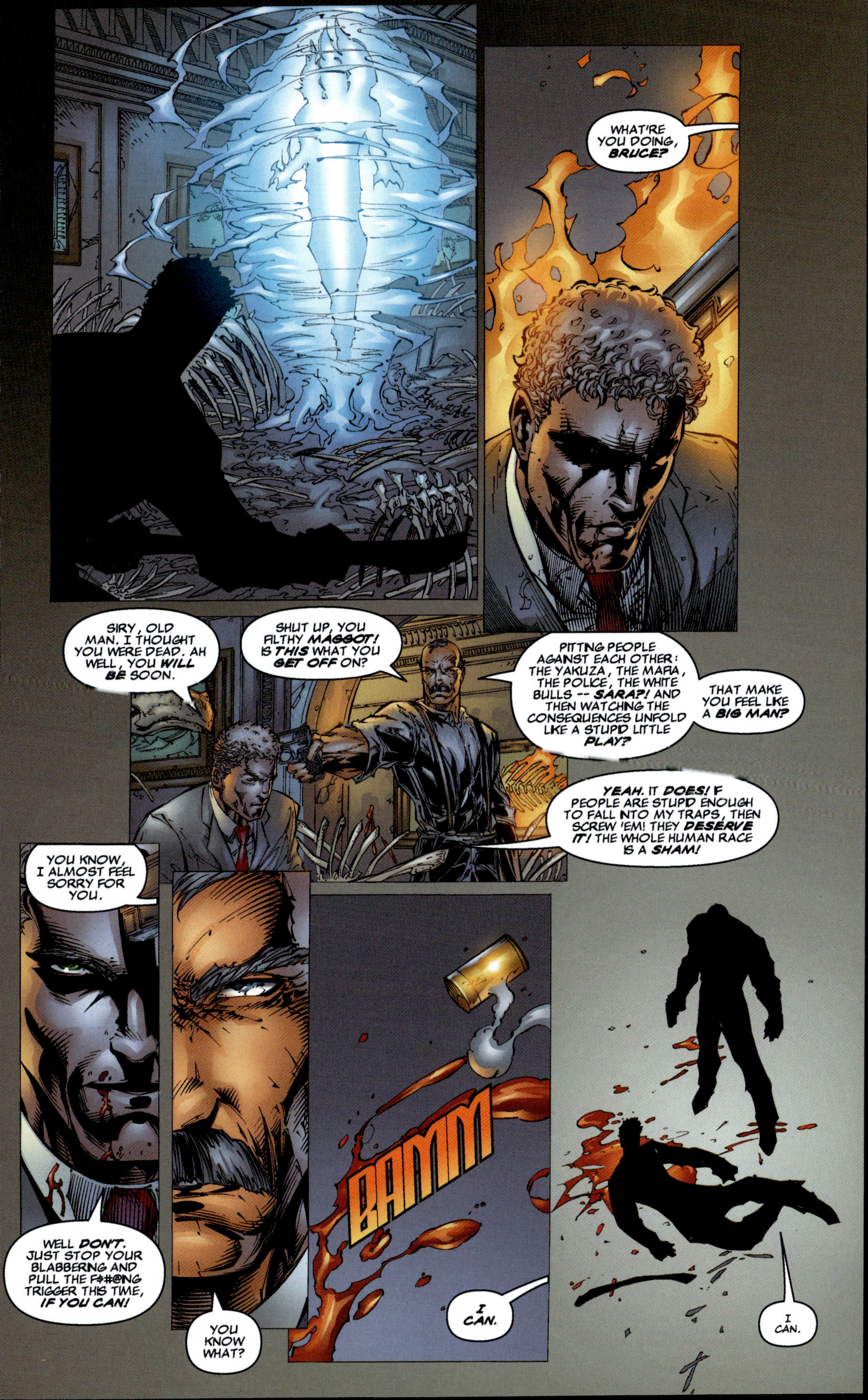

WHAT'RE YOU DOING, BRUCE?
SIRY, OLD MAN. I THOUGHT YOU WERE DEAD. AH WELL, YOU WILL BE SOON.
SHUT UP, YOU FILTHY MAGGOT! IS THIS WHAT YOU GET OFF ON?
PITTING PEOPLE AGAINST EACH OTHER: THE YAKUZA, THE MAFIA, THE POLICE, THE WHITE BULLS -- SARA?! AND THEN WATCHING THE CONSEQUENCES UNFOLD LIKE A STUPID LITTLE PLAY?
THAT MAKE YOU FEEL LIKE A BIG MAN?
YEAH. IT DOES! IF PEOPLE ARE STUPID ENOUGH TO FALL INTO MY TRAPS, THEN SCREW 'EM! THEY DESERVE IT! THE WHOLE HUMAN RACE IS A SHAM!
YOU KNOW, I ALMOST FEEL SORRY FOR YOU.
WELL DON'T. JUST STOP YOUR BLABBERING AND PULL THE F$#@ING TRIGGER THIS TIME, IF YOU CAN!
YOU KNOW WHAT?
I CAN.
BAMM
I CAN.

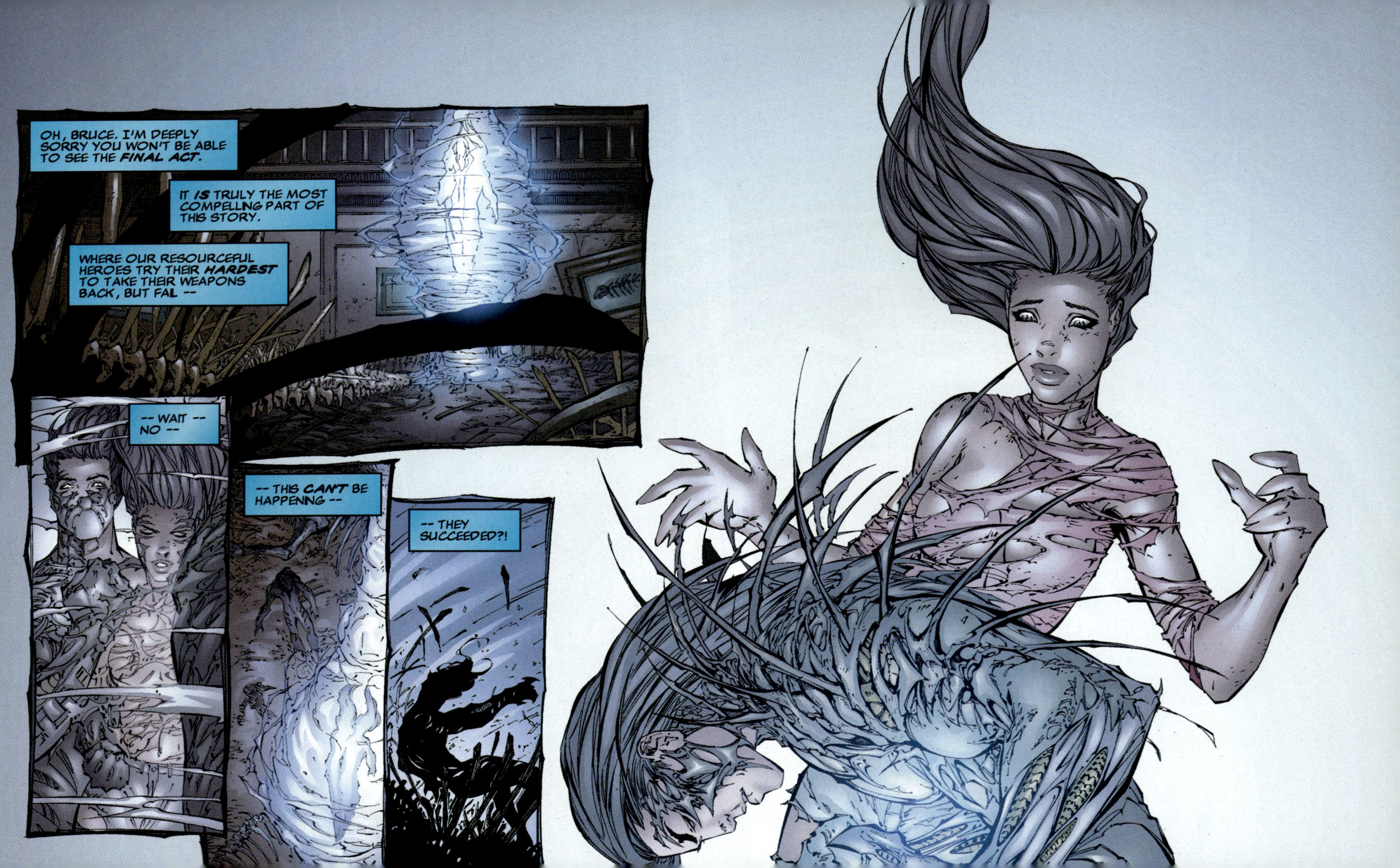
OH, BRUCE. I'M DEEPLY SORRY YOU WON'T BE ABLE TO SEE THE **FINAL ACT**.
IT **IS** TRULY THE MOST COMPELLING PART OF THIS STORY.
WHERE OUR RESOURCEFUL HEROES TRY THEIR **HARDEST** TO TAKE THEIR WEAPONS BACK, BUT FAIL --
-- WAIT -- NO --
-- THIS **CAN'T** BE HAPPENING --
-- THEY SUCCEEDED?!

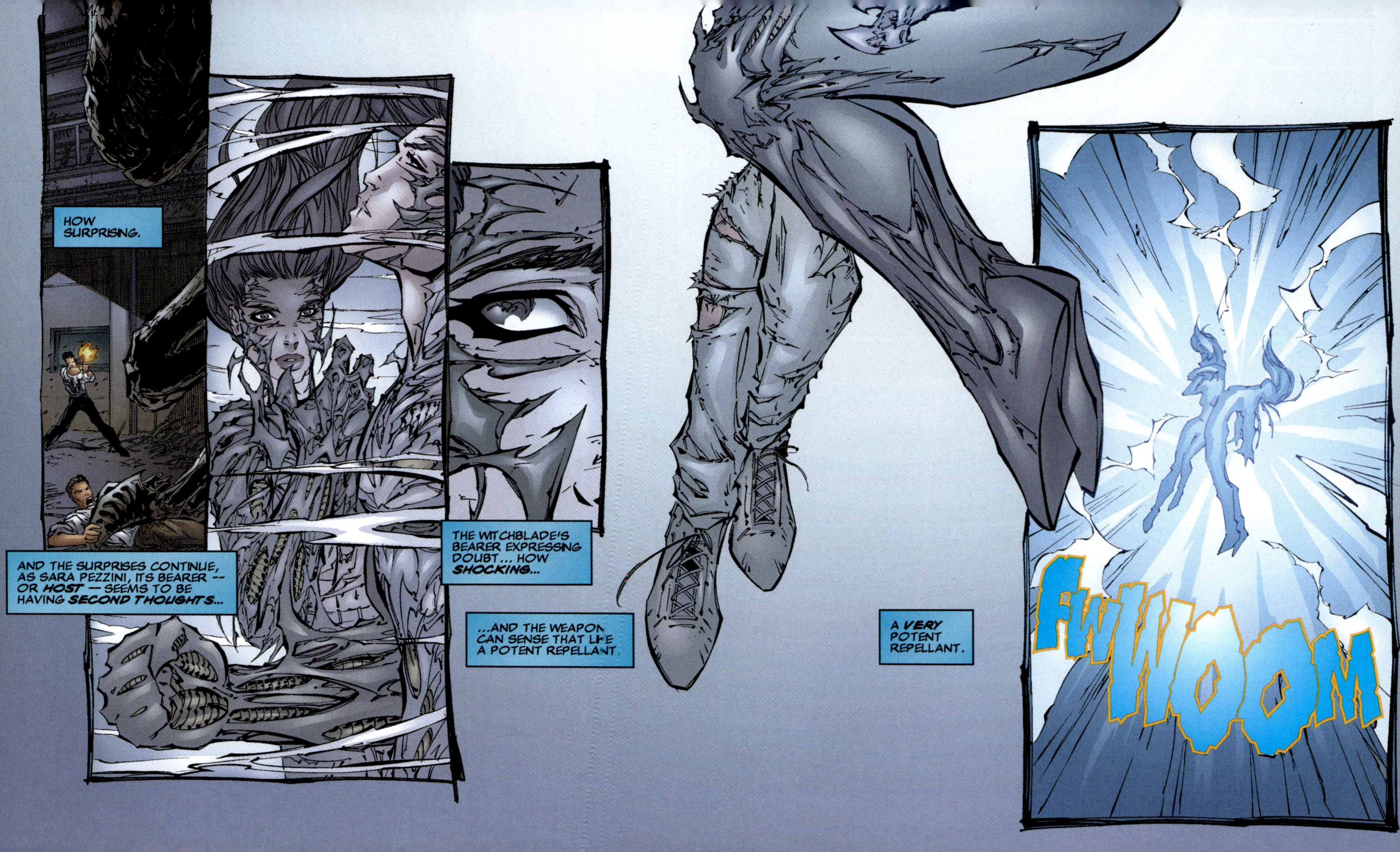
HOW SURPRISING.
AND THE SURPRISES CONTINUE, AS SARA PEZZINI, ITS BEARER -- OR *HOST* -- SEEMS TO BE HAVING *SECOND THOUGHTS...*
THE WITCHBLADE'S BEARER EXPRESSING DOUBT... HOW *SHOCKING...*
...AND THE WEAPON CAN SENSE THAT LIFE A POTENT REPELLANT.
A *VERY* POTENT REPELLANT.
FWWOOM

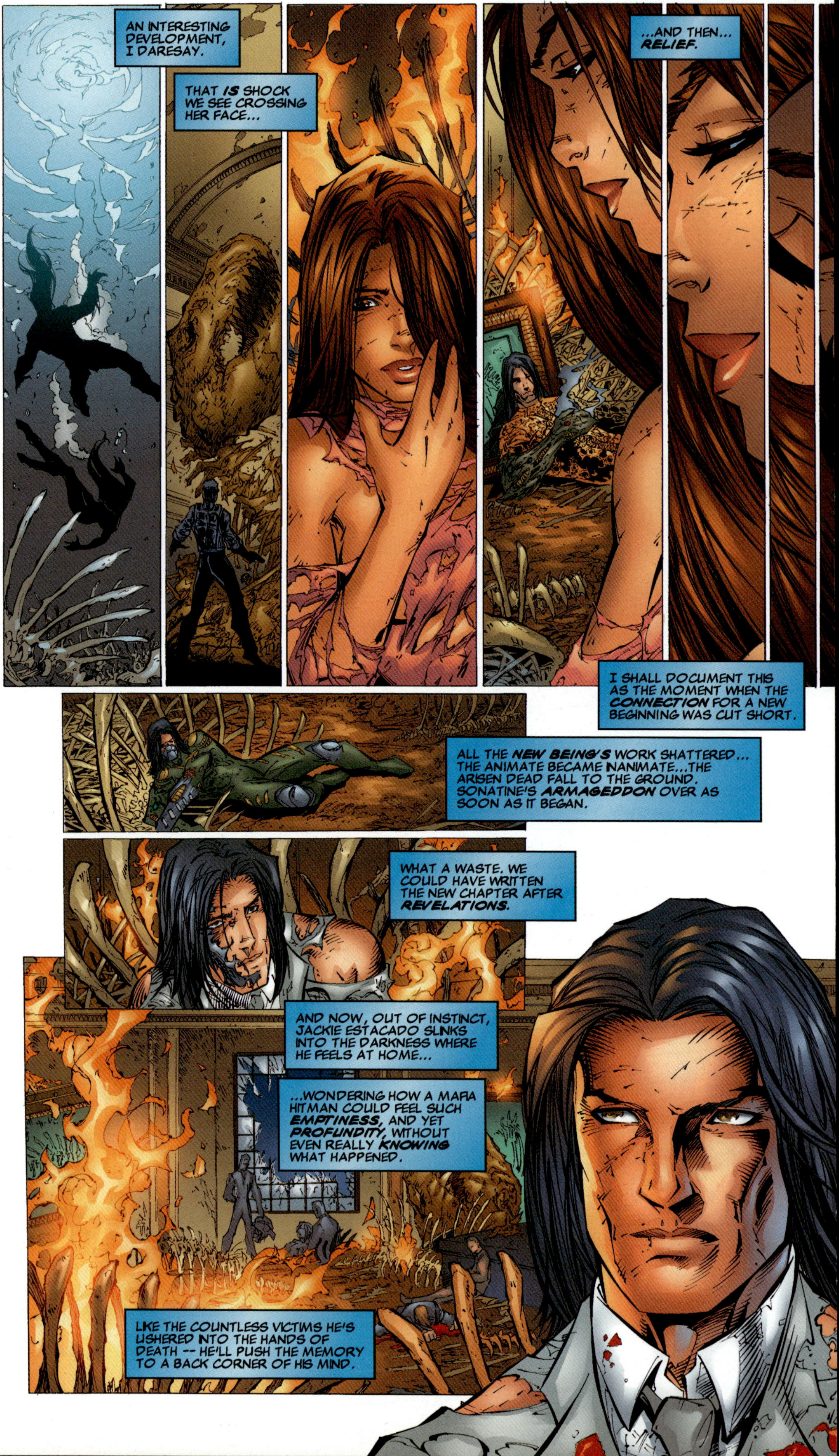
AN INTERESTING DEVELOPMENT, I DARESAY.
THAT IS SHOCK WE SEE CROSSING HER FACE...
...AND THEN... RELIEF.
I SHALL DOCUMENT THIS AS THE MOMENT WHEN THE CONNECTION FOR A NEW BEGINNING WAS CUT SHORT.
ALL THE NEW BEING'S WORK SHATTERED... THE ANIMATE BECAME INANIMATE...THE ARISEN DEAD FALL TO THE GROUND. SONATINE'S ARMAGEDDON OVER AS SOON AS IT BEGAN.
WHAT A WASTE. WE COULD HAVE WRITTEN THE NEW CHAPTER AFTER REVELATIONS.
AND NOW, OUT OF INSTINCT, JACKIE ESTACADO SLINKS INTO THE DARKNESS WHERE HE FEELS AT HOME...
...WONDERING HOW A MAFIA HITMAN COULD FEEL SUCH EMPTINESS, AND YET PROFUNDITY, WITHOUT EVEN REALLY KNOWING WHAT HAPPENED.
LIKE THE COUNTLESS VICTIMS HE'S USHERED INTO THE HANDS OF DEATH -- HE'LL PUSH THE MEMORY TO A BACK CORNER OF HIS MIND.

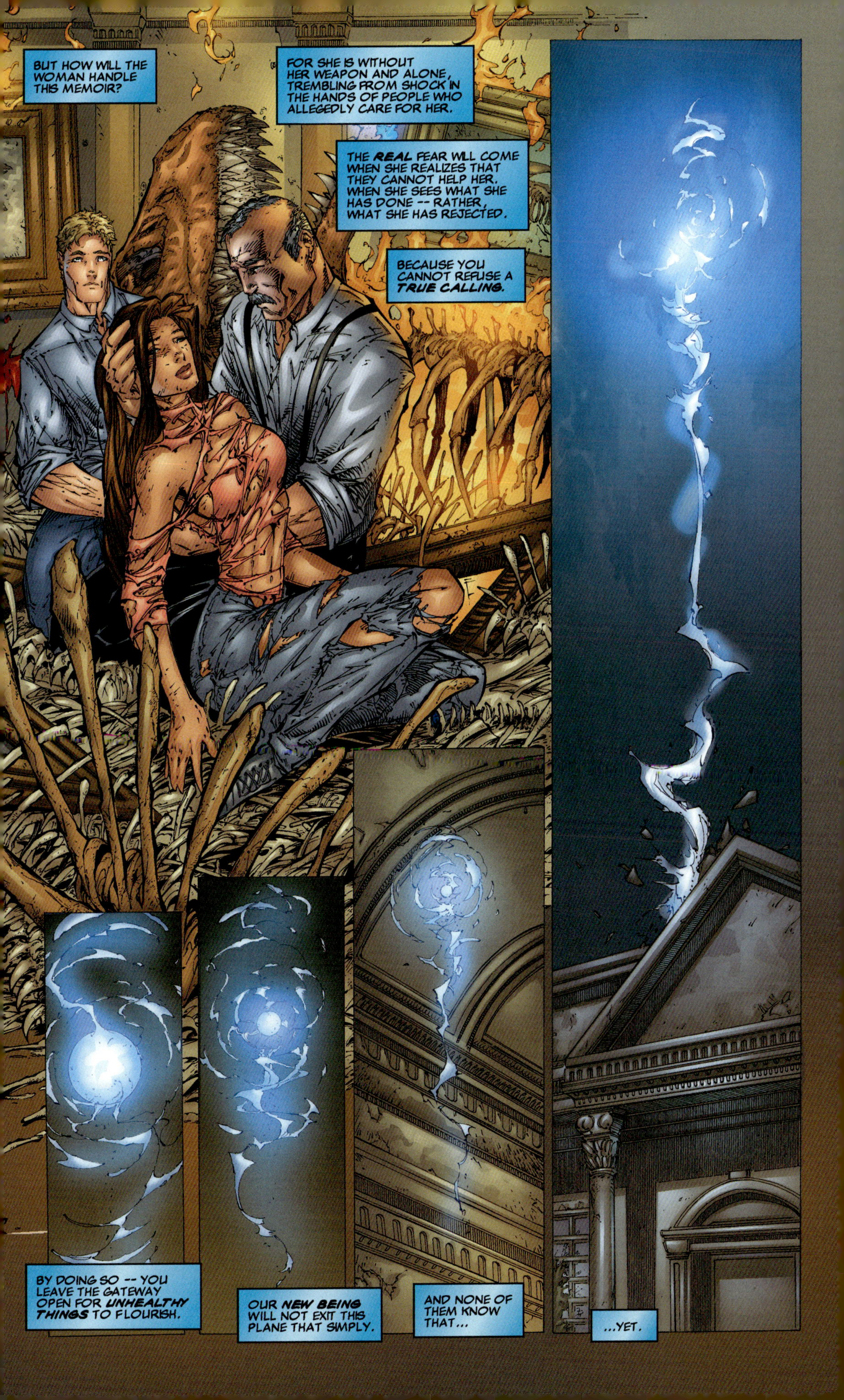
BUT HOW WILL THE WOMAN HANDLE THIS MEMOIR?
FOR SHE IS WITHOUT HER WEAPON AND ALONE, TREMBLING FROM SHOCK IN THE HANDS OF PEOPLE WHO ALLEGEDLY CARE FOR HER.
THE REAL FEAR WILL COME WHEN SHE REALIZES THAT THEY CANNOT HELP HER. WHEN SHE SEES WHAT SHE HAS DONE -- RATHER, WHAT SHE HAS REJECTED.
BECAUSE YOU CANNOT REFUSE A TRUE CALLING.
BY DOING SO -- YOU LEAVE THE GATEWAY OPEN FOR UNHEALTHY THINGS TO FLOURISH.
OUR NEW BEING WILL NOT EXIT THIS PLANE THAT SIMPLY.
AND NONE OF THEM KNOW THAT...
...YET.

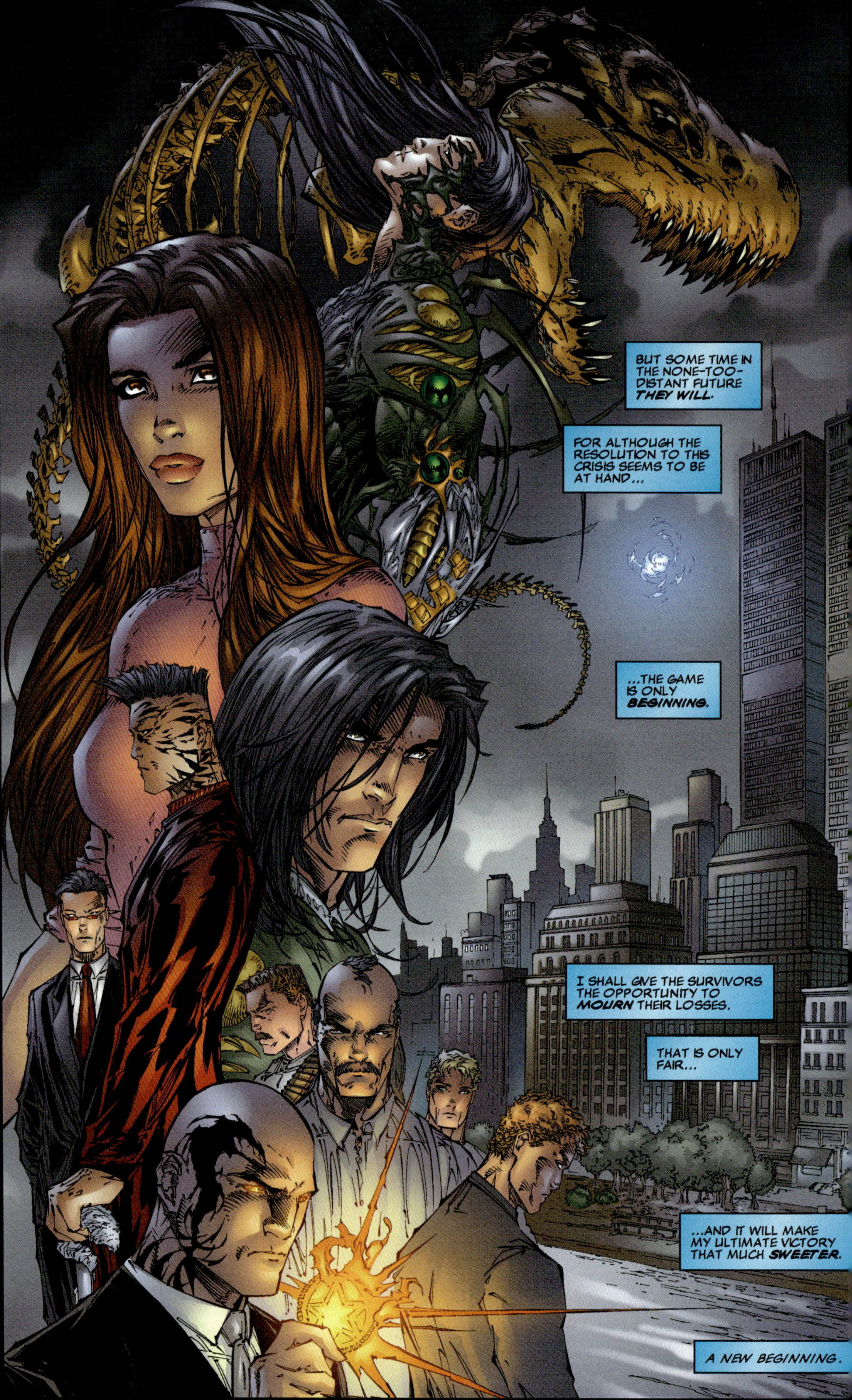
BUT SOME TIME IN THE NONE-TOO-DISTANT FUTURE THEY WILL.
FOR ALTHOUGH THE RESOLUTION TO THIS CRISIS SEEMS TO BE AT HAND...
...THE GAME IS ONLY BEGINNING.
I SHALL GIVE THE SURVIVORS THE OPPORTUNITY TO MOURN THEIR LOSSES.
THAT IS ONLY FAIR...
...AND IT WILL MAKE MY ULTIMATE VICTORY THAT MUCH SWEETER.
A NEW BEGINNING.

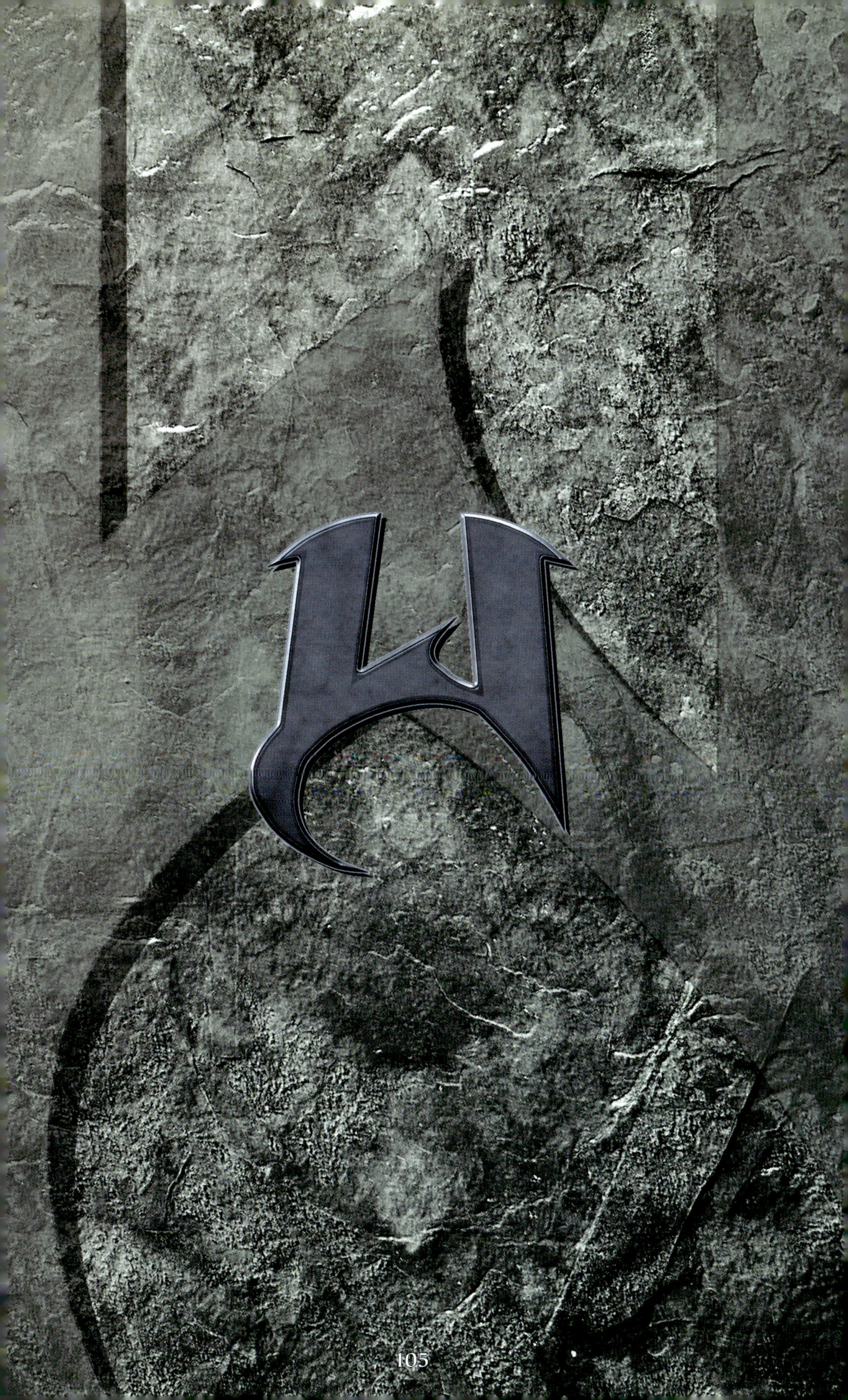

issue #20

plot: **David Wohl, Christina Z.** and **Michael Turner**
script: **David Wohl** and **Christina Z.**
pencils: **Michael Turner** and **Mat Broome**
inks: **D-Tron, Joe Weems V** and **Sean Parsons**
colors: **JD Smith**

ink assists: **Andy Kim, Marsha Chen, Jose "Jag" Guillen, Jeff De Los Santos**
and **Marco Galli**

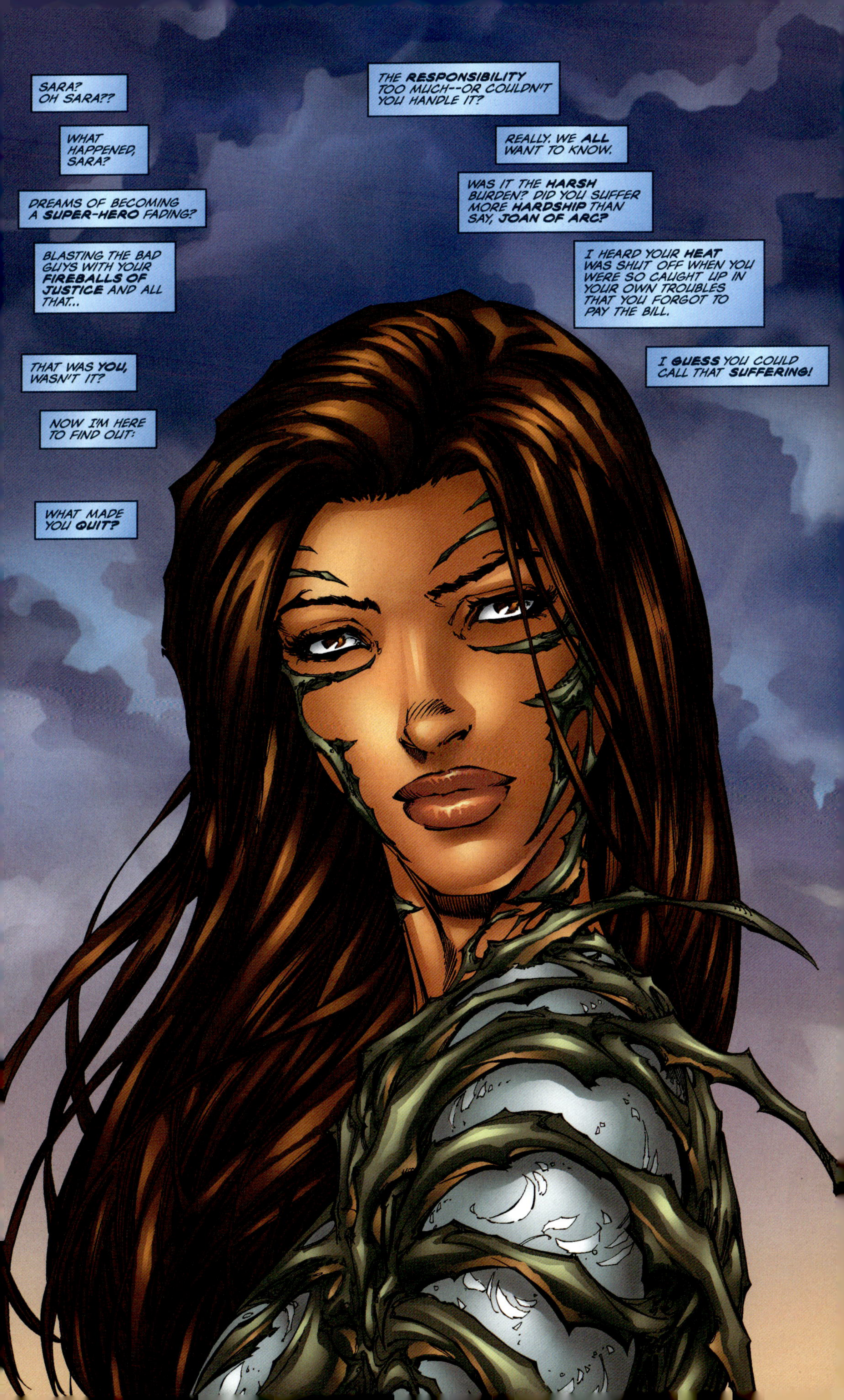

SARA? OH SARA??
WHAT HAPPENED, SARA?
DREAMS OF BECOMING A SUPER-HERO FADING?
BLASTING THE BAD GUYS WITH YOUR FIREBALLS OF JUSTICE AND ALL THAT...
THAT WAS YOU, WASN'T IT?
NOW I'M HERE TO FIND OUT:
WHAT MADE YOU QUIT?
THE RESPONSIBILITY TOO MUCH--OR COULDN'T YOU HANDLE IT?
REALLY. WE ALL WANT TO KNOW.
WAS IT THE HARSH BURDEN? DID YOU SUFFER MORE HARDSHIP THAN SAY, JOAN OF ARC?
I HEARD YOUR HEAT WAS SHUT OFF WHEN YOU WERE SO CAUGHT UP IN YOUR OWN TROUBLES THAT YOU FORGOT TO PAY THE BILL.
I GUESS YOU COULD CALL THAT SUFFERING!

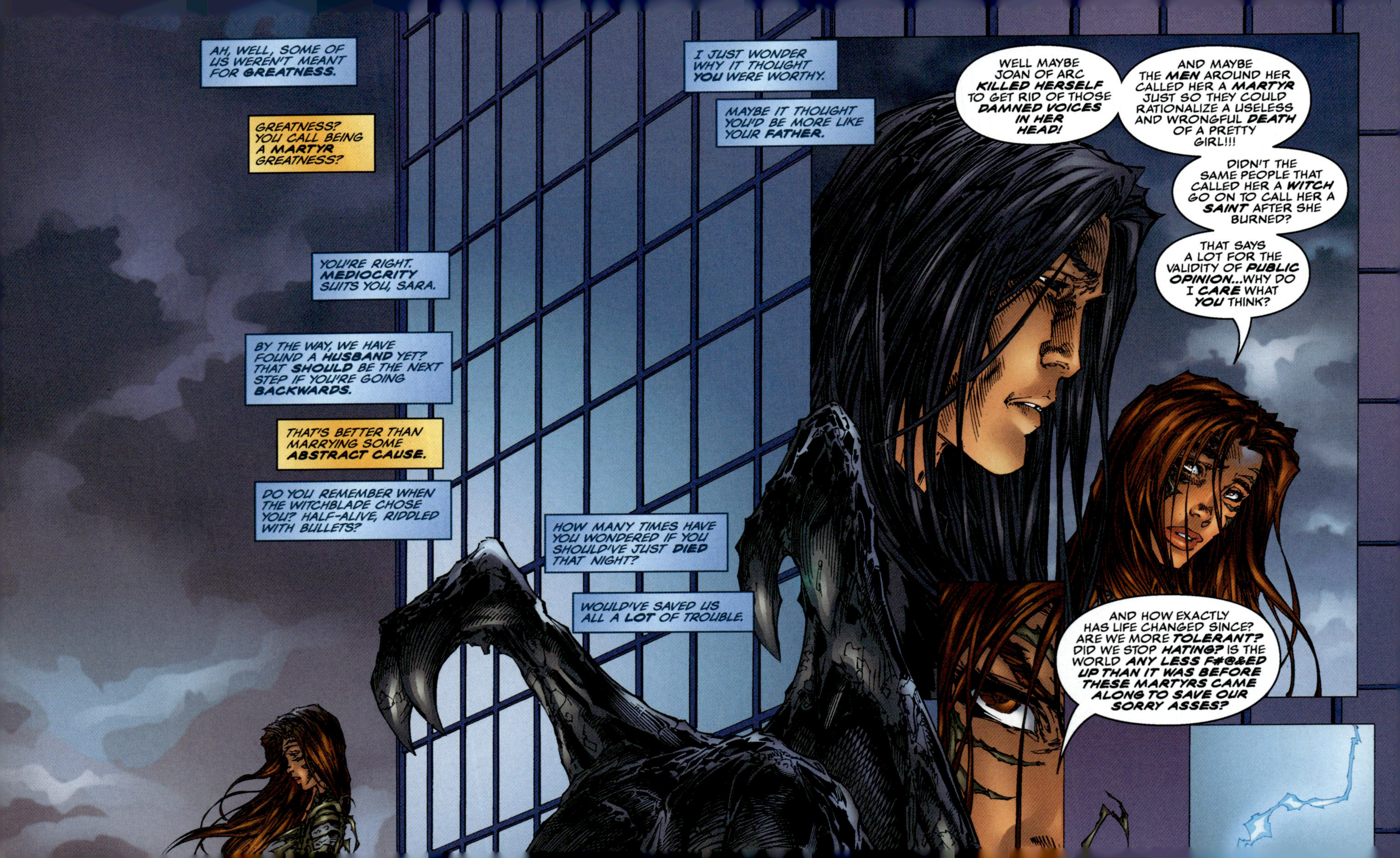
AH, WELL, SOME OF US WEREN'T MEANT FOR **GREATNESS.**
GREATNESS? YOU CALL BEING A **MARTYR** GREATNESS?
YOU'RE RIGHT. **MEDIOCRITY** SUITS YOU, SARA.
BY THE WAY, WE HAVE FOUND A **HUSBAND** YET? THAT **SHOULD** BE THE NEXT STEP IF YOU'RE GOING **BACKWARDS.**
THAT'S BETTER THAN MARRYING SOME **ABSTRACT CAUSE.**
DO YOU REMEMBER WHEN THE WITCHBLADE CHOSE YOU? HALF-ALIVE, RIDDLED WITH BULLETS?
I JUST WONDER WHY IT THOUGHT **YOU** WERE WORTHY.
MAYBE IT THOUGHT YOU'D BE MORE LIKE YOUR **FATHER.**
HOW MANY TIMES HAVE YOU WONDERED IF YOU SHOULD'VE JUST **DIED** THAT NIGHT?
WOULD'VE SAVED US ALL A **LOT** OF TROUBLE.
WELL MAYBE JOAN OF ARC **KILLED HERSELF** TO GET RID OF THOSE **DAMNED VOICES IN HER HEAD!**
AND MAYBE THE **MEN** AROUND HER CALLED HER A **MARTYR** JUST SO THEY COULD RATIONALIZE A USELESS AND WRONGFUL **DEATH** OF A PRETTY GIRL!!!
DIDN'T THE SAME PEOPLE THAT CALLED HER A **WITCH** GO ON TO CALL HER A **SAINT** AFTER SHE BURNED?
THAT SAYS A LOT FOR THE VALIDITY OF **PUBLIC OPINION**...WHY DO I **CARE** WHAT **YOU** THINK?
AND HOW EXACTLY HAS LIFE CHANGED SINCE? ARE WE MORE **TOLERANT?** DID WE STOP **HATING?** IS THE WORLD **ANY LESS F#@&ED UP THAN IT WAS BEFORE THESE MARTYRS CAME ALONG TO SAVE OUR SORRY ASSES?**

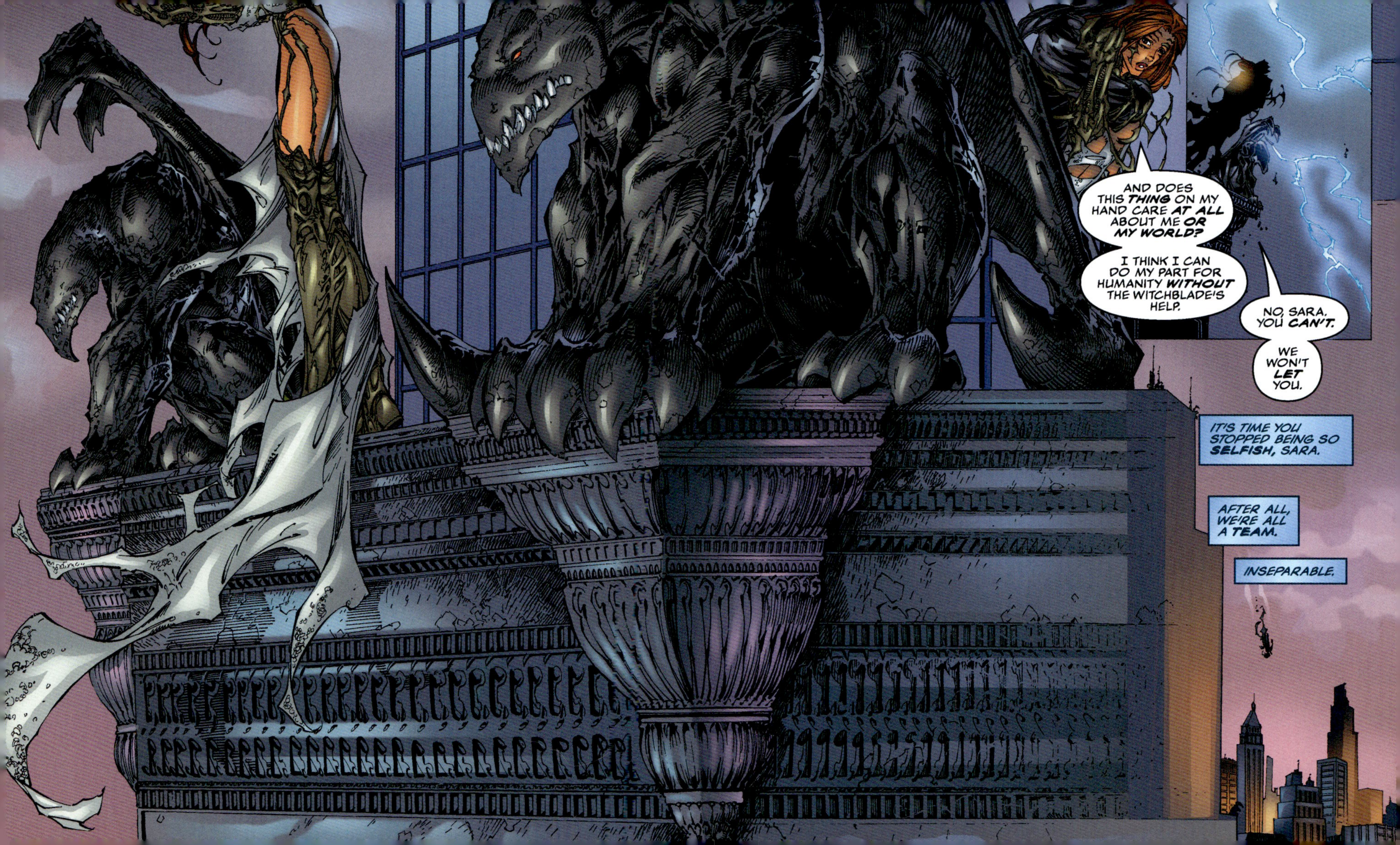
AND DOES THIS **THING** ON MY HAND CARE **AT ALL** ABOUT ME **OR MY WORLD?**
I THINK I CAN DO MY PART FOR HUMANITY **WITHOUT** THE WITCHBLADE'S HELP.
NO, SARA. YOU **CAN'T**.
WE WON'T **LET** YOU.
IT'S TIME YOU STOPPED BEING SO **SELFISH**, SARA.
AFTER ALL, WE'RE ALL A **TEAM**.
INSEPARABLE.

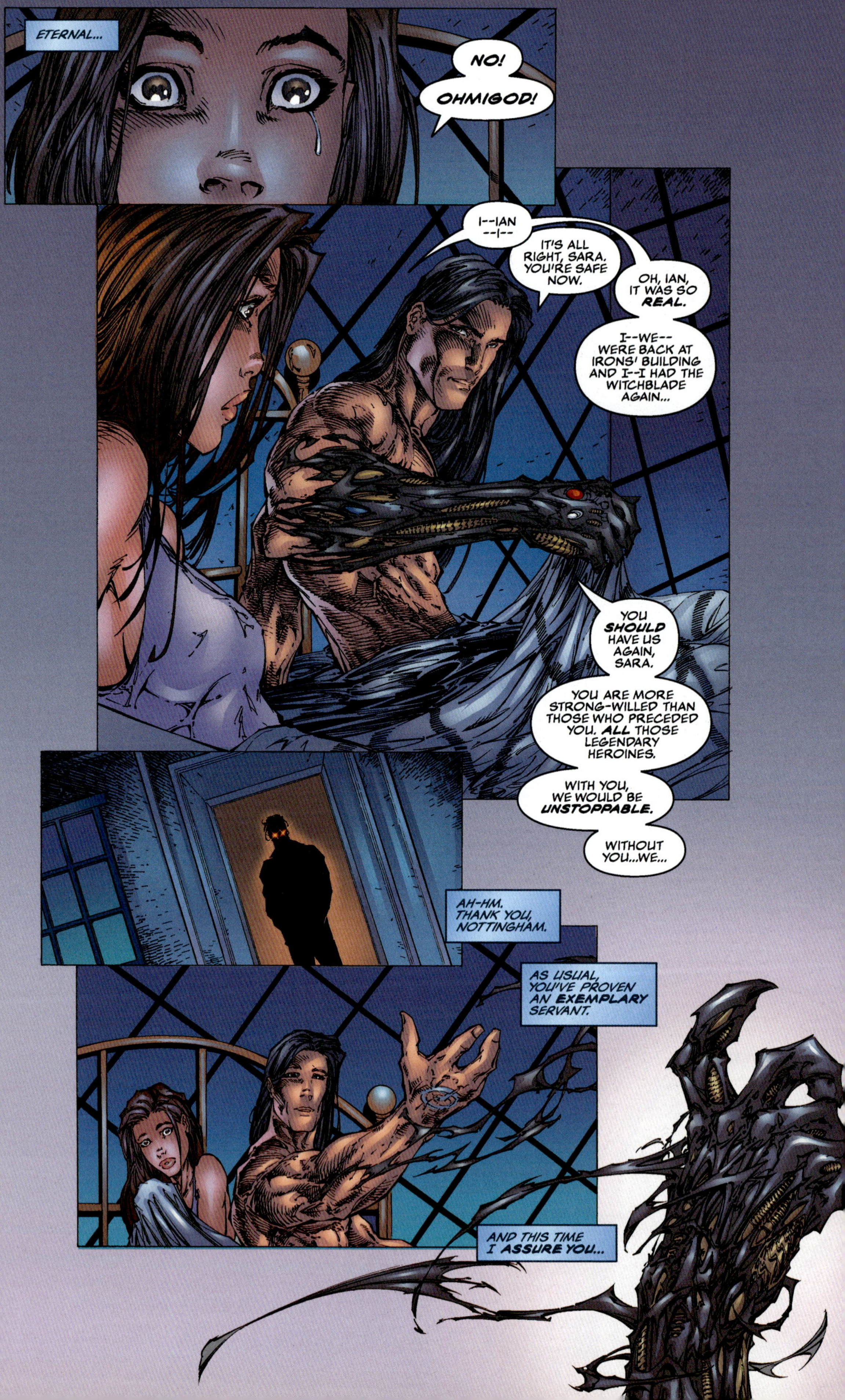

ETERNAL...
NO!
OHMIGOD!
I--IAN --I--
IT'S ALL RIGHT, SARA. YOU'RE SAFE NOW.
OH, IAN, IT WAS SO REAL.
I--WE--WERE BACK AT IRONS' BUILDING AND I--I HAD THE WITCHBLADE AGAIN...
YOU SHOULD HAVE US AGAIN, SARA.
YOU ARE MORE STRONG-WILLED THAN THOSE WHO PRECEDED YOU. ALL THOSE LEGENDARY HEROINES.
WITH YOU, WE WOULD BE UNSTOPPABLE.
WITHOUT YOU...WE...
AH-HM. THANK YOU, NOTTINGHAM.
AS USUAL, YOU'VE PROVEN AN EXEMPLARY SERVANT.
AND THIS TIME I ASSURE YOU...

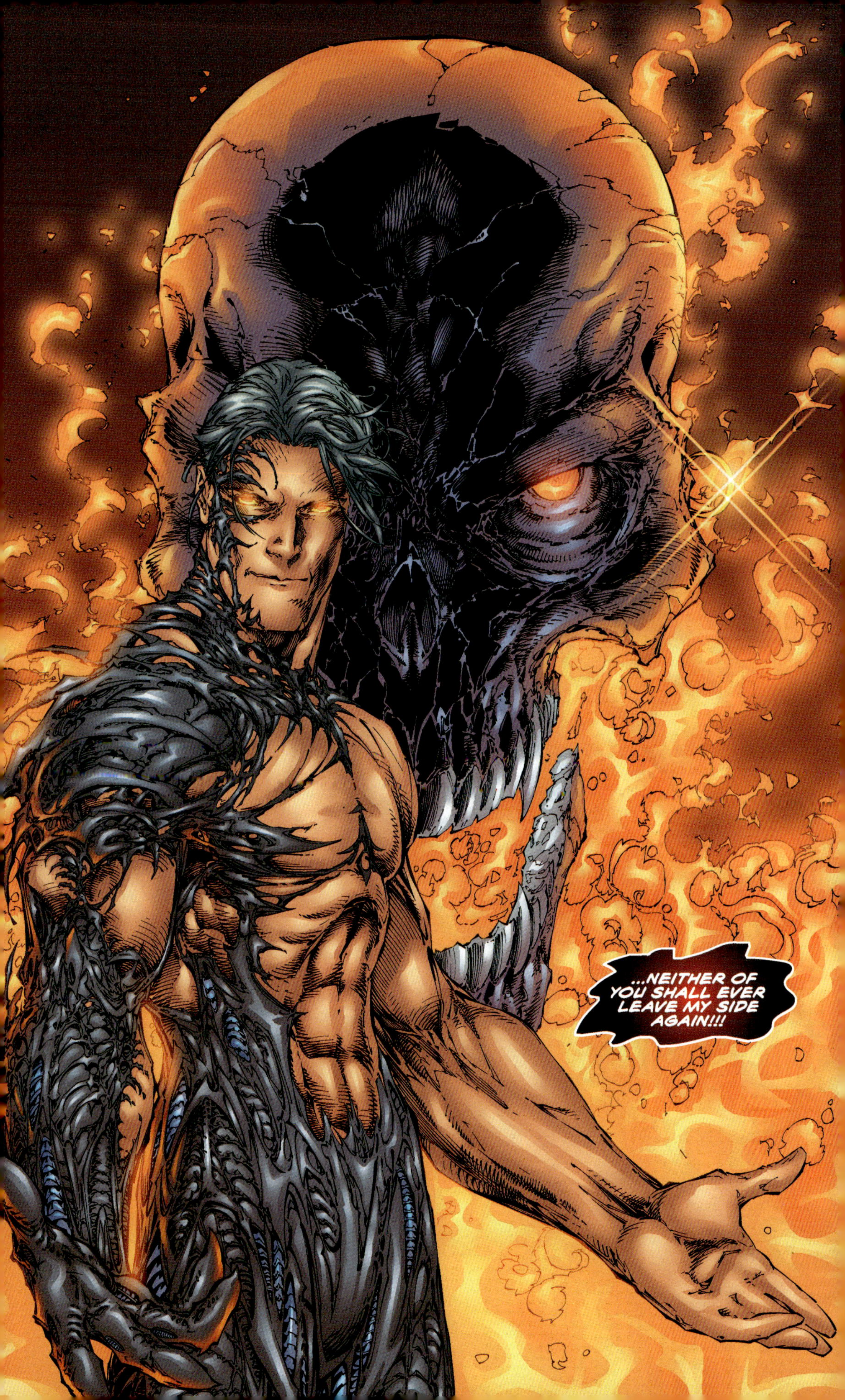
...NEITHER OF YOU SHALL EVER LEAVE MY SIDE AGAIN!!!

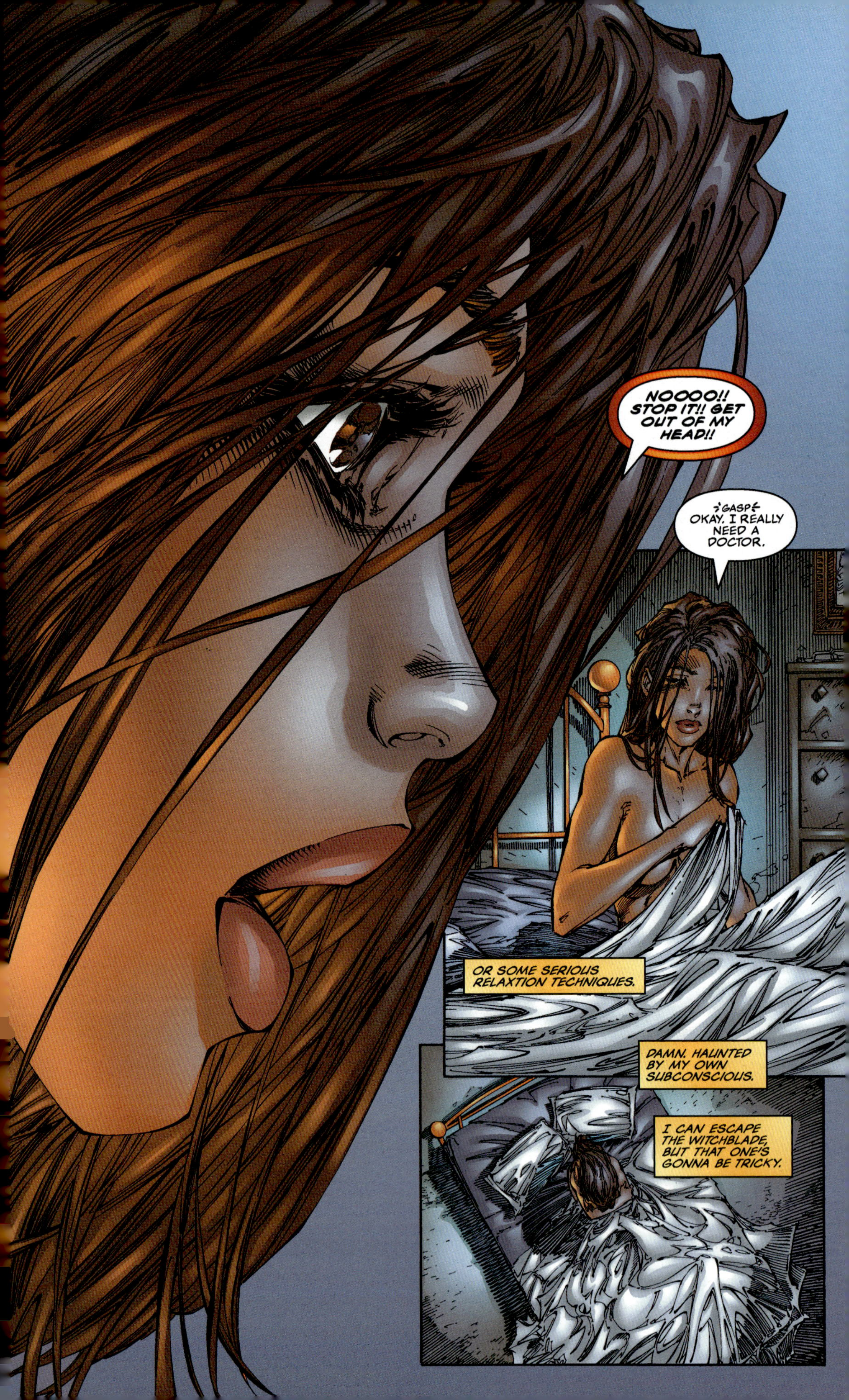

NOOOO!! STOP IT!! GET OUT OF MY HEAD!!
GASP OKAY. I REALLY NEED A DOCTOR.
OR SOME SERIOUS RELAXTION TECHNIQUES.
DAMN. HAUNTED BY MY OWN SUBCONSCIOUS.
I CAN ESCAPE THE WITCHBLADE, BUT THAT ONE'S GONNA BE TRICKY.

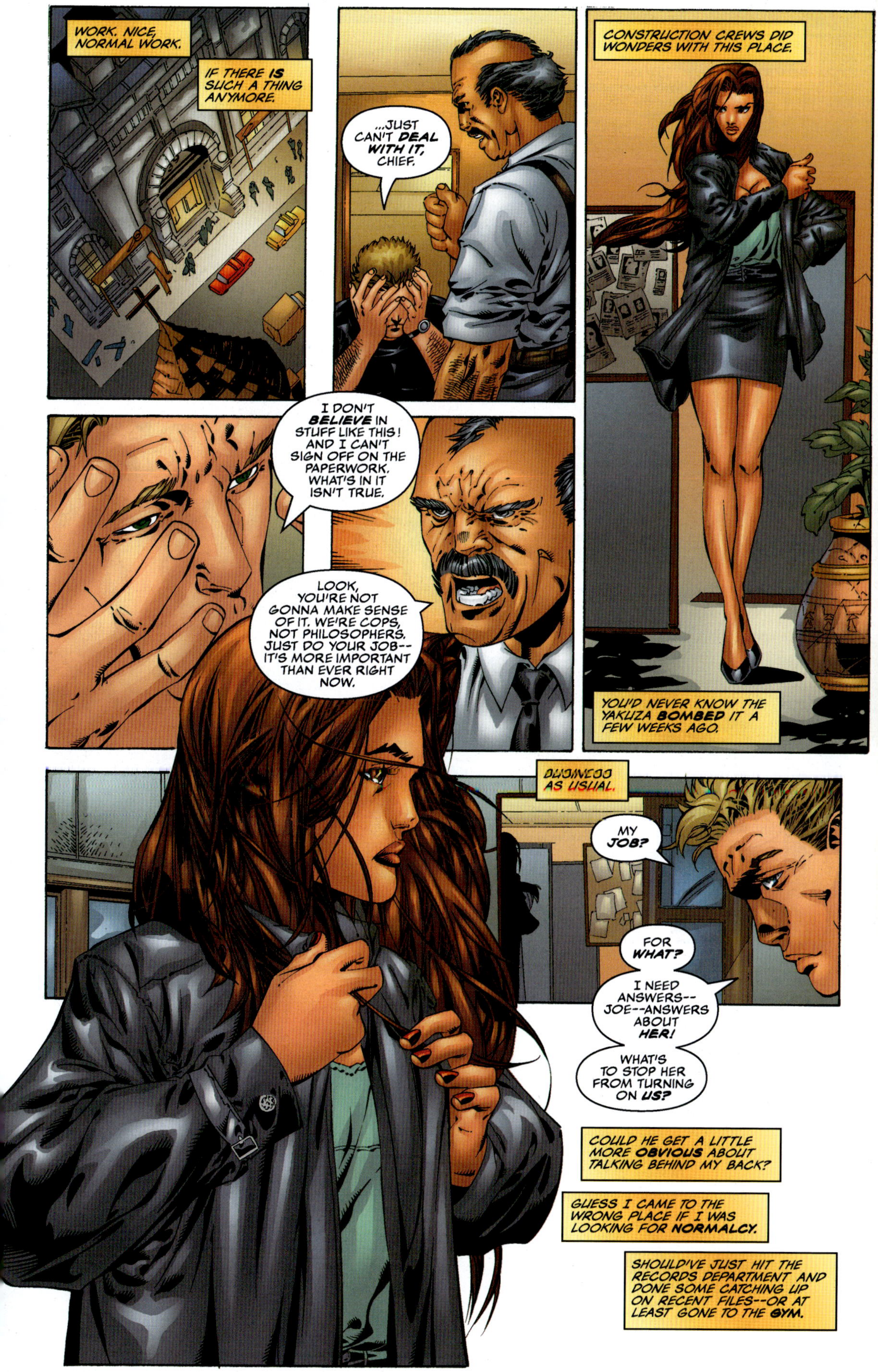
WORK. NICE, NORMAL WORK.
IF THERE IS SUCH A THING ANYMORE.
...JUST CAN'T DEAL WITH IT, CHIEF.
CONSTRUCTION CREWS DID WONDERS WITH THIS PLACE.
I DON'T BELIEVE IN STUFF LIKE THIS! AND I CAN'T SIGN OFF ON THE PAPERWORK. WHAT'S IN IT ISN'T TRUE.
LOOK, YOU'RE NOT GONNA MAKE SENSE OF IT. WE'RE COPS, NOT PHILOSOPHERS. JUST DO YOUR JOB-- IT'S MORE IMPORTANT THAN EVER RIGHT NOW.
YOU'D NEVER KNOW THE YAKUZA BOMBED IT A FEW WEEKS AGO.
AS USUAL.
MY JOB?
FOR WHAT?
I NEED ANSWERS-- JOE--ANSWERS ABOUT HER!
WHAT'S TO STOP HER FROM TURNING ON US?
COULD HE GET A LITTLE MORE OBVIOUS ABOUT TALKING BEHIND MY BACK?
GUESS I CAME TO THE WRONG PLACE IF I WAS LOOKING FOR NORMALCY.
SHOULD'VE JUST HIT THE RECORDS DEPARTMENT AND DONE SOME CATCHING UP ON RECENT FILES--OR AT LEAST GONE TO THE GYM.

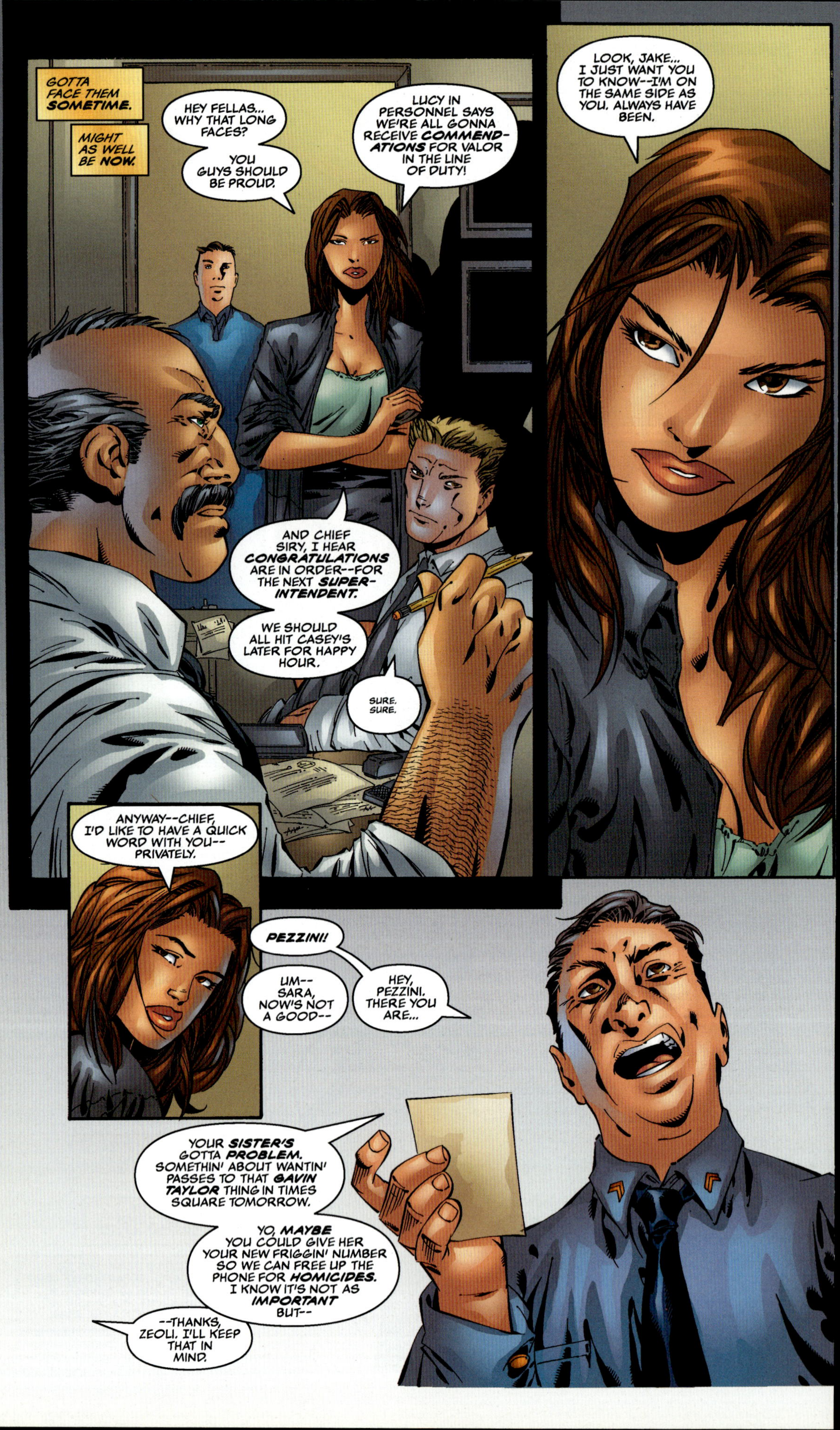
GOTTA FACE THEM SOMETIME.
MIGHT AS WELL BE NOW.
HEY FELLAS... WHY THAT LONG FACES?
YOU GUYS SHOULD BE PROUD.
LUCY IN PERSONNEL SAYS WE'RE ALL GONNA RECEIVE COMMEND-ATIONS FOR VALOR IN THE LINE OF DUTY!
AND CHIEF SIRY, I HEAR CONGRATULATIONS ARE IN ORDER--FOR THE NEXT SUPER-INTENDENT.
WE SHOULD ALL HIT CASEY'S LATER FOR HAPPY HOUR.
SURE. SURE.
LOOK, JAKE... I JUST WANT YOU TO KNOW--I'M ON THE SAME SIDE AS YOU. ALWAYS HAVE BEEN.
ANYWAY--CHIEF, I'D LIKE TO HAVE A QUICK WORD WITH YOU--PRIVATELY.
PEZZINI!
UM-- SARA, NOW'S NOT A GOOD--
HEY, PEZZINI. THERE YOU ARE...
YOUR SISTER'S GOTTA PROBLEM. SOMETHIN' ABOUT WANTIN' PASSES TO THAT GAVIN TAYLOR THING IN TIMES SQUARE TOMORROW.
YO, MAYBE YOU COULD GIVE HER YOUR NEW FRIGGIN' NUMBER SO WE CAN FREE UP THE PHONE FOR HOMICIDES. I KNOW IT'S NOT AS IMPORTANT BUT--
--THANKS, ZEOLI. I'LL KEEP THAT IN MIND.

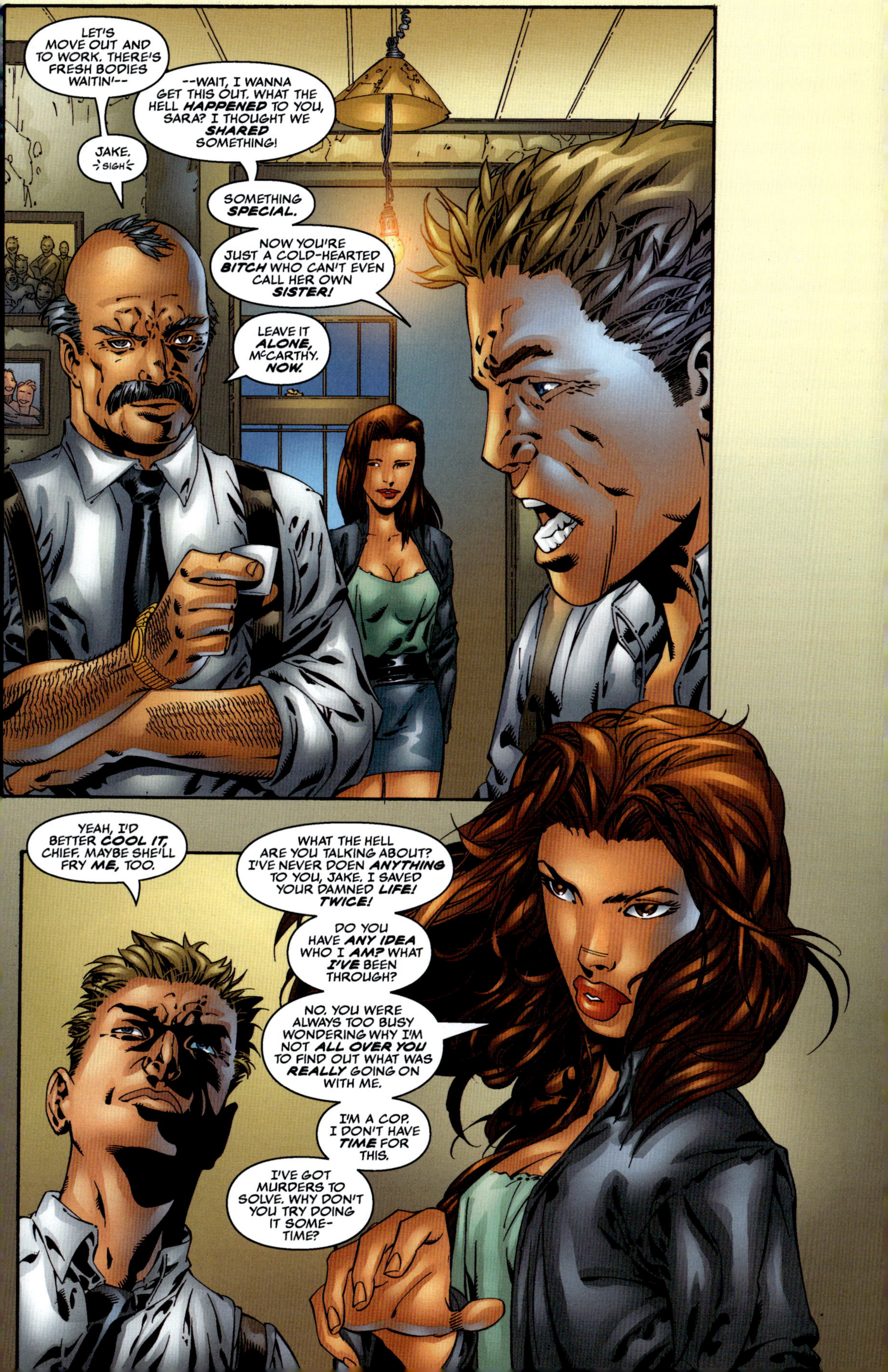
LET'S MOVE OUT AND TO WORK. THERE'S FRESH BODIES WAITIN'--
JAKE. SIGH
--WAIT, I WANNA GET THIS OUT. WHAT THE HELL HAPPENED TO YOU, SARA? I THOUGHT WE SHARED SOMETHING!
SOMETHING SPECIAL.
NOW YOU'RE JUST A COLD-HEARTED BITCH WHO CAN'T EVEN CALL HER OWN SISTER!
LEAVE IT ALONE, McCARTHY. NOW.
YEAH, I'D BETTER COOL IT, CHIEF. MAYBE SHE'LL FRY ME, TOO.
WHAT THE HELL ARE YOU TALKING ABOUT? I'VE NEVER DOEN ANYTHING TO YOU, JAKE. I SAVED YOUR DAMNED LIFE! TWICE!
DO YOU HAVE ANY IDEA WHO I AM? WHAT I'VE BEEN THROUGH?
NO. YOU WERE ALWAYS TOO BUSY WONDERING WHY I'M NOT ALL OVER YOU TO FIND OUT WHAT WAS REALLY GOING ON WITH ME.
I'M A COP. I DON'T HAVE TIME FOR THIS.
I'VE GOT MURDERS TO SOLVE. WHY DON'T YOU TRY DOING IT SOME-TIME?

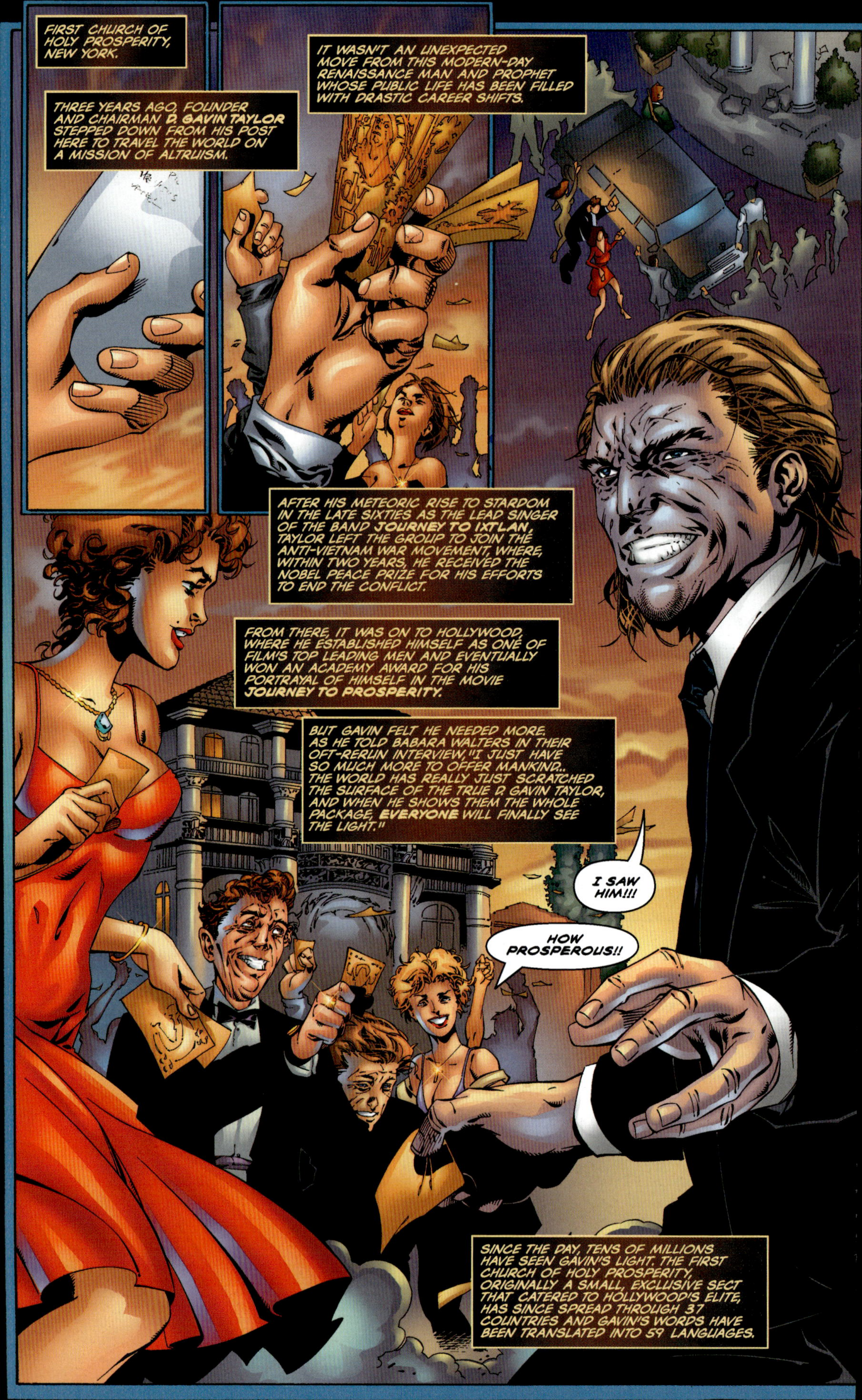
FIRST CHURCH OF HOLY PROSPERITY, NEW YORK.
THREE YEARS AGO, FOUNDER AND CHAIRMAN D. GAVIN TAYLOR STEPPED DOWN FROM HIS POST HERE TO TRAVEL THE WORLD ON A MISSION OF ALTRUISM.
IT WASN'T AN UNEXPECTED MOVE FROM THIS MODERN-DAY RENAISSANCE MAN AND PROPHET WHOSE PUBLIC LIFE HAS BEEN FILLED WITH DRASTIC CAREER SHIFTS.
AFTER HIS METEORIC RISE TO STARDOM IN THE LATE SIXTIES AS THE LEAD SINGER OF THE BAND JOURNEY TO IXTLAN, TAYLOR LEFT THE GROUP TO JOIN THE ANTI-VIETNAM WAR MOVEMENT, WHERE, WITHIN TWO YEARS, HE RECEIVED THE NOBEL PEACE PRIZE FOR HIS EFFORTS TO END THE CONFLICT.
FROM THERE, IT WAS ON TO HOLLYWOOD, WHERE HE ESTABLISHED HIMSELF AS ONE OF FILM'S TOP LEADING MEN AND EVENTUALLY WON AN ACADEMY AWARD FOR HIS PORTRAYAL OF HIMSELF IN THE MOVIE JOURNEY TO PROSPERITY.
BUT GAVIN FELT HE NEEDED MORE. AS HE TOLD BABARA WALTERS IN THEIR OFT-RERUN INTERVIEW, "I JUST HAVE SO MUCH MORE TO OFFER MANKIND.. THE WORLD HAS REALLY JUST SCRATCHED THE SURFACE OF THE TRUE D GAVIN TAYLOR, AND WHEN HE SHOWS THEM THE WHOLE PACKAGE, EVERYONE WILL FINALLY SEE THE LIGHT."
I SAW HIM!!!
HOW PROSPEROUS!!
SINCE THE DAY, TENS OF MILLIONS HAVE SEEN GAVIN'S LIGHT. THE FIRST CHURCH OF HOLY PROSPERITY, ORIGINALLY A SMALL, EXCLUSIVE SECT THAT CATERED TO HOLLYWOOD'S ELITE, HAS SINCE SPREAD THROUGH 37 COUNTRIES AND GAVIN'S WORDS HAVE BEEN TRANSLATED INTO 59 LANGUAGES.

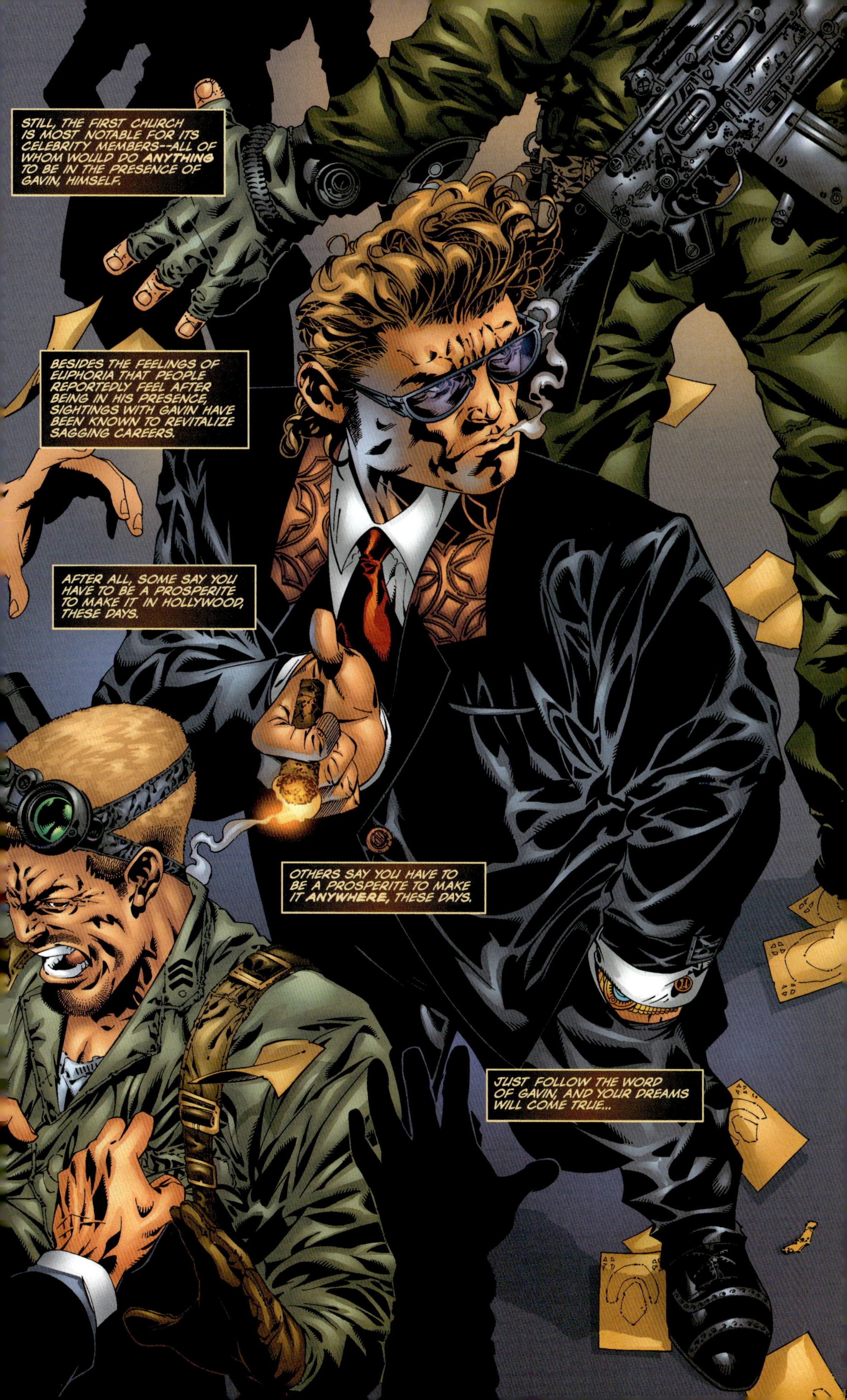
STILL, THE FIRST CHURCH IS MOST NOTABLE FOR ITS CELEBRITY MEMBERS--ALL OF WHOM WOULD DO **ANYTHING** TO BE IN THE PRESENCE OF GAVIN, HIMSELF.
BESIDES THE FEELINGS OF EUPHORIA THAT PEOPLE REPORTEDLY FEEL AFTER BEING IN HIS PRESENCE, SIGHTINGS WITH GAVIN HAVE BEEN KNOWN TO REVITALIZE SAGGING CAREERS.
AFTER ALL, SOME SAY YOU HAVE TO BE A PROSPERITE TO MAKE IT IN HOLLYWOOD, THESE DAYS.
OTHERS SAY YOU HAVE TO BE A PROSPERITE TO MAKE IT **ANYWHERE**, THESE DAYS.
JUST FOLLOW THE WORD OF GAVIN, AND YOUR DREAMS WILL COME TRUE...

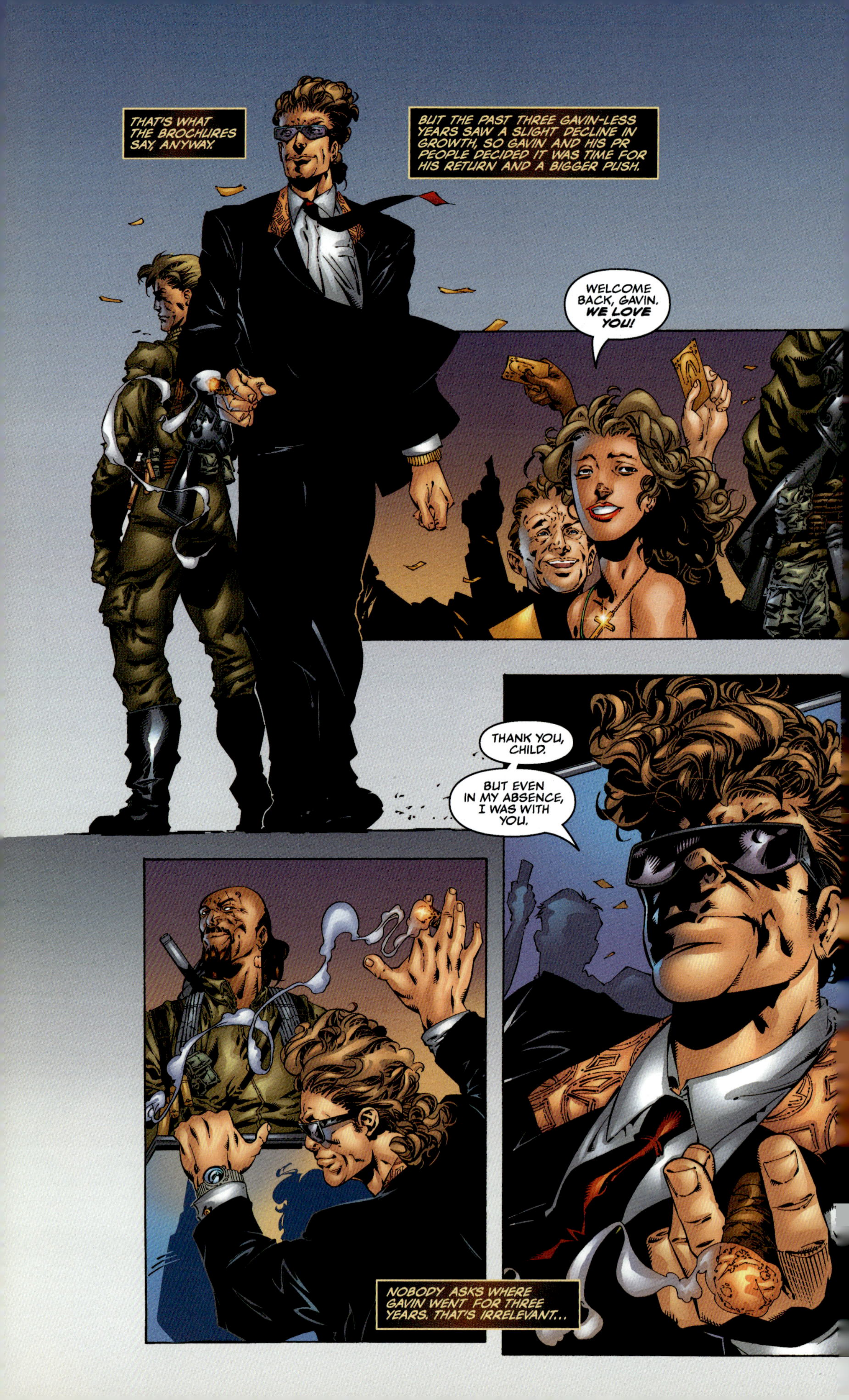
THAT'S WHAT THE BROCHURES SAY, ANYWAY.
BUT THE PAST THREE GAVIN-LESS YEARS SAW A SLIGHT DECLINE IN GROWTH, SO GAVIN AND HIS PR PEOPLE DECIDED IT WAS TIME FOR HIS RETURN AND A BIGGER PUSH.
WELCOME BACK, GAVIN. WE LOVE YOU!
THANK YOU, CHILD.
BUT EVEN IN MY ABSENCE, I WAS WITH YOU.
NOBODY ASKS WHERE GAVIN WENT FOR THREE YEARS. THAT'S IRRELEVANT...

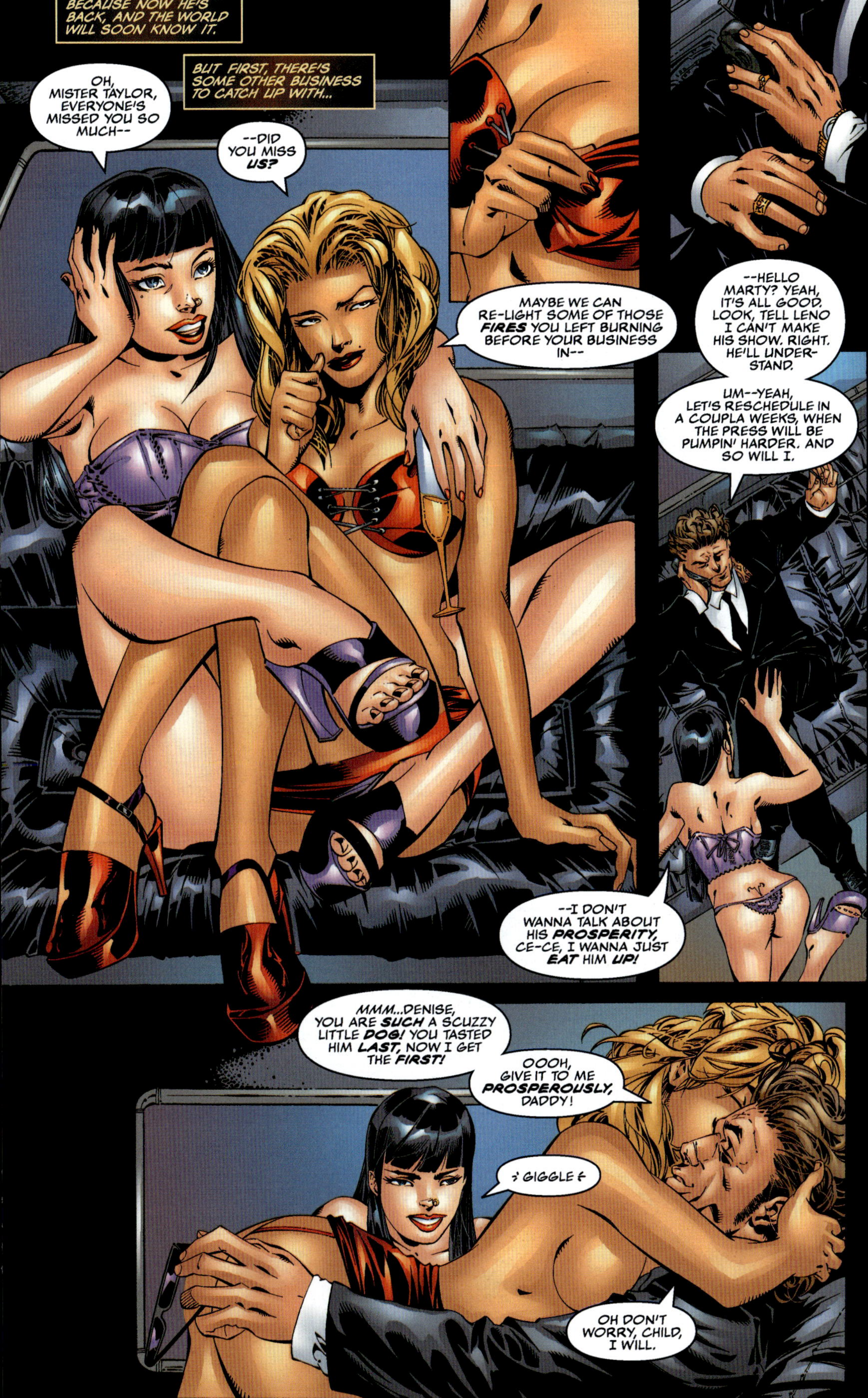
BECAUSE NOW HE'S BACK, AND THE WORLD WILL SOON KNOW IT.
BUT FIRST, THERE'S SOME OTHER BUSINESS TO CATCH UP WITH...
OH, MISTER TAYLOR, EVERYONE'S MISSED YOU SO MUCH--
--DID YOU MISS US?
MAYBE WE CAN RE-LIGHT SOME OF THOSE FIRES YOU LEFT BURNING BEFORE YOUR BUSINESS IN--
--HELLO MARTY? YEAH, IT'S ALL GOOD. LOOK, TELL LENO I CAN'T MAKE HIS SHOW. RIGHT. HE'LL UNDER-STAND.
UM--YEAH, LET'S RESCHEDULE IN A COUPLA WEEKS, WHEN THE PRESS WILL BE PUMPIN' HARDER. AND SO WILL I.
--I DON'T WANNA TALK ABOUT HIS PROSPERITY, CE-CE, I WANNA JUST EAT HIM UP!
MMM...DENISE, YOU ARE SUCH A SCUZZY LITTLE DOG! YOU TASTED HIM LAST, NOW I GET THE FIRST!
OOOH, GIVE IT TO ME PROSPEROUSLY, DADDY!
GIGGLE
OH DON'T WORRY, CHILD, I WILL.

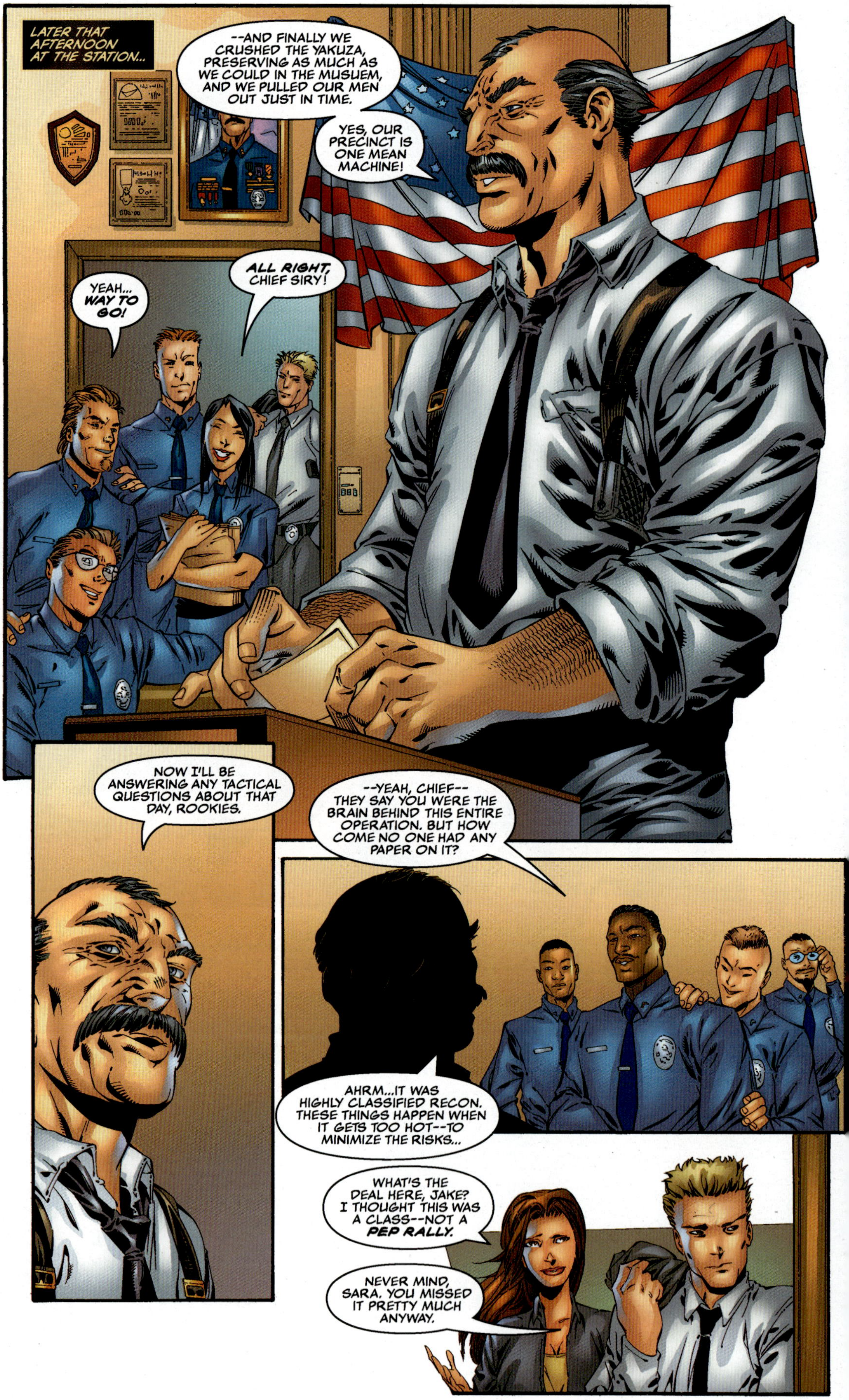

LATER THAT AFTERNOON AT THE STATION...
--AND FINALLY WE CRUSHED THE YAKUZA, PRESERVING AS MUCH AS WE COULD IN THE MUSUEM, AND WE PULLED OUR MEN OUT JUST IN TIME.
YES, OUR PRECINCT IS ONE MEAN MACHINE!
YEAH... WAY TO GO!
ALL RIGHT, CHIEF SIRY!
NOW I'LL BE ANSWERING ANY TACTICAL QUESTIONS ABOUT THAT DAY, ROOKIES.
--YEAH, CHIEF-- THEY SAY YOU WERE THE BRAIN BEHIND THIS ENTIRE OPERATION. BUT HOW COME NO ONE HAD ANY PAPER ON IT?
AHRM...IT WAS HIGHLY CLASSIFIED RECON. THESE THINGS HAPPEN WHEN IT GETS TOO HOT--TO MINIMIZE THE RISKS...
WHAT'S THE DEAL HERE, JAKE? I THOUGHT THIS WAS A CLASS--NOT A PEP RALLY.
NEVER MIND, SARA. YOU MISSED IT PRETTY MUCH ANYWAY.

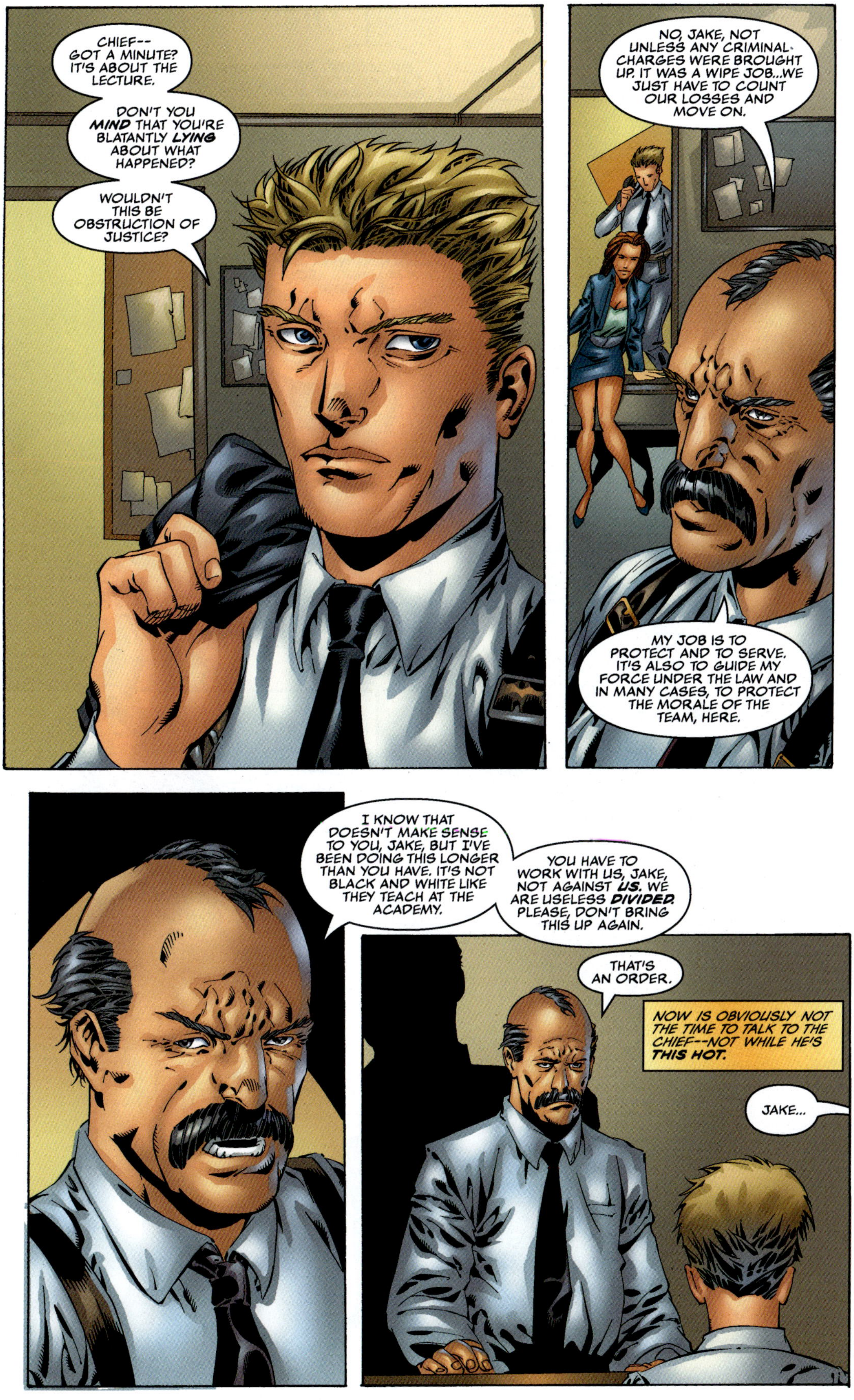
CHIEF-- GOT A MINUTE? IT'S ABOUT THE LECTURE.
DON'T YOU MIND THAT YOU'RE BLATANTLY LYING ABOUT WHAT HAPPENED?
WOULDN'T THIS BE OBSTRUCTION OF JUSTICE?
NO, JAKE, NOT UNLESS ANY CRIMINAL CHARGES WERE BROUGHT UP. IT WAS A WIPE JOB...WE JUST HAVE TO COUNT OUR LOSSES AND MOVE ON.
MY JOB IS TO PROTECT AND TO SERVE. IT'S ALSO TO GUIDE MY FORCE UNDER THE LAW AND IN MANY CASES, TO PROTECT THE MORALE OF THE TEAM, HERE.
I KNOW THAT DOESN'T MAKE SENSE TO YOU, JAKE, BUT I'VE BEEN DOING THIS LONGER THAN YOU HAVE. IT'S NOT BLACK AND WHITE LIKE THEY TEACH AT THE ACADEMY.
YOU HAVE TO WORK WITH US, JAKE, NOT AGAINST US. WE ARE USELESS DIVIDED. PLEASE, DON'T BRING THIS UP AGAIN.
THAT'S AN ORDER.
NOW IS OBVIOUSLY NOT THE TIME TO TALK TO THE CHIEF--NOT WHILE HE'S THIS HOT.
JAKE...

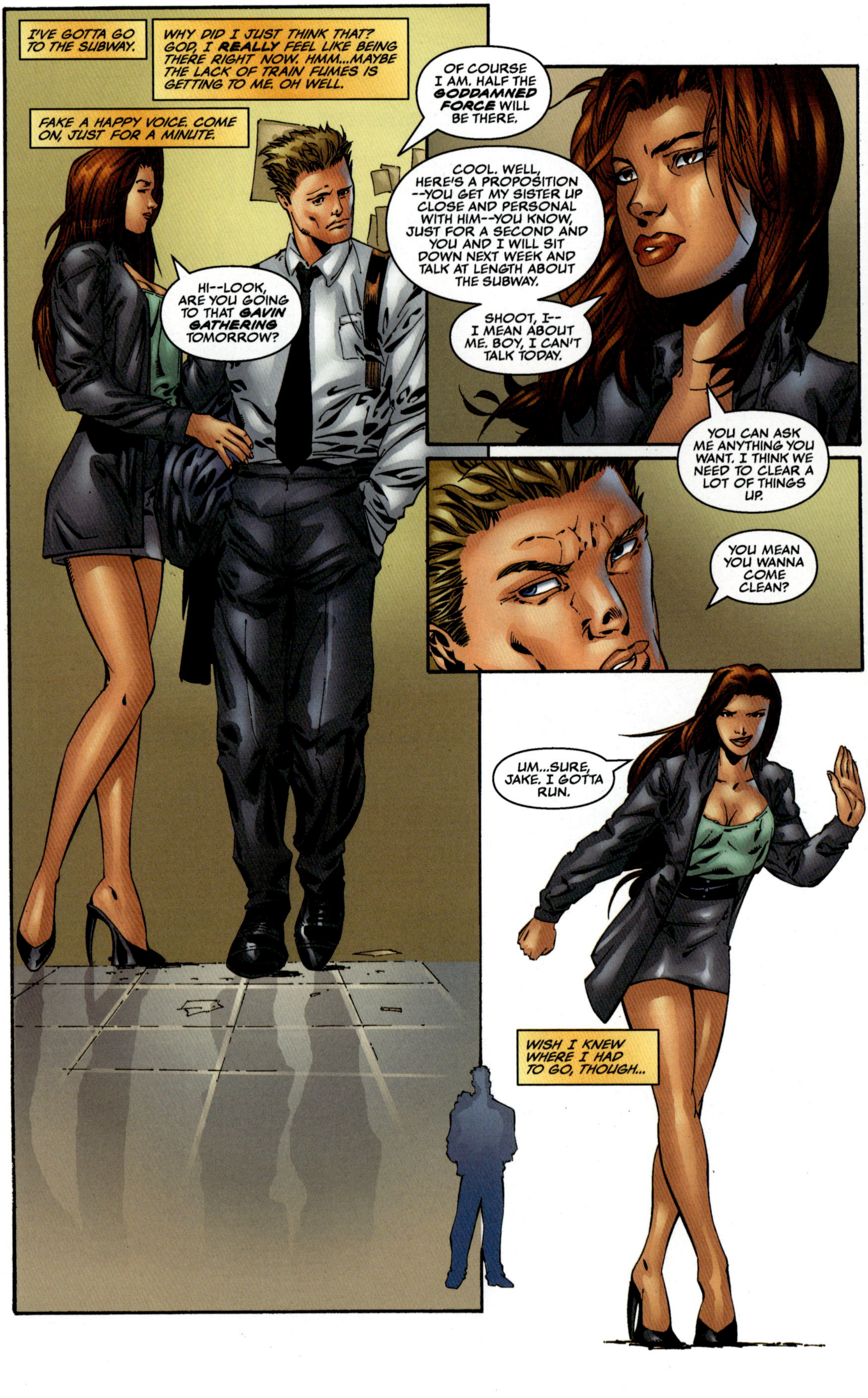
I'VE GOTTA GO TO THE SUBWAY.
WHY DID I JUST THINK THAT? GOD, I REALLY FEEL LIKE BEING THERE RIGHT NOW. HMM...MAYBE THE LACK OF TRAIN FUMES IS GETTING TO ME. OH WELL.
FAKE A HAPPY VOICE. COME ON, JUST FOR A MINUTE.
HI--LOOK, ARE YOU GOING TO THAT GAVIN GATHERING TOMORROW?
OF COURSE I AM. HALF THE GODDAMNED FORCE WILL BE THERE.
COOL. WELL, HERE'S A PROPOSITION --YOU GET MY SISTER UP CLOSE AND PERSONAL WITH HIM--YOU KNOW, JUST FOR A SECOND AND YOU AND I WILL SIT DOWN NEXT WEEK AND TALK AT LENGTH ABOUT THE SUBWAY.
SHOOT, I-- I MEAN ABOUT ME. BOY, I CAN'T TALK TODAY.
YOU CAN ASK ME ANYTHING YOU WANT. I THINK WE NEED TO CLEAR A LOT OF THINGS UP.
YOU MEAN YOU WANNA COME CLEAN?
UM...SURE, JAKE. I GOTTA RUN.
WISH I KNEW WHERE I HAD TO GO, THOUGH...

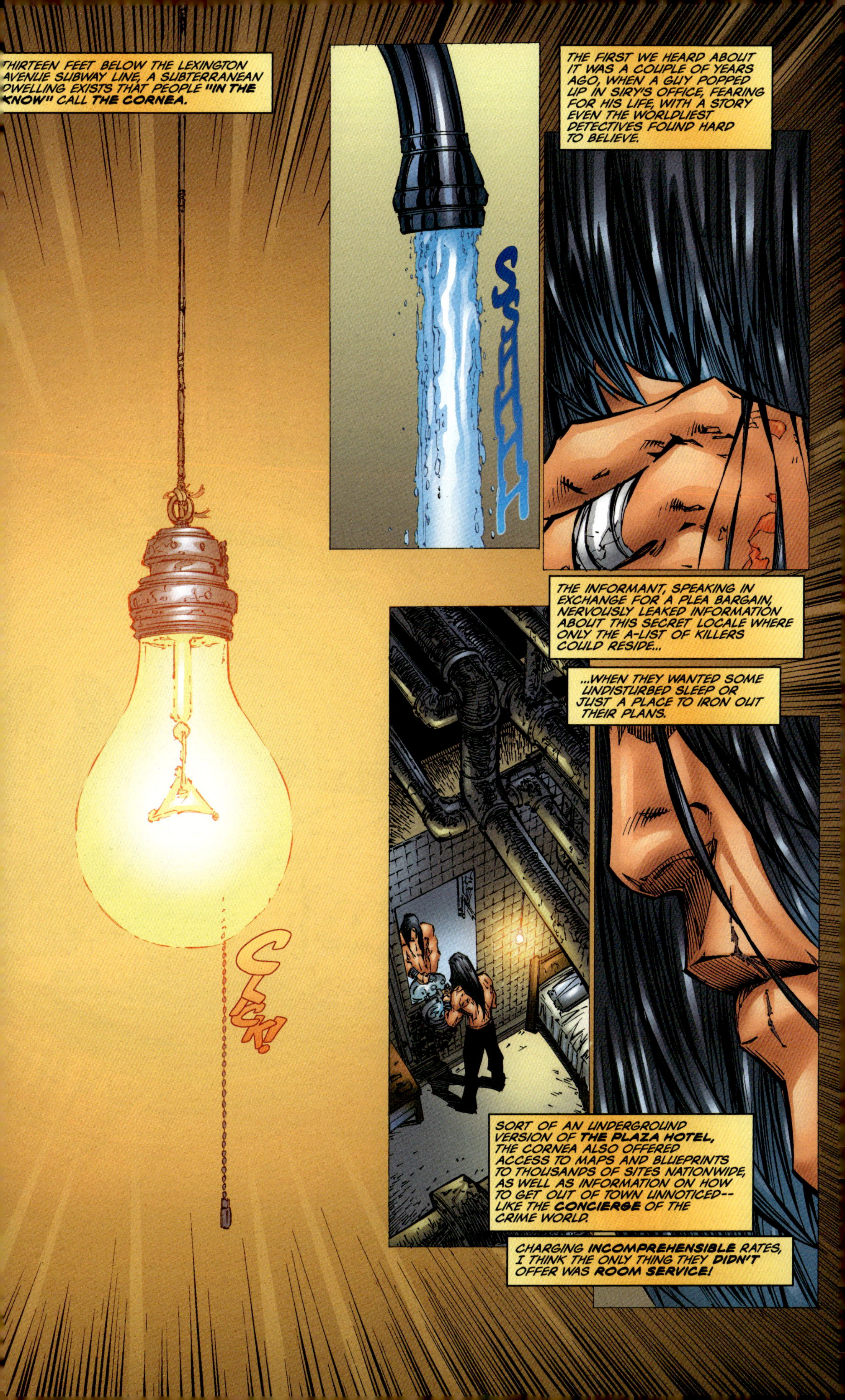
THIRTEEN FEET BELOW THE LEXINGTON AVENUE SUBWAY LINE, A SUBTERRANEAN DWELLING EXISTS THAT PEOPLE "IN THE KNOW" CALL THE CORNEA.
CLICK!
THE FIRST WE HEARD ABOUT IT WAS A COUPLE OF YEARS AGO, WHEN A GUY POPPED UP IN SIRY'S OFFICE, FEARING FOR HIS LIFE, WITH A STORY EVEN THE WORLDLIEST DETECTIVES FOUND HARD TO BELIEVE.
SSHHH
THE INFORMANT, SPEAKING IN EXCHANGE FOR A PLEA BARGAIN, NERVOUSLY LEAKED INFORMATION ABOUT THIS SECRET LOCALE WHERE ONLY THE A-LIST OF KILLERS COULD RESIDE...
...WHEN THEY WANTED SOME UNDISTURBED SLEEP OR JUST A PLACE TO IRON OUT THEIR PLANS.
SORT OF AN UNDERGROUND VERSION OF THE PLAZA HOTEL, THE CORNEA ALSO OFFERED ACCESS TO MAPS AND BLUEPRINTS TO THOUSANDS OF SITES NATIONWIDE, AS WELL AS INFORMATION ON HOW TO GET OUT OF TOWN UNNOTICED-- LIKE THE CONCIERGE OF THE CRIME WORLD.
CHARGING INCOMPREHENSIBLE RATES, I THINK THE ONLY THING THEY DIDN'T OFFER WAS ROOM SERVICE!

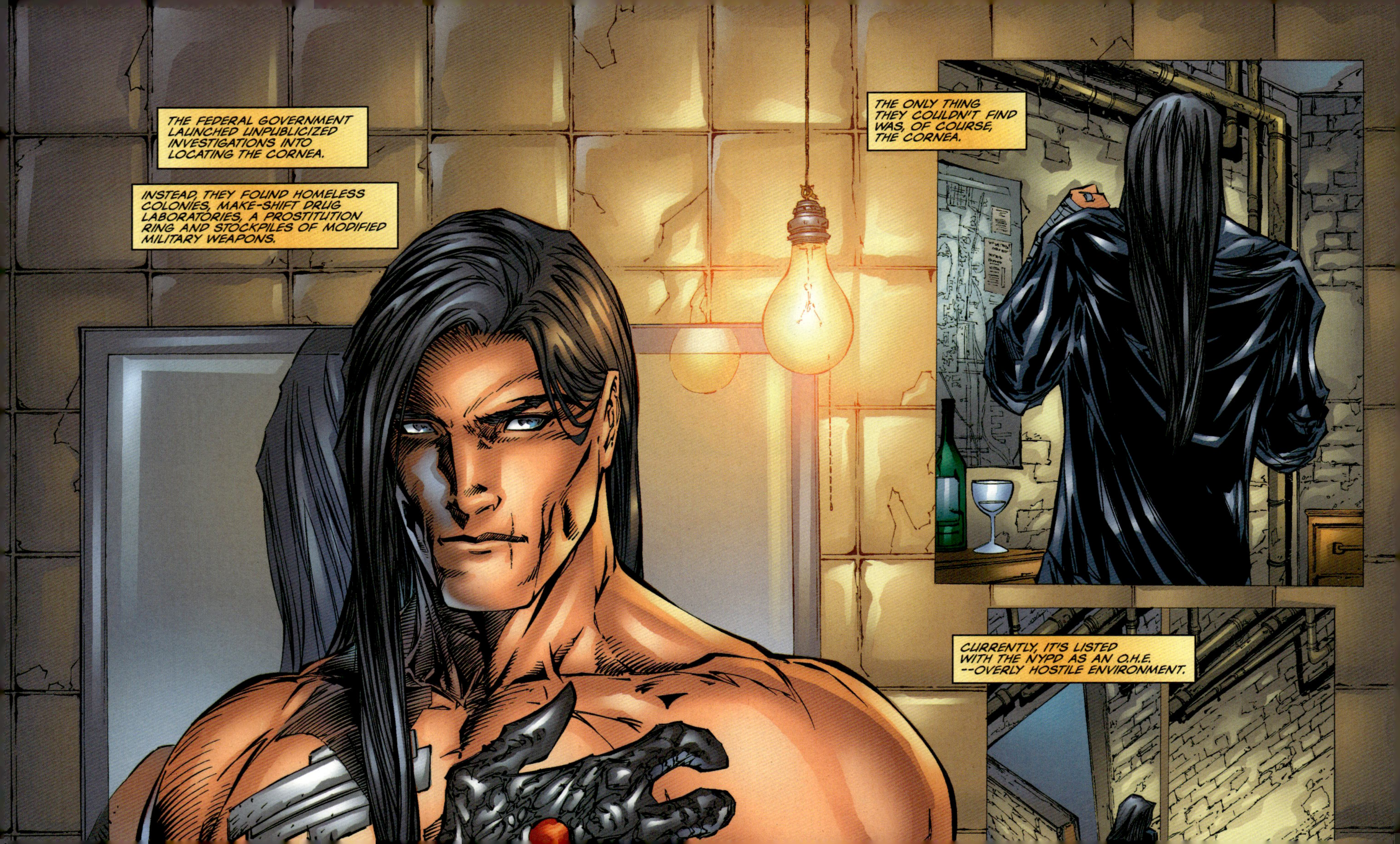
THE FEDERAL GOVERNMENT LAUNCHED UNPUBLICIZED INVESTIGATIONS INTO LOCATING THE CORNEA.
INSTEAD, THEY FOUND HOMELESS COLONIES, MAKE-SHIFT DRUG LABORATORIES, A PROSTITUTION RING AND STOCKPILES OF MODIFIED MILITARY WEAPONS.
THE ONLY THING THEY COULDN'T FIND WAS, OF COURSE, THE CORNEA.
CURRENTLY, IT'S LISTED WITH THE NYPD AS AN O.H.E. --OVERLY HOSTILE ENVIRONMENT.

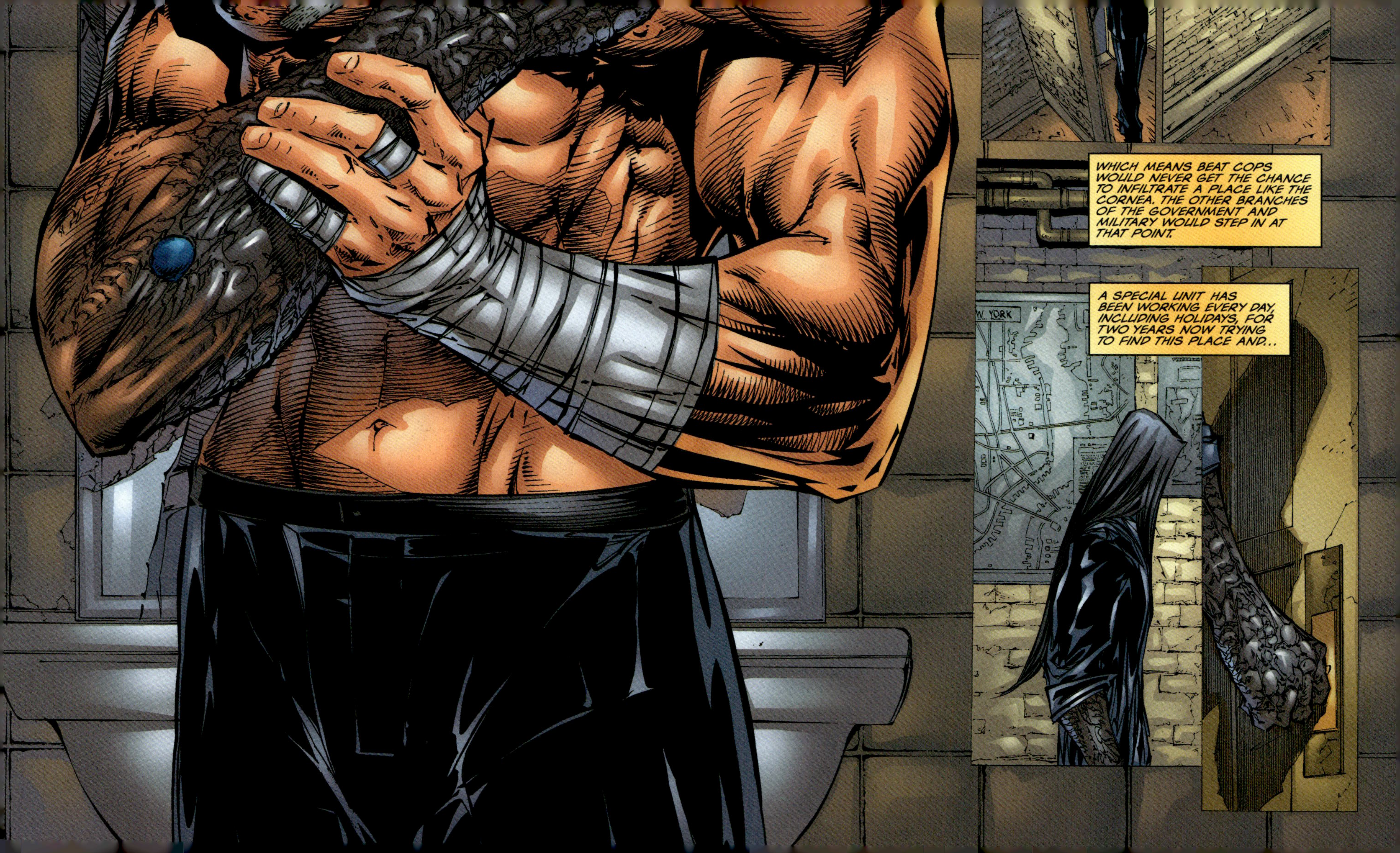
WHICH MEANS BEAT COPS WOULD NEVER GET THE CHANCE TO INFILTRATE A PLACE LIKE THE CORNEA. THE OTHER BRANCHES OF THE GOVERNMENT AND MILITARY WOULD STEP IN AT THAT POINT.
A SPECIAL UNIT HAS BEEN WORKING EVERY DAY, INCLUDING HOLIDAYS, FOR TWO YEARS NOW TRYING TO FIND THIS PLACE AND...
W. YORK

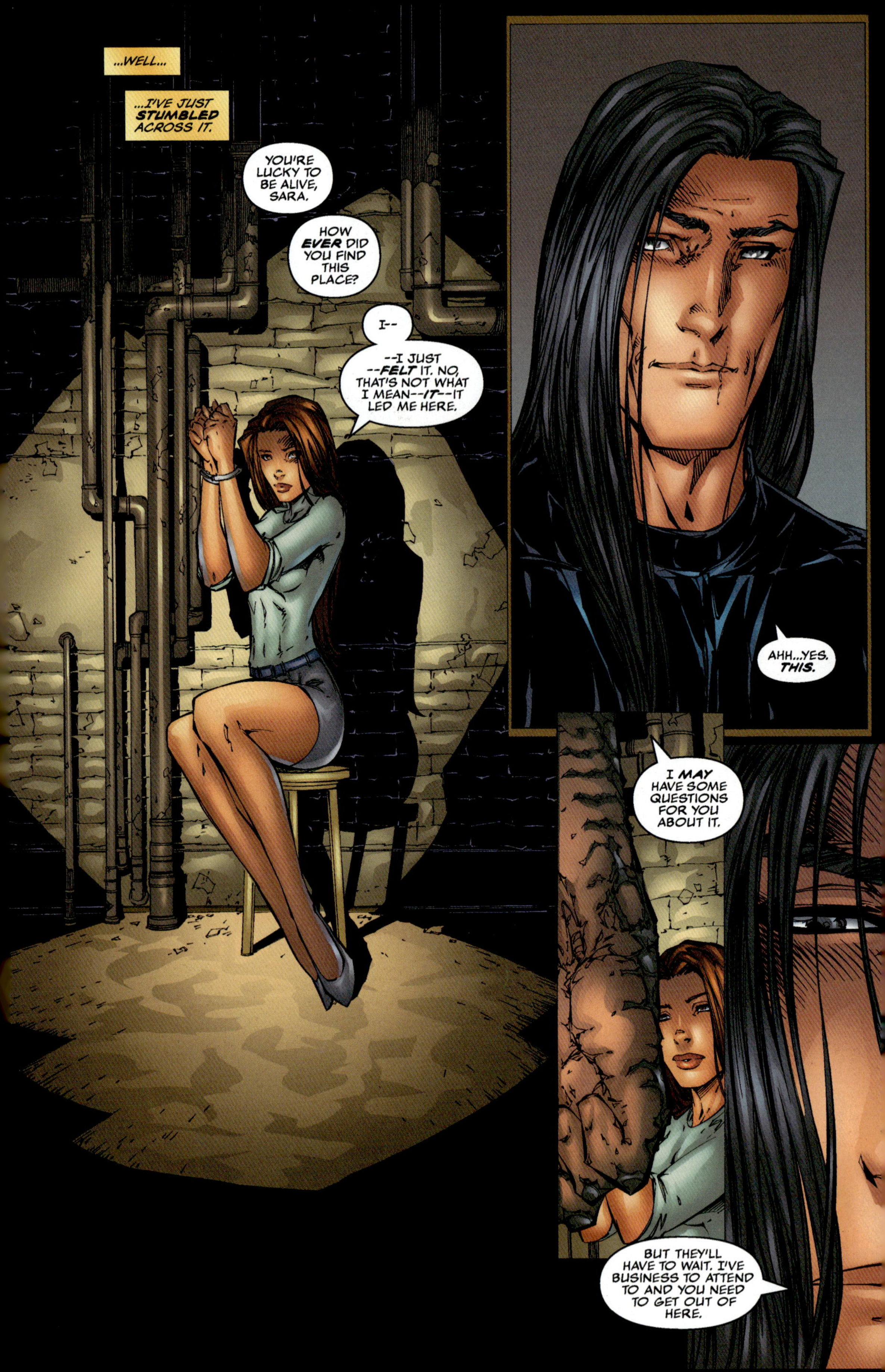
...WELL...
...I'VE JUST STUMBLED ACROSS IT.
YOU'RE LUCKY TO BE ALIVE, SARA.
HOW EVER DID YOU FIND THIS PLACE?
I--
--I JUST --FELT IT. NO, THAT'S NOT WHAT I MEAN--IT--IT LED ME HERE.
AHH...YES. THIS.
I MAY HAVE SOME QUESTIONS FOR YOU ABOUT IT.
BUT THEY'LL HAVE TO WAIT. I'VE BUSINESS TO ATTEND TO AND YOU NEED TO GET OUT OF HERE.

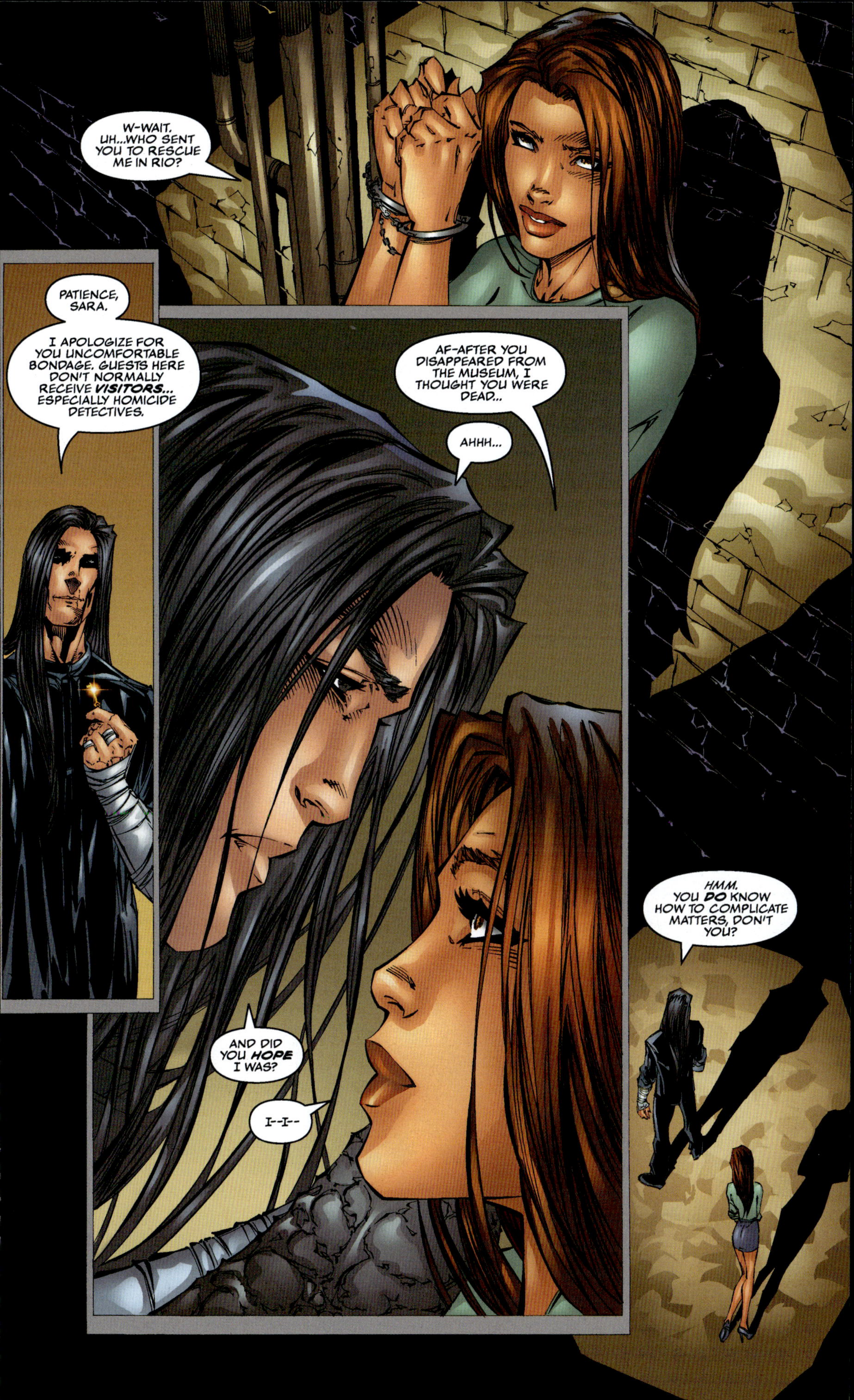
W-WAIT. UH...WHO SENT YOU TO RESCUE ME IN RIO?
PATIENCE, SARA.
I APOLOGIZE FOR YOU UNCOMFORTABLE BONDAGE. GUESTS HERE DON'T NORMALLY RECEIVE VISITORS... ESPECIALLY HOMICIDE DETECTIVES.
AF-AFTER YOU DISAPPEARED FROM THE MUSEUM, I THOUGHT YOU WERE DEAD...
AHHH...
AND DID YOU HOPE I WAS?
I-I-
HMM. YOU DO KNOW HOW TO COMPLICATE MATTERS, DON'T YOU?

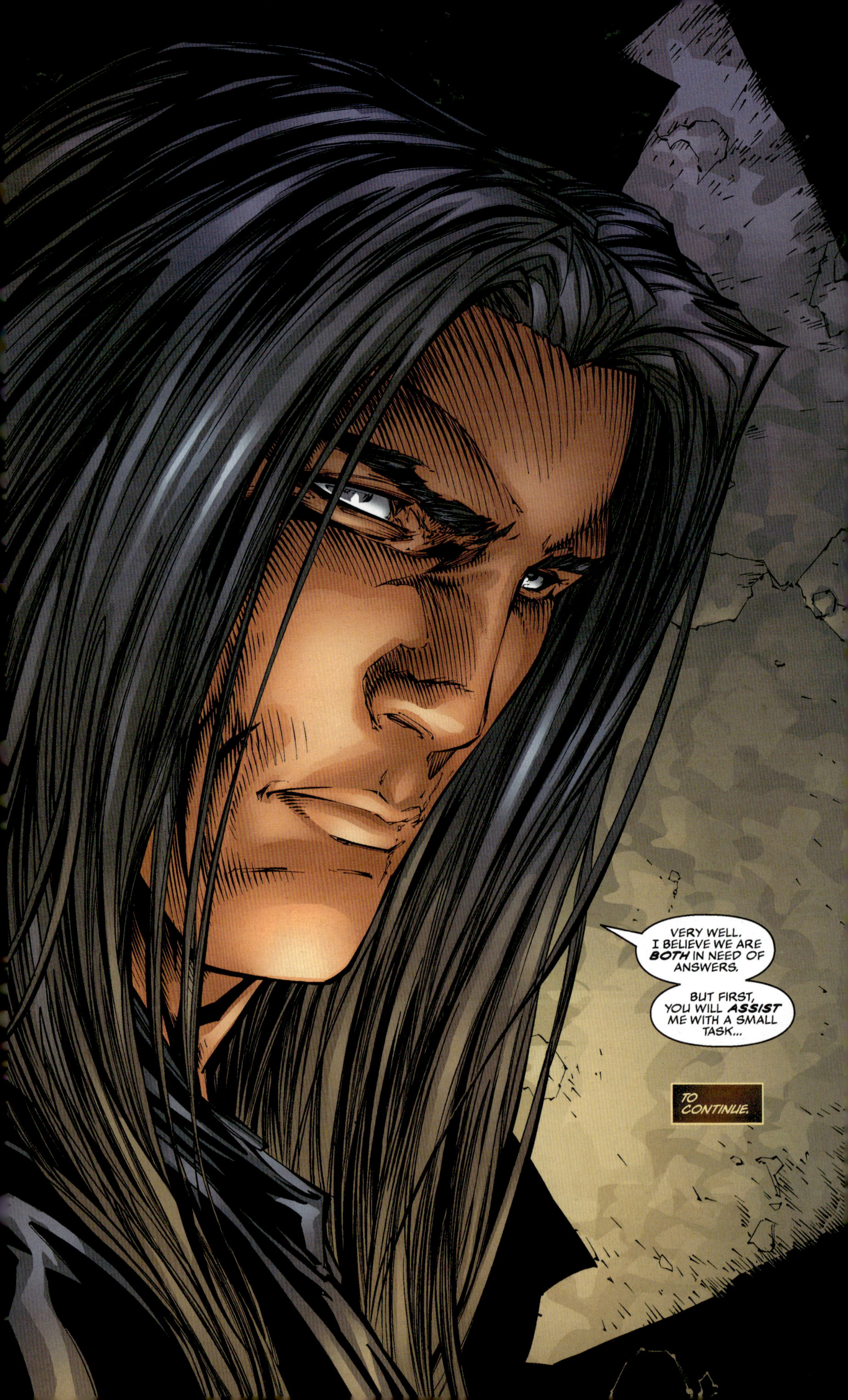
VERY WELL. I BELIEVE WE ARE BOTH IN NEED OF ANSWERS.
BUT FIRST, YOU WILL ASSIST ME WITH A SMALL TASK...
TO CONTINUE.

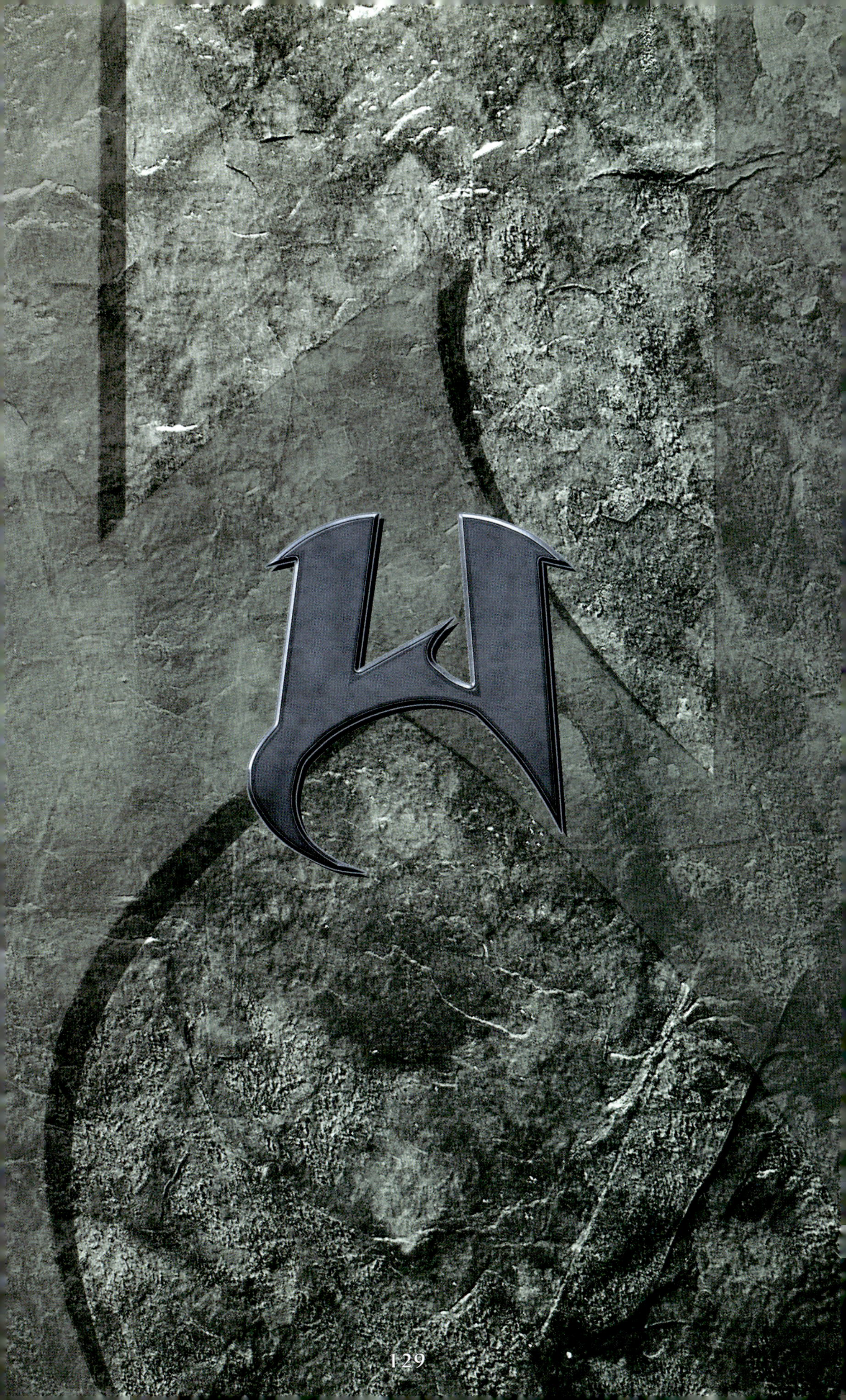

issue #21

story: **David Wohl** and **Christina Z.**
pencils: **Michael Turner, Brian Ching** and **Clarence Lansang**
inks: **D-Tron**
colors: **JD Smith**

ink assists: **Andy Kim, Marsha Chen, Jose "Jag" Guillen** and **Jeff De Los Santos**

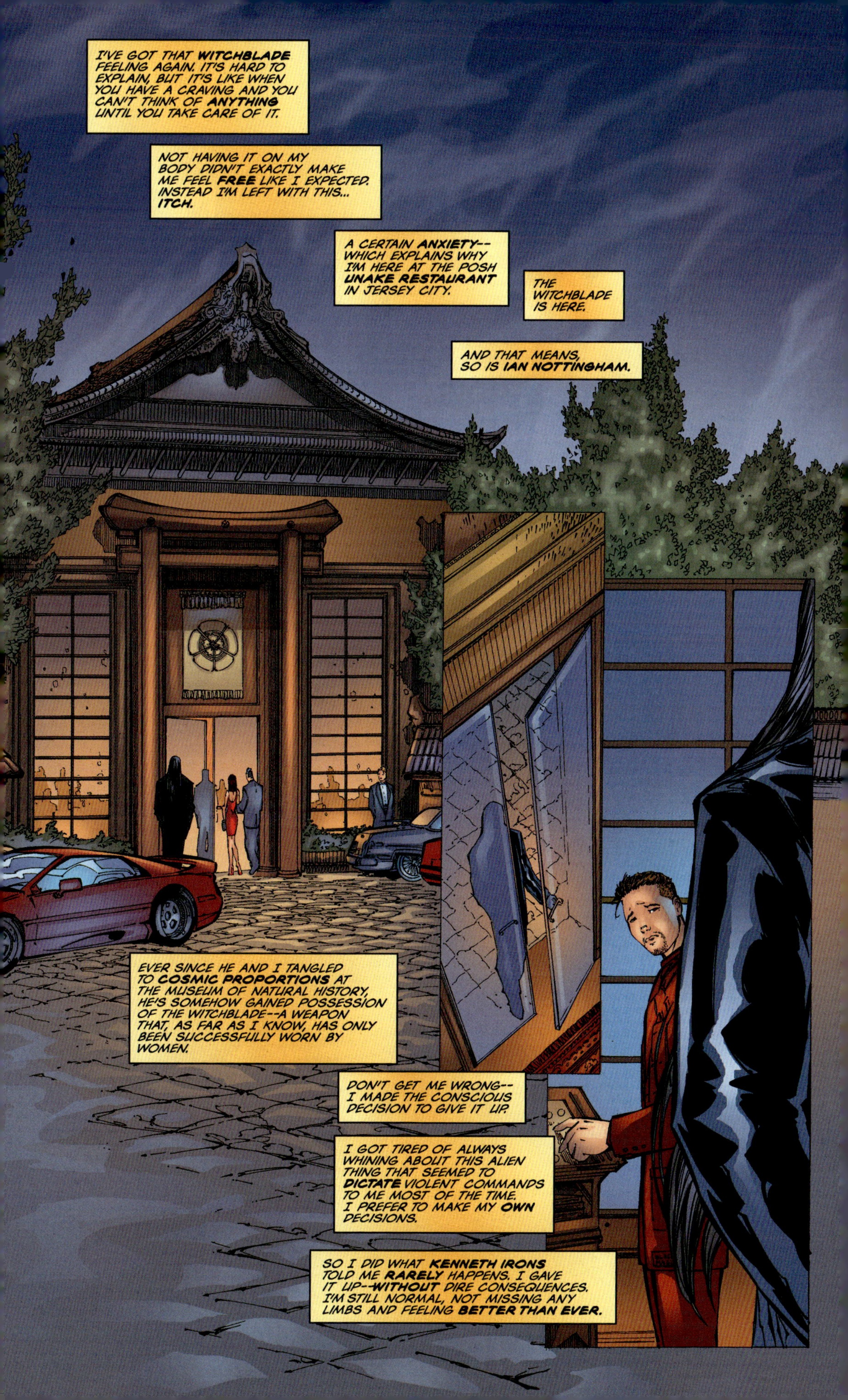
I'VE GOT THAT WITCHBLADE FEELING AGAIN. IT'S HARD TO EXPLAIN, BUT IT'S LIKE WHEN YOU HAVE A CRAVING AND YOU CAN'T THINK OF ANYTHING UNTIL YOU TAKE CARE OF IT.
NOT HAVING IT ON MY BODY DIDN'T EXACTLY MAKE ME FEEL FREE LIKE I EXPECTED. INSTEAD I'M LEFT WITH THIS... ITCH.
A CERTAIN ANXIETY-- WHICH EXPLAINS WHY I'M HERE AT THE POSH UNAKE RESTAURANT IN JERSEY CITY.
THE WITCHBLADE IS HERE.
AND THAT MEANS, SO IS IAN NOTTINGHAM.
EVER SINCE HE AND I TANGLED TO COSMIC PROPORTIONS AT THE MUSEUM OF NATURAL HISTORY, HE'S SOMEHOW GAINED POSSESSION OF THE WITCHBLADE--A WEAPON THAT, AS FAR AS I KNOW, HAS ONLY BEEN SUCCESSFULLY WORN BY WOMEN.
DON'T GET ME WRONG-- I MADE THE CONSCIOUS DECISION TO GIVE IT UP.
I GOT TIRED OF ALWAYS WHINING ABOUT THIS ALIEN THING THAT SEEMED TO DICTATE VIOLENT COMMANDS TO ME MOST OF THE TIME. I PREFER TO MAKE MY OWN DECISIONS.
SO I DID WHAT KENNETH IRONS TOLD ME RARELY HAPPENS. I GAVE IT UP--WITHOUT DIRE CONSEQUENCES. I'M STILL NORMAL, NOT MISSING ANY LIMBS AND FEELING BETTER THAN EVER.

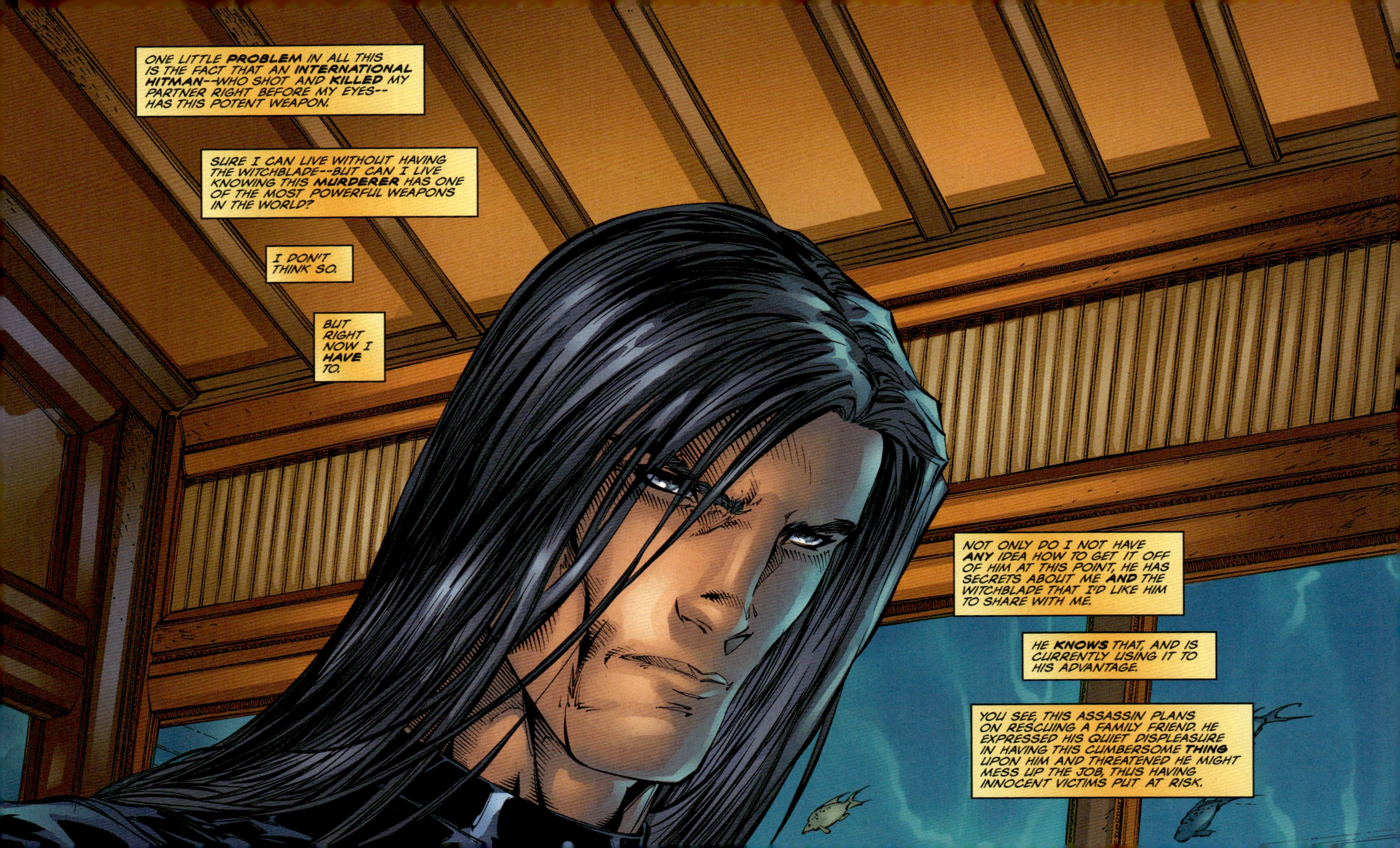
ONE LITTLE **PROBLEM** IN ALL THIS IS THE FACT THAT AN **INTERNATIONAL HITMAN**--WHO SHOT AND **KILLED** MY PARTNER RIGHT BEFORE MY EYES--HAS THIS POTENT WEAPON.
SURE I CAN LIVE WITHOUT HAVING THE WITCHBLADE--BUT CAN I LIVE KNOWING THIS **MURDERER** HAS ONE OF THE MOST POWERFUL WEAPONS IN THE WORLD?
I DON'T THINK SO.
BUT RIGHT NOW I **HAVE** TO.
NOT ONLY DO I NOT HAVE **ANY** IDEA HOW TO GET IT OFF OF HIM AT THIS POINT, HE HAS SECRETS ABOUT ME **AND** THE WITCHBLADE THAT I'D LIKE HIM TO SHARE WITH ME.
HE **KNOWS** THAT, AND IS CURRENTLY USING IT TO HIS ADVANTAGE.
YOU SEE, THIS ASSASSIN PLANS ON RESCUING A FAMILY FRIEND. HE EXPRESSED HIS QUIET DISPLEASURE IN HAVING THIS CUMBERSOME **THING** UPON HIM AND THREATENED HE MIGHT MESS UP THE JOB, THUS HAVING INNOCENT VICTIMS PUT AT RISK.

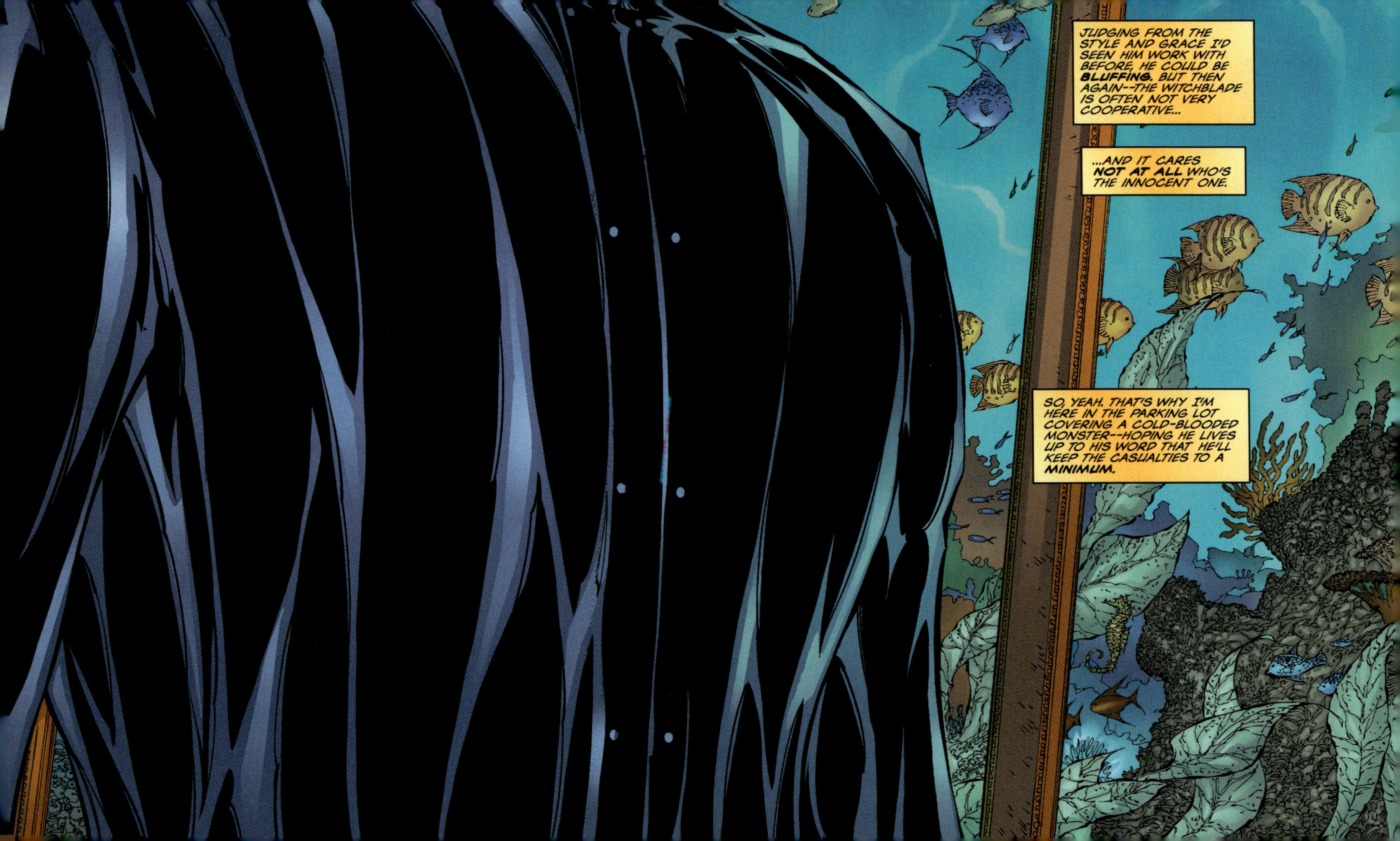
JUDGING FROM THE STYLE AND GRACE I'D SEEN HIM WORK WITH BEFORE, HE COULD BE **BLUFFING**. BUT THEN AGAIN--THE WITCHBLADE IS OFTEN NOT VERY COOPERATIVE...
...AND IT CARES **NOT AT ALL** WHO'S THE INNOCENT ONE.
SO, YEAH. THAT'S WHY I'M HERE IN THE PARKING LOT COVERING A COLD-BLOODED MONSTER--HOPING HE LIVES UP TO HIS WORD THAT HE'LL KEEP THE CASUALTIES TO A **MINIMUM**.

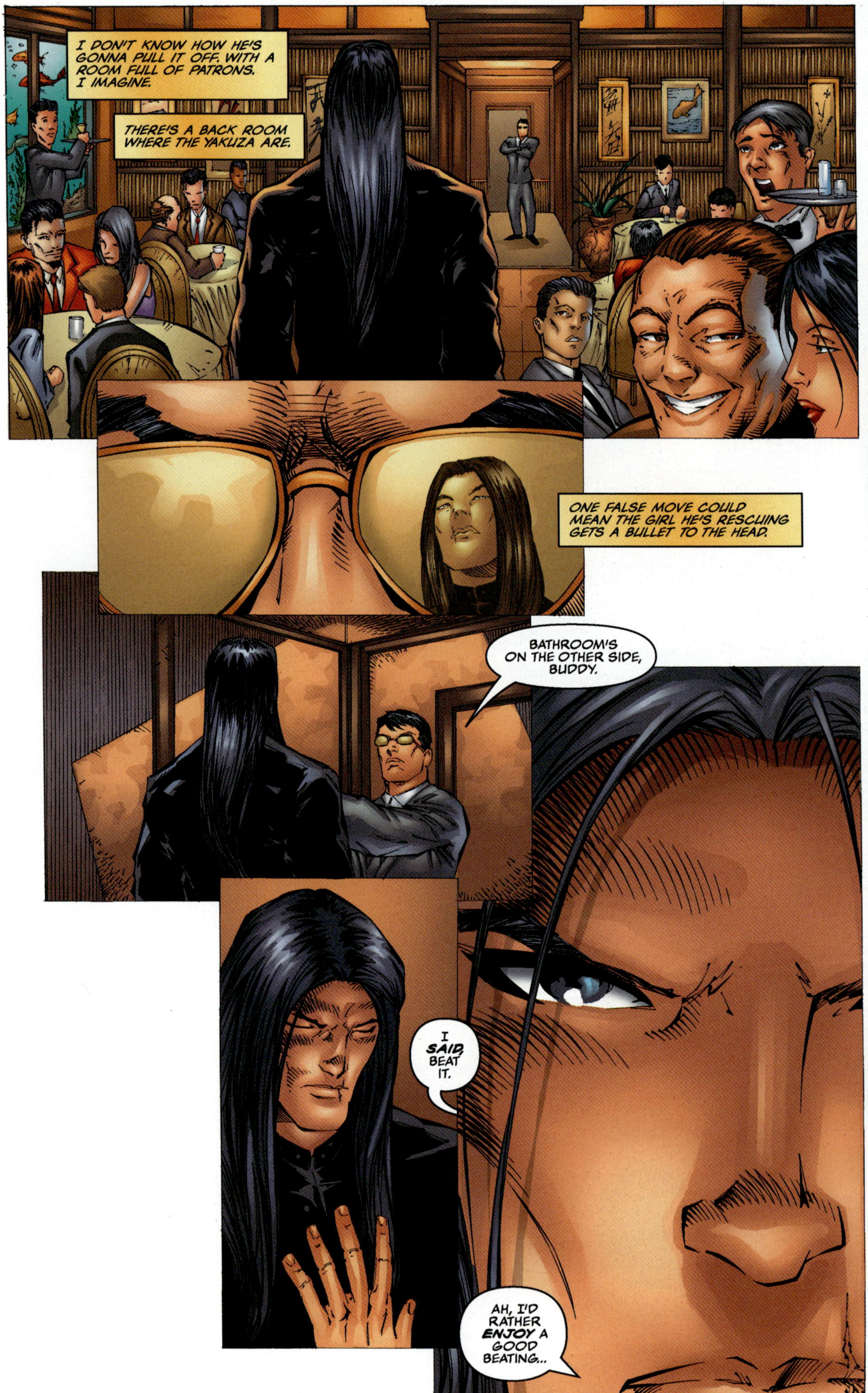
I DON'T KNOW HOW HE'S GONNA PULL IT OFF. WITH A ROOM FULL OF PATRONS, I IMAGINE.
THERE'S A BACK ROOM WHERE THE YAKUZA ARE.
ONE FALSE MOVE COULD MEAN THE GIRL HE'S RESCUING GETS A BULLET TO THE HEAD.
BATHROOM'S ON THE OTHER SIDE, BUDDY.
I SAID, BEAT IT.
AH, I'D RATHER ENJOY A GOOD BEATING...

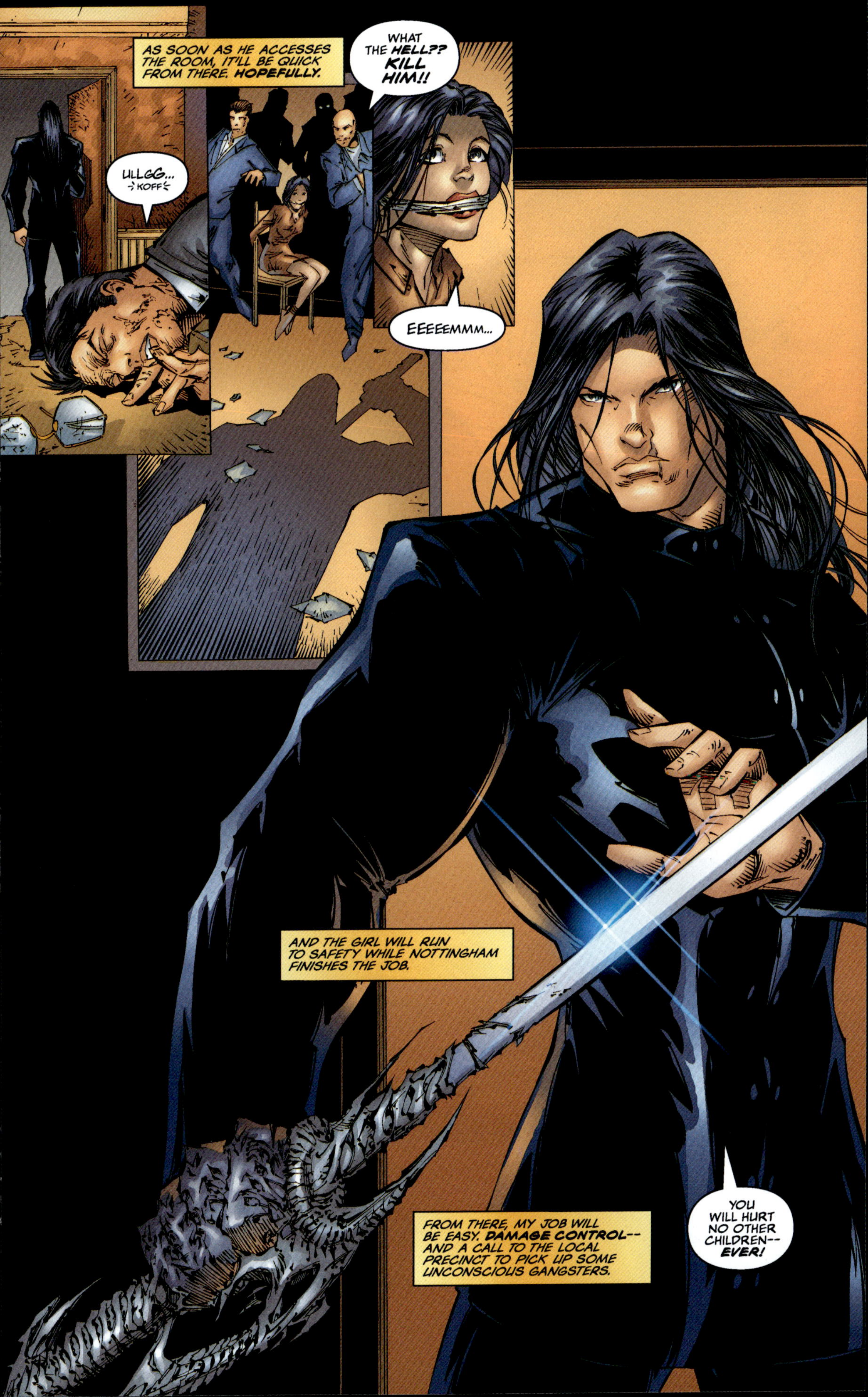
AS SOON AS HE ACCESSES THE ROOM, IT'LL BE QUICK FROM THERE. HOPEFULLY.
ULLGG... KOFF
WHAT THE HELL?? KILL HIM!!
EEEEEMMM...
AND THE GIRL WILL RUN TO SAFETY WHILE NOTTINGHAM FINISHES THE JOB.
FROM THERE, MY JOB WILL BE EASY. DAMAGE CONTROL-- AND A CALL TO THE LOCAL PRECINCT TO PICK UP SOME UNCONSCIOUS GANGSTERS.
YOU WILL HURT NO OTHER CHILDREN-- EVER!

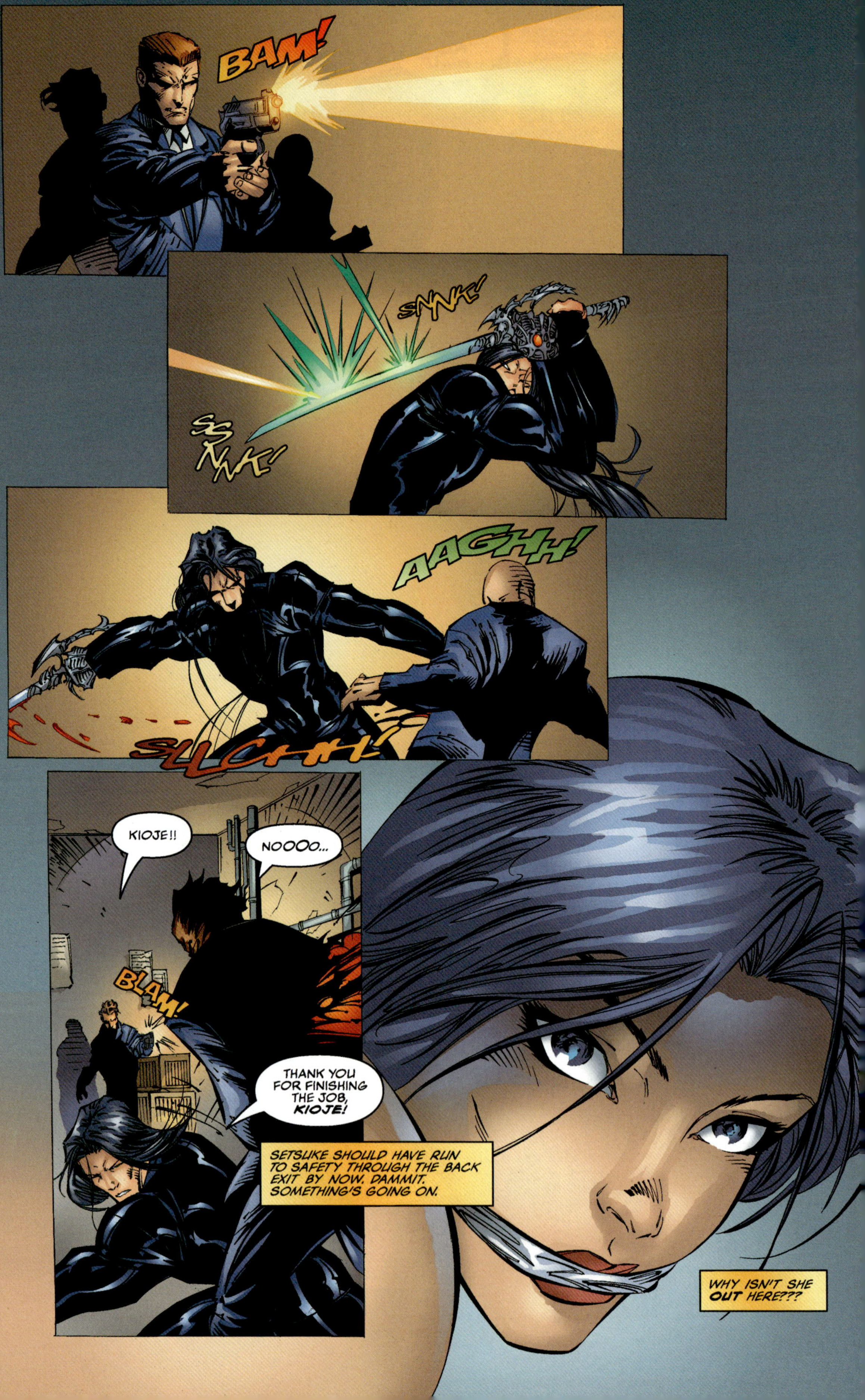
BAM!
SNNK!
SSNNK!
AAGHH!
SLLCHHH!
KIOJE!!
NOOOO...
BLAM!
THANK YOU FOR FINISHING THE JOB, KIOJE!
SETSUKE SHOULD HAVE RUN TO SAFETY THROUGH THE BACK EXIT BY NOW. DAMMIT. SOMETHING'S GOING ON.
WHY ISN'T SHE OUT HERE???

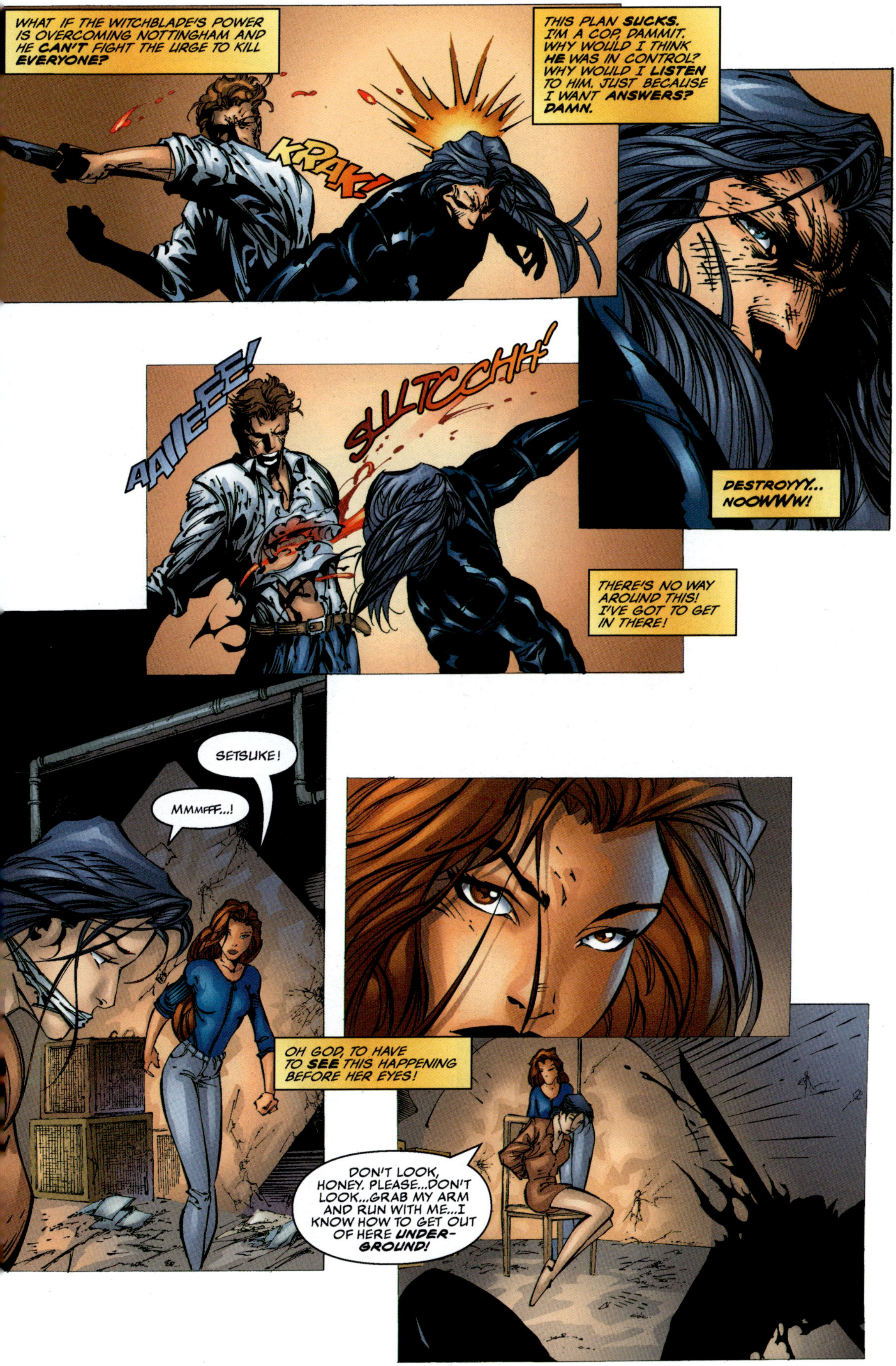

WHAT IF THE WITCHBLADE'S POWER IS OVERCOMING NOTTINGHAM AND HE CAN'T FIGHT THE URGE TO KILL EVERYONE?
KRAK!
THIS PLAN SUCKS. I'M A COP, DAMMIT. WHY WOULD I THINK HE WAS IN CONTROL? WHY WOULD I LISTEN TO HIM, JUST BECAUSE I WANT ANSWERS? DAMN.
DESTROYYY... NOOWWW!
AAIIEEE!
SLLLTCCHH!
THERE'S NO WAY AROUND THIS! I'VE GOT TO GET IN THERE!
SETSUKE!
MMMFFF...!
OH GOD, TO HAVE TO SEE THIS HAPPENING BEFORE HER EYES!
DON'T LOOK, HONEY. PLEASE...DON'T LOOK...GRAB MY ARM AND RUN WITH ME...I KNOW HOW TO GET OUT OF HERE UNDER-GROUND!

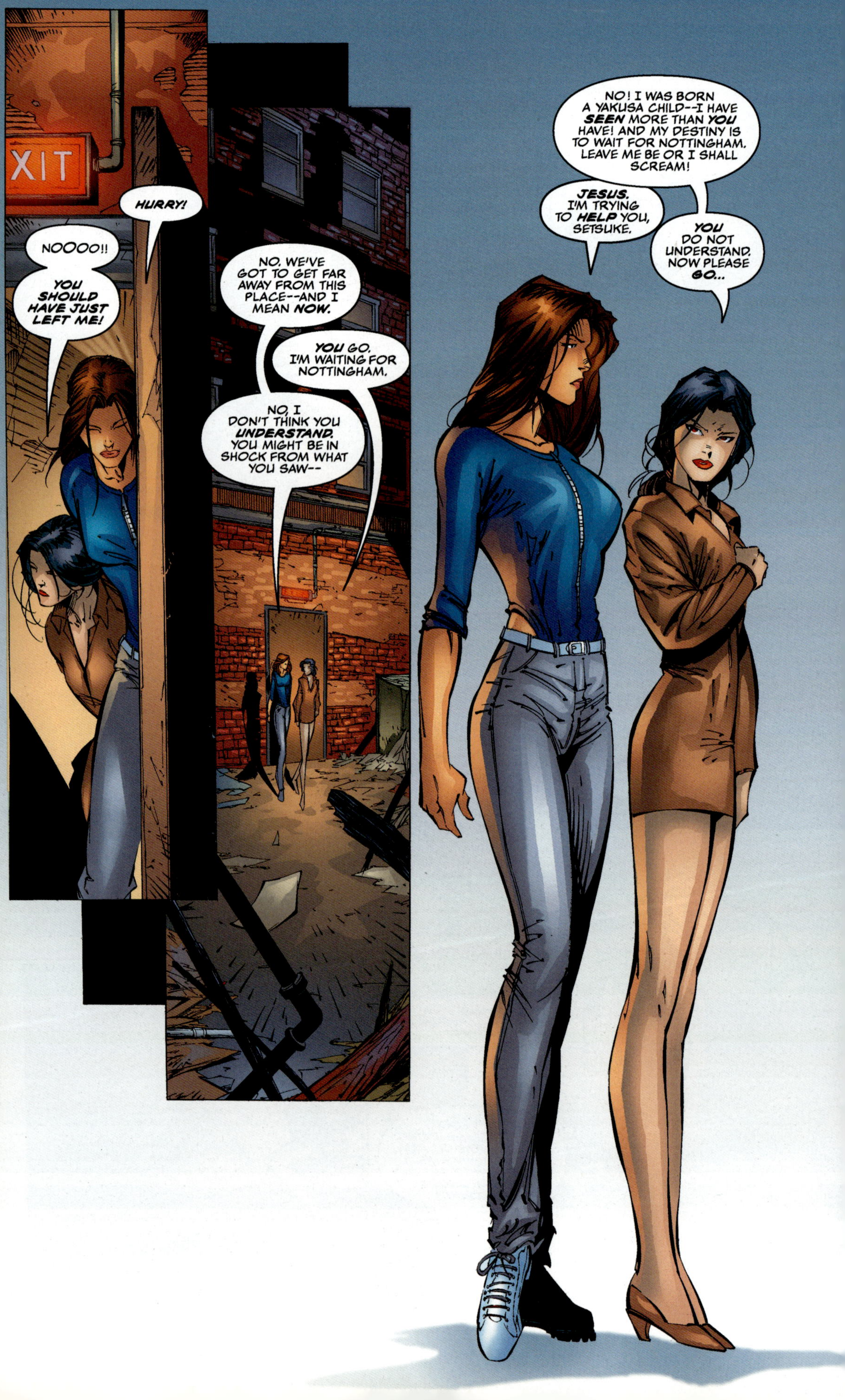

XIT
HURRY!
NOOOO!!
YOU SHOULD HAVE JUST LEFT ME!
NO, WE'VE GOT TO GET FAR AWAY FROM THIS PLACE--AND I MEAN NOW.
YOU GO. I'M WAITING FOR NOTTINGHAM.
NO, I DON'T THINK YOU UNDERSTAND. YOU MIGHT BE IN SHOCK FROM WHAT YOU SAW--
NO! I WAS BORN A YAKUSA CHILD--I HAVE SEEN MORE THAN YOU HAVE! AND MY DESTINY IS TO WAIT FOR NOTTINGHAM. LEAVE ME BE OR I SHALL SCREAM!
JESUS. I'M TRYING TO HELP YOU, SETSUKE.
YOU DO NOT UNDERSTAND. NOW PLEASE GO...

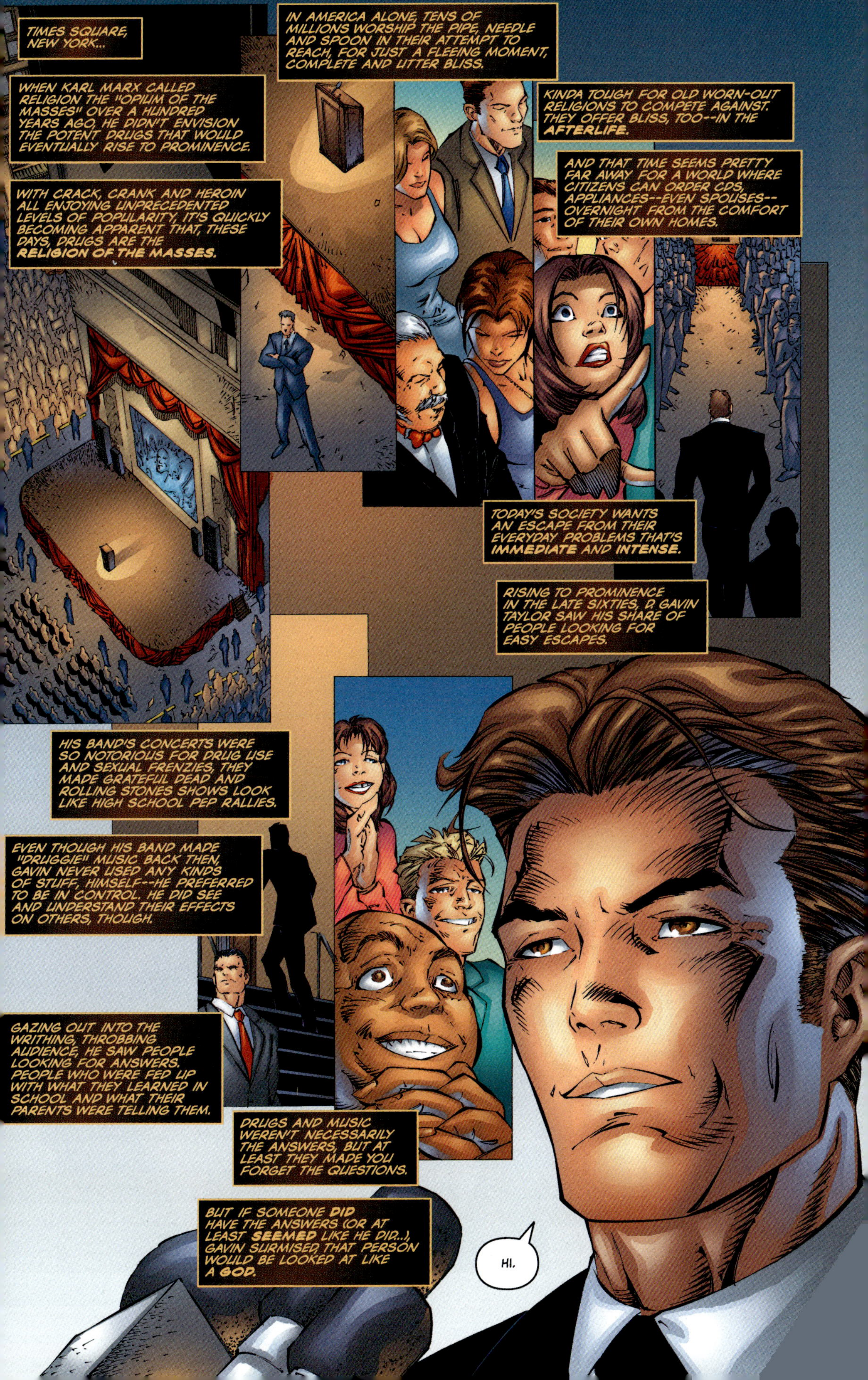
TIMES SQUARE, NEW YORK...
WHEN KARL MARX CALLED RELIGION THE "OPIUM OF THE MASSES" OVER A HUNDRED YEARS AGO, HE DIDN'T ENVISION THE POTENT DRUGS THAT WOULD EVENTUALLY RISE TO PROMINENCE.
WITH CRACK, CRANK AND HEROIN ALL ENJOYING UNPRECEDENTED LEVELS OF POPULARITY, IT'S QUICKLY BECOMING APPARENT THAT, THESE DAYS, DRUGS ARE THE RELIGION OF THE MASSES.
IN AMERICA ALONE, TENS OF MILLIONS WORSHIP THE PIPE, NEEDLE AND SPOON IN THEIR ATTEMPT TO REACH, FOR JUST A FLEEING MOMENT, COMPLETE AND UTTER BLISS.
KINDA TOUGH FOR OLD WORN-OUT RELIGIONS TO COMPETE AGAINST. THEY OFFER BLISS, TOO--IN THE AFTERLIFE.
AND THAT TIME SEEMS PRETTY FAR AWAY FOR A WORLD WHERE CITIZENS CAN ORDER CDS, APPLIANCES--EVEN SPOUSES--OVERNIGHT FROM THE COMFORT OF THEIR OWN HOMES.
TODAY'S SOCIETY WANTS AN ESCAPE FROM THEIR EVERYDAY PROBLEMS THAT'S IMMEDIATE AND INTENSE.
RISING TO PROMINENCE IN THE LATE SIXTIES, D GAVIN TAYLOR SAW HIS SHARE OF PEOPLE LOOKING FOR EASY ESCAPES.
HIS BAND'S CONCERTS WERE SO NOTORIOUS FOR DRUG USE AND SEXUAL FRENZIES, THEY MADE GRATEFUL DEAD AND ROLLING STONES SHOWS LOOK LIKE HIGH SCHOOL PEP RALLIES.
EVEN THOUGH HIS BAND MADE "DRUGGIE" MUSIC BACK THEN, GAVIN NEVER USED ANY KINDS OF STUFF, HIMSELF--HE PREFERRED TO BE IN CONTROL. HE DID SEE AND UNDERSTAND THEIR EFFECTS ON OTHERS, THOUGH.
GAZING OUT INTO THE WRITHING, THROBBING AUDIENCE, HE SAW PEOPLE LOOKING FOR ANSWERS. PEOPLE WHO WERE FED UP WITH WHAT THEY LEARNED IN SCHOOL AND WHAT THEIR PARENTS WERE TELLING THEM.
DRUGS AND MUSIC WEREN'T NECESSARILY THE ANSWERS, BUT AT LEAST THEY MADE YOU FORGET THE QUESTIONS.
BUT IF SOMEONE DID HAVE THE ANSWERS (OR AT LEAST SEEMED LIKE HE DID...), GAVIN SURMISED, THAT PERSON WOULD BE LOOKED AT LIKE A GOD.
HI.

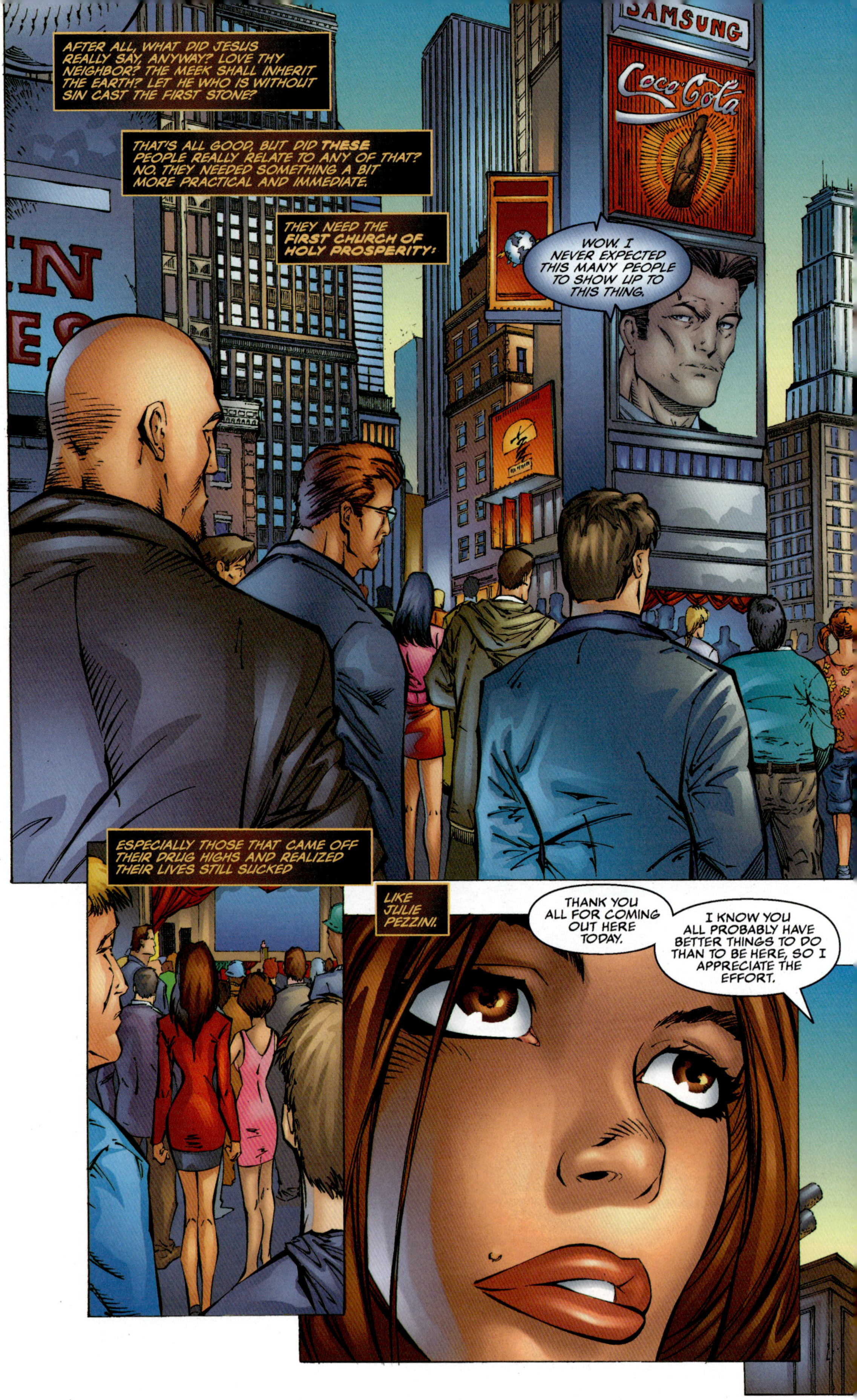
AFTER ALL, WHAT DID JESUS REALLY SAY, ANYWAY? LOVE THY NEIGHBOR? THE MEEK SHALL INHERIT THE EARTH? LET HE WHO IS WITHOUT SIN CAST THE FIRST STONE?
THAT'S ALL GOOD, BUT DID **THESE** PEOPLE REALLY RELATE TO ANY OF THAT? NO. THEY NEEDED SOMETHING A BIT MORE PRACTICAL AND IMMEDIATE.
THEY NEED THE **FIRST CHURCH OF HOLY PROSPERITY:**
SAMSUNG
Coca-Cola
WOW. I NEVER EXPECTED THIS MANY PEOPLE TO SHOW UP TO THIS THING.
ESPECIALLY THOSE THAT CAME OFF THEIR DRUG HIGHS AND REALIZED THEIR LIVES STILL SUCKED
LIKE JULIE PEZZINI.
THANK YOU ALL FOR COMING OUT HERE TODAY.
I KNOW YOU ALL PROBABLY HAVE BETTER THINGS TO DO THAN TO BE HERE, SO I APPRECIATE THE EFFORT.

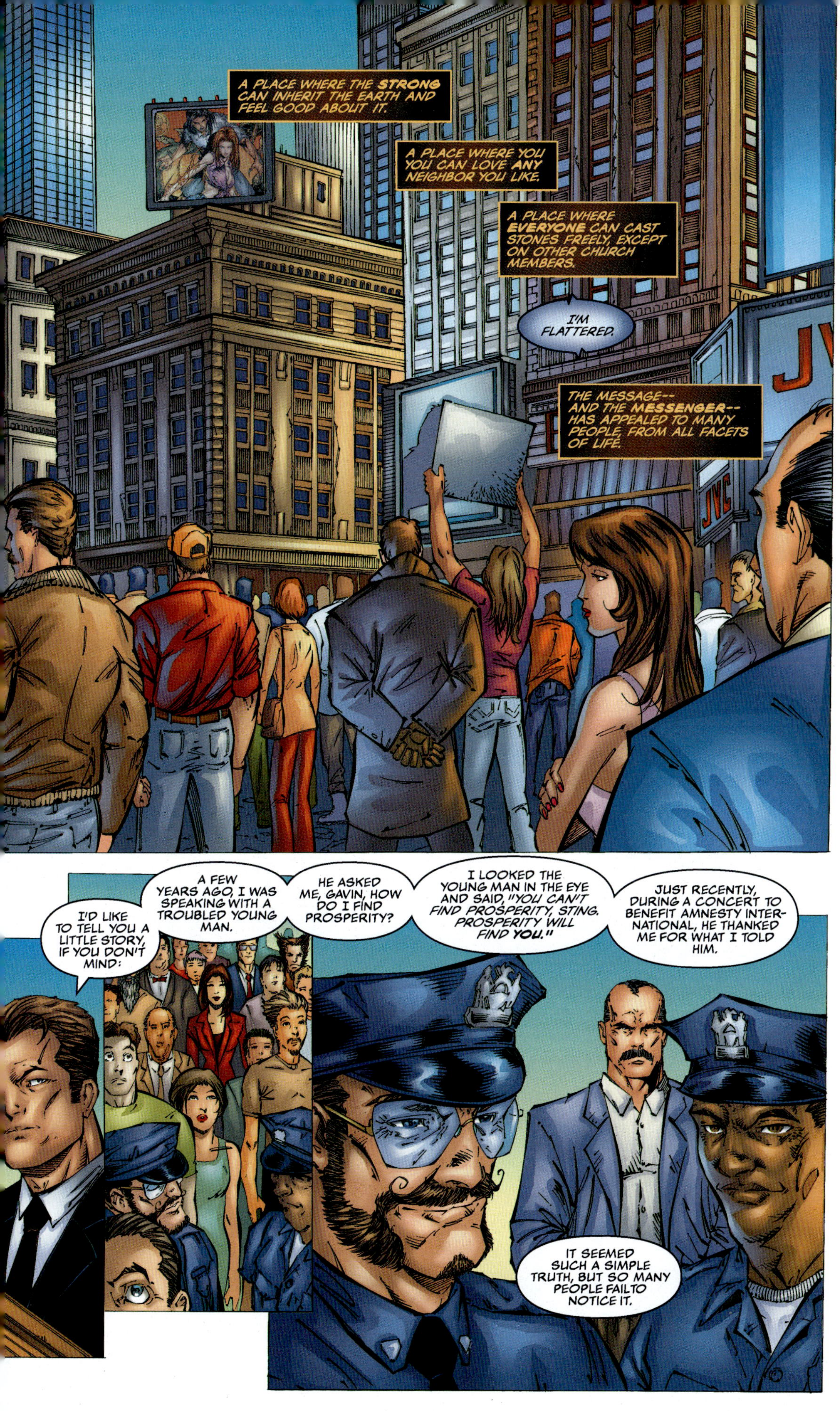
A PLACE WHERE THE STRONG CAN INHERIT THE EARTH AND FEEL GOOD ABOUT IT.
A PLACE WHERE YOU YOU CAN LOVE ANY NEIGHBOR YOU LIKE.
A PLACE WHERE EVERYONE CAN CAST STONES FREELY, EXCEPT ON OTHER CHURCH MEMBERS.
I'M FLATTERED.
THE MESSAGE-- AND THE MESSENGER-- HAS APPEALED TO MANY PEOPLE, FROM ALL FACETS OF LIFE.
I'D LIKE TO TELL YOU A LITTLE STORY, IF YOU DON'T MIND:
A FEW YEARS AGO, I WAS SPEAKING WITH A TROUBLED YOUNG MAN.
HE ASKED ME, GAVIN, HOW DO I FIND PROSPERITY?
I LOOKED THE YOUNG MAN IN THE EYE AND SAID, "YOU CAN'T FIND PROSPERITY, STING. PROSPERITY WILL FIND YOU."
JUST RECENTLY, DURING A CONCERT TO BENEFIT AMNESTY INTERNATIONAL, HE THANKED ME FOR WHAT I TOLD HIM.
IT SEEMED SUCH A SIMPLE TRUTH, BUT SO MANY PEOPLE FAIL TO NOTICE IT.

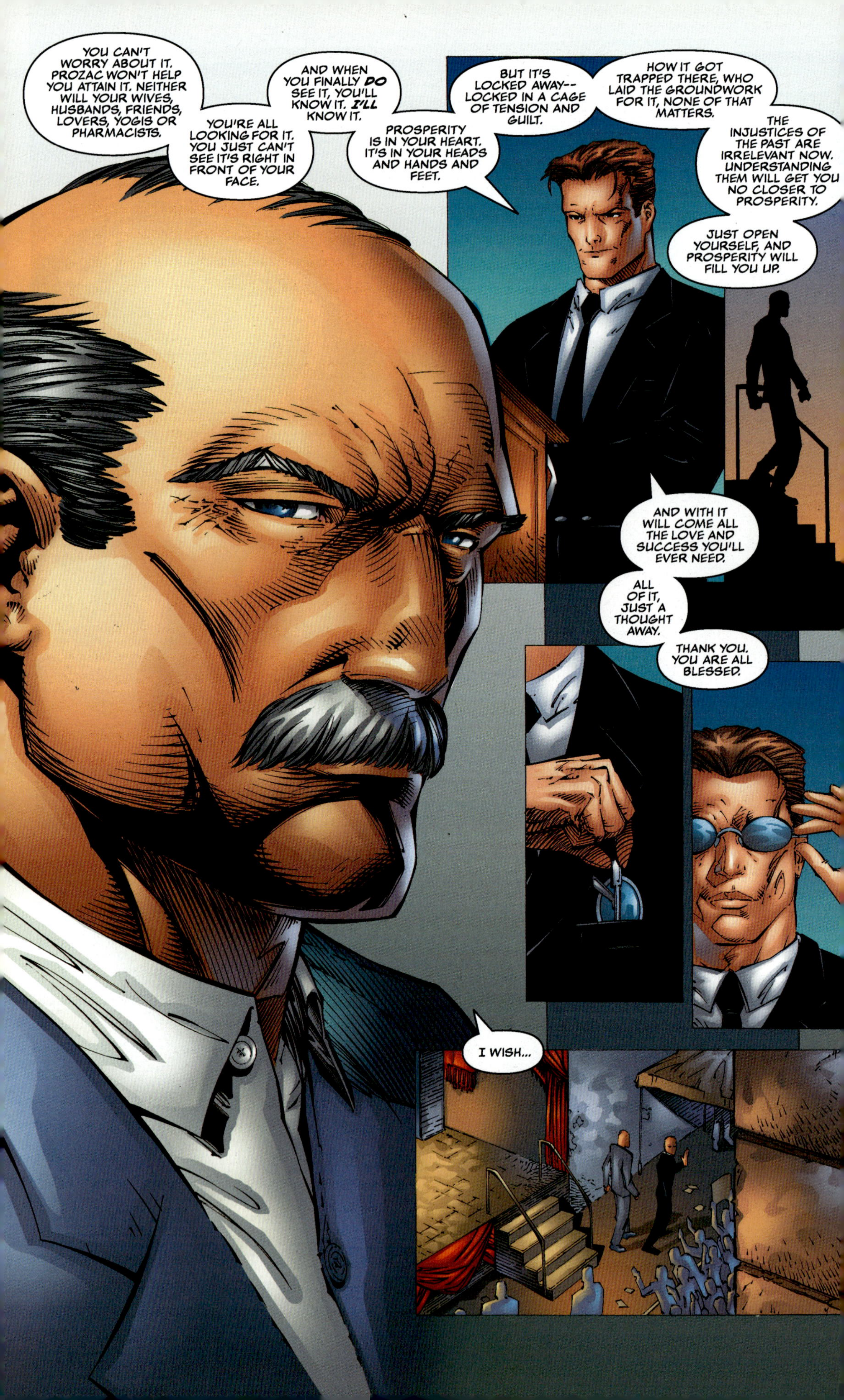

YOU CAN'T WORRY ABOUT IT. PROZAC WON'T HELP YOU ATTAIN IT. NEITHER WILL YOUR WIVES, HUSBANDS, FRIENDS, LOVERS, YOGIS OR PHARMACISTS.
YOU'RE ALL LOOKING FOR IT. YOU JUST CAN'T SEE IT'S RIGHT IN FRONT OF YOUR FACE.
AND WHEN YOU FINALLY *DO* SEE IT, YOU'LL KNOW IT. *I'LL* KNOW IT.
PROSPERITY IS IN YOUR HEART. IT'S IN YOUR HEADS AND HANDS AND FEET.
BUT IT'S LOCKED AWAY-- LOCKED IN A CAGE OF TENSION AND GUILT.
HOW IT GOT TRAPPED THERE, WHO LAID THE GROUNDWORK FOR IT, NONE OF THAT MATTERS.
THE INJUSTICES OF THE PAST ARE IRRELEVANT NOW. UNDERSTANDING THEM WILL GET YOU NO CLOSER TO PROSPERITY.
JUST OPEN YOURSELF, AND PROSPERITY WILL FILL YOU UP.
AND WITH IT WILL COME ALL THE LOVE AND SUCCESS YOU'LL EVER NEED.
ALL OF IT, JUST A THOUGHT AWAY.
THANK YOU. YOU ARE ALL BLESSED.
I WISH...

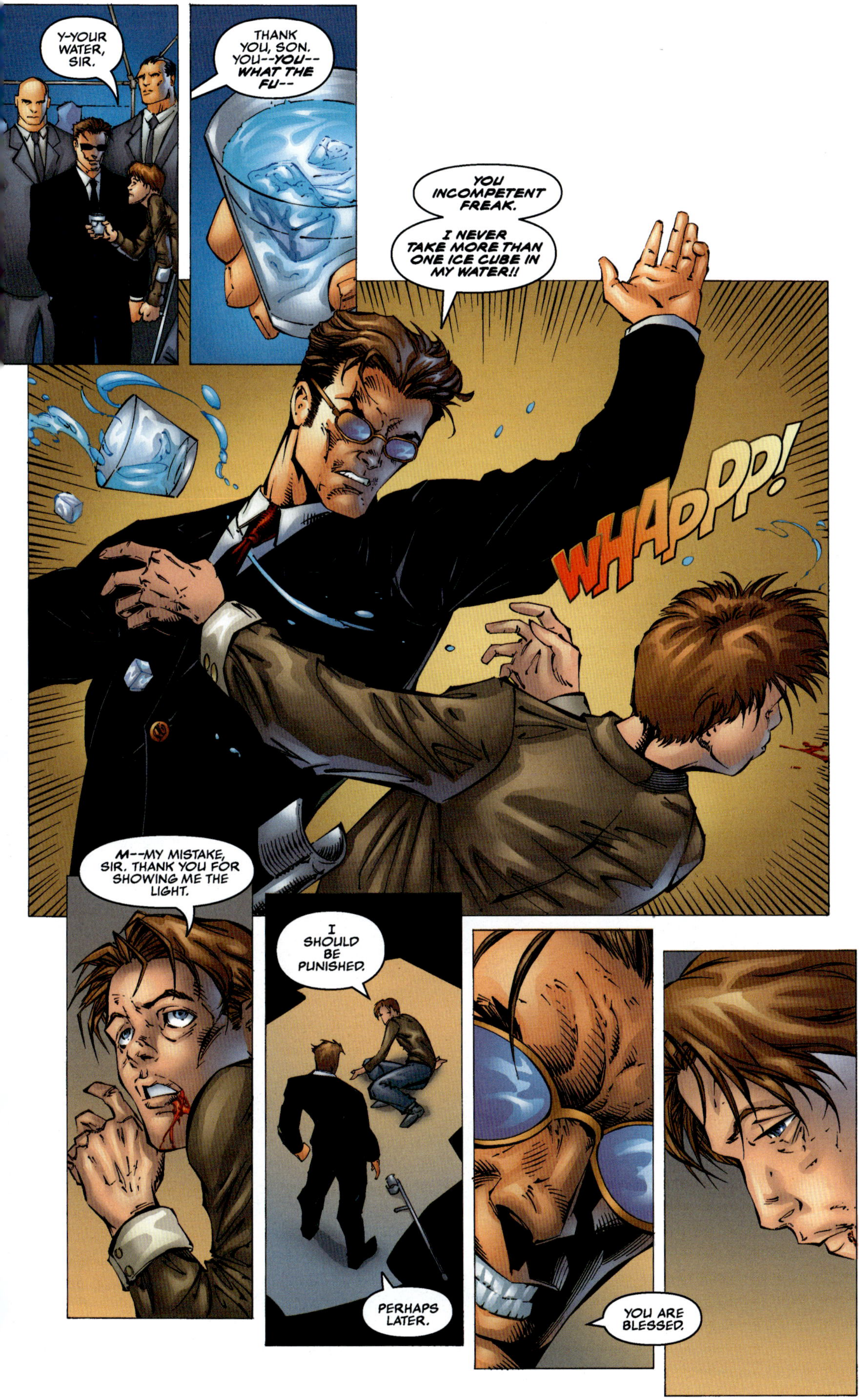
Y-YOUR WATER, SIR.
THANK YOU, SON. YOU--YOU-- WHAT THE FU--
YOU INCOMPETENT FREAK.
I NEVER TAKE MORE THAN ONE ICE CUBE IN MY WATER!!
WHAPPP!
M--MY MISTAKE, SIR. THANK YOU FOR SHOWING ME THE LIGHT.
I SHOULD BE PUNISHED.
PERHAPS LATER.
YOU ARE BLESSED.

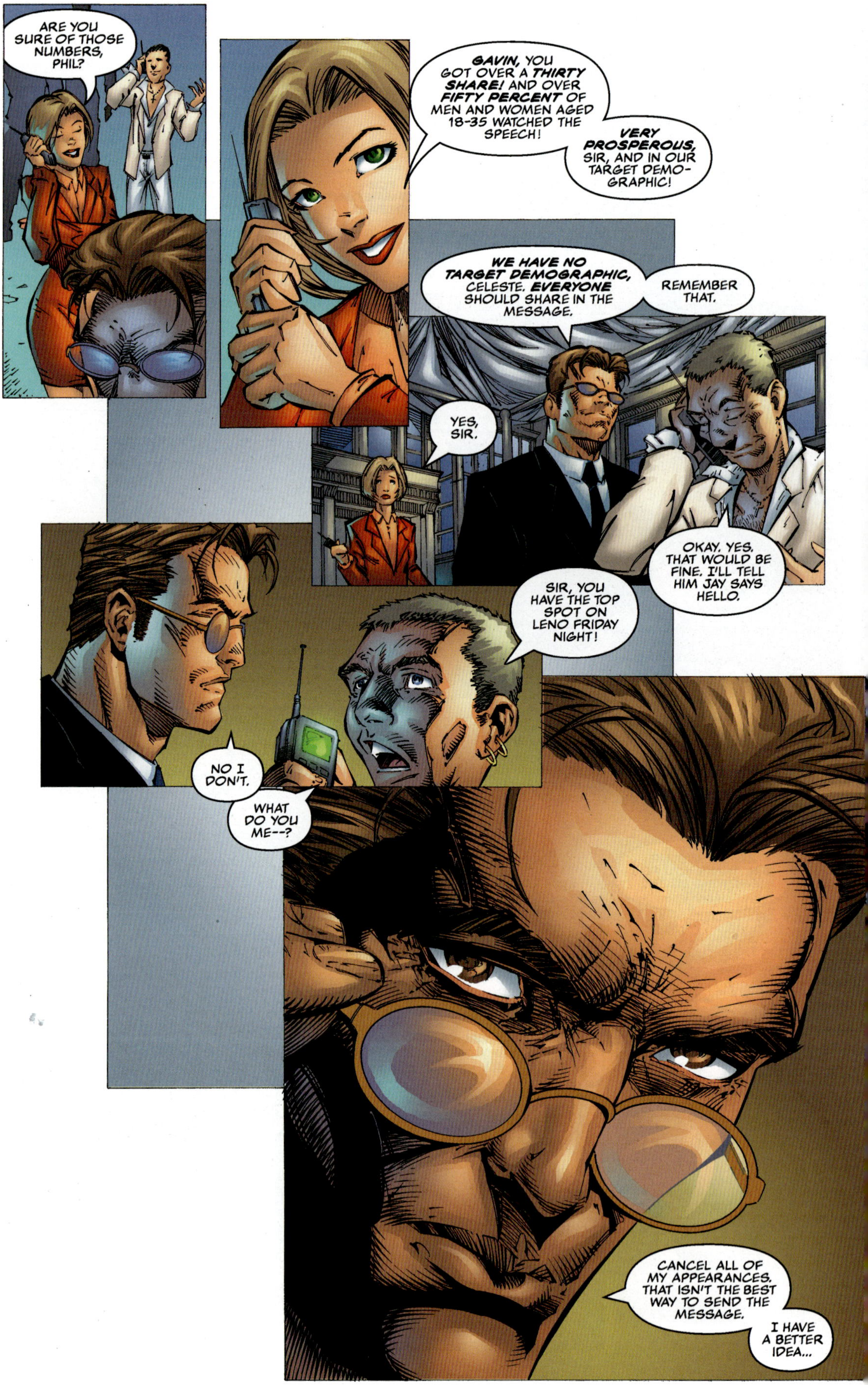
ARE YOU SURE OF THOSE NUMBERS, PHIL?
GAVIN, YOU GOT OVER A ***THIRTY SHARE!*** AND OVER ***FIFTY PERCENT*** OF MEN AND WOMEN AGED 18-35 WATCHED THE SPEECH!
VERY PROSPEROUS, SIR, AND IN OUR TARGET DEMO-GRAPHIC!
WE HAVE NO TARGET DEMOGRAPHIC, CELESTE. ***EVERYONE*** SHOULD SHARE IN THE MESSAGE.
REMEMBER THAT.
YES, SIR.
OKAY. YES. THAT WOULD BE FINE. I'LL TELL HIM JAY SAYS HELLO.
SIR, YOU HAVE THE TOP SPOT ON LENO FRIDAY NIGHT!
NO I DON'T.
WHAT DO YOU ME--?
CANCEL ALL OF MY APPEARANCES. THAT ISN'T THE BEST WAY TO SEND THE MESSAGE.
I HAVE A BETTER IDEA...

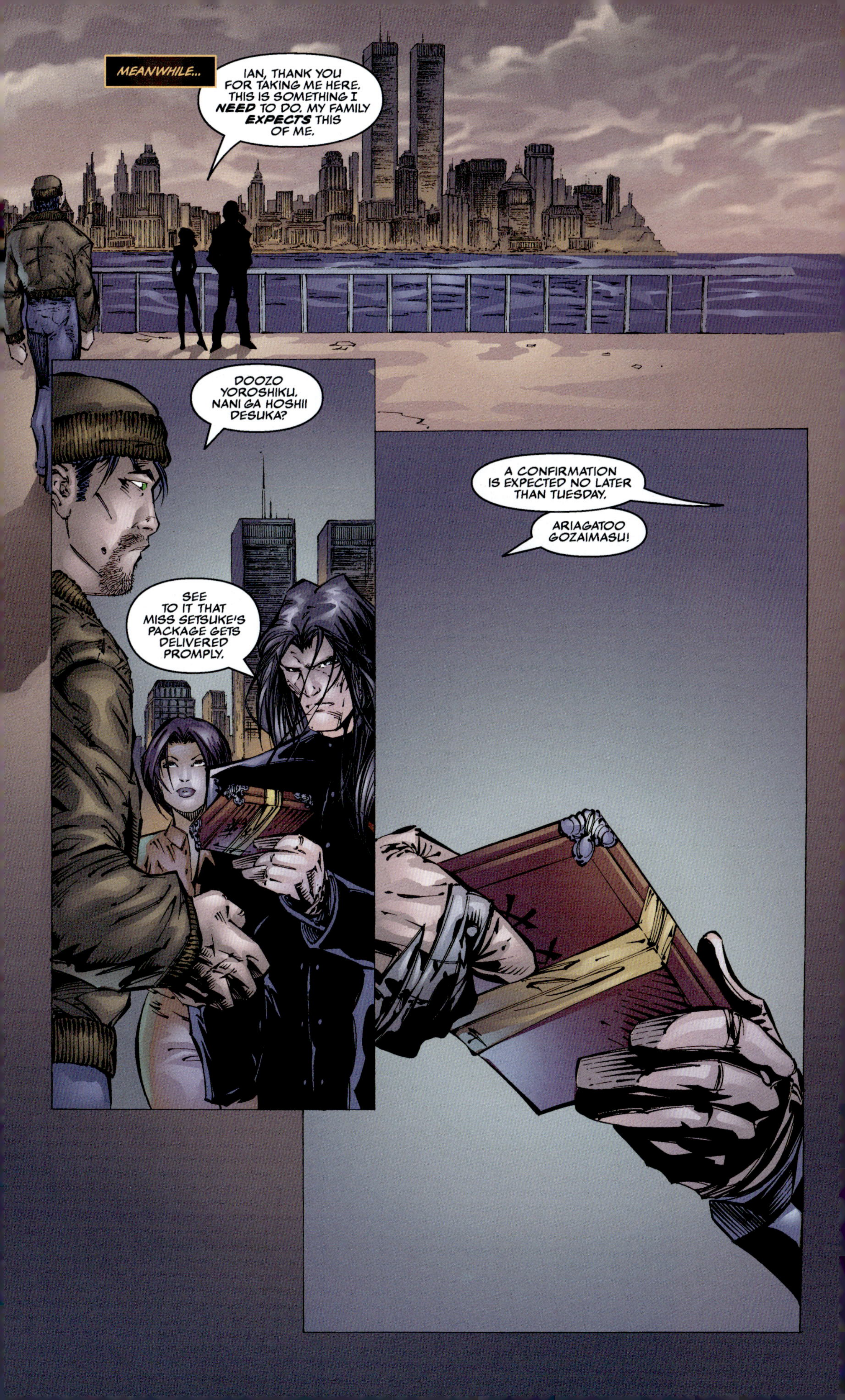
MEANWHILE...
IAN, THANK YOU FOR TAKING ME HERE. THIS IS SOMETHING I NEED TO DO. MY FAMILY EXPECTS THIS OF ME.
DOOZO YOROSHIKU. NANI GA HOSHII DESUKA?
SEE TO IT THAT MISS SETSUKE'S PACKAGE GETS DELIVERED PROMPLY.
A CONFIRMATION IS EXPECTED NO LATER THAN TUESDAY.
ARIAGATOO GOZAIMASU!

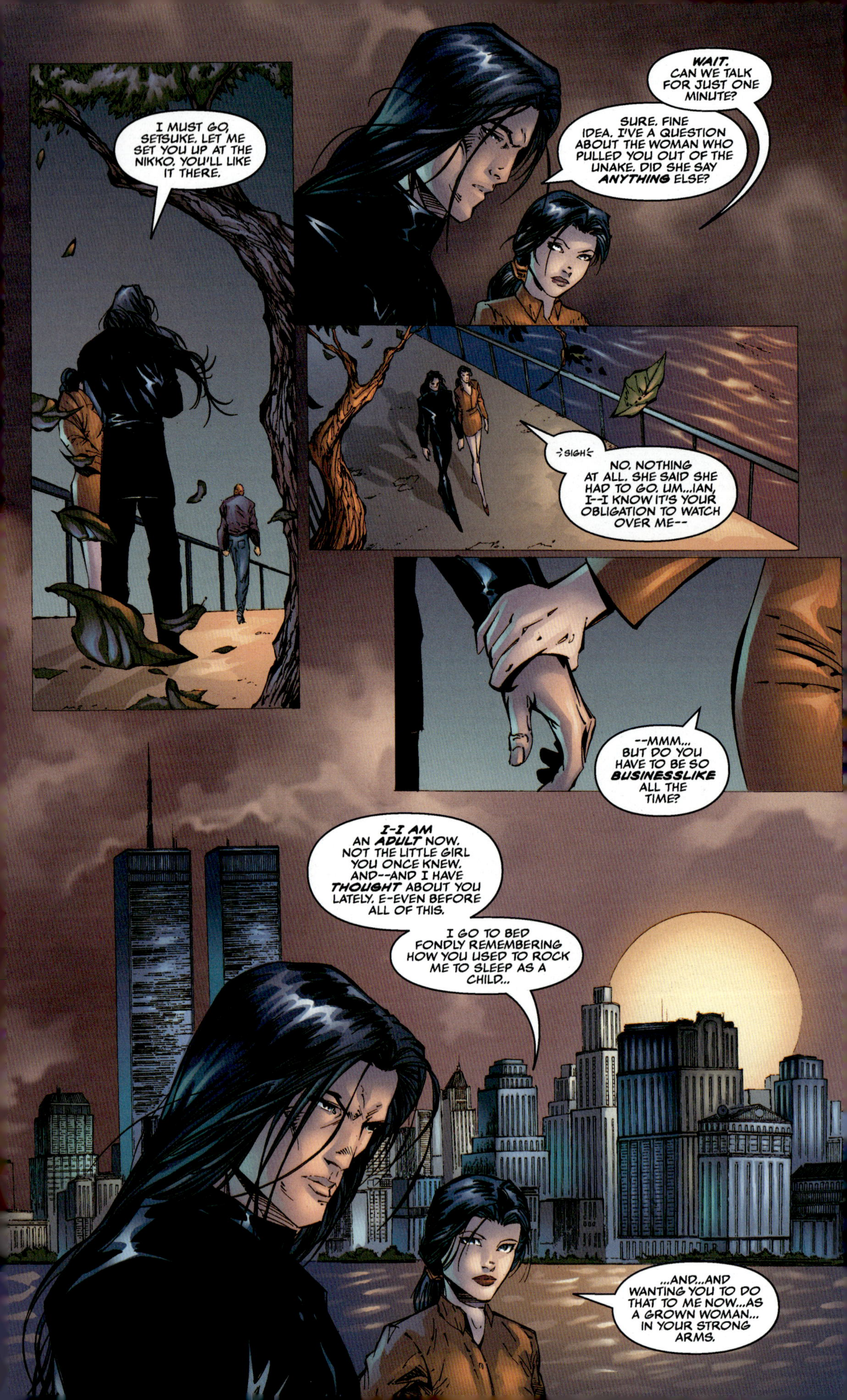
I MUST GO, SETSUKE. LET ME SET YOU UP AT THE NIKKO. YOU'LL LIKE IT THERE.
WAIT. CAN WE TALK FOR JUST ONE MINUTE?
SURE. FINE IDEA. I'VE A QUESTION ABOUT THE WOMAN WHO PULLED YOU OUT OF THE UNAKE. DID SHE SAY ANYTHING ELSE?
SIGH
NO, NOTHING AT ALL. SHE SAID SHE HAD TO GO. UM...IAN, I--I KNOW IT'S YOUR OBLIGATION TO WATCH OVER ME--
--MMM... BUT DO YOU HAVE TO BE SO BUSINESSLIKE ALL THE TIME?
I-I AM AN ADULT NOW. NOT THE LITTLE GIRL YOU ONCE KNEW. AND--AND I HAVE THOUGHT ABOUT YOU LATELY. E-EVEN BEFORE ALL OF THIS.
I GO TO BED FONDLY REMEMBERING HOW YOU USED TO ROCK ME TO SLEEP AS A CHILD...
...AND...AND WANTING YOU TO DO THAT TO ME NOW...AS A GROWN WOMAN... IN YOUR STRONG ARMS.

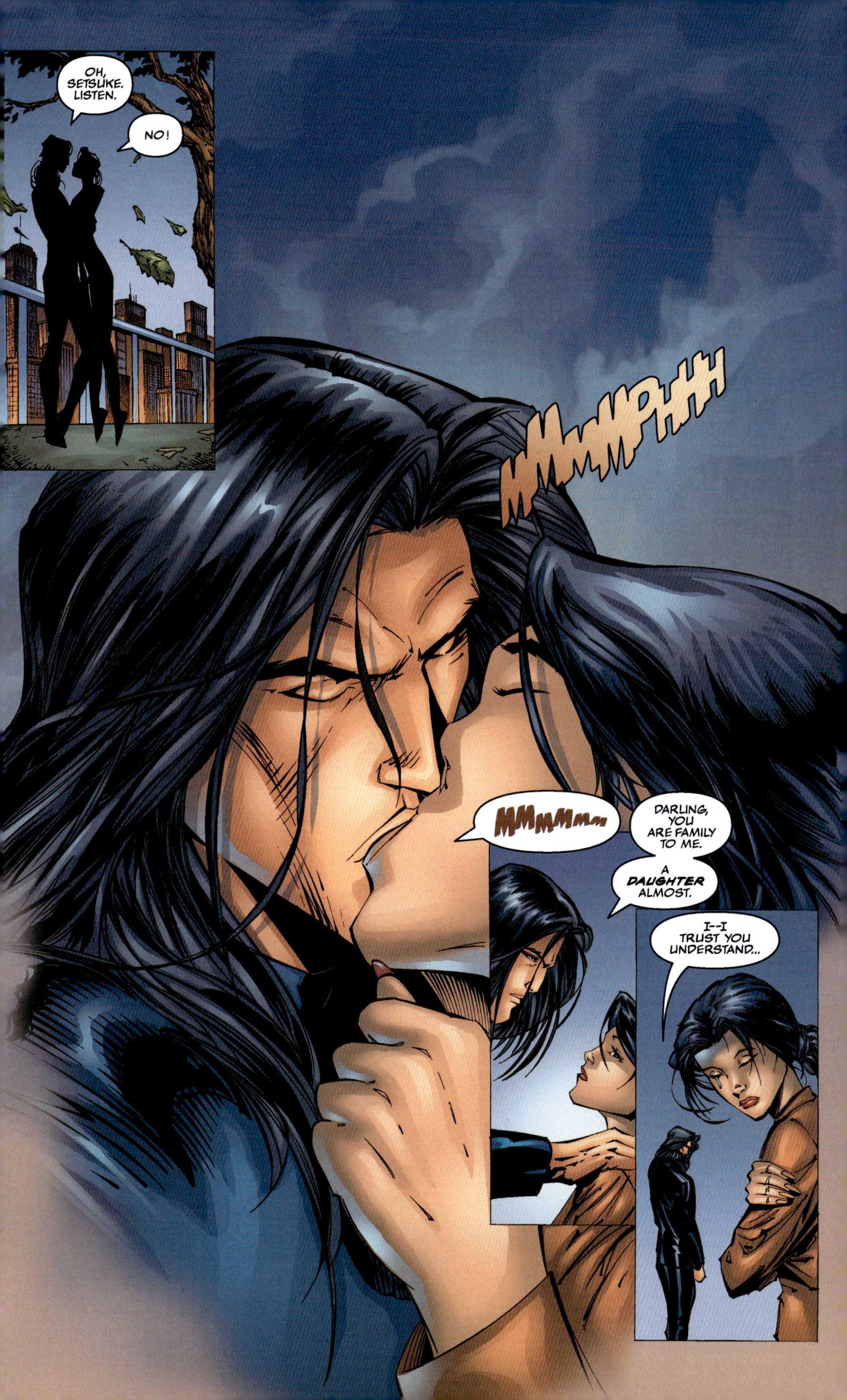

OH, SETSUKE. LISTEN.
NO!
MMMMPHHH
MMMMMM
DARLING, YOU ARE FAMILY TO ME.
A *DAUGHTER* ALMOST.
I--I TRUST YOU UNDERSTAND...

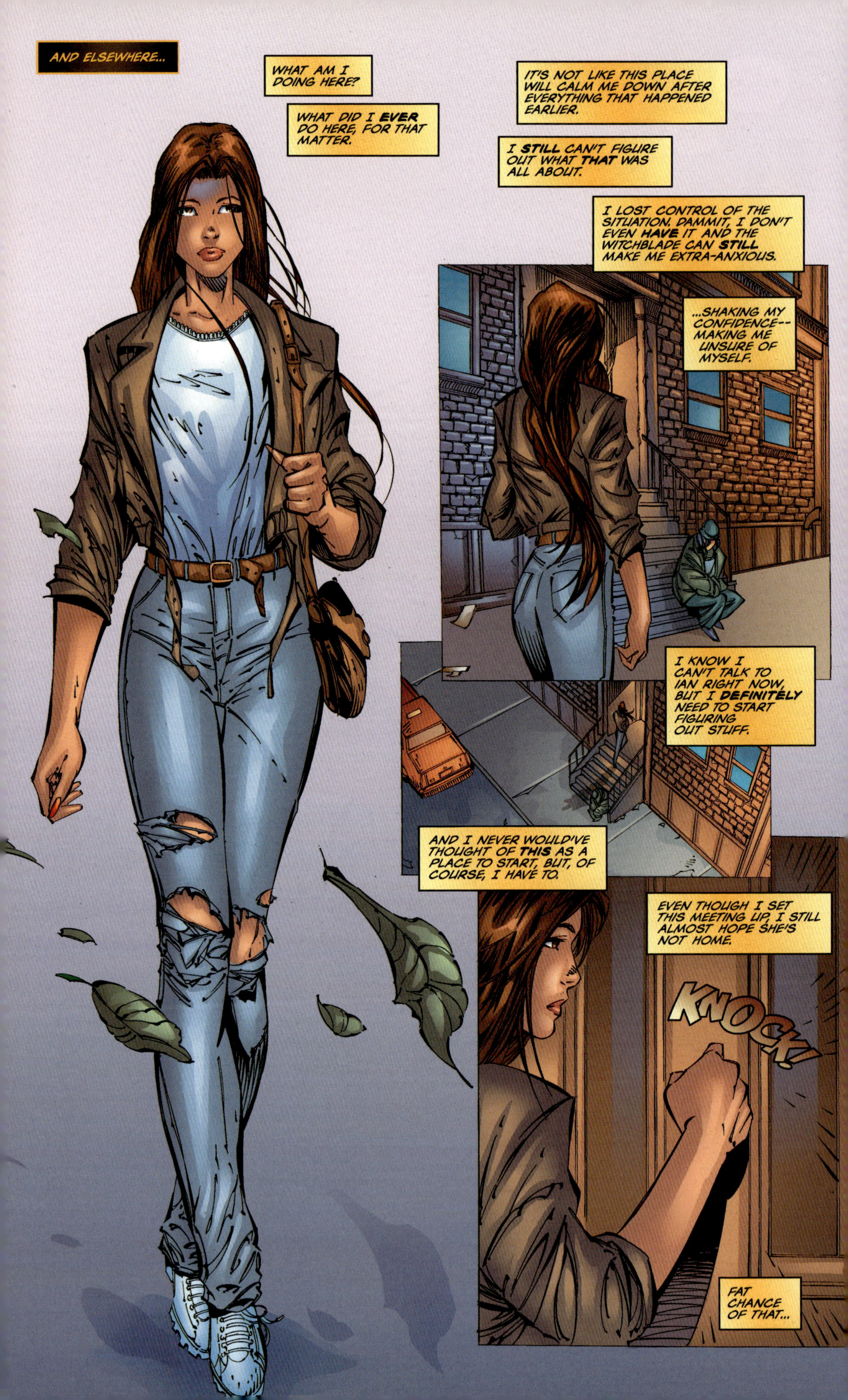

AND ELSEWHERE...
WHAT AM I DOING HERE?
WHAT DID I EVER DO HERE, FOR THAT MATTER.
IT'S NOT LIKE THIS PLACE WILL CALM ME DOWN AFTER EVERYTHING THAT HAPPENED EARLIER.
I STILL CAN'T FIGURE OUT WHAT THAT WAS ALL ABOUT.
I LOST CONTROL OF THE SITUATION. DAMMIT, I DON'T EVEN HAVE IT AND THE WITCHBLADE CAN STILL MAKE ME EXTRA-ANXIOUS.
...SHAKING MY CONFIDENCE-- MAKING ME UNSURE OF MYSELF.
I KNOW I CAN'T TALK TO IAN RIGHT NOW, BUT I DEFINITELY NEED TO START FIGURING OUT STUFF.
AND I NEVER WOULD'VE THOUGHT OF THIS AS A PLACE TO START, BUT, OF COURSE, I HAVE TO.
EVEN THOUGH I SET THIS MEETING UP, I STILL ALMOST HOPE SHE'S NOT HOME.
KNOCK!
FAT CHANCE OF THAT...

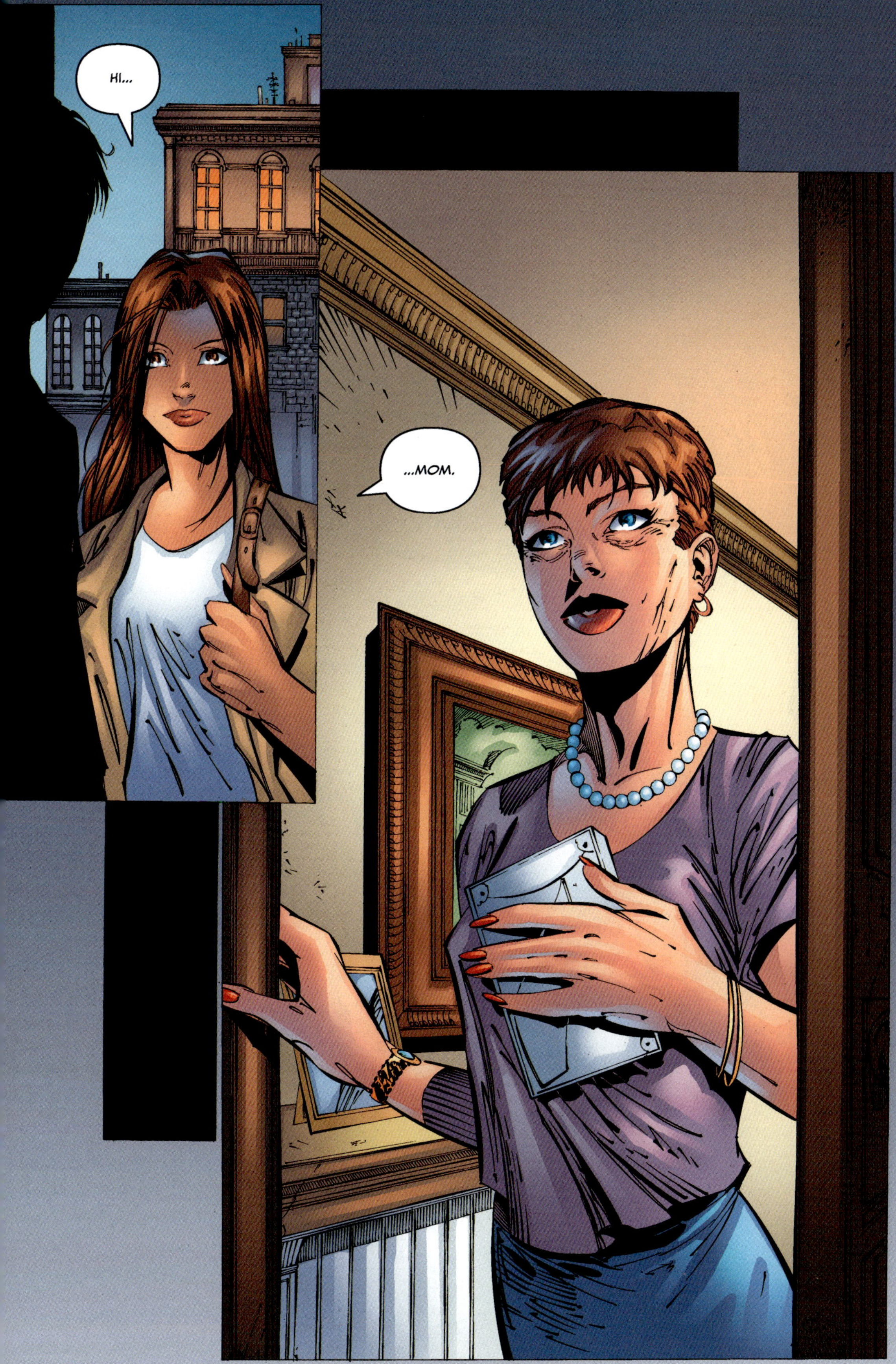
HI...
...MOM.

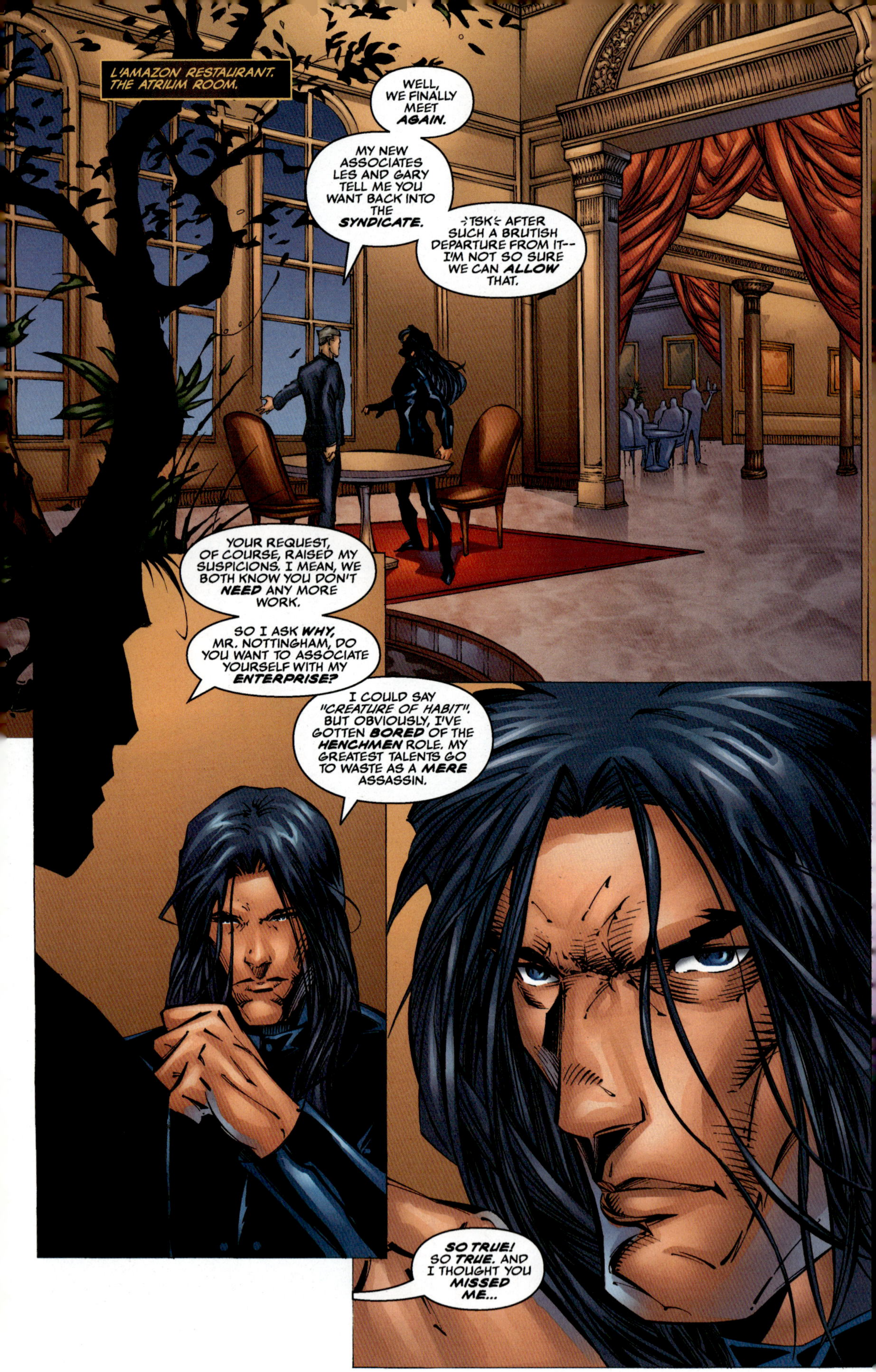
L'AMAZON RESTAURANT. THE ATRIUM ROOM.
WELL, WE FINALLY MEET AGAIN.
MY NEW ASSOCIATES LES AND GARY TELL ME YOU WANT BACK INTO THE SYNDICATE.
TSK AFTER SUCH A BRUTISH DEPARTURE FROM IT-- I'M NOT SO SURE WE CAN ALLOW THAT.
YOUR REQUEST, OF COURSE, RAISED MY SUSPICIONS. I MEAN, WE BOTH KNOW YOU DON'T NEED ANY MORE WORK.
SO I ASK WHY, MR. NOTTINGHAM, DO YOU WANT TO ASSOCIATE YOURSELF WITH MY ENTERPRISE?
I COULD SAY "CREATURE OF HABIT", BUT OBVIOUSLY, I'VE GOTTEN BORED OF THE HENCHMEN ROLE. MY GREATEST TALENTS GO TO WASTE AS A MERE ASSASSIN.
SO TRUE! SO TRUE. AND I THOUGHT YOU MISSED ME...

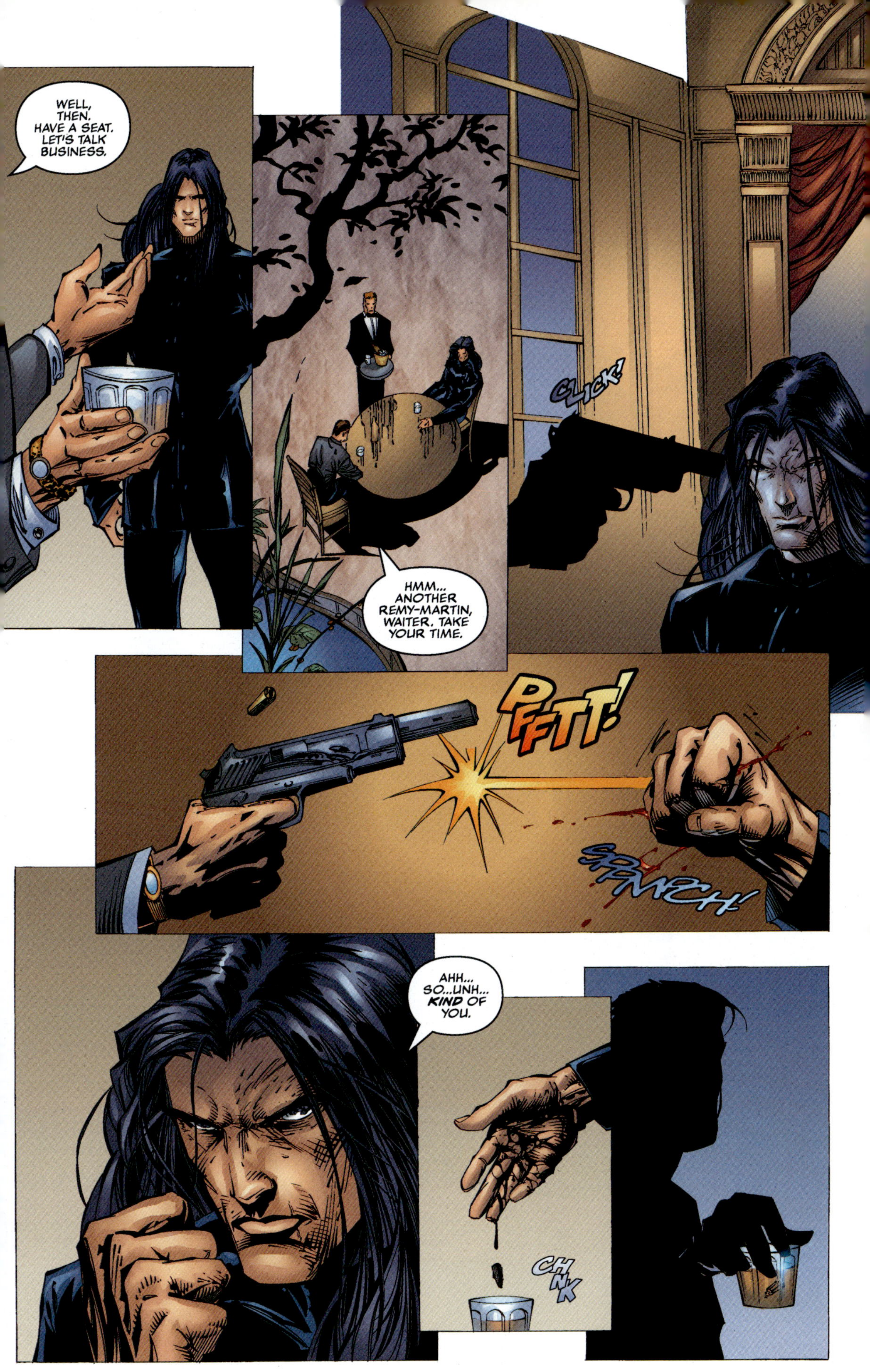
WELL, THEN. HAVE A SEAT. LET'S TALK BUSINESS.
HMM... ANOTHER REMY-MARTIN, WAITER. TAKE YOUR TIME.
CLICK!
PFFTT!
SPMCH!
AHH... SO...UNH... KIND OF YOU.
CHNK

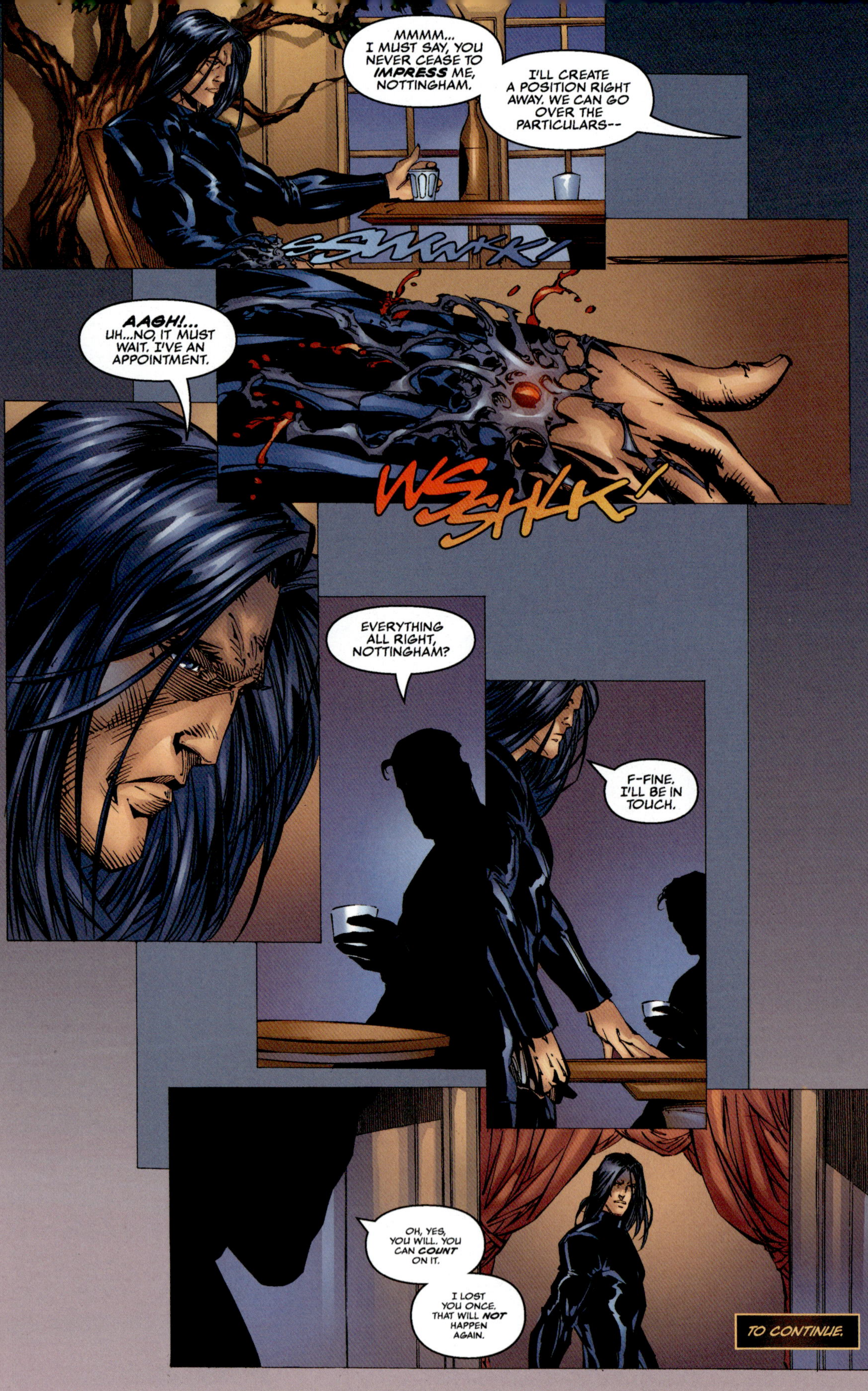
MMMM... I MUST SAY, YOU NEVER CEASE TO IMPRESS ME, NOTTINGHAM.
I'LL CREATE A POSITION RIGHT AWAY. WE CAN GO OVER THE PARTICULARS--
AAGH!... UH...NO, IT MUST WAIT. I'VE AN APPOINTMENT.
WSSHKK!
EVERYTHING ALL RIGHT, NOTTINGHAM?
F-FINE. I'LL BE IN TOUCH.
OH, YES, YOU WILL. YOU CAN COUNT ON IT.
I LOST YOU ONCE. THAT WILL NOT HAPPEN AGAIN.
TO CONTINUE.

issue #22

story: **David Wohl** and **Christina Z.**
pencils: **Randy Green**
layouts: **Michael Turner** pages 1-8 and 16-22
pencil finishes: **Brian Ching, Dan Fraga** and **Clarence Lansang**
inks: **D-Tron**
colors: **JD Smith**

ink assists: **Andy Kim, Marsha Chen, Jose "Jag" Guillen**
and **Jeff De Los Santos**

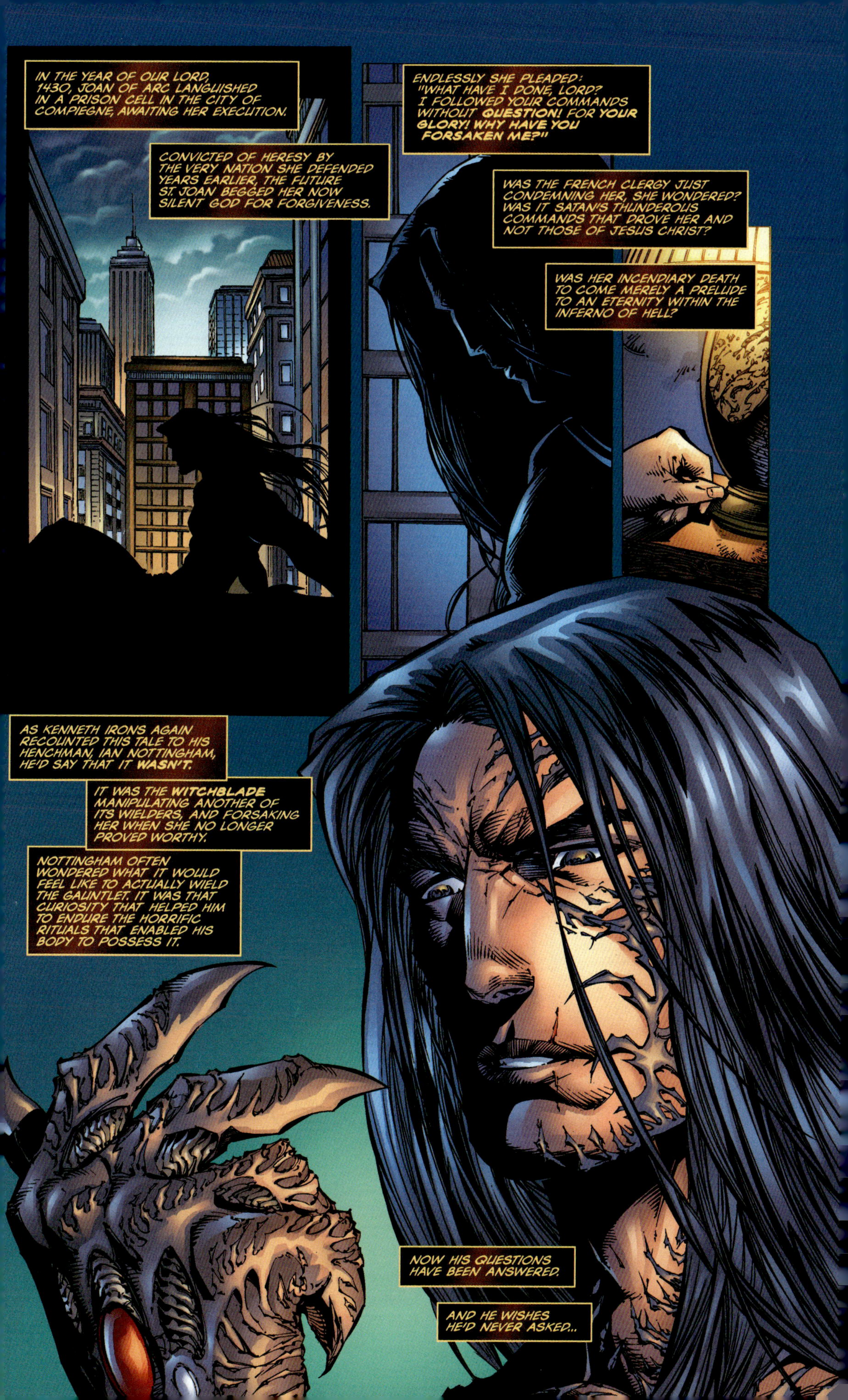
IN THE YEAR OF OUR LORD, 1430, JOAN OF ARC LANGUISHED IN A PRISON CELL IN THE CITY OF COMPIEGNE, AWAITING HER EXECUTION.
CONVICTED OF HERESY BY THE VERY NATION SHE DEFENDED YEARS EARLIER, THE FUTURE ST. JOAN BEGGED HER NOW SILENT GOD FOR FORGIVENESS.
ENDLESSLY SHE PLEADED: "WHAT HAVE I DONE, LORD? I FOLLOWED YOUR COMMANDS WITHOUT QUESTION! FOR YOUR GLORY! WHY HAVE YOU FORSAKEN ME?"
WAS THE FRENCH CLERGY JUST CONDEMNING HER, SHE WONDERED? WAS IT SATAN'S THUNDEROUS COMMANDS THAT DROVE HER AND NOT THOSE OF JESUS CHRIST?
WAS HER INCENDIARY DEATH TO COME MERELY A PRELUDE TO AN ETERNITY WITHIN THE INFERNO OF HELL?
AS KENNETH IRONS AGAIN RECOUNTED THIS TALE TO HIS HENCHMAN, IAN NOTTINGHAM, HE'D SAY THAT IT WASN'T.
IT WAS THE WITCHBLADE MANIPULATING ANOTHER OF ITS WIELDERS, AND FORSAKING HER WHEN SHE NO LONGER PROVED WORTHY.
NOTTINGHAM OFTEN WONDERED WHAT IT WOULD FEEL LIKE TO ACTUALLY WIELD THE GAUNTLET. IT WAS THAT CURIOSITY THAT HELPED HIM TO ENDURE THE HORRIFIC RITUALS THAT ENABLED HIS BODY TO POSSESS IT.
NOW HIS QUESTIONS HAVE BEEN ANSWERED.
AND HE WISHES HE'D NEVER ASKED...

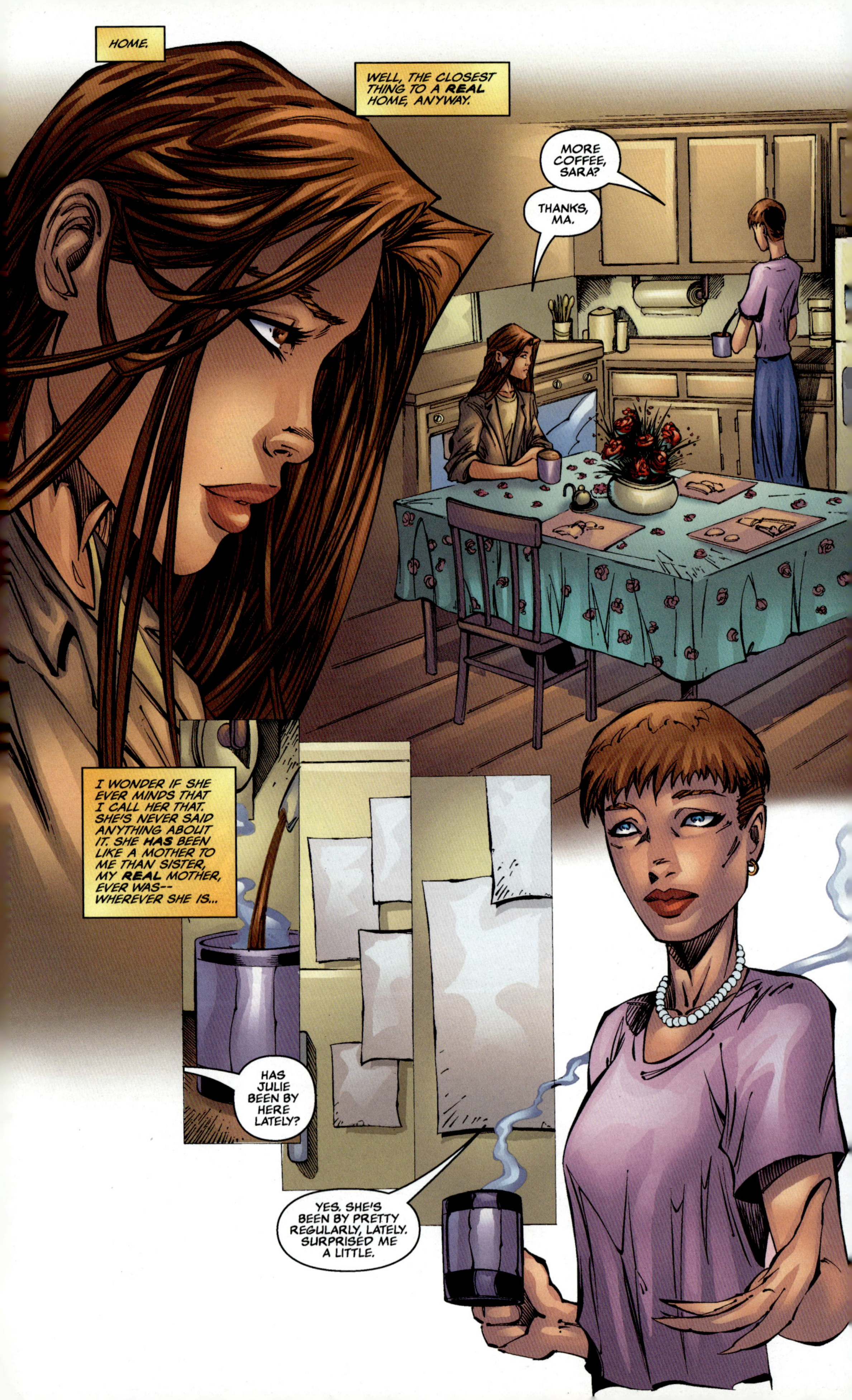
HOME.
WELL, THE CLOSEST THING TO A REAL HOME, ANYWAY.
MORE COFFEE, SARA?
THANKS, MA.
I WONDER IF SHE EVER MINDS THAT I CALL HER THAT. SHE'S NEVER SAID ANYTHING ABOUT IT. SHE HAS BEEN LIKE A MOTHER TO ME THAN SISTER, MY REAL MOTHER, EVER WAS-- WHEREVER SHE IS...
HAS JULIE BEEN BY HERE LATELY?
YES. SHE'S BEEN BY PRETTY REGULARLY, LATELY. SURPRISED ME A LITTLE.

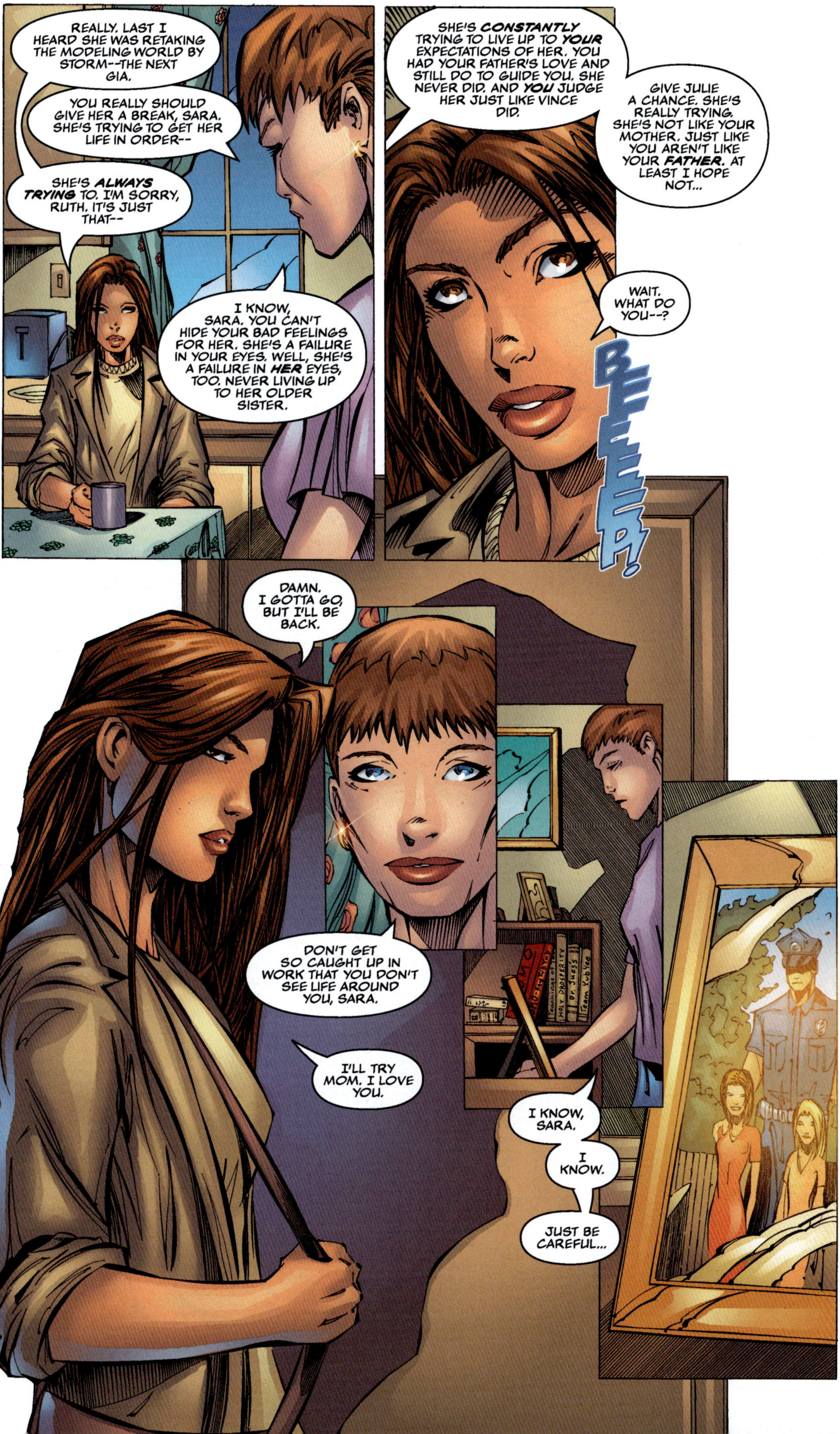
REALLY. LAST I HEARD SHE WAS RETAKING THE MODELING WORLD BY STORM--THE NEXT GIA.
YOU REALLY SHOULD GIVE HER A BREAK, SARA. SHE'S TRYING TO GET HER LIFE IN ORDER--
SHE'S ALWAYS TRYING TO. I'M SORRY, RUTH. IT'S JUST THAT--
I KNOW, SARA. YOU CAN'T HIDE YOUR BAD FEELINGS FOR HER. SHE'S A FAILURE IN YOUR EYES. WELL, SHE'S A FAILURE IN HER EYES, TOO. NEVER LIVING UP TO HER OLDER SISTER.
SHE'S CONSTANTLY TRYING TO LIVE UP TO YOUR EXPECTATIONS OF HER. YOU HAD YOUR FATHER'S LOVE AND STILL DO TO GUIDE YOU. SHE NEVER DID. AND YOU JUDGE HER JUST LIKE VINCE DID.
GIVE JULIE A CHANCE. SHE'S REALLY TRYING. SHE'S NOT LIKE YOUR MOTHER. JUST LIKE YOU AREN'T LIKE YOUR FATHER. AT LEAST I HOPE NOT...
WAIT. WHAT DO YOU--?
BEEEEP!
DAMN. I GOTTA GO, BUT I'LL BE BACK.
DON'T GET SO CAUGHT UP IN WORK THAT YOU DON'T SEE LIFE AROUND YOU, SARA.
I'LL TRY MOM. I LOVE YOU.
I KNOW, SARA.
I KNOW.
JUST BE CAREFUL...

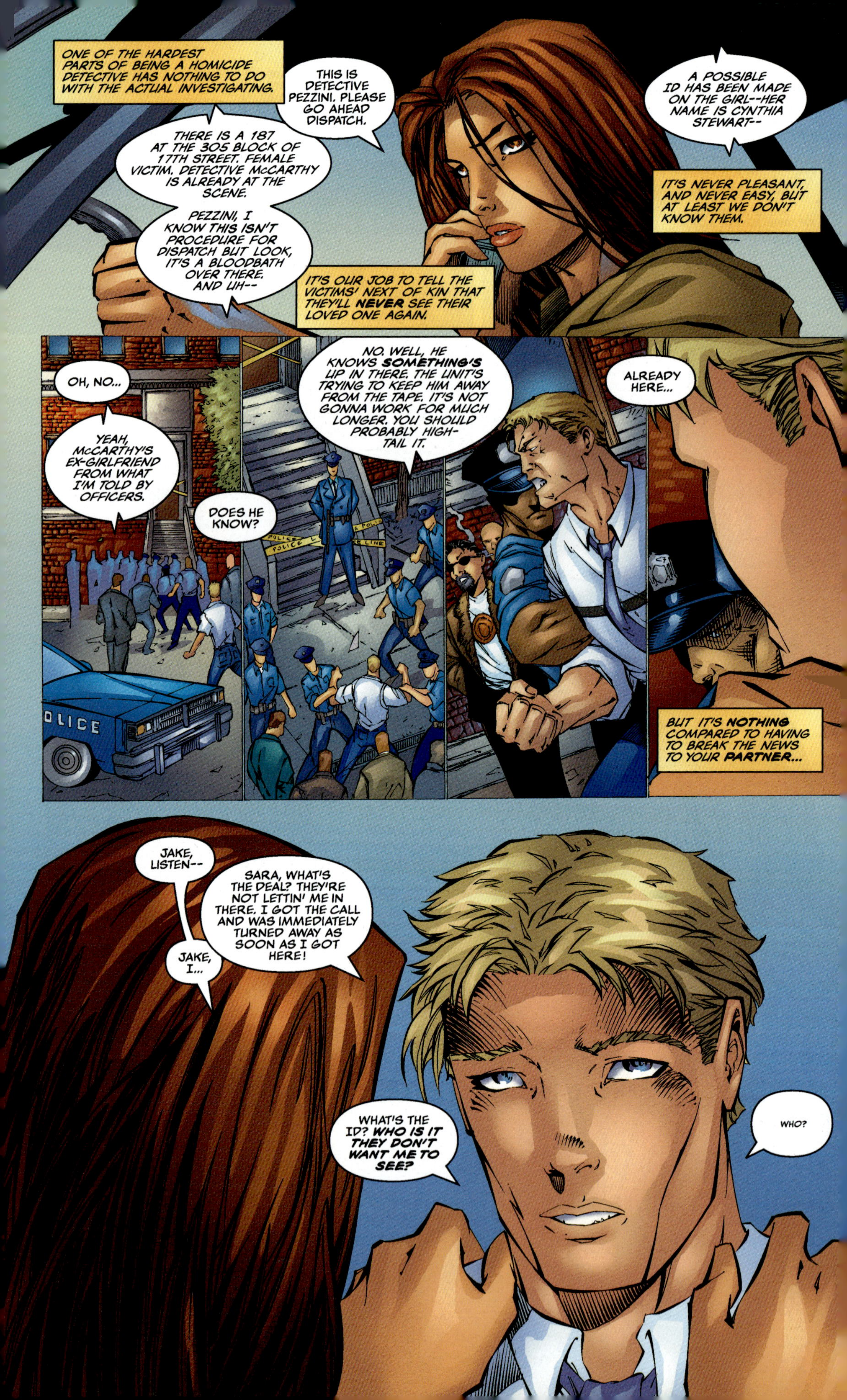

ONE OF THE HARDEST PARTS OF BEING A HOMICIDE DETECTIVE HAS NOTHING TO DO WITH THE ACTUAL INVESTIGATING.
THIS IS DETECTIVE PEZZINI. PLEASE GO AHEAD DISPATCH.
THERE IS A 187 AT THE 305 BLOCK OF 17TH STREET. FEMALE VICTIM. DETECTIVE McCARTHY IS ALREADY AT THE SCENE.
PEZZINI, I KNOW THIS ISN'T PROCEDURE FOR DISPATCH BUT LOOK, IT'S A BLOODBATH OVER THERE. AND UH--
IT'S OUR JOB TO TELL THE VICTIMS' NEXT OF KIN THAT THEY'LL NEVER SEE THEIR LOVED ONE AGAIN.
A POSSIBLE ID HAS BEEN MADE ON THE GIRL--HER NAME IS CYNTHIA STEWART--
IT'S NEVER PLEASANT, AND NEVER EASY, BUT AT LEAST WE DON'T KNOW THEM.
OH, NO...
YEAH, McCARTHY'S EX-GIRLFRIEND FROM WHAT I'M TOLD BY OFFICERS.
DOES HE KNOW?
NO. WELL, HE KNOWS SOMETHING'S UP IN THERE. THE UNIT'S TRYING TO KEEP HIM AWAY FROM THE TAPE. IT'S NOT GONNA WORK FOR MUCH LONGER. YOU SHOULD PROBABLY HIGH-TAIL IT.
POLICE LINE
OLICE
ALREADY HERE...
BUT IT'S NOTHING COMPARED TO HAVING TO BREAK THE NEWS TO YOUR PARTNER...
JAKE, LISTEN--
SARA, WHAT'S THE DEAL? THEY'RE NOT LETTIN' ME IN THERE. I GOT THE CALL AND WAS IMMEDIATELY TURNED AWAY AS SOON AS I GOT HERE!
JAKE, I...
WHAT'S THE ID? WHO IS IT THEY DON'T WANT ME TO SEE?
WHO?

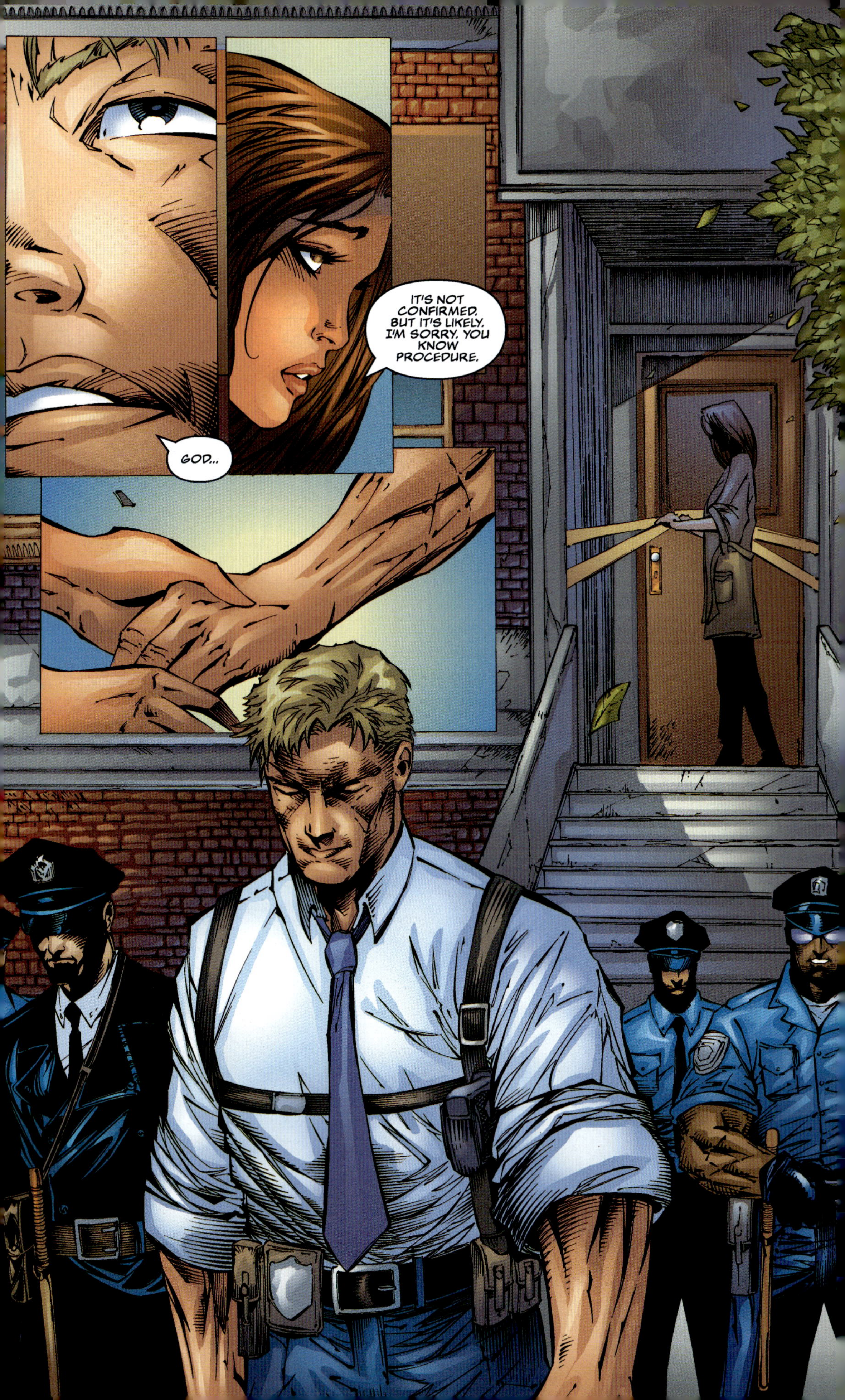
IT'S NOT CONFIRMED, BUT IT'S LIKELY. I'M SORRY. YOU KNOW PROCEDURE.
GOD...

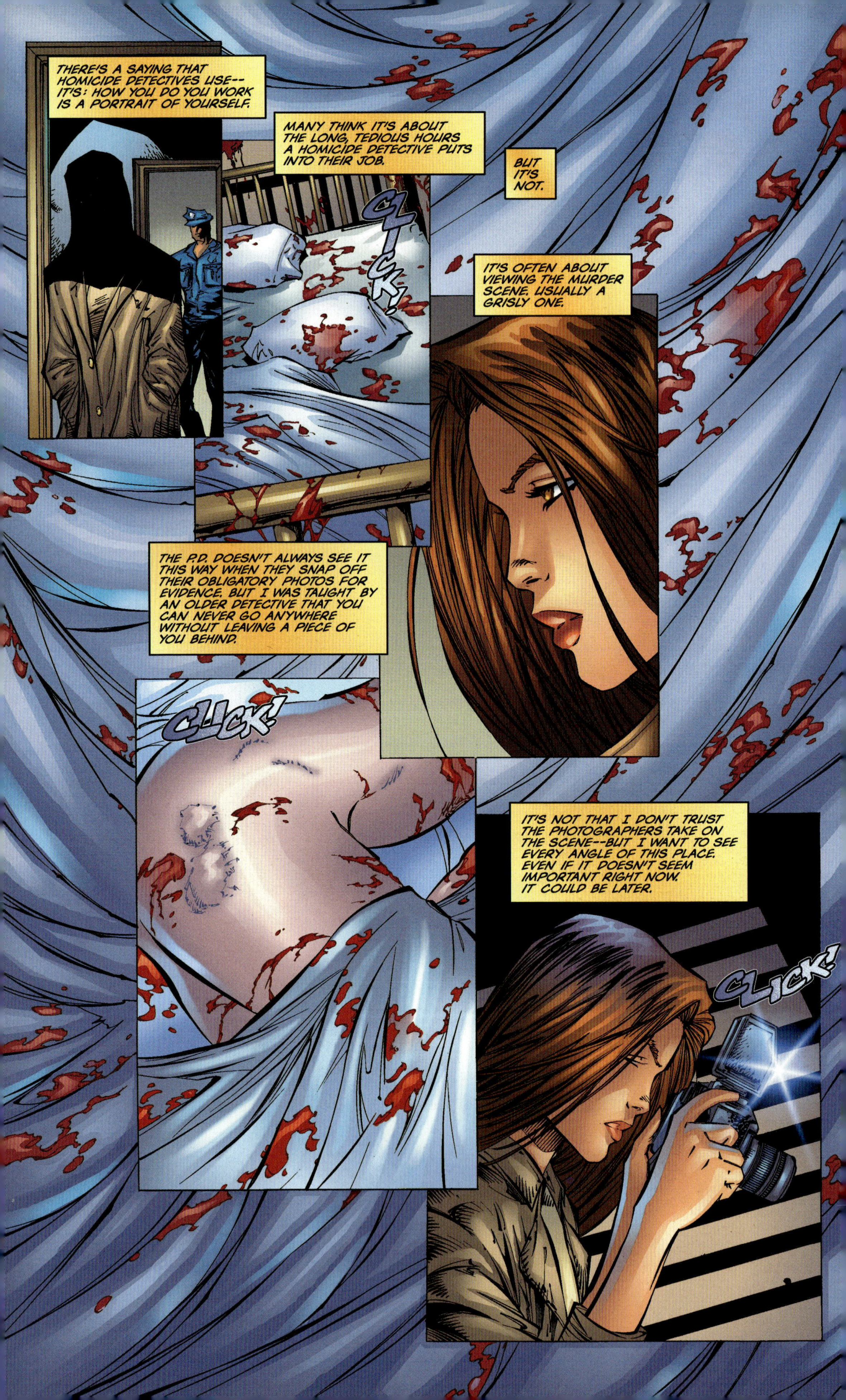
THERE'S A SAYING THAT HOMICIDE DETECTIVES USE-- IT'S: HOW YOU DO YOU WORK IS A PORTRAIT OF YOURSELF.
MANY THINK IT'S ABOUT THE LONG, TEDIOUS HOURS A HOMICIDE DETECTIVE PUTS INTO THEIR JOB.
CLICK!
BUT IT'S NOT.
IT'S OFTEN ABOUT VIEWING THE MURDER SCENE. USUALLY A GRISLY ONE.
THE P.D. DOESN'T ALWAYS SEE IT THIS WAY WHEN THEY SNAP OFF THEIR OBLIGATORY PHOTOS FOR EVIDENCE. BUT I WAS TAUGHT BY AN OLDER DETECTIVE THAT YOU CAN NEVER GO ANYWHERE WITHOUT LEAVING A PIECE OF YOU BEHIND.
CLICK!
IT'S NOT THAT I DON'T TRUST THE PHOTOGRAPHERS TAKE ON THE SCENE--BUT I WANT TO SEE EVERY ANGLE OF THIS PLACE. EVEN IF IT DOESN'T SEEM IMPORTANT RIGHT NOW. IT COULD BE LATER.
CLICK!

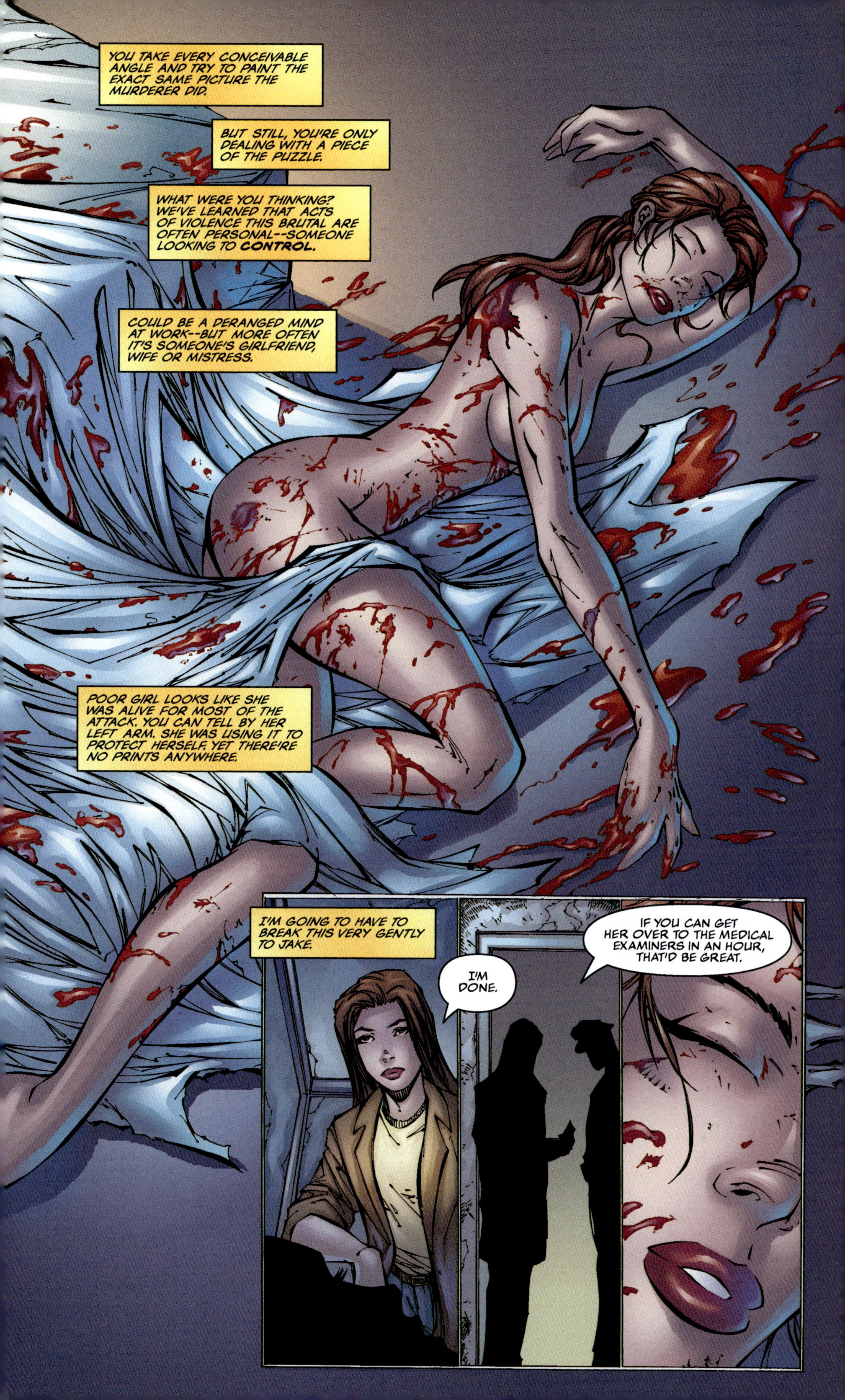
YOU TAKE EVERY CONCEIVABLE ANGLE AND TRY TO PAINT THE EXACT SAME PICTURE THE MURDERER DID.
BUT STILL, YOU'RE ONLY DEALING WITH A PIECE OF THE PUZZLE.
WHAT WERE YOU THINKING? WE'VE LEARNED THAT ACTS OF VIOLENCE THIS BRUTAL ARE OFTEN PERSONAL--SOMEONE LOOKING TO CONTROL.
COULD BE A DERANGED MIND AT WORK--BUT MORE OFTEN IT'S SOMEONE'S GIRLFRIEND, WIFE OR MISTRESS.
POOR GIRL LOOKS LIKE SHE WAS ALIVE FOR MOST OF THE ATTACK. YOU CAN TELL BY HER LEFT ARM. SHE WAS USING IT TO PROTECT HERSELF, YET THERE'RE NO PRINTS ANYWHERE.
I'M GOING TO HAVE TO BREAK THIS VERY GENTLY TO JAKE.
I'M DONE.
IF YOU CAN GET HER OVER TO THE MEDICAL EXAMINERS IN AN HOUR, THAT'D BE GREAT.

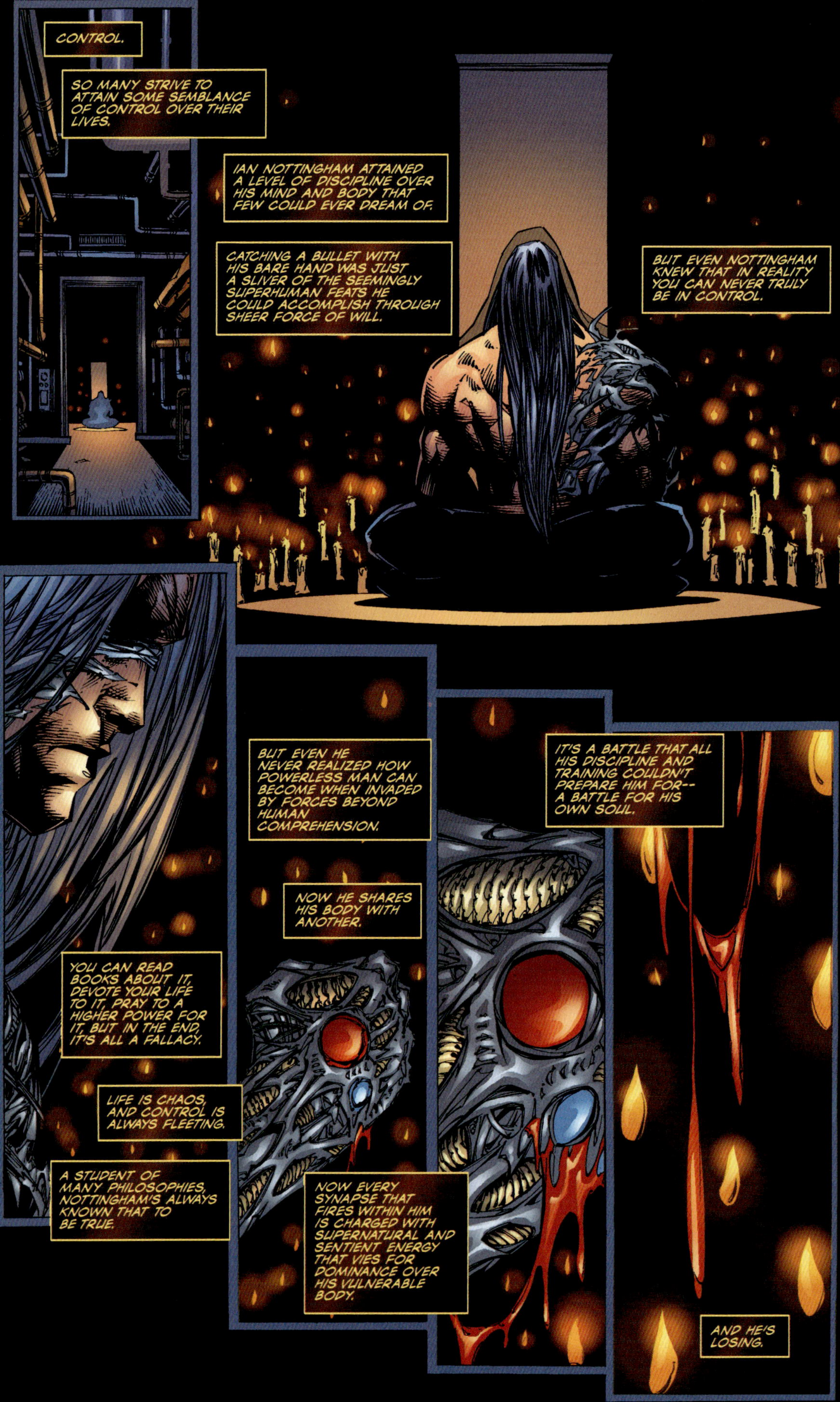
CONTROL.
SO MANY STRIVE TO ATTAIN SOME SEMBLANCE OF CONTROL OVER THEIR LIVES.
IAN NOTTINGHAM ATTAINED A LEVEL OF DISCIPLINE OVER HIS MIND AND BODY THAT FEW COULD EVER DREAM OF.
CATCHING A BULLET WITH HIS BARE HAND WAS JUST A SLIVER OF THE SEEMINGLY SUPERHUMAN FEATS HE COULD ACCOMPLISH THROUGH SHEER FORCE OF WILL.
BUT EVEN NOTTINGHAM KNEW THAT IN REALITY YOU CAN NEVER TRULY BE IN CONTROL.
YOU CAN READ BOOKS ABOUT IT, DEVOTE YOUR LIFE TO IT, PRAY TO A HIGHER POWER FOR IT, BUT IN THE END, IT'S ALL A FALLACY.
LIFE IS CHAOS, AND CONTROL IS ALWAYS FLEETING.
A STUDENT OF MANY PHILOSOPHIES, NOTTINGHAM'S ALWAYS KNOWN THAT TO BE TRUE.
BUT EVEN HE NEVER REALIZED HOW POWERLESS MAN CAN BECOME WHEN INVADED BY FORCES BEYOND HUMAN COMPREHENSION.
NOW HE SHARES HIS BODY WITH ANOTHER.
NOW EVERY SYNAPSE THAT FIRES WITHIN HIM IS CHARGED WITH SUPERNATURAL AND SENTIENT ENERGY THAT VIES FOR DOMINANCE OVER HIS VULNERABLE BODY.
IT'S A BATTLE THAT ALL HIS DISCIPLINE AND TRAINING COULDN'T PREPARE HIM FOR-- A BATTLE FOR HIS OWN SOUL.
AND HE'S LOSING.

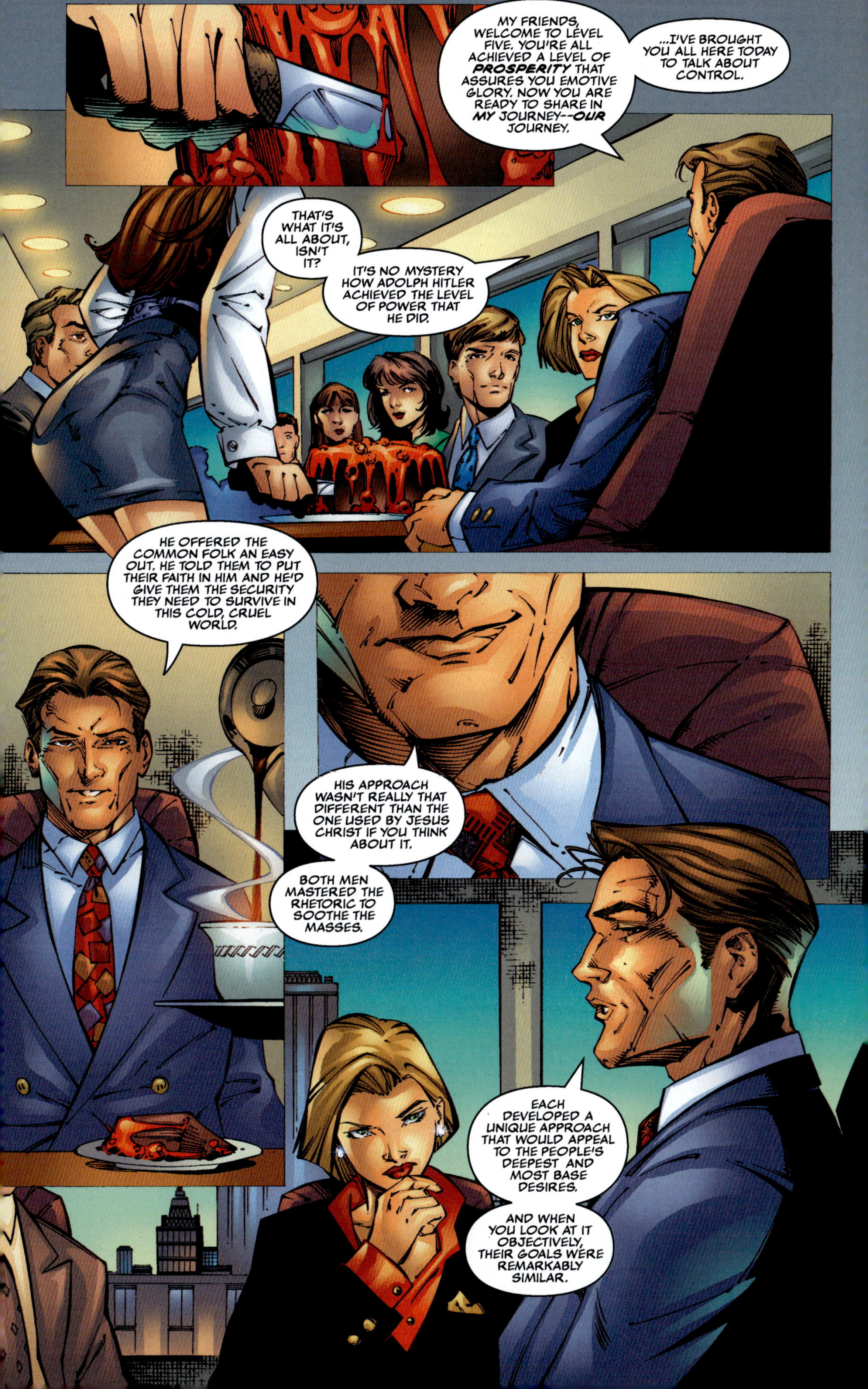
MY FRIENDS, WELCOME TO LEVEL FIVE. YOU'RE ALL ACHIEVED A LEVEL OF **PROSPERITY** THAT ASSURES YOU EMOTIVE GLORY. NOW YOU ARE READY TO SHARE IN **MY** JOURNEY--**OUR** JOURNEY.
...I'VE BROUGHT YOU ALL HERE TODAY TO TALK ABOUT CONTROL.
THAT'S WHAT IT'S ALL ABOUT, ISN'T IT?
IT'S NO MYSTERY HOW ADOLPH HITLER ACHIEVED THE LEVEL OF POWER THAT HE DID.
HE OFFERED THE COMMON FOLK AN EASY OUT. HE TOLD THEM TO PUT THEIR FAITH IN HIM AND HE'D GIVE THEM THE SECURITY THEY NEED TO SURVIVE IN THIS COLD, CRUEL WORLD.
HIS APPROACH WASN'T REALLY THAT DIFFERENT THAN THE ONE USED BY JESUS CHRIST IF YOU THINK ABOUT IT.
BOTH MEN MASTERED THE RHETORIC TO SOOTHE THE MASSES.
EACH DEVELOPED A UNIQUE APPROACH THAT WOULD APPEAL TO THE PEOPLE'S DEEPEST AND MOST BASE DESIRES.
AND WHEN YOU LOOK AT IT OBJECTIVELY, THEIR GOALS WERE REMARKABLY SIMILAR.

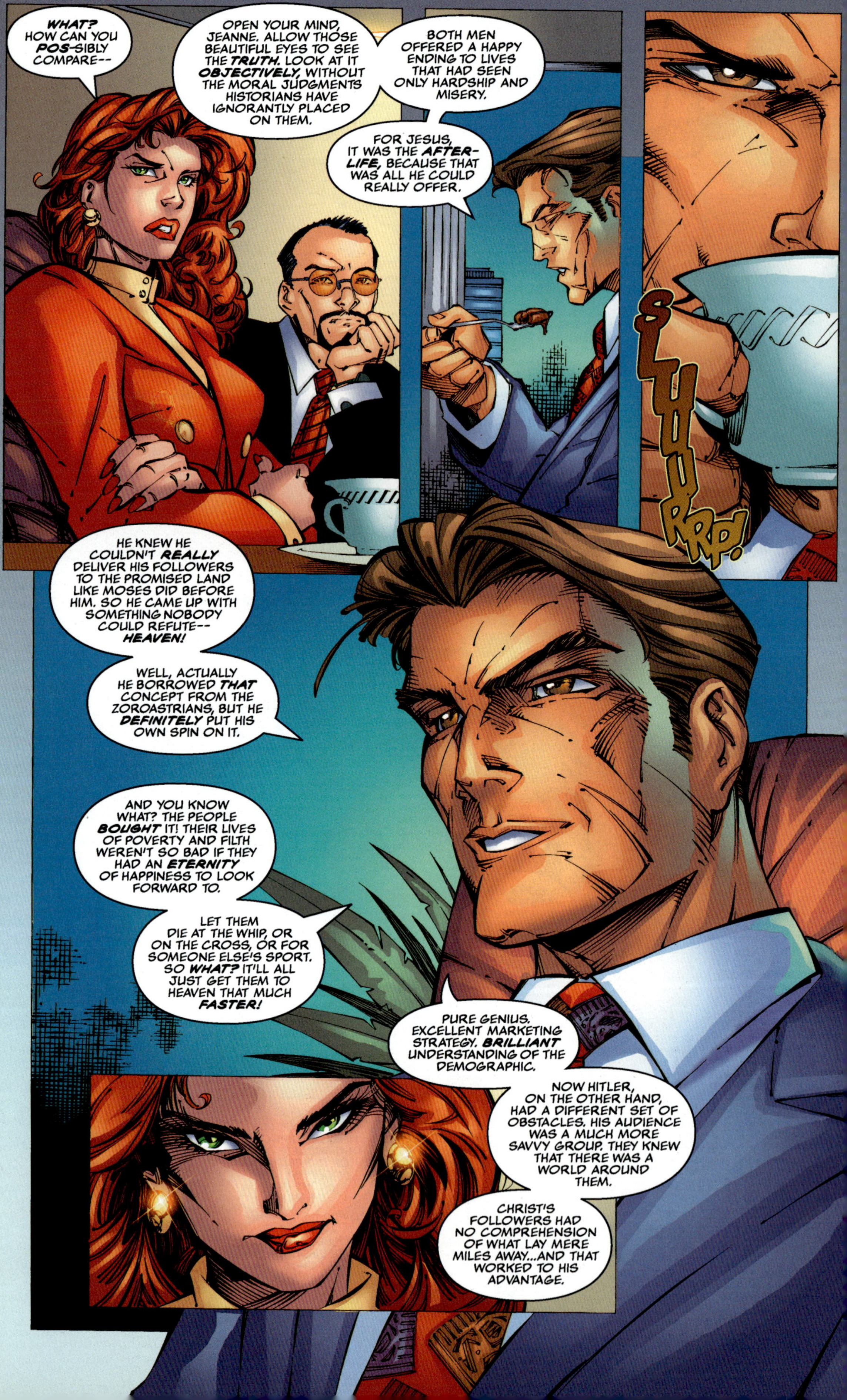
WHAT? HOW CAN YOU POS-SIBLY COMPARE--
OPEN YOUR MIND, JEANNE. ALLOW THOSE BEAUTIFUL EYES TO SEE THE TRUTH. LOOK AT IT OBJECTIVELY, WITHOUT THE MORAL JUDGMENTS HISTORIANS HAVE IGNORANTLY PLACED ON THEM.
BOTH MEN OFFERED A HAPPY ENDING TO LIVES THAT HAD SEEN ONLY HARDSHIP AND MISERY.
FOR JESUS, IT WAS THE AFTER-LIFE, BECAUSE THAT WAS ALL HE COULD REALLY OFFER.
SLUURRP!
HE KNEW HE COULDN'T REALLY DELIVER HIS FOLLOWERS TO THE PROMISED LAND LIKE MOSES DID BEFORE HIM. SO HE CAME UP WITH SOMETHING NOBODY COULD REFUTE-- HEAVEN!
WELL, ACTUALLY HE BORROWED THAT CONCEPT FROM THE ZOROASTRIANS, BUT HE DEFINITELY PUT HIS OWN SPIN ON IT.
AND YOU KNOW WHAT? THE PEOPLE BOUGHT IT! THEIR LIVES OF POVERTY AND FILTH WEREN'T SO BAD IF THEY HAD AN ETERNITY OF HAPPINESS TO LOOK FORWARD TO.
LET THEM DIE AT THE WHIP, OR ON THE CROSS, OR FOR SOMEONE ELSE'S SPORT. SO WHAT? IT'LL ALL JUST GET THEM TO HEAVEN THAT MUCH FASTER!
PURE GENIUS. EXCELLENT MARKETING STRATEGY. BRILLIANT UNDERSTANDING OF THE DEMOGRAPHIC.
NOW HITLER, ON THE OTHER HAND, HAD A DIFFERENT SET OF OBSTACLES. HIS AUDIENCE WAS A MUCH MORE SAVVY GROUP. THEY KNEW THAT THERE WAS A WORLD AROUND THEM.
CHRIST'S FOLLOWERS HAD NO COMPREHENSION OF WHAT LAY MERE MILES AWAY...AND THAT WORKED TO HIS ADVANTAGE.

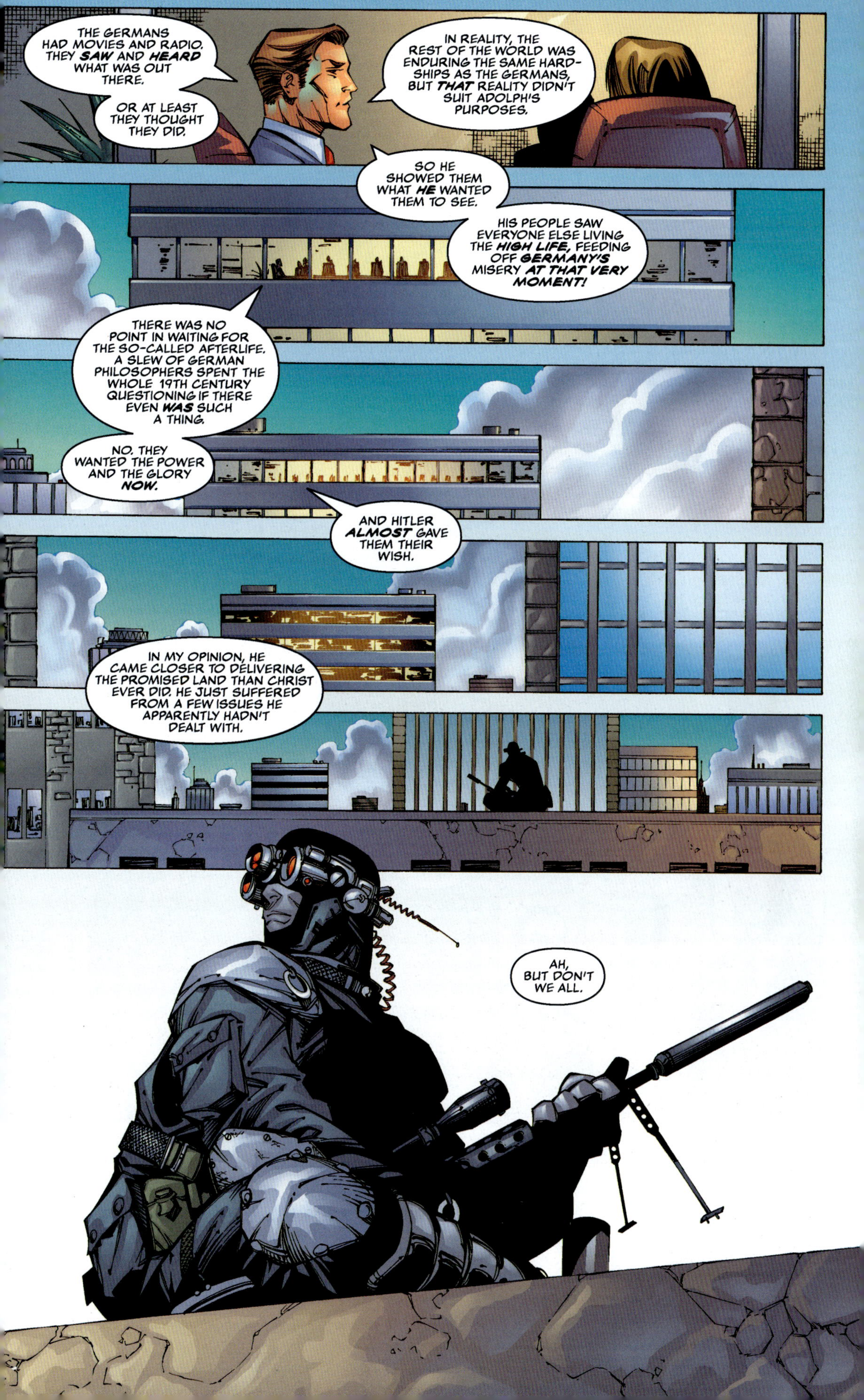
THE GERMANS HAD MOVIES AND RADIO. THEY SAW AND HEARD WHAT WAS OUT THERE.
OR AT LEAST THEY THOUGHT THEY DID.
IN REALITY, THE REST OF THE WORLD WAS ENDURING THE SAME HARDSHIPS AS THE GERMANS, BUT THAT REALITY DIDN'T SUIT ADOLPH'S PURPOSES.
SO HE SHOWED THEM WHAT HE WANTED THEM TO SEE.
HIS PEOPLE SAW EVERYONE ELSE LIVING THE HIGH LIFE, FEEDING OFF GERMANY'S MISERY AT THAT VERY MOMENT!
THERE WAS NO POINT IN WAITING FOR THE SO-CALLED AFTERLIFE. A SLEW OF GERMAN PHILOSOPHERS SPENT THE WHOLE 19TH CENTURY QUESTIONING IF THERE EVEN WAS SUCH A THING.
NO. THEY WANTED THE POWER AND THE GLORY NOW.
AND HITLER ALMOST GAVE THEM THEIR WISH.
IN MY OPINION, HE CAME CLOSER TO DELIVERING THE PROMISED LAND THAN CHRIST EVER DID. HE JUST SUFFERED FROM A FEW ISSUES HE APPARENTLY HADN'T DEALT WITH.
AH, BUT DON'T WE ALL.

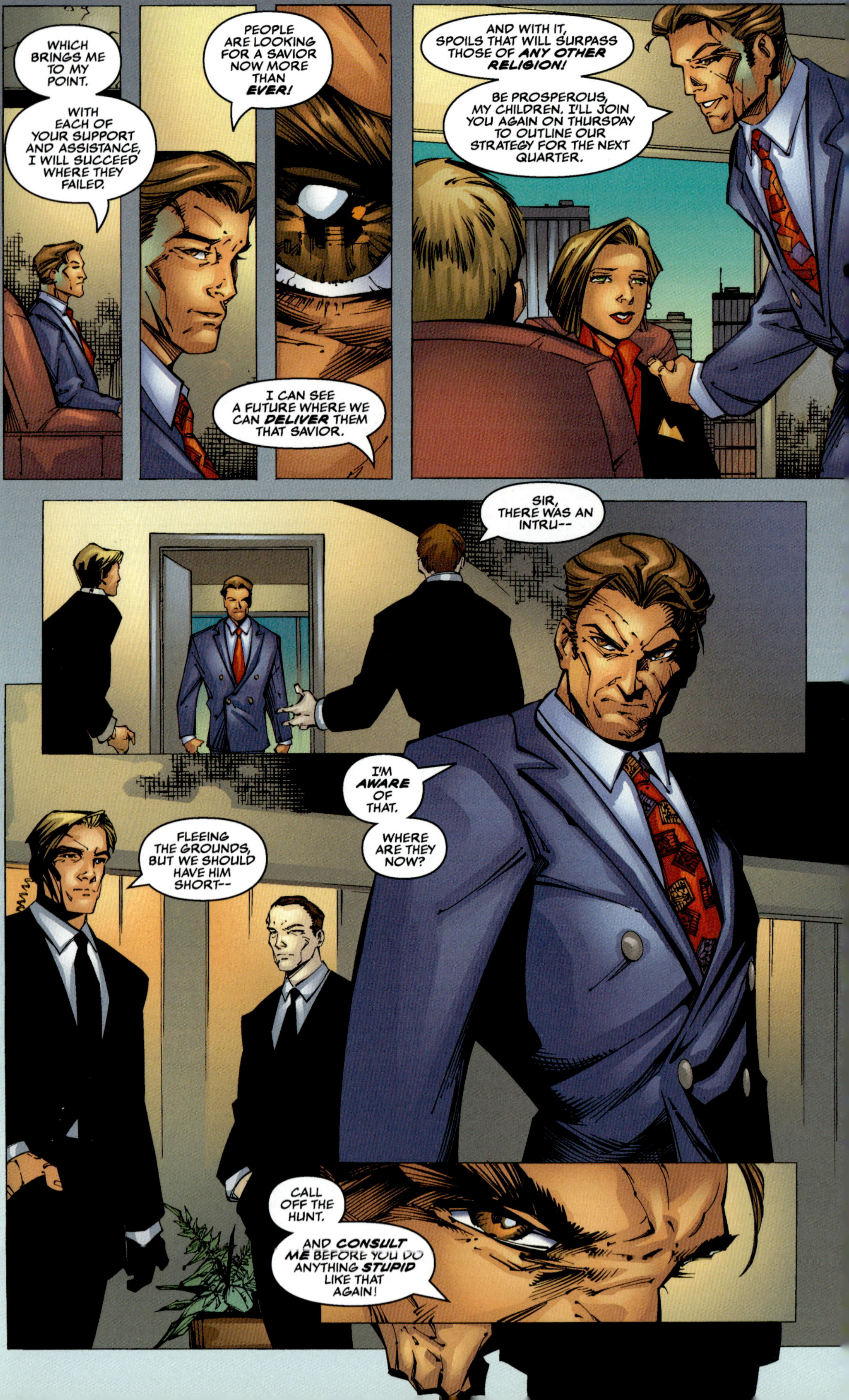
WHICH BRINGS ME TO MY POINT.
WITH EACH OF YOUR SUPPORT AND ASSISTANCE, I WILL SUCCEED WHERE THEY FAILED.
PEOPLE ARE LOOKING FOR A SAVIOR NOW MORE THAN EVER!
I CAN SEE A FUTURE WHERE WE CAN DELIVER THEM THAT SAVIOR.
AND WITH IT, SPOILS THAT WILL SURPASS THOSE OF ANY OTHER RELIGION!
BE PROSPEROUS, MY CHILDREN. I'LL JOIN YOU AGAIN ON THURSDAY TO OUTLINE OUR STRATEGY FOR THE NEXT QUARTER.
SIR, THERE WAS AN INTRU--
I'M AWARE OF THAT.
WHERE ARE THEY NOW?
FLEEING THE GROUNDS, BUT WE SHOULD HAVE HIM SHORT--
CALL OFF THE HUNT.
AND CONSULT ME BEFORE YOU DO ANYTHING STUPID LIKE THAT AGAIN!

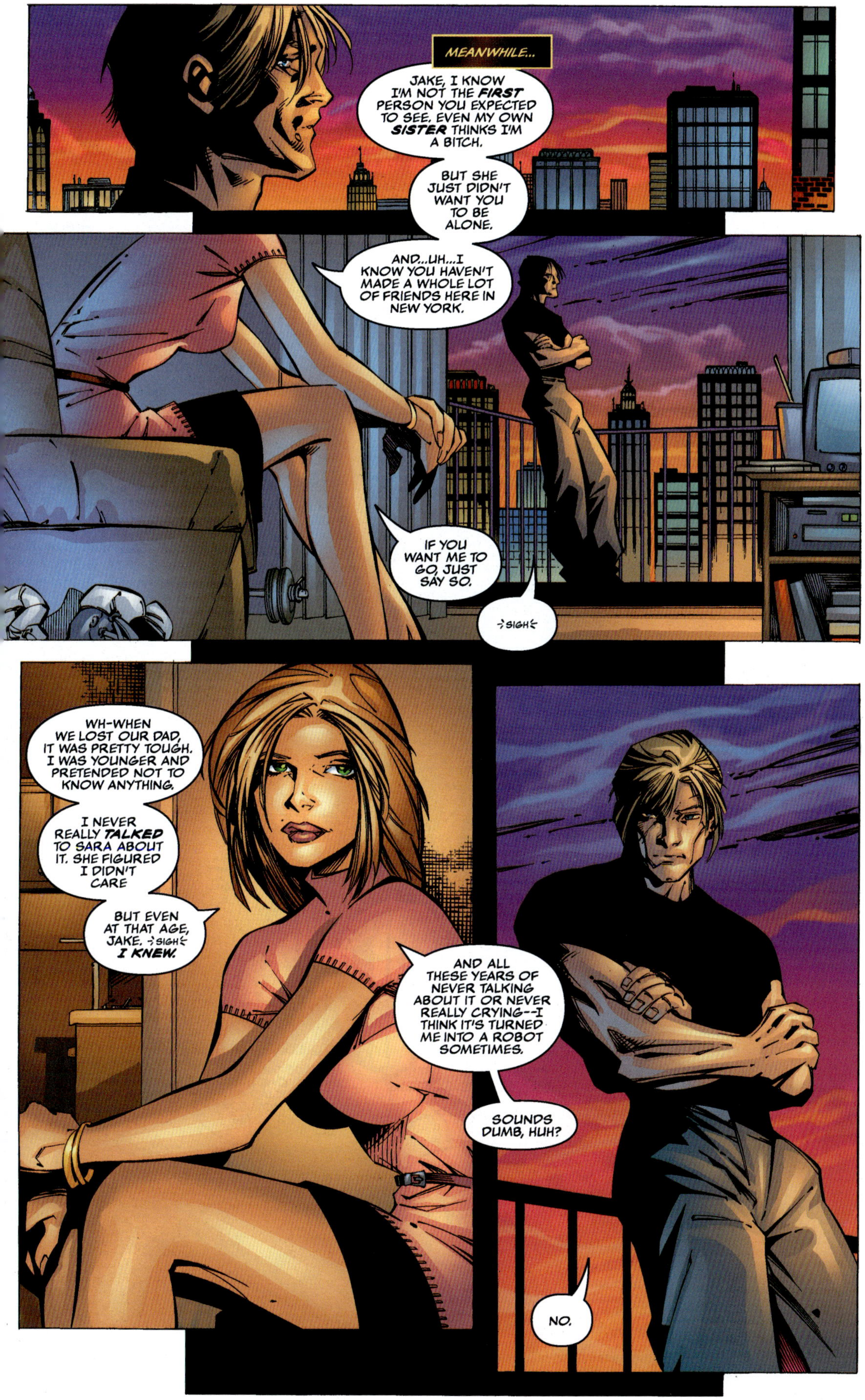
MEANWHILE...
JAKE, I KNOW I'M NOT THE FIRST PERSON YOU EXPECTED TO SEE. EVEN MY OWN SISTER THINKS I'M A BITCH.
BUT SHE JUST DIDN'T WANT YOU TO BE ALONE.
AND...UH...I KNOW YOU HAVEN'T MADE A WHOLE LOT OF FRIENDS HERE IN NEW YORK.
IF YOU WANT ME TO GO, JUST SAY SO.
SIGH
WH-WHEN WE LOST OUR DAD, IT WAS PRETTY TOUGH. I WAS YOUNGER AND PRETENDED NOT TO KNOW ANYTHING.
I NEVER REALLY TALKED TO SARA ABOUT IT. SHE FIGURED I DIDN'T CARE
BUT EVEN AT THAT AGE, JAKE. *SIGH* I KNEW.
AND ALL THESE YEARS OF NEVER TALKING ABOUT IT OR NEVER REALLY CRYING--I THINK IT'S TURNED ME INTO A ROBOT SOMETIMES.
SOUNDS DUMB, HUH?
NO.

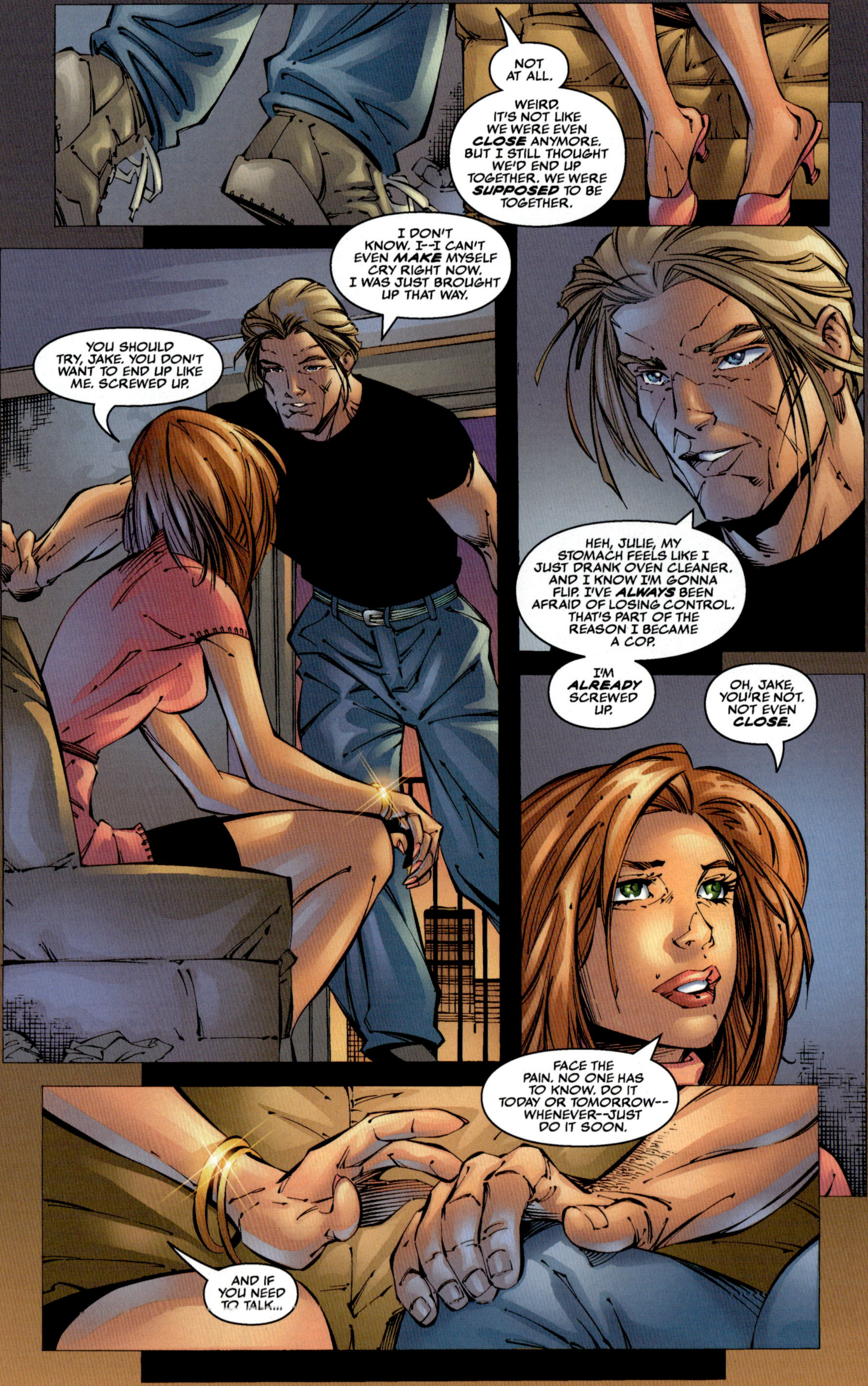
NOT AT ALL.
WEIRD. IT'S NOT LIKE WE WERE EVEN CLOSE ANYMORE. BUT I STILL THOUGHT WE'D END UP TOGETHER. WE WERE SUPPOSED TO BE TOGETHER.
I DON'T KNOW. I--I CAN'T EVEN MAKE MYSELF CRY RIGHT NOW. I WAS JUST BROUGHT UP THAT WAY.
YOU SHOULD TRY, JAKE. YOU DON'T WANT TO END UP LIKE ME. SCREWED UP.
HEH, JULIE, MY STOMACH FEELS LIKE I JUST DRANK OVEN CLEANER. AND I KNOW I'M GONNA FLIP. I'VE ALWAYS BEEN AFRAID OF LOSING CONTROL. THAT'S PART OF THE REASON I BECAME A COP.
I'M ALREADY SCREWED UP.
OH, JAKE, YOU'RE NOT. NOT EVEN CLOSE.
FACE THE PAIN. NO ONE HAS TO KNOW. DO IT TODAY OR TOMORROW-- WHENEVER--JUST DO IT SOON.
AND IF YOU NEED TO TALK...

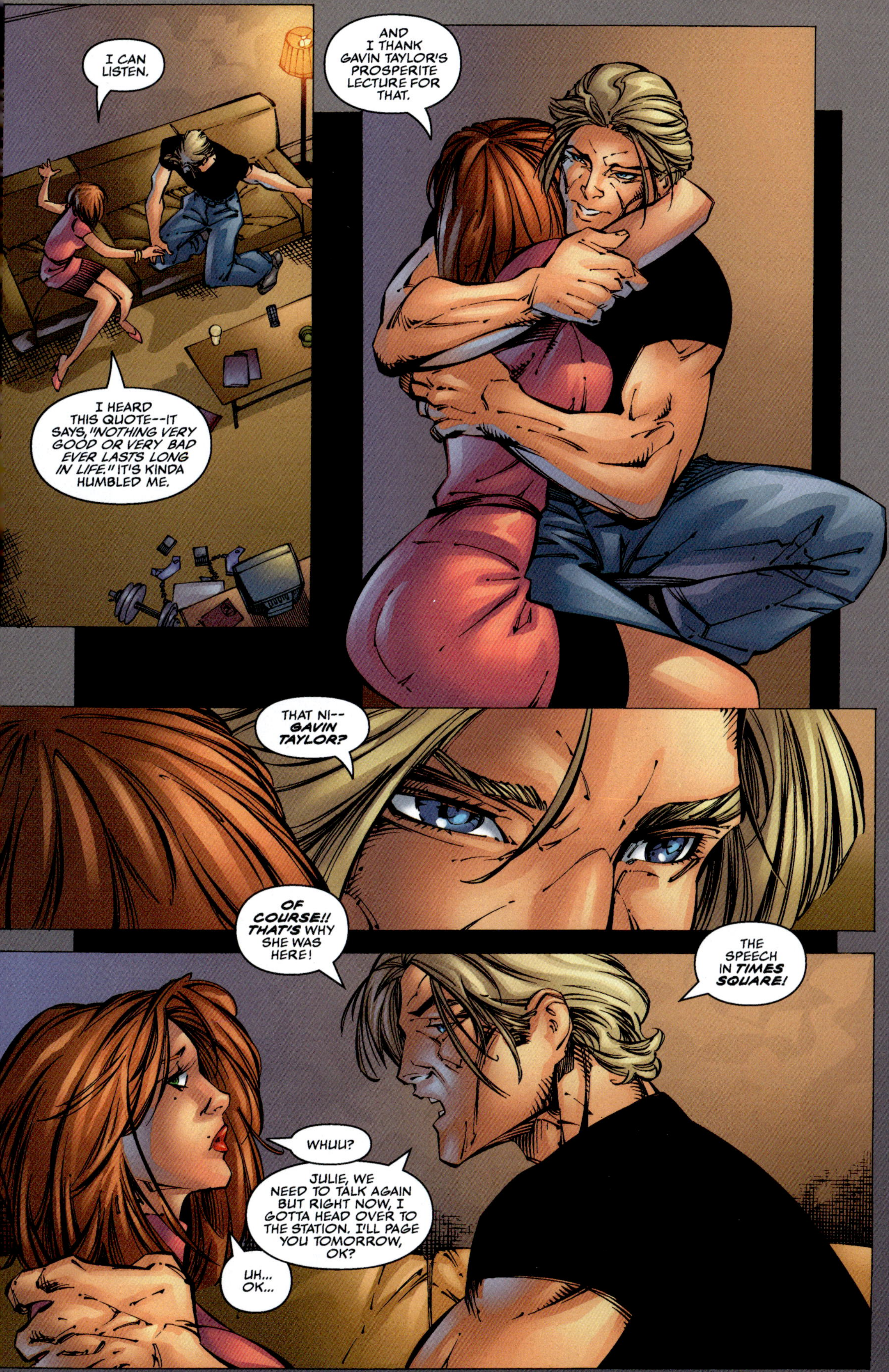
I CAN LISTEN.
I HEARD THIS QUOTE--IT SAYS, "NOTHING VERY GOOD OR VERY BAD EVER LASTS LONG IN LIFE." IT'S KINDA HUMBLED ME.
AND I THANK GAVIN TAYLOR'S PROSPERITE LECTURE FOR THAT.
THAT NI-- GAVIN TAYLOR?
OF COURSE!! THAT'S WHY SHE WAS HERE!
THE SPEECH IN TIMES SQUARE!
WHUU?
JULIE, WE NEED TO TALK AGAIN BUT RIGHT NOW, I GOTTA HEAD OVER TO THE STATION. I'LL PAGE YOU TOMORROW, OK?
UH... OK...

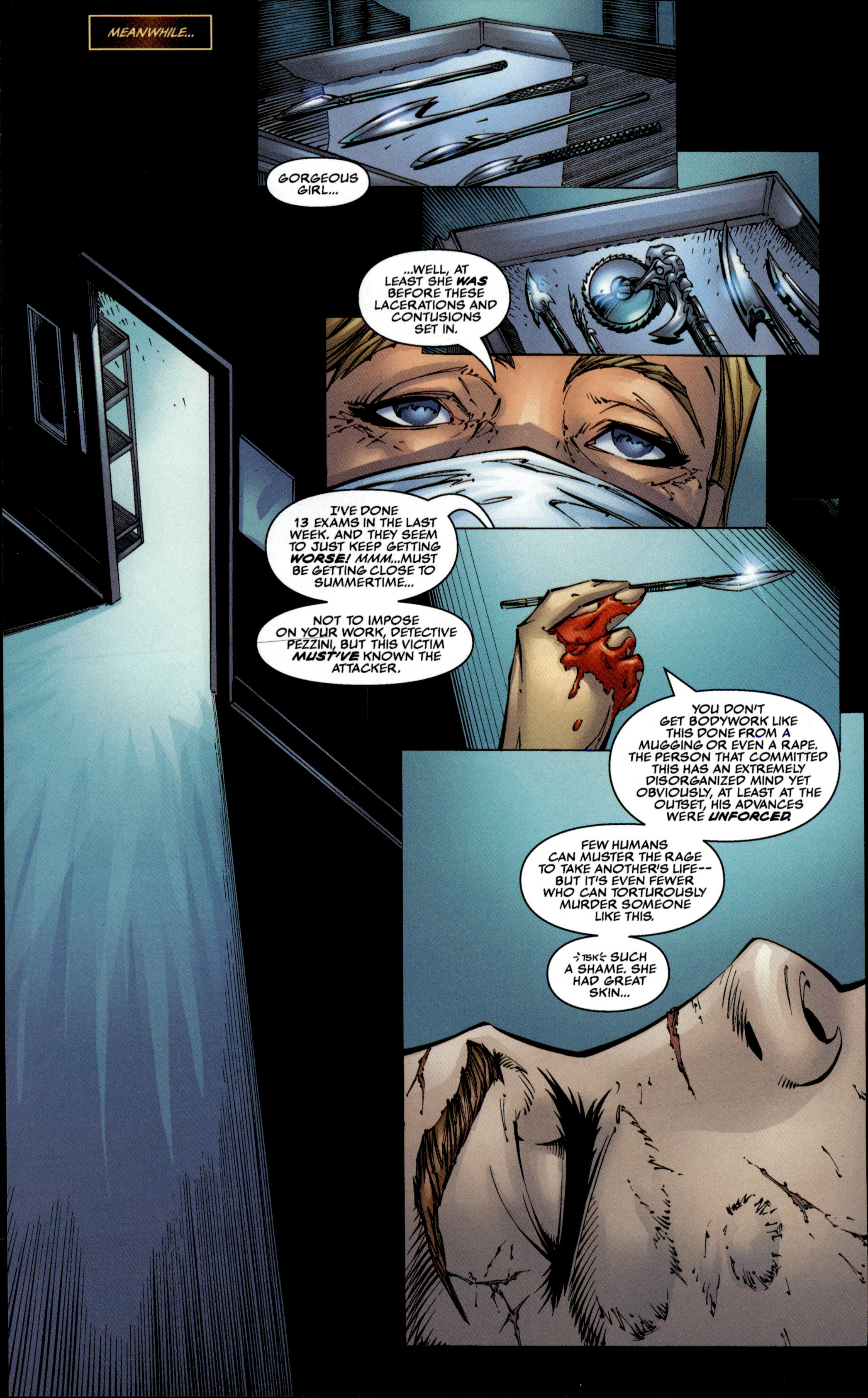
MEANWHILE...
GORGEOUS GIRL...
...WELL, AT LEAST SHE WAS BEFORE THESE LACERATIONS AND CONTUSIONS SET IN.
I'VE DONE 13 EXAMS IN THE LAST WEEK, AND THEY SEEM TO JUST KEEP GETTING WORSE! MMM...MUST BE GETTING CLOSE TO SUMMERTIME...
NOT TO IMPOSE ON YOUR WORK, DETECTIVE PEZZINI, BUT THIS VICTIM MUST'VE KNOWN THE ATTACKER.
YOU DON'T GET BODYWORK LIKE THIS DONE FROM A MUGGING OR EVEN A RAPE. THE PERSON THAT COMMITTED THIS HAS AN EXTREMELY DISORGANIZED MIND YET OBVIOUSLY, AT LEAST AT THE OUTSET, HIS ADVANCES WERE UNFORCED.
FEW HUMANS CAN MUSTER THE RAGE TO TAKE ANOTHER'S LIFE-- BUT IT'S EVEN FEWER WHO CAN TORTUROUSLY MURDER SOMEONE LIKE THIS.
TSK SUCH A SHAME. SHE HAD GREAT SKIN...

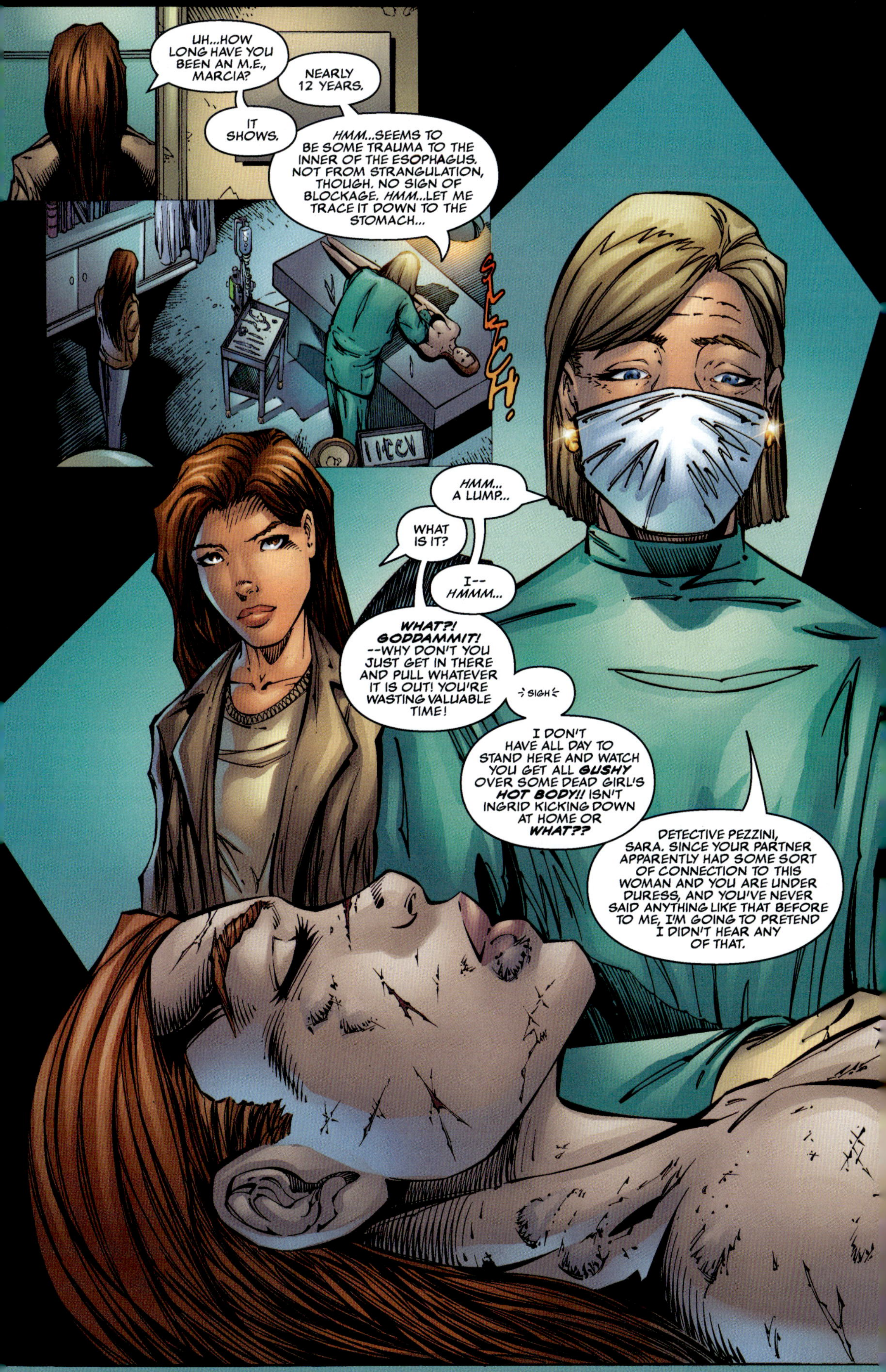
UH...HOW LONG HAVE YOU BEEN AN M.E., MARCIA?
NEARLY 12 YEARS.
IT SHOWS.
HMM...SEEMS TO BE SOME TRAUMA TO THE INNER OF THE ESOPHAGUS. NOT FROM STRANGULATION, THOUGH. NO SIGN OF BLOCKAGE. HMM...LET ME TRACE IT DOWN TO THE STOMACH...
SLLCCH!
HMM... A LUMP...
WHAT IS IT?
I-- HMMM...
WHAT?! GODDAMMIT! --WHY DON'T YOU JUST GET IN THERE AND PULL WHATEVER IT IS OUT! YOU'RE WASTING VALUABLE TIME!
SIGH
I DON'T HAVE ALL DAY TO STAND HERE AND WATCH YOU GET ALL GUSHY OVER SOME DEAD GIRL'S HOT BODY!! ISN'T INGRID KICKING DOWN AT HOME OR WHAT??
DETECTIVE PEZZINI, SARA. SINCE YOUR PARTNER APPARENTLY HAD SOME SORT OF CONNECTION TO THIS WOMAN AND YOU ARE UNDER DURESS, AND YOU'VE NEVER SAID ANYTHING LIKE THAT BEFORE TO ME, I'M GOING TO PRETEND I DIDN'T HEAR ANY OF THAT.

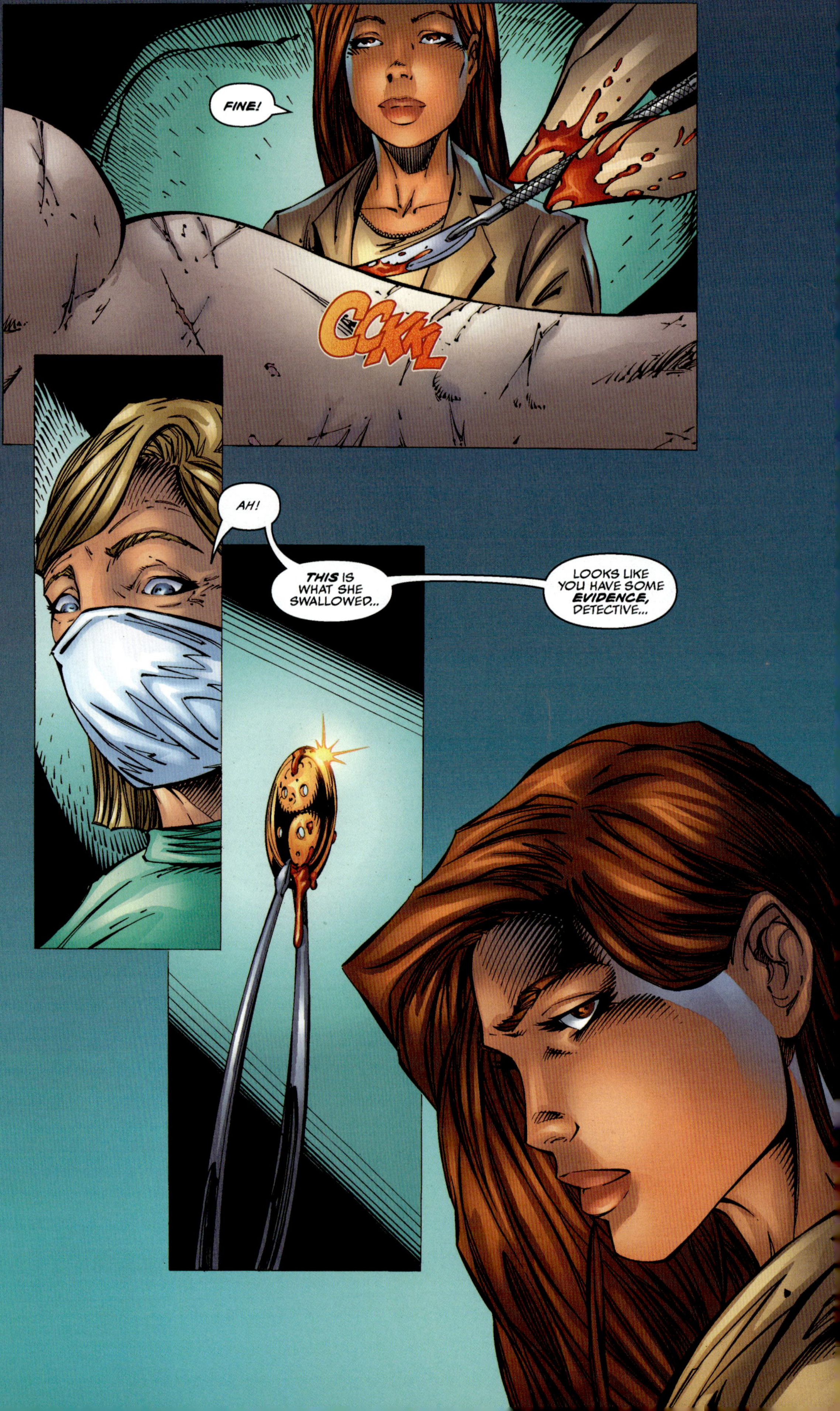
FINE!
CCKKL
AH!
THIS IS WHAT SHE SWALLOWED...
LOOKS LIKE YOU HAVE SOME EVIDENCE, DETECTIVE...

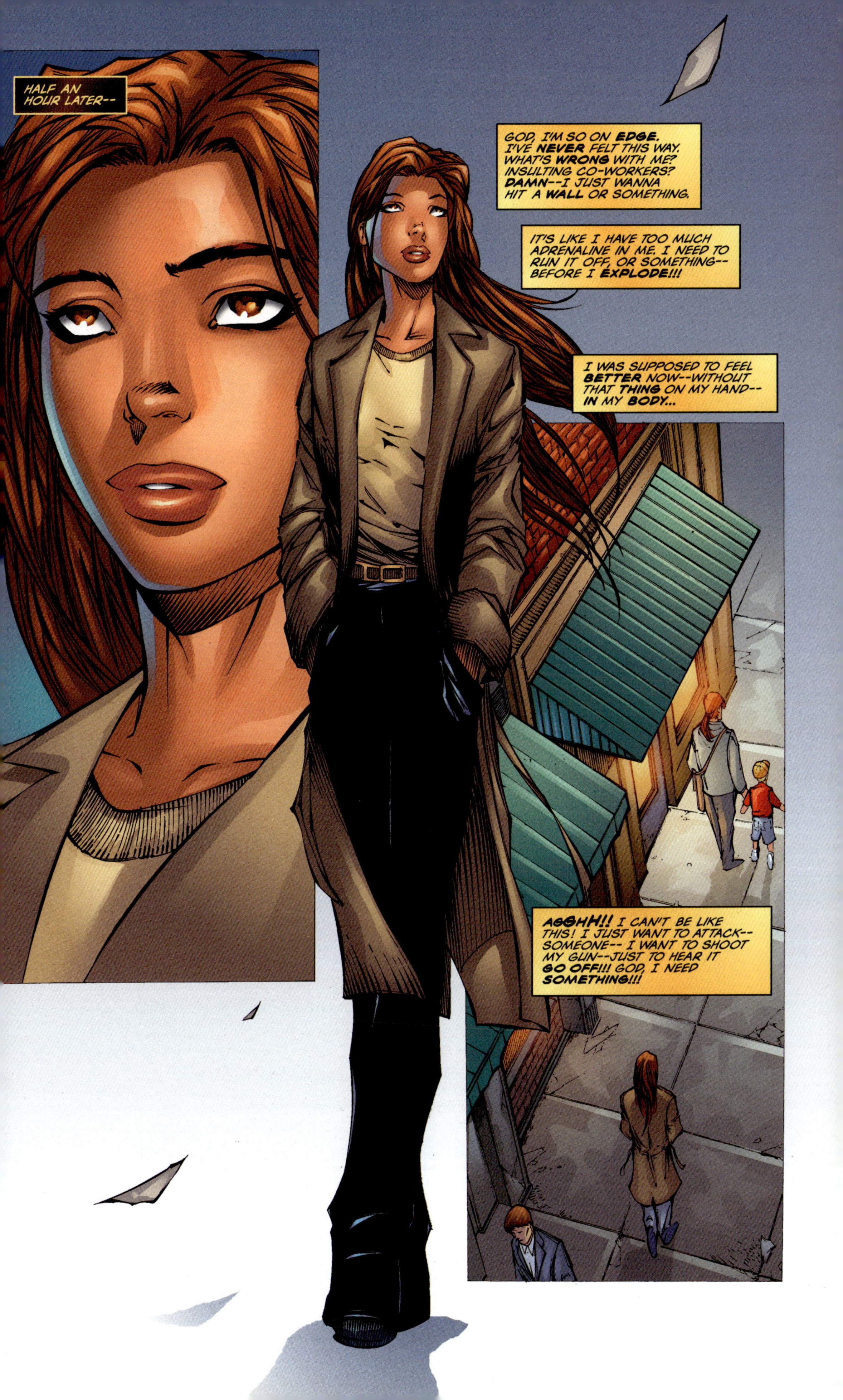
HALF AN HOUR LATER--
GOD, I'M SO ON EDGE. I'VE NEVER FELT THIS WAY. WHAT'S WRONG WITH ME? INSULTING CO-WORKERS? DAMN--I JUST WANNA HIT A WALL OR SOMETHING.
IT'S LIKE I HAVE TOO MUCH ADRENALINE IN ME. I NEED TO RUN IT OFF, OR SOMETHING--BEFORE I EXPLODE!!!
I WAS SUPPOSED TO FEEL BETTER NOW--WITHOUT THAT THING ON MY HAND--IN MY BODY...
AGGHH!! I CAN'T BE LIKE THIS! I JUST WANT TO ATTACK--SOMEONE-- I WANT TO SHOOT MY GUN--JUST TO HEAR IT GO OFF!!! GOD, I NEED SOMETHING!!!

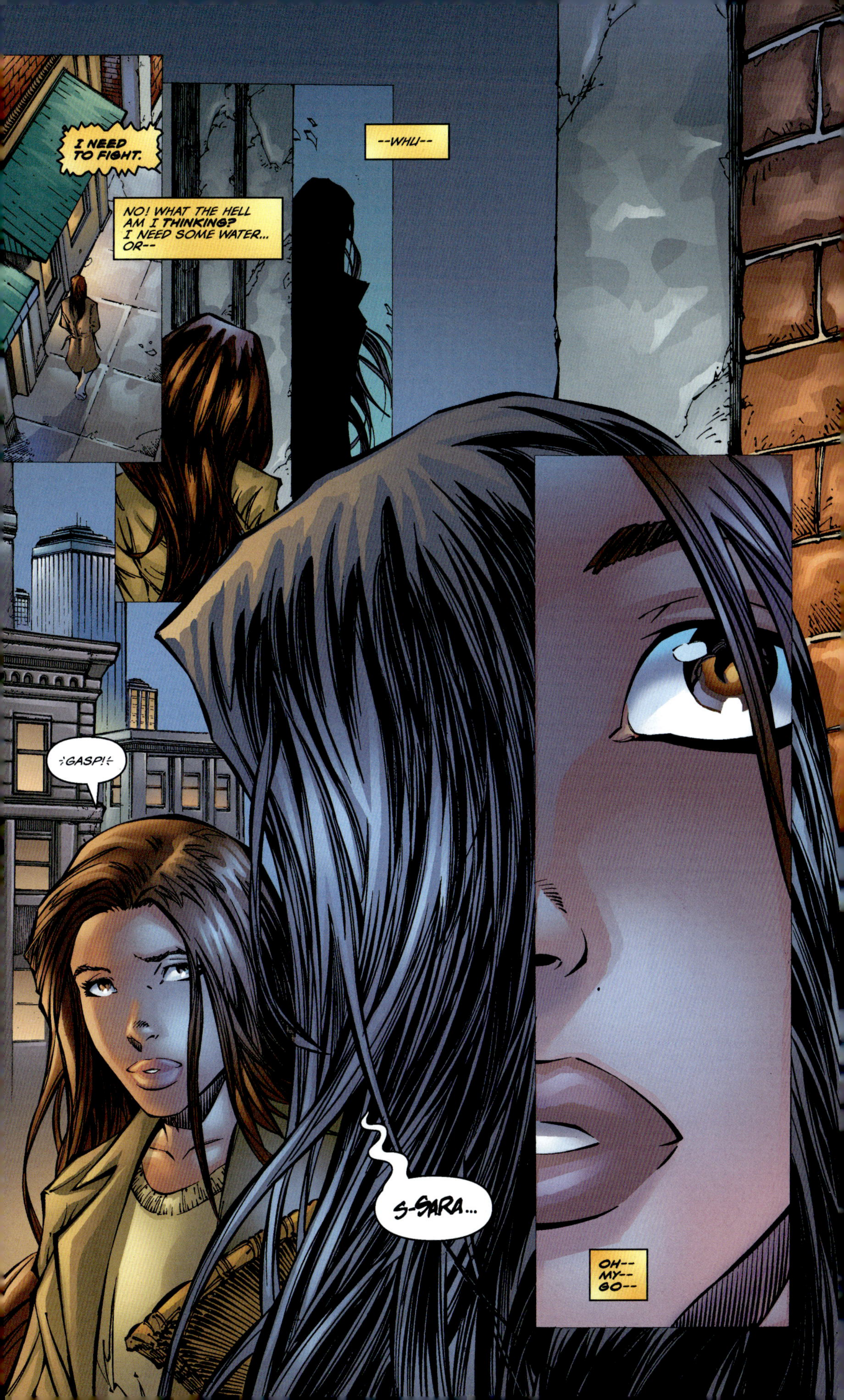
I NEED TO FIGHT.
NO! WHAT THE HELL AM I THINKING? I NEED SOME WATER... OR--
--WHU--
GASP!
S-SARA...
OH-- MY-- GO--

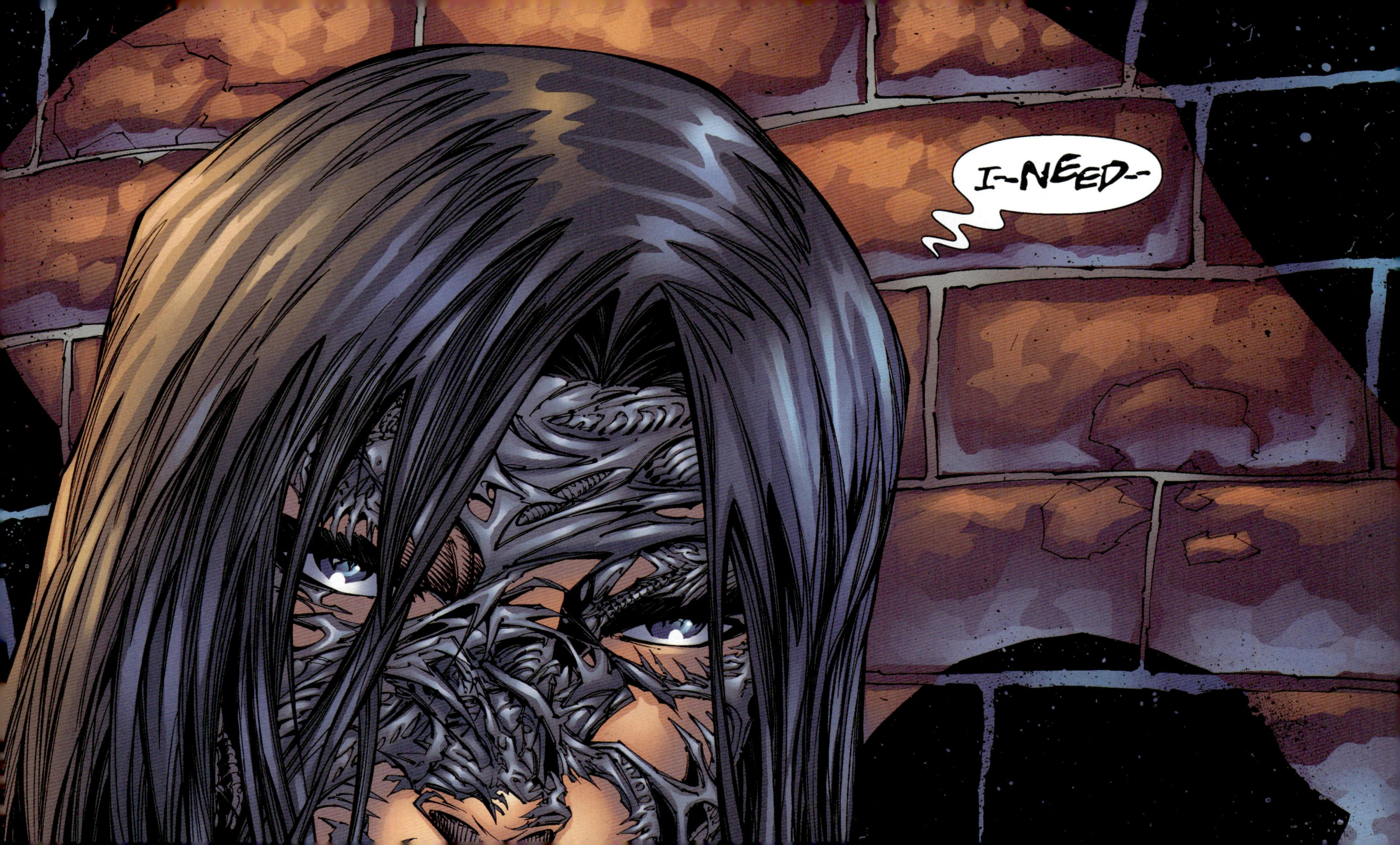
I--NEED--

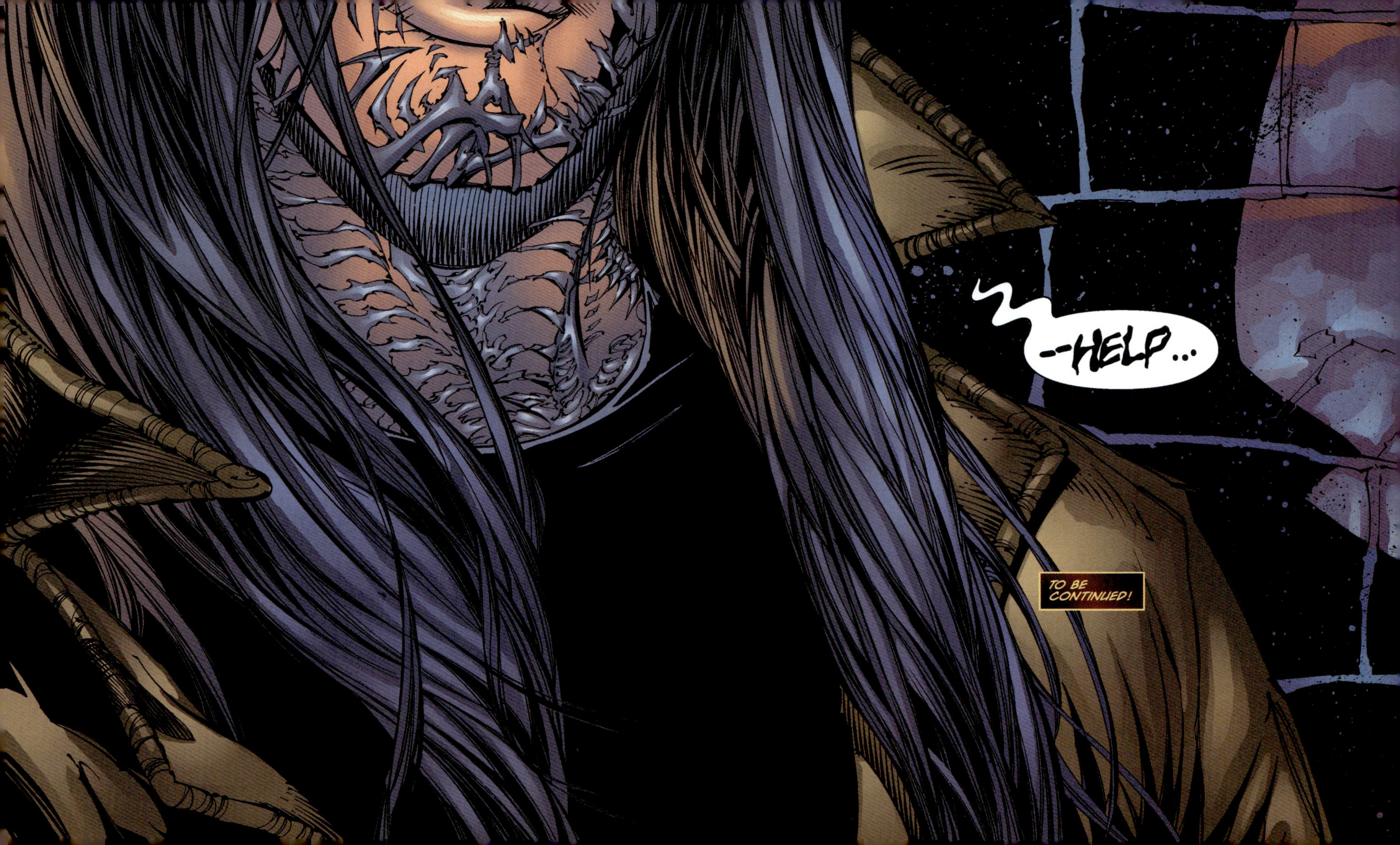
--HELP...
TO BE CONTINUED!

issue #23

story: **David Wohl** and **Christina Z.**
pencils: **Randy Green** pages 7-11, 21 and 22
layouts: **Michael Turner** pages 1-6 and 12-20
pencil finishes: **Dan Fraga** and **Clarence Lansang**
inks: **D-Tron**
colors: **JD Smith**

ink assists: **Andy Kim, Marsha Chen, Jose "Jag" Guillen**
and **Jeff De Los Santos**

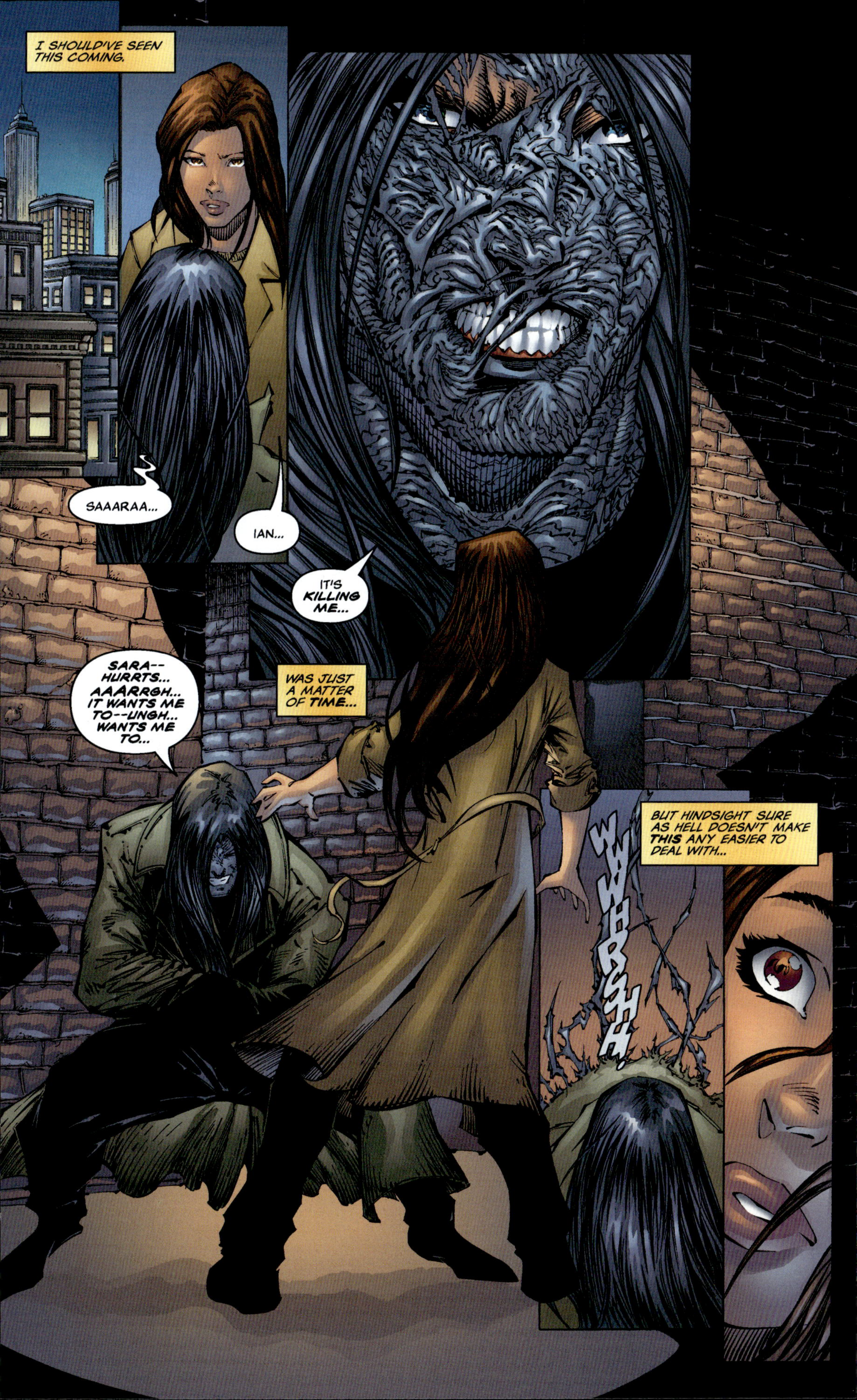
I SHOULD'VE SEEN THIS COMING.
SAAARAA...
IAN...
IT'S KILLING ME...
SARA-- HURRTS... AAARRGH... IT WANTS ME TO--UNGH... WANTS ME TO...
WAS JUST A MATTER OF TIME...
BUT HINDSIGHT SURE AS HELL DOESN'T MAKE THIS ANY EASIER TO DEAL WITH...
WWHRSHH!

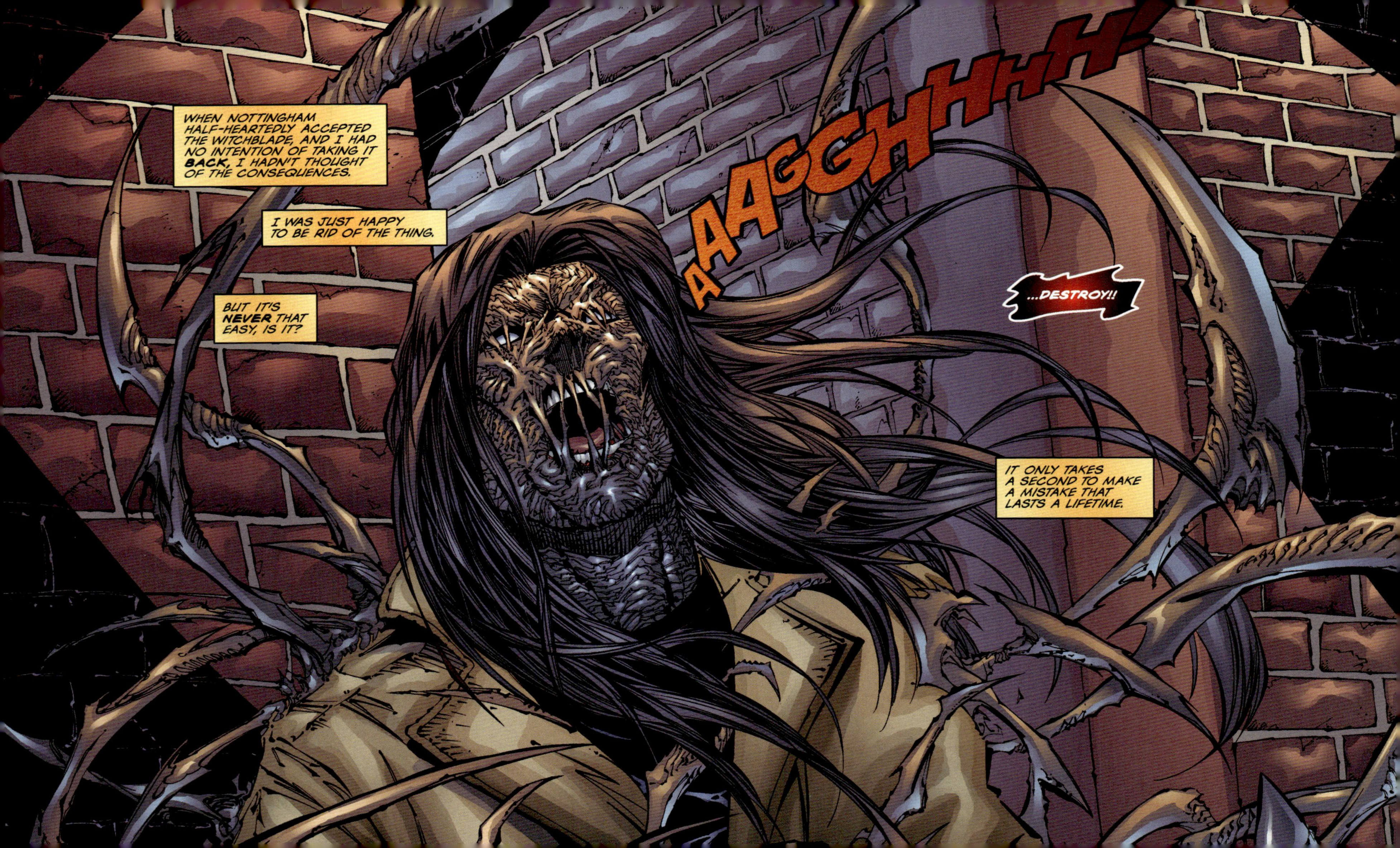
WHEN NOTTINGHAM HALF-HEARTEDLY ACCEPTED THE WITCHBLADE, AND I HAD NO INTENTION OF TAKING IT **BACK**, I HADN'T THOUGHT OF THE CONSEQUENCES.
I WAS JUST HAPPY TO BE RID OF THE THING.
BUT IT'S **NEVER** THAT EASY, IS IT?
AAAGGHHHHH!
...DESTROY!!
IT ONLY TAKES A SECOND TO MAKE A MISTAKE THAT LASTS A LIFETIME.

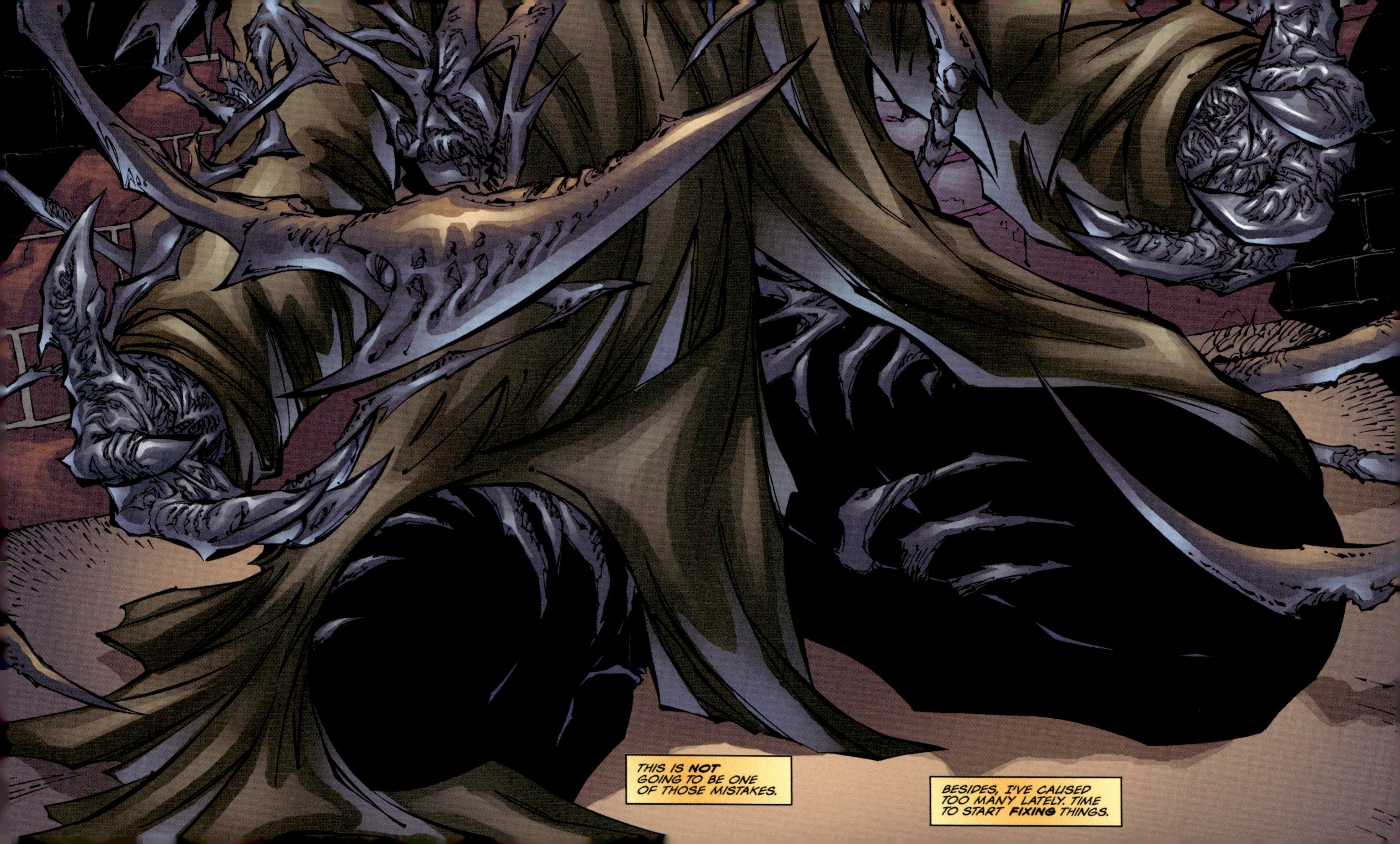
THIS IS **NOT** GOING TO BE ONE OF THOSE MISTAKES.
BESIDES, I'VE CAUSED TOO MANY LATELY. TIME TO START **FIXING** THINGS.

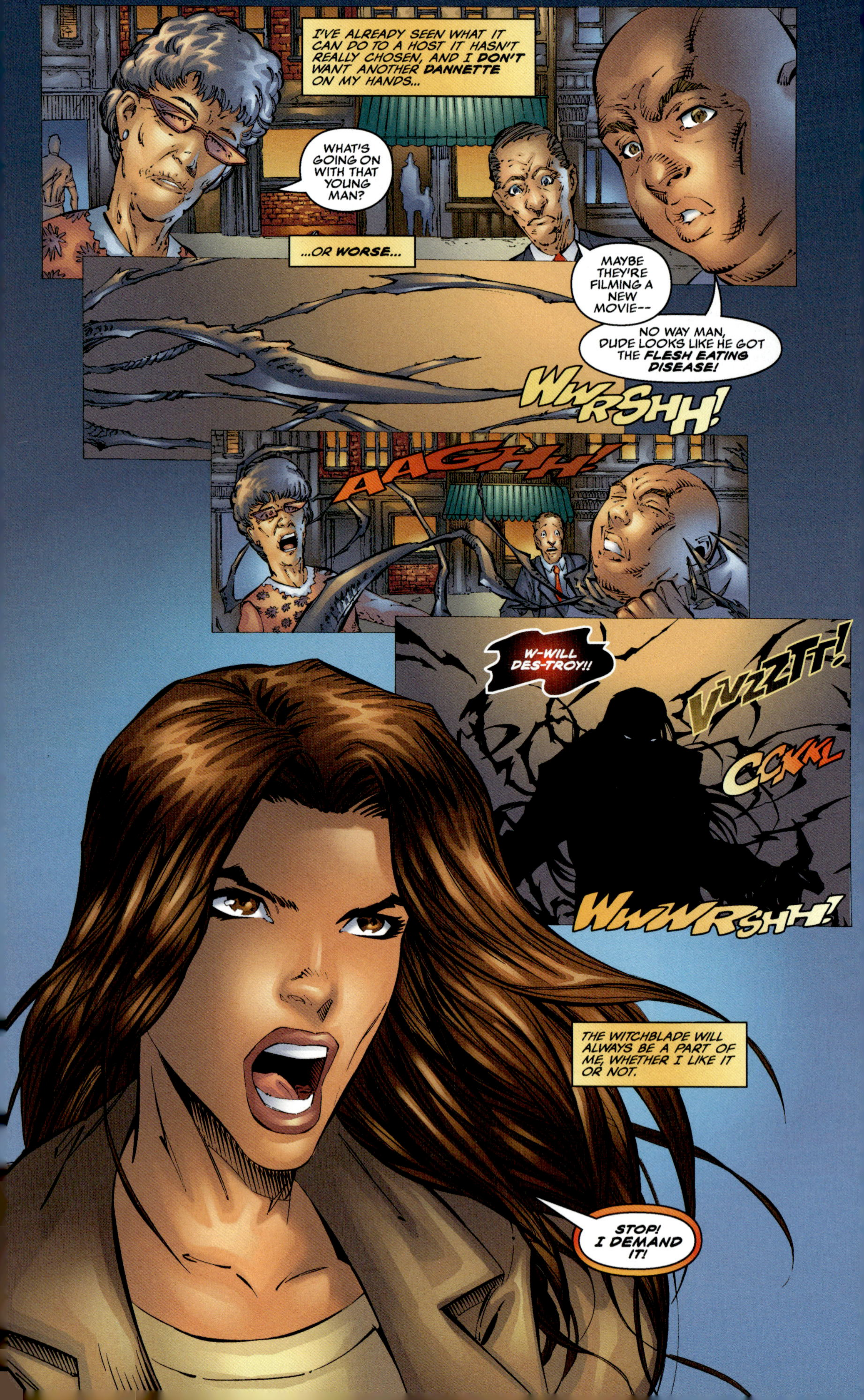

I'VE ALREADY SEEN WHAT IT CAN DO TO A HOST IT HASN'T REALLY CHOSEN, AND I DON'T WANT ANOTHER DANNETTE ON MY HANDS...
WHAT'S GOING ON WITH THAT YOUNG MAN?
...OR WORSE...
MAYBE THEY'RE FILMING A NEW MOVIE--
NO WAY MAN, DUDE LOOKS LIKE HE GOT THE FLESH EATING DISEASE!
WWRSHH!
AACHH!
W-WILL DES-TROY!!
VVZZTT!
CCKKL
WWWRSHH!
THE WITCHBLADE WILL ALWAYS BE A PART OF ME, WHETHER I LIKE IT OR NOT.
STOP! I DEMAND IT!

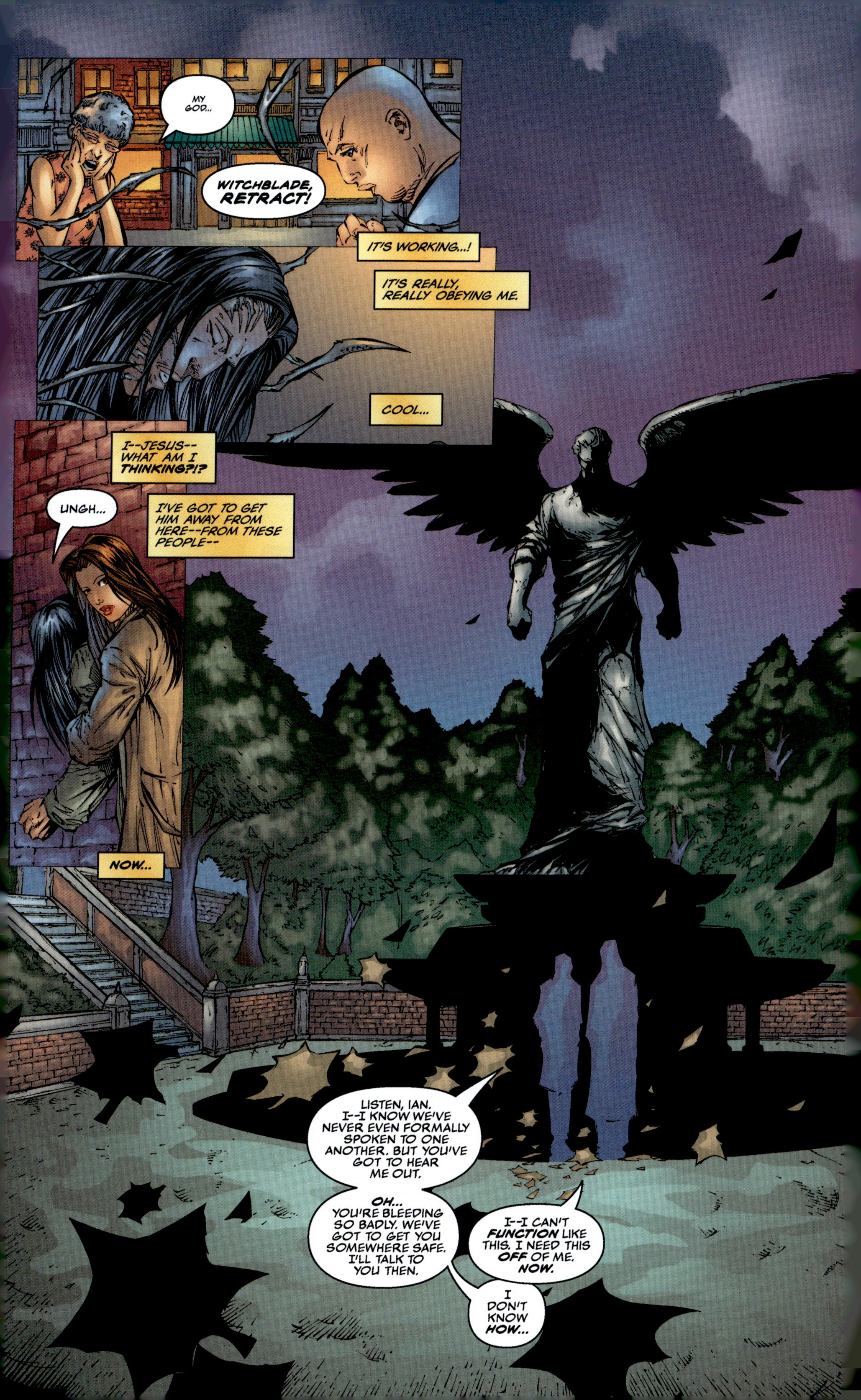

MY GOD...
WITCHBLADE, RETRACT!
IT'S WORKING...!
IT'S REALLY, REALLY OBEYING ME.
COOL...
I--JESUS-- WHAT AM I THINKING?!?
UNGH...
I'VE GOT TO GET HIM AWAY FROM HERE--FROM THESE PEOPLE--
NOW...
LISTEN, IAN. I--I KNOW WE'VE NEVER EVEN FORMALLY SPOKEN TO ONE ANOTHER. BUT YOU'VE GOT TO HEAR ME OUT.
OH... YOU'RE BLEEDING SO BADLY. WE'VE GOT TO GET YOU SOMEWHERE SAFE. I'LL TALK TO YOU THEN.
I--I CAN'T FUNCTION LIKE THIS. I NEED THIS OFF OF ME. NOW.
I DON'T KNOW HOW...

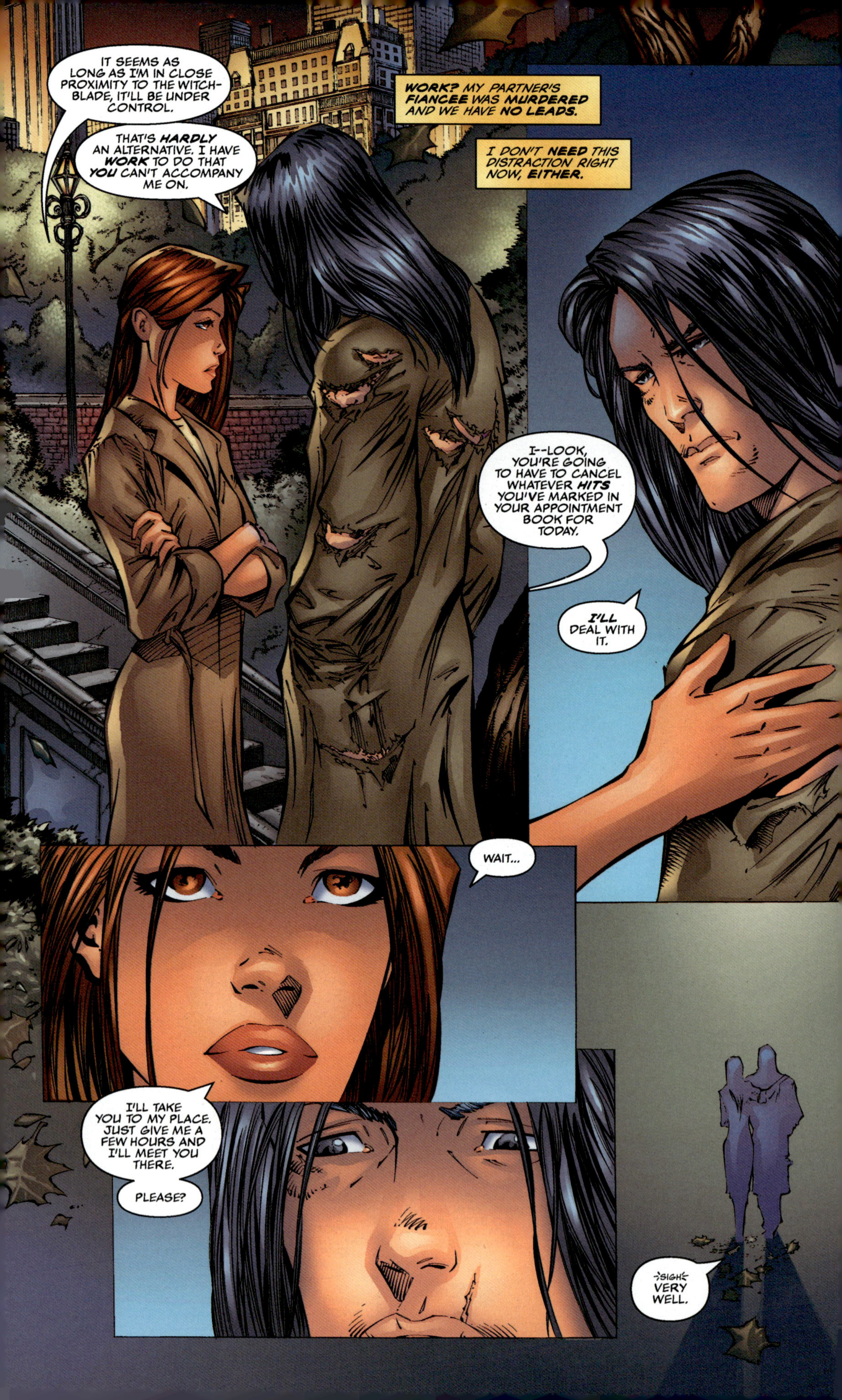
IT SEEMS AS LONG AS I'M IN CLOSE PROXIMITY TO THE WITCH-BLADE, IT'LL BE UNDER CONTROL.
THAT'S HARDLY AN ALTERNATIVE. I HAVE WORK TO DO THAT YOU CAN'T ACCOMPANY ME ON.
WORK? MY PARTNER'S FIANCEE WAS MURDERED AND WE HAVE NO LEADS.
I DON'T NEED THIS DISTRACTION RIGHT NOW, EITHER.
I--LOOK, YOU'RE GOING TO HAVE TO CANCEL WHATEVER HITS YOU'VE MARKED IN YOUR APPOINTMENT BOOK FOR TODAY.
I'LL DEAL WITH IT.
WAIT...
I'LL TAKE YOU TO MY PLACE. JUST GIVE ME A FEW HOURS AND I'LL MEET YOU THERE.
PLEASE?
SIGH
VERY WELL.

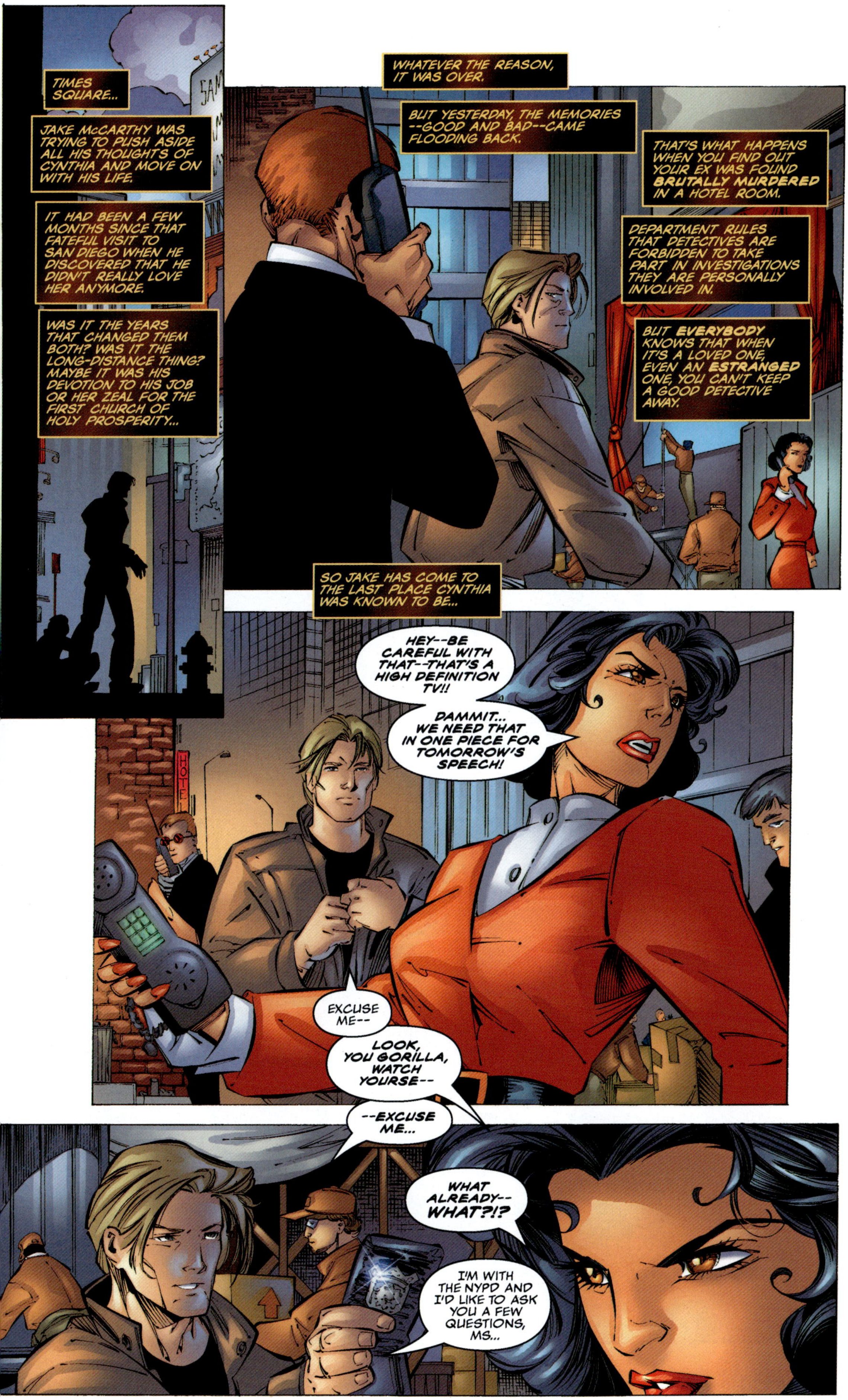
TIMES SQUARE...
JAKE McCARTHY WAS TRYING TO PUSH ASIDE ALL HIS THOUGHTS OF CYNTHIA AND MOVE ON WITH HIS LIFE.
IT HAD BEEN A FEW MONTHS SINCE THAT FATEFUL VISIT TO SAN DIEGO WHEN HE DISCOVERED THAT HE DIDN'T REALLY LOVE HER ANYMORE.
WAS IT THE YEARS THAT CHANGED THEM BOTH? WAS IT THE LONG-DISTANCE THING? MAYBE IT WAS HIS DEVOTION TO HIS JOB OR HER ZEAL FOR THE FIRST CHURCH OF HOLY PROSPERITY...
WHATEVER THE REASON, IT WAS OVER.
BUT YESTERDAY, THE MEMORIES --GOOD AND BAD--CAME FLOODING BACK.
THAT'S WHAT HAPPENS WHEN YOU FIND OUT YOUR EX WAS FOUND BRUTALLY MURDERED IN A HOTEL ROOM.
DEPARTMENT RULES THAT DETECTIVES ARE FORBIDDEN TO TAKE PART IN INVESTIGATIONS THEY ARE PERSONALLY INVOLVED IN.
BUT EVERYBODY KNOWS THAT WHEN IT'S A LOVED ONE, EVEN AN ESTRANGED ONE, YOU CAN'T KEEP A GOOD DETECTIVE AWAY.
SO JAKE HAS COME TO THE LAST PLACE CYNTHIA WAS KNOWN TO BE...
HEY--BE CAREFUL WITH THAT--THAT'S A HIGH DEFINITION TV!!
DAMMIT... WE NEED THAT IN ONE PIECE FOR TOMORROW'S SPEECH!
EXCUSE ME--
LOOK, YOU GORILLA, WATCH YOURSE--
--EXCUSE ME...
WHAT ALREADY--WHAT?!?
I'M WITH THE NYPD AND I'D LIKE TO ASK YOU A FEW QUESTIONS, MS...

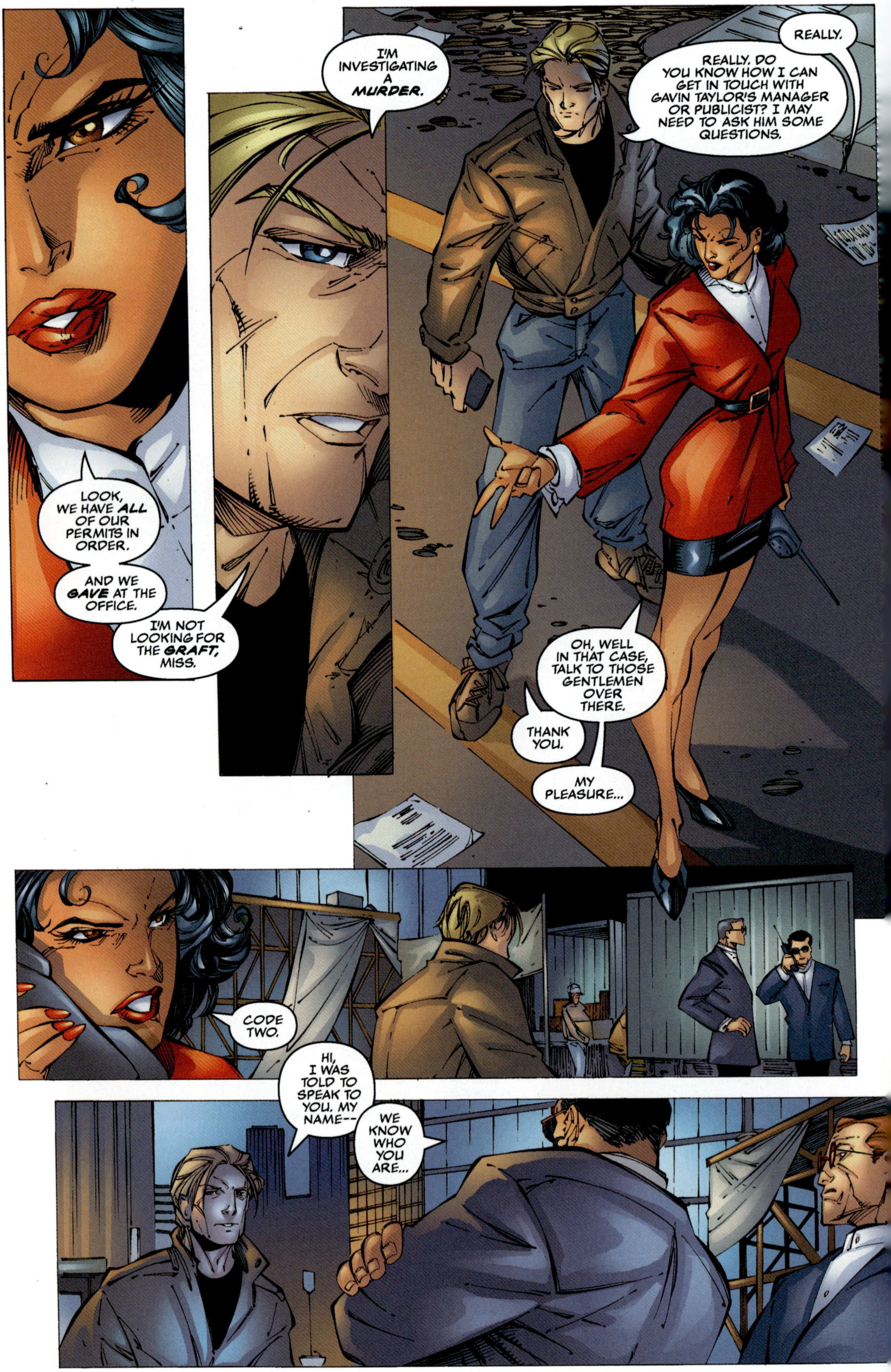

I'M INVESTIGATING A MURDER.
REALLY.
REALLY. DO YOU KNOW HOW I CAN GET IN TOUCH WITH GAVIN TAYLOR'S MANAGER OR PUBLICIST? I MAY NEED TO ASK HIM SOME QUESTIONS.
LOOK, WE HAVE ALL OF OUR PERMITS IN ORDER.
AND WE GAVE AT THE OFFICE.
I'M NOT LOOKING FOR THE GRAFT, MISS.
OH, WELL IN THAT CASE, TALK TO THOSE GENTLEMEN OVER THERE.
THANK YOU.
MY PLEASURE...
CODE TWO.
HI, I WAS TOLD TO SPEAK TO YOU. MY NAME--
WE KNOW WHO YOU ARE...

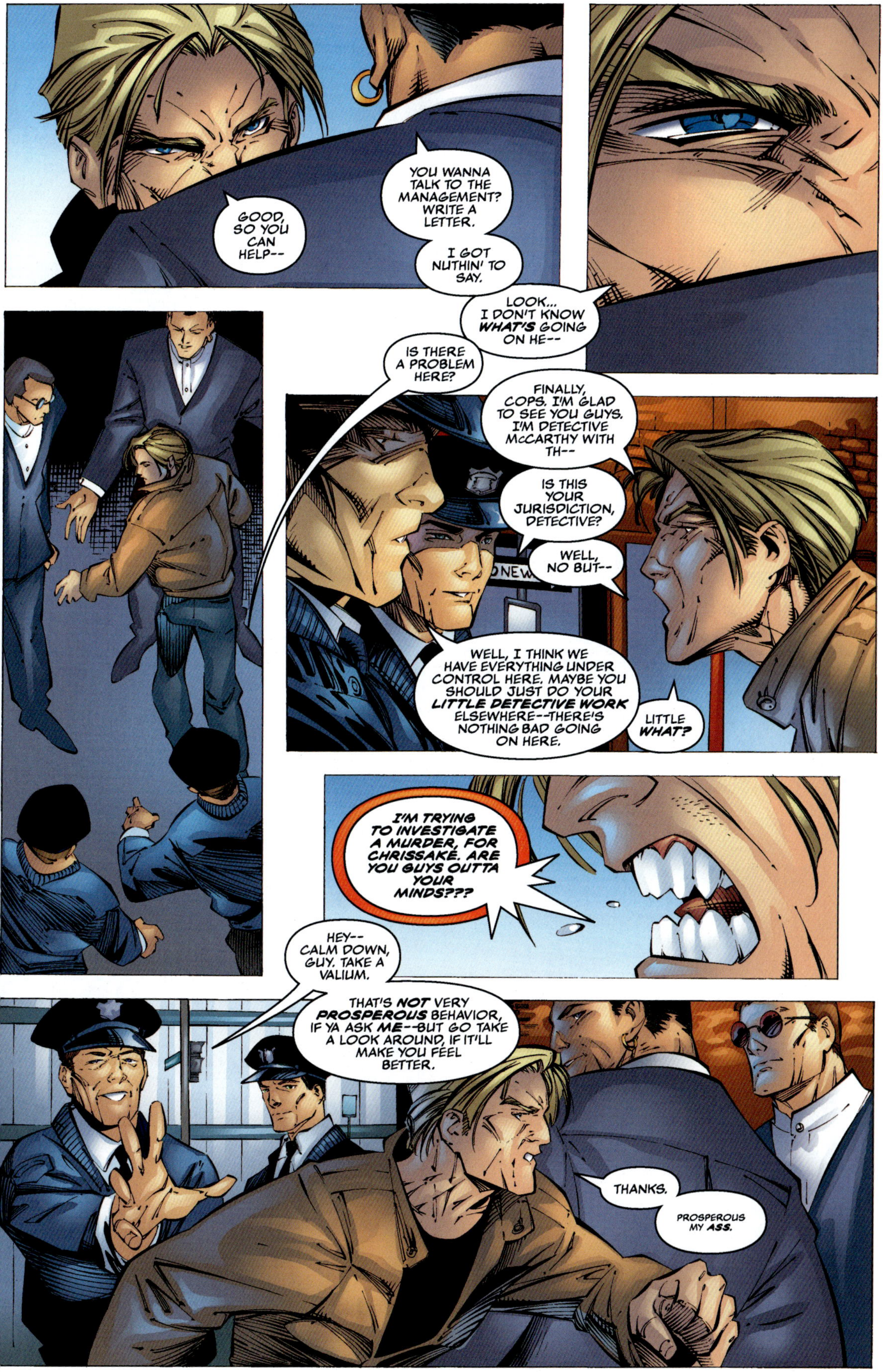
YOU WANNA TALK TO THE MANAGEMENT? WRITE A LETTER.
GOOD, SO YOU CAN HELP--
I GOT NUTHIN' TO SAY.
LOOK... I DON'T KNOW WHAT'S GOING ON HE--
IS THERE A PROBLEM HERE?
FINALLY, COPS. I'M GLAD TO SEE YOU GUYS. I'M DETECTIVE McCARTHY WITH TH--
IS THIS YOUR JURISDICTION, DETECTIVE?
WELL, NO BUT--
WELL, I THINK WE HAVE EVERYTHING UNDER CONTROL HERE. MAYBE YOU SHOULD JUST DO YOUR LITTLE DETECTIVE WORK ELSEWHERE--THERE'S NOTHING BAD GOING ON HERE.
LITTLE WHAT?
I'M TRYING TO INVESTIGATE A MURDER, FOR CHRISSAKE. ARE YOU GUYS OUTTA YOUR MINDS???
HEY-- CALM DOWN, GUY. TAKE A VALIUM.
THAT'S NOT VERY PROSPEROUS BEHAVIOR, IF YA ASK ME--BUT GO TAKE A LOOK AROUND, IF IT'LL MAKE YOU FEEL BETTER.
THANKS.
PROSPEROUS MY ASS.

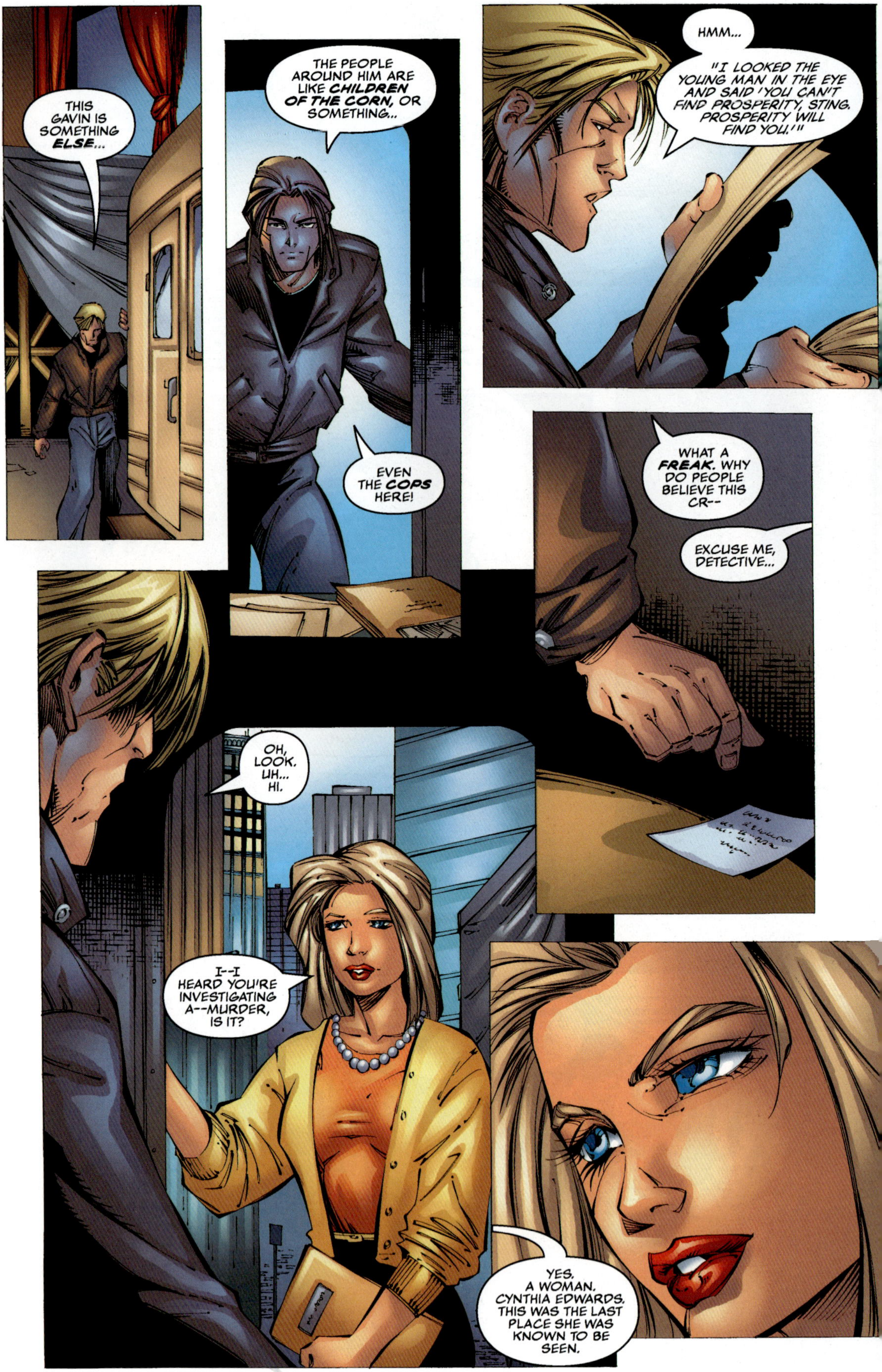
THIS GAVIN IS SOMETHING ELSE...
THE PEOPLE AROUND HIM ARE LIKE CHILDREN OF THE CORN, OR SOMETHING...
EVEN THE COPS HERE!
HMM...
"I LOOKED THE YOUNG MAN IN THE EYE AND SAID 'YOU CAN'T FIND PROSPERITY, STING. PROSPERITY WILL FIND YOU.'"
WHAT A FREAK. WHY DO PEOPLE BELIEVE THIS CR--
EXCUSE ME, DETECTIVE...
OH, LOOK. UH... HI.
I--I HEARD YOU'RE INVESTIGATING A--MURDER, IS IT?
YES. A WOMAN. CYNTHIA EDWARDS. THIS WAS THE LAST PLACE SHE WAS KNOWN TO BE SEEN.

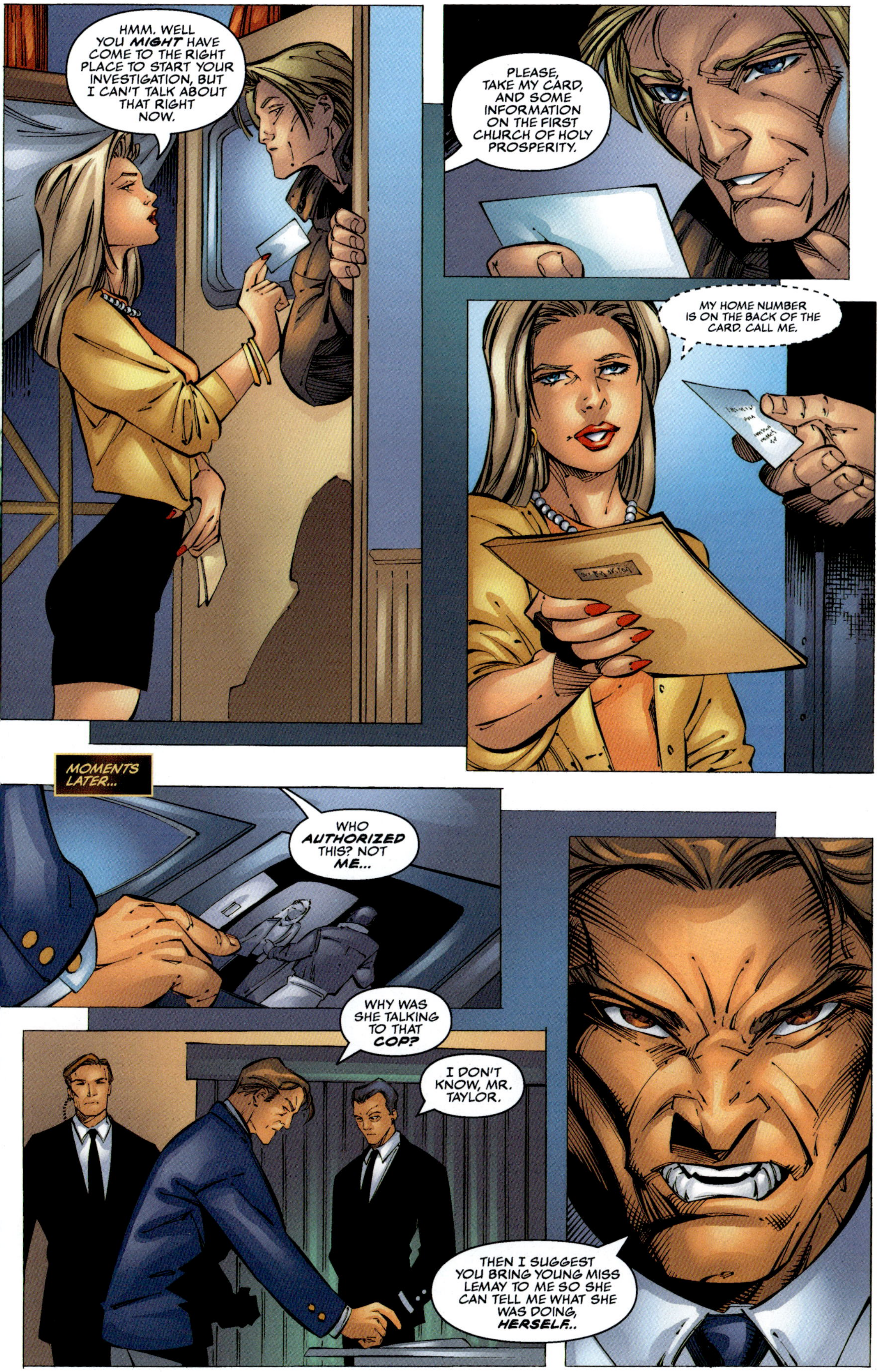
HMM. WELL YOU MIGHT HAVE COME TO THE RIGHT PLACE TO START YOUR INVESTIGATION, BUT I CAN'T TALK ABOUT THAT RIGHT NOW.
PLEASE, TAKE MY CARD, AND SOME INFORMATION ON THE FIRST CHURCH OF HOLY PROSPERITY.
MY HOME NUMBER IS ON THE BACK OF THE CARD. CALL ME.
MOMENTS LATER...
WHO AUTHORIZED THIS? NOT ME...
WHY WAS SHE TALKING TO THAT COP?
I DON'T KNOW, MR. TAYLOR.
THEN I SUGGEST YOU BRING YOUNG MISS LEMAY TO ME SO SHE CAN TELL ME WHAT SHE WAS DOING, HERSELF..

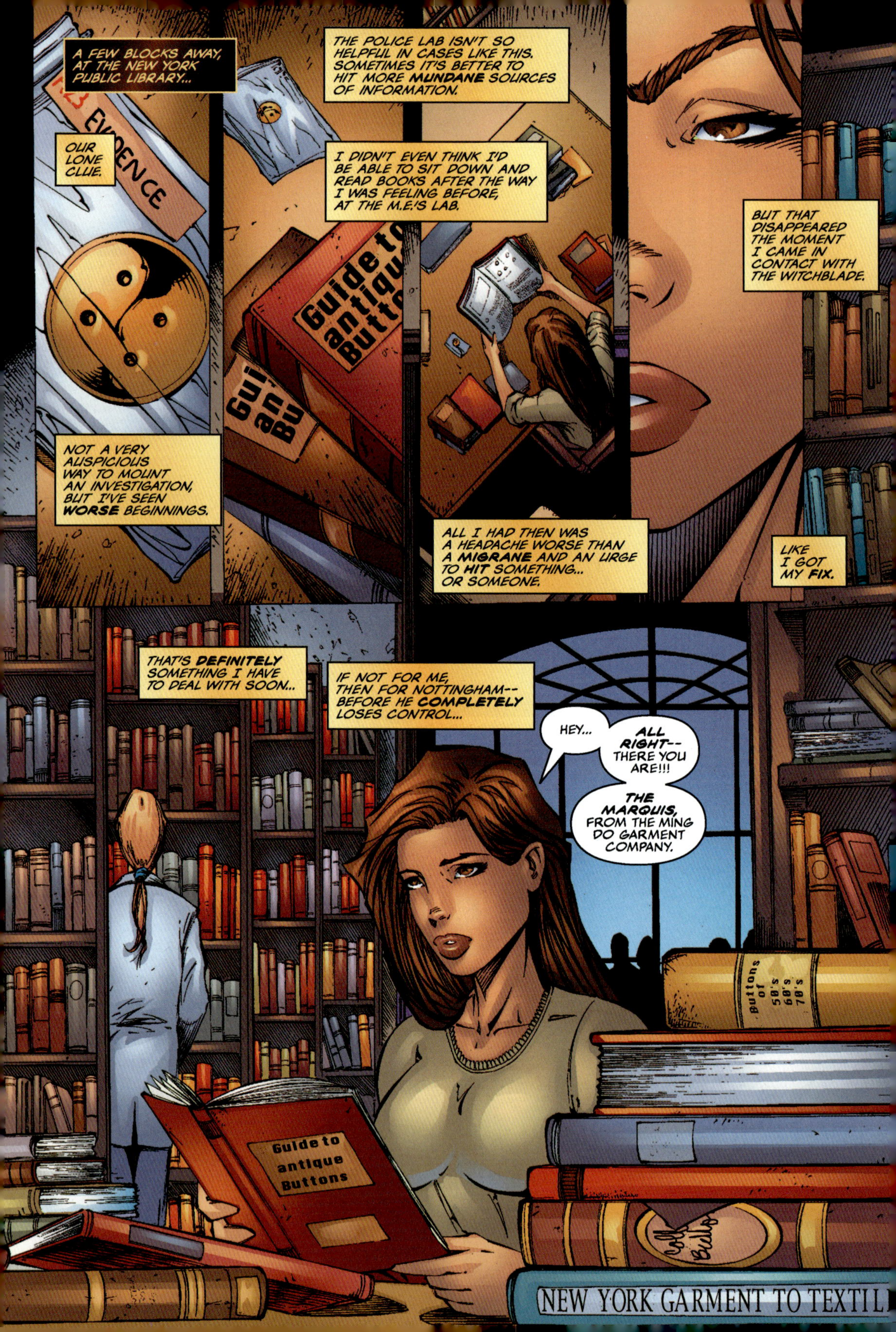

A FEW BLOCKS AWAY, AT THE NEW YORK PUBLIC LIBRARY...
EVIDENCE
OUR LONE CLUE.
NOT A VERY AUSPICIOUS WAY TO MOUNT AN INVESTIGATION, BUT I'VE SEEN WORSE BEGINNINGS.
THE POLICE LAB ISN'T SO HELPFUL IN CASES LIKE THIS. SOMETIMES IT'S BETTER TO HIT MORE MUNDANE SOURCES OF INFORMATION.
I DIDN'T EVEN THINK I'D BE ABLE TO SIT DOWN AND READ BOOKS AFTER THE WAY I WAS FEELING BEFORE, AT THE M.E.'S LAB.
ALL I HAD THEN WAS A HEADACHE WORSE THAN A MIGRANE AND AN URGE TO HIT SOMETHING... OR SOMEONE.
BUT THAT DISAPPEARED THE MOMENT I CAME IN CONTACT WITH THE WITCHBLADE.
LIKE I GOT MY FIX.
THAT'S DEFINITELY SOMETHING I HAVE TO DEAL WITH SOON...
IF NOT FOR ME, THEN FOR NOTTINGHAM-- BEFORE HE COMPLETELY LOSES CONTROL...
HEY...
ALL RIGHT-- THERE YOU ARE!!!
THE MARQUIS, FROM THE MING DO GARMENT COMPANY.
Guide to antique Buttons
Buttons of 50's 60's 70's
NEW YORK GARMENT TO TEXTIL

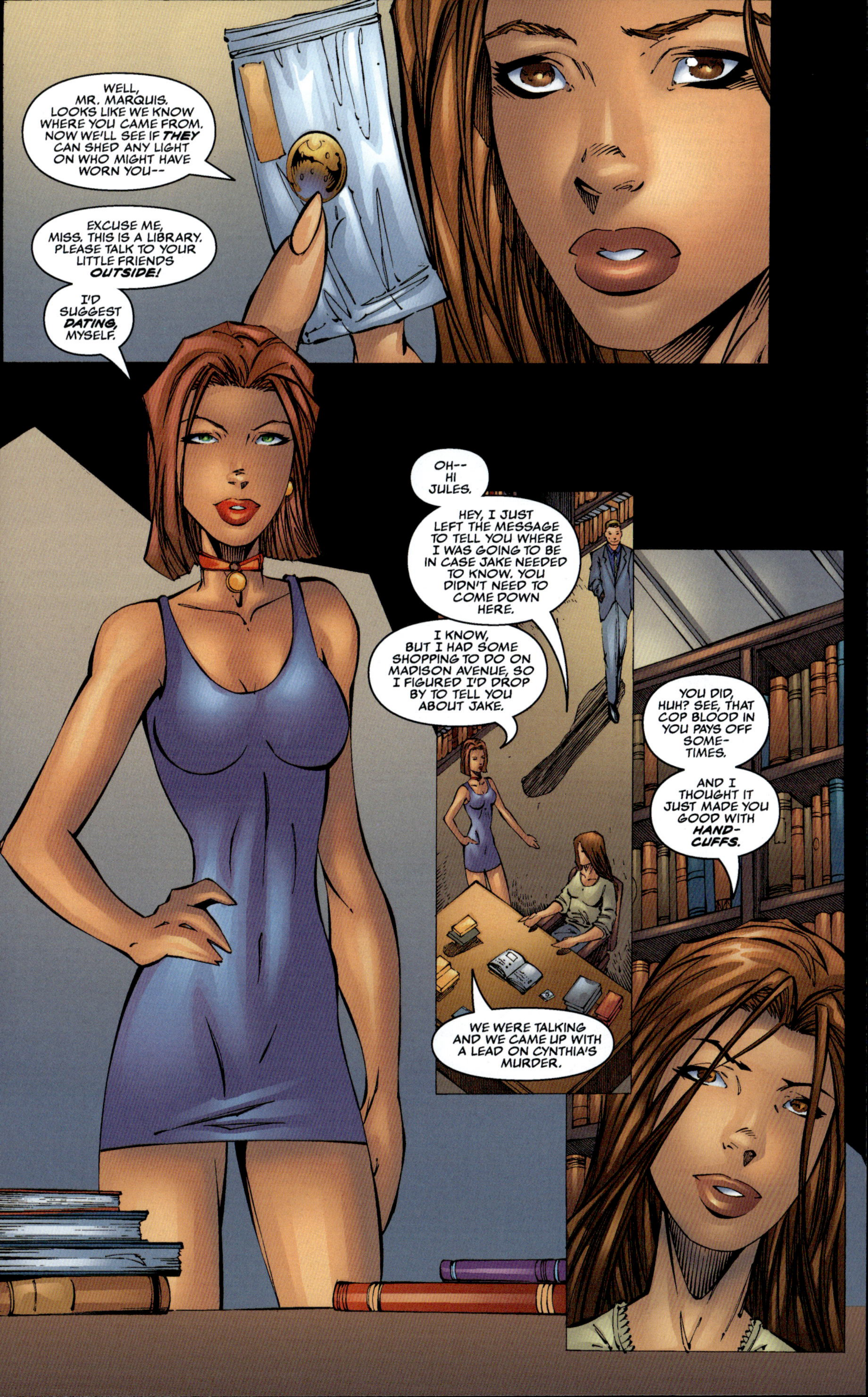
WELL, MR. MARQUIS. LOOKS LIKE WE KNOW WHERE YOU CAME FROM. NOW WE'LL SEE IF THEY CAN SHED ANY LIGHT ON WHO MIGHT HAVE WORN YOU--
EXCUSE ME, MISS. THIS IS A LIBRARY. PLEASE TALK TO YOUR LITTLE FRIENDS OUTSIDE!
I'D SUGGEST DATING, MYSELF.
OH-- HI JULES.
HEY, I JUST LEFT THE MESSAGE TO TELL YOU WHERE I WAS GOING TO BE IN CASE JAKE NEEDED TO KNOW. YOU DIDN'T NEED TO COME DOWN HERE.
I KNOW, BUT I HAD SOME SHOPPING TO DO ON MADISON AVENUE, SO I FIGURED I'D DROP BY TO TELL YOU ABOUT JAKE.
WE WERE TALKING AND WE CAME UP WITH A LEAD ON CYNTHIA'S MURDER.
YOU DID, HUH? SEE, THAT COP BLOOD IN YOU PAYS OFF SOME-TIMES.
AND I THOUGHT IT JUST MADE YOU GOOD WITH HAND-CUFFS.

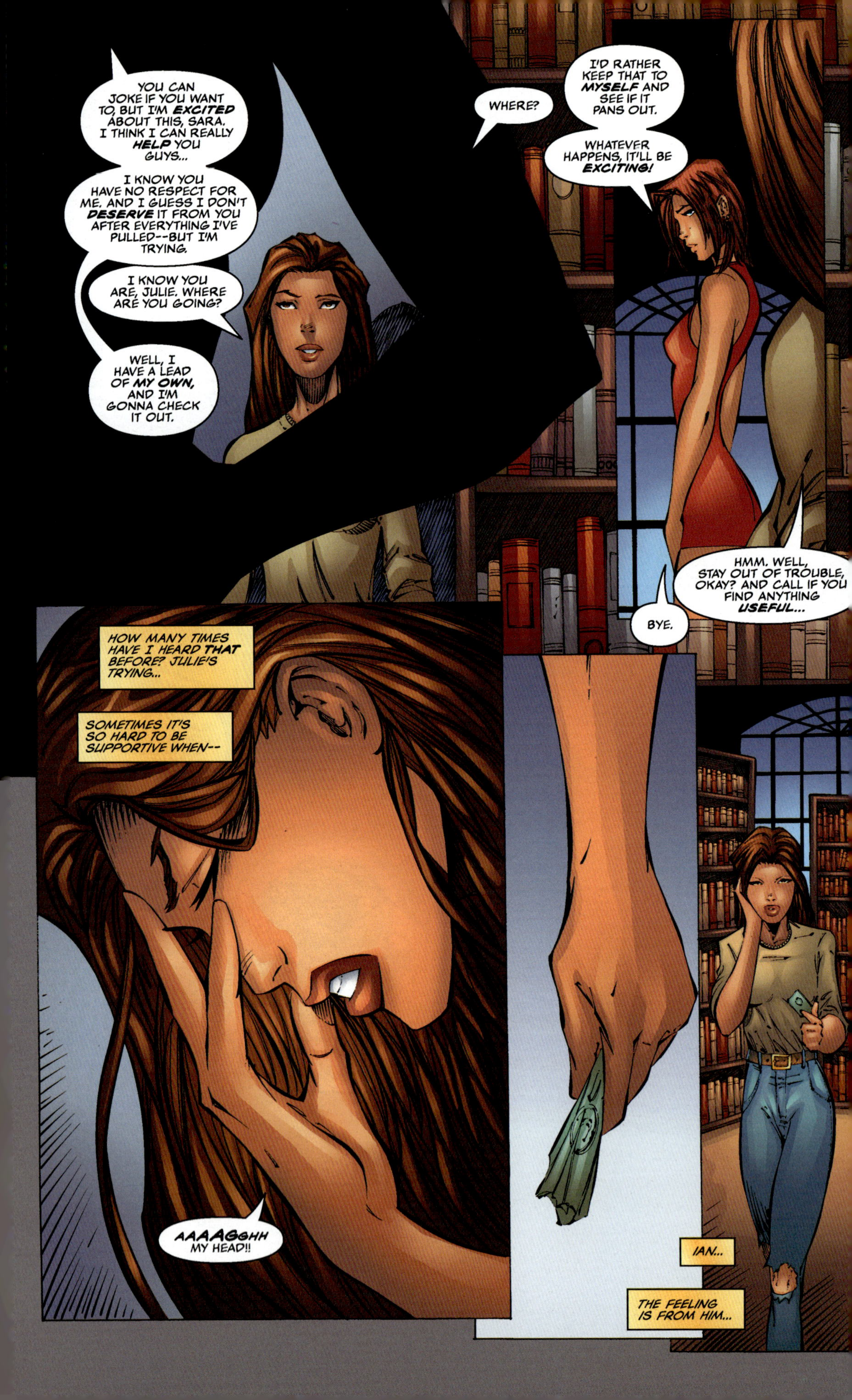
YOU CAN JOKE IF YOU WANT TO, BUT I'M EXCITED ABOUT THIS, SARA. I THINK I CAN REALLY HELP YOU GUYS...
I KNOW YOU HAVE NO RESPECT FOR ME. AND I GUESS I DON'T DESERVE IT FROM YOU AFTER EVERYTHING I'VE PULLED--BUT I'M TRYING.
I KNOW YOU ARE, JULIE. WHERE ARE YOU GOING?
WELL, I HAVE A LEAD OF MY OWN, AND I'M GONNA CHECK IT OUT.
WHERE?
I'D RATHER KEEP THAT TO MYSELF AND SEE IF IT PANS OUT.
WHATEVER HAPPENS, IT'LL BE EXCITING!
HMM. WELL, STAY OUT OF TROUBLE, OKAY? AND CALL IF YOU FIND ANYTHING USEFUL...
BYE.
HOW MANY TIMES HAVE I HEARD THAT BEFORE? JULIE'S TRYING...
SOMETIMES IT'S SO HARD TO BE SUPPORTIVE WHEN--
AAAAAGGHH MY HEAD!!
IAN...
THE FEELING IS FROM HIM...

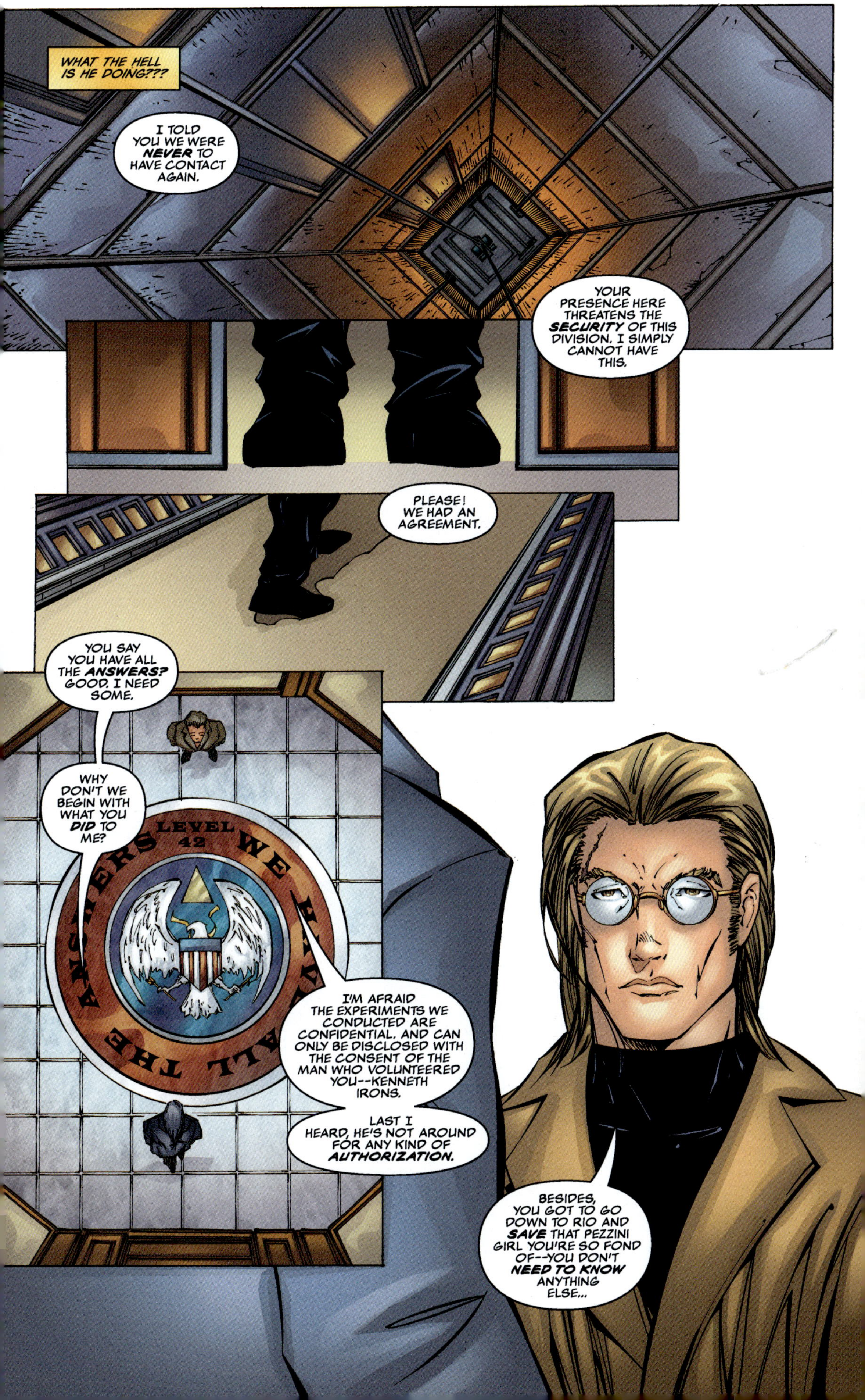
WHAT THE HELL IS HE DOING???
I TOLD YOU WE WERE NEVER TO HAVE CONTACT AGAIN.
YOUR PRESENCE HERE THREATENS THE SECURITY OF THIS DIVISION. I SIMPLY CANNOT HAVE THIS.
PLEASE! WE HAD AN AGREEMENT.
YOU SAY YOU HAVE ALL THE ANSWERS? GOOD. I NEED SOME.
WHY DON'T WE BEGIN WITH WHAT YOU DID TO ME?
LEVEL 42
WE HAVE ALL THE ANSWERS
I'M AFRAID THE EXPERIMENTS WE CONDUCTED ARE CONFIDENTIAL, AND CAN ONLY BE DISCLOSED WITH THE CONSENT OF THE MAN WHO VOLUNTEERED YOU--KENNETH IRONS.
LAST I HEARD, HE'S NOT AROUND FOR ANY KIND OF AUTHORIZATION.
BESIDES, YOU GOT TO GO DOWN TO RIO AND SAVE THAT PEZZINI GIRL YOU'RE SO FOND OF--YOU DON'T NEED TO KNOW ANYTHING ELSE...

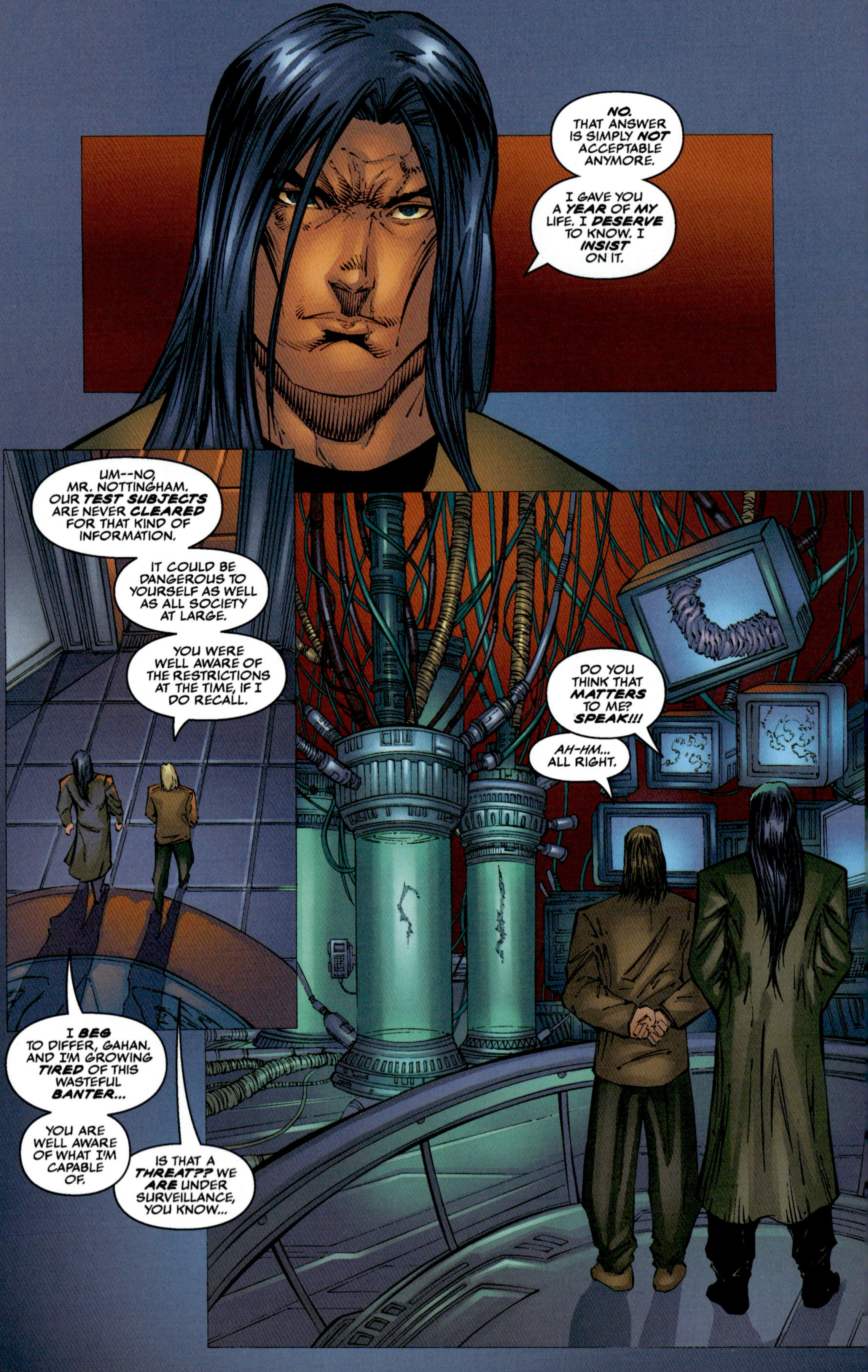
NO. THAT ANSWER IS SIMPLY NOT ACCEPTABLE ANYMORE.
I GAVE YOU A YEAR OF MY LIFE. I DESERVE TO KNOW. I INSIST ON IT.
UM--NO, MR. NOTTINGHAM. OUR TEST SUBJECTS ARE NEVER CLEARED FOR THAT KIND OF INFORMATION.
IT COULD BE DANGEROUS TO YOURSELF AS WELL AS ALL SOCIETY AT LARGE.
YOU WERE WELL AWARE OF THE RESTRICTIONS AT THE TIME, IF I DO RECALL.
DO YOU THINK THAT MATTERS TO ME? SPEAK!!!
AH-HM... ALL RIGHT.
I BEG TO DIFFER, GAHAN, AND I'M GROWING TIRED OF THIS WASTEFUL BANTER...
YOU ARE WELL AWARE OF WHAT I'M CAPABLE OF.
IS THAT A THREAT?? WE ARE UNDER SURVEILLANCE, YOU KNOW...

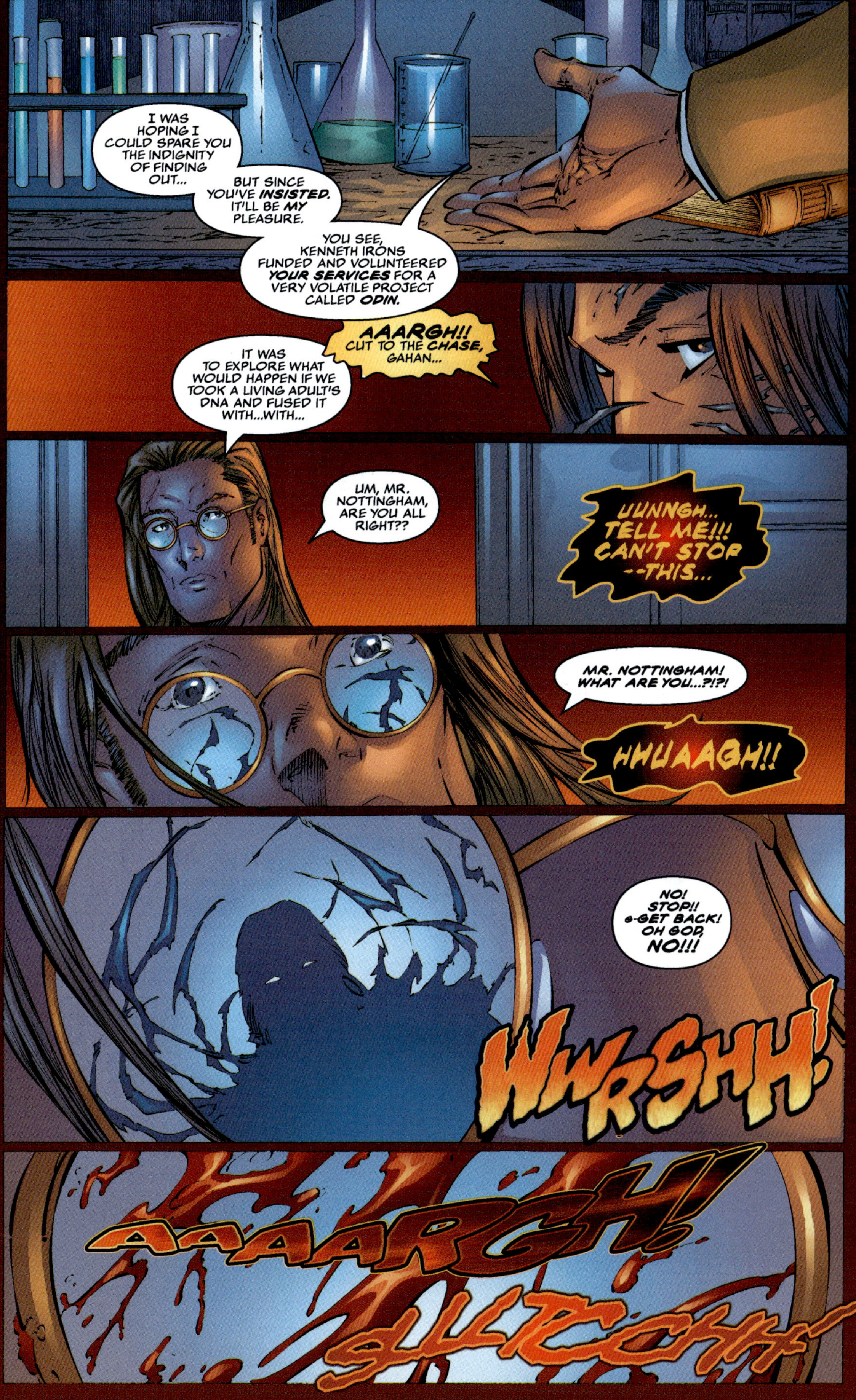
I WAS HOPING I COULD SPARE YOU THE INDIGNITY OF FINDING OUT...
BUT SINCE YOU'VE INSISTED, IT'LL BE MY PLEASURE.
YOU SEE, KENNETH IRONS FUNDED AND VOLUNTEERED YOUR SERVICES FOR A VERY VOLATILE PROJECT CALLED ODIN.
AAARGH!! CUT TO THE CHASE, GAHAN...
IT WAS TO EXPLORE WHAT WOULD HAPPEN IF WE TOOK A LIVING ADULT'S DNA AND FUSED IT WITH...WITH...
UM, MR. NOTTINGHAM, ARE YOU ALL RIGHT??
UUNNGH... TELL ME!!! CAN'T STOP --THIS...
MR. NOTTINGHAM! WHAT ARE YOU...?!?!
HHUAAGH!!
NO! STOP!! G-GET BACK! OH GOD, NO!!!
WWRSHH!
AAAAARGH!!
SHLRCHH!

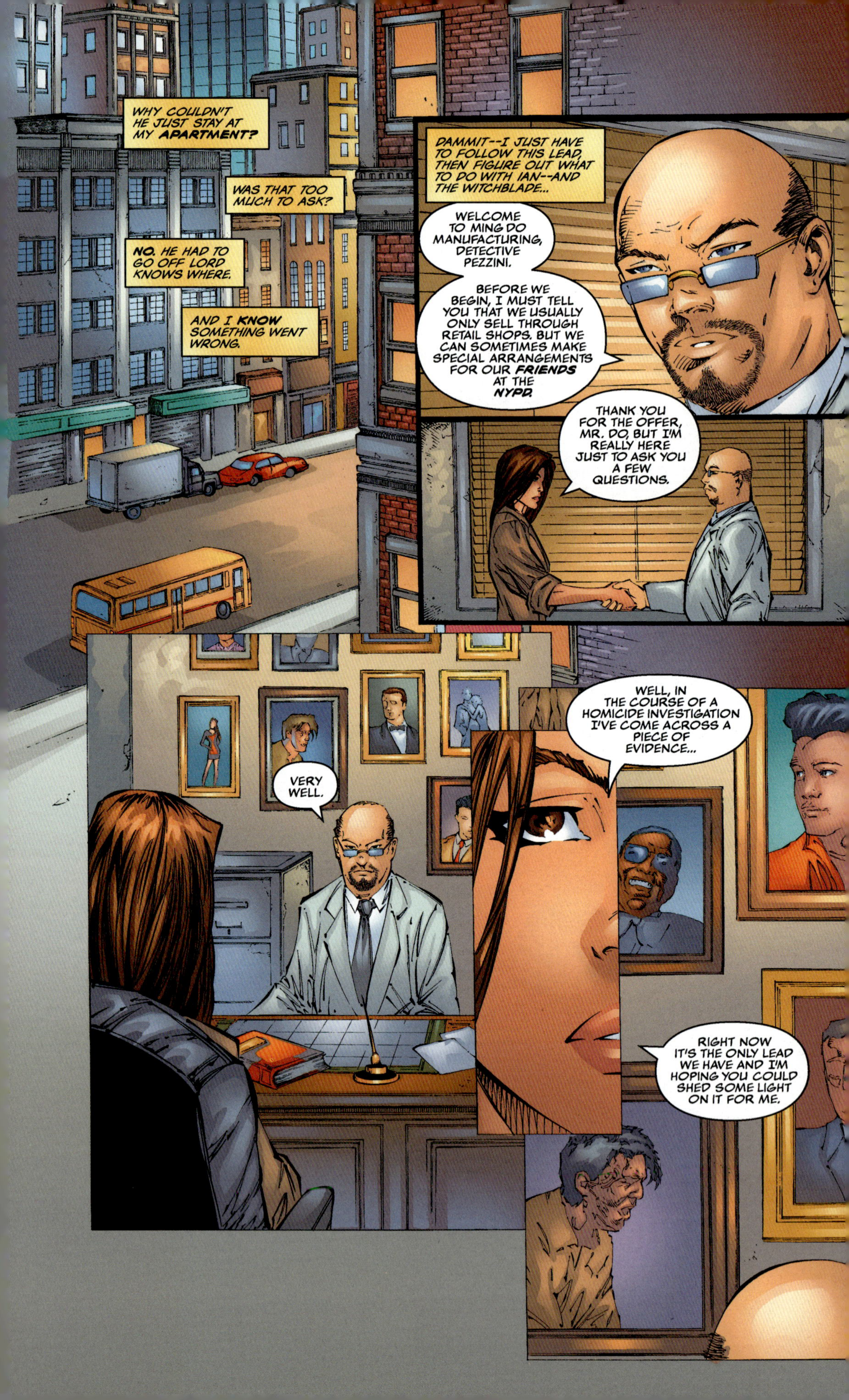
WHY COULDN'T HE JUST STAY AT MY APARTMENT?
WAS THAT TOO MUCH TO ASK?
NO. HE HAD TO GO OFF LORD KNOWS WHERE.
AND I KNOW SOMETHING WENT WRONG.
DAMMIT--I JUST HAVE TO FOLLOW THIS LEAD, THEN FIGURE OUT WHAT TO DO WITH IAN--AND THE WITCHBLADE...
WELCOME TO MING DO MANUFACTURING, DETECTIVE PEZZINI.
BEFORE WE BEGIN, I MUST TELL YOU THAT WE USUALLY ONLY SELL THROUGH RETAIL SHOPS. BUT WE CAN SOMETIMES MAKE SPECIAL ARRANGEMENTS FOR OUR FRIENDS AT THE NYPD.
THANK YOU FOR THE OFFER, MR. DO, BUT I'M REALLY HERE JUST TO ASK YOU A FEW QUESTIONS.
VERY WELL.
WELL, IN THE COURSE OF A HOMICIDE INVESTIGATION I'VE COME ACROSS A PIECE OF EVIDENCE...
RIGHT NOW IT'S THE ONLY LEAD WE HAVE AND I'M HOPING YOU COULD SHED SOME LIGHT ON IT FOR ME.

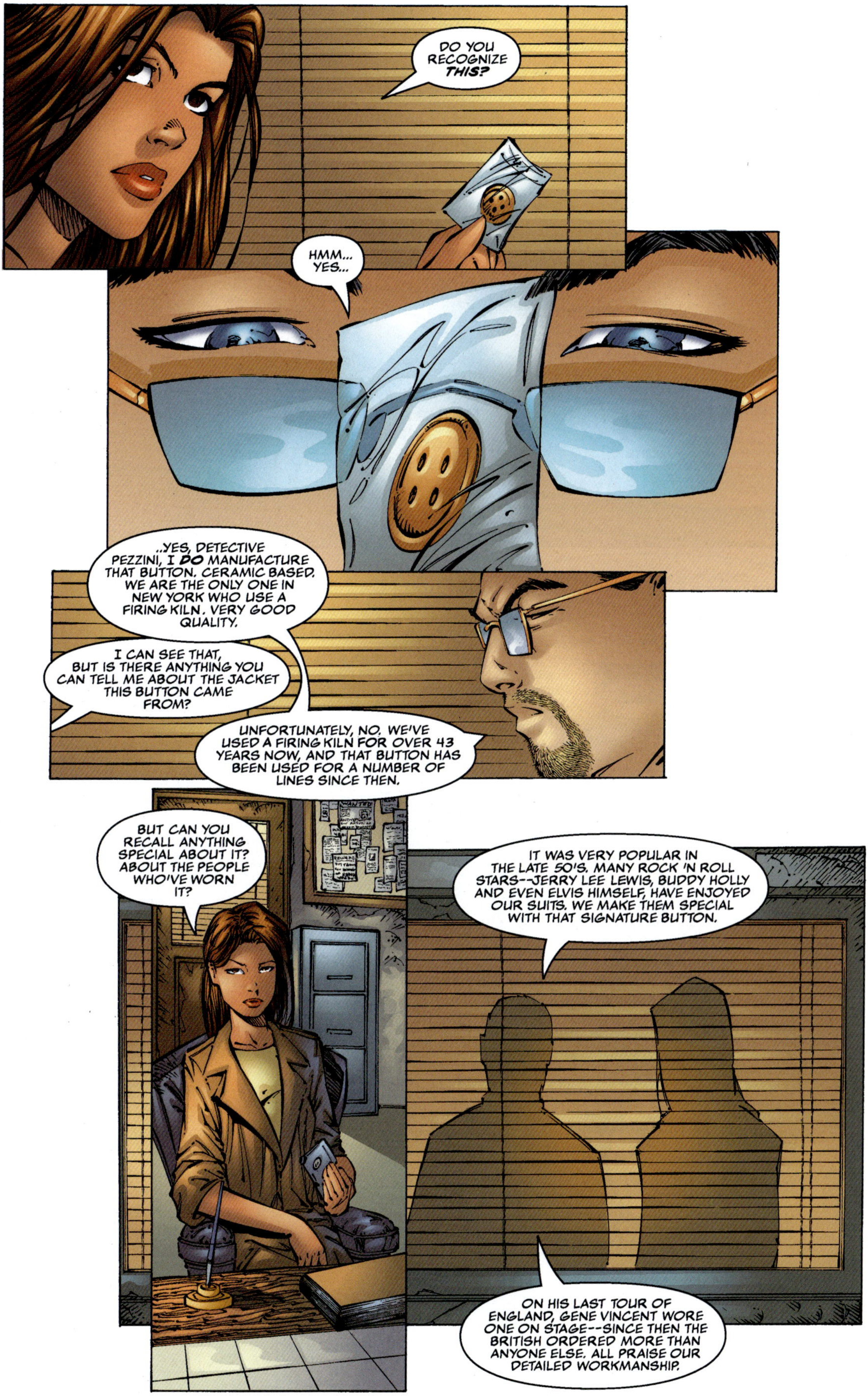
DO YOU RECOGNIZE THIS?
HMM... YES...
..YES, DETECTIVE PEZZINI, I DO MANUFACTURE THAT BUTTON. CERAMIC BASED. WE ARE THE ONLY ONE IN NEW YORK WHO USE A FIRING KILN. VERY GOOD QUALITY.
I CAN SEE THAT, BUT IS THERE ANYTHING YOU CAN TELL ME ABOUT THE JACKET THIS BUTTON CAME FROM?
UNFORTUNATELY, NO. WE'VE USED A FIRING KILN FOR OVER 43 YEARS NOW, AND THAT BUTTON HAS BEEN USED FOR A NUMBER OF LINES SINCE THEN.
BUT CAN YOU RECALL ANYTHING SPECIAL ABOUT IT? ABOUT THE PEOPLE WHO'VE WORN IT?
IT WAS VERY POPULAR IN THE LATE 50'S. MANY ROCK 'N ROLL STARS--JERRY LEE LEWIS, BUDDY HOLLY AND EVEN ELVIS HIMSELF, HAVE ENJOYED OUR SUITS. WE MAKE THEM SPECIAL WITH THAT SIGNATURE BUTTON.
ON HIS LAST TOUR OF ENGLAND, GENE VINCENT WORE ONE ON STAGE--SINCE THEN THE BRITISH ORDERED MORE THAN ANYONE ELSE. ALL PRAISE OUR DETAILED WORKMANSHIP.

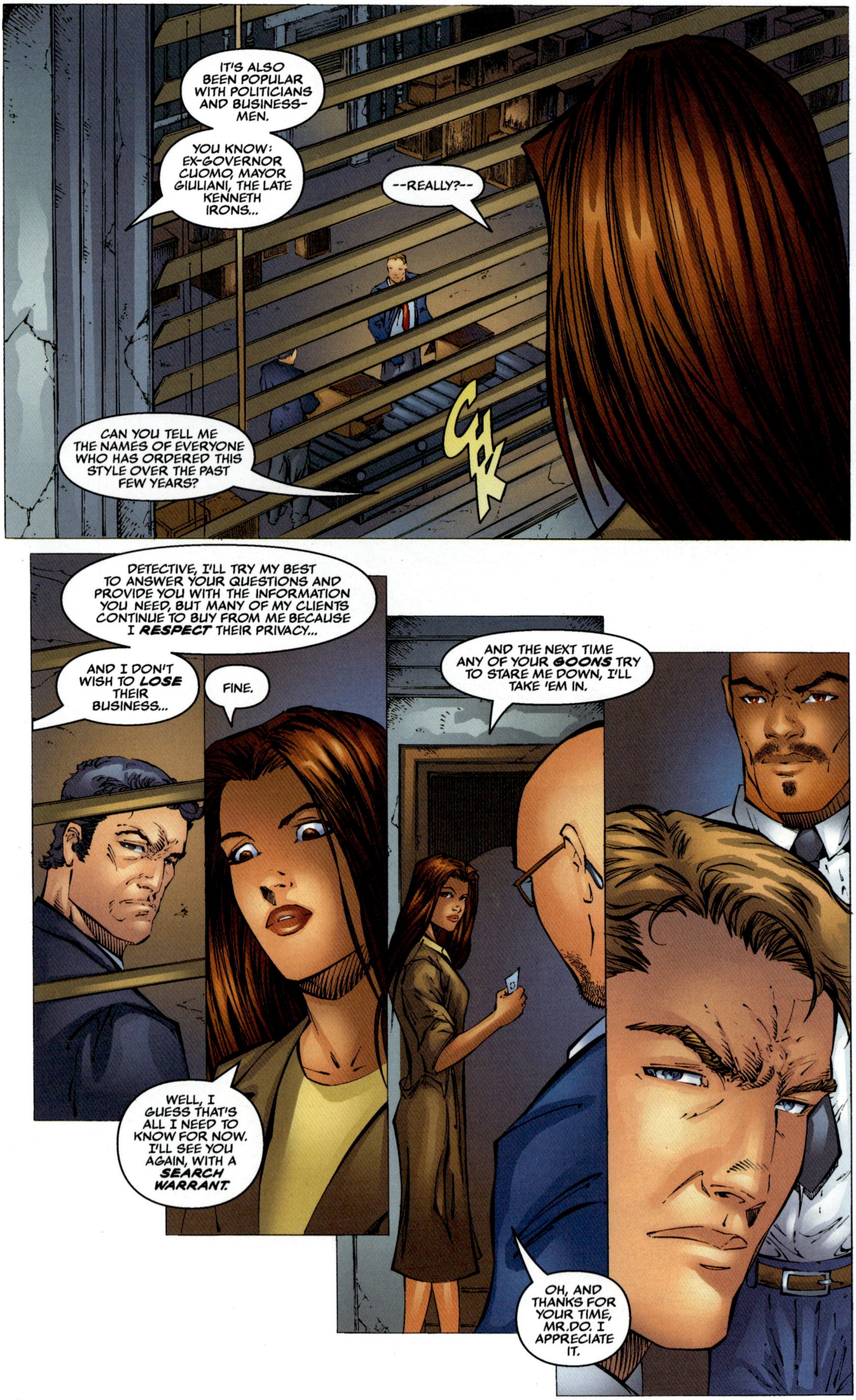
IT'S ALSO BEEN POPULAR WITH POLITICIANS AND BUSINESS-MEN.
YOU KNOW: EX-GOVERNOR CUOMO, MAYOR GIULIANI, THE LATE KENNETH IRONS...
--REALLY?--
CAN YOU TELL ME THE NAMES OF EVERYONE WHO HAS ORDERED THIS STYLE OVER THE PAST FEW YEARS?
CHK
DETECTIVE, I'LL TRY MY BEST TO ANSWER YOUR QUESTIONS AND PROVIDE YOU WITH THE INFORMATION YOU NEED, BUT MANY OF MY CLIENTS CONTINUE TO BUY FROM ME BECAUSE I RESPECT THEIR PRIVACY...
AND I DON'T WISH TO LOSE THEIR BUSINESS...
FINE.
WELL, I GUESS THAT'S ALL I NEED TO KNOW FOR NOW. I'LL SEE YOU AGAIN, WITH A SEARCH WARRANT.
AND THE NEXT TIME ANY OF YOUR GOONS TRY TO STARE ME DOWN, I'LL TAKE 'EM IN.
OH, AND THANKS FOR YOUR TIME, MR. DO. I APPRECIATE IT.

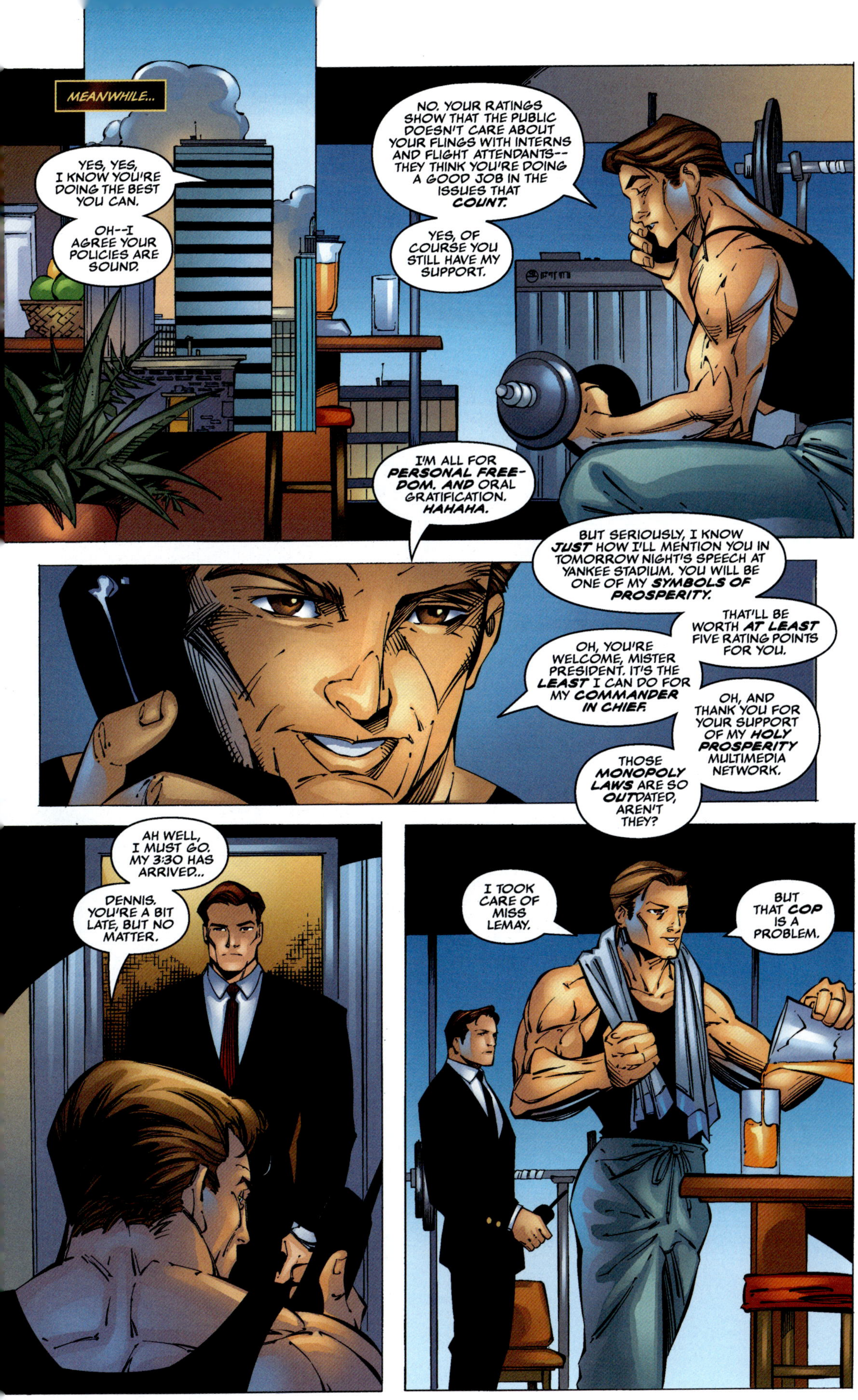
MEANWHILE...
YES, YES, I KNOW YOU'RE DOING THE BEST YOU CAN.
OH--I AGREE YOUR POLICIES ARE SOUND.
NO, YOUR RATINGS SHOW THAT THE PUBLIC DOESN'T CARE ABOUT YOUR FLINGS WITH INTERNS AND FLIGHT ATTENDANTS-- THEY THINK YOU'RE DOING A GOOD JOB IN THE ISSUES THAT COUNT.
YES, OF COURSE YOU STILL HAVE MY SUPPORT.
I'M ALL FOR PERSONAL FREE-DOM. AND ORAL GRATIFICATION. HAHAHA.
BUT SERIOUSLY, I KNOW JUST HOW I'LL MENTION YOU IN TOMORROW NIGHT'S SPEECH AT YANKEE STADIUM. YOU WILL BE ONE OF MY SYMBOLS OF PROSPERITY.
THAT'LL BE WORTH AT LEAST FIVE RATING POINTS FOR YOU.
OH, YOU'RE WELCOME, MISTER PRESIDENT. IT'S THE LEAST I CAN DO FOR MY COMMANDER IN CHIEF.
OH, AND THANK YOU FOR YOUR SUPPORT OF MY HOLY PROSPERITY MULTIMEDIA NETWORK.
THOSE MONOPOLY LAWS ARE SO OUTDATED, AREN'T THEY?
AH WELL, I MUST GO. MY 3:30 HAS ARRIVED...
DENNIS. YOU'RE A BIT LATE, BUT NO MATTER.
I TOOK CARE OF MISS LEMAY.
BUT THAT COP IS A PROBLEM.

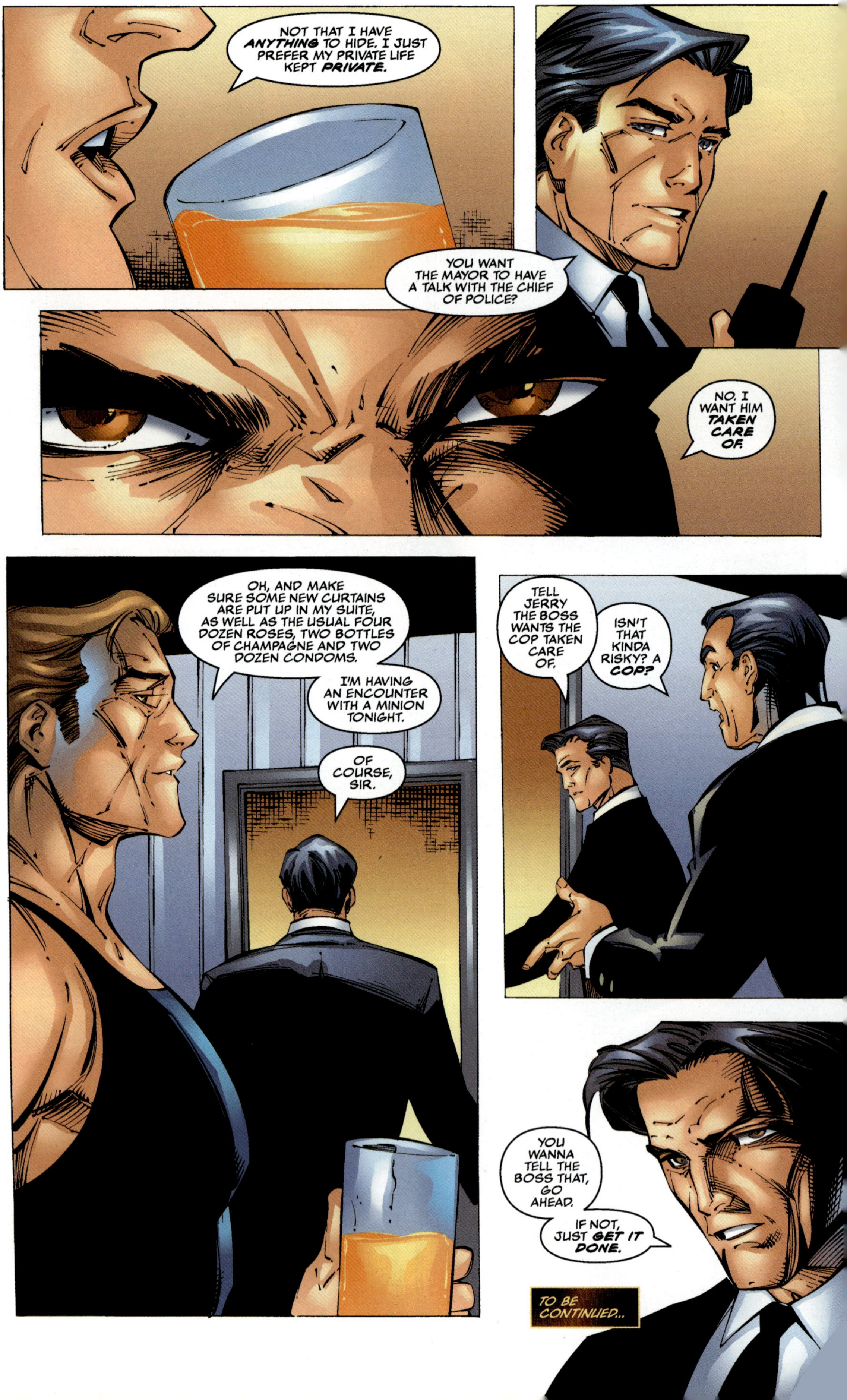
NOT THAT I HAVE ANYTHING TO HIDE. I JUST PREFER MY PRIVATE LIFE KEPT PRIVATE.
YOU WANT THE MAYOR TO HAVE A TALK WITH THE CHIEF OF POLICE?
NO. I WANT HIM TAKEN CARE OF.
OH, AND MAKE SURE SOME NEW CURTAINS ARE PUT UP IN MY SUITE, AS WELL AS THE USUAL FOUR DOZEN ROSES, TWO BOTTLES OF CHAMPAGNE AND TWO DOZEN CONDOMS.
I'M HAVING AN ENCOUNTER WITH A MINION TONIGHT.
OF COURSE, SIR.
TELL JERRY THE BOSS WANTS THE COP TAKEN CARE OF.
ISN'T THAT KINDA RISKY? A COP?
YOU WANNA TELL THE BOSS THAT, GO AHEAD.
IF NOT, JUST GET IT DONE.
TO BE CONTINUED...

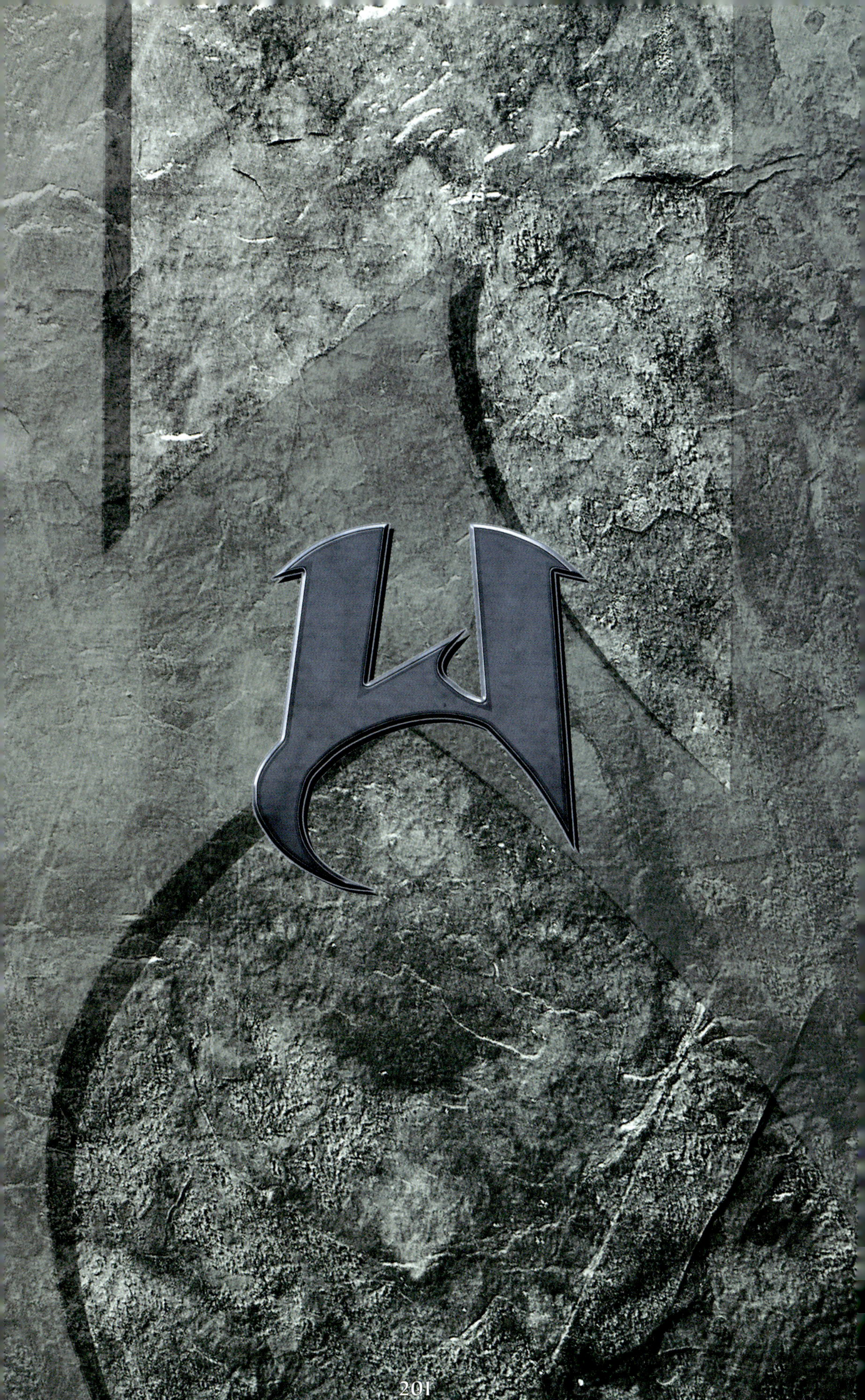

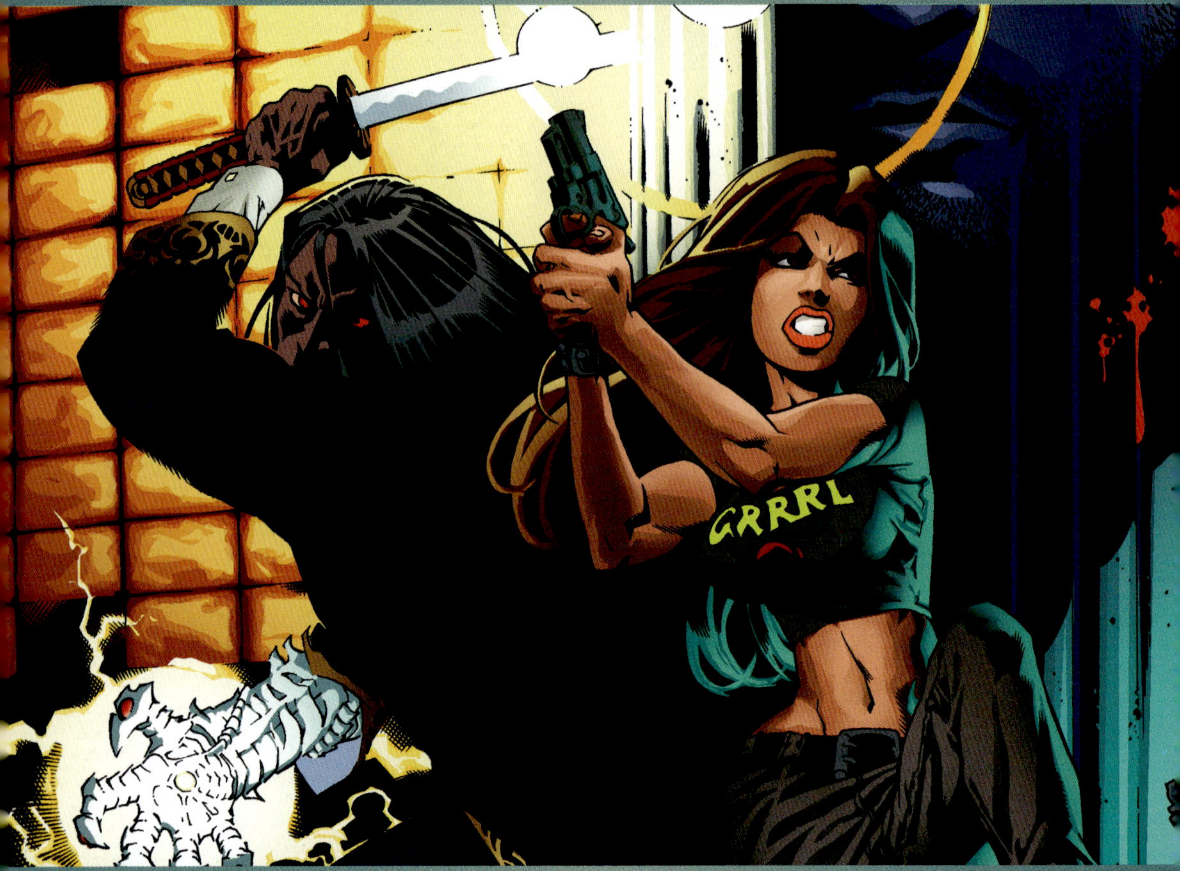
GRRRL

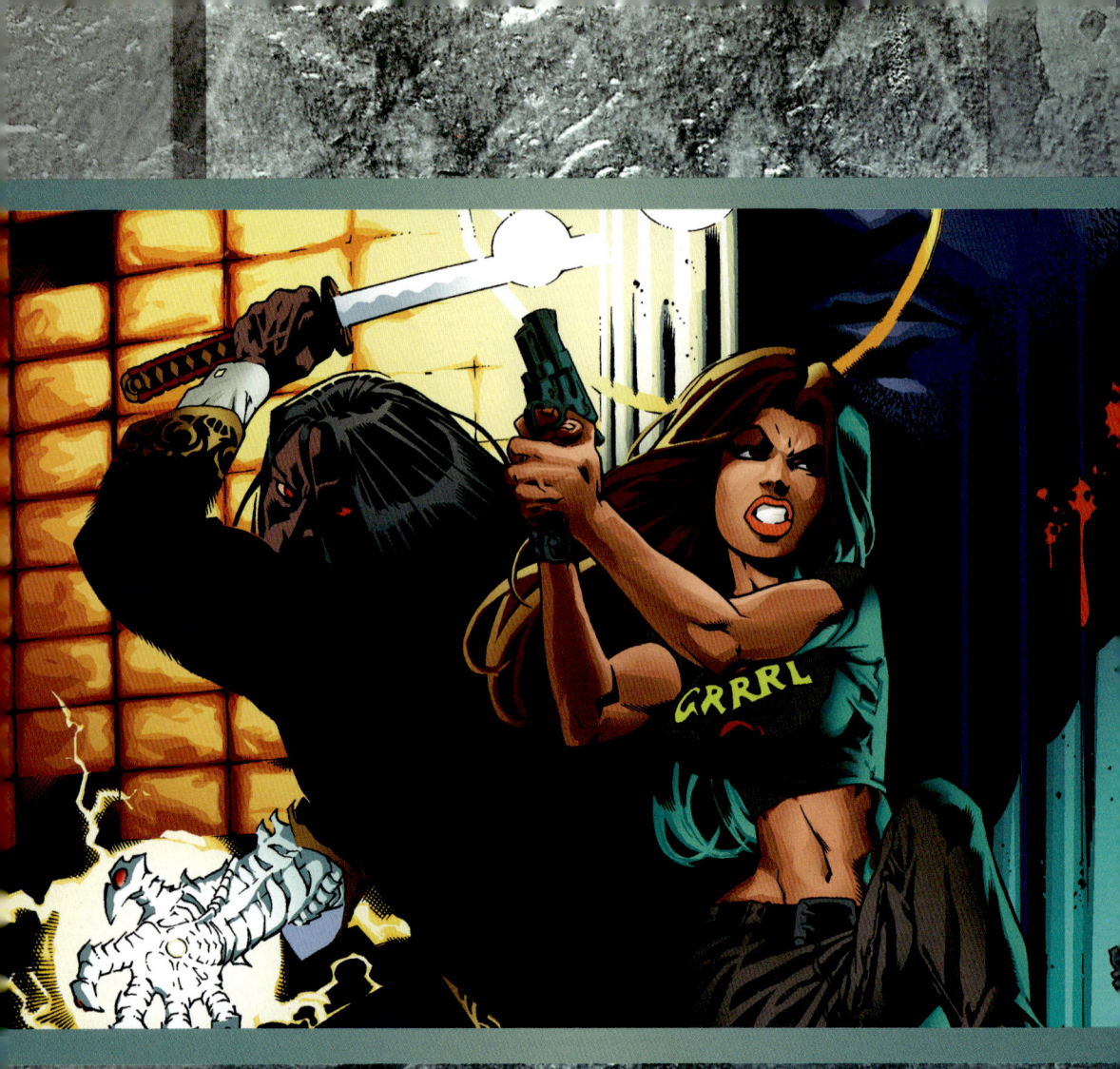

ISSUE #24

story: **David Wohl** and **Christina Z.**
pencils: **Jason Pearson** pages 1-15
Randy Green pages 16-22
inks: **Jason Martin** pages 1-15
Jonathan Sibal pages 16-22
colors: **JD Smith** pages 1-15
Richard Isanove pages 16-22

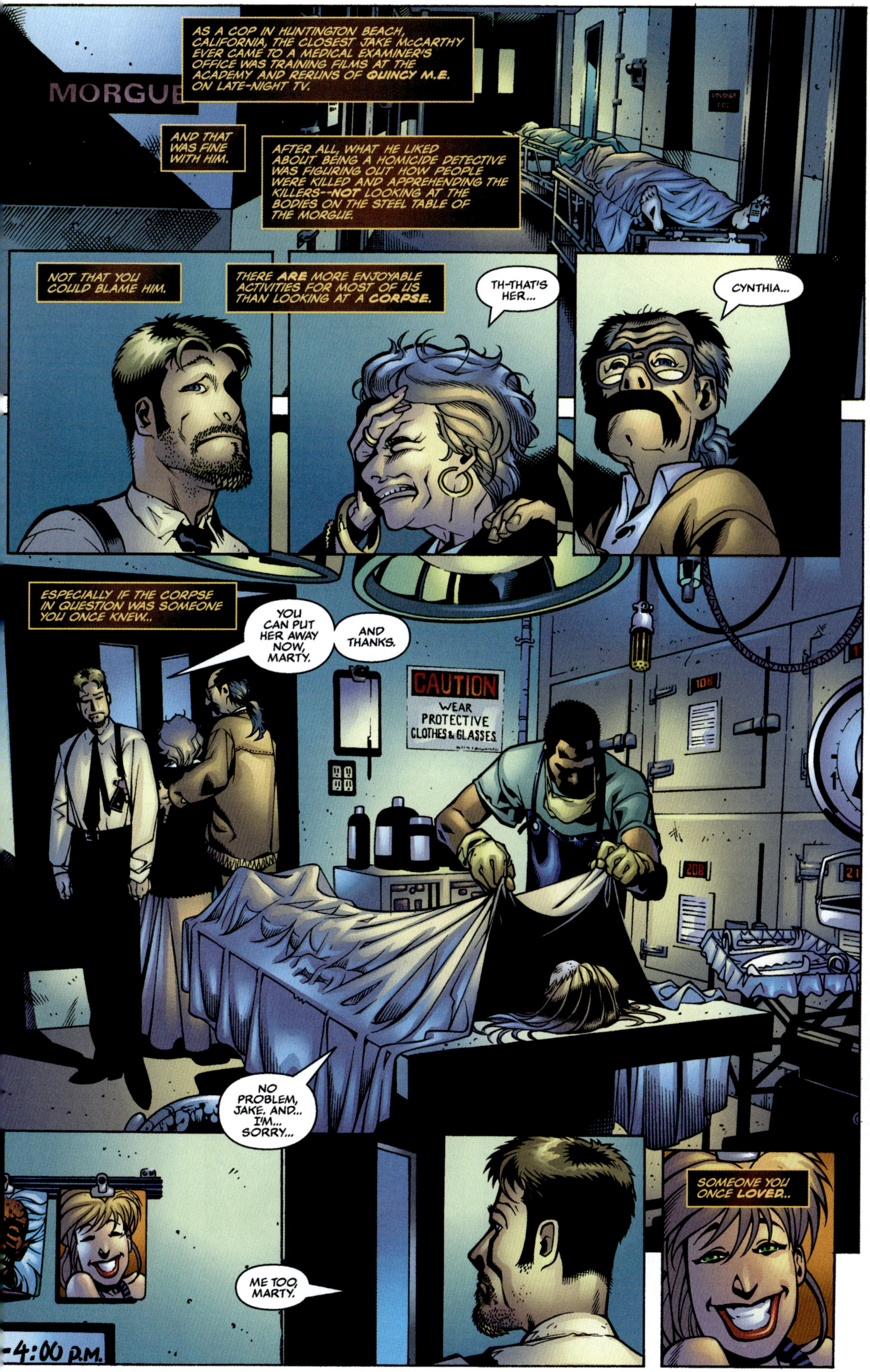
MORGUE
AS A COP IN HUNTINGTON BEACH, CALIFORNIA, THE CLOSEST JAKE McCARTHY EVER CAME TO A MEDICAL EXAMINER'S OFFICE WAS TRAINING FILMS AT THE ACADEMY AND RERUNS OF QUINCY M.E. ON LATE-NIGHT TV.
AND THAT WAS FINE WITH HIM.
AFTER ALL, WHAT HE LIKED ABOUT BEING A HOMICIDE DETECTIVE WAS FIGURING OUT HOW PEOPLE WERE KILLED AND APPREHENDING THE KILLERS--NOT LOOKING AT THE BODIES ON THE STEEL TABLE OF THE MORGUE.
NOT THAT YOU COULD BLAME HIM.
THERE ARE MORE ENJOYABLE ACTIVITIES FOR MOST OF US THAN LOOKING AT A CORPSE.
TH-THAT'S HER...
CYNTHIA...
ESPECIALLY IF THE CORPSE IN QUESTION WAS SOMEONE YOU ONCE KNEW...
YOU CAN PUT HER AWAY NOW, MARTY.
AND THANKS.
CAUTION
WEAR PROTECTIVE CLOTHES & GLASSES
108
208
NO PROBLEM, JAKE. AND... I'M... SORRY...
ME TOO, MARTY.
-4:00 P.M.
SOMEONE YOU ONCE LOVED...

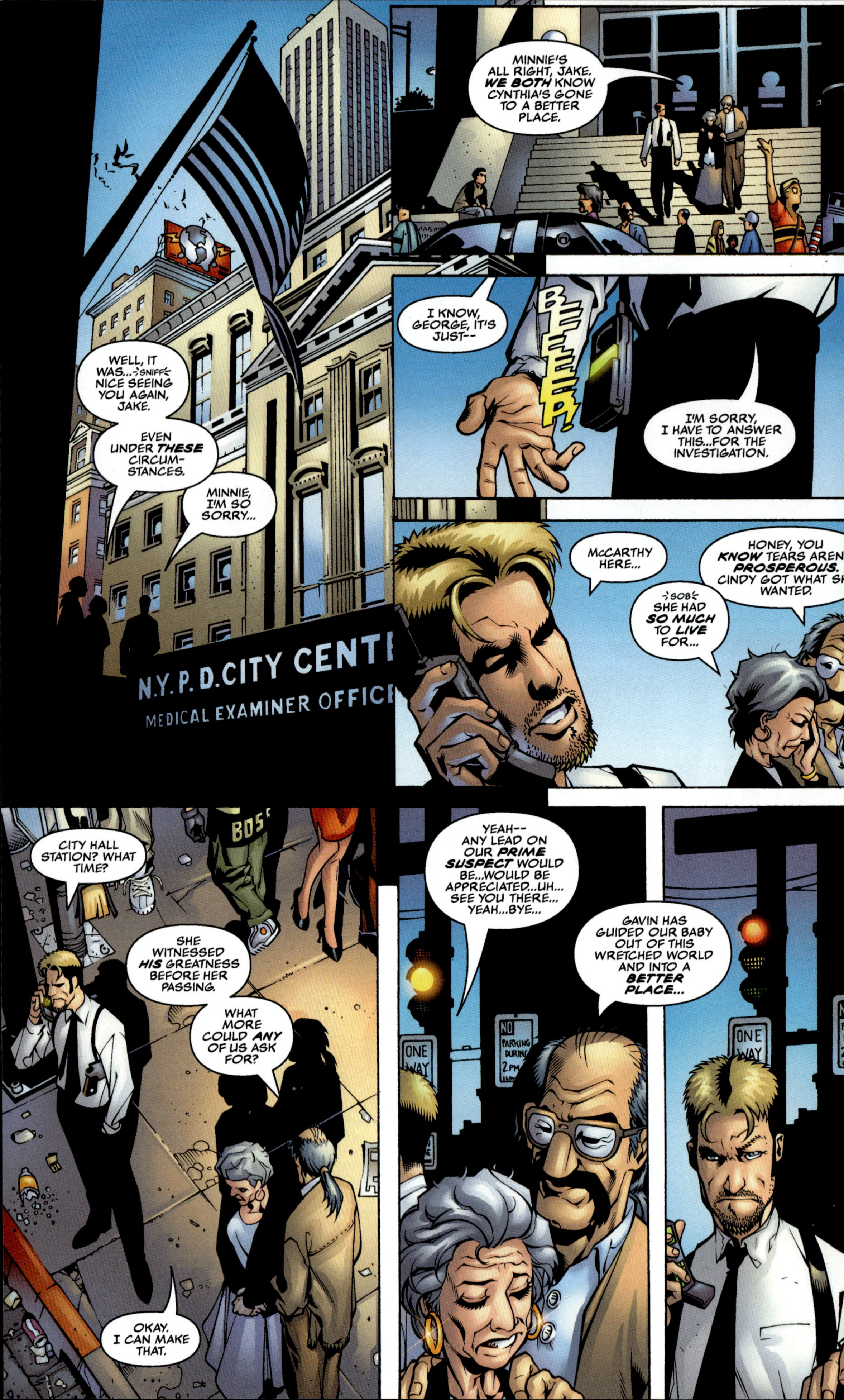
WELL, IT WAS... SNIFF NICE SEEING YOU AGAIN, JAKE.
EVEN UNDER THESE CIRCUM-STANCES.
MINNIE, I'M SO SORRY...
N.Y.P.D. CITY CENT
MEDICAL EXAMINER OFFIC
MINNIE'S ALL RIGHT, JAKE. WE BOTH KNOW CYNTHIA'S GONE TO A BETTER PLACE.
I KNOW, GEORGE, IT'S JUST--
BEEEEP!
I'M SORRY, I HAVE TO ANSWER THIS...FOR THE INVESTIGATION.
McCARTHY HERE...
HONEY, YOU KNOW TEARS AREN PROSPEROUS. CINDY GOT WHAT SH WANTED.
SOB SHE HAD SO MUCH TO LIVE FOR...
CITY HALL STATION? WHAT TIME?
SHE WITNESSED HIS GREATNESS BEFORE HER PASSING.
WHAT MORE COULD ANY OF US ASK FOR?
OKAY. I CAN MAKE THAT.
YEAH-- ANY LEAD ON OUR PRIME SUSPECT WOULD BE...WOULD BE APPRECIATED...UH... SEE YOU THERE... YEAH...BYE...
GAVIN HAS GUIDED OUR BABY OUT OF THIS WRETCHED WORLD AND INTO A BETTER PLACE...
ONE WAY
NO PARKING DURING 2PM
ONE WAY

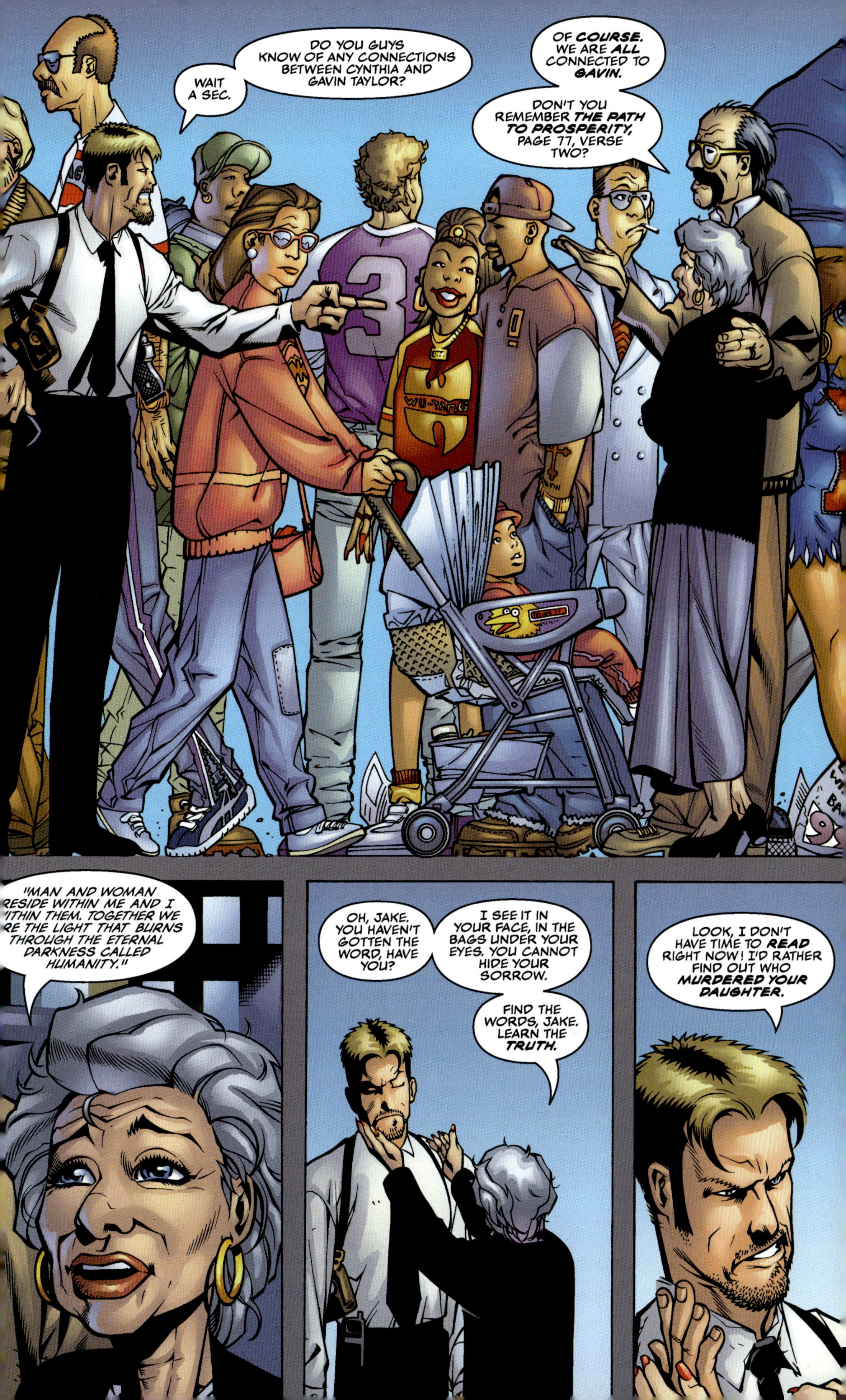
WAIT A SEC.
DO YOU GUYS KNOW OF ANY CONNECTIONS BETWEEN CYNTHIA AND GAVIN TAYLOR?
OF COURSE. WE ARE ALL CONNECTED TO GAVIN.
DON'T YOU REMEMBER THE PATH TO PROSPERITY, PAGE 77, VERSE TWO?
WU-TANG
"MAN AND WOMAN RESIDE WITHIN ME AND I WITHIN THEM. TOGETHER WE ARE THE LIGHT THAT BURNS THROUGH THE ETERNAL DARKNESS CALLED HUMANITY."
OH, JAKE. YOU HAVEN'T GOTTEN THE WORD, HAVE YOU?
I SEE IT IN YOUR FACE, IN THE BAGS UNDER YOUR EYES. YOU CANNOT HIDE YOUR SORROW.
FIND THE WORDS, JAKE. LEARN THE TRUTH.
LOOK, I DON'T HAVE TIME TO READ RIGHT NOW! I'D RATHER FIND OUT WHO MURDERED YOUR DAUGHTER.

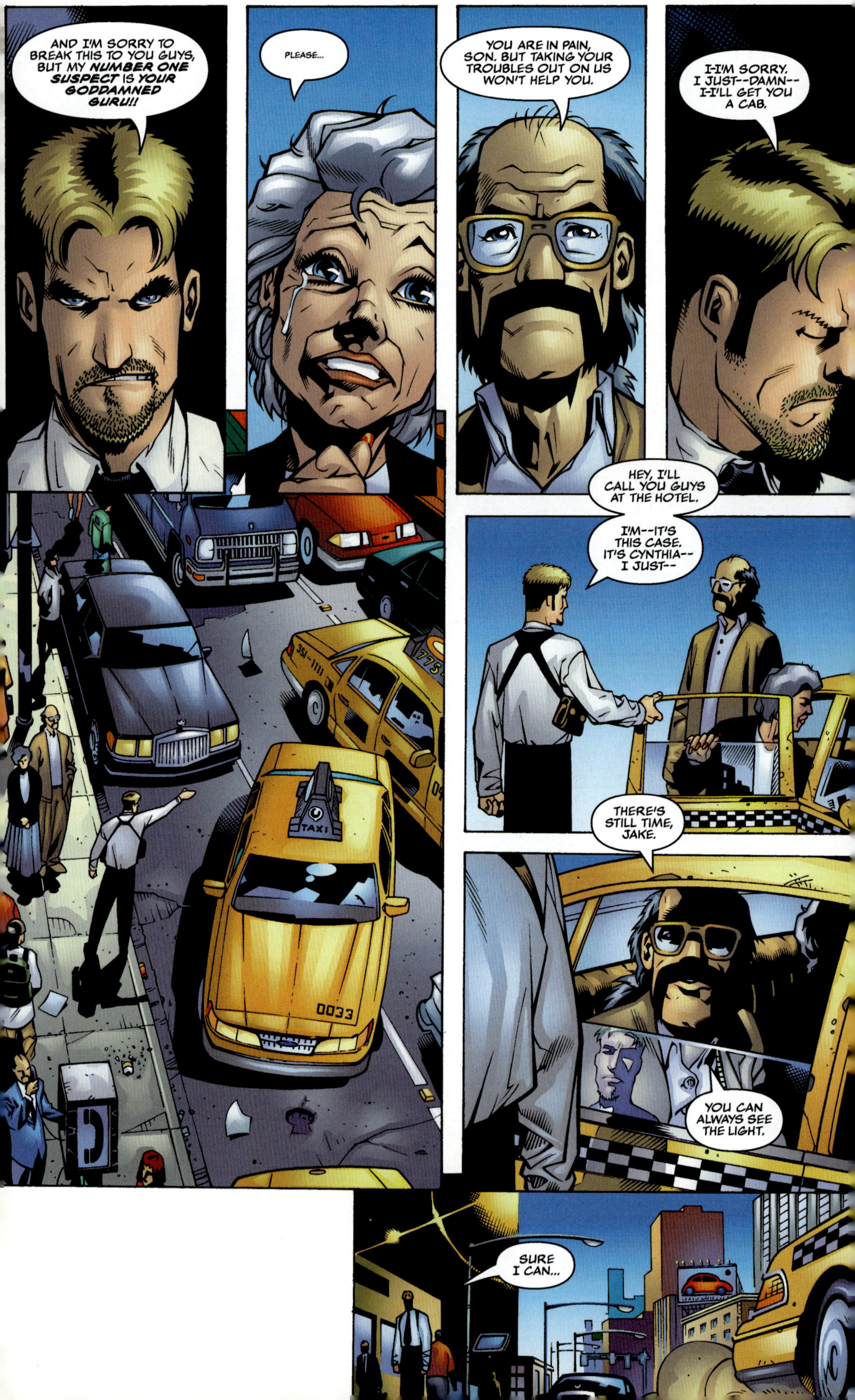
AND I'M SORRY TO BREAK THIS TO YOU GUYS, BUT MY NUMBER ONE SUSPECT IS YOUR GODDAMNED GURU!!
PLEASE...
YOU ARE IN PAIN, SON. BUT TAKING YOUR TROUBLES OUT ON US WON'T HELP YOU.
I-I'M SORRY. I JUST--DAMN-- I-I'LL GET YOU A CAB.
HEY, I'LL CALL YOU GUYS AT THE HOTEL.
I'M--IT'S THIS CASE. IT'S CYNTHIA-- I JUST--
THERE'S STILL TIME, JAKE.
YOU CAN ALWAYS SEE THE LIGHT.
SURE I CAN...

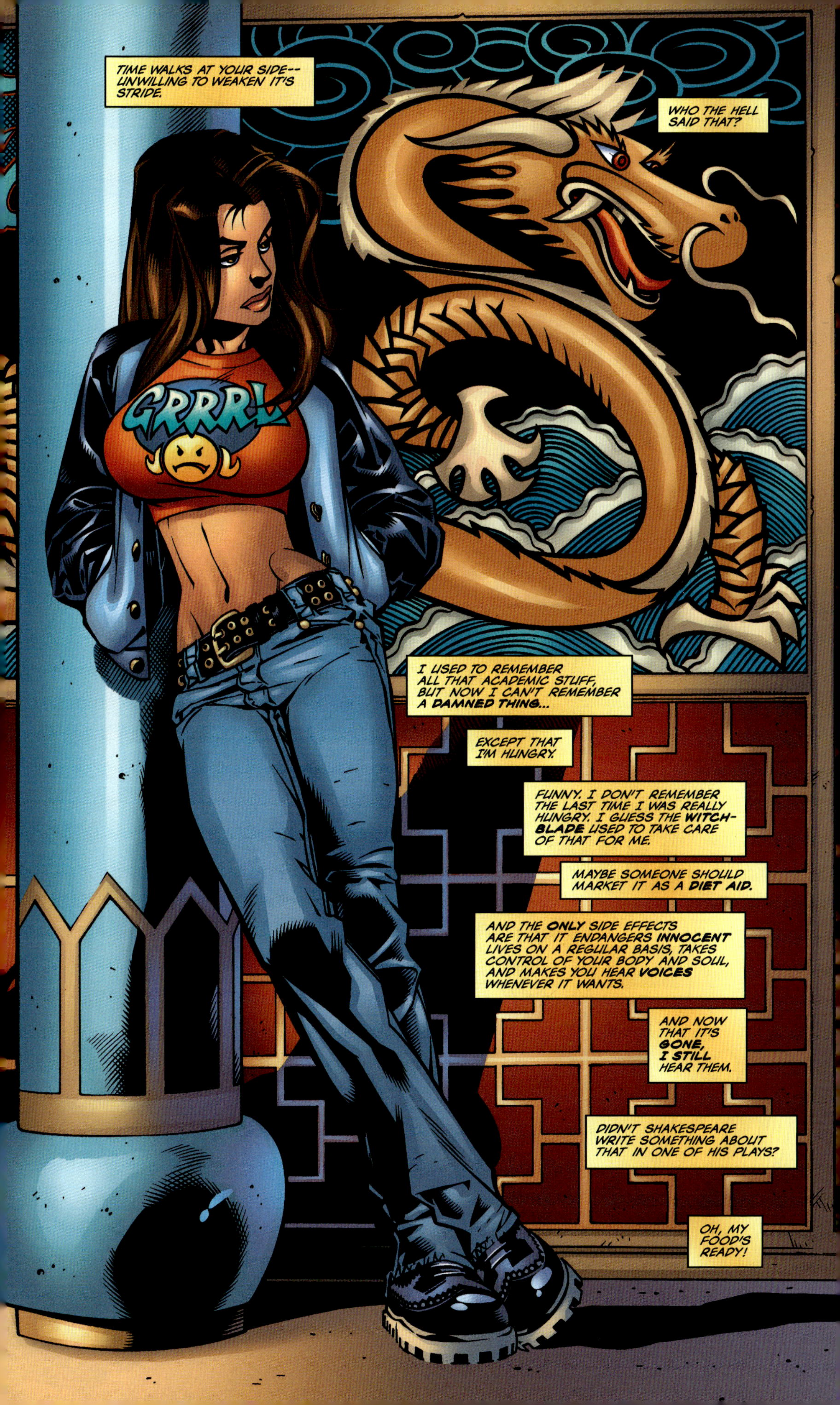
TIME WALKS AT YOUR SIDE-- UNWILLING TO WEAKEN IT'S STRIDE.
WHO THE HELL SAID THAT?
GRRRL
I USED TO REMEMBER ALL THAT ACADEMIC STUFF, BUT NOW I CAN'T REMEMBER A DAMNED THING...
EXCEPT THAT I'M HUNGRY.
FUNNY. I DON'T REMEMBER THE LAST TIME I WAS REALLY HUNGRY. I GUESS THE WITCHBLADE USED TO TAKE CARE OF THAT FOR ME.
MAYBE SOMEONE SHOULD MARKET IT AS A DIET AID.
AND THE ONLY SIDE EFFECTS ARE THAT IT ENDANGERS INNOCENT LIVES ON A REGULAR BASIS, TAKES CONTROL OF YOUR BODY AND SOUL, AND MAKES YOU HEAR VOICES WHENEVER IT WANTS.
AND NOW THAT IT'S GONE, I STILL HEAR THEM.
DIDN'T SHAKESPEARE WRITE SOMETHING ABOUT THAT IN ONE OF HIS PLAYS?
OH, MY FOOD'S READY!

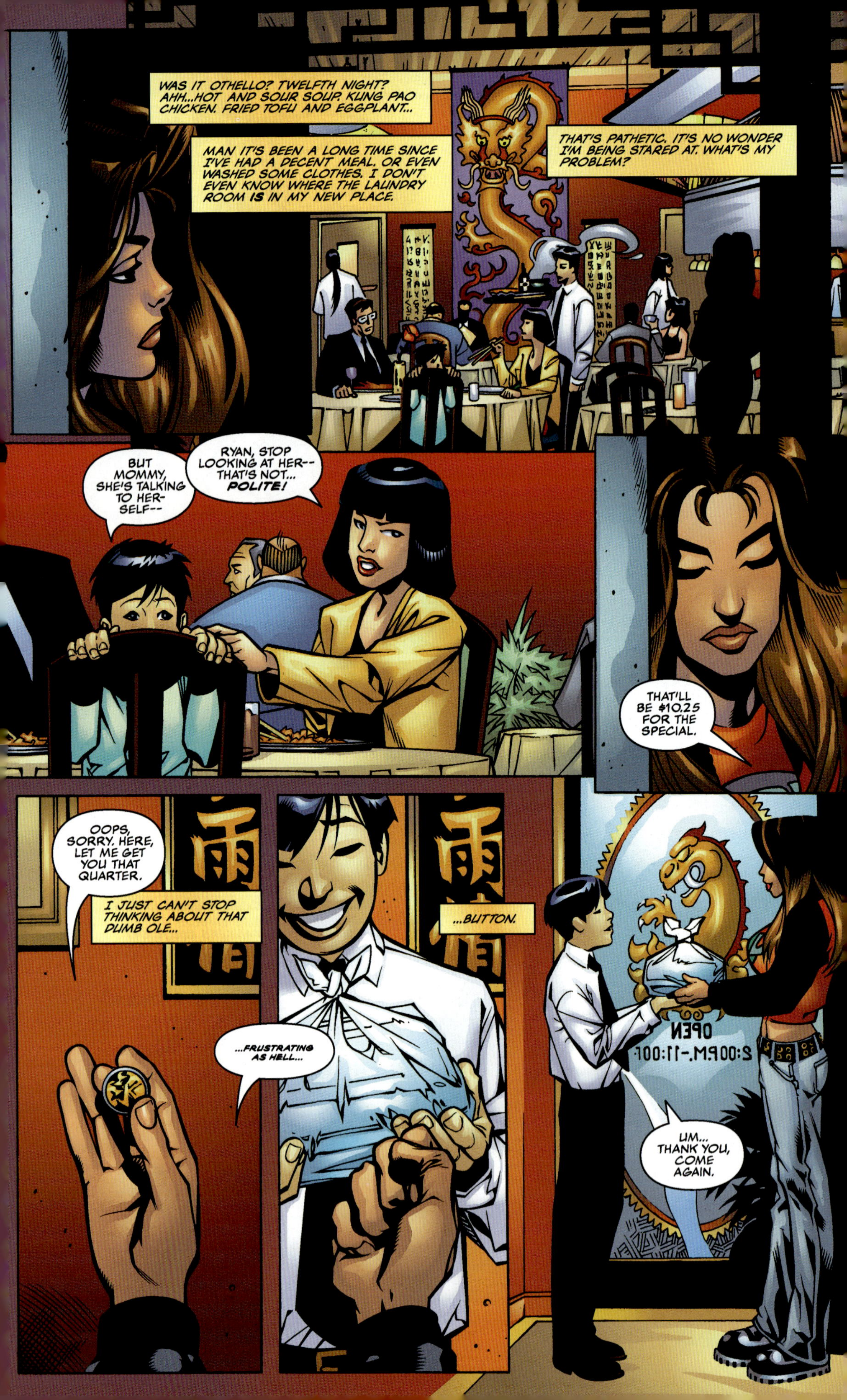

WAS IT OTHELLO? TWELFTH NIGHT? AHH...HOT AND SOUR SOUP. KUNG PAO CHICKEN. FRIED TOFU AND EGGPLANT...
MAN IT'S BEEN A LONG TIME SINCE I'VE HAD A DECENT MEAL. OR EVEN WASHED SOME CLOTHES. I DON'T EVEN KNOW WHERE THE LAUNDRY ROOM IS IN MY NEW PLACE.
THAT'S PATHETIC. IT'S NO WONDER I'M BEING STARED AT. WHAT'S MY PROBLEM?
BUT MOMMY, SHE'S TALKING TO HER-SELF--
RYAN, STOP LOOKING AT HER--THAT'S NOT... POLITE!
THAT'LL BE $10.25 FOR THE SPECIAL.
OOPS, SORRY. HERE, LET ME GET YOU THAT QUARTER.
I JUST CAN'T STOP THINKING ABOUT THAT DUMB OLE...
...BUTTON.
...FRUSTRATING AS HELL...
UM... THANK YOU, COME AGAIN.

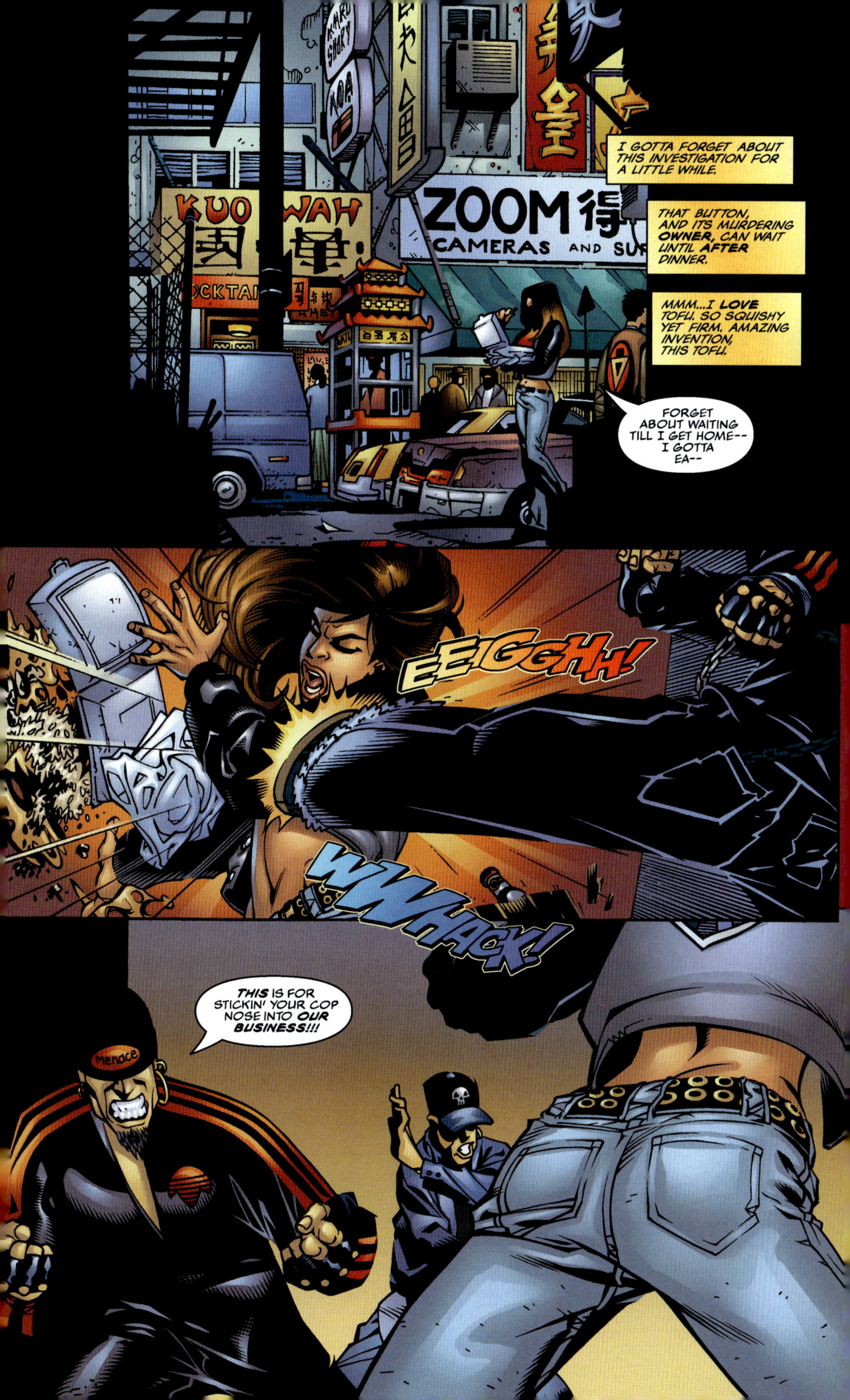
I GOTTA FORGET ABOUT THIS INVESTIGATION FOR A LITTLE WHILE.
THAT BUTTON, AND ITS MURDERING OWNER, CAN WAIT UNTIL AFTER DINNER.
MMM...I LOVE TOFU. SO SQUISHY YET FIRM. AMAZING INVENTION, THIS TOFU.
FORGET ABOUT WAITING TILL I GET HOME-- I GOTTA EA--
EEIGGHH!
WWHACK!
THIS IS FOR STICKIN' YOUR COP NOSE INTO OUR BUSINESS!!!

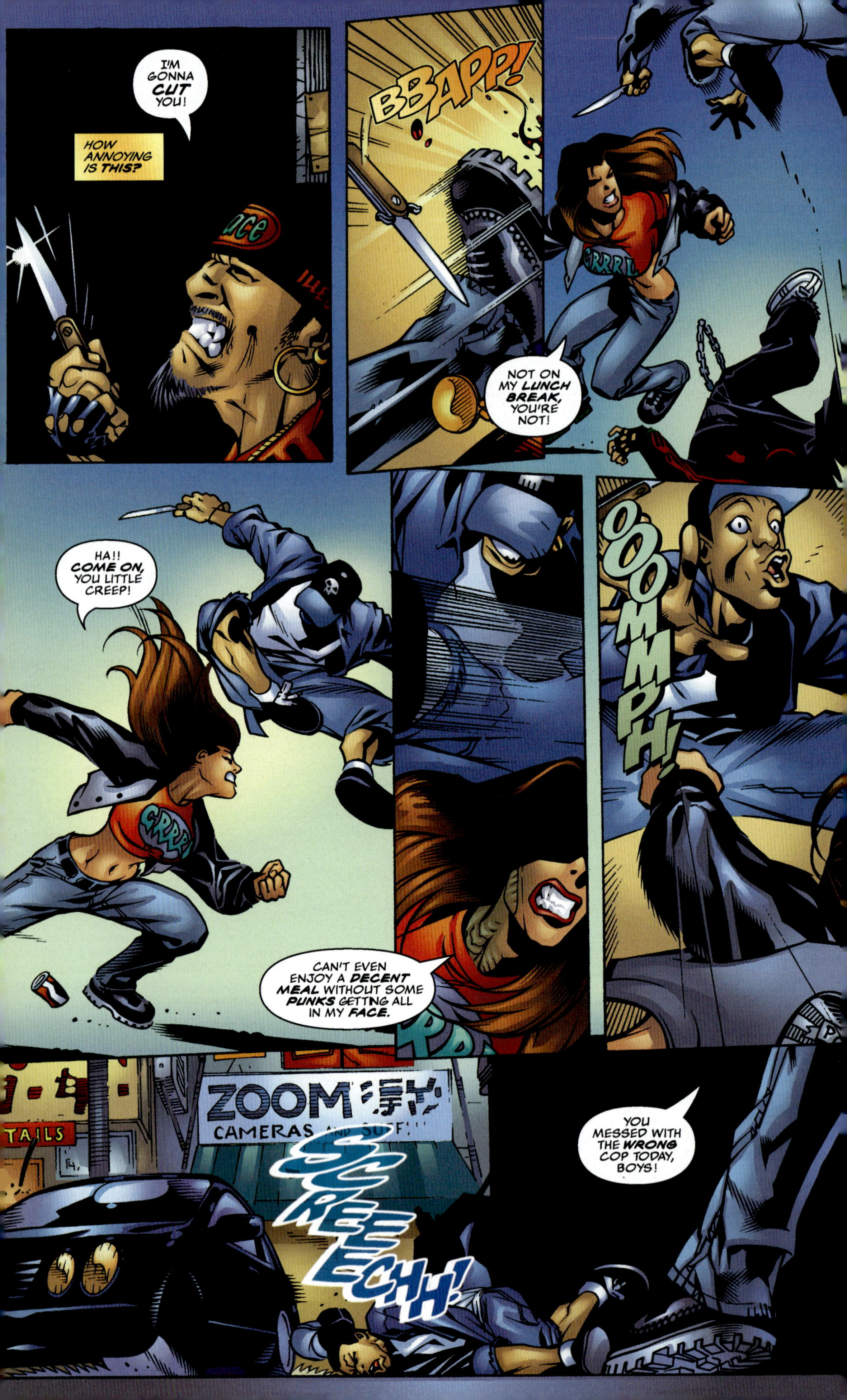
I'M GONNA CUT YOU!
HOW ANNOYING IS THIS?
BBAPP!
NOT ON MY LUNCH BREAK, YOU'RE NOT!
HA!! COME ON, YOU LITTLE CREEP!
CAN'T EVEN ENJOY A DECENT MEAL WITHOUT SOME PUNKS GETTING ALL IN MY FACE.
OOOMMMPH!
ZOOM
CAMERAS AND STUFF
SCREEECHH!
YOU MESSED WITH THE WRONG COP TODAY, BOYS!

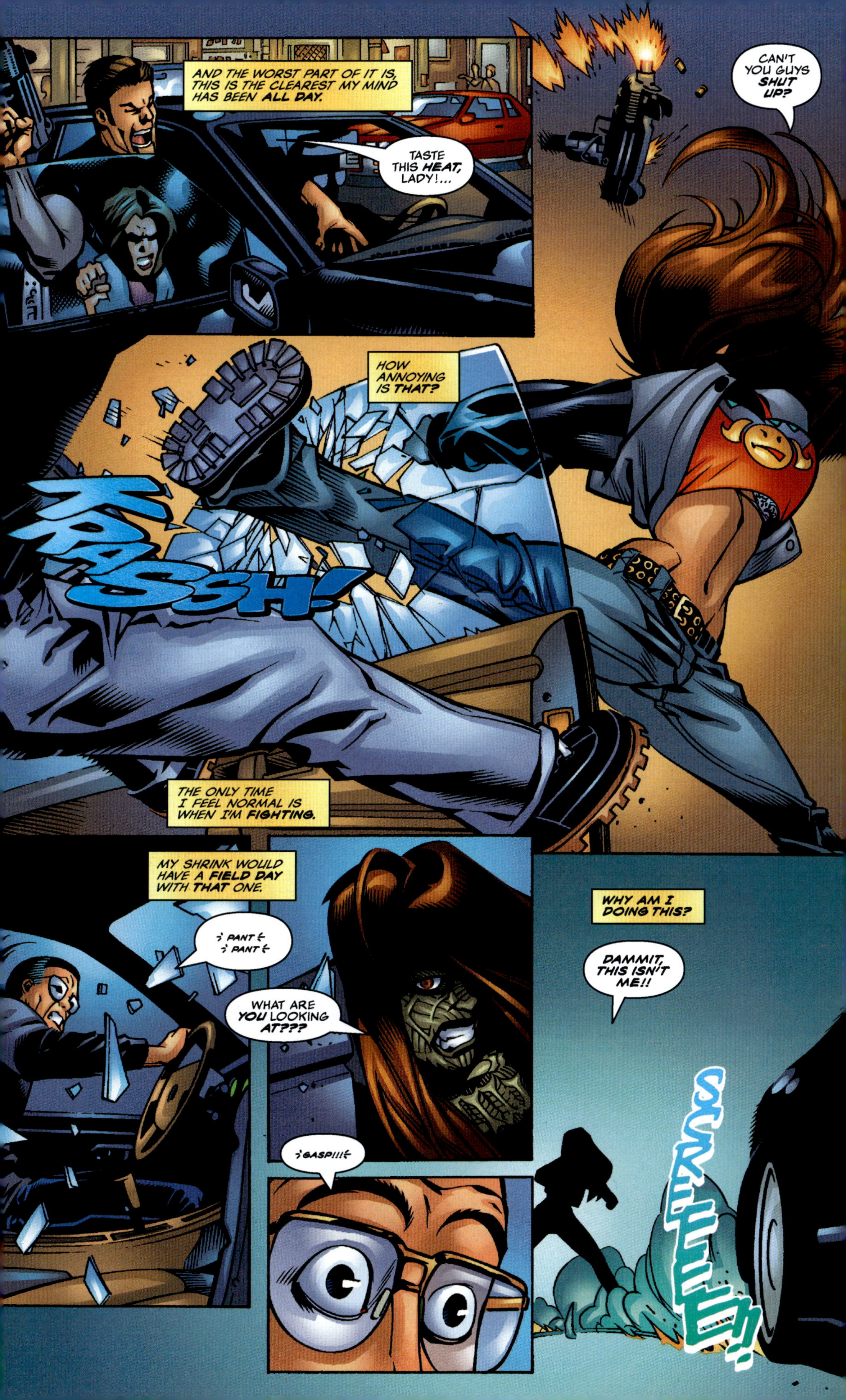
AND THE WORST PART OF IT IS, THIS IS THE CLEAREST MY MIND HAS BEEN ALL DAY.
TASTE THIS HEAT, LADY!...
CAN'T YOU GUYS SHUT UP?
HOW ANNOYING IS THAT?
KRASSH!
THE ONLY TIME I FEEL NORMAL IS WHEN I'M FIGHTING.
MY SHRINK WOULD HAVE A FIELD DAY WITH THAT ONE.
PANT PANT
WHAT ARE YOU LOOKING AT???
GASP!!!
WHY AM I DOING THIS?
DAMMIT, THIS ISN'T ME!!
SCREEEE!!

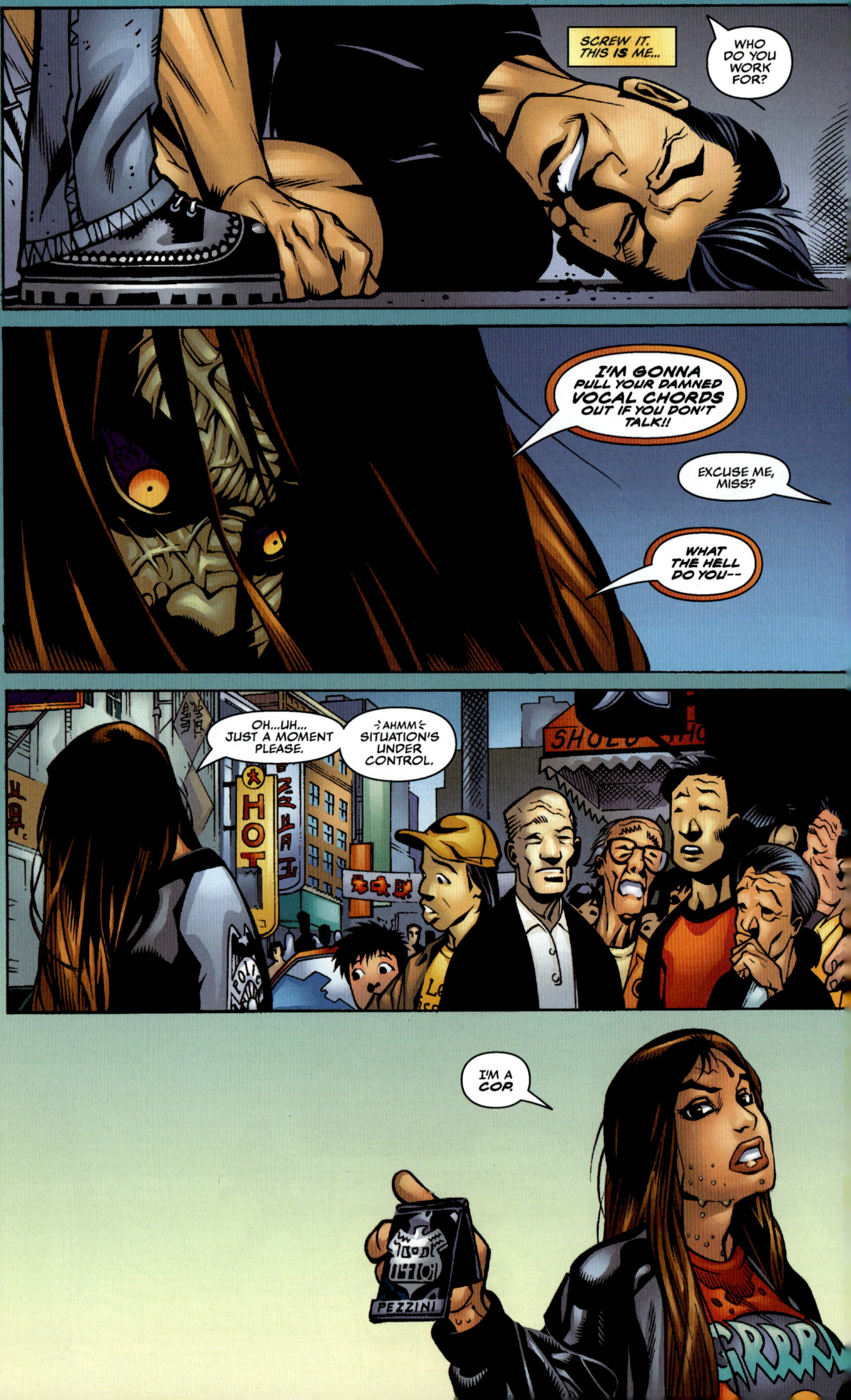
SCREW IT. THIS IS ME...
WHO DO YOU WORK FOR?
I'M GONNA PULL YOUR DAMNED VOCAL CHORDS OUT IF YOU DON'T TALK!!
EXCUSE ME, MISS?
WHAT THE HELL DO YOU--
OH...UH... JUST A MOMENT PLEASE.
AHMM SITUATION'S UNDER CONTROL.
I'M A COP.
PEZZINI

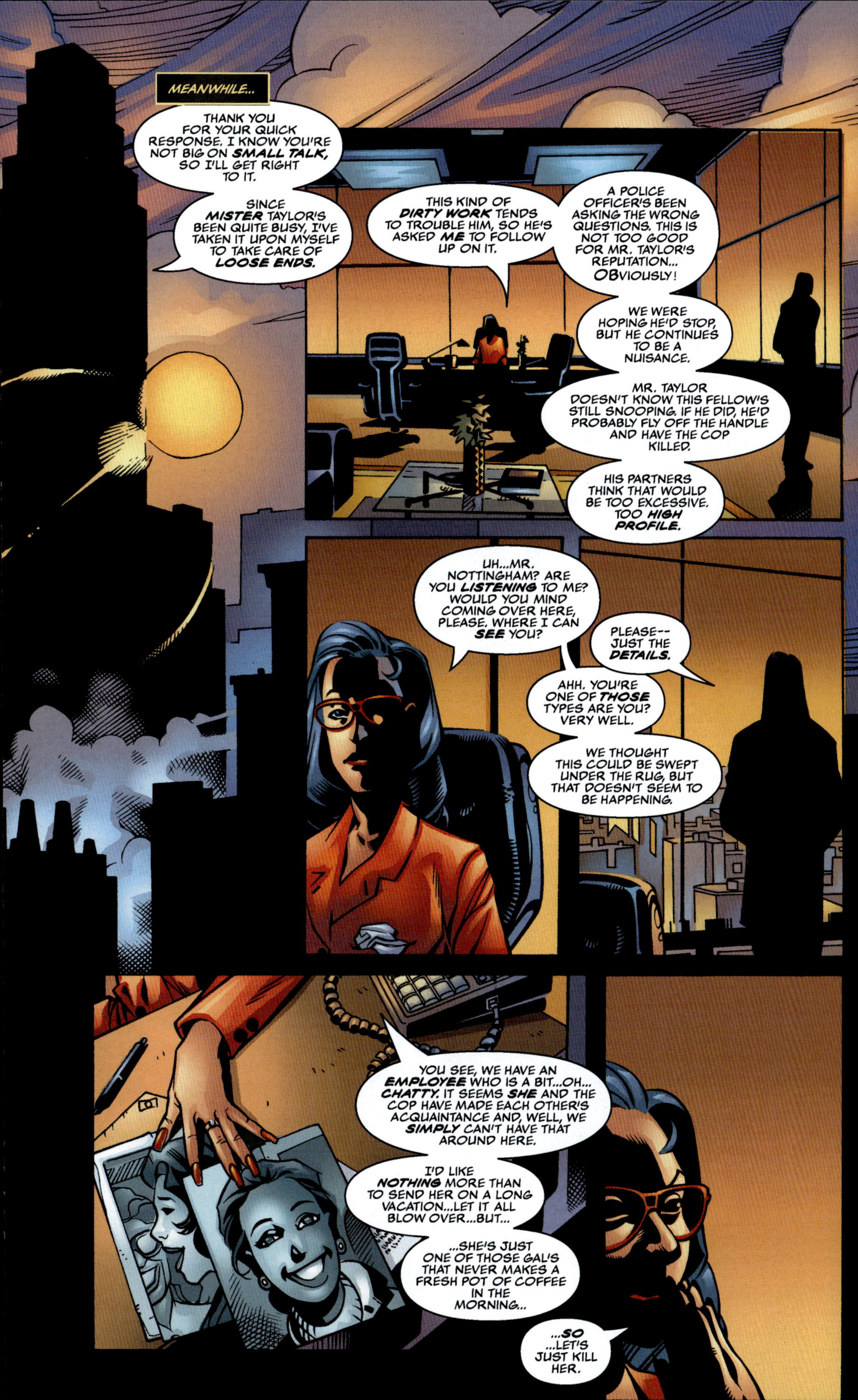
MEANWHILE...
THANK YOU FOR YOUR QUICK RESPONSE. I KNOW YOU'RE NOT BIG ON SMALL TALK, SO I'LL GET RIGHT TO IT.
SINCE MISTER TAYLOR'S BEEN QUITE BUSY, I'VE TAKEN IT UPON MYSELF TO TAKE CARE OF LOOSE ENDS.
THIS KIND OF DIRTY WORK TENDS TO TROUBLE HIM, SO HE'S ASKED ME TO FOLLOW UP ON IT.
A POLICE OFFICER'S BEEN ASKING THE WRONG QUESTIONS. THIS IS NOT TOO GOOD FOR MR. TAYLOR'S REPUTATION... OBVIOUSLY!
WE WERE HOPING HE'D STOP, BUT HE CONTINUES TO BE A NUISANCE.
MR. TAYLOR DOESN'T KNOW THIS FELLOW'S STILL SNOOPING. IF HE DID, HE'D PROBABLY FLY OFF THE HANDLE AND HAVE THE COP KILLED.
HIS PARTNERS THINK THAT WOULD BE TOO EXCESSIVE. TOO HIGH PROFILE.
UH...MR. NOTTINGHAM? ARE YOU LISTENING TO ME? WOULD YOU MIND COMING OVER HERE, PLEASE, WHERE I CAN SEE YOU?
PLEASE-- JUST THE DETAILS.
AHH. YOU'RE ONE OF THOSE TYPES ARE YOU? VERY WELL.
WE THOUGHT THIS COULD BE SWEPT UNDER THE RUG, BUT THAT DOESN'T SEEM TO BE HAPPENING.
YOU SEE, WE HAVE AN EMPLOYEE WHO IS A BIT...OH... CHATTY. IT SEEMS SHE AND THE COP HAVE MADE EACH OTHER'S ACQUAINTANCE AND, WELL, WE SIMPLY CAN'T HAVE THAT AROUND HERE.
I'D LIKE NOTHING MORE THAN TO SEND HER ON A LONG VACATION...LET IT ALL BLOW OVER...BUT...
...SHE'S JUST ONE OF THOSE GAL'S THAT NEVER MAKES A FRESH POT OF COFFEE IN THE MORNING...
...SO ...LET'S JUST KILL HER.

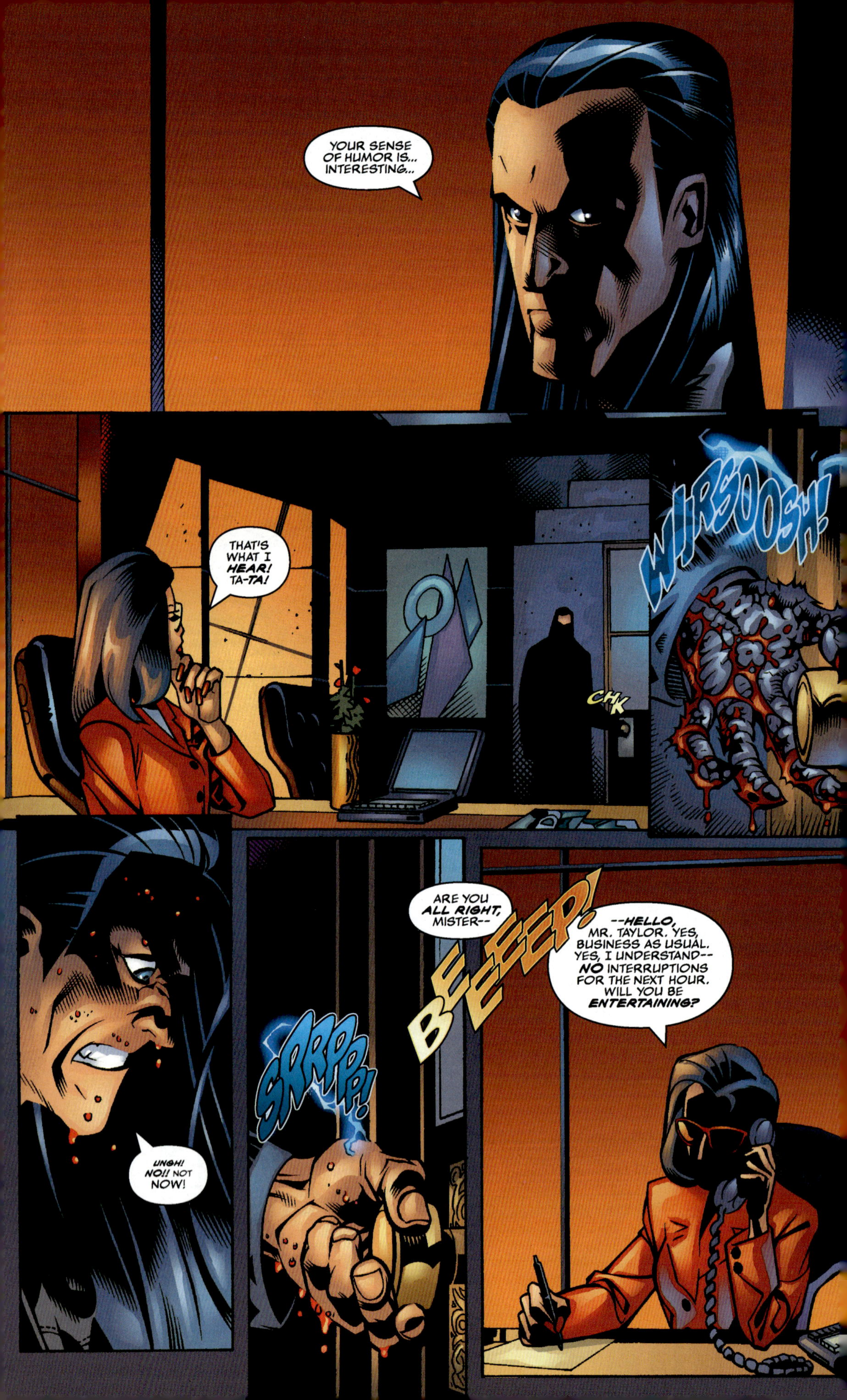
YOUR SENSE OF HUMOR IS... INTERESTING...
THAT'S WHAT I HEAR! TA-TA!
WIRSOOSH!
CHK
UNGH! NO!! NOT NOW!
SRRPPP!
ARE YOU ALL RIGHT, MISTER--
BEEEEP!
--HELLO, MR. TAYLOR. YES, BUSINESS AS USUAL. YES, I UNDERSTAND-- NO INTERRUPTIONS FOR THE NEXT HOUR. WILL YOU BE ENTERTAINING?

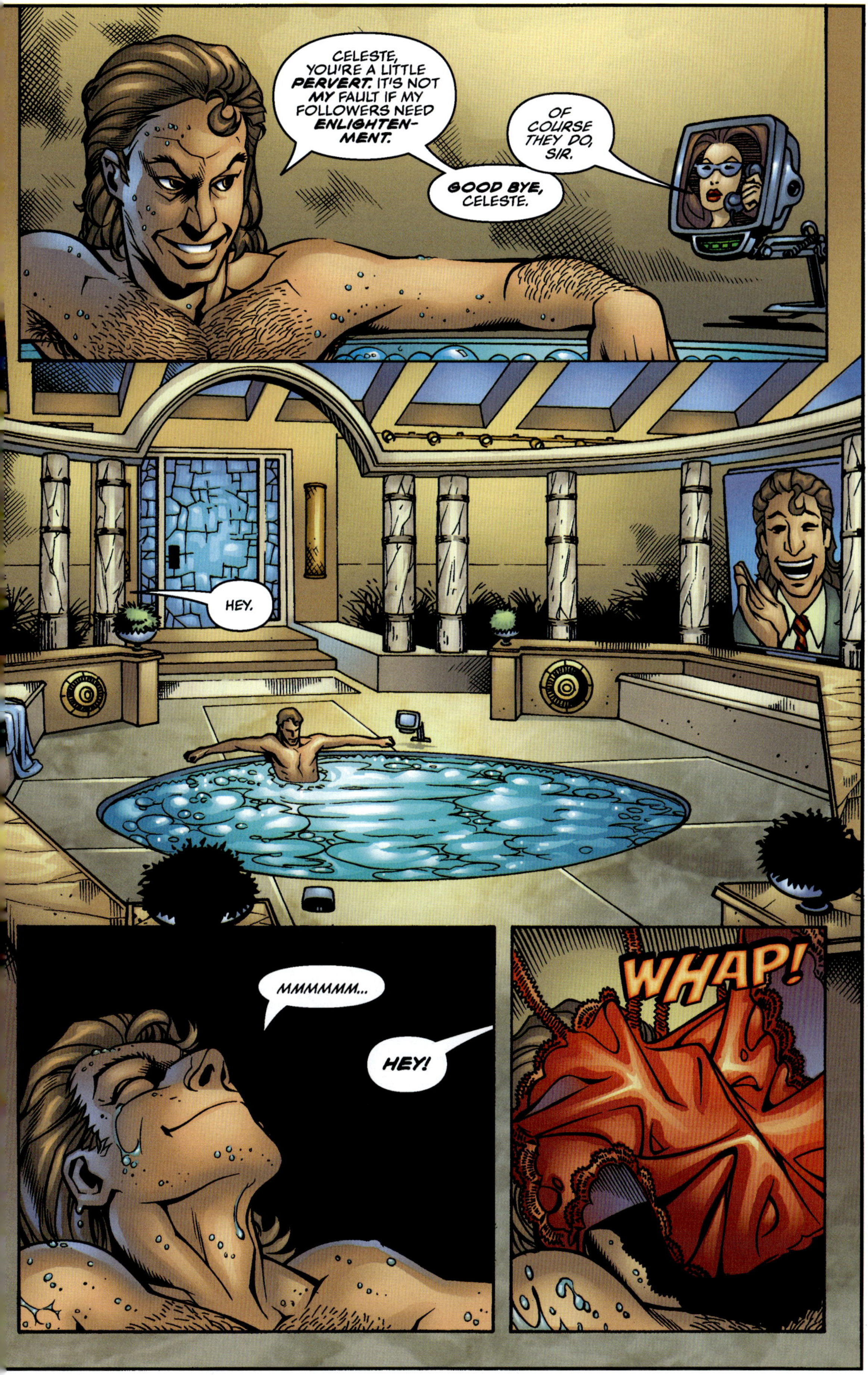
CELESTE, YOU'RE A LITTLE **PERVERT.** IT'S NOT **MY** FAULT IF MY FOLLOWERS NEED **ENLIGHTENMENT.**
OF COURSE THEY DO, SIR.
GOOD BYE, CELESTE.
HEY.
MMMMMM...
HEY!
WHAP!

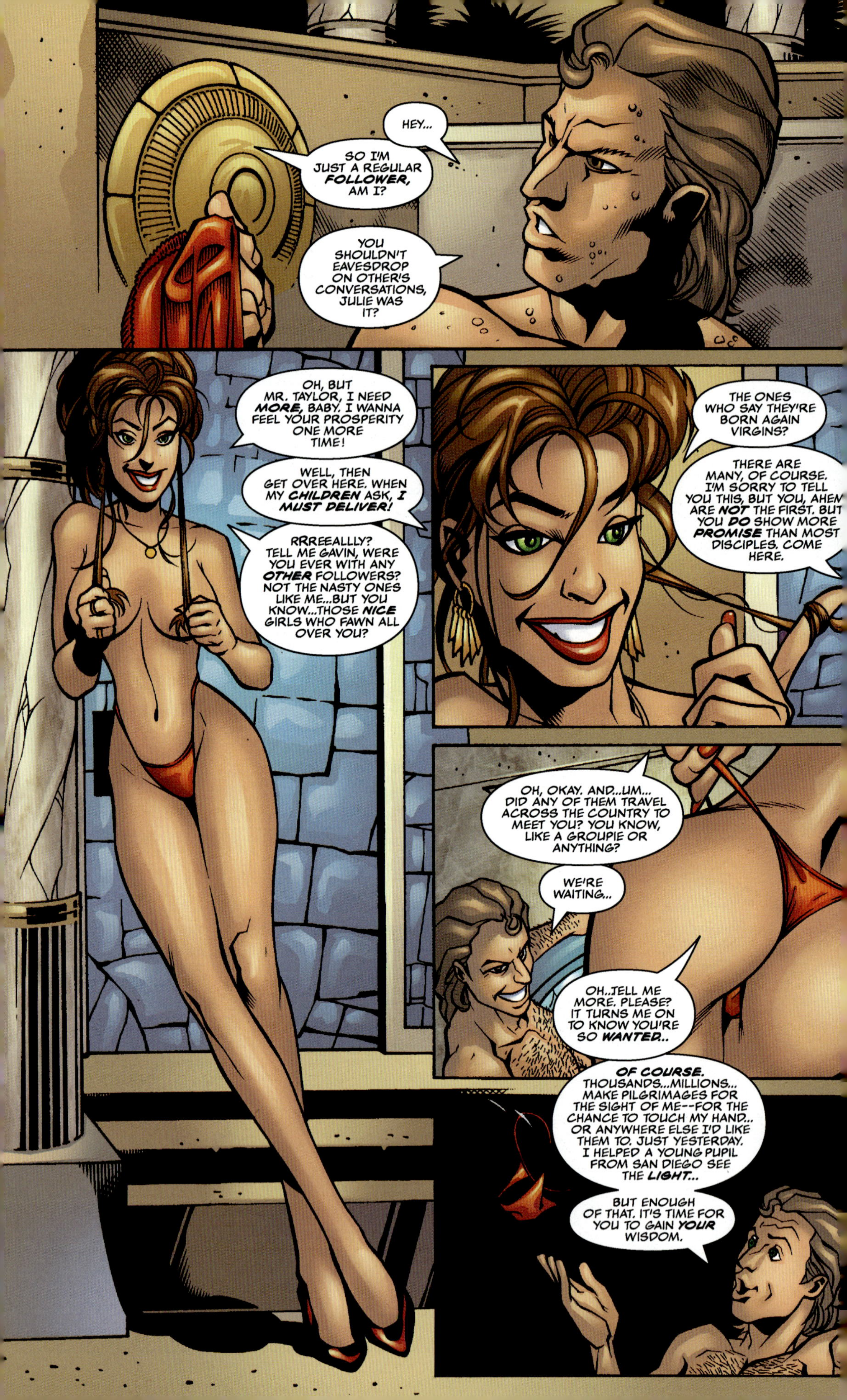
HEY...
SO I'M JUST A REGULAR FOLLOWER, AM I?
YOU SHOULDN'T EAVESDROP ON OTHER'S CONVERSATIONS, JULIE WAS IT?
OH, BUT MR. TAYLOR, I NEED MORE, BABY. I WANNA FEEL YOUR PROSPERITY ONE MORE TIME!
WELL, THEN GET OVER HERE. WHEN MY CHILDREN ASK, I MUST DELIVER!
RRREEALLLY? TELL ME GAVIN, WERE YOU EVER WITH ANY OTHER FOLLOWERS? NOT THE NASTY ONES LIKE ME...BUT YOU KNOW...THOSE NICE GIRLS WHO FAWN ALL OVER YOU?
THE ONES WHO SAY THEY'RE BORN AGAIN VIRGINS?
THERE ARE MANY, OF COURSE. I'M SORRY TO TELL YOU THIS, BUT YOU, AHEM ARE NOT THE FIRST. BUT YOU DO SHOW MORE PROMISE THAN MOST DISCIPLES. COME HERE.
OH, OKAY. AND...UM... DID ANY OF THEM TRAVEL ACROSS THE COUNTRY TO MEET YOU? YOU KNOW, LIKE A GROUPIE OR ANYTHING?
WE'RE WAITING...
OH..TELL ME MORE. PLEASE? IT TURNS ME ON TO KNOW YOU'RE SO WANTED..
OF COURSE. THOUSANDS...MILLIONS... MAKE PILGRIMAGES FOR THE SIGHT OF ME--FOR THE CHANCE TO TOUCH MY HAND... OR ANYWHERE ELSE I'D LIKE THEM TO. JUST YESTERDAY, I HELPED A YOUNG PUPIL FROM SAN DIEGO SEE THE LIGHT...
BUT ENOUGH OF THAT. IT'S TIME FOR YOU TO GAIN YOUR WISDOM.

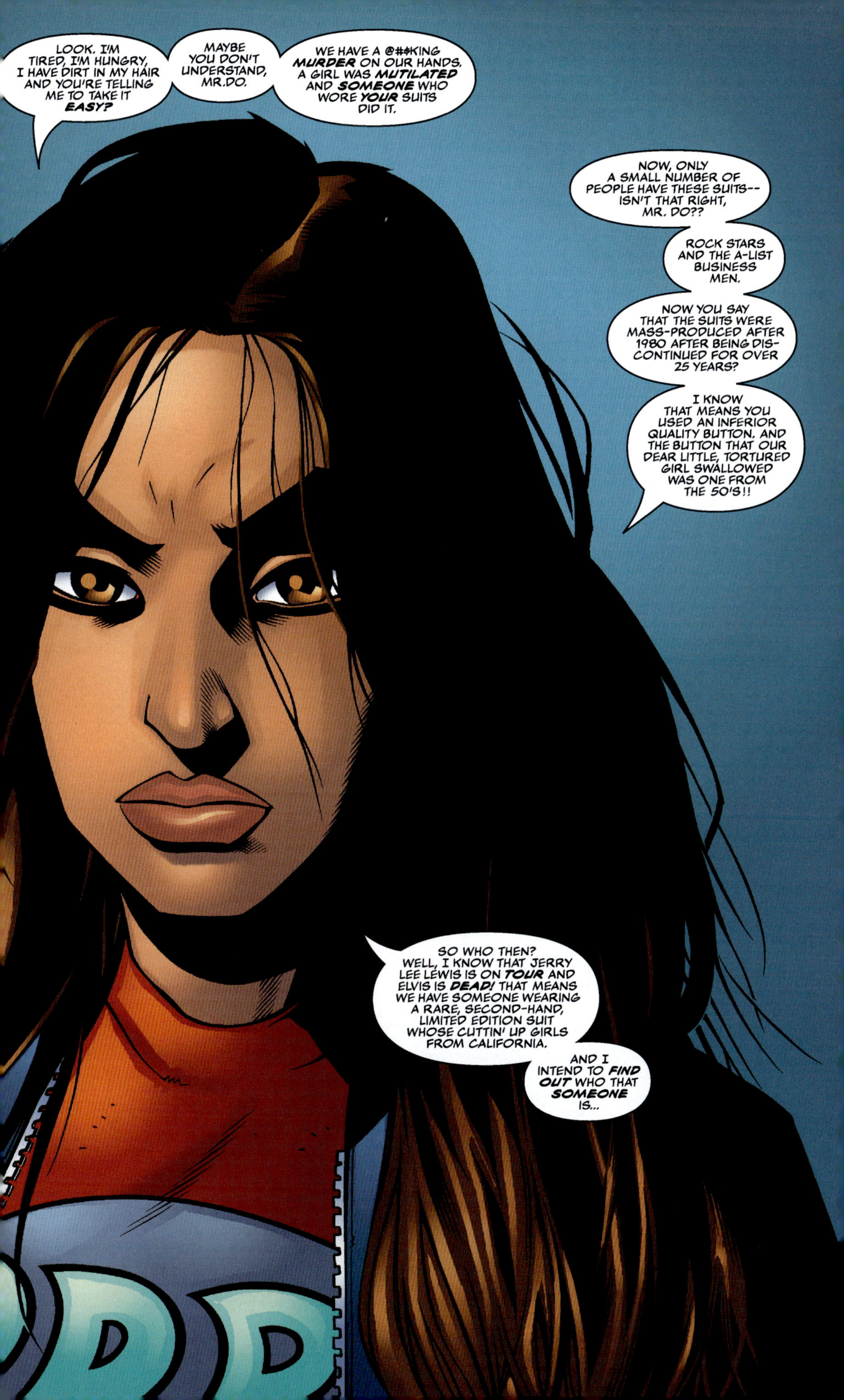
LOOK, I'M TIRED, I'M HUNGRY, I HAVE DIRT IN MY HAIR AND YOU'RE TELLING ME TO TAKE IT EASY?
MAYBE YOU DON'T UNDERSTAND, MR.DO.
WE HAVE A @##KING MURDER ON OUR HANDS. A GIRL WAS MUTILATED AND SOMEONE WHO WORE YOUR SUITS DID IT.
NOW, ONLY A SMALL NUMBER OF PEOPLE HAVE THESE SUITS-- ISN'T THAT RIGHT, MR. DO??
ROCK STARS AND THE A-LIST BUSINESS MEN.
NOW YOU SAY THAT THE SUITS WERE MASS-PRODUCED AFTER 1980 AFTER BEING DISCONTINUED FOR OVER 25 YEARS?
I KNOW THAT MEANS YOU USED AN INFERIOR QUALITY BUTTON, AND THE BUTTON THAT OUR DEAR LITTLE, TORTURED GIRL SWALLOWED WAS ONE FROM THE 50'S!!
SO WHO THEN? WELL, I KNOW THAT JERRY LEE LEWIS IS ON TOUR AND ELVIS IS DEAD! THAT MEANS WE HAVE SOMEONE WEARING A RARE, SECOND-HAND, LIMITED EDITION SUIT WHOSE CUTTIN' UP GIRLS FROM CALIFORNIA.
AND I INTEND TO FIND OUT WHO THAT SOMEONE IS...

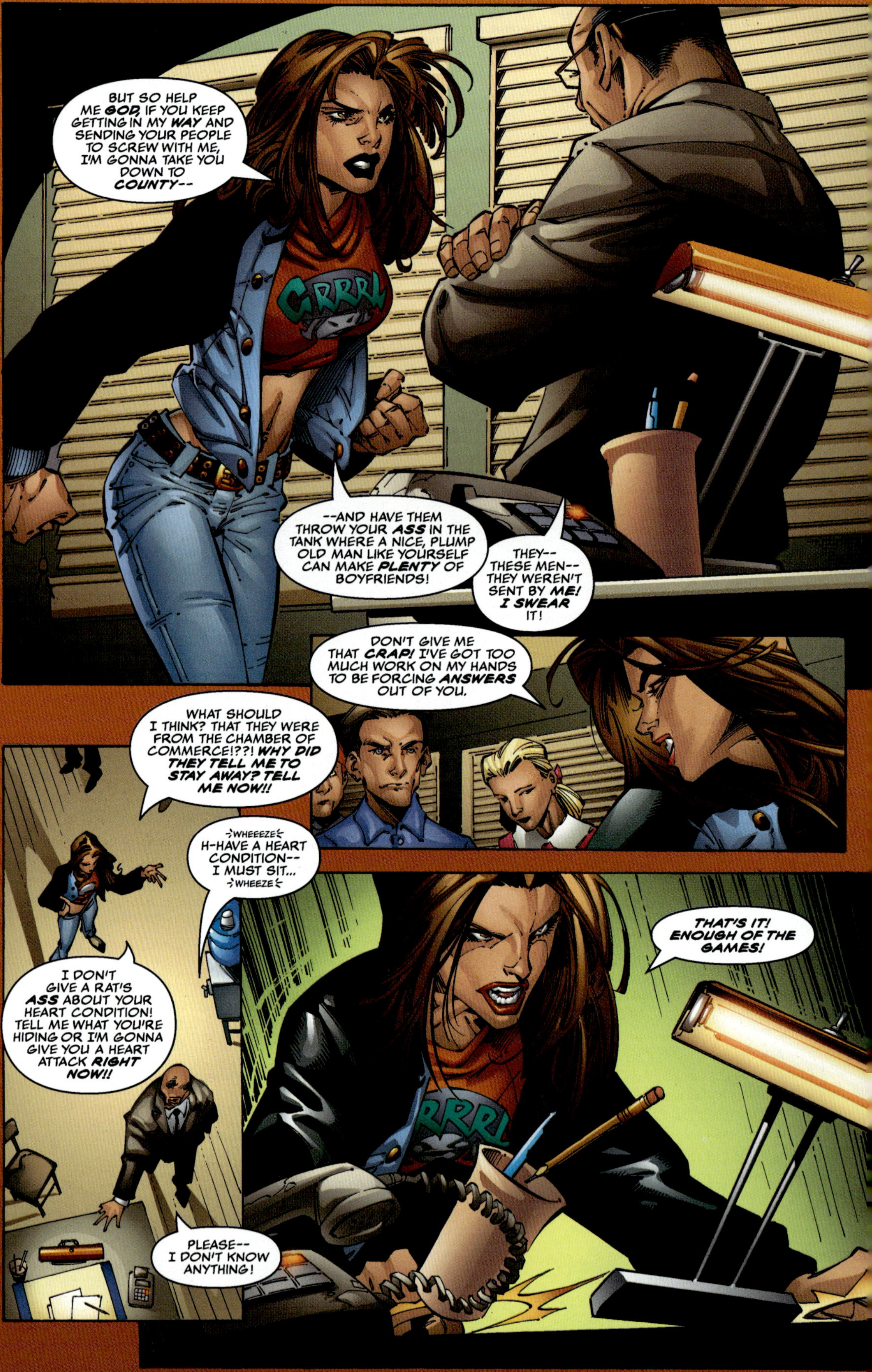
BUT SO HELP ME GOD, IF YOU KEEP GETTING IN MY WAY AND SENDING YOUR PEOPLE TO SCREW WITH ME, I'M GONNA TAKE YOU DOWN TO COUNTY--
--AND HAVE THEM THROW YOUR ASS IN THE TANK WHERE A NICE, PLUMP OLD MAN LIKE YOURSELF CAN MAKE PLENTY OF BOYFRIENDS!
THEY-- THESE MEN-- THEY WEREN'T SENT BY ME! I SWEAR IT!
DON'T GIVE ME THAT CRAP! I'VE GOT TOO MUCH WORK ON MY HANDS TO BE FORCING ANSWERS OUT OF YOU.
WHAT SHOULD I THINK? THAT THEY WERE FROM THE CHAMBER OF COMMERCE!??! WHY DID THEY TELL ME TO STAY AWAY? TELL ME NOW!!
WHEEEZE H-HAVE A HEART CONDITION-- I MUST SIT... WHEEZE
I DON'T GIVE A RAT'S ASS ABOUT YOUR HEART CONDITION! TELL ME WHAT YOU'RE HIDING OR I'M GONNA GIVE YOU A HEART ATTACK RIGHT NOW!!
PLEASE-- I DON'T KNOW ANYTHING!
THAT'S IT! ENOUGH OF THE GAMES!

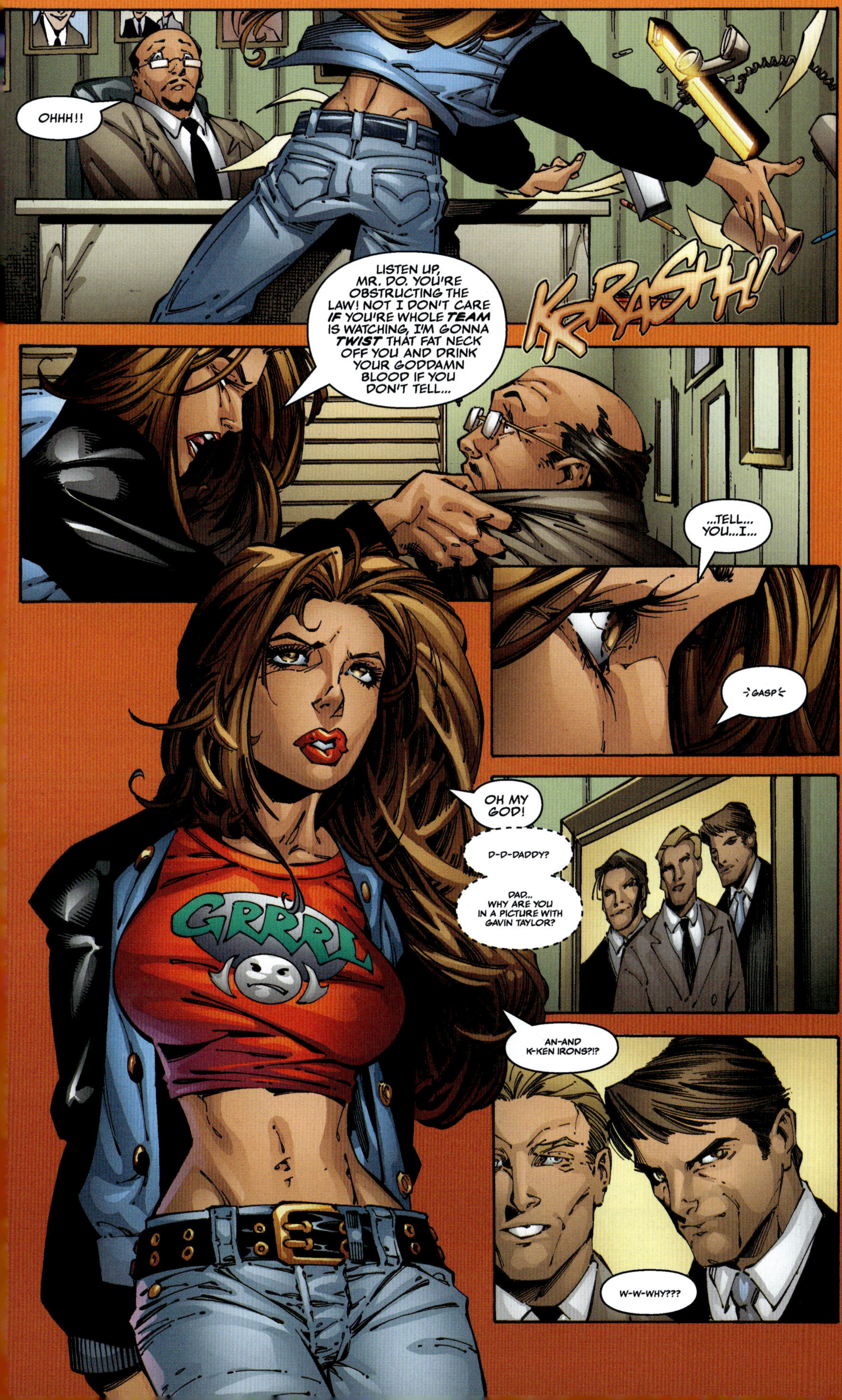
OHHH!!
LISTEN UP, MR. DO. YOU'RE OBSTRUCTING THE LAW! NOT I DON'T CARE IF YOU'RE WHOLE TEAM IS WATCHING, I'M GONNA TWIST THAT FAT NECK OFF YOU AND DRINK YOUR GODDAMN BLOOD IF YOU DON'T TELL...
K-RASHH!
...TELL... YOU...I...
GASP
OH MY GOD!
D-D-DADDY?
DAD... WHY ARE YOU IN A PICTURE WITH GAVIN TAYLOR?
AN-AND K-KEN IRONS?!?
W-W-WHY???

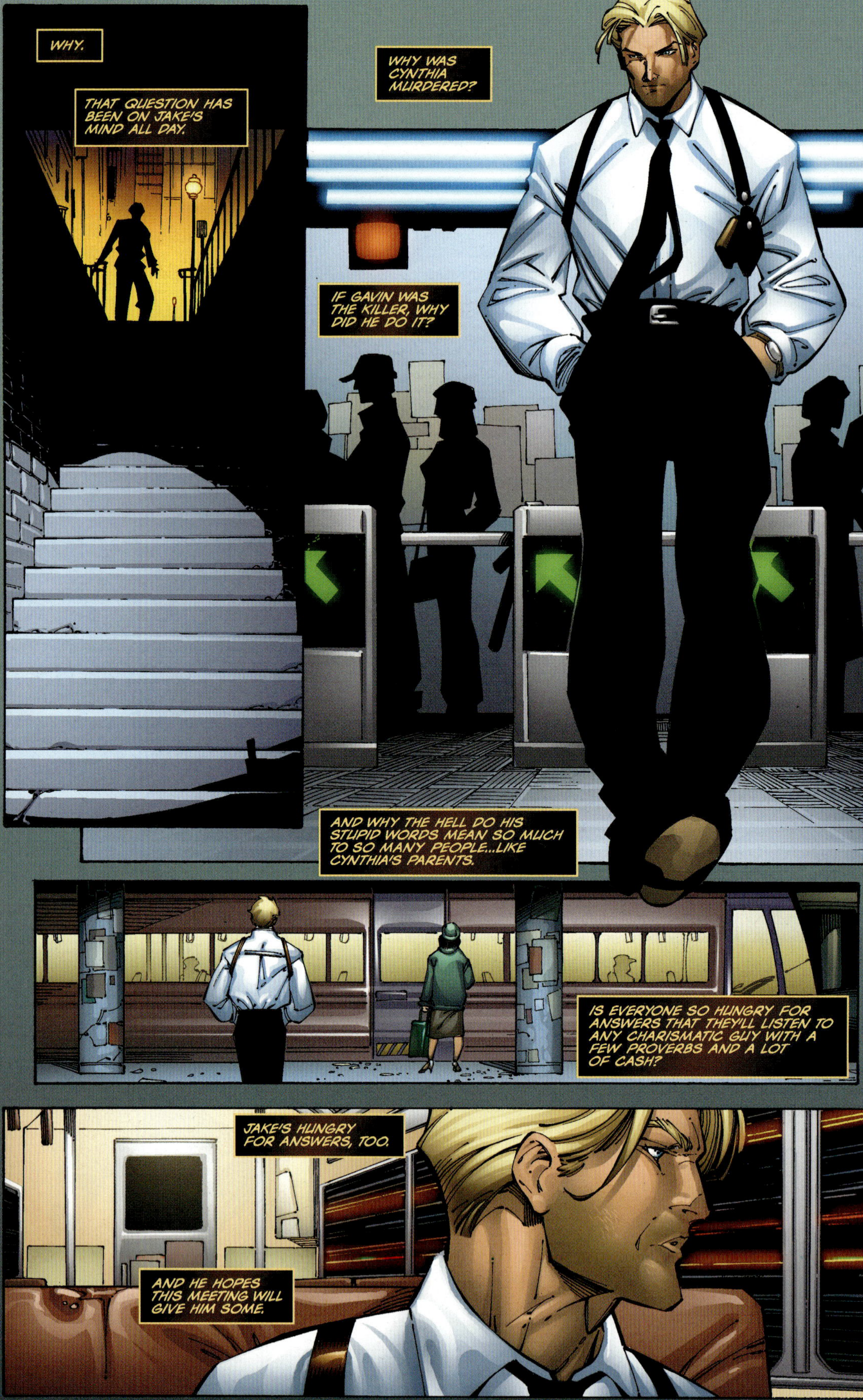
WHY.
THAT QUESTION HAS BEEN ON JAKE'S MIND ALL DAY.
WHY WAS CYNTHIA MURDERED?
IF GAVIN WAS THE KILLER, WHY DID HE DO IT?
AND WHY THE HELL DO HIS STUPID WORDS MEAN SO MUCH TO SO MANY PEOPLE...LIKE CYNTHIA'S PARENTS.
IS EVERYONE SO HUNGRY FOR ANSWERS THAT THEY'LL LISTEN TO ANY CHARISMATIC GUY WITH A FEW PROVERBS AND A LOT OF CASH?
JAKE'S HUNGRY FOR ANSWERS, TOO.
AND HE HOPES THIS MEETING WILL GIVE HIM SOME.

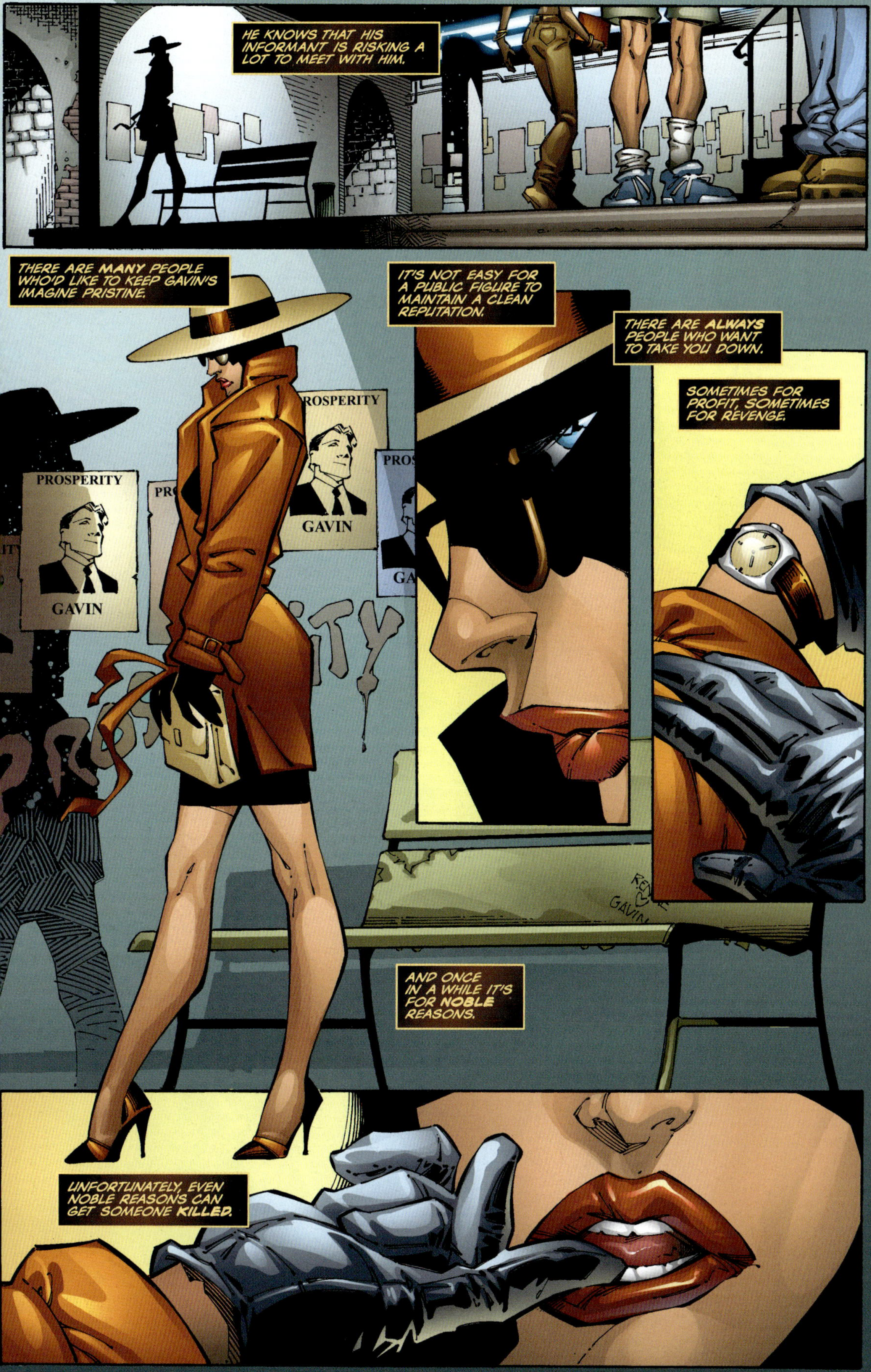

HE KNOWS THAT HIS INFORMANT IS RISKING A LOT TO MEET WITH HIM.
THERE ARE MANY PEOPLE WHO'D LIKE TO KEEP GAVIN'S IMAGINE PRISTINE.
PROSPERITY
GAVIN
PROSPERITY
GAVIN
IT'S NOT EASY FOR A PUBLIC FIGURE TO MAINTAIN A CLEAN REPUTATION.
THERE ARE ALWAYS PEOPLE WHO WANT TO TAKE YOU DOWN.
SOMETIMES FOR PROFIT, SOMETIMES FOR REVENGE.
AND ONCE IN A WHILE IT'S FOR NOBLE REASONS.
UNFORTUNATELY, EVEN NOBLE REASONS CAN GET SOMEONE KILLED.

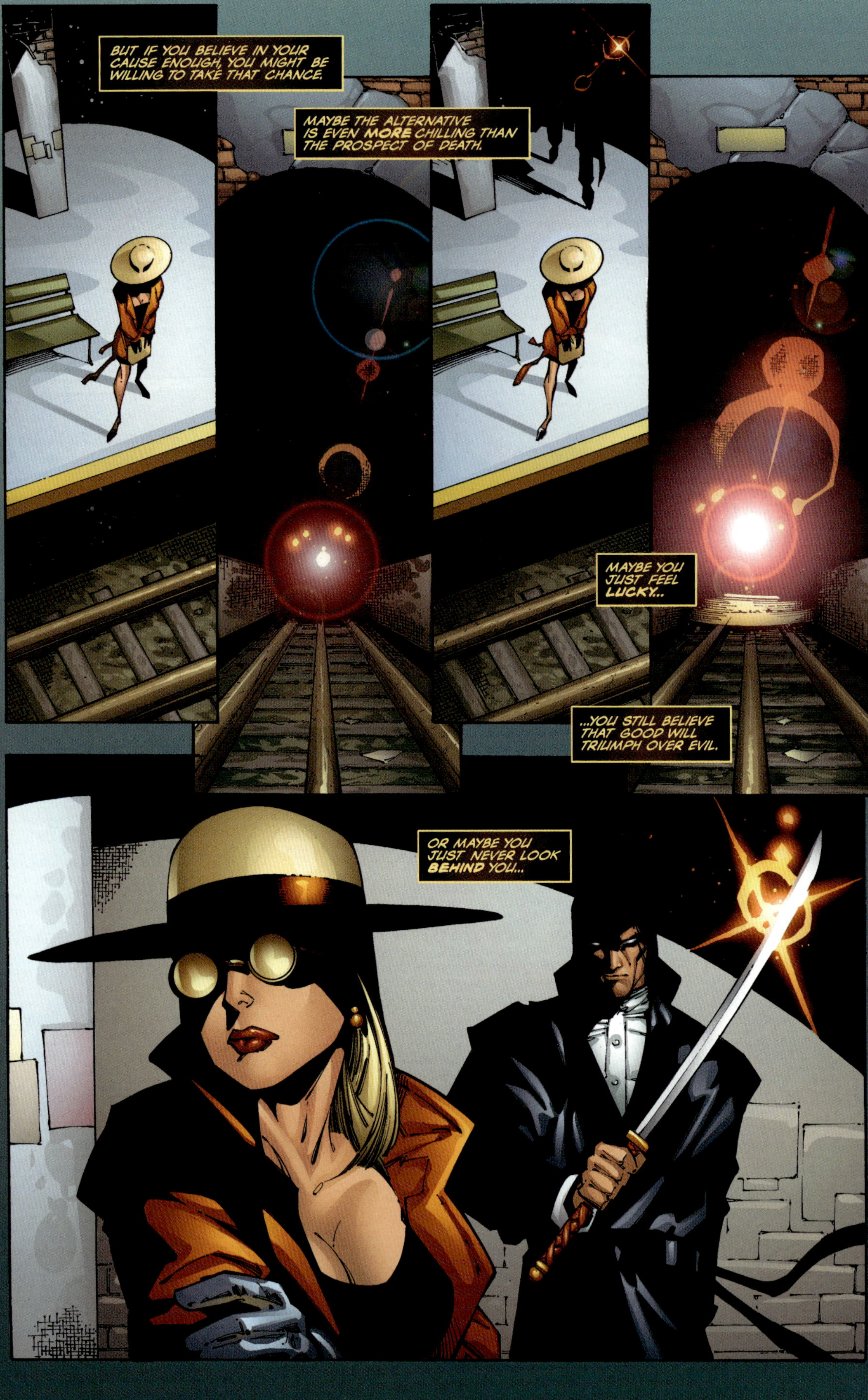
BUT IF YOU BELIEVE IN YOUR CAUSE ENOUGH, YOU MIGHT BE WILLING TO TAKE THAT CHANCE.
MAYBE THE ALTERNATIVE IS EVEN MORE CHILLING THAN THE PROSPECT OF DEATH.
MAYBE YOU JUST FEEL LUCKY...
...YOU STILL BELIEVE THAT GOOD WILL TRIUMPH OVER EVIL.
OR MAYBE YOU JUST NEVER LOOK BEHIND YOU...

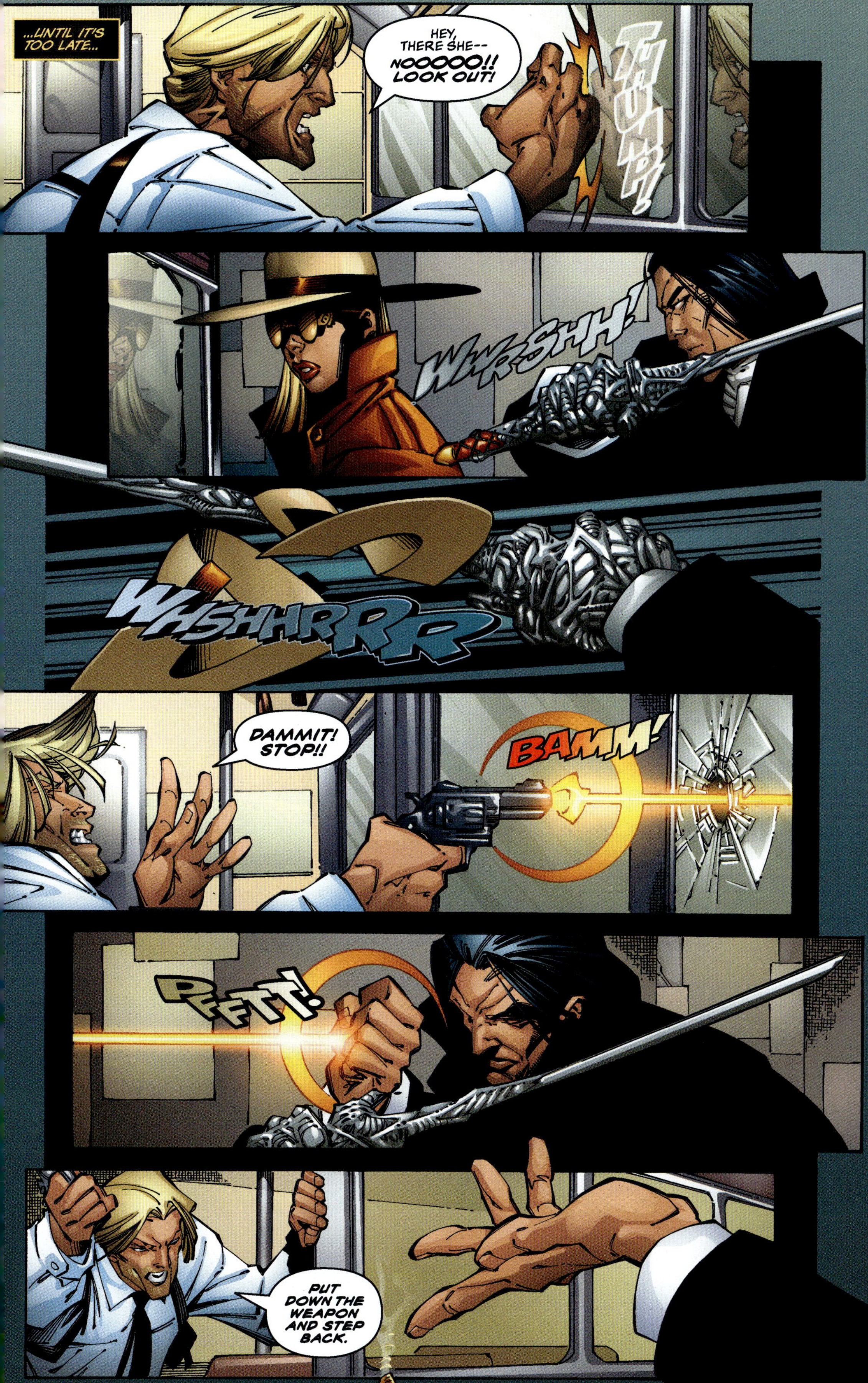
...UNTIL IT'S TOO LATE...
HEY, THERE SHE-- NOOOOO!! LOOK OUT!
THUMP!
WHR-SHH!
WHSHHRRR
DAMMIT! STOP!!
BAMM!
PFFT!
PUT DOWN THE WEAPON AND STEP BACK.

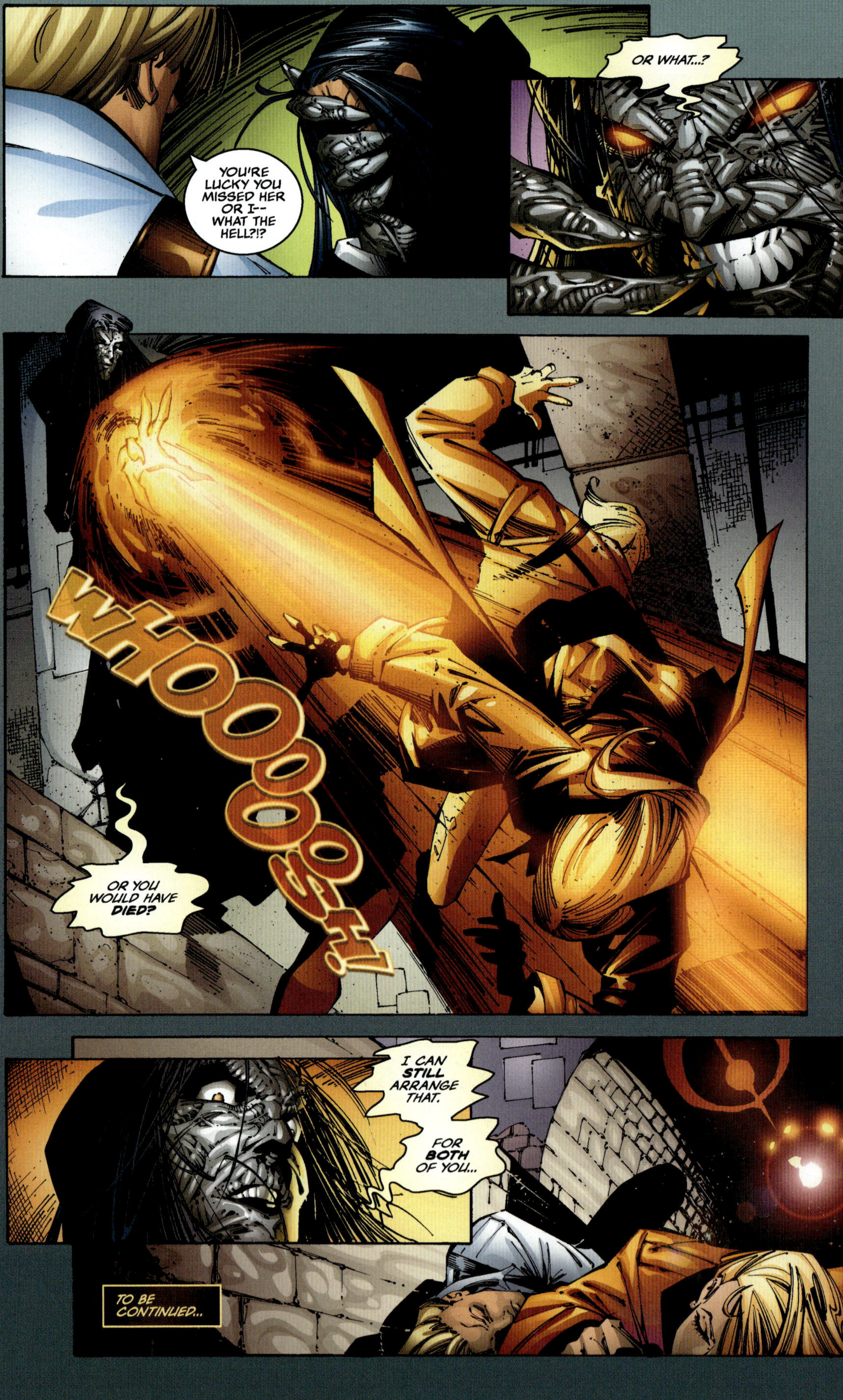
YOU'RE LUCKY YOU MISSED HER OR I-- WHAT THE HELL?!?
OR WHAT...?
WHOOOOOSH!
OR YOU WOULD HAVE DIED?
I CAN STILL ARRANGE THAT.
FOR BOTH OF YOU...
TO BE CONTINUED...

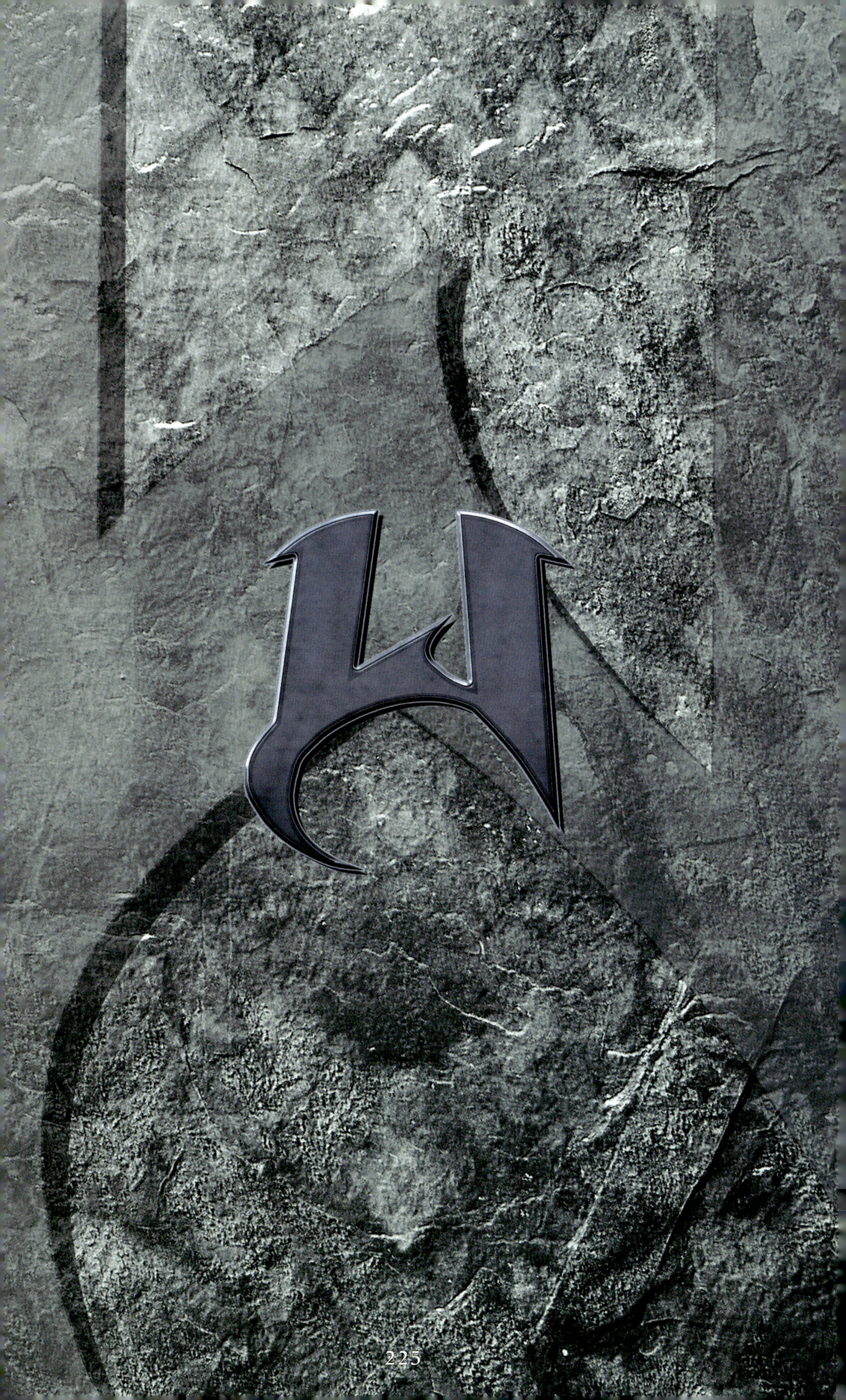

issue #25

story: David Wohl and Christina Z.
pencils: Michael Turner
inks: D-Tron
colors: JD Smith

pencil assists: Keu Cha
ink assists: Andy Kim, Jeff De Los Santos, Marcia Chen
and Jose "Jag" Guillen

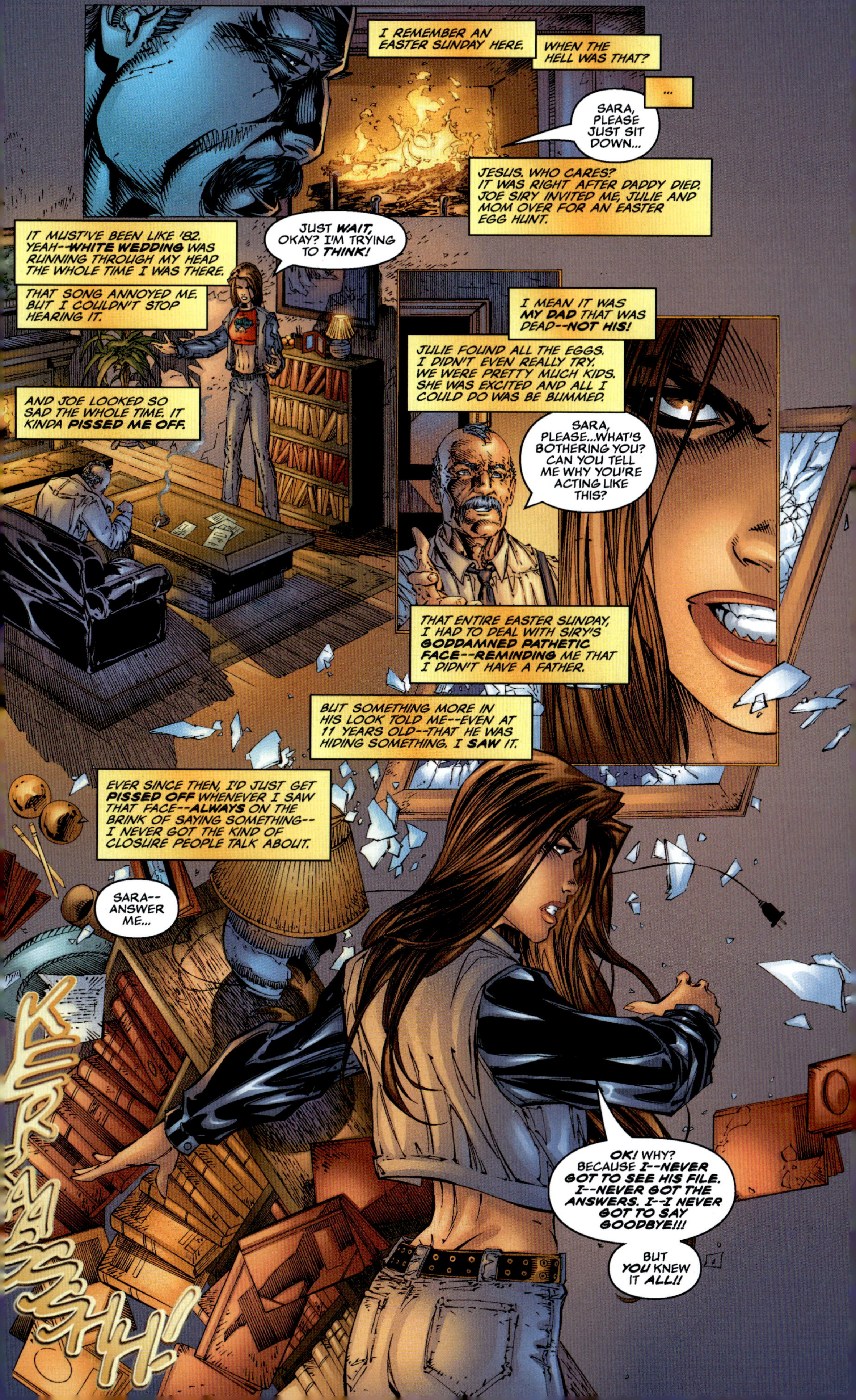

I REMEMBER AN EASTER SUNDAY HERE.
WHEN THE HELL WAS THAT?
...
SARA, PLEASE JUST SIT DOWN...
JESUS. WHO CARES? IT WAS RIGHT AFTER DADDY DIED. JOE SIRY INVITED ME, JULIE AND MOM OVER FOR AN EASTER EGG HUNT.
IT MUST'VE BEEN LIKE '82. YEAH--WHITE WEDDING WAS RUNNING THROUGH MY HEAD THE WHOLE TIME I WAS THERE.
JUST WAIT, OKAY? I'M TRYING TO THINK!
THAT SONG ANNOYED ME. BUT I COULDN'T STOP HEARING IT.
AND JOE LOOKED SO SAD THE WHOLE TIME. IT KINDA PISSED ME OFF.
I MEAN IT WAS MY DAD THAT WAS DEAD--NOT HIS!
JULIE FOUND ALL THE EGGS. I DIDN'T EVEN REALLY TRY. WE WERE PRETTY MUCH KIDS. SHE WAS EXCITED AND ALL I COULD DO WAS BE BUMMED.
SARA, PLEASE...WHAT'S BOTHERING YOU? CAN YOU TELL ME WHY YOU'RE ACTING LIKE THIS?
THAT ENTIRE EASTER SUNDAY, I HAD TO DEAL WITH SIRY'S GODDAMNED PATHETIC FACE--REMINDING ME THAT I DIDN'T HAVE A FATHER.
BUT SOMETHING MORE IN HIS LOOK TOLD ME--EVEN AT 11 YEARS OLD--THAT HE WAS HIDING SOMETHING. I SAW IT.
EVER SINCE THEN, I'D JUST GET PISSED OFF WHENEVER I SAW THAT FACE--ALWAYS ON THE BRINK OF SAYING SOMETHING-- I NEVER GOT THE KIND OF CLOSURE PEOPLE TALK ABOUT.
SARA-- ANSWER ME...
KERRAASSHH!
OK! WHY? BECAUSE I--NEVER GOT TO SEE HIS FILE. I--NEVER GOT THE ANSWERS. I--I NEVER GOT TO SAY GOODBYE!!!
BUT YOU KNEW IT ALL!!

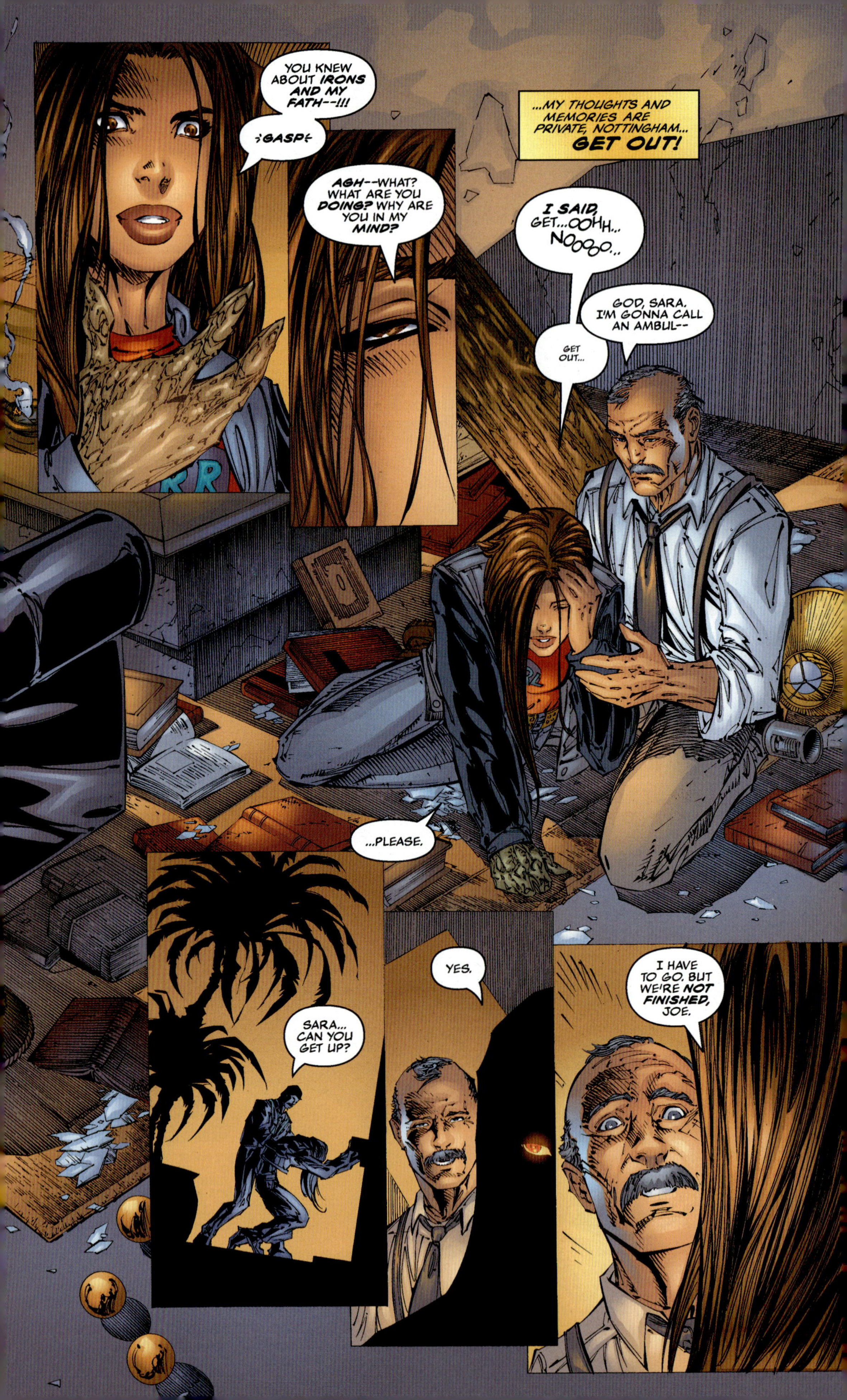
YOU KNEW ABOUT IRONS AND MY FATH--!!!
:GASP:
AGH--WHAT? WHAT ARE YOU DOING? WHY ARE YOU IN MY MIND?
...MY THOUGHTS AND MEMORIES ARE PRIVATE, NOTTINGHAM... GET OUT!
I SAID, GET...OOHH... NOOOOO...
GOD, SARA. I'M GONNA CALL AN AMBUL--
GET OUT...
...PLEASE.
SARA... CAN YOU GET UP?
YES.
I HAVE TO GO, BUT WE'RE NOT FINISHED, JOE.

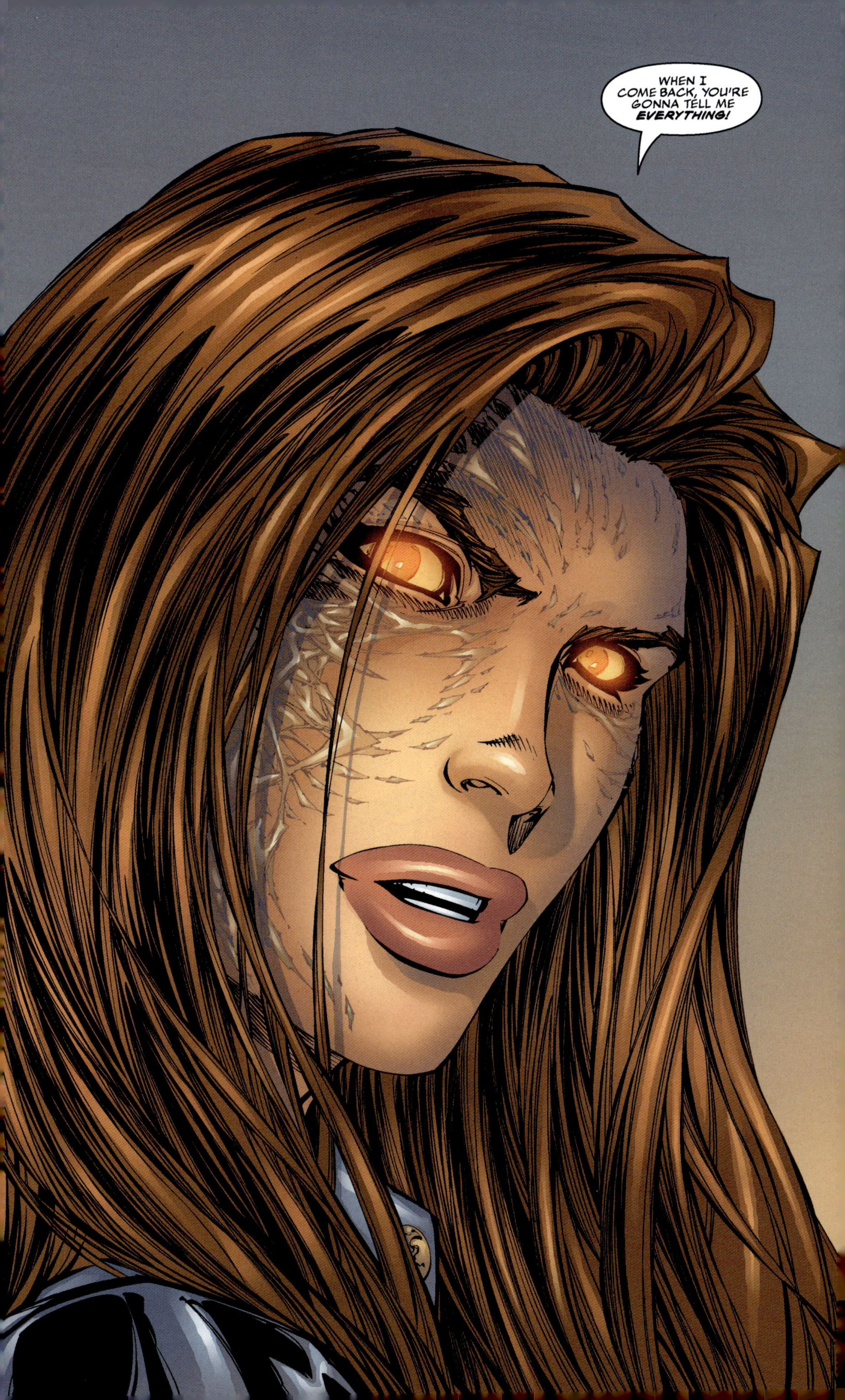
WHEN I COME BACK, YOU'RE GONNA TELL ME *EVERYTHING!*

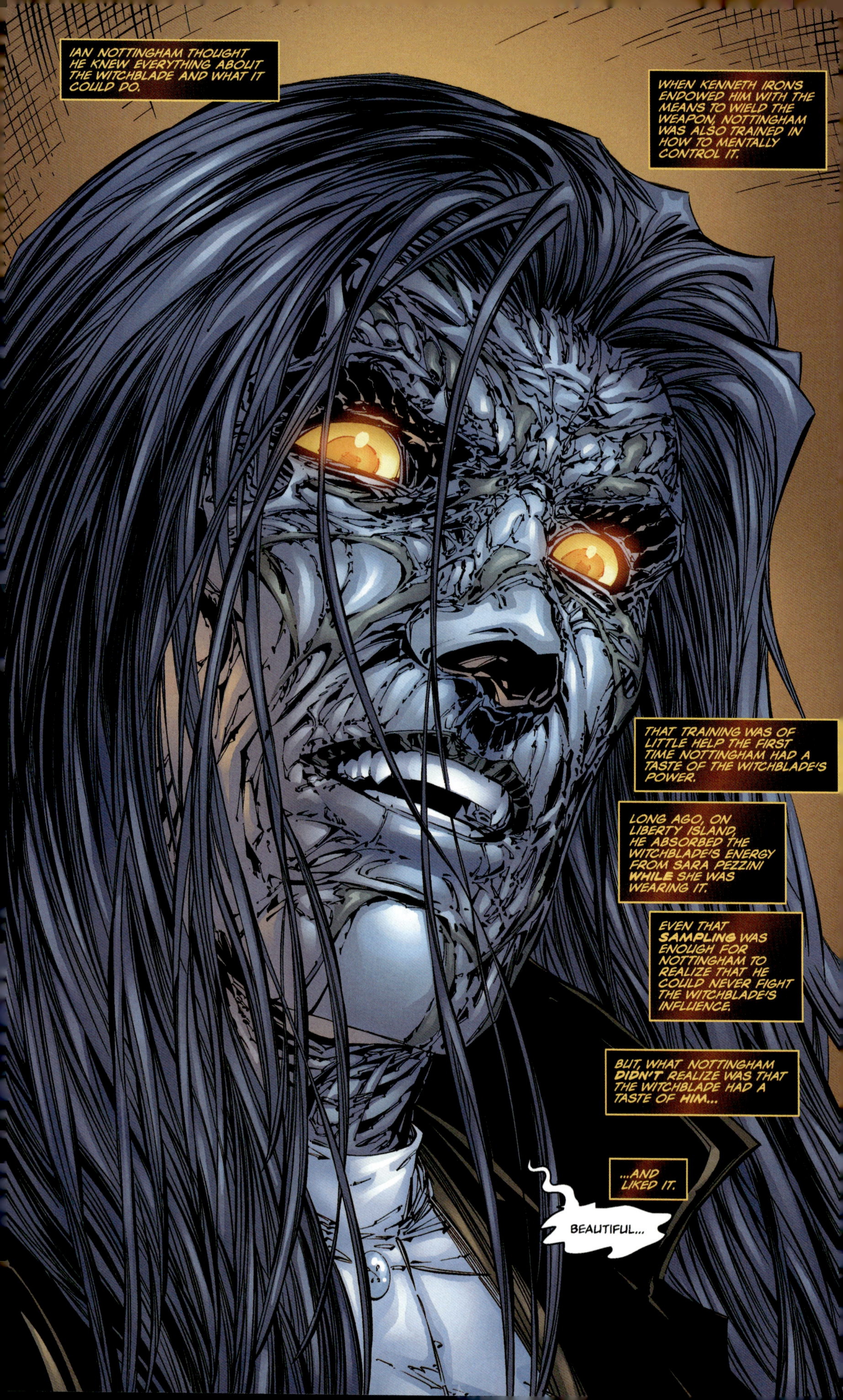
IAN NOTTINGHAM THOUGHT HE KNEW EVERYTHING ABOUT THE WITCHBLADE AND WHAT IT COULD DO.
WHEN KENNETH IRONS ENDOWED HIM WITH THE MEANS TO WIELD THE WEAPON, NOTTINGHAM WAS ALSO TRAINED IN HOW TO MENTALLY CONTROL IT.
THAT TRAINING WAS OF LITTLE HELP THE FIRST TIME NOTTINGHAM HAD A TASTE OF THE WITCHBLADE'S POWER.
LONG AGO, ON LIBERTY ISLAND, HE ABSORBED THE WITCHBLADE'S ENERGY FROM SARA PEZZINI **WHILE** SHE WAS WEARING IT.
EVEN THAT **SAMPLING** WAS ENOUGH FOR NOTTINGHAM TO REALIZE THAT HE COULD NEVER FIGHT THE WITCHBLADE'S INFLUENCE.
BUT, WHAT NOTTINGHAM **DIDN'T** REALIZE WAS THAT THE WITCHBLADE HAD A TASTE OF **HIM**...
...AND LIKED IT.
BEAUTIFUL...

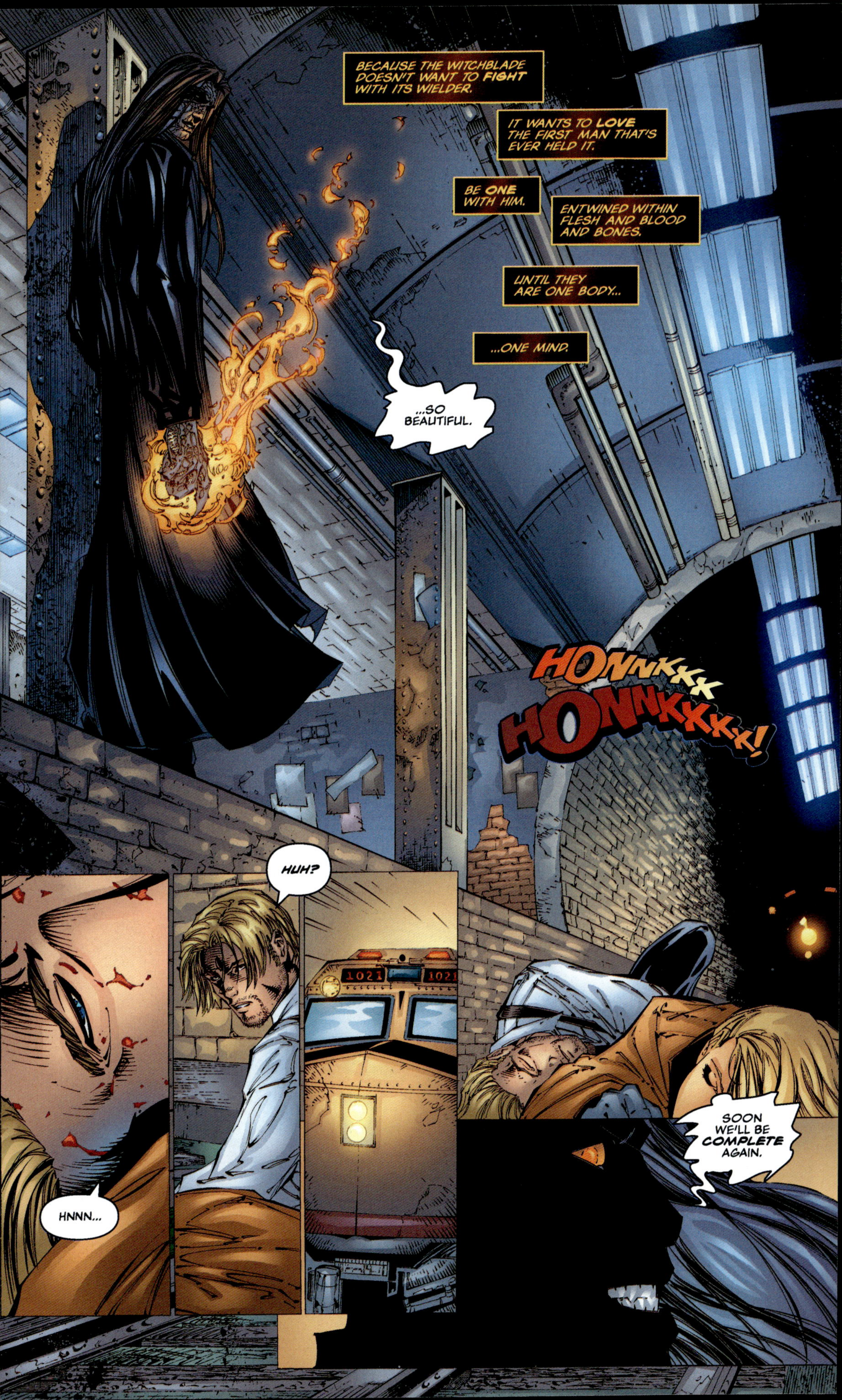

BECAUSE THE WITCHBLADE DOESN'T WANT TO FIGHT WITH ITS WIELDER.
IT WANTS TO LOVE THE FIRST MAN THAT'S EVER HELD IT.
BE ONE WITH HIM.
ENTWINED WITHIN FLESH AND BLOOD AND BONES.
UNTIL THEY ARE ONE BODY...
...ONE MIND.
...SO BEAUTIFUL.
HONNKKKK
HONNKKKKK!
HNNN...
HUH?
1021
SOON WE'LL BE COMPLETE AGAIN.

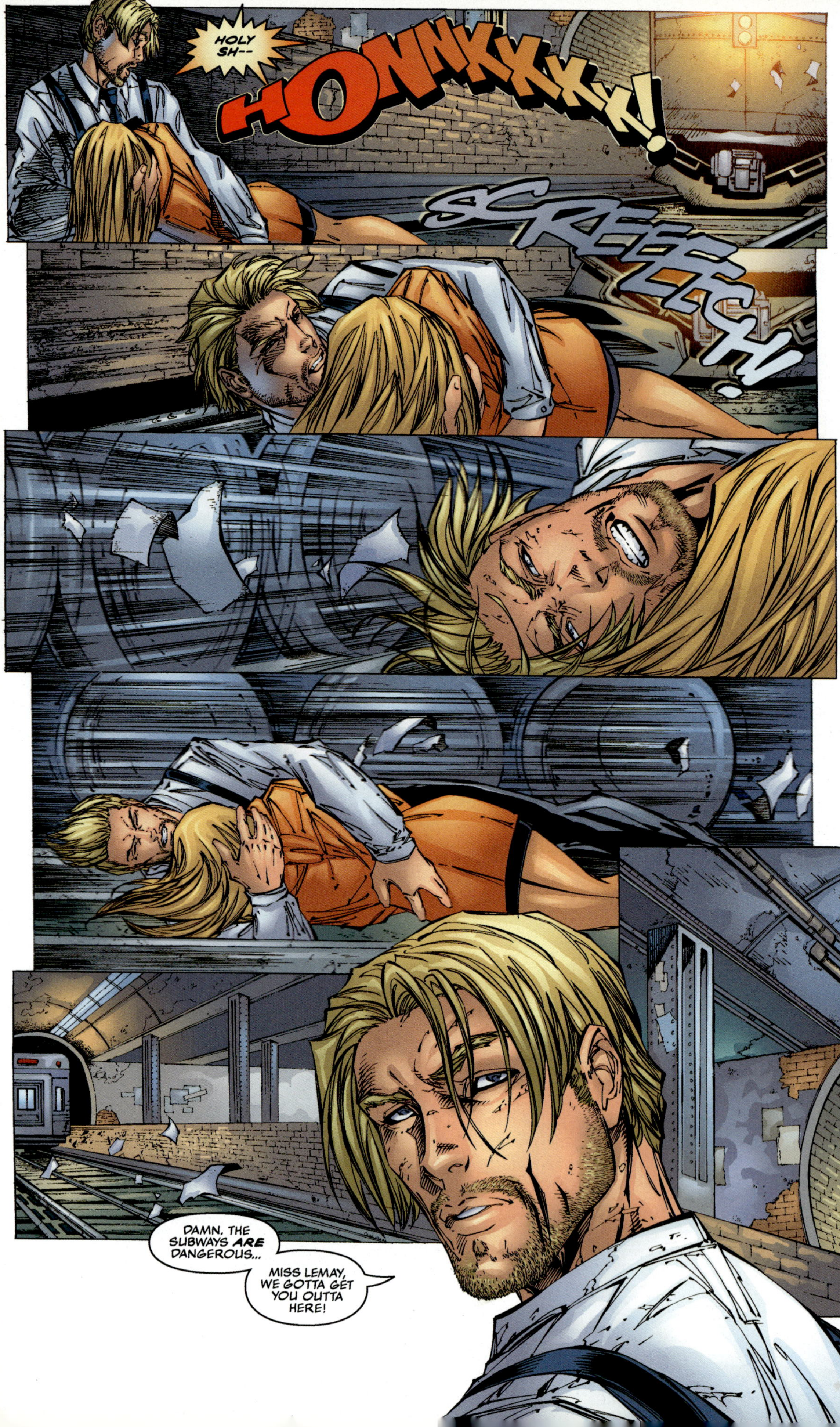
HOLY SH--
HONNKKKKK!
SCREEEECH!
DAMN, THE SUBWAYS ARE DANGEROUS...
MISS LEMAY, WE GOTTA GET YOU OUTTA HERE!

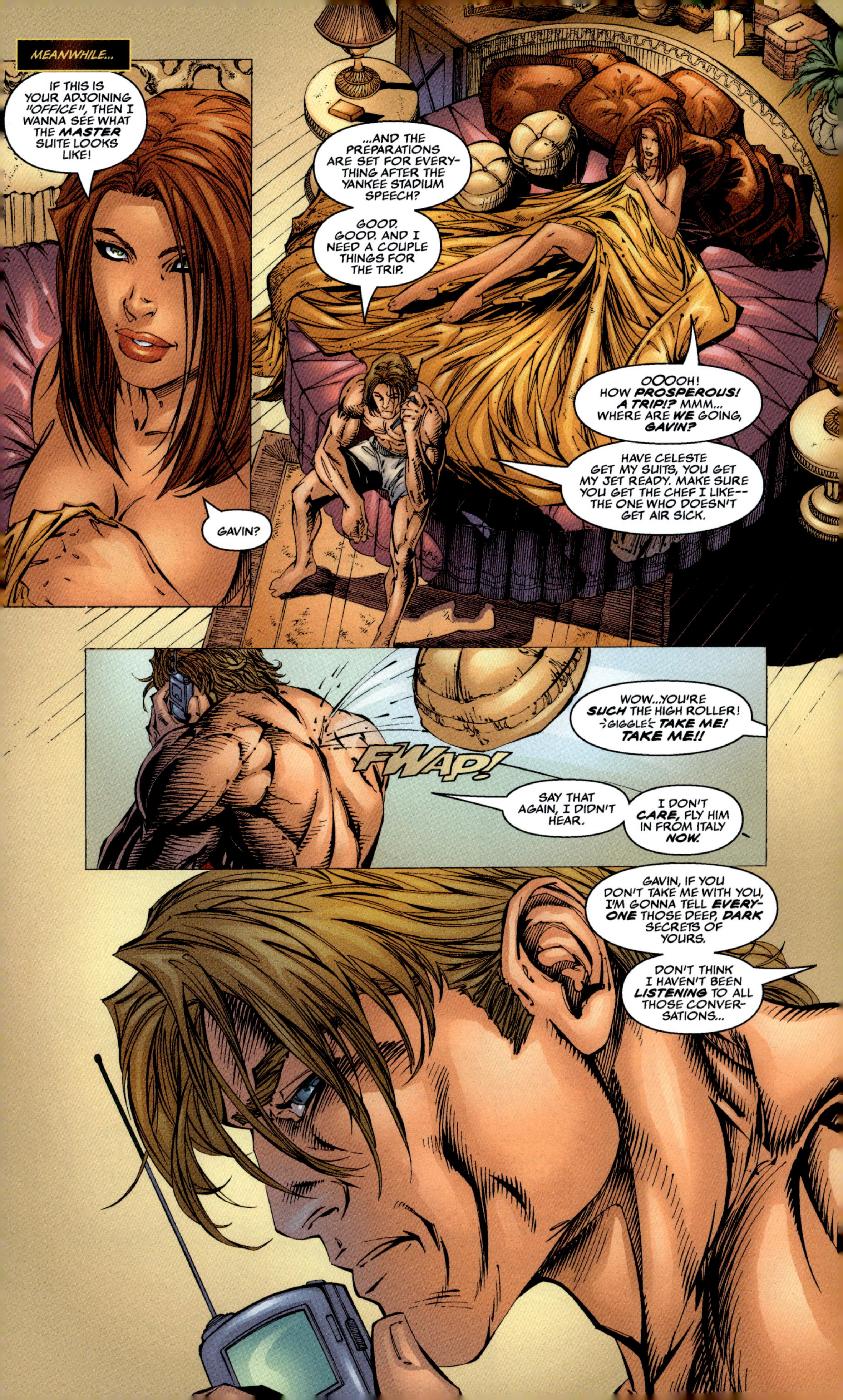
MEANWHILE...
IF THIS IS YOUR ADJOINING "OFFICE", THEN I WANNA SEE WHAT THE MASTER SUITE LOOKS LIKE!
...AND THE PREPARATIONS ARE SET FOR EVERYTHING AFTER THE YANKEE STADIUM SPEECH?
GOOD. GOOD. AND I NEED A COUPLE THINGS FOR THE TRIP.
GAVIN?
OOOOH! HOW PROSPEROUS! A TRIP!? MMM... WHERE ARE WE GOING, GAVIN?
HAVE CELESTE GET MY SUITS, YOU GET MY JET READY. MAKE SURE YOU GET THE CHEF I LIKE-- THE ONE WHO DOESN'T GET AIR SICK.
WOW...YOU'RE SUCH THE HIGH ROLLER! -GIGGLE- TAKE ME! TAKE ME!!
FWAP!
SAY THAT AGAIN, I DIDN'T HEAR.
I DON'T CARE, FLY HIM IN FROM ITALY NOW.
GAVIN, IF YOU DON'T TAKE ME WITH YOU, I'M GONNA TELL EVERYONE THOSE DEEP, DARK SECRETS OF YOURS.
DON'T THINK I HAVEN'T BEEN LISTENING TO ALL THOSE CONVERSATIONS...

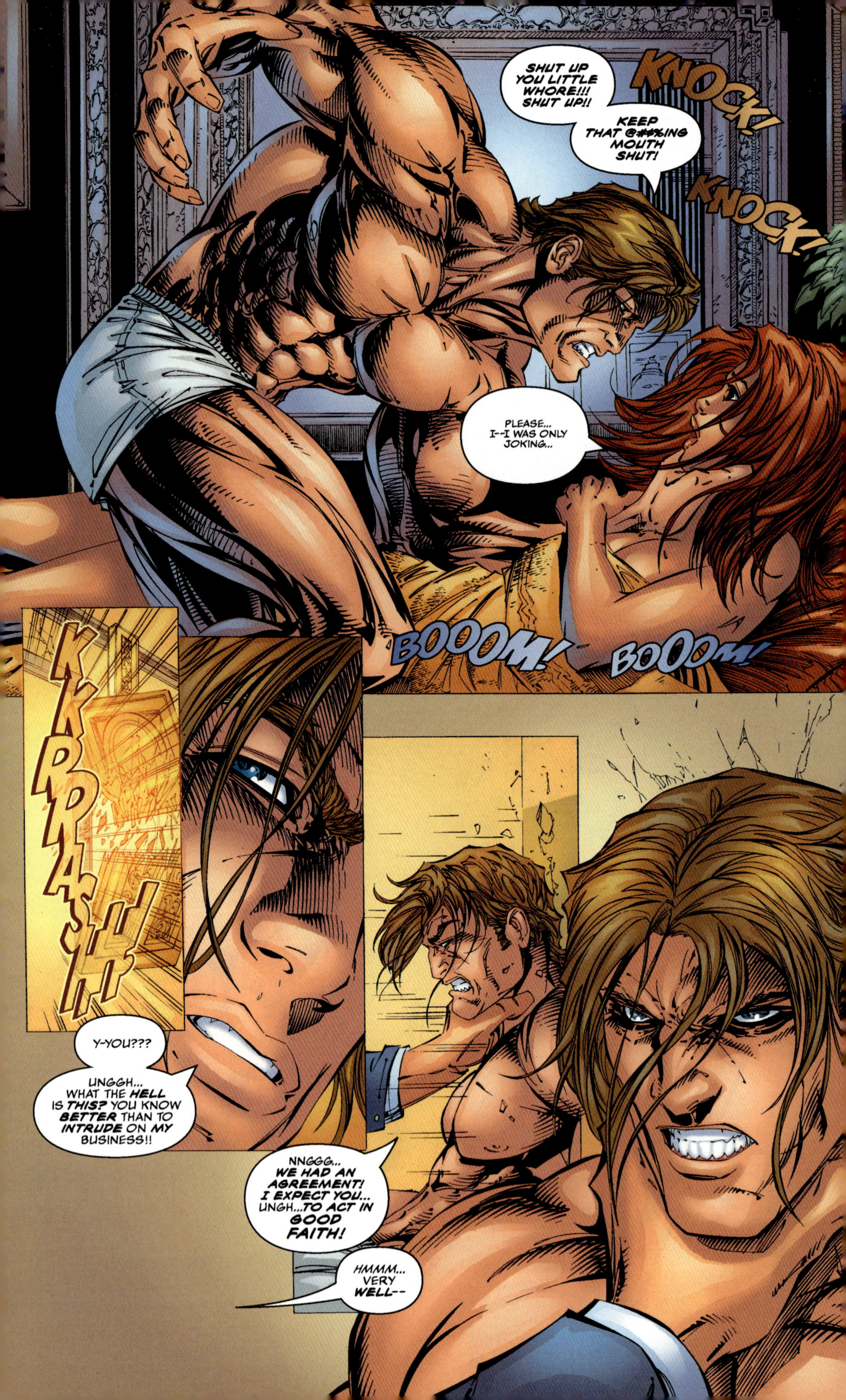
SHUT UP YOU LITTLE WHORE!!! SHUT UP!!
KNOCK!
KEEP THAT @##%ING MOUTH SHUT!
KNOCK!
PLEASE... I--I WAS ONLY JOKING...
BOOOM!
BOOOM!
KKRRASHH
Y-YOU???
UNGGH... WHAT THE HELL IS THIS? YOU KNOW BETTER THAN TO INTRUDE ON MY BUSINESS!!
NNGGG... WE HAD AN AGREEMENT! I EXPECT YOU... UNGH...TO ACT IN GOOD FAITH!
HMMM... VERY WELL--

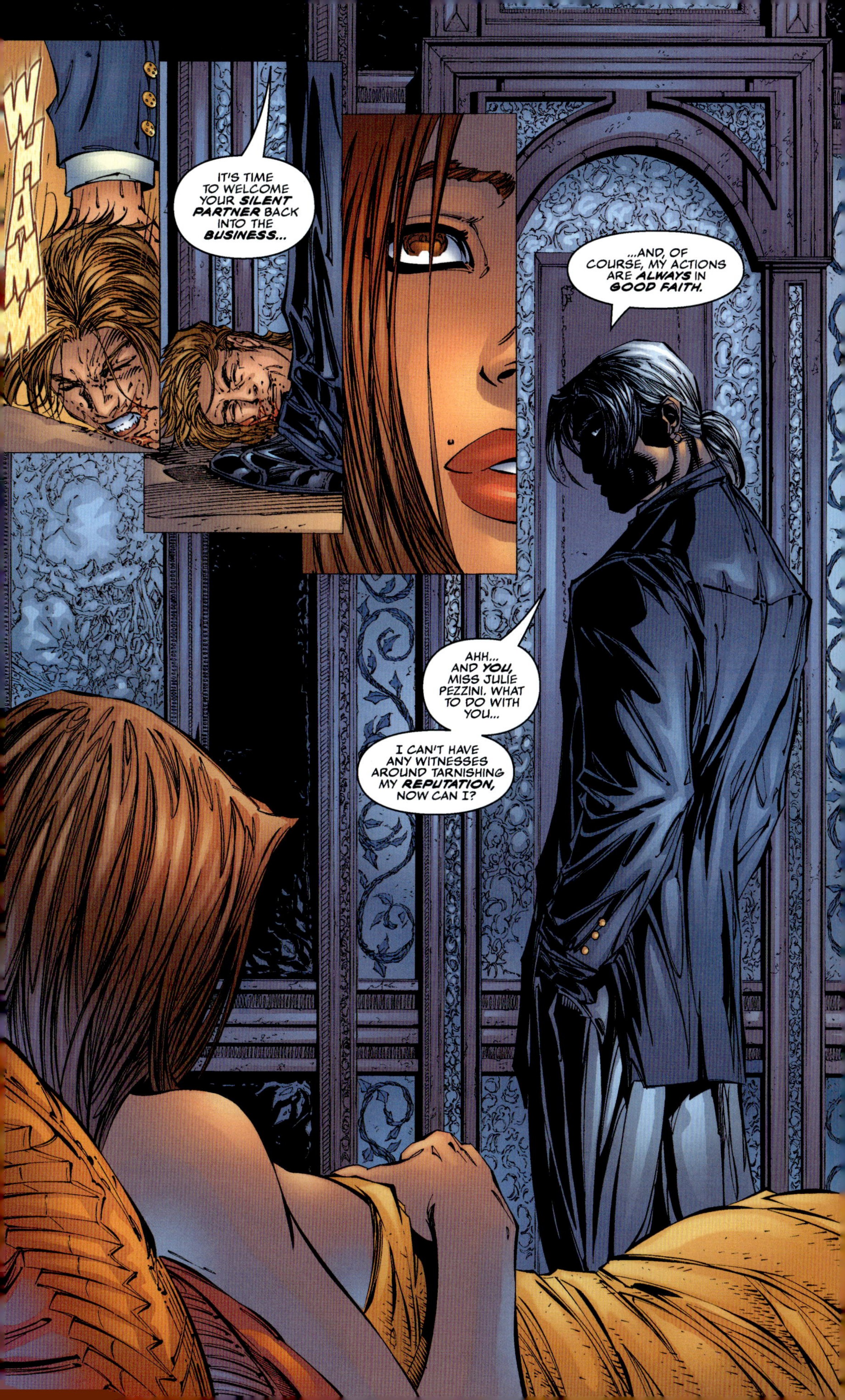
WHAM
IT'S TIME TO WELCOME YOUR SILENT PARTNER BACK INTO THE BUSINESS...
...AND, OF COURSE, MY ACTIONS ARE ALWAYS IN GOOD FAITH.
AHH... AND YOU, MISS JULIE PEZZINI. WHAT TO DO WITH YOU...
I CAN'T HAVE ANY WITNESSES AROUND TARNISHING MY REPUTATION, NOW CAN I?

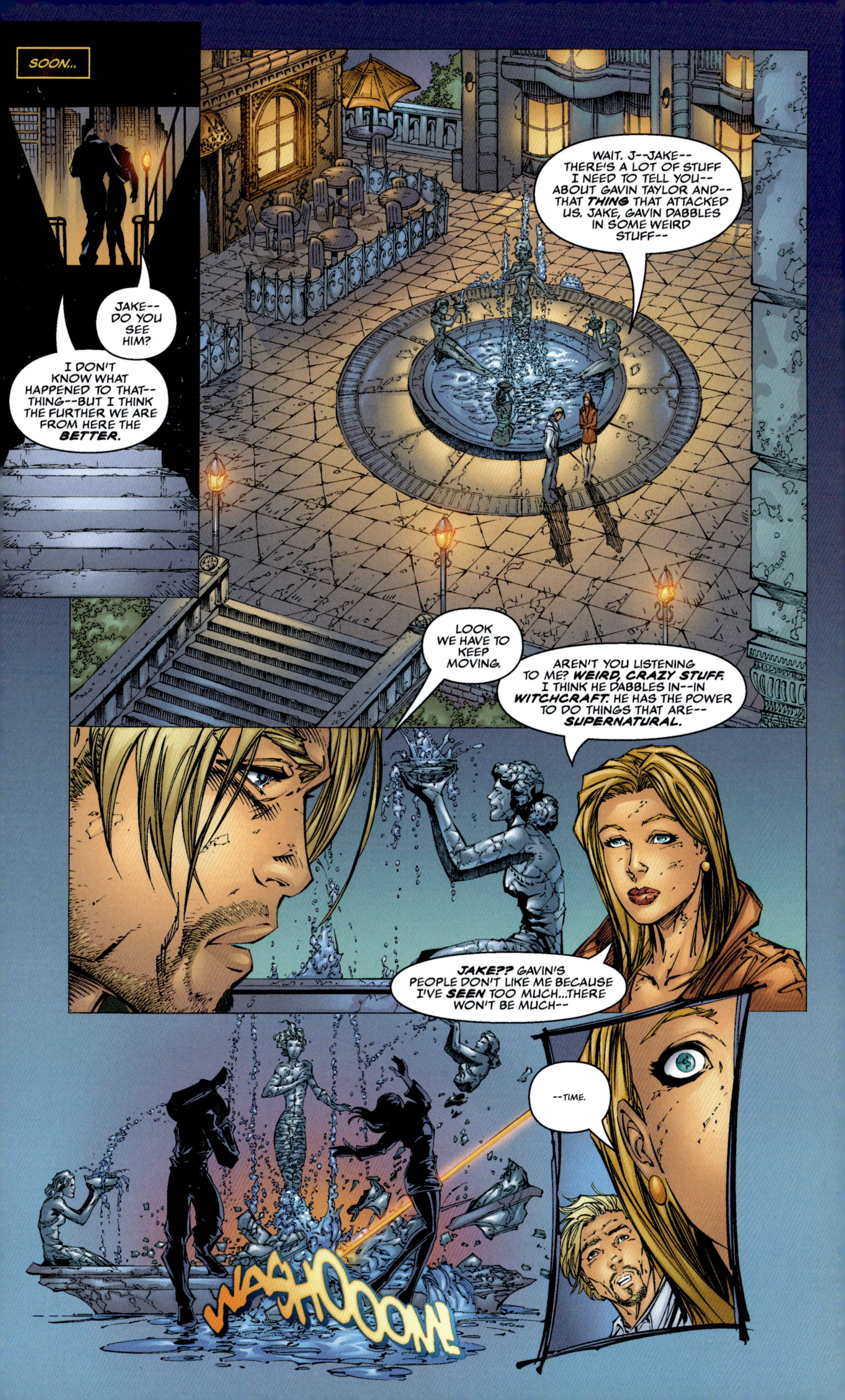

SOON...
JAKE-- DO YOU SEE HIM?
I DON'T KNOW WHAT HAPPENED TO THAT-- THING--BUT I THINK THE FURTHER WE ARE FROM HERE THE BETTER.
WAIT. J--JAKE-- THERE'S A LOT OF STUFF I NEED TO TELL YOU-- ABOUT GAVIN TAYLOR AND-- THAT THING THAT ATTACKED US. JAKE, GAVIN DABBLES IN SOME WEIRD STUFF--
LOOK WE HAVE TO KEEP MOVING.
AREN'T YOU LISTENING TO ME? WEIRD, CRAZY STUFF. I THINK HE DABBLES IN--IN WITCHCRAFT. HE HAS THE POWER TO DO THINGS THAT ARE-- SUPERNATURAL.
JAKE?? GAVIN'S PEOPLE DON'T LIKE ME BECAUSE I'VE SEEN TOO MUCH...THERE WON'T BE MUCH--
--TIME.
WASHOOOOM!

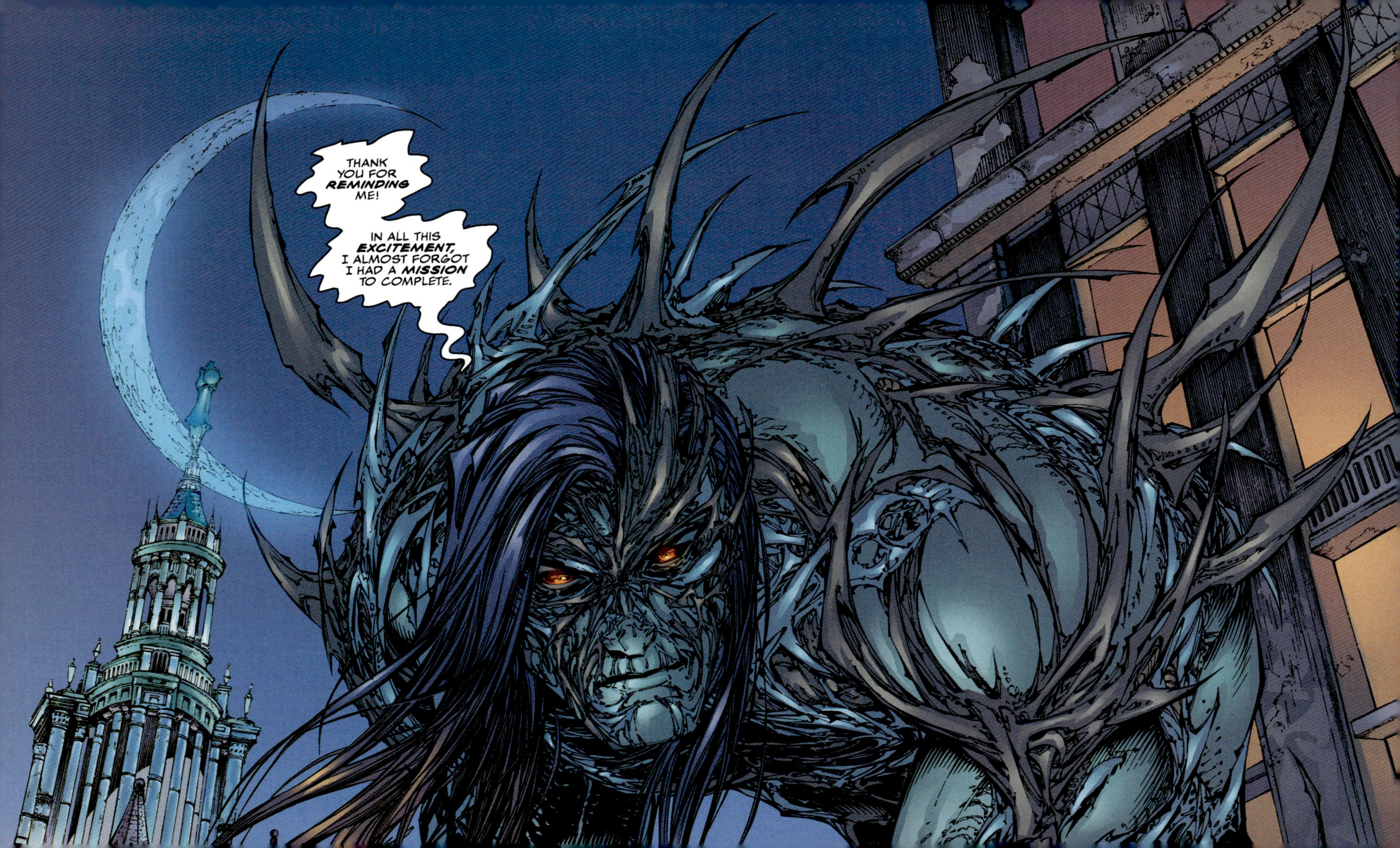
THANK YOU FOR **REMINDING** ME!
IN ALL THIS **EXCITEMENT,** I ALMOST FORGOT I HAD A **MISSION** TO COMPLETE.

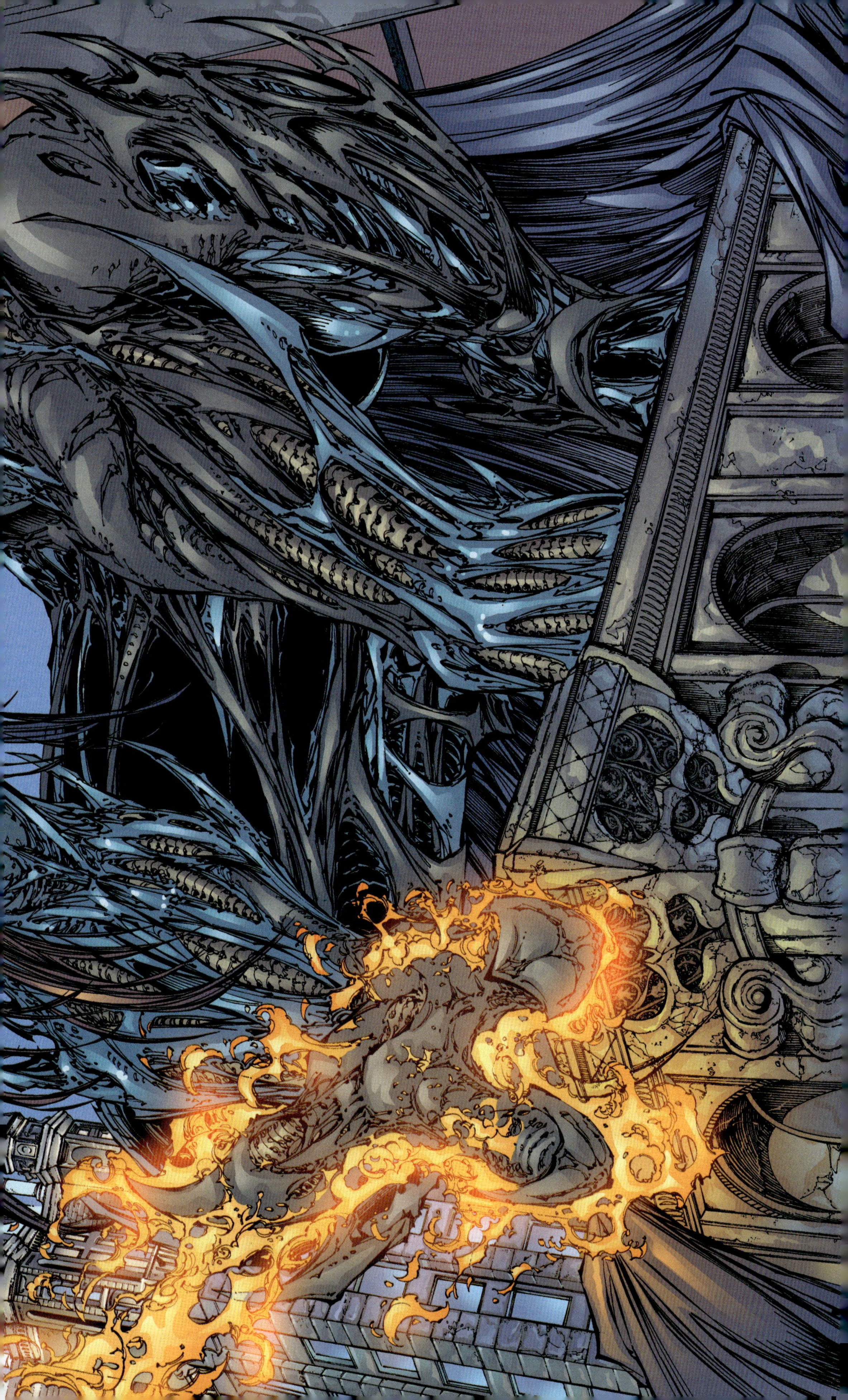

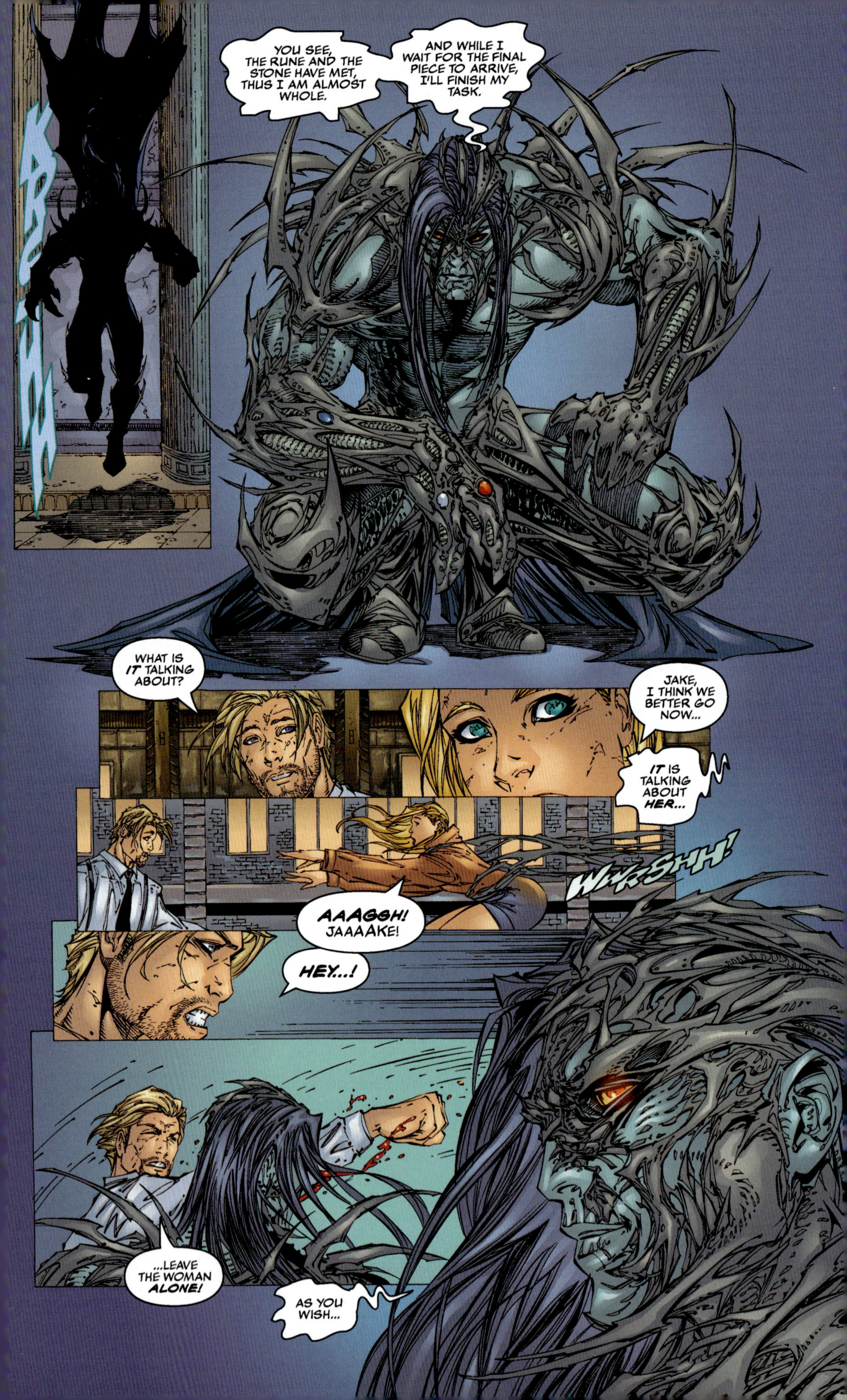
KRUSHHH
YOU SEE, THE RUNE AND THE STONE HAVE MET, THUS I AM ALMOST WHOLE.
AND WHILE I WAIT FOR THE FINAL PIECE TO ARRIVE, I'LL FINISH MY TASK.
WHAT IS *IT* TALKING ABOUT?
JAKE, I THINK WE BETTER GO NOW...
IT IS TALKING ABOUT *HER*...
WHASHH!
AAAGGH! JAAAAKE!
HEY...!
...LEAVE THE WOMAN *ALONE!*
AS YOU WISH...

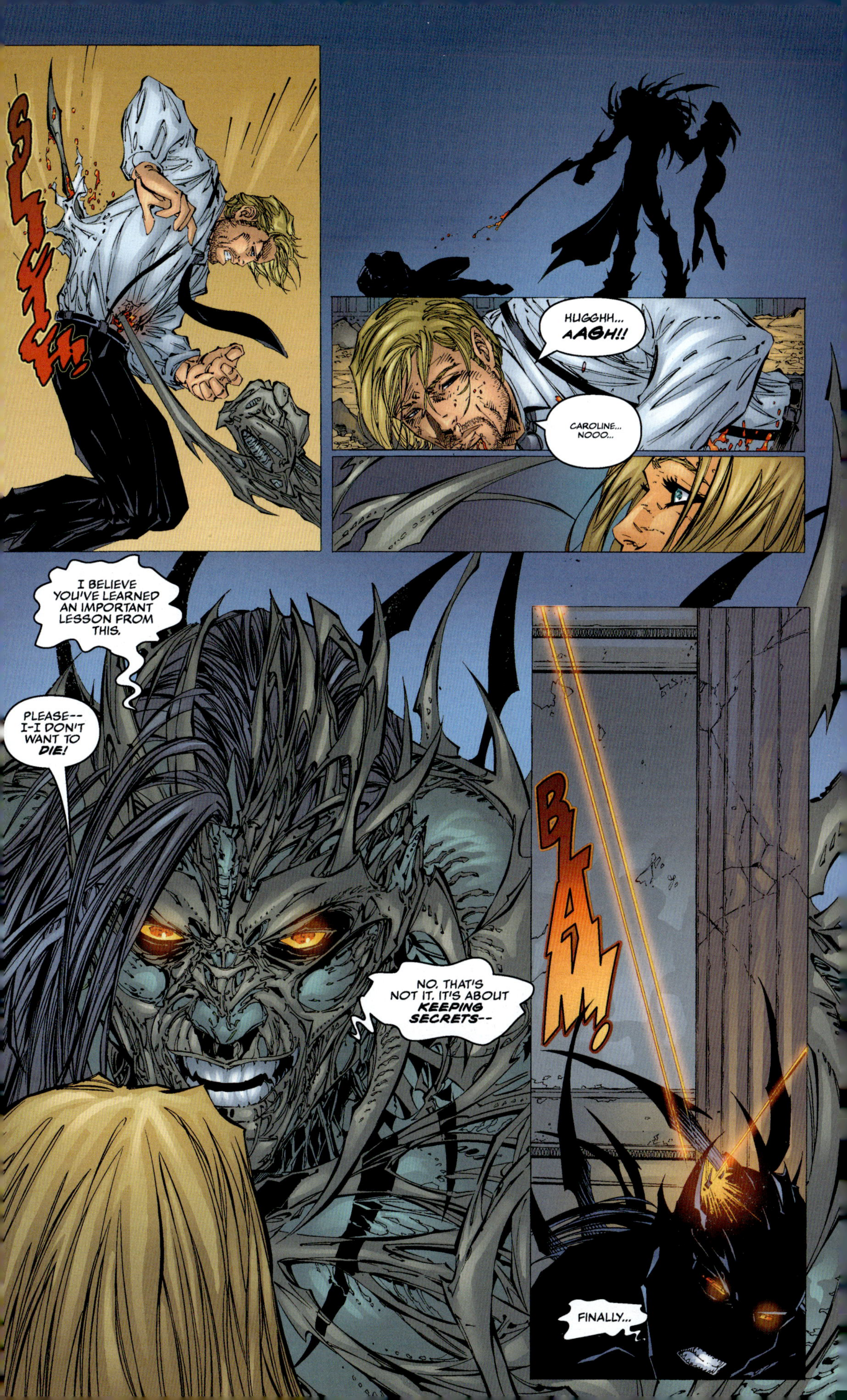
SLUNCH!
HUGGHH... AAGH!!
CAROLINE... NOOO...
I BELIEVE YOU'VE LEARNED AN IMPORTANT LESSON FROM THIS.
PLEASE-- I-I DON'T WANT TO DIE!
NO, THAT'S NOT IT. IT'S ABOUT KEEPING SECRETS--
BLAM!
FINALLY...

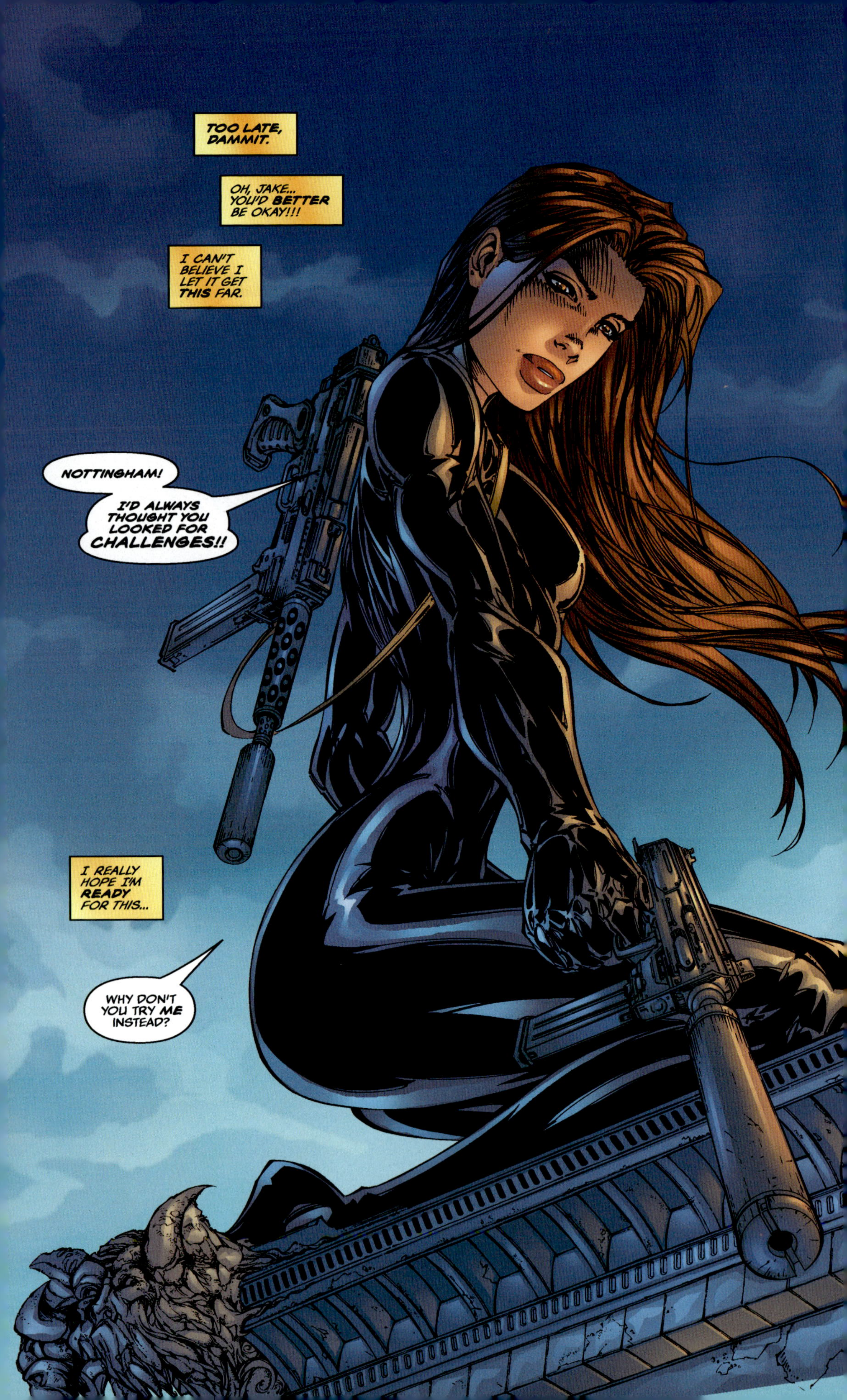
TOO LATE, DAMMIT.
OH, JAKE... YOU'D **BETTER** BE OKAY!!!
I CAN'T BELIEVE I LET IT GET **THIS** FAR.
NOTTINGHAM!
I'D ALWAYS THOUGHT YOU LOOKED FOR **CHALLENGES!!**
I REALLY HOPE I'M **READY** FOR THIS...
WHY DON'T YOU TRY **ME** INSTEAD?

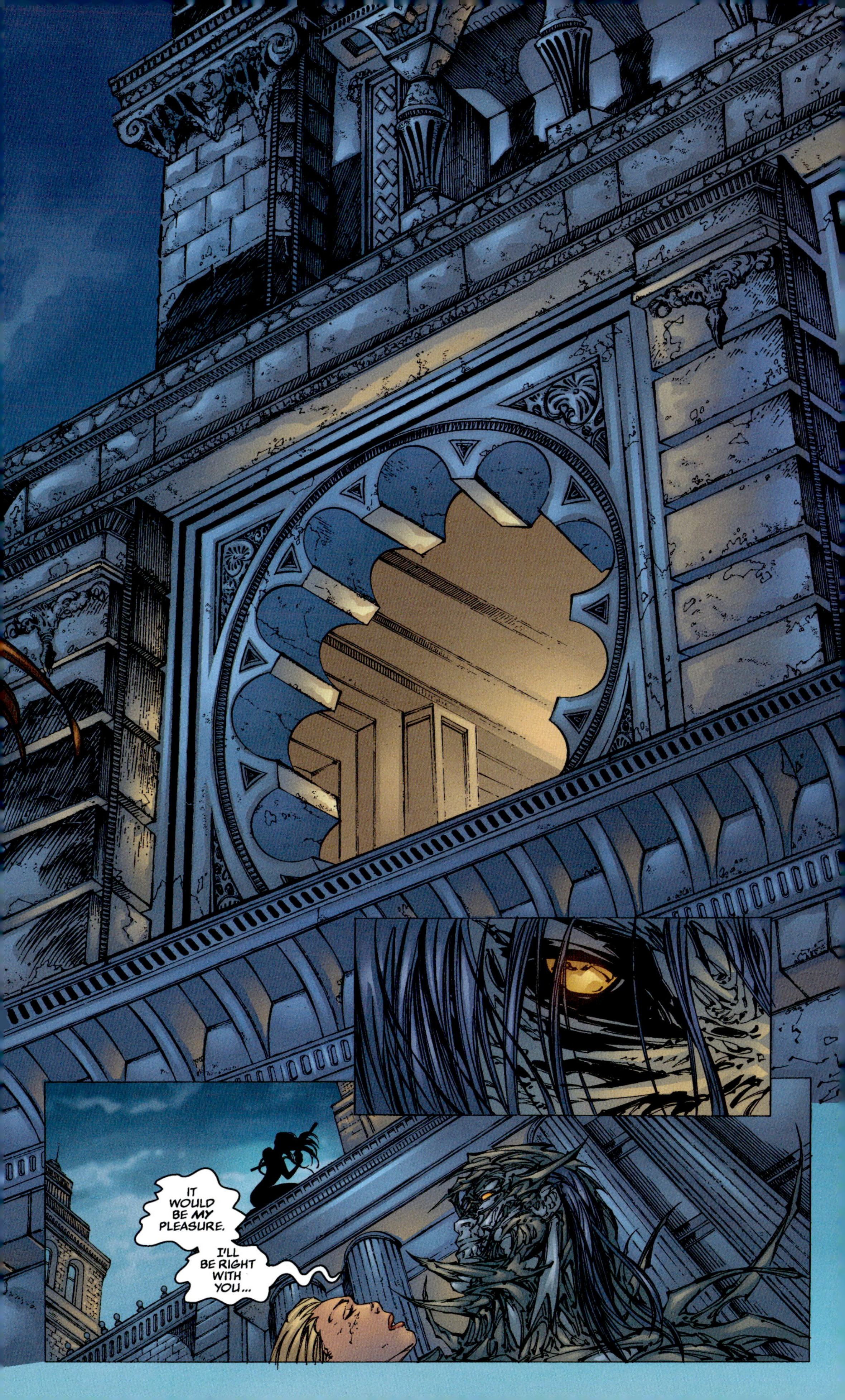
IT WOULD BE MY PLEASURE.
I'LL BE RIGHT WITH YOU...

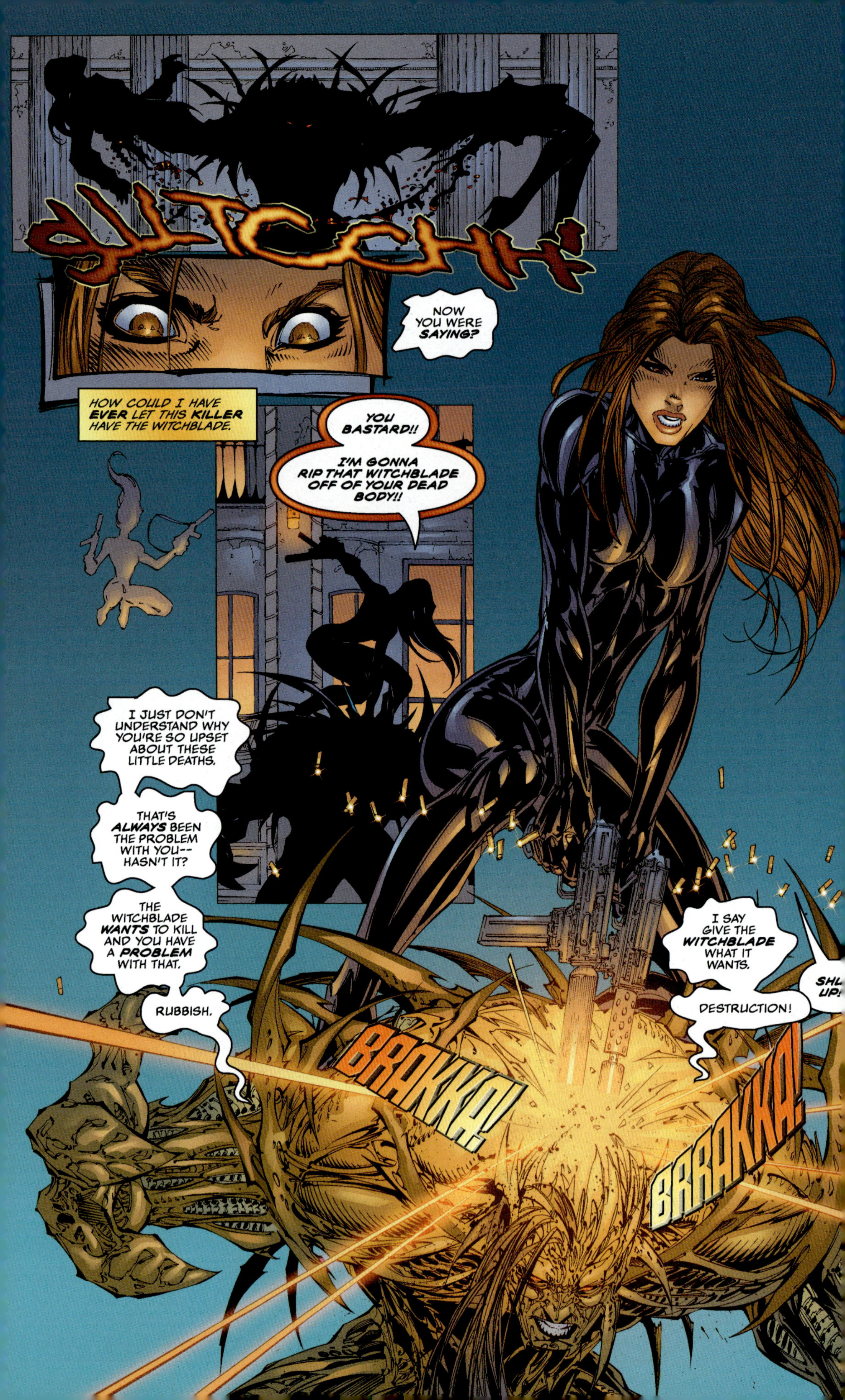
NOW YOU WERE SAYING?
HOW COULD I HAVE EVER LET THIS KILLER HAVE THE WITCHBLADE.
YOU BASTARD!!
I'M GONNA RIP THAT WITCHBLADE OFF OF YOUR DEAD BODY!!
I JUST DON'T UNDERSTAND WHY YOU'RE SO UPSET ABOUT THESE LITTLE DEATHS.
THAT'S ALWAYS BEEN THE PROBLEM WITH YOU-- HASN'T IT?
THE WITCHBLADE WANTS TO KILL AND YOU HAVE A PROBLEM WITH THAT.
RUBBISH.
I SAY GIVE THE WITCHBLADE WHAT IT WANTS.
DESTRUCTION!
BRAKKA!
BRAKKA!

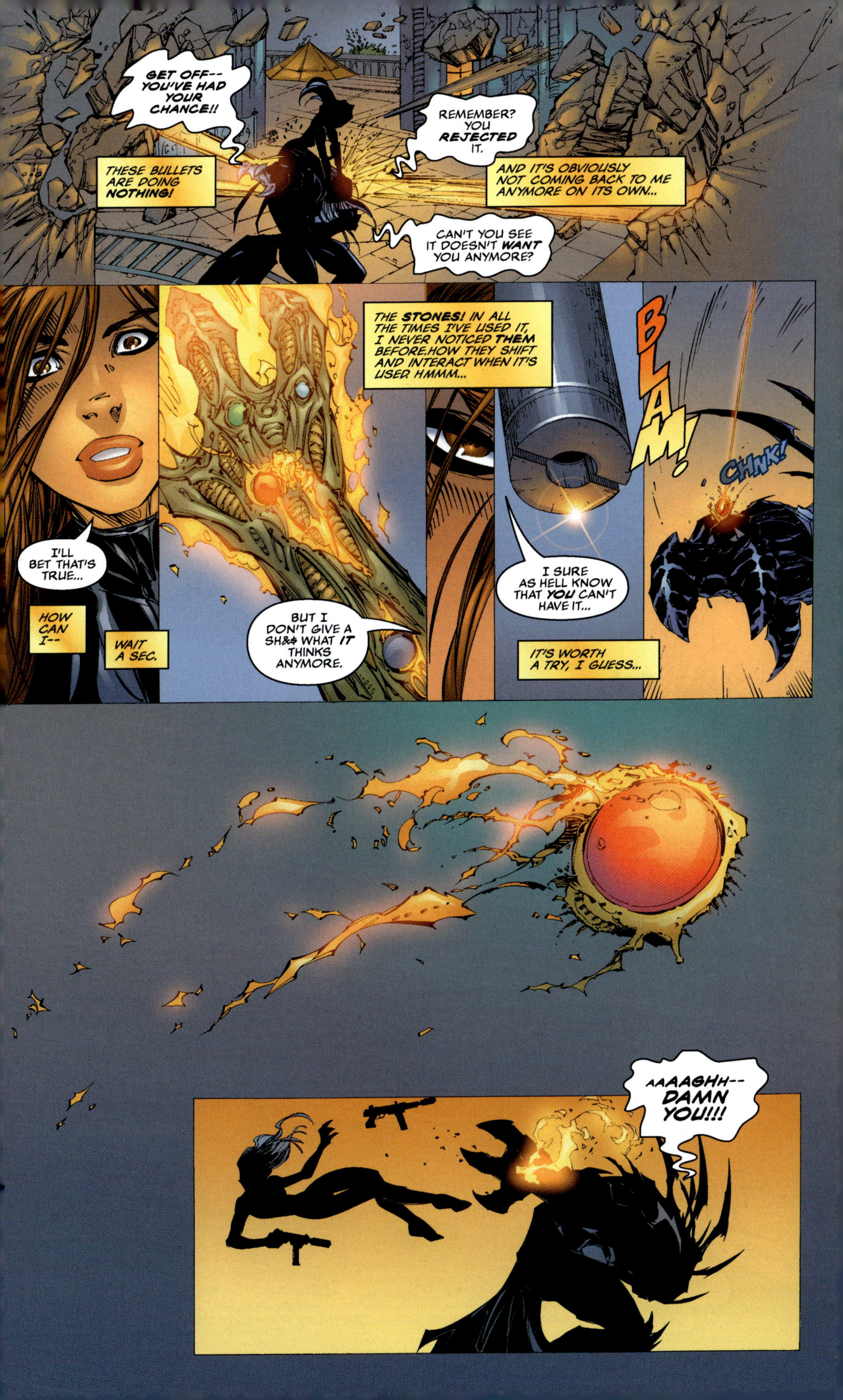
GET OFF-- YOU'VE HAD YOUR CHANCE!!
THESE BULLETS ARE DOING NOTHING!
REMEMBER? YOU REJECTED IT.
AND IT'S OBVIOUSLY NOT COMING BACK TO ME ANYMORE ON ITS OWN...
CAN'T YOU SEE IT DOESN'T WANT YOU ANYMORE?
I'LL BET THAT'S TRUE...
HOW CAN I--
WAIT A SEC.
BUT I DON'T GIVE A SH&$ WHAT IT THINKS ANYMORE.
THE STONES! IN ALL THE TIMES I'VE USED IT, I NEVER NOTICED THEM BEFORE. HOW THEY SHIFT AND INTERACT WHEN IT'S USED. HMMM...
I SURE AS HELL KNOW THAT YOU CAN'T HAVE IT...
IT'S WORTH A TRY, I GUESS...
BLAM!
CHINK!
AAAAGHH-- DAMN YOU!!!

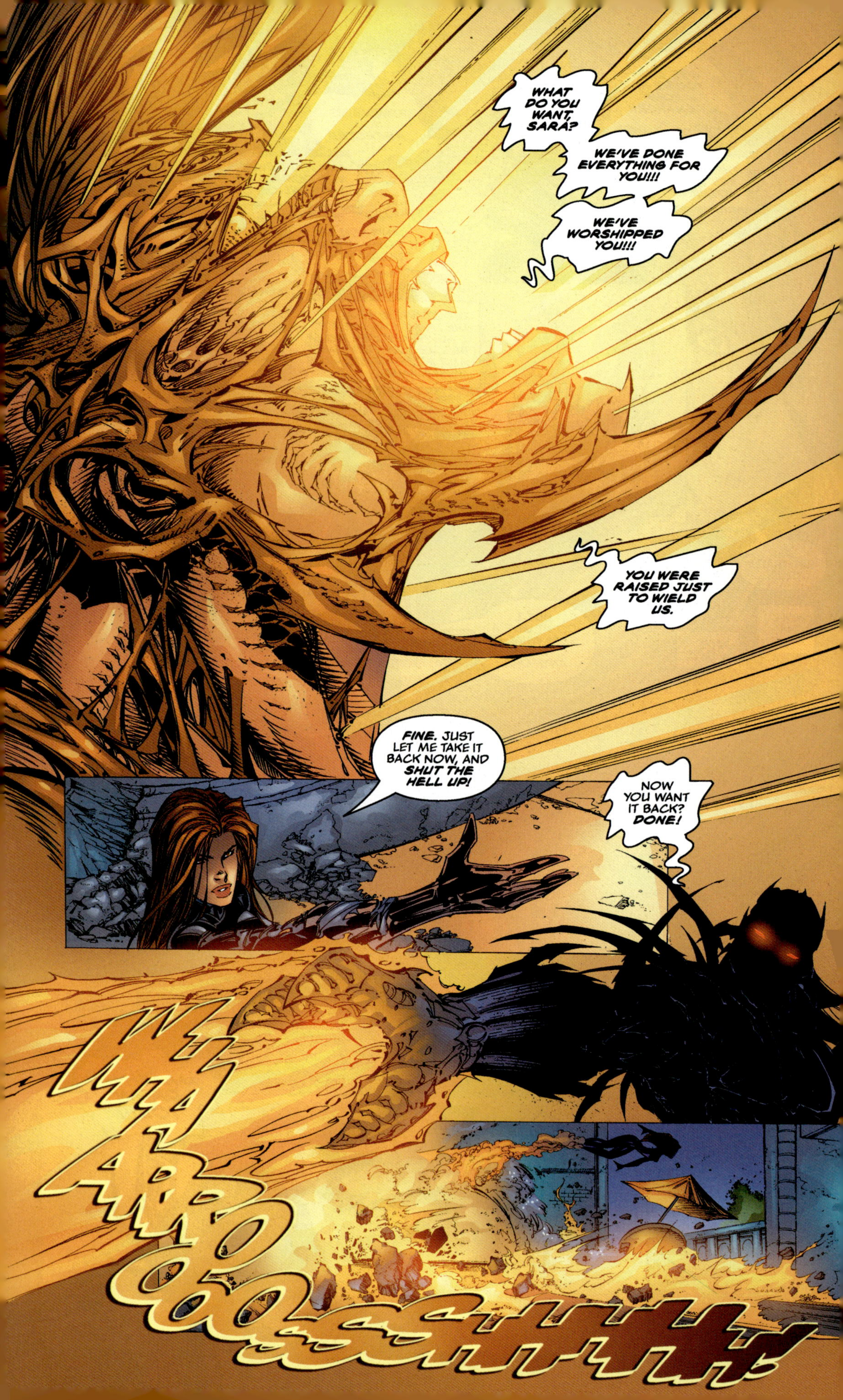
WHAT DO YOU WANT, SARA?
WE'VE DONE EVERYTHING FOR YOU!!!
WE'VE WORSHIPPED YOU!!!
YOU WERE RAISED JUST TO WIELD US.
FINE. JUST LET ME TAKE IT BACK NOW, AND SHUT THE HELL UP!
NOW YOU WANT IT BACK? DONE!
WHAROOOSHHHH!

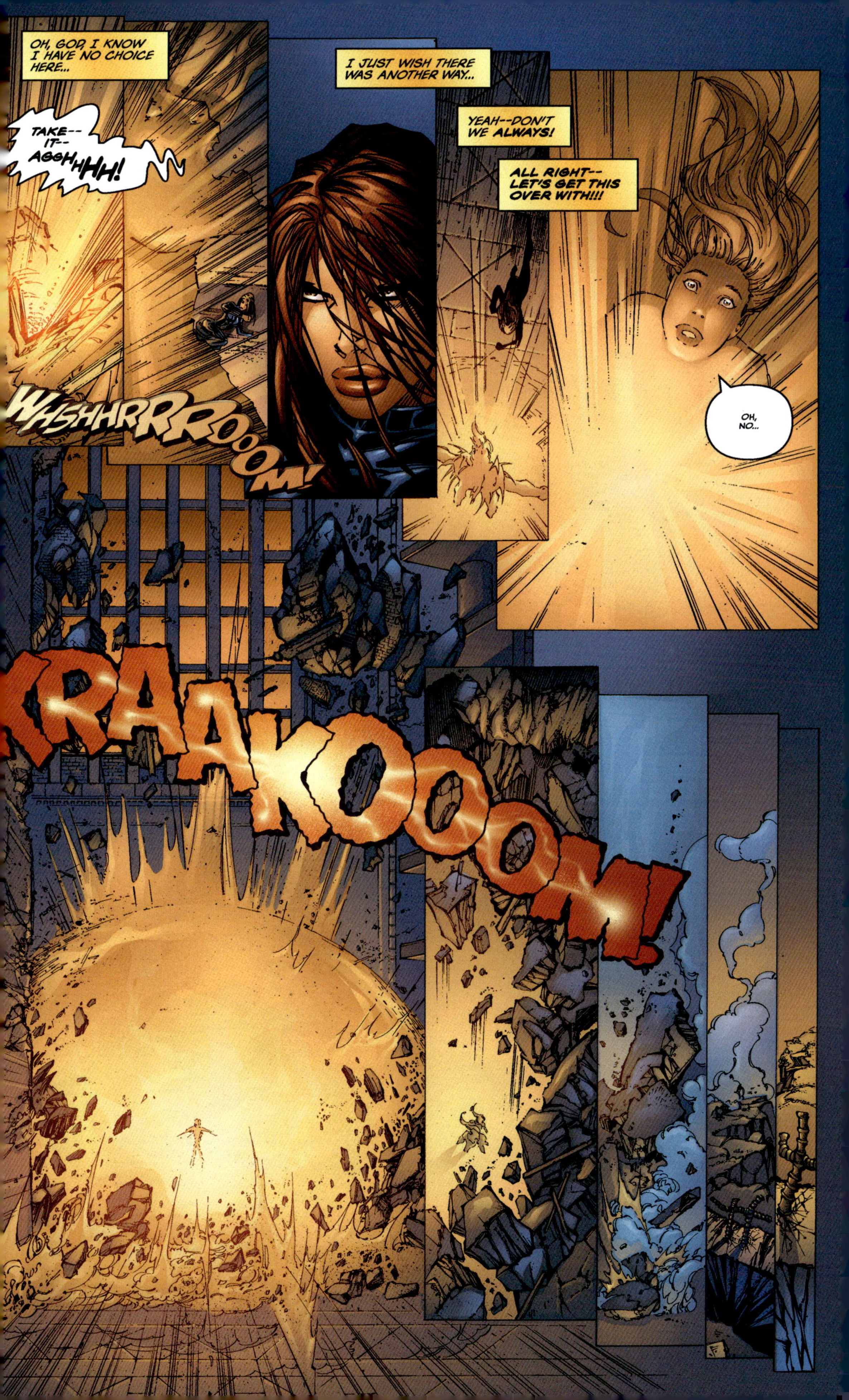
OH, GOD, I KNOW I HAVE NO CHOICE HERE...
TAKE-- IT-- AGGHHHH!
WHSHHRRROOOM!
I JUST WISH THERE WAS ANOTHER WAY...
YEAH--DON'T WE ALWAYS!
ALL RIGHT-- LET'S GET THIS OVER WITH!!!
OH, NO...
KRAAKOOOOM!

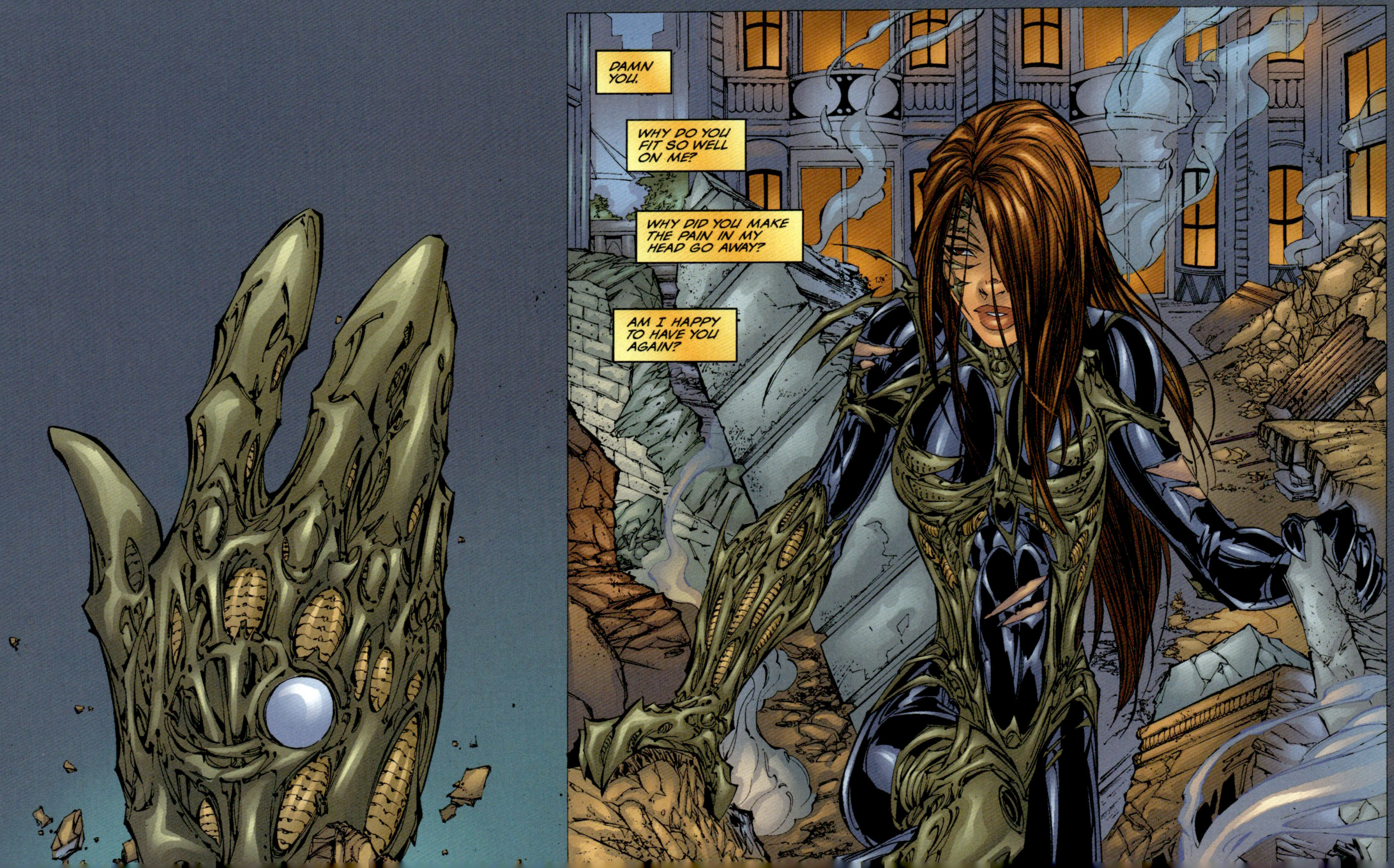
DAMN YOU.
WHY DO YOU FIT SO WELL ON ME?
WHY DID YOU MAKE THE PAIN IN MY HEAD GO AWAY?
AM I HAPPY TO HAVE YOU AGAIN?

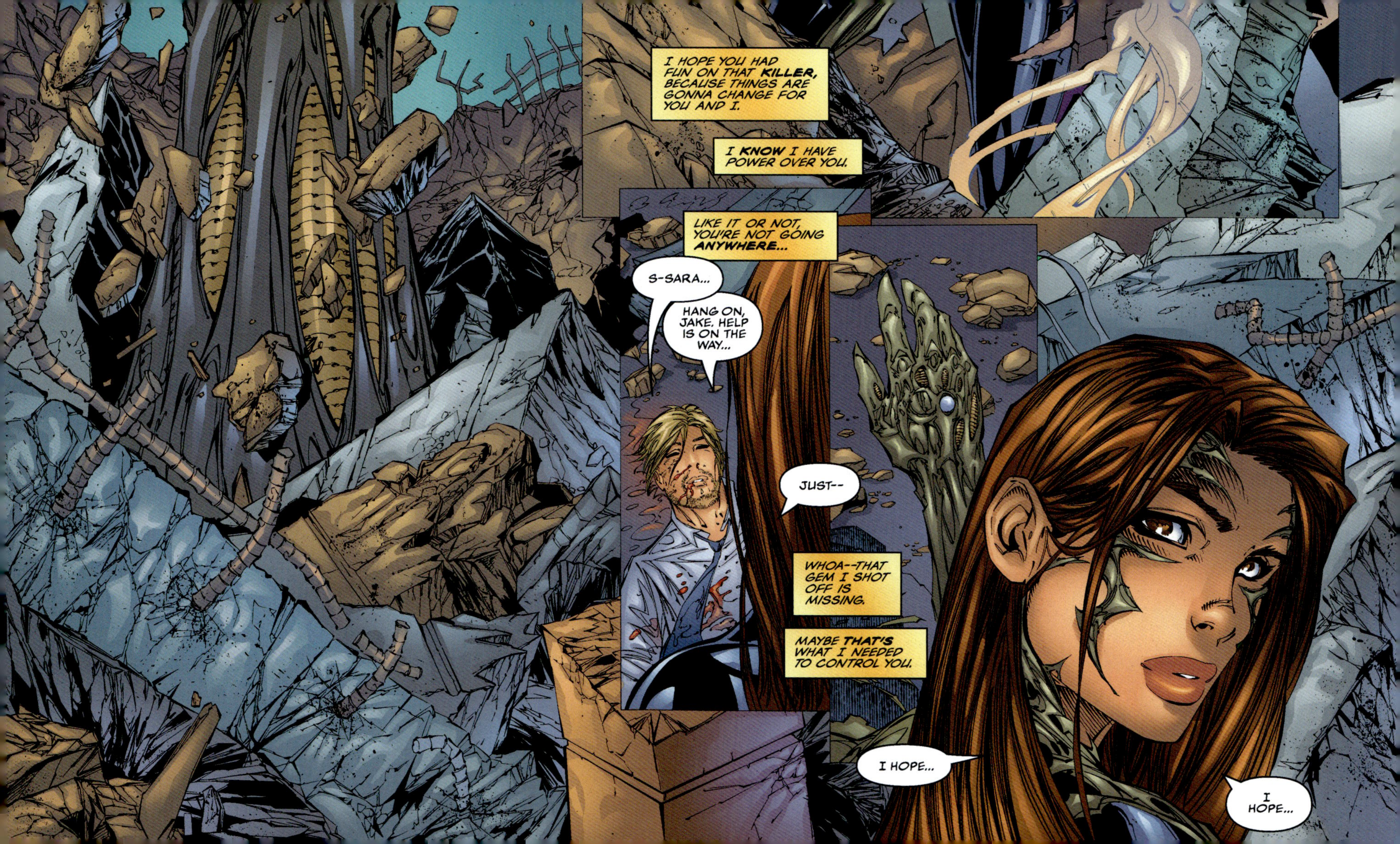
I HOPE YOU HAD FUN ON THAT KILLER, BECAUSE THINGS ARE GONNA CHANGE FOR YOU AND I.
I KNOW I HAVE POWER OVER YOU.
LIKE IT OR NOT, YOU'RE NOT GOING ANYWHERE...
S-SARA...
HANG ON, JAKE. HELP IS ON THE WAY...
JUST--
WHOA--THAT GEM I SHOT OFF IS MISSING.
MAYBE THAT'S WHAT I NEEDED TO CONTROL YOU.
I HOPE...
I HOPE...

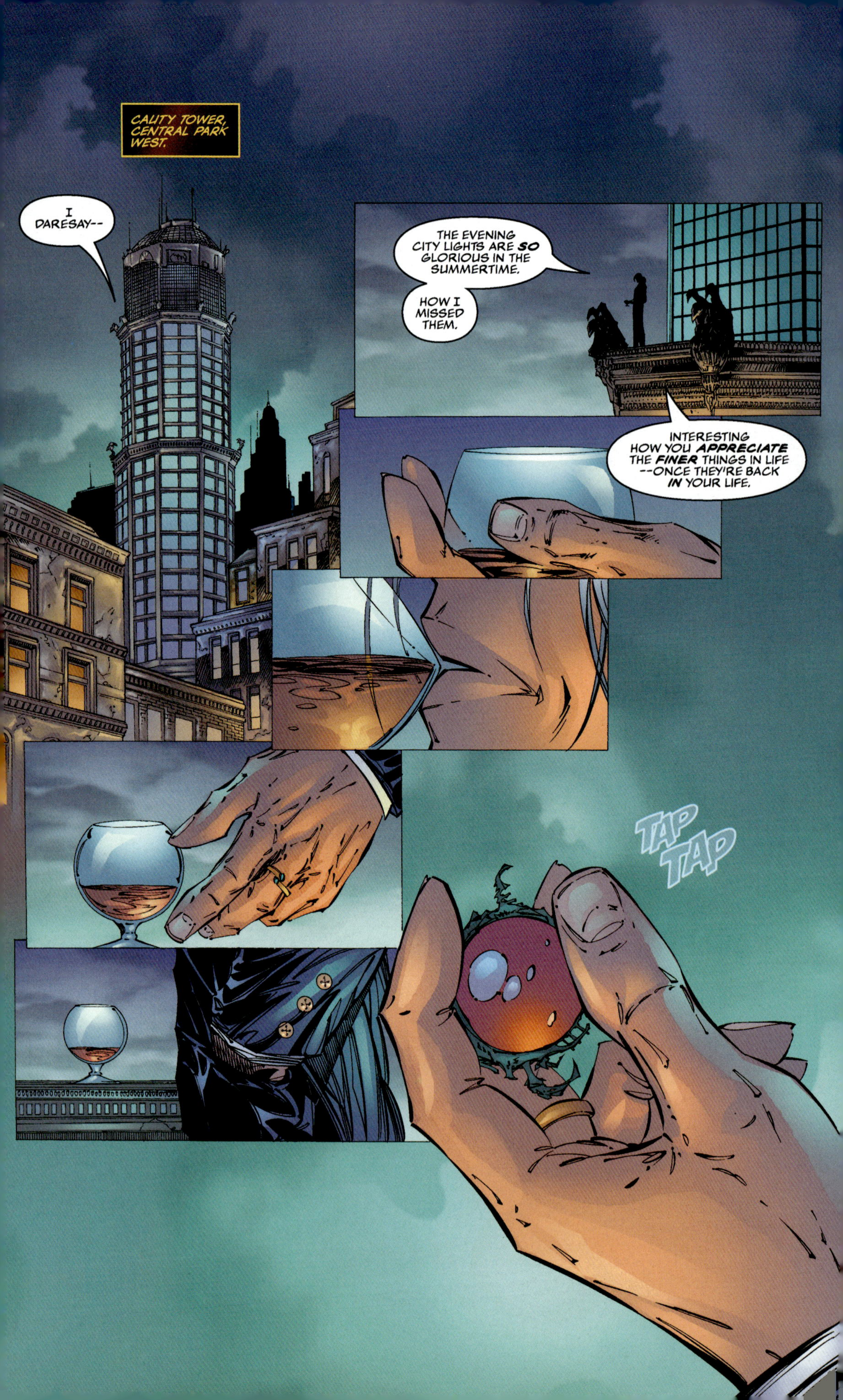

CAUTY TOWER, CENTRAL PARK WEST.
I DARESAY--
THE EVENING CITY LIGHTS ARE SO GLORIOUS IN THE SUMMERTIME.
HOW I MISSED THEM.
INTERESTING HOW YOU APPRECIATE THE FINER THINGS IN LIFE --ONCE THEY'RE BACK IN YOUR LIFE.
TAP TAP

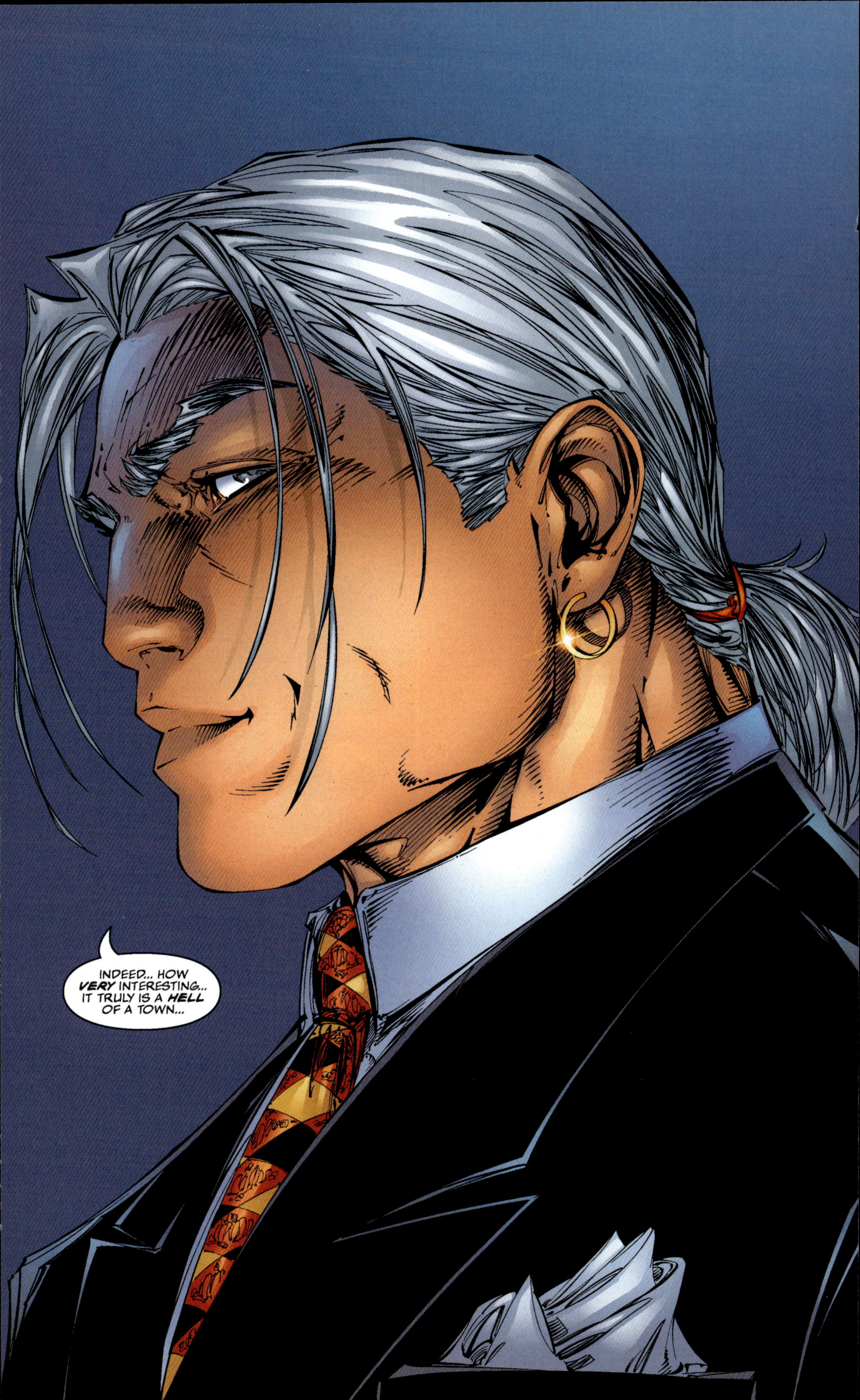
INDEED... HOW VERY INTERESTING... IT TRULY IS A HELL OF A TOWN...

Witchblade: Origins VOLUME 3

Cover Gallery

 *Witchblade* issue #18 cover A
art by: **Michael Turner,
D-Tron** and **JD Smith**

 *Witchblade* issue #18, Alternate cover
art by: **Michael Turner, Marc Silvestri
D-Tron, Matt "Batt" Banning
Steve Firchow** and **JD Smith**

 *Witchblade* issue #18
American Entertainment alternate cover
art by: **Michael Turner, D-Tron**
and **JD Smith**

 *The Darkness* issue #9
art by: **Marc Silvestri,
Matt "Batt" Banning**
and **Liquid!**

 *The Darkness* issue #10
art by: **Marc Silvestri,
Matt "Batt" Banning**
and **Richard Isanove**

 *Witchblade* issue #19
art by: **Michael Turner, D-Tron**
and **JD Smith**

 *Family Ties* trade paperback vol. 1
art by: **Marc Silvestri,
Danny Miki**
and **Steve Firchow**

 *Witchblade* issue #20
art by: **Michael Turner, D-Tron**
and **JD Smith**

 *Witchblade* issue #21
art by: **Michael Turner, D-Tron**
and **JD Smith**

 *Witchblade* issue #22
art by: **Michael Turner, D-Tron**
and **JD Smith**

 *Witchblade* issue #23
art by: **Clarence Lansang, D-Tron**
and **JD Smith**

 *Witchblade* issue #24
art by: **Jason Pearson**

 *Witchblade* issue #24 alternate cover
art by: **Randy Green, D-Tron**
and **JD Smith**

 *Witchblade* issue #25
art by: **Michael Turner, D-Tron**
and **JD Smith**

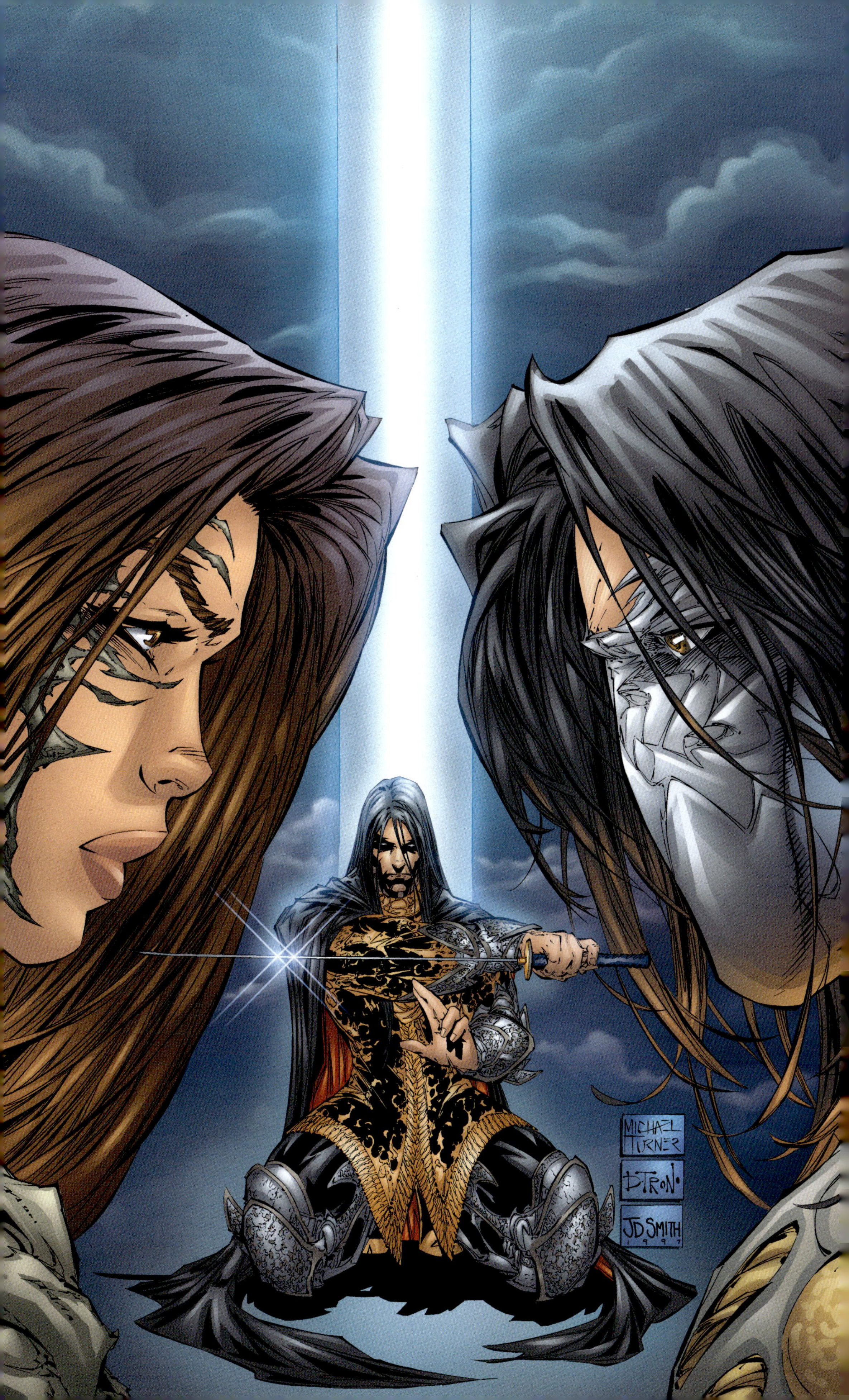
MICHAEL TURNER
JD SMITH 1997

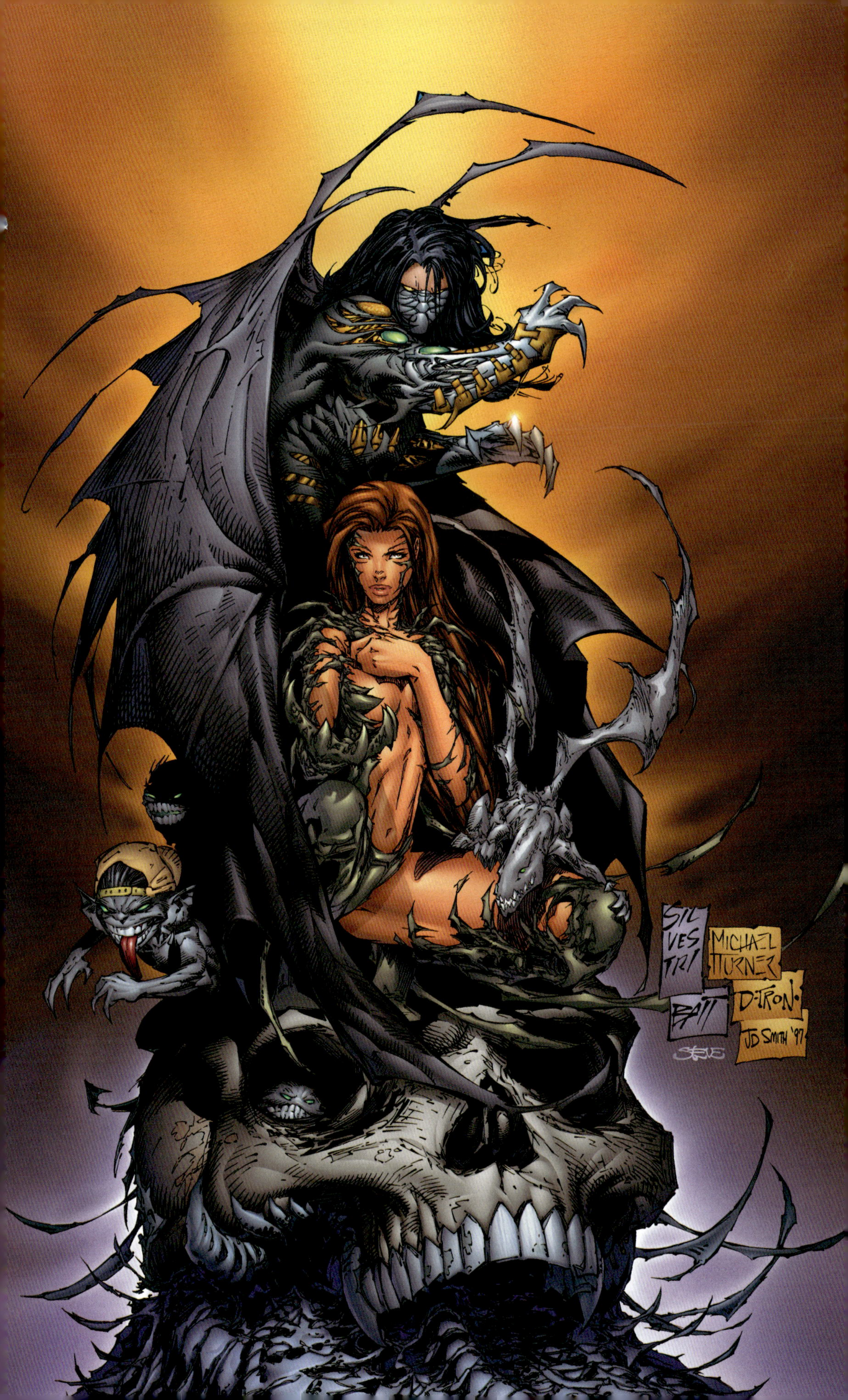
SILVESTRI
MICHAEL TURNER
BATT
D-TRON
JD SMITH '97
STEVE

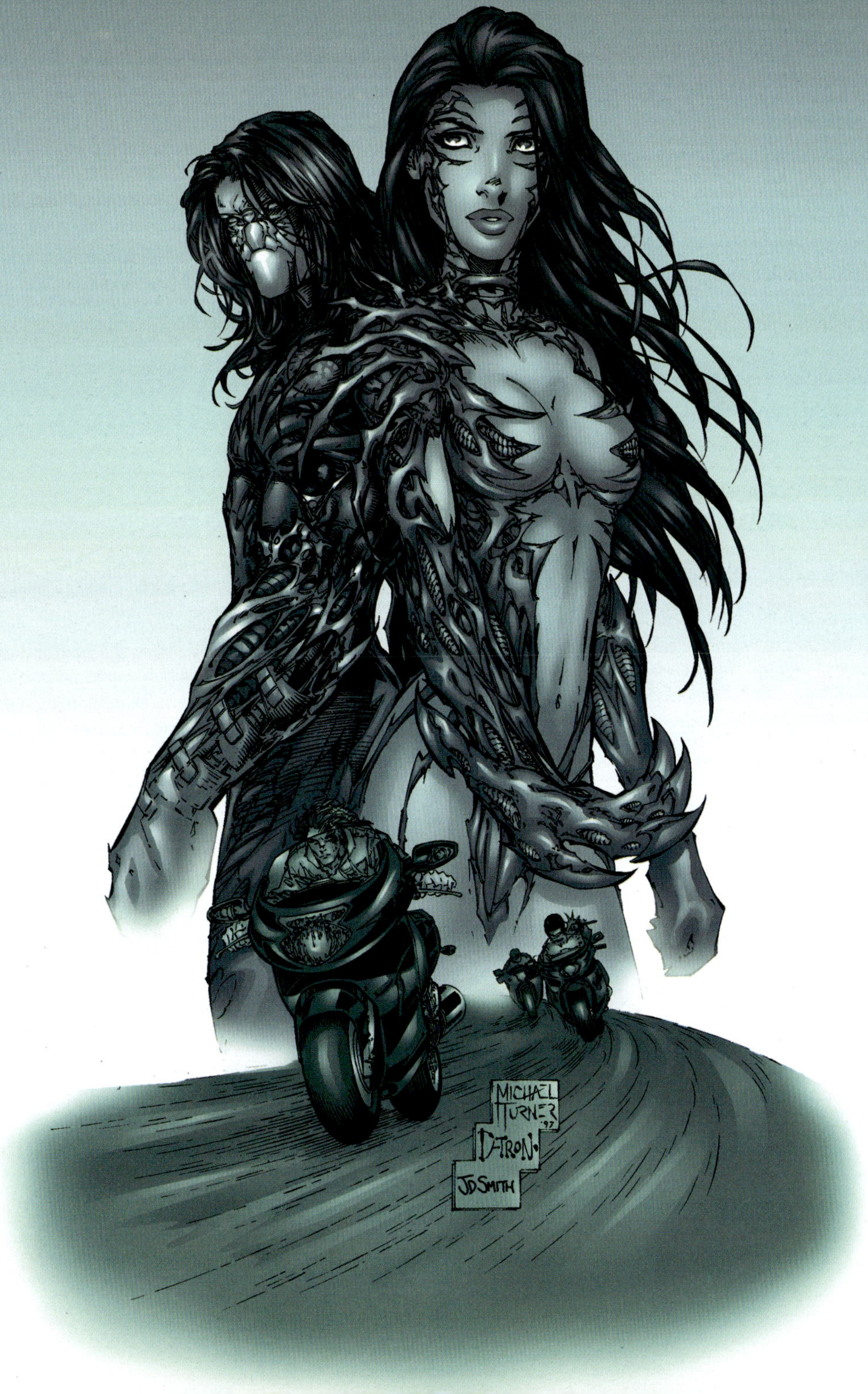
MICHAEL TURNER '97
D-TRON
JD SMITH

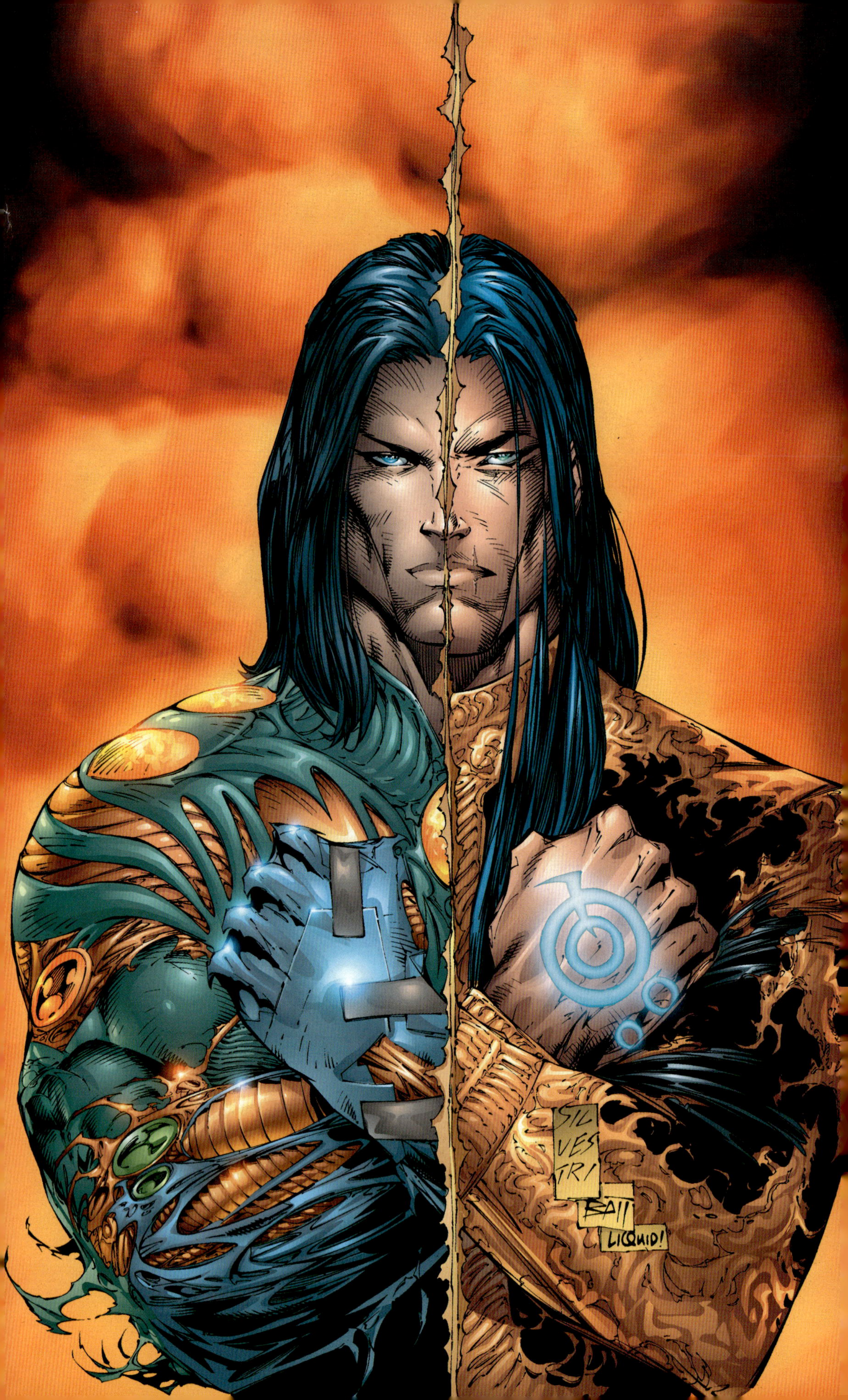
SIL
VES
TRI
LIQUID!

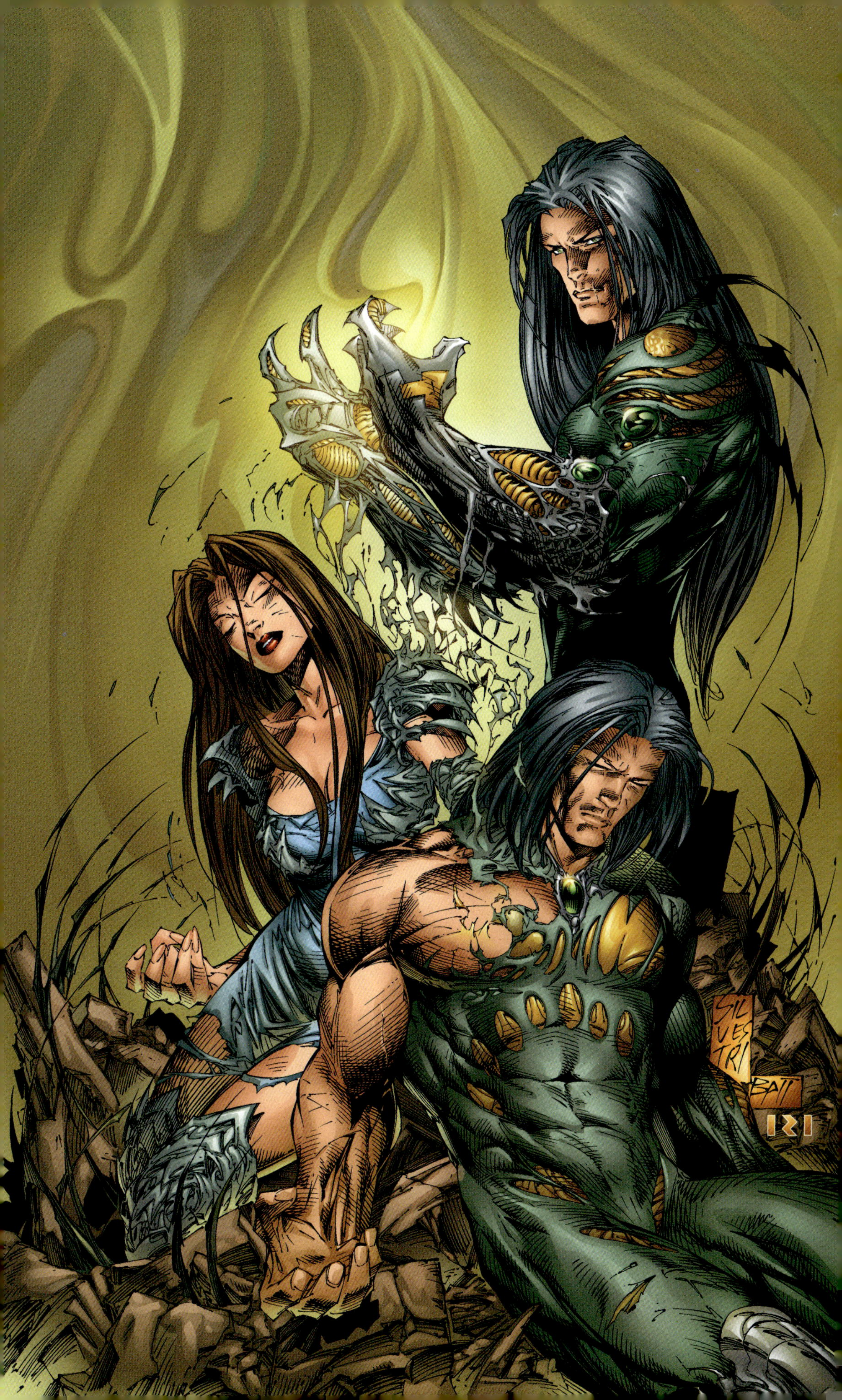

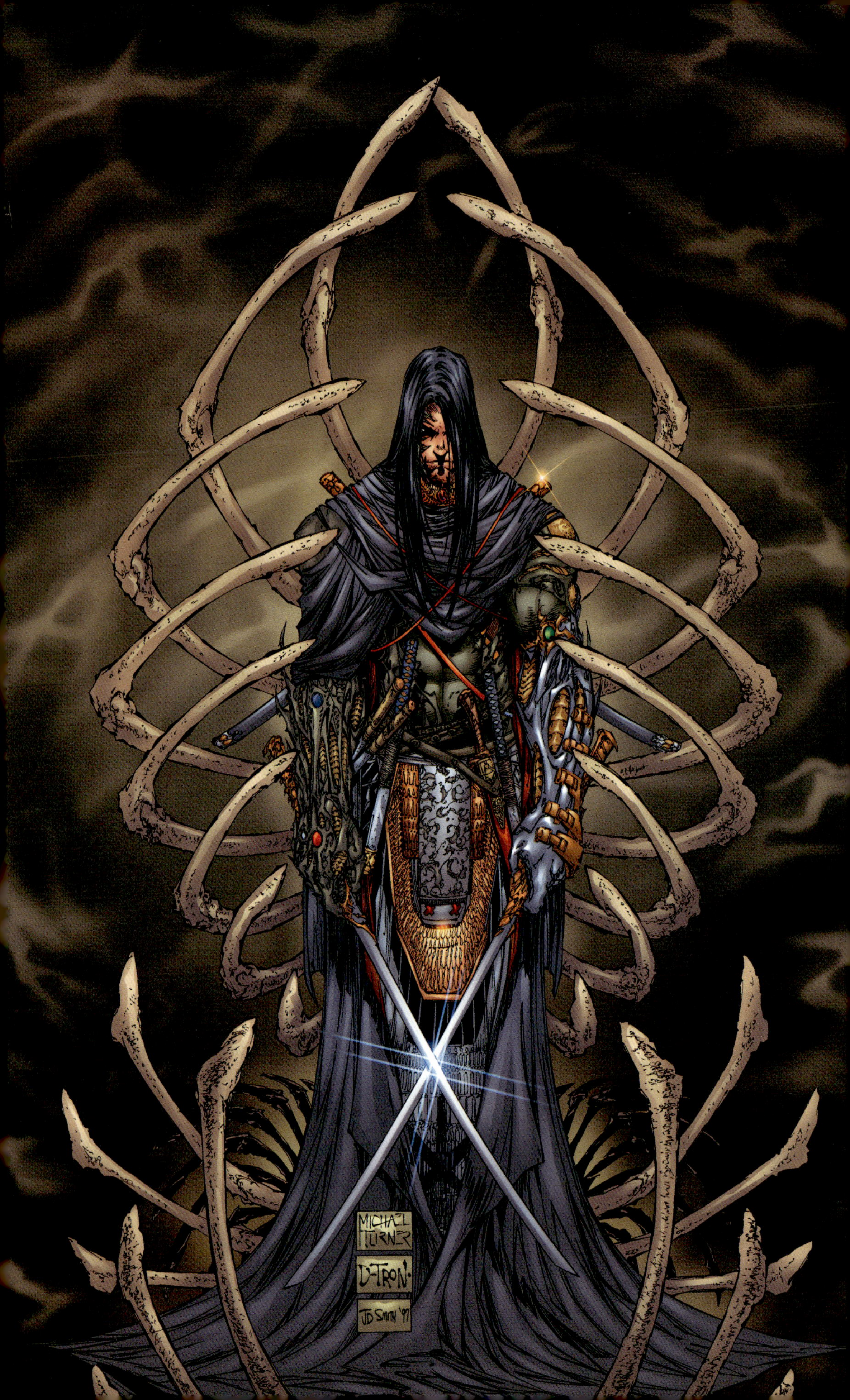
MICHAEL TURNER
D-TRON
JD Smith '97

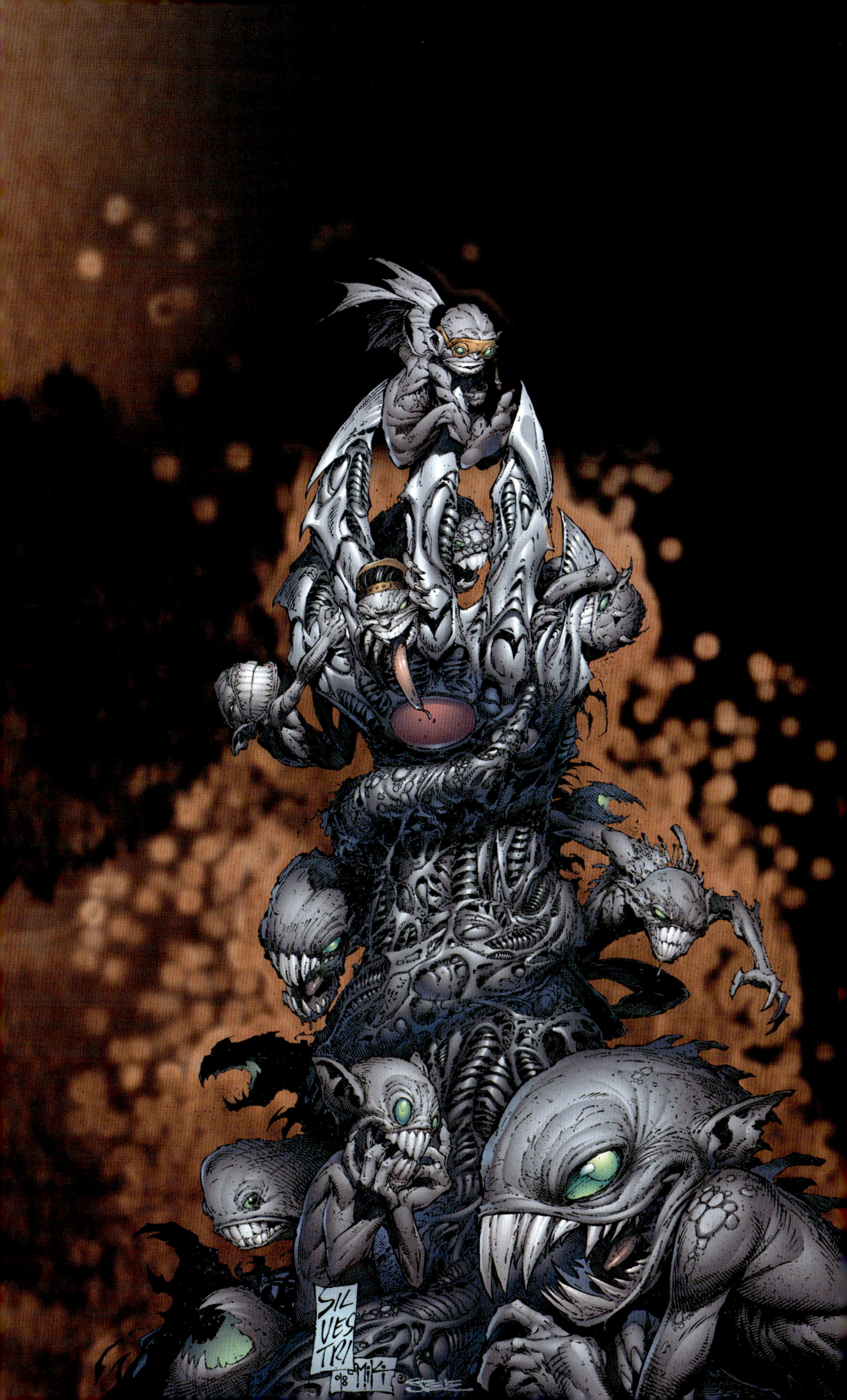

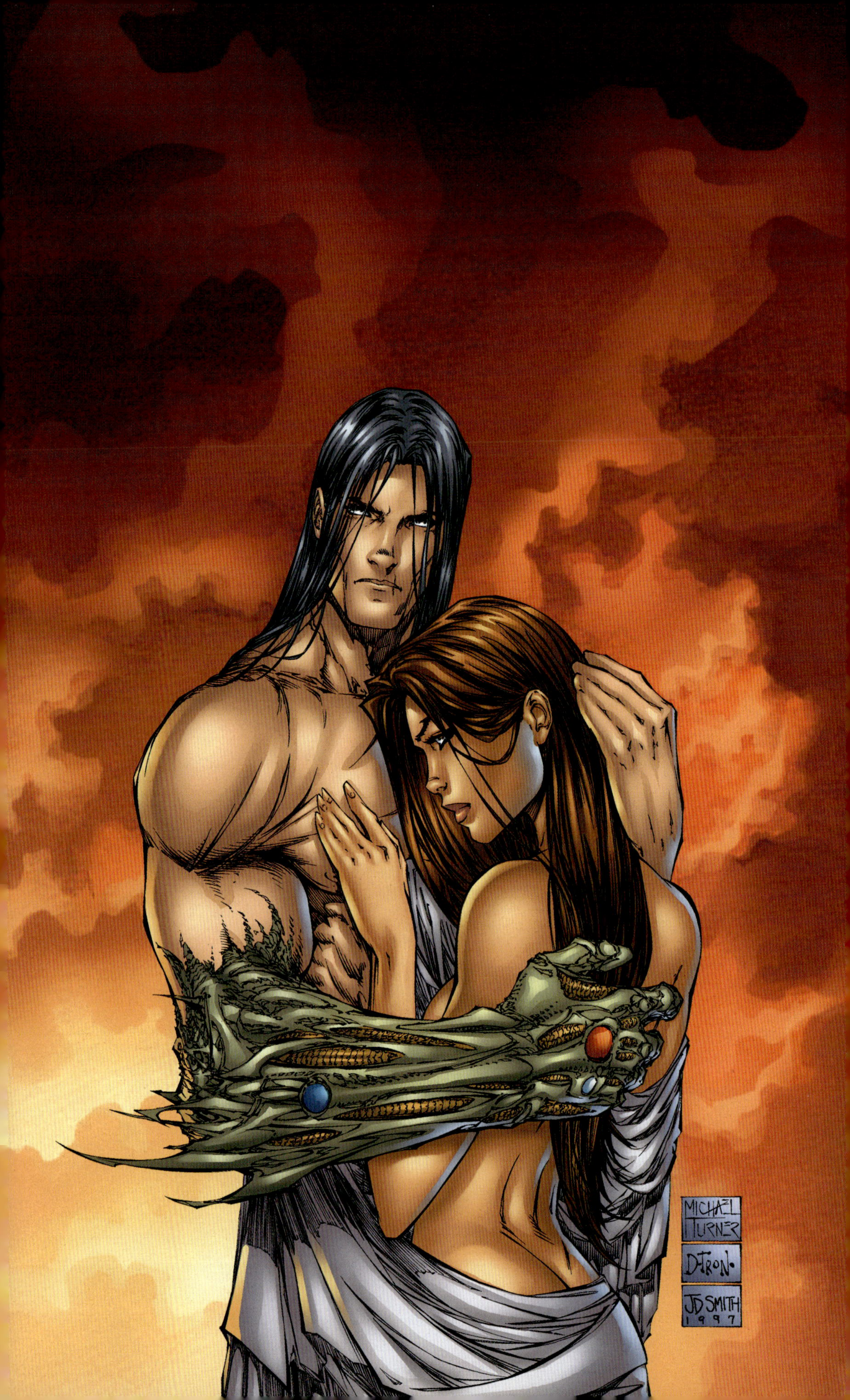
MICHAEL TURNER
D-TRON
JD SMITH 1997

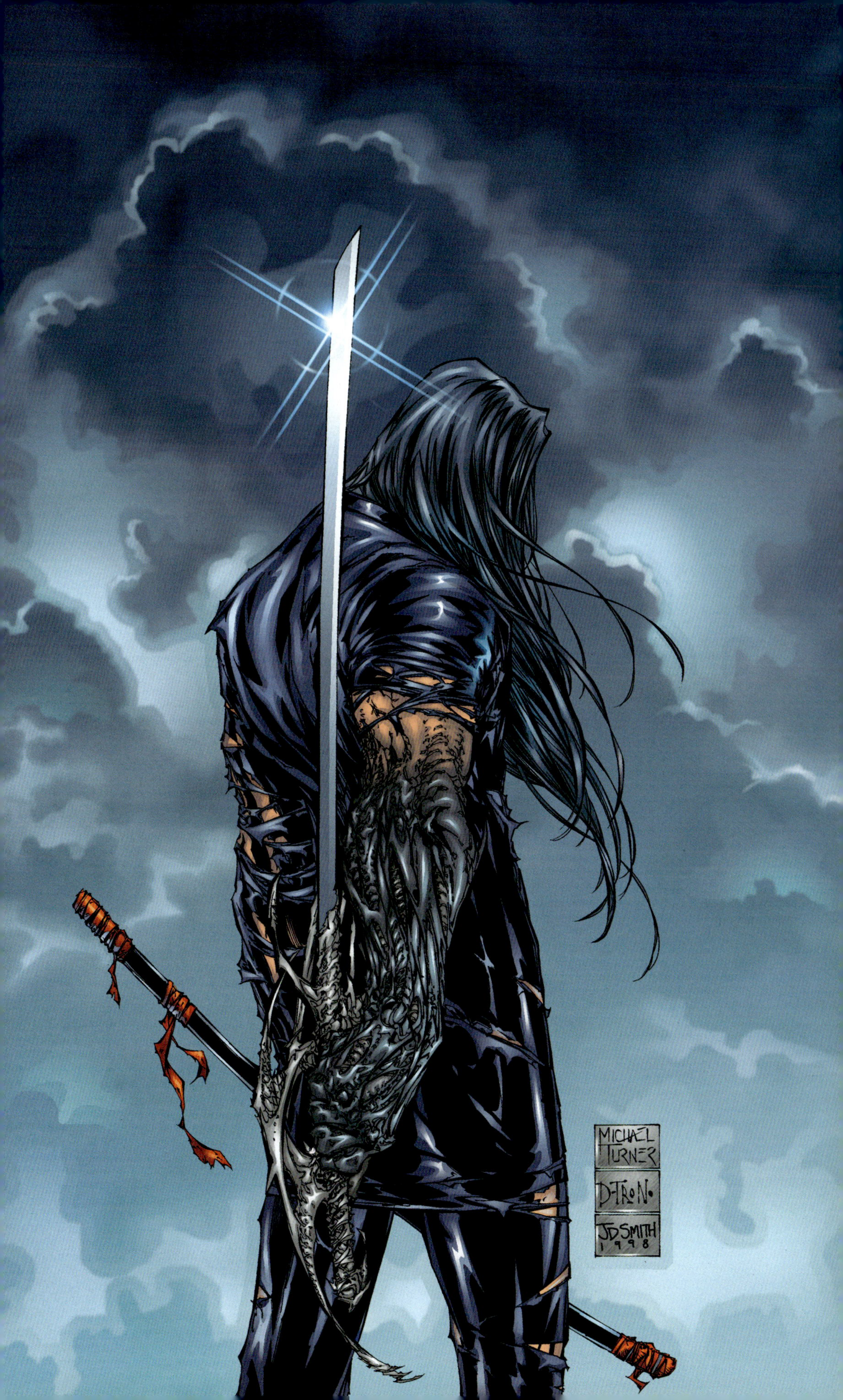
MICHAEL TURNER
D-TRON
JD SMITH 1998

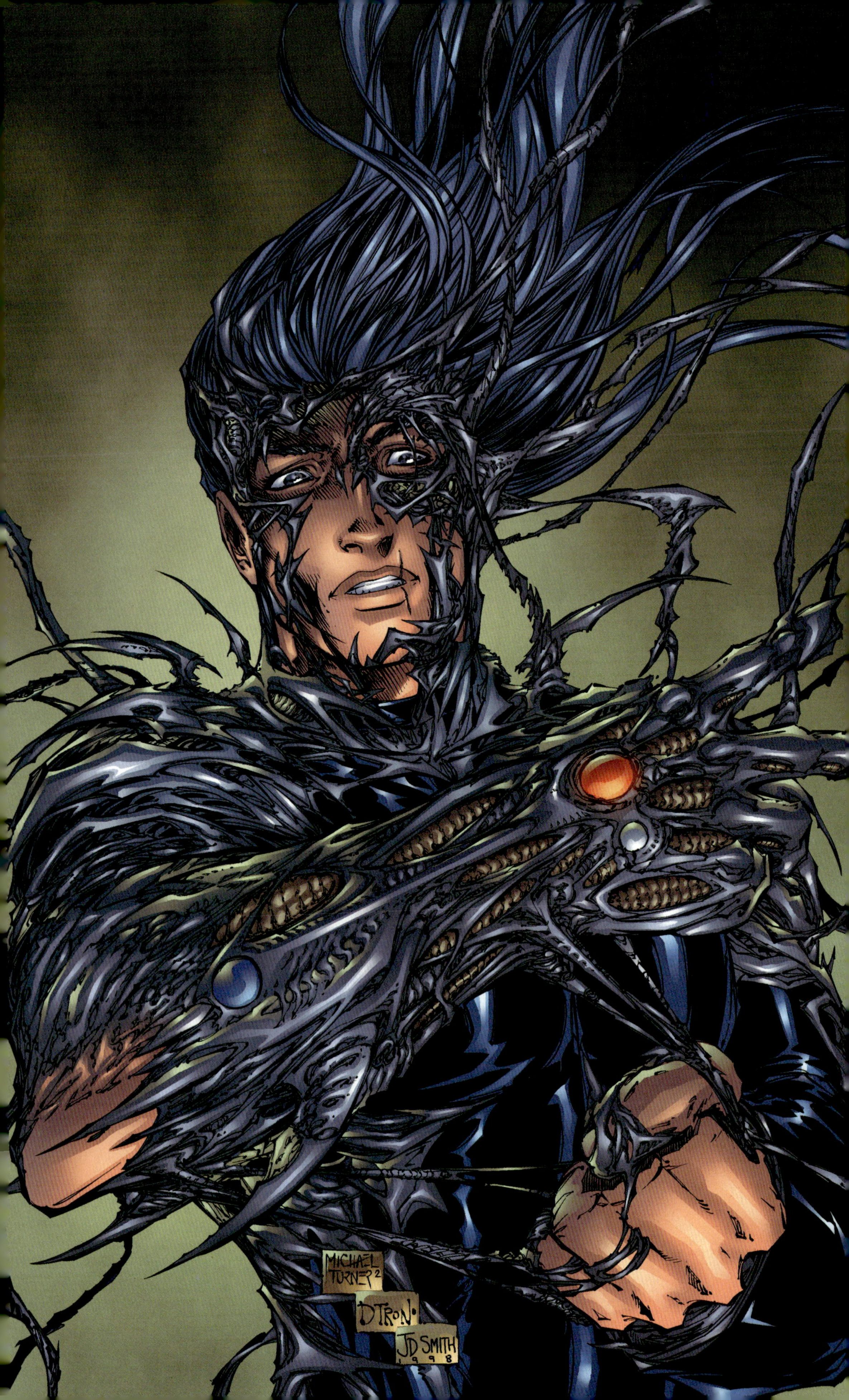

MICHAEL TURNER²
D'TRON
JD SMITH
1998

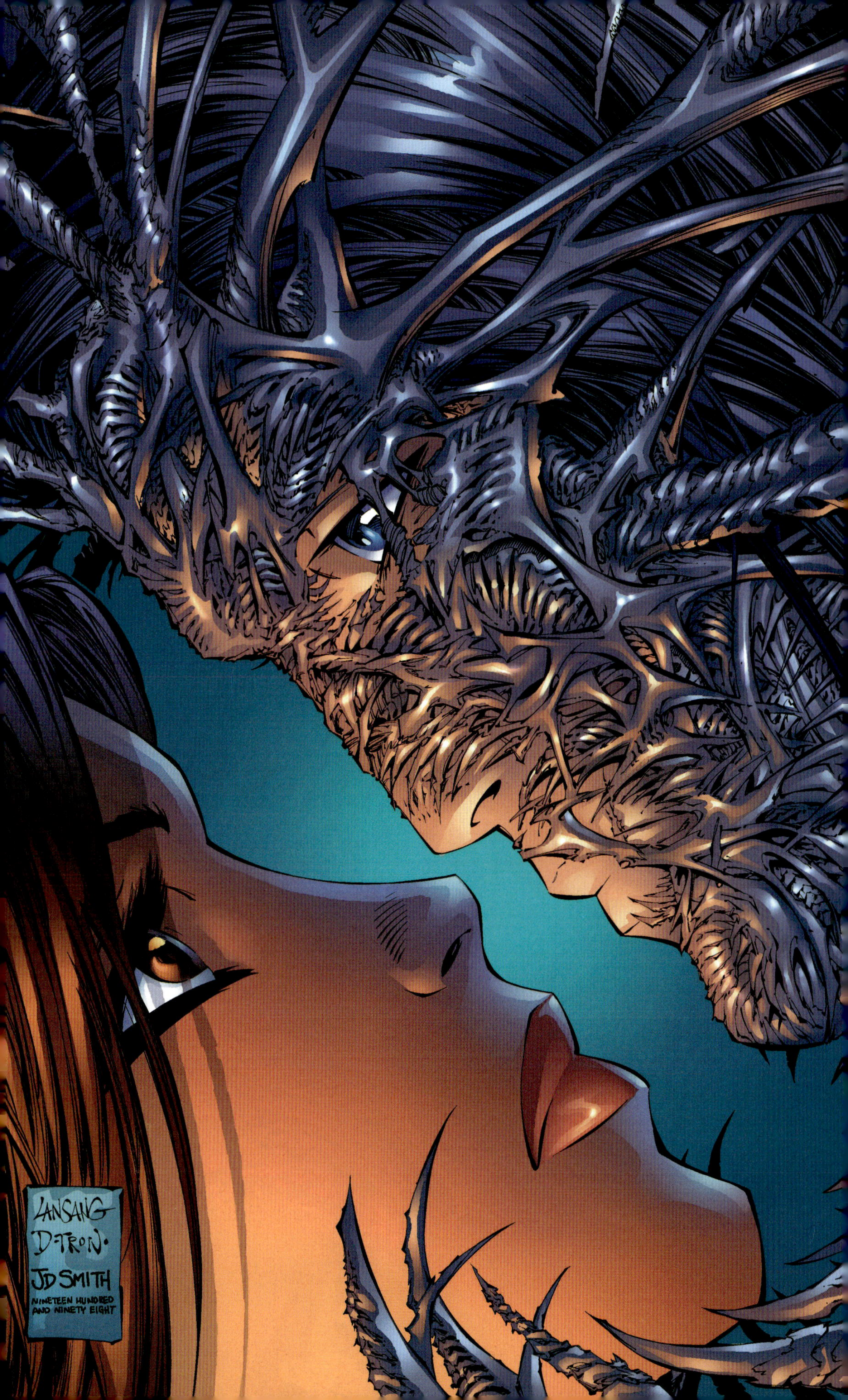
LANSANG
D-TRON.
JD SMITH
NINETEEN HUNDRED AND NINETY EIGHT

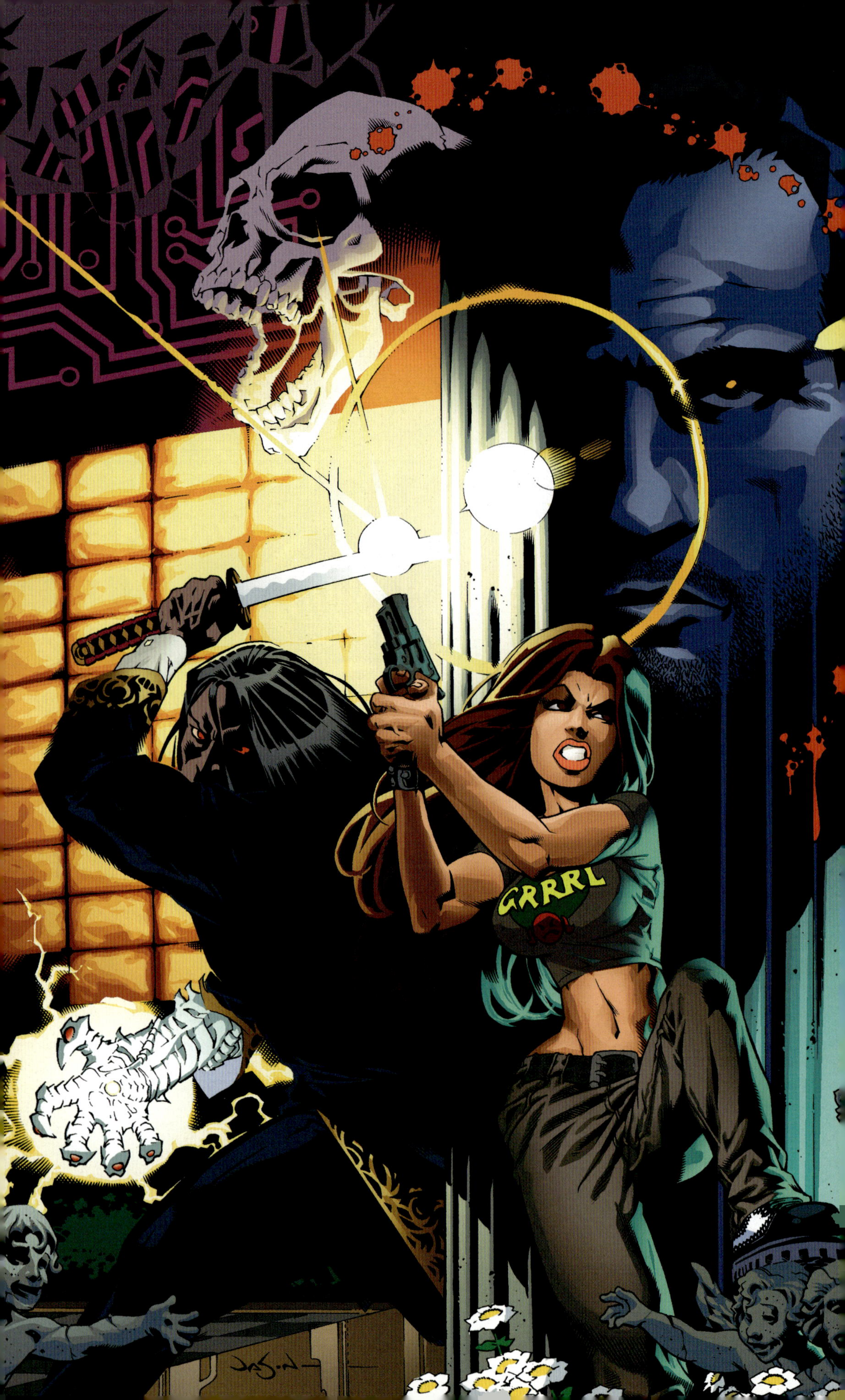
GRRRL

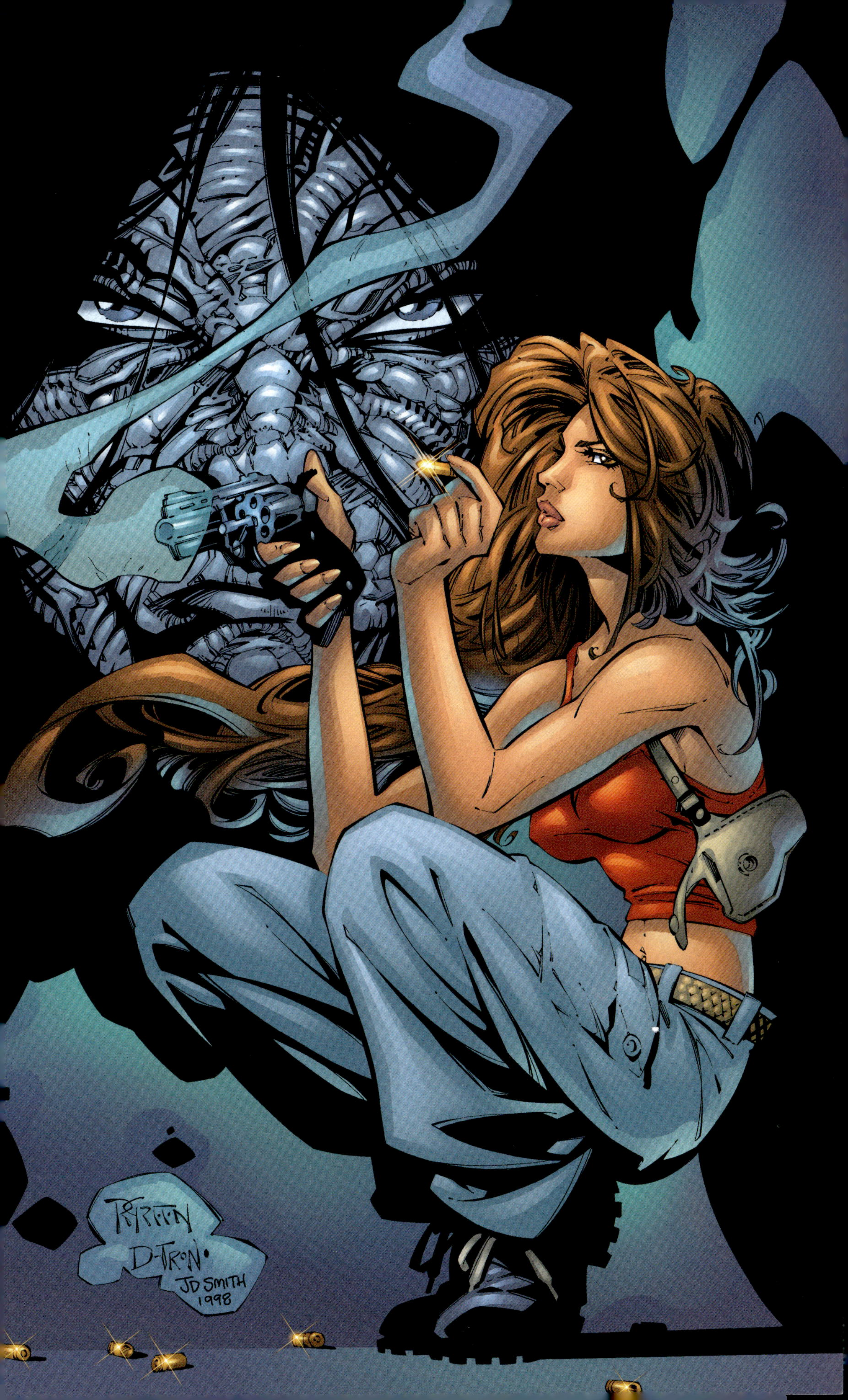
D-TRON
JD SMITH
1998

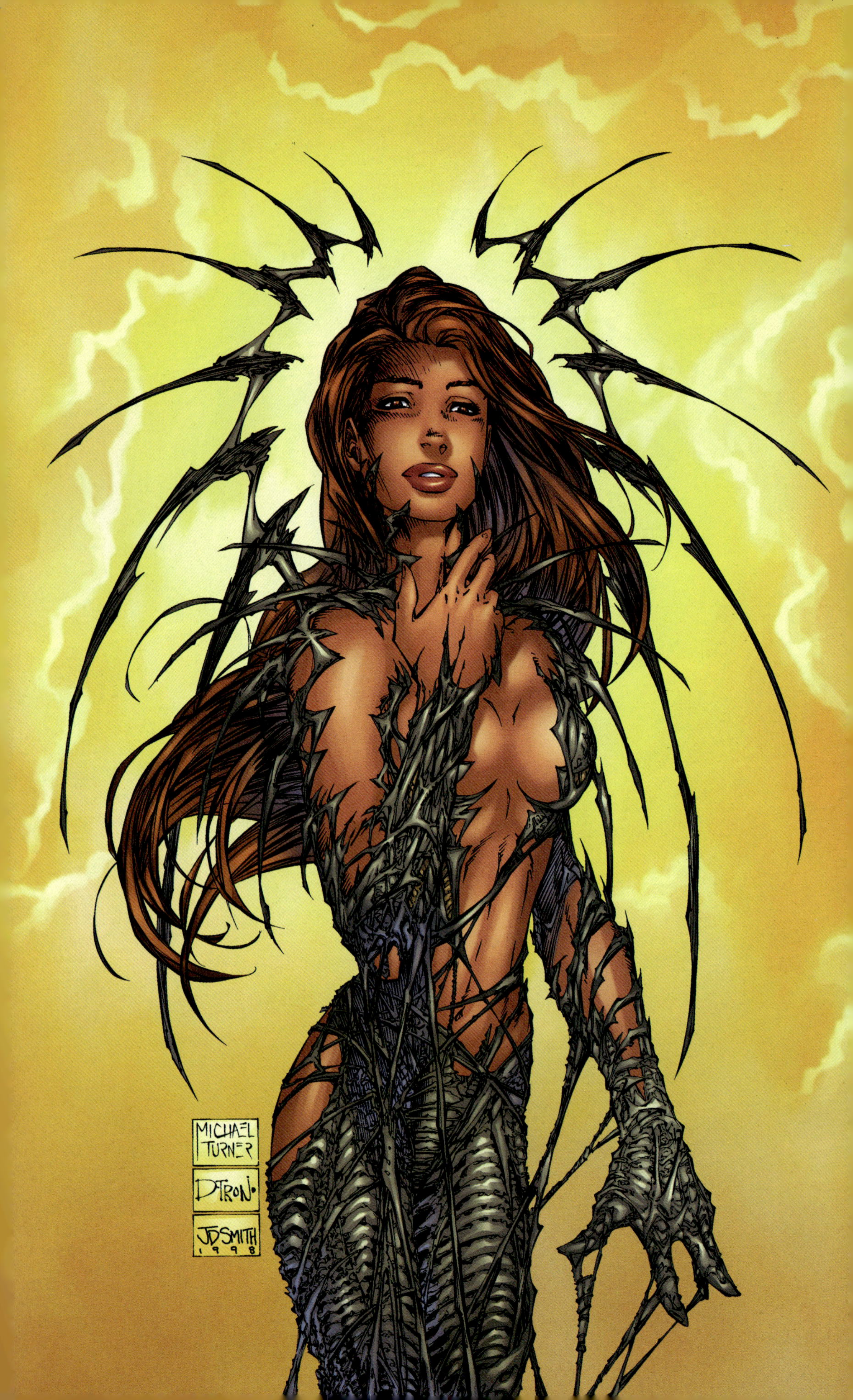
MICHAEL TURNER
D-TRON
JDSMITH 1998

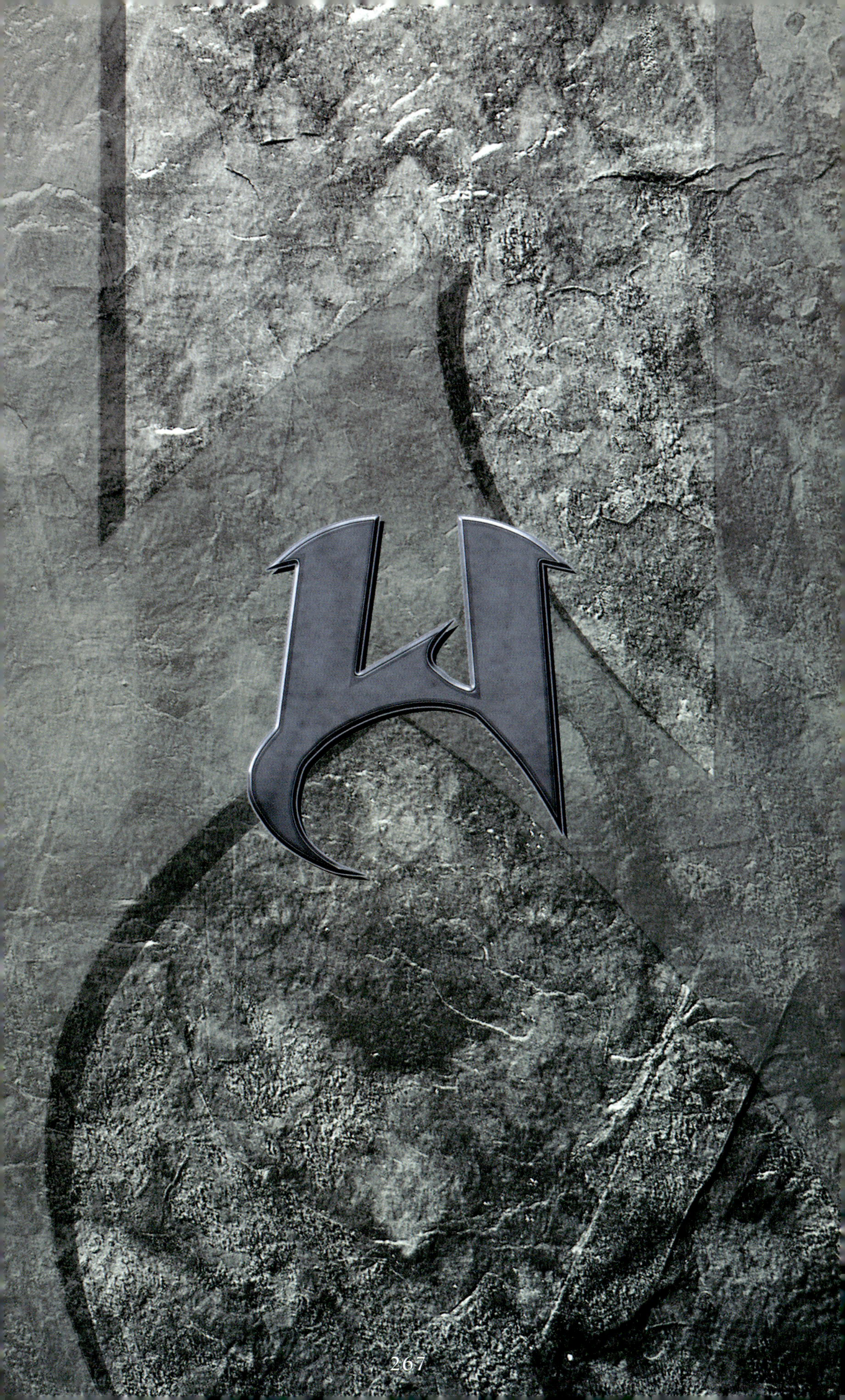

Read more *Witchblade* in these trade paperback collections.

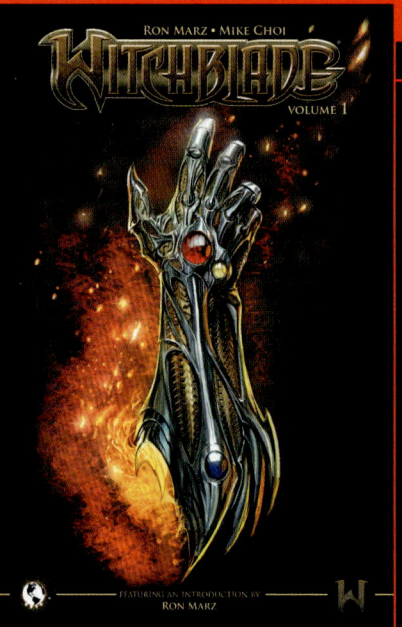

Ron Marz • Mike Choi
Witchblade
Volume 1
Featuring an introduction by
Ron Marz

Witchblade

volume 1 - volume 5

written by:
Ron Marz
pencils by:
Mike Choi, Stephen Sadowski, Keu Cha, Chris Bachalo, Stjepan Sejic and more!

Get in on the ground floor of Top Cow's flagship title with these affordable trade paperback collections from Ron Marz's series-redefining run on Witchblade! Each volume collects a key story arc in the continuing adventures of Sara Pezzini and the Witchblade.

volume 1
collects issues #80-#85
(ISBN: 978-1-58240-906-1) $9.99

Ron Marz • Mike Choi • Chris Bachalo • Keu Cha
Witchblade
Volume 2
Featuring an introduction by
Phil Hester

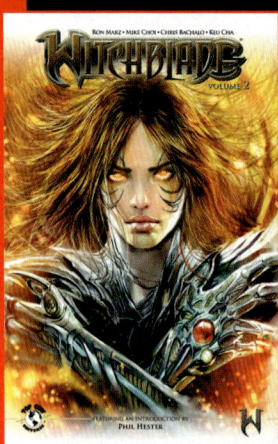

volume 2
collects issues #86-#92
(ISBN: 978-1-58240-886-6)
U.S.D. $14.99

Witchblade
Volume 3

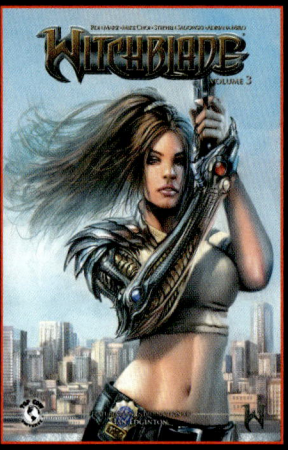

volume 3
collects issues #93-#100
(ISBN: 978-1-58240-887-3)
U.S.D. $14.99

Ron Marz • Adriana Melo • Stjepan Sejic • Sami Basri
Witchblade
Volume 4
Marc Bernardin

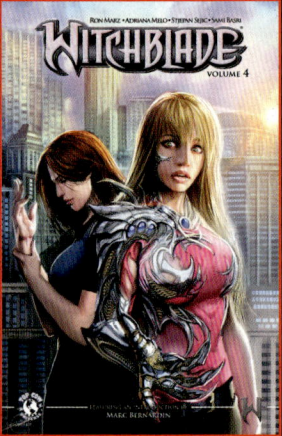

volume 4
collects issues #101-109
(ISBN: 978-1-58240-898-9)
U.S.D. $17.99

Ron Marz • Stjepan Sejic • Sami Basri
Witchblade
Volume 5
Featuring an introduction by
Robert Kirkman

volume 5
collects issues #110-115,
First Born issues #1-3
(ISBN: 978-1-58240-899-6)
U.S.D. $17.99

Witchblade

volume 6
collects issues #116-#120
(ISBN: 978-1-60706-041-3)
U.S.D. $14.99

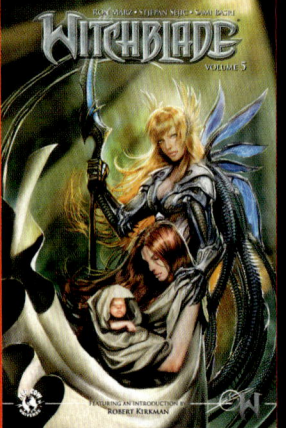

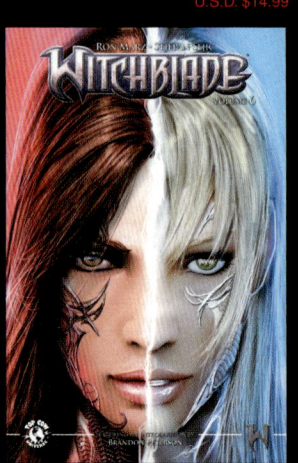

New York City Police Detective Sara Pezzini is the bearer of the Witchblade, a mysterious artifact that takes the form of a deadly and powerful gauntlet. Now Sara must try to control the Witchblade and learn its secrets, even as she investigates the city's strangest, most supernatural crimes.

Check out our new "Art of" collections now available from Top Cow!

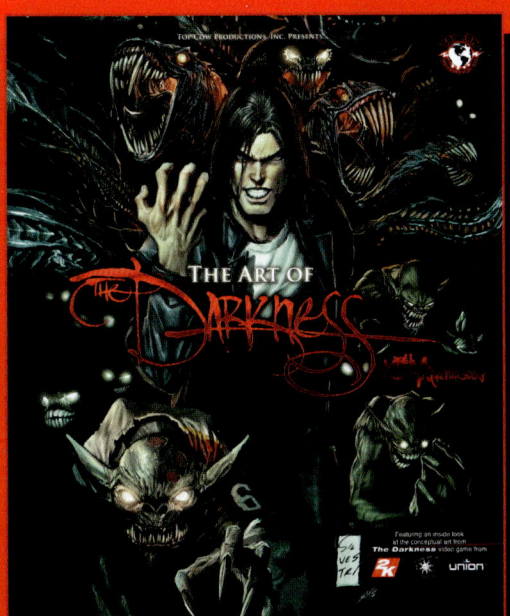
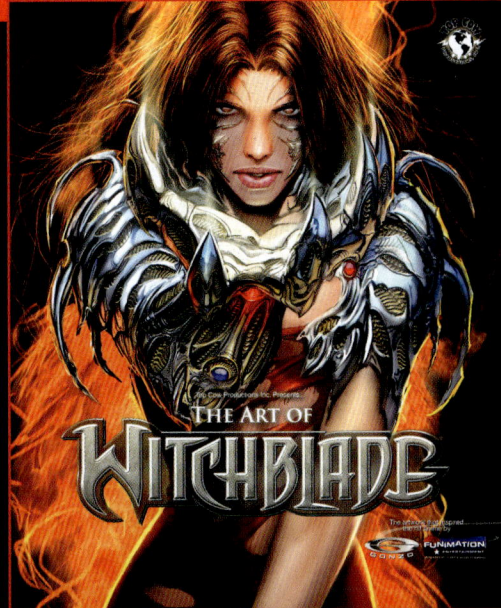

The Art of The Darkness

The Art of Witchblade

Celebrate the ongoing saga of *The Darkness* and *Witchblade* with these deluxe edition art collections! Inspired by "Art of" books for video games and films, these over-sized art books feature glorious illustrations and commentary from the original creators, all contained in a glossy, thick-papered, beautifully designed book. Covers, splash pages, collectible cards, sketches--the very best art from *The Darkness and Witchblade* collected in one place! See it here in its unadulterated form. A decade of work to choose from, these are the definitive "Art of" books for *The Darkness and Witchblade*! Featuring art by the top names in comics including:

Marc Silvestri, Michael Turner, Dale Keown, Jae Lee, Stjepan Sejic, Dave Finch, Whilce Portacio and many more!

The Art of The Darkness, (ISBN 13: 978-1-58240-649-7) $14.99

The Art of Witchblade, (ISBN 13: 978-1-58240-857-6) $19.99

The Art of Marc Silvestri

From his humble beginnings as penciler on Marvel's *Conan*, Marc Silvestri understood what it meant to produce a quality comic book. Driven by his commitment to excellence, Silvestri gained a huge following in the late 1980s on such titles as *Uncanny X-Men* and *Wolverine*. His popularity continued to grow when he founded Top Cow Productions and had breakout successes with *Cyberforce* and *The Darkness*. Under his guidance, Top Cow has grown from comic books into a company with ongoing development of video games, anime and feature films.

Silvestri's decades-spanning career has taught him not only the importance of producing quality work, but also the need to foster the next generation of artists by maintaining one of the few working art studio environments in the industry.

Softcover (ISBN 13: 978-1-58240-903-0) $19.99
Hardcover (ISBN 13: 978-1-58240-904-7) $29.99

Jump into the Top Cow Universe with The Darkness!

The Darkness
Accursed vol.1

written by:
Phil Hester

pencils by:
Michael Broussard

Mafia hitman Jackie Estacado was both blessed and cursed on his 21st birthday when he became the bearer of The Darkness, an elemental force that allows those who wield it access to an otherwordly dimension and control over the demons who dwell there. Forces for good in the world rise up to face Jackie and the evil his gift represents, but there is one small problem. In this story...they are the bad guys.

Now's your chance to read "Empire," the first storyline by the new creative team of **Phil Hester** (*Firebreather, Green Arrow*) and **Michael Broussard** (*Unholy Union*) that marked the shocking return of *The Darkness* to the Top Cow Universe!

Book Market Edition
(ISBN 13: 978-1-58240-958-0) $9.99

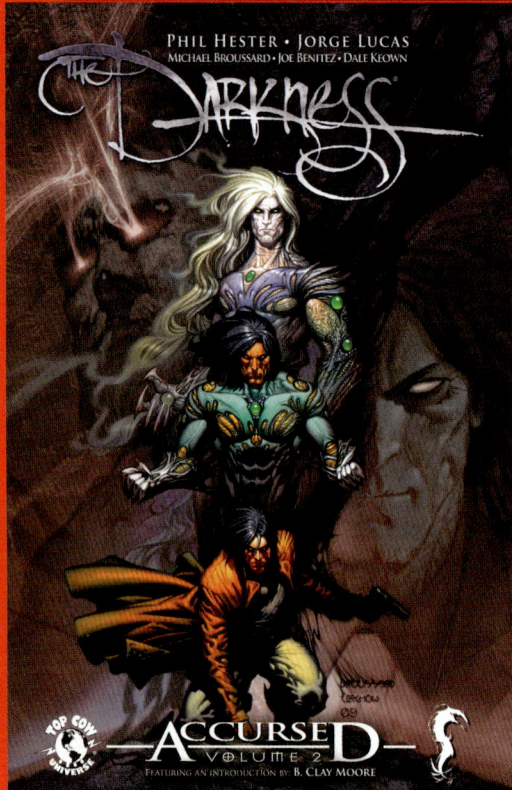

The Darkness
Accursed vol.2

written by:
Phil Hester

pencils by:
Jorge Lucas, Dale Keown, Joe Benitez, Michael Broussard and more!

But the road home is no easy journey as he runs afoul of Mexican witches, wannabe gangsters and even Aphrodite IV! Jackie soon discovers his battle with The Darkness cast his soul into Hell while leaving his body and mind on Earth. Enter The Sovereign, an arch-demon who promises to reunite Jackie's body and soul, but at a price that may be worse than Hell itself. Plus, witness a possible future ruled by The Darkness run amok in a spectacular story drawn by a list of all-star artists!

Collects *The Darkness* Vol. 3 #7-10 and the double-sized *The Darkness* #75 (issue #11 before the Legacy Numbering took effect), plus a cover gallery and behind-the-scenes extras!

(ISBN 13: 978-1-60706-044-4) $9.99

Premium collected editions

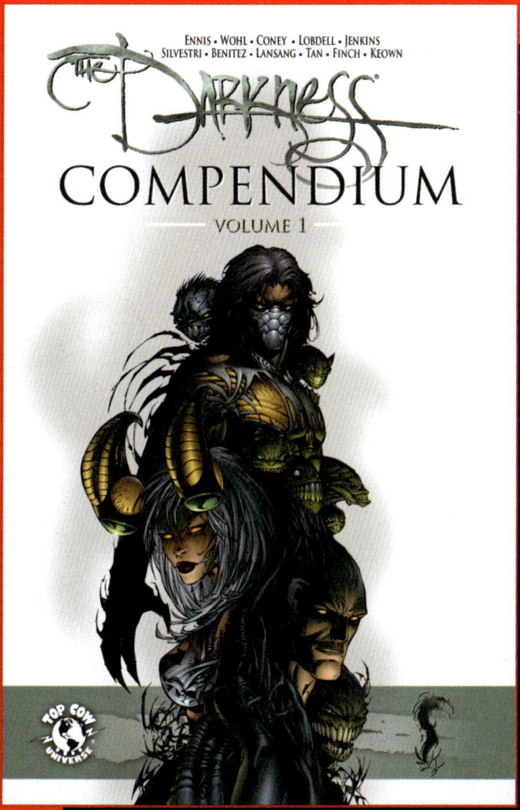
ENNIS • WOHL • CONEY • LOBDELL • JENKINS
SILVESTRI • BENITEZ • LANSANG • TAN • FINCH • KEOWN
The Darkness
COMPENDIUM
VOLUME 1

The Darkness
Compendium vol.1

written by:
Garth Ennis, Paul Jenkins,
Scott Lobdell
pencils by:
Marc Silvestri, Joe Benitez and more!

On his 21st birthday, the awesome and terrible powers of the Darkness awaken within Jackie Estacado, a mafia hitman for the Franchetti crime family. There's nothing like going back to the beginning and reading it all over again-- issues #1-40, plus the complete run of the *Tales of the Darkness* series collected into one trade paperback. See how the Darkness first appeared and threw Jackie into the chaotic world of the supernatural. Get the first appearances of The Magdalena and more!

SC (ISBN 13: 978-1-58240-643-5) $59.99
HC (ISBN 13: 978-1-58240-992-7) $99.99

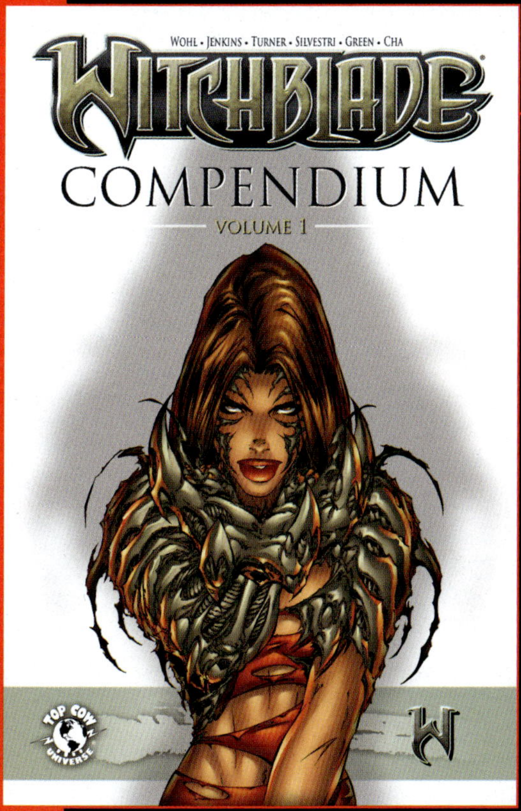
WOHL • JENKINS • TURNER • SILVESTRI • GREEN • CHA
WITCHBLADE
COMPENDIUM
VOLUME 1

Witchblade
Compendium vol.1

written by:
David Wohl, Christina Z.,
Paul Jenkins
pencils by:
Michael Turner, Randy Green
Keu Cha and more!

From the hit live-action television series to the current Japanese anime, *Witchblade* has been Top Cow's flagship title for over a decade. There's nothing like going back to the beginning and reading it all over again. This massive collection houses issues #1-50 in a single edition for the first time. See how the Witchblade chose Sara and threw her into the chaotic world of the supernatural. Get the first appearances of Sara Pezzini, Ian Nottingham, Kenneth Irons and Jackie Estacado in one handy tome!

SC (ISBN 13: 978-1-58240-634-3) $59.99
HC (ISBN 13: 978-1-58240-798-2) $99.99

Premium collected editions

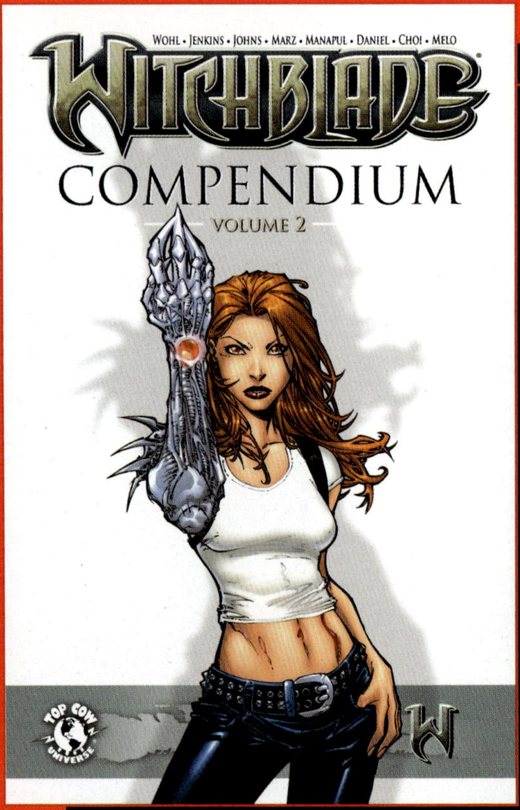
WOHL • JENKINS • JOHNS • MARZ • MANAPUL • DANIEL • CHOI • MELO
WITCHBLADE
COMPENDIUM
VOLUME 2

Witchblade
Compendium vol.2

written by:
David Wohl, Christina Z., Paul Jenkins and Ron Marz
pencils by:
Michael Turner, Randy Green Keu Cha, Mike Choi and more!

From the "Death Pool" story arc featuring the death of a major Witchblade character to heading up the NYPD's Special Cases Unit, Witchblade bearer Sara Pezzini and her new partner Patrick Gleason find themselves with more questions than answers as their investigations lead them from haunted museums, dark alleys and forgotten tunnels beneath New York City. Meanwhile, the enigmatic Curator leaves a trails of clues for Sara, ultimately leading her to the explosive origin of the Witchblade itself!

Collects Witchblade issues #51-100

SC (ISBN 13: 978-1-58240-731-9) $59.99
HC (ISBN 13: 978-1-58240-960-3) $99.99

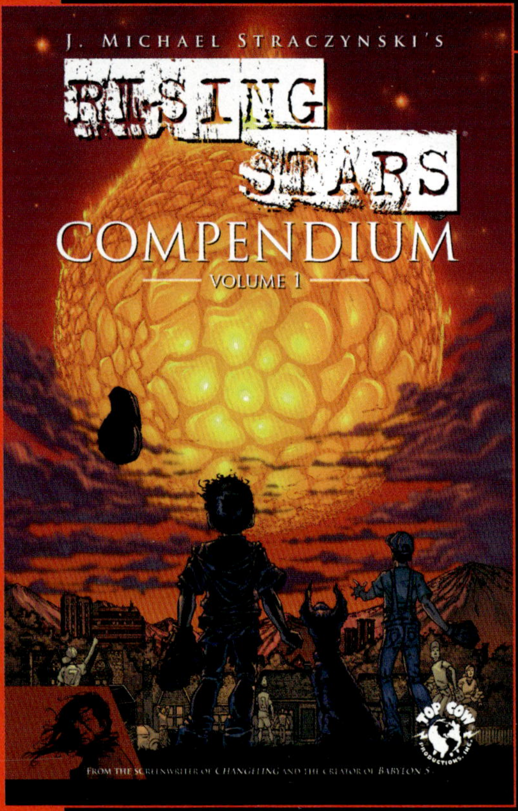
J. MICHAEL STRACZYNSKI'S
RISING STARS
COMPENDIUM
VOLUME 1
FROM THE SCREENWRITER OF CHANGELING AND THE CREATOR OF BABYLON 5

Rising Stars
Compendium vol.1

written by:
J. Michael Straczynski

pencils by:
Keu Cha, Ken Lashley Gary Frank, Brent Anderson and more!

The *Rising Stars* Compendium Edition collects the entire saga of the Pederson Specials, including the entire original series written by series creator **J. Michael Straczynski**, (*Supreme Power/Midnight Nation*) as well as the three limited series Bright, Voices of the Dead and Untouchable written by **Fiona Avery**, (*Amazing Fantasy/No Honor*).

Collects *Rising Stars* issues #0, #1/2, #1-24, Prelude, the short story "Initiations", the limited series *Bright* issues #1-3, *Voices of the Dead* issues #1-6 and *Untouchable* issues #1-5

SC (ISBN 13: 978-1-58240-802-6) $59.99
HC (ISBN 13: 978-1-58240-032-1) $99.99